During the annual celebration of the Order of the Garter, Sir Michael Devereaux arrives in King Henry VIII's court on a mission for his benefactor. The celebration's endless feats and sumptuous women delight the charismatic newcomer, who becomes captivated by the enigmatic Princess Renée of France. But evil, it seems, has followed Michael to the court. Shortly after his arrival, an unknown killer claims several victims, including the queen's lady-in-waiting, and the powerful Cardinal Wolsey asks Michael to help with the investigation. As he searches for the killer, Michael is haunted by disturbing images of the victims—flashes of violence that lead him to doubt his own sanity. Michael soon realizes that the key to solving the crime is connected to both the pope's imperial vault in Rome and a mystery from Michael's own past—revealing a secret that is so damning, it could forever alter the future of mankind.

Powerfully evocative and steeped with detail from the breathtaking era of the Tudors, *Royal Blood* is historical storytelling at its richest—an unforgettable tale of intrigue, passion, and danger.

Books by Rona Sharon:

MY WICKED PIRATE

ONCE A RAKE

ROYAL BLOOD

Published by Kensington Publishing Corp.

ROYAL BLOOD

RONA SHARON

KENSINGTON BOOKS

KENSINGTON BOOKS are published by

Kensington Publishing Corp.
850 Third Avenue
New York, NY 10022

All Kensington titles, imprints, and distributed lines are available at special quantity discounts for bulk purchases for sales promotion, premiums, fund-raising, educational, or institutional use.

Special book excerpts or customized printings can also be created to fit specific needs. For details, write or phone the office of the Kensington Special Sales Manager: Kensington Publishing Corp., 850 Third Avenue, New York, NY 10022. Attn. Special Sales Department. Phone: 1-800-221-2647.

Kensington and the K logo Reg. U.S. Pat. & TM Off.

ISBN-13: 978-1-60751-912-6

Printed in the United States of America

For Dana and Zeev—
With all the love and gratitude in my heart

In memory of my friend, Niza

❧ 1 ❧

In front—a precipice;
Behind—wolves.

—an ancient Roman aphorism

Tiltyard at Castle Tyrone, Ireland, 1518

"Again!"

The command was followed by a clap of thunder.

Michael slammed his visor shut and stormed into combat. Rain sheeted the marshy, torchlit lists, rendering him near blind. After hours of training, his arms throbbed from holding the lance and shield, his leg muscles burned with the effort of keeping his hot-blooded destrier at a straight gallop. The earth shook beneath the thundering stallions as mighty hoofs plowed through sludge. Dreading the collision and despising his fear, Michael couched his lance at his sinister opponent, armored in black steel cap-à-pie and bearing down on him like a dark chthonic force.

Aim low, then at the last moment strike the helm, the Earl of Tyrone's instructions resounded in Michael's head. *Strike the helm, the helm . . .*

The shocking blow to his own helmet prized Michael out of the saddle. He crashed into the squelchy ground, whence he had risen moments before, in an ungainly heap of armored limbs.

Mud splotched the grille of his visor as massive hoofs reached his sprawled form and reared up, threatening to fossilize him in the midden. With an oath, Michael recoiled on capped elbows and spurs, glaring up at Sir Ferdinand, Lord Tyrone's shadow. "Blood from a stone!" the raspy voice mocked him. The raven visor turned toward the shrouded figure observing the joust from a recess inside the barbican. "Your incompetent sunflower is not ready! He will never be ready!"

Michael felt murderous. Yes, he had lost, again. But he could cudgel Ferdinand for drubbing him and then deprecating him to the great lord who had reared him as his own son and legal heir. Only killing Sir Ferdinand would be akin to slaying a mountain; the knight was indestructible.

Michael fell back on the pulpy alluvium, exhausted and dispirited. Rain drummed his visor; cool rivulets sluiced his face. The storm was gathering force. Dusk bled into night. Squinting at the donjon, its diamond panes glowing brightly beneath the darkening welkin, he fancied a long hot bucking by a roaring fire, a flagon of mulled wine, a juicy hunch of mutton, a pliant wench . . .

"Again!"

The terse order sliced through his aching head, jolting his battered bones. The varlets' strong hands hauled him up and set him aright. He wrenched himself free from their steadying grip and trudged, clanking, to the end of the course. Pippin, his manservant, bridled his horse. Archangel snorted, shook its armored head, and stomped its feet in protest, fetlocks deep in mud.

Michael gentled the destrier with petting and praise. "One last time, and we will have done, O great one. My word upon it."

He swung onto his weary horse with a metallic clang, his muscles groaning at the ongoing torture like rheumatic joints on a withered nun. Pippin handed him the lance and buckler with his usual word of encouragement. "You will fell him this time, master. I know you will."

"The left shoulder." Michael eyed his complacent adversary. "He protects his heart."

"A delicate heart, eh? Forsooth, that is a point in his favor, for I doubted he had one."

"Aye, 'tis black as his suit of armor—and his soul."

"God smite him," Pippin muttered scathingly.

Michael steered Archangel to the starting line. The signal was given, and he was hurtling up the rain-battered course at full tilt, the sloughy ground quaking beneath Archangel's hoofs. *The heart, the heart*, Michael thought, focusing on the magnificently wrought black breastplate.

A heartbeat later, he was on his back in the muddy puddles. His left shoulder hurt as if it had been ripped from his body. He shut his eyes tightly. He felt . . . routed, peppered, unworthy.

Sir Ferdinand drew rein, laughing viciously. "Mind your own heart next time, sunflower!"

The authoritative voice in the tower rumbled, "Put him on his feet and bring him to me!"

Michael, divested of his armor and a good deal of aplomb, leaked mud at the threshold to the castle's eyrie at the top of the bastion. His noble protector's preferred haunt was constructed after the Pantheon in Rome, an architectural marvel with a rounded dome and a skylight carved out of its center that formed an interior waterfall when it rained. A gilt gridiron set in the black marble floor drained the rainwater into the support pillar around which the tower stairwell spiraled and straight into the castle's water reservoir. Here, the Earl of Tyrone, Lord Lieutenant of Ireland and England's bulwark against a Celtic uprising, came to study the heavens through his *teleskopos*.

A plethora of horn lanterns set in the rotund wall paid homage to marble busts of gods and emperors and to the arms man had wielded on battlefields since the birth of time: The twenty foot long *sarissa* Alexander the Great conquered Asia withal; the Roman *gladius* that taught the old Greek world Latin; the *francisca* that shattered the shields of the legionaries and catapulted the Roman Empire into darkness; the crushing Norse *mjolnir*, the bane of the Saxons, the Celts, the Franks, and the Iberians; the Mongol short bow that kept vast territories under Genghis Khan's thumb; and Don Álvaro de Zúñiga's innovative *espada ropera*, the light blade ushering the future.

Tonight, as it rained, instead of standing beneath the center skylight, training a rock crystal on a comet, the earl prowled round the cascade. "Trounced today, battered yesterday, and barely held your own with the sword the day before. You outwit your tutors in every discipline. Why can you not outmaneuver Sir Ferdinand in combat?

The annual chapter of the Noble Order of the Garter approaches, Michael. My honor is at stake here, as is the future of my house!"

Michael shifted restlessly, his gaze on his toecaps, his conscience trammeled by unpalatable failure. It took all he had to drudge up the galling admission. "He is stronger."

"Brains carry a man further than might, Michael! It would behoove you to know this!"

Setting his jaw, Michael lifted his eyes. "He knows my next move before I make it."

"Then outthink him, damn you! Can you not keep your thoughts under lock and key? Must the secrets of your mind be an open tome? Did I waste two decades of my life teaching you the quadrivium, training and instructing you in the games of kings to be thusly disillusioned?"

Michael remained silent.

"Ferdinand knows that the future of my house depends upon you. He pushes you to excel."

Michael bristled. "He pushes me to commit murder, my lord."

"Alas, my only son was destroyed on a foreign battlefield years gone, and the gods have not blessed me with other offspring— until you came along. Your noble sire, who fought like a lion and died for his king at Blackheath during the Cornish rebellion, had sworn me to take his son, begotten off a second wife, and raise him as I would mine own, for fear his heir would reject a half sibling. He did not swear me to embrace you to my loving bosom and set you up as my legal heir, but I saw a bright-eyed lad, quick and sharp and steeled. I thought, 'Here be my son, here be the man unto whom I shall bequeath my lands, chattels, and the honor of my name, my heart and soul and all that I am! Here be my future'!" The earl circled the waterfall, hands clasped behind his back. "I did not expect you to fell Sir Ferdinand. He *is* stronger, a bloody-minded bull who would sooner crush a lit candle than snuff it out. He has fought a thousand battles and lived. I expected you to persist! To take his blows and jolt his confidence! That was the point of the exercise! Now you come to me with your head downcast, all pity-pleading and beaten . . . ."

Stoically Michael straightened his back. He had his lord's inches now, yet, heart-burned, he felt shorter than a mouse. Tyrone gazed at him grumpily, fondly. "Ferdinand has his weaknesses, greater than yours. I want you to attend this year's knightly chapter. It is important to me."

Michael blinked in surprise. "You would still send me to court?"

"I would send a champion!" Tyrone's dark eyes glinted. "Swift, cunning, and ruthless in his devotion to me! Indomitable. Unstoppable. Relentless. Are you this man? Or has the precocious boy I have nurtured to become the Seventh Earl of Tyrone traded his tiger spots for a plumule?"

Michael sensed without being told that his lord and mentor expected more than words from him, an assurance of sorts, some proof of his commitment and wherewithal.

"The greatest battles are not won on battlefields, Michael. They are predetermined in council chambers and ladies' beds, in courtly banquets and tournaments, in the nursery and . . . up here!" He tapped his temple with a finger. "An illustrious general may win the battle and lose the war. In contrast, a downtrodden soldier who takes the worst punishment and rallies for another battle will triumph in the end. Remember the Battle of Cannae, Michael. When the Carthaginian army led by Hannibal slaughtered Varro's army on Italian soil, the Romans, incapable of stomaching defeat, withdrew, recovered, and returned at full strength to ultimately obliterate Carthage to all eternity. Survival is the key. If beaten, retreat, regroup, and rally—and never *ever* give!"

"Give what, my lord?"

"Give up, give in, give out . . . Never! Till your last drop of blood! Do you understand?"

"I do." Michael swallowed. "Command me to London, my lord. I will do you credit."

"You will pledge it? You will do for me as I did for you?"

"More. I swear it."

"Upon your honor, you will serve none but me and let not temptation lead you astray?"

"Temptation, my lord? What could possibly tempt me to violate my pledge to you?"

Tyrone's mouth twisted wryly. "Think you I am ignorant of how you soothe your mind and body at night? You spill your vigor into wenches and souse your head with wine. You grin?"

Michael schooled his features. He could have sworn he had curbed the very emergence of a grin. Yet his lord was a master at diving thoughts. "I had as lief die than fail you, my lord."

"Attend me, Michael. The rule at court is simple: Enthrall but do not love; be loved but do not become any man or woman's thrall. Be a Spartan in an Athenian pelt, or all will be lost."

"I know my duty." Michael drew his dagger and knelt before the earl. "In blood I pledge my ever-binding fealty to you." He fisted the sharp-edged blade and was about to wrench it hard.

"Spare your hand. You will have need of it." Tyrone seized the dagger and walked over to a table laden with a gold chalice. "Come. Let us observe the proper rite of initiation. My son."

Pain and desiccation harbingered the sunrise. Michael came awake parched, sweaty, and in a state of excruciating agony. He shivered violently with cold, his skin burned, his heart palpitated madly, his brain screamed in torment, as if a thousand heated pokers cut through his flesh, and he was overcome with irrational terror. A roar of anguish tore from his throat to echo throughout the vaulted passageways, halls, staircases, and chambers of the vast castle.

The door to his bedchamber opened. Cáit, the pretty maid he bedded on occasion, rushed in to light candles. Pippin barrowed in an iron casket on a pulley and left it by the bedside. An old man marched over to examine Michael. He wore a black houppelande, a hoary beard masked half his face, silvery hair flew down his back. Dark eyes gleamed at Michael. "Hold him down!" he told the servants. "Laddy, my name is Donough O'Hickey. I will make you well again."

Michael thrashed wildly, flinging battle-hardened limbs pell-mell and arching fitfully off the mattress. Semidelirious, he fought the invisible hellhounds tearing him to shreds from the inside out like a baited bear. His two attendants lost the battle in restraining him.

"Jesu, he is burning up!" cried Cáit.

The old man took charge with superior strength. He jabbed one of Michael's eyelids open, felt his forehead, and probed at his mouth. "As I thought, food poisoning, same as His Lordship."

"Food poisoning?" Cáit exclaimed disbelievingly. "Looks more like the Sweat to me."

"I will give him a physic to cleanse his bowels of venom. Leave us. You may return later to clean him up. But mind, his ailment may not pass for a sennight. Food and drink are prohibited. He may only drink my physic until he is fit."

Michael howled in frustration. "Seven nights like this?" Cursing at the violent pain ravaging his mind and body, he glared at the old healer and growled, "Get this thing out of me now!"

Cáit patted his arm tentatively. "My dearest lord—"

"Come away, Cáit. Master O'Hickey knows his business." Pippin towed her out, the mere mention of the sweating sickness sprouting wings on his back.

The Irish healer removed a precious Italian glass bottle from the casket. "Alack, the serving wench had the right of it. I did not care to stir up panic and mayhem, for you and His Lordship are afflicted with the sweating sickness. This is the second stage of the disease. Cold shivers, aches and burns, apprehension, perspiration, delirium, megrim, heart palpitations, and intense thirst."

"The Sweat!" Michael lunged up, mad with terror. "You dotant! Why conceal the truth from my servants? They will infect the vill! Have you no care for babes, Celtic tinker?"

"Fables! The contagion is in the blood. The old sages knew it, but their wisdom was torched by savages. The disease is *venerius vīrulentus*. Know you Latin? What is *vīrus*, lordling?"

"Poison," Michael chocked, agitated, feverish.

"Precisely. You have consumed natural venom that had been put in your food, such as blood of a sickly rodent. See, I was partially untruthful with the tasty wench. You cannot infect others with your breath. Nor with skin contact. The illness lives within you. Your blood is dying. If it is not treated, you will perish in three days. Recovery may take seven nights. What is your choice?"

"Life!" A stab of pain arched Michael off the bed. When it subsided, icy tremors seized him.

"Interesting. That is the usual preference among my patients." The motley-minded O'Hickey shoved a hand beneath Michael's head and put the mouth of the bottle to his lips. "Drink this."

Panting, Michael complied. His first gulp of the medicament nearly ripped the inside of his throat. "Hell's broth! What is it? Blood and *uisce*?" Instantly he craved more.

"The blood of Grendel's mum! *He-he-he* . . . Lick your throat, did it?" O'Hickey cackled. "It is dragon's blood, a cordial of sweet wines, crushed pearls, lead powder, marshmallows, salt of Amen, coral, elder leaves, sorrel, linseed vinegar, worms, marigold, meadow plant, feverfew—"

"Enough!" The old rook's imbecility of mind was exacerbating his sufferance.

"Certes, if my potion is not to your taste, I could leech you. That is what they did last year in London when the plague smote them. They bled the sick three days afore they burned them."

Michael snatched the glass bottle and drained it in a long swallow. Sweetness suffused him. He fell back on the pillow, gasping for air, and closed his eyes as the palliative effect of the thick brew spread through his tormented body, soothing his flesh, his mind, his spirit . . .

"You will want to sleep now, little lord, but harken well. My lord of Tyrone says you are to England for the St. George's tournaments."

"I doubt I will partake of aught but my own funeral . . ." Michael heaved.

"In a sennight you will be as good as new. Better than new. You have a casketful of bottles and will need every drop to carry you through your adventures. Once a day you will have a fierce thirst on you, mayhap twice. Drink and be merry but do not let anyone find you out, nor transfer the contents into another vessel, for the elements will lose their curative qualities if not contained in glass. You may feed and drink properly but do not wet your drouth with aught else."

Michael realized the dotard had the right of it. None could know he had the plague, not even Pippin, who was to accompany him to court. His thoughts drifted. Through the mist he heard the Irishman say, "Ah, the forest of dreams beckons, and the worst to affright now lives within. . . ."

Michael's eyes flicked open at the sharp pricking at his gullet. Darkness filled his vision, but within two heartbeats he gained focus. A polished blade of a sword reflected silvery moonbeams. A shadowy form loomed over his bed. "Cockcrow in two hours, sunflower," Ferdinand informed him, malevolence thickening his raspy voice. "King Henry's court awaits your incompetence."

A woman moaned sleepily; a rounded bottom wiggled against his naked hip. Ah, Cáit. After seven days and nights of sweaty delirium, of ravaging pain inflicted by inner fire and imaginary stropped blades, of fighting off the effects of the poison with the remedy prescribed by the Irish healer, Michael emerged from his sickbed hungry for life. However, his fête was premature. He felt ill and thirsty all over again. He ached for O'Hickey's draught.

"Healed, sunflower?" snarled the bane of his existence, his sword point intentionally keeping Michael away from the glass bottles stored in the cupboard. "You are swyving harlots while your liege lord is dying."

"There is no shame in living, you spayed ox!" Michael growled. His triumph over death was eclipsed by his lord's ongoing battle with the disease. But what could he do? Tyrone would not see him. Stealthily he wound his hand in the sheet and reached for the dagger stashed under the mattress. Of a sudden he lunged up, deflecting the sword from his neck and pressing the dagger to his archrival's black heart. He met Sir Ferdinand's stunned gaze at eye level. "Rouse me at the tip of a blade again, and I will execute you, with or without my Lord Tyrone's permission."

"A harmless thunderbolt, a vain threat, a voice and nothing besides! We will meet again on the combat field upon your return from court! I will not be merciful as I have been hitherto!"

Michael shoved past him and sauntered to the cupboard across the spacious bedchamber. He ripped the doors open, grabbed a bottle, unsealed it with his teeth, and poured its contents down his throat. Cool air blew on his bare back.

"My lord would see you!" Sir Ferdinand growled from the entryway, and slammed the door.

Gasping for air, Michael leaned back against the wall and savored the sweet relief flowing in his body. His skin felt hot and febrile, the once pale complexion resembled a roasted swine. He knew he should be thankful, for few who were struck down with the Sweat survived it. It was a marvel he lived at all. Yet how could he journey to England, knowing his noble protector might never recover and that he might never see him again? And how would he prevail over the king's champions in his dismal state? He would not last a single course in the lists. He would disgrace his lord's insignia, lose Ireland to some trencher-knight, and make a laughingstock of himself.

Fortune favors the brave, Tyrone had taught him. Michael's mind cleaved to the maxim as the Irish villagers drew faith from their crucifix and weeping deities. Moments ago he had bested his archrival for the first time. Mayhap his luck was changing. He had to believe it.

"Come back to bed," Cáit whispered drowsily. "I'll give you a proper send-off."

His thirst slaked, a familiar hunger awakened. Michael came over and flung the bed linen off her curvaceous softness. He flattened his hands on either side of her and climbed in between her warm, parted thighs. "We'll have to be fast," he murmured, and invaded her lush country.

A mere shadow of a great man, the formidable Earl of Tyrone looked deathlike in the tawny candlelight silting his bedchamber. Tapestries depicting ancient battles swathed the stone walls. Swords, axes, and chieftain shields hung over the cold fireplace. Michael had not seen his worthy lord since the night he had gone up to the eyrie, the night they had both contracted the Sweat.

"Michael." Tyrone extended a feeble hand.

Michael knelt down beside the bed and clasped the veined

hand in his. His gaze darkened on the ugly incisions marring the skin along Tyrone's wrist. "O'Hickey leeched you? Why?"

"Make me proud at King Henry's court. Bring honor and glory to my house . . . and all that is mine shall be yours, riches and power beyond your wildest imaginings."

Terrible sorrow possessed Michael. "You are dying. . . ."

Tyrone found the observation amusing. "I am old. Certes I am dying. I have been dying for a long time. Pale death kicks with impartial foot at the hovels of the poor and the towers of kings. Oh, if only Jupiter could restore to me the years gone by. . . . I vow I shan't depart this life ere I see you again."

Michael drew a breath. "My lord, any words of wisdom to see me through the games?"

"Words of caution: practice modesty, gallantry, and reserve. Invite not the probing minds to meddle in your affairs. Conceal your purpose. Let no man discover your malady, nor its remedy. Keep your own counsel. Love not. Trust your senses and do not be afeared. I have given you the best of mine, my knowledge, my strength. Use my gifts wisely, discreetly. Here, take my ring. It will be your amulet. It belonged to my great Roman forebear who came to Britannia with the Ninth Legion and conquered a future under the golden standard."

Emotion choked Michael. He had never seen the ring leave the earl's forefinger before. The Tyrone arms under which he would compete in the tournaments displayed a rampant red eagle with golden talons over black. The emblem etched in the gold ring was of a serpent with the head and breasts of a woman and the wings of a dragon. Reverently he removed it from the anemic hand and slid it onto his. Anticipation flavored with apprehension urged him to be on his way.

"I suggest you conceal this ring from the eyes of the court, for the pagan symbol may offend their Christian sensibilities and condemn you to suspicion and reproach. Remember, you are no fondling, Michael Devereaux, future Earl of Tyrone, though you may seem so. Appearances may deceive, words may deceive, and even actions deceive. You will see what others cannot. You will know their lies. You will taste their fears and desires. Use them, beguile them, but never let yourself be fooled. Let not idle pursuits deflect you from the course you are on. I took a fearless boy and forged him into a fearsome man. What you most desire is always within your grasp."

"I'm your liege man. I feal to you in all things, my noble lord. Your desires are my desires."

The earl's dark, sunken eyes gleamed with pride and affection as he patted Michael's head. "My golden boy. You are a good son, dutiful and clever. You know what you have to do."

❧ 2 ❧

Splendidly false, nobly untruthful.

—Horace: *Odes III*

The Royal Château in Amboise, France

"Move your feet, little whore!"

Princess Renée de Valois of France, wishing the varmint taking her by the arm ten fathoms deep, staggered out of her apartment with a sheet wrapped around her nude body. Mortification cooled her fury as she caught sight of the sea of goggling eyes, noble and common, enjoying the spectacle: the late King Louis's youngest daughter being dragged in dishabille along the gallery like a condemned prisoner to the execution block. Bedraggled, quivering, ebony tresses tumbling in a tangle to her waist, she lacked only the crown of nettles to complete her shame.

Behind her, her beloved Raphael was being marched by the royal guards, his untidy clothes smeared with multihued paints, for he had been interrupted while creating a new masterpiece for which she provided the subject matter: Froward Renée, whom the court would henceforth dub "the wanton princess who shamed the Valois," had been posing for a Venus.

The Duke de Soubise, her tormentor, smiled with cruel satisfaction as the crowd parted to clear a path for them toward King Francis's apartment. Renée held her head high, deploying the majesty impressed upon her by Queen Anne of France, Duchess of Brittany, her dearly departed mother. She disregarded the leering faces marveling at her degradation; she ignored the orphaned girl inside her, desperate to crawl into a hole and weep. She had none to blame but herself.

Soubise had merely taken advantage of her foolish temerity. It never occurred to her that the besotted old lecher, whom she deemed an innocuous pest, would burst upon her with guards issued by Long-Nose. Alas, while she had been savoring her first affaire de coeur, the great love of her life, Soubise had been plotting his coup de grâce down to the last detail. She was doomed.

Renée remembered the sweet-tempered, dutiful little princess she had once been. That girl would never have conceived of taking a pauper for a lover, but she had not been herself since her mother passed away three winters hence. She loved her sweet mother, heart and soul, and would gladly have traded places with her rather than endure the pain of watching her waste away of an illness. King Louis, upon glimpsing his youngest daughter's grief the first day of her mother's funeral, ruthlessly commanded Renée to compose herself, muttering in her ear, "If a single tear should roll upon your cheek in the common gaze, you will cease to be a daughter of mine."

Queen Anne's funeral lasted forty days. Forty days of hell during which Renée mourned her mother's demise in secret, in terror of discovery, and in absolute solitude. Afterward, in the spirit of her mother's fiercely independent nature, she cut the reins imposed on her by a heartless sire, becoming refractory, bold, and feisty insomuch that King Louis felt hard-pressed to contract an immediate new marriage alliance for his fifteen-year-old shrew of a daughter. As her betrothed, Prince Andres of Navarre, had died in battle, her royal sire settled on the aged Duke of Lorraine, who thereupon accommodated Renée in passing away before the ink dried on the settlement. Oh, he could have married her against her will, but he knew she would be back within the month and that he would have to bear the brunt of whatever trickery and mischief she had applied to be free.

She distinctly remembered her father telling her that she would be the death of him when no other groom could be found to take her off his hands. A war had been declared between them. To wear her spirit down and convince her to seek refuge in the arms of a

husband, he kept her at his side, employing her in all sorts of te-
dious matters of state that tested her fortitude and patience.

Two years later he had lost the battle and perished. Of exasperation, Renée presumed, albeit others claimed that his aged body
expired from "overexertion in the bedchamber" while in the
throes of his last desperate attempt at begetting a male heir off his
third and very young wife, Lady Mary Tudor, King Henry VIII of
England's sister, who had become Renée's bosom friend.

"Froward Renée," King Louis called her at his deathbed, an epithet that had somehow found itself into the mouths of the court
and stayed with her. "You think you take after your mother, but it
is I you resemble. Were it not for Salic Law, which precludes
women from ascending to the throne of France, I would see you
on mine, my daughter."

"My sister Claude is the eldest," Renée reminded him. "She
has precedence."

"And the wits God gave a cow," her father stated with disgust.
"Claude the Cow."

Not once did Renée miss him after his death.

Lamentably, as soon as Long-Nose inherited the crown, she had
a new betrothed. A German prince, rumored to be crablike and
malformed. She disposed of him easily. Well-placed whispers as
regards poison effectively put him off the idea of marrying her.
King Francis was outraged.

"You look fetching, Renée, a veritable goddess of love," said the
decrepit Soubise, smacking his lips. "Although I prefer you nude,
as you were a moment ago. A feast to mine eyes."

"Your eyes will be the first items I cut out, imbecile!"

"This is the Lady Marguerite's influence. She has odd notions
of a woman's place at court. All that free thinking and free spirituality and free love . . ."

Renée shot Soubise a sulfurous glare. Lady Marguerite of Angoulême, King Francis's older sister, was a patroness of the arts, of
humanists and reformers, a poetess and an author of plays. Her ac-
claimed salon, the New Parnassus, had become Renée's haven
after losing her royal parents to God and her older sister Claude to
a new husband and an elevation to the throne of France. There

she had transformed from a lonely, malcontent, introverted girl to the lady she was meant to be. "I am certain His Majesty will be interested in your opinion on his lady sister, Soubise."

"You mistake me, *ma petite*. I'm grateful to my king's lady sister for delivering you into my clutches. Fear not, we'll continue to practice her notions of love indefatigably. They would say at court, 'The radiant young princess of the violet-blue eyes has become the loving lady wife of—'"

"An ancient wittol with maggots for brains!" She let out a cry as tentacles bit into her flesh.

"Better me than no man, for no illustrious prince would have you for a wife, Princess Lust."

She made the mistake of glancing at him—seeing the covetous lust in his rheumy eyes, the spittle foaming in the corners of his mouth, the sagging dewlaps of his pockmarked visage—and almost retched. A more repulsive creature did not exist at court.

Her bare feet pattering along the cold stone, Renée looked back at the swarthy young man prodded onward by pikes at his back. *Raphael, save us!* Her eyes spoke in silent supplication. Her lover's head wilted. Was he crying? His frailty incensed her, disgusted her. As much as she admired his artistic gentleness, at that moment she needed him to be the stronger of the two of them. Then it dawned on her that his penance would be much worse than a hair shirt, for he, a common painter, had dared to carnally know a princess of the blood.

As a rule, a lady caught with a lover who was not her husband was banished to a nunnery—a lady caught in bed with her spouse became an object of ridicule—and the lover paid his dues in a duel instigated by either the horned husband or the enraged father. As for princesses of the blood, the matter was a trifle more complicated. Certes, daughters were less welcome to their royal sires than sons, but they were useful currency in acquiring thrones and land, as in the case of Renée's mother. A princess's maidenhood was a valuable national asset.

Renée, an unwed princess, was setting a precedent in taking a lover, and a nonentity at that. Custom dictated that her defiler be charged with high treason and put to death. Poor Raphael. What did he know of court intrigue, power plays, and betrayed confidences? He was but a poor painter from a village in Perugia, who carved out a life for himself by the skill of his brush. She would have to defend him, but how? Would King Francis spare Raphael if she surrendered the two boons he was after—her body and a renunciation of her claims to the duchy of Brittany?

You fool, she could hear her royal sire berating her, *have I taught you nothing?*

"Here we are," the Duke of Soubise announced as the royal bodyguard thrust open the doors to the king's privy chamber. Keeping her spine ramrod straight, Renée walked in.

King Francis sat at a table with his sister Lady Marguerite. Cardinal Medici lounged in the bay window. Renée's sister, Queen Claude, was conspicuously absent. Soubise nudged Renée to the center of the luxurious chamber, genuflected fulsomely, and launched into a detailed account of the compromising scene he had come upon. Explaining about the painting would be pointless, Renée knew, for she would be subjected to a physical examination. The king and his sister wore flinty expressions. Suspicion buzzed in her head. In his peroration, the toadying, impudent duke magnanimously offered himself as her savior in marriage. King Francis dismissed Soubise with an ambiguous promise to consider his suit and ordered the guards to place Raphael under arrest. Lady Marguerite sent a page to fetch Renée a cloak and shoes, for which Renée was grateful.

Still their dignified astonishment did not ring true.

King Francis cleared the chamber of his attendants so that only Marguerite, Cardinal Medici, and Renée remained. "We are appalled!" he blasted away at her. "Your wantonness shames us in the eyes of the world! Neither maid nor wife, your name a scandal, your honor slain—we are of a mind to exercise the severest form of penalty. Henceforward your ample dowry and annuities are revoked, your defiler will be trialed for high treason, and you will marry the Duke of Soubise!"

Renée, practicing the sangfroid bequeathed to her by her royal sire, listened and wondered how Long-Nose expected to govern France when a child could see through this charade. The son of a minor French prince, Francis of Valois came to the throne by right of birth strengthened with his marriage to Claude. Though he was generally considered a humanist and a man of letters, Renée knew him to be a man of slight morals. Her father once told her that when something looked like a trap and smelled like a trap, it was a trap. Soubise's catching her *en flagrante delicto* was no accident.

"Your Majesty." She sank to her knees, head bowed penitently. "She who is undeserving of your bounty and grace kneels before you in shame, humbled by your benevolence."

Her quiet submission threw her spectators into a confused silence. Cardinal Medici stepped away from the bay window. "Does she speak English?"

"She is fluent in English, Latin, Greek, Spanish, and Italian," Lady Marguerite replied.

The cardinal lifted Renée's chin. "Are you intimate with personages at the English court?"

Renée studied him charily. Pope Leo X's first cousin and designated successor, raised by his uncle, Lorenzo Il Magnifico of Florence, the godfather of the illuminated era they lived in, was not the transparent buffoon Long-Nose was but of her sire's ilk. "I correspond with the Dowager Queen of France, the newly remarried Duchess of Suffolk. Lady Mary and I are friends."

The cardinal helped her to her feet. "Show me your teeth."

Renée was taken aback. "Am I a horse—"

"Do as His Grace bids you, insolent girl!" Lady Marguerite scolded.

Renée's amazement doubled. So, she thought, Soubise spoke the truth. Lady Marguerite had a hand in this. Sweet Jesu! Was Raphael involved as well? No, his petrifaction had been genuine. He loved her; he would never betray her. In contrast, Lady Marguerite was low and deceitful. Simmering with resentment, Renée offered the cardinal a toothy smile.

"Good, good." He nodded. "Now remove the portmanteau. . . ."

Her eyes narrowed into slits. "I am cold."

"It would take a minute, no more."

Reluctantly, she dropped the cloak.

"And the bedsheet."

Renée felt her jaw slackening. She jutted her chin defiantly. "I refuse."

"Then we will summon a guard to do it for you." The Lady Marguerite snapped her fingers.

Renée flushed. She wasn't timid—she was livid! How dare they insult a princess of France? Thoughts flew like darts through her head. She glowered scornfully at King Francis. The lustful degenerate had untiringly attempted to unclothe her for months. It galled her that he should now get his wish, leastways part of it. "By the rood, what is this about?" she demanded to know.

"None of your concern, at the moment," the cardinal replied calmly. "The sheet."

"Guards!" Marguerite called, jolting Renée.

"Call them off!" Renée hissed. She did not stir until she heard the doors close. If these three jades insisted on examining her as one would a broodmare, she would give them a good show of backbone. Her revenge would be all the sweeter for it in the end. They truly had no idea whom they were dealing with. She leveled a cool gaze at the cardinal, burying her humiliation in a dark place, and, with a smile of contemptuous superiority, efficiently divested herself of the sheet. It sashayed off her body to pile at her ankles. "There." She straightened her spine unabashedly, a gesture that made her small breasts jut. She wanted to die. "Do I please Your Graces?"

Cardinal Medici perused her swiftly and looked away. "Tell me of her character."

King Francis, who short of rape had done everything within his power to lay her and failed, scrutinized her at length. She felt his lascivious gaze slide over her breasts, belly, *mons veneris*, thighs, and legs like unwanted hands. "She has all the wiles and guiles of an expensive whore—"

A gasp of indignation escaped Renée's lips. The lying cur!

"—the proud willfulness of her mother, and the deceitful practices, tricks, and stratagems of her sire," King Francis added bitterly, his eyes on Renée's body.

The cardinal searched her eyes. "How many lovers have you had, Renée?"

She sucked in her breath. "I am not a whore!" she ground out emphatically, not the least bit cowed yet exceedingly froward. "If you think to push me into the bed of a poxed—"

"Just the one," Marguerite replied for her. "She fancies herself in love with the painter."

Cardinal Medici shot Francis a glare. "Experienced in the art as a professional *cortigiana*?" What false promises had Long-Nose made the cardinal and why? Renée cared to know. "Mayhap it is better this way. Men can tell the millage on women. Pure-looking is good."

"Pure!" Lady Marguerite huffed. In millage she surpassed a hackney—and knew it.

"I am chilled," Renée clipped. "I would be of no use to you if I died of lung rot."

"You may cover yourself," the cardinal permitted. As she wrapped the sheet and cloak about her, he said, "The Florentine ambassador described you as a delightfully witty, educated girl of angelic beauty and grace, a replica of the queen your mother, which you are. He said you were not for the distaff and praised you for knowing the secrets of diplomacy. Has she talents, skills?"

"She declaims playwrights, philosophers, poets, and theologians from memory," Marguerite replied curtly. "She dances and sings skillfully and accompanies her singing on the lute. She has an eye for art and is a sharp cardplayer. There is no end to her artful accomplishments."

A direct hit! Renée could have strangled the woman she had hereto considered her doting benefactress.

"Convent-bred?" asked the cardinal.

"Fah!" Marguerite fleered. "Queen Anne refused to part with her little talisman. After Her Grace died, King Louis took an interest in the girl. He called her 'my precocious child, created in my image.' She became the keeper of his secrets and a shrewd dissembler. I do not know what he hoped to gain by sowing her mind with needless information. He created a most disagreeable creature no prince would have. A woman to be treated with caution, Your Grace."

Renée seethed. She was *nothing* like her father! She was her mother's daughter! "Jesu, pity! What is it you want from me? Let us speak of it and be done!"

"Pray do not expect her loyalty," Marguerite added. "She keeps faith with no one."

"I kept faith with you!" Renée cried bitterly. "How confoundedly imbecilic of me!"

"Her loyalty is the least of my concerns, for that can easily be bought." The cardinal took a seat behind the table and filled a goblet with wine. "She is very young. That is my sole concern. Albeit . . . her purity and inexperience make her the perfect instrument, for who would suspect a fresh young thing to be anything other than what she appears to be?"

King Francis looked pleased as a swine in mud. "Sister, we should like to offer you a way to redeem yourself in our eyes and regain our favor."

Aha! The negotiation part, at last! "Am I to be sent to a nunnery?" Renée asked tartly.

"The good Lord offers sinners countless ways to redeem themselves," Cardinal Medici said. "A girl who wishes to atone for the sin of licentiousness takes the veil, but you are not penitent, are you? You regret getting caught."

Renée smiled pertly. "Mayhap I should atone for my sin of incompetence." She was already in so much trouble she doubted her insolence could exacerbate her situation.

"You shall have ample opportunities to atone for that, my dear."

"Install you in a nunnery!" Long-Nose, as always a step behind, scoffed. "How long before you escape to your mother's relatives in Brittany and raise an army against me, *hein?*"

"I would never commit treason against France!" Renée vowed, and meant it.

"Let us discuss your reward."

"My reward?" Renée blinked in surprise at the cardinal. What had she missed?

"Should you succeed," he clarified.

"In what?"

"I will double your annuity," Long-Nose announced.

"As payment for doing what?" she dogged. This could not be good for her health.

"And your lover will be spared," the cardinal interposed. "Upon your successful return."

"My return? From England?" Her heart drummed wildly. "But Your Graces will not tell me until we have set a price and I pledged my collaboration."

"Very good," the cardinal praised.

"I told you she was shrewd."

"I am not a whore!"

"This is not an office for a whore," Cardinal Medici assured her.

"I refuse regardless."

"Refuse now and your punishment will be as I have decreed," Francis replied. "Soubise, the death of your lover, and the loss of your annuity and dowry, mayhap even a charge of treason."

"Consent and you will profit. However"—Cardinal Medici's enticing tone turned flinty—"should you accept our offer and renege at a later date, your punishment will be death."

"You expect me to state my price and make my decision before I know the particulars?"

"Once our negotiation is concluded, we will have passed the point of no return," Cardinal Medici emphasized. "Should you fail and try to flee . . ."

"I never fail," Renée muttered dismissively, her mind feverishly weighing the pros and cons. How far would she go to secure her future? "Would I be asked to commit a mortal sin?"

"You will be asked to perform a holy duty," Medici asserted.

"Is spying on the English a holy duty?" she countered challengingly. She was aware of the risks she was running in conducting herself in this fashion, yet they were testing her.

"We are not asking you to spy," muttered the cardinal. "Yes or no? Decide now."

"If I am caught, the English will execute me. If I refuse, you will execute Raphael. If I fail, you will kill me. So, in effect, my only recourse is to accept your assignment and succeed."

"Yes!" the cardinal and the king responded cheerfully as one.

"In that case, I demand the duchy of Brittany and Raphael's freedom as my reward."

"You cannot have Brittany!" Francis thundered as Marguerite cried, "The nerve of this girl!"

Renée glared unflinchingly at Marguerite. "You are not the one being *asked* to risk her life." She regarded the king and the cardinal. "Whatever you would have me do, I set Brittany as my prize. Once my 'holy duty' is performed to your satisfaction, the queen my mother's titles and estates will be restored to me with a royal assurance that the right of succession will be passed to my issue, in female line. I will then leave your court and your realm."

An angry muscle twitched in King Francis's jaw. "The duchy of Brittany is within my realm, as it was within the realm of the king your father!"

"As decreed by Semi-Salic Law, the duchy of Brittany belonged to the queen my mother." Renée listed all the arguments her mother had plagued her father with before and after they were married. Her sire, resolved to absorb the duchy into his dominion, bribed Pope Alexander VI for a dispensation to put aside his wife, Queen Joan, and bullied Anne of Brittany into marrying him. Queen Anne refused until death to sanction the marriage of Claude to Louis's heir, pushing instead for an alliance with Luxembourg and for Brittany to go to Renée. Nevertheless, with his single-minded ruthlessness, Louis saw to it that the marriage of Claude and Francis took place in the year following Anne's death and kept Brittany within the grasp of the French monarchy.

"You cannot have Brittany," King Francis repeated decisively. "You shall be paid in gold."

"One has no use for gold within a prison. I would have my independence or nothing at all."

"This nothing includes Soubise," he reminded her. "And the death of your lover."

"So be it." Renée fixed him with her notoriously stubborn glare.

Cardinal Medici seemed displeased with King Francis's maladroit handling of the matter. "I should like to remind Your Majesty that his contract . . . with the Medici Bank—"

"My dear Cardinal Protector of France!" cried Francis. "I won't pay for your triple tiara with civil war. For all her false vows of loyalty, once this malapert has Brittany, she will recoup her mother's sovereignty and break from France. I will lose a considerable share of my taxes and have a Franco-Breton war on my hands. No amount of Florentine gold is worth the trouble."

Renée smiled. Medici gold in exchange for trebucheting Medici into the chair of St. Peter's. She was eager to see which one of them would cave in first. Her purse was on the buffoon.

"You may have the duchy of Chartres," Long-Nose relented, as expected.

Pedantically she replied, "His Majesty has already dowered me with Chartres."

"Revoked! But, if you are satisfactorily obedient, we shall let you keep it."

"May I be excused?" Renée stared him in the eye. "Soubise is waiting."

The cardinal glared at Francis, who grudgingly offered, "Chartres and lands near Nantes."

Was it his last ditch-stand, Renée wondered, or would the millions in gold the Medici Bank of Florence was willing to pay to instate another Medici pope after Pope Leo X moved to higher pastures prove too tempting to refuse? "Your Graces, I fear me you have placed too great a store in my capabilities. I am but a woman—frail, docile, meek, ignorant of the world—"

"Fah!" said Marguerite. "A headstrong trickster is what you are!"

"What if I were to disappear somewhere between France and England and never return?"

"You could, but then you will have forfeited Brittany, as well as your lover, and be forever on the run," the cardinal reasoned softly.

Renée plunged on. "If I refuse, I die. If I fail, I die. If I succeed, I shall be in mortal danger. Your Graces leave me with little to lose. Anything short of Brittany is not worth the trouble."

Long-Nose addressed the cardinal. "How will you compensate me for Brittany?"

"Double the figure we agreed upon."

"Treble it."

"Done." The cardinal beamed. "My dear girl, you will travel to England, perform your holy duty, and upon your return, you shall be vested Duchess of Brittany."

"And Chartres," Renée amended. "I require this in writing, validated with Your Graces' seals, and I will be vested *before* my departure." She smiled prettily. "If it please Your Graces."

Marguerite's face turned beet red. "You . . . impudent, insubordinate, froward girl!"

Yes, always froward. Renée sighed, dreading to hear what precisely she had agreed to.

Cardinal Medici offered her a wine cup. "Here's to the success of your mission, *Your Grace*!"

Renée forced herself to sip, not gulp the calming rosé and prayed she would not become the shortest-living duchess in the history of Brittany and Chartres. "Your Graces, now that all is settled between us, I should like to know the particulars of my assignment. Surely you would not be so generous were I to merely spy on the English, for I am confident you have ambassadors aplenty."

"All in good time," said the cardinal, and sent for one Lieutenant Armado Baglioni.

What could it be? Renée's brain spun with possibilities. "Am I to steal the queen's jewels? The Great Seal of England, perchance?"

"I would send a thief for that."

"Poison the Lord Chancellor?"

The cardinal laughed. "I would send a poisoner. Ah, Lieutenant Armado. Madame, meet the commander of your personal bodyguard."

The Italian officer bowed. A pendant dangled from his neck. It was a gold cross over black. Renée eyed it with interest. "Your family emblem, Lieutenant?"

"No, madame. The insignia—" A hiss from Cardinal Medici hushed him.

She snorted. "If the emblem is so secretive, I suggest you leave it behind, Lieutenant."

"Sound advice," the cardinal agreed. "I have made ready special quarters for Your Grace at my chateau. I suggest you depart now."

"Who is to be my official escort to England?" she queried. "I must arrive with an embassy."

The overlords of her universe exchanged baffled looks. They had not considered this detail.

"Choose whomever you want," the king granted peevishly.

"The Marquis de Rougé, with a caveat."

"What caveat?" the king, the cardinal, and the king's lady sister demanded in unison.

"A little one."

❧ 3 ❧

We have all played the fool once. . . .

—Mantuanus: *Eclogues*

Greenwich Palace, London, April 1518

The Yeomen of the Guard, fine-looking giants armed with great swords, silver breastplates, and gilt halberds, stood to attention as Cardinal Wolsey entered the king's state apartments with a purposeful stride. The doors to the guard room, the presence chamber, and the privy chamber were flung open, one after the other, as if blown ajar by his stormy frame of mind.

The grooms of the chamber, supervised by the sergeant of the hall, ceased their labors—scrubbing the oaken floors of leakages and dried mud, replenishing the fire pans with faggots, unfurling fresh saffron-scented rush matting, and airing the rooms before the king arose—to bow to His Grace. The ushers guarding the privy chamber announced him to the gentlemen outside the royal bedchamber, waiting to array King Henry with freshly brushed clothes, and those alerted the esquires sleeping on palliasses in the anteroom.

Richard Pace, Wolsey's erstwhile secretary who now sedulously served the king, met him outside the bedchamber door. "Carew is back. By commandment. Too soon, after mine opinion."

"Most unfortunate," replied the cardinal *sotto voce*, an undertone he and Pace had perfected during the years the secretary was formally in his employ. "He is working against me, I know it. Keep me apprised of his utterances. Unfortunately, greater evils are descending upon us, next to which Carew is but a pesky gadfly. Mind, a thousand eyes and ears open, Pace. No detail is too small for my scrutiny." Without further ado, he proceeded inside the royal bedchamber.

Ordinarily Wolsey would send a message to King Henry requesting a private audience to discuss state business and to inquire where his king would receive him. Not this time.

"Wolsey!" His young master, a strapping, auburn-haired man of seven and twenty summers, whom the cardinal had not seen since January, was wearing naught but his slops, having just risen, and a jolly countenance. "Good morrow, my good cardinal! How have you done since last we saw at Christmas? We have wondrous tidings, my lord!" Of a sudden the king's cheer ebbed. "What is it, Wolsey? Why the ashen face? Tell me now!" The doors opened as a pair of knights, replacements of the night esquires, arrived to assist the king in his morning ablutions. "Out!"

With apologetic murmurings, the doors closed. The cardinal bowed humbly. "Your Majesty, I give you good day and beg Your Grace's pardon that I need must upset—"

"Pray, to the point, my Lord Chancellor."

"Your Majesty, I have it on good authority that some unknown evildoers are plotting against Your Grace. My Lord Bishop of Worcester, who is traveling on the continent, reports that during his visit to an astrologer the French king is wont to consult on occasion, three tall men, English, he supposed, came into the astrologer's chamber on some mysterious errand, stayed there briefly, and then left by a secret way. Shortly thereafter my lord bishop heard that these men went to King Francis and offered to kill Your Grace for him."

"The devil!" cried his king, outraged. "You shall find these knaves and bring them to me!"

"Yes, Your Majesty. I have already sent able men to find them. As for the second rumor."

"God's teeth! There is more?"

"My spy at Lyons testifies in an urgent dispatch that he has seen the pretender Richard de la Pole riding together with King Francis, deep in conversation. He relates a most disturbing tale that King Francis is determined to send assassins to Your Grace's court to set fire by crafty and cautelous means within the house wherein Your Majesty shall be abiding, to the intent, which God forbid, to destroy His Grace's most noble person and all other there being present. De la Pole has promised the malefactors a reward of four thousand francs."

King Henry swore through fine, clenched teeth. "Is that all?"

"Alack, no, Your Majesty, I regret to say. Further investigation on my part suggests another assassin is on his way from an unspecified harbor with instructions to infiltrate the ranks of those coming to partake of the Order of the Garter's celebrations and harm Your Grace's person. This account frays me the most, for it reveals careful planning and a strong intent. As of yet, I have not been able to determine whether the sinister author of the foul plot is foreign or domestic, although I suspect he retains insidious sympathizers among Your Grace's companions, persons desirous of usurping your rightful throne, ready to aid and abet the assassin on English soil."

"The pox to them!" King Henry bellowed. "You must discover the subversive elements in my court, Wolsey, so that I will make an example of them for others entertaining like designs!"

"I would advise Your Majesty to restrict the numbers attending at court. Howbeit, as such measures may not be possible during the annual chapter, I have taken it upon myself to compose a list of individuals who may have sufficient cause to conspire against Your Grace."

The king waited, his light blue eyes, inherited from his grandam's grandsire, Prince John of Gaunt, King Edward III's son, ablaze with royal effrontery and Plantagenet wrath.

"I suggest we make good watch on the Duke of Buckingham, my Lord Northumberland, my Lord Derby, my Lord Wiltshire, and on others whom Your Grace may think suspect."

"Buckingham! That warmongering, bilious malcontent! He runs his domains like a kingdom within my kingdom, maintains an army twice the size of mine own, and has his henchmen kiss his ringed hand before speaking to him! I shall have him banished from court!"

"If he is the mastermind, as I suspect he is, it will be wiser to keep him close and watched."

"Yes, of course. You are the coolheaded betwixt us, Wolsey. Apply yourself to spying on His Grace and report to me of your findings. As for Northumberland, why suspect him?"

"My Lord Northumberland was recently fined for swelling his retinue and thus exceeding the tolerable number of armed retainers. He did not like it and was heard muttering treason."

"Pestilent traitors! I was about to tell you privily that the queen my wife is with child!"

Wolsey, unhappy bearer of bad tidings, feigned utter and joyful astonishment. "*Ave Maria gratia plena! Benedictine*, Your Highness! England shall rejoice to no end! Please allow me to be among the first to congratulate Your Graces." He bowed effusively in a puddle of scarlet robes.

"I thank you for the good wishes, Cardinal. *Deo gratias*, I shall have a son. Alack, your news now hangs over mine own as a black cloud that eclipses all happiness."

"My beloved king, I am aggrieved that my haunting worries have destroyed such happiness. The reasons for my mistrust, to which none are privy but Your Majesty and me, are so grave and secret that I could not, in good faith, keep still. But now I think upon it, mayhap Her Majesty, God give her health, ought to repair to a safer place until the other matter is resolved."

The King of England planted fists on hips, his glare as formidable as his person. "*We* do not dance to the piping of traitors, Wolsey. You find them. I shall hang, draw, and quarter them."

Traffic was heavy on the river Thames. Dignitaries coming to attend the opening feast of the annual chapter of the Order of the Garter poured out of spruced barges in their colorful silks and satins, gold-trimmed velvets and brocades, fur-lined cloaks, and extravagant jewels.

Sitting atop Archangel at the head of a small retinue, Michael observed officious mothers reminding their youthful daughters to smile, dance, and flirt with influential personages and do their best to attract the attention of Their Majesties. He saw courtiers re-

newing acquaintances and forming new alliances, making over-
tures at the ladies and boasting of their successes in the hunt, in
money schemes, and in the tourneys of the bedchamber. Gossip
spiced serious topics, such as quarrels, marriages, deaths, obtaining
patronages, offices, lands, preferments, and privileges.

Michael, feeling acutely incongruous, was nevertheless aware
he had one thing in common with the rest of them. He, too, had
come to court in search of something.

His lord had assured him that his superior combat skills and
comprehensive education would compensate for minor deficien-
cies, such as his not being familiar with a single soul at court, and
that his presence would command attention by sheer merit. His
trunks carried the richest clothes, the finest armor, premium uten-
sils, a treasure in coin, and his secret potion. "And you have you,"
his lord had said with a confident gleam in his eye. "One may lose
all and regain tenfold, so long as one has faith in one's abilities. Be
true to the man you are, Michael. You may surprise yourself."

Michael stirred his horse and retinue toward the palace courtyard, where armed guards in red and black uniform struggled to
repel a swarm of petitioners begging entrance, shouting names, titles, affiliations to this and that, the mighty men of the court, as
well as wide-eyed Londoners jostling for a peek at the lords and
ladies of the realm, and create a path for the dignitaries to traverse.
An officer assessed Michael's flaunts, horse, and attendants, and
shouted to let the great lord through. Pleased, Michael herded his
small cavalcade through a whirlwind of bad odors—the fetid stench
of the ragged poor mingling with the cloying perfumes of the overscented—into the chaotic middle court. Servants displaying various liveries and badges rushed hither and yon, carrying trunks,
walking horses to the stables, and endeavoring not to tramp on
their betters.

Michael swung off Archangel's back and tossed the reins to his
groom. His first business was with the king's receiver. King Henry,
having been crowned on St. George's Day, considered it his official
birthday. Lord Tyrone, conscious of this fact, had sent the king a
precious, delicate, and very garrulous gift. A survey of the courtyard pointed Michael in the right direction, for he was not the only

one who was come bearing gifts. He beckoned two of his hired porters to follow him with the canvas-wrapped cage and approached one of the clerks sitting behind a long table.

"Good-den, I am Michael Devereaux. I bring a gift for His Majesty, courtesy of the Earl of Tyrone, Lord Lieutenant of Ireland."

"Please state the contents of His Lordship's gift, sir."

With a flick of his wrist, Michael unveiled the cage, causing quite a stir, inside and beyond. "Gerfalcons, goshawks, peregrines, tiercels, sparrowhawks, and merlins. Two of each."

The clerk grinned. "Like Noah's Ark."

Who the pox was Noah? Michael wondered as he noted with satisfaction the numerous faces crowding to have a look at the valuable items. The falcons, wearing tiny hoods and bells, their talons ribboned with red silk jesses, perched on fetter-locks and were heatedly discussing the weather. Michael was well aware the earl's gifts surpassed all others, in market value and style. As soon as Lord Tyrone got wind that King Henry, a renowned sportsman, had built a mews at Greenwich right next to his privy lodgings, the die was cast. The king would love his new birds.

Michael returned to his retinue in good cheer. Now for his second task: lodging. He stopped an idle stable hand. "Pray, lad, who assigns quarters in the palace?"

"Your Worship will want to see Riggs of the household." He indicated the man standing at the entrance to the palace, wearing a green badge, his nose buried in a ledger. The queue leading to Riggs was mostly composed of an influx of knights of the shire coming to pay homage to the king and hopefully to make an impression in the tournaments. Riggs turned most of them away. Not all the guests—who owned neither mansions in the Strand or near Westminster or Whitehall nor houses in the vicinity—were entitled to lodging at court for the duration of the chapter. Only those who had the patronage of powerful men, such as Michael's protector, Lord Tyrone.

"Conn." Michael beckoned his groom and gave him ale money. "See to Archangel."

The stable hand raised an expectant eyebrow. When naught occurred, he muttered peevishly, "Your Worship may bestow your men-at-arms at the inn down at the wharf. Attendants sleep with their masters, grooms in the public chambers in the undercroft. Come with me, Conn. We'll find this fine fellow a clean stall with fresh feed and get a jack of ale for us at the buttery hatch."

Aside from Conn and Pippin, who was supervising the porters unloading his trunks, Michael had no other retainers. When he voiced his qualms about traveling without men-at-arms, his lord laughed heartily and made an enigmatic remark about unfortunate pirates and highwaymen.

Michael set off toward the sergeant of the household when the sound of glass bottles clinking brought him to a halt. He could not, however, in all fairness, upbraid the porters for mishandling the casket, for he could tell they moved it with care. Still the resounding ring fried his nerves. Journeying with delicate breakables was a nuisance. Italian glass was costly and rare because of the hassle involved in transporting it. Only the wealthy owned such pieces, and they dared not roam the countryside with boxfuls of them. It would have been sensible to empty the bottles into a barrel, but O'Hickey had insisted the physic would lose its remedial qualities if contained in a nonvitreous vessel. Michael had no choice but to adhere to the crazed graybeard's dictate.

His increasing dependency on the medicament was another nuisance. He was able to abstain for most hours of the day, but when the drouth came upon him moments before sunrise, his body demanded instant relief and would not be denied. If only he knew how long the vile, lingering effects of the Sweat would last so that he could regulate his consumption habits for the duration of the chapter and maybe longer. He had great things to accomplish and tremendous obstacles to overcome. Good health did not ensure his success; feeling poorly would guarantee his failure.

The sudden ringing crash sent his heart plummeting to his feet. He whipped around and saw one of the porters flat on the ground, embracing the large casket to his chest. His helper stood by, looking guilty and frightened. "Your pardon, sir. The great burden slipped my hand."

Crouching beside the casket, Michael yanked off a leather cord from around his neck and inserted a small key into the lock. "All of you, around me in a circle, backs to me, eyes ahead."

The men clustered around him, no one daring to steal a look, not even the porter cushioning the casket. Terrified that his arsenal of dragon's blood was destroyed, Michael lifted the lid and pushed a gentle hand beneath the batch of straw to stroke each felt-padded bottle. No cracks, no leakage. Relief surged through him—then disgust. What wretched, pitiful weakness, to be thusly enamored of a cordial! The very idea of living in a bottle's thralldom like the Irishmen with their *uisce* contrasted with the principle of self-discipline and the sense of purpose his noble lord had instilled in him since boyhood. To need something was demeaning; *craving* something, as if his life depended on it, was torment. Once he fulfilled his pledge to the dying earl, Michael vowed, he would cleanse his mind and body of this imprecation or die trying!

He locked the casket and retied the leather cord around his neck. He looked at the sprawled porter. "How now, man? Still breathing?"

"Aye, sir." The man smiled faintly. The casket was perched on his muscled abdomen.

Michael made a mental note to reward the man for rescuing his bottles. First, however, he should liberate him. He clasped the iron handles, braced himself, and carefully lifted the casket with the intention of placing it on the ground. He had a moment of shock. Nonplussed, he glared at the maladroit porter who had dropped the casket. Great burden his arse! Scheming laggard! Did he think to fleece him for extra coin? He hoisted the casket effortlessly and shifted it to ride on his hip. The porters staggered back, round-eyed. Fools! They never imagined he might handle the casket himself and discover how light it was. With an oath, he paced off toward the sergeant.

Someone shoved past him. "What hoa!" the man bellowed, fingering a tear in his popinjay-colored, gilt-embroidered, knops-cluttered, fur-lined sleeve. It was a fashion Michael detested. The man shot him a fuming glare. "One-trunk-inheriting, out-of-town clod! Mind your step!"

"Apologies." Michael bowed stiffly, mindful of the bottles rattling on his hip.

"Apologize to your Maker, blockhead! I demand an angel for the damage you've wreaked!"

"You should not try to push by a man with a load, regardless of your eagerness to make your obeisance to the king. Find a wench to stitch you up."

The popinjay blocked his path, his dander up. "I find this an occasion to withdraw unto some private place where we might settle our differences."

Michael took the man's measures. A few inches shorter, a few years older, his light fair hair shorn close to the scalp, as seemed to be the fashion with the courtiers swaggering about. His eyes were a light brown, and there was something familiar about him. "Have we met before?"

The man's expression switched from livid to circumspect. "I do not think so!"

"Stop pothering, Walter. What is amiss?" A woman, fair and tall, wedged herself between them. She examined the rip in the eyesore of a doublet. "Oh, it is nothing. I shall beg needle and thread from the queen's ladies and stitch it for you."

"There you go!" Michael smirked at the peacock.

The woman lifted light brown eyes to Michael and blinked in bewilderment. "Hello."

The physical resemblance between her and the surly popinjay told Michael they were brother and sister. He sketched a careful bow. "My lady."

Walter looked apoplectic. He took her arm. "Come away, Meg!"

Meg stood pat, perusing Michael with curiosity. "Pray, sir, what may I call your name?"

"Michael Devereaux, your servant, lady." He inclined his head, liking her vivaciousness.

"Devereaux!" brother and sister exclaimed in unison.

Walter demanded sharply, "Whence are you, sir?"

"From Ireland, not that it is any of your business. I do not recall hearing your name, sir."

Meg opened her mouth to speak. Walter shushed her curtly.

Pinning Michael in his glare, he wrapped Meg's hand around his arm and said, "Come, Margaret."

Towed toward the palace entry, Meg called out over her shoulder, "I was pleased to make your acquaintance, Michael Devereaux. Hopefully we shall speak anon. Adieu for now!"

"Adieu," Michael murmured, staring after her with a puzzled frown.

"Why so rude?" Meg snapped at her brother. "I wanted to know him better. He might be—"

"You are not to speak to that man again, Meg. I forbid it!" Years of humiliation, frustration, and poverty welled up in Walter with a vengeance. "You know I know best."

"No, I do not think you do, but I am not disposed to arguing with you now."

That was a first, he mused as they walked past Greedy Riggs. How he pitied those waiting in line for lodging, out-of-towners, nobodies, as he used to be afore securing the good lordship of the Duke of Norfolk. He remembered shabby hostels, rooms crammed with others like himself, sword arms for hire. But that was water under the bridge. Nowadays he and Meg occupied lavish chambers in Norfolk's demesne on the Strand. He hoped His Grace would make good on his word to obtain him a knighthood of the Garter as a first step in Walter's reclamation of his baronetcy of Chartley—which his fool of a father had lost in an act of attainder— and set his sister, recently widowed, among Queen Katherine's ladies. Meg was sweet, attractive, and clever. As a lady-in-waiting, her prospects of making a sensible match should increase tenfold. Abruptly he let go of her arm and retracted his steps to the shadows of the entryway. Concealed behind Riggs, Walter studied the so-called Michael Devereaux. He stood in line like a mannerly lad, gazing about him, hungering for every detail. Jolthead. "How now, Riggs," Walter murmured at the man's back.

Riggs did not lift his eyes from the ledger, though he probably knew exactly where his next lodger should be installed. Riggs enjoyed making his betters wait, plead, and break into a sweat at his scowling. It gave him a sense of power. It also lined his pockets with coin. "I give you good day, His Grace of Norfolk's master of the horse." Riggs snickered. "How may I serve you?"

"See the lumbering jackanapes at the end of the line, the one carrying his own trunk? He is new to this court, an Irishman. How would you like to practice pranks on him, my treat?"

His eyes still on the same page in the ledger, Riggs opened his hand behind his back.

Walter dropped a testril into it. "Good man, Riggs." His mood improved, he returned to his sister, and together they continued toward the king's presence chamber.

Michael was appalled. Mean was one word to describe the space he was allotted: stark brick walls blackened with soot, an earthen floor, meagerly furnished with a truckle bed covered with a rank palliasse, straw sticking out, and a three-legged stool. An anchorite cell, in the undercroft beneath the palace, where wine barrels were stored and servants quartered in public rooms.

Michael, standing at the threshold, the trunks containing his equipage stacked one atop the other beside him, his manservant and the porters pretending not to notice his discomfiture, refused to accept this was where he would be spending his nights. "But I'm on the list! Knights of the Garter are entitled to single or double lodgings at court for the duration of the chapter."

"Oh, I beg Your Worship's pardon! Sir Michael, was it? Or mayhap Earl Devereaux?" The sergeant perused his ledger again. "No. I have one Master Michael Devereaux." The ledger closed with a thud. The glint of mocking triumph in the sergeant's eyes bellied his innocent expression.

That drew blood. "While I am not yet bestowed with the cross of St. George, I act for my noble benefactor, the Earl of Tyrone, Lord Lieutenant of Ireland, who *is* a Knight Companion *and* a direct issue of the first lord ever to be vested Knight of the Garter by King Edward the Third!" When Riggs shrugged, maintaining the blank stare, frustration gnawed at Michael. He knew no one at court, none he could take this up with. "I am entitled to certain perquisites!"

"Your Worship is entitled to bouche of court, logs and toadstools for fire lighting, and a bed. This is a bed." He indicated the truckle bed nestling in the gloomy shadows of the sooty room. "Pray do not take it in a snuff, sir. I shall dispatch a lad with firewood posthaste."

In a snuff! "Wherefore should I have need of firewood, pray? I have no fireplace!"

The sergeant stuck his head inside the cell. It came out smiling. "Aren't you the sharp-eyed jack! I reckon Your Worship will break many a lance in the tournaments. Right. Won't be needing logs or faggots." He penciled a line in the ledger: *Master Devereaux will do without fire. No need to bother with him.*

Michael was lugubriously conscious of the fact that he was not especially fear-provoking. Pretty as a girl and fights like a girl, was Ferdinand's favorite gibe. Nevertheless, he was a grown man and a large one at that. One thing he had learned from his nemesis was that size alone had the power to intimidate. He loomed over the nasty man. "The accommodation is unacceptable to me. I would not bestow a dog in this pothole. Why should I put up with it my-self?"

The sergeant stilled for a heartbeat, but when he realized the great flaxen hound was all bark and no bite, he relaxed somewhat. "If Your Worship is discontented—"

"Supremely discontented!"

"Then I heartily recommend the Greyhound Inn. Howbeit"— he scratched his capped pate—"it may be overcharged and over-crowded, filled to capacity with foreign lords and ambassadors. It is the same everywhere this time of year. Every room snatched up by His Majesty's illustrious knights. Perhaps after the tournaments. The games are quite brutal, for some." He considered the men shuffling their feet nearby. "Your servants may sleep in the public chambers on this level, sir, and if the public haunts are over-stuffed, you had best bestow them at the wharf."

Michael considered relocating to a public room or to the wharf, himself. There, however, privacy would be nonexistent. How would he protect his bottles or excuse his fever fits at dawn? King Henry was reputedly terrified of death and disease. If word got out that Michael was ailing and dependent on dubious medicine, he would find himself in worse places than this room.

"Personages wishing to participate in this even's masque may see Sir Thomas Carwarden, master of the revels. The feast of the Garter is at nightfall, the masque at midnight. Godgigoden." Riggs fled, leaving Michael, his manservant, the porters, and a mountain of oaken trunks in the rat-infested corridor in the vaulted undercroft, standing under a smoking wall sconce.

There must be someone he could take this up with, Michael reflected in indignation. He had no intention of residing underground like a troll. Moreover, there would be no amusing dalliances in these woeful conditions. This and the fact that cleanliness would be nigh on impossible—was he expected to buck in the conduit in the courtyard?—rankled him. This being his first venture to court did not imply he was a churl and therefore undeserving of decent quarters. His attendance at the annual chapter was approved months ago. He was the legal heir to an earldom, the future de facto ruler of a country. His noble lord's primogenitor had been King Edward's most trusted ally in an overthrow of a usurper centuries ago, and in recognition of his invaluable contribution, his steadfastness and valor, King Edward had rewarded his friend the earldom of Tyrone and the first knighthood of the Garter. Michael's pride rebelled at the indignity. The dark fetid cell was unfit for a servant, let alone a future earl. Evading Pippin's gaze, he paid the porters. He was sourly tempted to try his luck at the overstuffed Greyhound Inn. Yet living at court was still in his best interest. He could hear Tyrone say: *The baser the beginning, the more praiseworthy the ascent to glory shall be.* So be it, Michael thought. From here the only way was up.

The downward stone steps, meanly lit and infested with rodents, spiraled hazardously under Renée's soft leather slippers as she furtively flew after Lady Anne Hastings's moving shadow. A truly pious lady-in-waiting who cleaved to her beads with perpetual Aves and Paternosters on her breath did not sneak into palace undercrofts like a thief in the night. Then again, according to the gossipmongers, Lady Anne had not always been a paragon of saintliness. The tattle on her was the stuff that kept tongues clacking for years. Apparently, when Anne came to court as the young bride of Sir George Hastings, she efficiently secured a position among the highest-ranking ladies in the queen's service and wormed her way into the king's bed. When her sister, Lady Elizabeth Stafford, a favorite of Queen Katherine's, discovered the love intrigue, she confided the truth to their brother, the mightiest lord and high steward of England. The Duke of Buckingham, proud, cantankerous, and feudally pugnacious, spewed his profane wrath on Sir William Compton, the king's erstwhile page and groom of the bedchamber who had negotiated the illicit assignations and had since risen to become one of the king's minions. Compton then hastened to find refuge under the wing of his royal master. The king, one leman short and out of favor with his indignant wife over the affair, chased off the irascible Buckingham with a flea in his ear and banished Lady Elizabeth from court very harshly, with scabs on her nose, labeling her an insidious spy. The horned Sir George Hastings installed his faithless wife in a nunnery and left court thereafter.

The affair had occurred three years ago. Now Lady Anne was back from her spiritual exile, using her newfangled godliness to play up to the devout queen, and skulking in murky cellars. It was Anne's furtive escape from the queen's grace in the privy garden that prompted Renée to go after the lady and spy out her business. One never knew what one might uncover. A child of the court, Renée was well aware that others' secrets were one's best currency, to be used in various enterprises to one's own advantage. Holding her heavy skirts high above the ground, she tiptoed in Anne's footsteps along the convoluted, torchlit tunnels and listened for sounds.

"Anne, in here," whispered a culture male voice, beckoning Anne into an alcove. So, Renée thought, the lady was up to her old tricks. "Did you make sure no one followed you?"

"Hello, Ned." Anne's tone was sulky. "What is it you wish to discuss with me so secretly?"

"Is this the greeting I get? No thanks for convincing your bitter-minded husband to take pity on you and let you out of the holy cage you have inhabited for the past three years?"

"You put me there!"

"'Twas your husband's doing. Hastings did not appreciate the horns you put on his head."

"It was your bloody-minded meddling that sent me to St. Mary's! What a nightmare! Three years of my life chafing my knees on cold stone to convince a flock of spiteful, decrepit virgins I was duly, penitently reformed! I shall never forgive you for this. Never!"

Renée, curious as to the identity of the man, peeked into the alcove. Ha! She knew it!

"You expect me to look the other way when you strumpet yourself in this brothel court with the usurper of my throne? He never cared for you, Anne. Making my lady sister his whore was another means wherewith to make me eat humble pie, to bring me to heel, to demonstrate to the court and to the entire world, for that matter, that we—the Lancastrians, the White Roses, the Poles, Abergavenny, progeny of purer Plantagenet blood—are nothing! That I am nothing! And now his henchman in scarlet robes, that overreaching venomous fox! That bawd! He has stolen my rightful role of chief adviser, curtails my policies, mocks and opposes everything I do on principle. He told his king that 'certain personages' were behaving in a manner that was not commensurate with the dignity and honor of the council. Fah! He spits in my face and is trawling for excuses to strike against me. How I disdain his ostentation, his presumptuousness. His very presence reviles me! He insults me openly, knowing his false king would protect him from my vengeance. I have sworn to rid myself—and England!—of them both, two boars in one valley."

"Ned!" Anne gasped, horrified. "Remember our father!"

"Our noble sire thought to play kingmaker, Anne. That was his error. He deposed a boy to make Richard of Gloucester king, and only when the deed was done, when he heard the shouts, *Verus rex, Rex Ricardus!* for Dickon, did it occur to him he had as much right to succeed Ned."

"Hush, brother, 'tis high treason you speak, and I would fain be excluded from your plots. Your hatred is showing. You are dangerous to be around." Anne made to leave.

Renée jumped back and froze. Ned's delaying his lady sister

with affectionate cajolery was not what fixed her to the spot—it was the fair-haired giant leaning against the wall beam across from her on the opposite edge of the alcove. He tipped his head in greeting, grinning lopsidedly.

Sweet Jesu, he was handsome: pleasingly proportioned, well groomed, with golden hair to his shoulders, bright eyes, and there was something very appealing about his mouth as he smiled at her. Saints, what was she thinking? She had been caught! But by whom?

Michael could not remove his eyes from the oval face and the gemlike eyes studying him in the dimness. Lavender and ambergris, her seductive fragrance misted his brain till he no longer cared what treason was being whispered inside the niche. She was young, wispy, parceled in a décolleté gown, diamonds glittering on her collarbones, glossy dark locks cascading to her waist.

Sweet tension gripped his body as she perused him with boldness, wariness, and calculation, trying to divine his identity and purpose in spying on the couple, as she was clearly doing.

Would she believe he had happened upon the intriguers by mistake? Having sent Pippin to the public haunts, locked his anchoritic dwelling—if the door hadn't had a lock, he would never have stayed—he had gotten drattedly lost navigating the stale, dim, subterranean passageways.

"Should he die without male heir, I shall easily take the throne," Ned was saying.

"Queen Katherine is pregnant again. Twice the sheet has come clean. Maria de Salinas says it's a boy. The king rejoices in secret and tomcats after Bessie Blount. Her Majesty spends every waking hour before her prie-dieu, afraid of a recurrence of the last time a prince was conceived."

Ned cursed venomously. "Who else knows of this?"

"Two, mayhap three of her closest women."

"Then I shan't wait. I will do it tonight, at the midnight masque, and you will help me."

"Me?" Anne cried in fright.

"Yes, you, the lady sister of the future king of England. Hark, Anne, I was told by a worthy prognosticator, a Carthusian monk by the name of Nicholas Hopkins, that the stars are aligned in *my* favor. He prophesies that the usurper of my throne should have no son and that I will succeed him. Already, I have begun to amass armed fighting men on the Welsh border. I bribed several of the yeomen of the royal guard with bales of cloth of gold and silver to do my bidding when the time is ripe. And that time is now. I am high on the public's mind in London and throughout my holdings. Anne, I tell you, the love this country has borne its king has been tempered by plague, taxes, and Henry's inability to produce a male heir. Discontent is rife amongst the nobles as well as among the common folk, for how could anyone trust a sovereign who lets inferiors serve in the work of governing? Look at his minions. Charles Brandon, the son of a standard bearer with a vein of ambition a mile wide, wields more influence over the usurper than any of us, nobles of ancient ancestry, vessels of true Plantagenet blood. William Compton, another minion, an orphan of the court. Who is he to garner offices and rake a fortune? Abergavenny and the Poles have sworn their allegiance to me. We would rather die than be ordered as we are now."

"Ned, our sire was attainted and decapitated for rebelling against Richard the Third. I beg you, brother, reconsider!"

High treason, Michael mouthed to his alluring cospy. She cocked an eyebrow in response, divulging none of her thoughts. Who was she? And who was this Ned, plotting to assassinate the king as if it were the solution to his quandary? The White Rose Lords were scions of the Plantagenet House of York, Michael knew, survivors of the gory civil wars that had raged between the royal houses of Lancaster and York for decades, ripping the country apart. Henry Tudor, a distant claimant to the throne on the Lancastrian side and the present king's royal sire, had defeated the last Yorkist king, Richard III, Dickon of Gloucester, and married his niece, the best surviving Yorkist claimant, thereby uniting the two royal houses and their arms.

"Henry Tudor will meet his Maker tonight," Ned stated decisively, "and the Right Reverend Cardinal of York will fall with him. The council disdains his grandiloquent vanity. In the taverns they say he would destroy this realm. Once I dispatch his false king, there will be no protection for the cardinal, no absolution, no quarter given to the lowborn arriviste. He will lose all his power and authority and be left exposed to suffer the vengeful hand of my wrath."

"How will you do it? Nay, do not tell me. I do not care to know."

Anne's arrant dismay roused Michael's preservation instinct. Conspirators were a volatile, desperate, highly strung lot, running a most hazardous gamble. Hadn't Brutus talked Cassius out of running his gladius through the flighty, clever, pusillanimous Cicero during a row wherein the great agitator tried to wash out of the scheme he himself had contrived to slay Julius Caesar days before the Ides of March? Yet the one thing more dangerous than eavesdropping on the traitors hatching the plot was to come into the attention of a mysterious third party. A very pretty third party, to be sure, but dangerous just the same, for she would blab on him to her masters.

"Tonight, at the midnight masque, after the mock fighting, there will be dancing. Lure him to a dalliance in the gallery. There is a bay behind the Venus tapestry. Keep his back to the arras. Henry Tudor will meet the ignominious death of a lecher."

So, Michael thought, as Anne continued to plead with her brother. This was to be his trial by fire. Self-preservation and prudence, badges of cowardice and lack of vision, would not have the reins of him. Bound by duty and honor, mindful of the fact that his presence had been noted by the jewel-eyed spy watching him in the shadows, he knew there was no way out. Even if he did nothing, said nothing, he was enmeshed in this to the bitter end. Fortune favors the brave.

"Choose whom you serve, dear sister—your lord brother . . . or Our Lady St. Mary de Pratis!"

4

Hidden hostilities are more to be feared
than open ones.

—Cicero: *In Verrem II*

Renée flounced upstairs in a mad dash. She had heard enough;
she dared not risk exposure. Reaching ground level, she stomped
her feet to dispose of dirt pellets, dusted her person of spiderwebs,
and walked briskly toward the royal chambers, where she could
disappear in the throng. The Duke of Buckinghamshire—descendent of King Edward III, King Henry's heir presumptive, the lord
high steward of England, the premier and wealthiest peer in the
realm, richer than King Henry, holder of seats in twelve counties,
and allied by blood and marriage to the oldest echelons of the nobility—planned to assassinate the King of England. Was that good
or bad for her?

There were no rights and wrongs in politics, her royal sire would
say, only implications. One had to analyze the situation from every
angle, take into consideration the players, bear in mind one's objectives, and astutely determine how best to manipulate the events
to suit one's purpose.

The king lived, the king died: which occurrence benefitted her
the most?

If King Henry lived, naught would differ; expect perhaps the
future of the house of Stafford. If King Henry died, Cardinal Wolsey would lose his buckler; Edward Stafford, the third Duke of
Buckingham, would seize the crown. Buckingham was the leader

of the disaffected nobles, a faction composed of Wolsey's victims—nobles of the highest, longest, and proudest pedigrees who had lost time-honored positions and the king's favor because of the up-and-rising son of an Ipswich butcher. Ergo, Buckingham's first order of the day as king would be to depose the reviled lord chancellor. Two boars in one valley. But he was unaware of the card of ten Wolsey had up his sleeve, a card he would not hesitate to use should his royal master die. It was this card Renée was after.

Hitherto, her scheming had come to naught. Cardinal Wolsey had abjured her presentation to Their Majesties; the banquet he had planned in honor of the king and the Knights of the Garter in the gardens of his new palace of Hampton Court had been postponed. Her quiver of tricks and plots was empty. Should Buckingham assassinate the king, the cardinal would have no choice but to play his trump card, and all future occasions for snatching it would be lost to her. *Unless . . .*

Unless she struck at the opportune moment—the occasion of misrule! What better time than when news of the king's murder reached the cardinal? Mayhem, fear, lawless confusion . . .

Hence, King Henry VIII must die.

Renée stopped in her peregrinations, unmindful of the perspiring bodies occluding the royal gallery. The last of her suspicions regarding the role she was destined to play in this treacherous game were dashed. Her puppeteers, King Francis and Cardinal Medici, had not been looking to retain the services of a spy or a thief or an assassin or a sophisticated harlot—they required all!

People had secrets. Knowledge was power. One person's rise meant another's downfall. At court one either lived on her wits or perished by stupidity. It was that simple. And as it turned out, her impulse had been correct. She had followed the king's former mistress to a meeting with the third most powerful man in England to discuss the king's assassination.

By whatever means, had been Cardinal Medici's valediction before she boarded his ship, the luxurious caravel now docking at Gravesend. They had not chosen her by a roll of the dice. King Francis, believing her to be the reincarnation of his perfidious predecessor—a master at the art of high confidence—had handpicked her to suit Cardinal Medici's needs. They accoutred her with trappings befitting her station, supplementing her already handsome wardrobe with extravagant jewels and gowns, assigned her a platoon of highly trained soldiers, signed all the documents she required, and attached her the marquis of her choice. In truth, she was on her own: an instrument masquerading as a princess on a peace mission, her position at court unspecified, even her sullied reputation a conducive factor in establishing her credibility as a featherheaded girl, one who had destroyed her chances of becoming queen somewhere by dallying with a nobody. No one would suspect her of possessing the guile necessary to aid the assassination of a king. Truth be told, she doubted she possessed it herself. But facilitate this assassination she must. So how did one assist conspirators without joining their ranks? By subtly removing obstacles from their path.

The duke's plan was elementary yet efficient. Anne might need prodding. Who was the fair man? Whom was he spying for? He had seen her. He had her life in his hands. As she had his.

"Froward Renée, the royal French whore," a man said behind her. "I wager you that in a fortnight the queen's new maid of honor shall become the king's well-ridden lady-in-waiting."

Renée moved away. The day before she had heard a knight in the Duke of Norfolk's retinue say to his mate: "If I had a drop of French blood in my body, I'd cut myself open to get rid of it, but I would not mind invading this morsel of France." And his pewfellow had replied: "Were I you, Devereaux, I'd ride the spirited French mare all the way to a double dukedom."

The gossip had arrived in England before she had, and true to the old adage, rumor gathered strength as it went. They thought her a wild piece, a wanton slut, and were speculating on the value of her dowry in gold, land, and demesnes. The men ogled her covetously. The ladies were gracious to her face and buzzed behind her back. Queen Katherine welcomed her with courteous wariness, as the Spanish distrusted all things French. King Henry was impassively hospitable; he weighed her in his male balance and decided to pass. Which suited her fine. She had no intention of entangling herself with another king. The only person she might partly confide in was due to arrive today: her bosom friend, the Lady Mary, the new Duchess of Suffolk.

Renée halted outside the king's watching chamber, locally christened as the Guard Room. Sir Henry Marney, Vice Chamberlain of England and Captain of the Guard, was conversing with the officer in charge. "Keep good watch on the king's grace and mind foreign fellows."

The officer, a handsome colossus with a carrot mane and alert green eyes—Renée suspected all the yeomen responsible for safeguarding the king at all times were chosen for their height and pleasing countenances—nodded and resumed his perambulation among his subordinates.

She peeked inside the chamber. King Henry, immured in gaudy opulence and presiding over a busy swarm of ambitious sycophants, was joshing with his favorite gallants, receiving the out-of-town knights coming to attend the chapter, gulping wine, and polishing off a fruit platter. She spotted a pair of conspicuously scarlet ecclesiastical robes. Two cardinals? One was the supreme Lord Chancellor, Cardinal Wolsey. Who was the other? Cardinal Campeggio? Still in London?

His Excellency the French ambassador, Monsieur Pierre-François le Marquis de Rougé, was conferring with the septuagenarian Duke of Norfolk, His Grace's son, Earl of Surrey, and the rude, Gallophobic Sir Devereaux of the duke's retinue. As she observed them, reading Rougé's lips and disliking what she fathomed, the Duke of Buckingham bawled past her toward the king, a score of dashing, scabbard-rattling noble retainers forming his wake. Scornful of Wolsey's ostentation, the duke was flamboyance personified in gilt crimson, with the heavy gold chains of his lineage and offices slung across his shoulders. She saw heads turning, men bowing, the king scowling. The duke flourished a pompous bow that smacked of malicious condescension and launched into an exchange with his soon-to-be slain sovereign. Was he already picturing himself on the throne?

Renée, stanching a sneer, delayed the jaunty page carrying in another fruit platter. "Robin."

He glanced aside. His eyes lit up. "My lady."

She was grooming the bright youth, a son of an officer of the guard, to be her eyes and ears in this morass of a court. She gestured for him to come away and whispered, "Pray, the French ambassador standing with His Grace of Norfolk, tell him I would speak with him privily."

"Right fast, my lady. Hmm . . ." He looked down, color spreading from high cheekbones to a downy chin. "Nan, my sweeting, she prized the silk scarf and consented to go walking with me."

Smiling, Renée magicked a gold angel. "Squire Nan to a clean cookshop in the city, feed her hen pastries and mead, buy her a sugared animal and a nosegay. On the way back, you shall have a kiss, I trow." As his arms were burdened with a chased silver platter heaped with apples, pears, damsons, cherries, plums, apricots, strawberries, and the oranges she had brought from France as a gift for Their Majesties, she slipped the coin into his sleeve with a wink. *"Bonne chance!"*

Robin beamed. "Thank you, my lady." He headed toward the doors, halted, rearranged his grip, and tossed her a perfect purple plum beneath the grinning eyes of the hulking sentries.

Then she saw him—the fair stranger from the undercroft—forging through the multitudes that packed the gallery in hopes of gaining admittance to the presence. He was singularly tall, golden, and beautiful, a magnificent Nordic tangling with bronzed skin. Turquoise eyes studded strong, clean features, absorbing everything, missing nothing. His leonine mane, unfashionably long, brushed broad shoulders draped with a gold collar. His attire was sober, immaculate, and of the finest quality: snowy sleeves burst out of gilt-trimmed slashes in an inky velvet doublet with matching hose; the cut of the raiment molding a strapping, athletic frame. He stood out among the hectic brocades of the rich merchants and the somber apparels of the aldermen, guildsmen, and lawyers milling about. Instinctively she knew he was not from around here. Who was he?

He perceived her, the sudden intensity of his gaze a shock. He changed direction. Instead of heading toward the watched over entrance to the guard room, he approached her.

The Marquis of Rougé stepped between them. "You summoned me."

"Where may we speak without interruption?" She put the plum in her purse.

"In the closet outside the chapel." Rougé took her elbow and steered her away.

Sashaying alongside the marquis, Renée glanced past her shoulder. The stranger remained outside the guard room, watching her. With a rakish grin, he inclined his head in greeting.

They would talk, soon, she decided, with a little tremor of excitement in her belly.

Rougé squired her into an antechamber adjoining the royal chapel. Redolent of frankincense and myrrh, aglow with beeswax candles, the room was furnished with a prie-dieu, stools, ornate silver reliquaries, paned cupboards displaying chryselephantine prayer books, crucifixes, jeweled chalices, and a precious collection of sacred relics. A snap of the marquis's fingers dismissed the priest standing by to shrive sinners. The marquis closed the door and leaned back against it.

Renée had his undivided attention. One of the reasons she had specifically begged Rougé for an escort was his fluency in Breton French, an argot few could follow. Privacy was preferable, though, for what she had to say. "Who is the second cardinal, the gray-beard?"

He folded his arms across his chest. "Lorenzo Cardinal Campeggio. Aught else?"

Renée scrutinized his dark eyes. A man of two score years, Pierre-François de Rougé was of medium build, raven-haired, with silver streaks at his temples, had an aristocratic beaked nose, and was considered a handsome man. He was a widower, much sought after by the ladies of their court, particularly the widows looking to net a second husband. He was a capable military leader, a rich landholder, an expert courtier, and unscrupulously driven by self-interest. He enjoyed the hunt, kept several mistresses, lived in splendor, and considered it his rightful due. Curiously, he was not loved by his kings, something that rankled with him, and although he possessed a nose for peril and a talent for survival, ambition girdled his intelligence, making him predictable and safe.

Renée knew he disliked her, distrusted her, and resented her for holding the leading rein of this expedition. He was conscripted into her service, compelled to jump at her beck and call and do her bidding without questioning her decisions. Mostly he begrudged her for being entrusted with a secret office he knew naught about. "I am no more an ambassador of peace than you are a companion to the queen," he had told her upon their departure, an admonition she had ignored.

His looks and bearing reminded her of a raptor. Hence, she must play the falconer. Already he was blindfolded with a hood and wearing her bells, and she possessed the silk jesses to tether him to her sleeve. That was the reason she had chosen the marquis. "Tell me about him."

"Campeggio? Nearly half a century old and more virtuous than an ugly virgin. What do you want with him? Do not tell me they sent you to seduce him."

This was going to be a long conversation. She sighed. "Pray, answer the question."

"There is not much to tell. He came to preach for another crusade against the Turks, hoping to stir the old flame in the young lion's heart. A mendicant beggar, like the rest of his ilk."

"Where does he lodge?"

"At York Place, Cardinal Wolsey's palace in the city."

York Place! Blessed Lady, finally she was getting somewhere!

"*Eh bien*, now that we are on the subject, I suppose I ought to inform you that I am moving out of the Greyhound Inn and into His Grace of Norfolk's house on the Strand, should you have need of me. . . . His Grace invited me to be his houseguest, and I graciously accepted."

You sybaritic fool. He would use you. "I need you at court. The inn is in close proximity to the palace. The Strand is a good hour away by boat, depending on the weather. We are not here to play at tennez. If you must try out Norfolk's new court, I suggest you visit, not move in."

Rougé gawked. "How did you know?" *Little witch*, he mouthed silently. He set his jaw and launched a sortie. "What need have you of me? To serve as your handmaiden? Have you been to the Greyhound? Stuffed with ink-bespotted Italian gossips who cluck and cackle about their dukes' illustrious courts from dawn to dusk and rouse the household ten times a-night for more tapers and more wine and more food. I am sick of that place!"

"Be reasonable, Rougé. Why do you suppose all the ambassadors reside there? They wish to be at the heart of things, to hear what their colleagues may have heard that they did not. Norfolk will wine and dine you, lull you into confidences, and bleed you for promises. Do you not see his intent? He despises Wolsey and seeks to establish personal relations with King Francis."

"Your point, madame?"

"Why alienate the Lord Chancellor of England?" *Cretin.* She wondered what impaired his judgment, which was usually sound. His injured pride or promises from Norfolk? "So long as we labor in our king's business, it would be impolitic to establish close friendships with personages of this court. You would be wise to refrain from associating yourself with Wolsey's enemies."

He leaned forward, gripped her wrist, and jerked her up against him. "Impudent brat! Do not presume to lecture me on court politics!" His eyes fell on her modest cleavage. "Why are we in England? Whose bed are you ordered to crawl into?"

"Unhand me, monsieur," she said flintily. "Lest you should like to be relieved of your post."

His black eyes glinted murderously. Undaunted, she lifted a hand to the pendant suspended from a collar of gold cockleshells sprawled over his shoulders. It depicted St. Michael slaying the Serpent. "Must I remind you whose collar you are wearing, Pierre?" she inquired softly.

He put his chin on his chest to see which of his chains she laid claim to. At first he looked relieved that she had not chosen the one displaying the arms of his house, for she could argue a maternal birthright to his bequest, but when her implication hit him, his eyes narrowed into vindictive slits. The pendant clasped in her hand portrayed the illustrious *Ordre de Saint-Michel*, created by King Louis XI, the Spider King, as the highest chivalric order of France, to mark an allegiance between the dukes of Brittany, Berry, and Orléans, the three potentates of the time. Significant though the alliance had been, it was her noble sire, the onetime Duke of Orléans and then King Louis XII, who unified the French dominions under his house, his rule, his banner.

"If you recognize the value and weight of this badge, which I admit was bestowed on me by the king your father, then you must also know that the three dozen knights of the Order of St. Michael are amongst the strongest nobles in France and are strictly in the king's power."

"Yes, that is true. But the lucrative iron mine you operate in the Loire in Brittany, whereon you rely heavily for your proceeds, is in my power."

"The devil!" he snarled, disbelieving.

"I had it shut down until I return to France successful in my peace mission."

His eyes turned into black cartwheels. "You lie!"

"I have a copy of His Majesty's writ in my apartment. Would you like to view it with your own eyes or employ what precious time we have in ensuring your solvency?"

A muscle ticked in his jaw; his expression was one of impotent rage. She read the struggle in his eyes as he questioned her sincerity and fretted over which cataclysm she might deliver next if he should be so disrespectful as to demand to see this proof. "What do you require of me?"

Renée was calm. Her fears were many and varied, but the marquis was not one of them. "To begin with, I require you unhand me." Instantly he let go. "Now." She affected a charming smile. "The Cardinal of York, I would meet him. It should be an informal audience and—"

"Is that where the wind blows?" Rougé scoffed. "To ply state secrets, send a royal whore."

She slapped him, catching him unawares.

"Madame, you try my patience," he rasped with barely leashed fury. As he stared at her, his spleen abated. He smirked. "Usually when a woman hits a man, she is asking to be bedded. Is that what you want from me? A quick tumble on the prie-dieu?"

"Rude, violent, and blasphemous withal. No, I thank you. I do not care for a tumble. I want you to arrange an audience for me with the Lord Chancellor. Are you capable of accomplishing this great feat?" As she studied his face, it occurred to her he might be in need of a carrot. "Yes, I did take certain precautions to guarantee your goodwill, knowing you are not the sort of man who would gladly accept a woman's lordship, but I specifically begged you for this peace mission."

He looked stunned—again. "You asked for me specifically?"

"Do not be shocked, monsieur. We are alike in many ways, though you have much to learn."

His complexion crimsoned. Heretofore he had considered her a confounded nuisance and an awkward diplomatic embassy. Now he viewed her differently, as if a blindfold were ripped from his eyes. Respect mingled with resentment. Thin lips stretched over even teeth in a vulpine smile. "Allow me to recant and rephrase. To ply state secrets, send a royal sword—sharp, beautiful, and lethal. Congratulations, madame. I am duly impressed. I did not think our king was blessed in his relations, but of course you are the king your father's daughter." He took her gloved hand and kissed its back. "I bow to you in all matters on this embassy. As for the Cardinal of York . . ."

"I should like to meet the cardinal and convey our king's personal message to him."

His expression hardened. "What message?"

She smiled, thinking of silk jesses. "The secret behind this peace mission, the true reason."

"Tell me," he begged in a whisper, his face and body taut with curiosity.

"King Francis"—she tormented him with her slowness—"is of a mind to bring France and England into peaceful unity by uniting his sister-by-marriage with an eligible English husband."

"You?"

She could see the wheels turning in his head. Ah, ambition, she thought. How obvious he was. "Surely the good cardinal should have several candidates in mind, a young English duke, or son of a duke. . . . I am well dowered." She shrugged dismissively, easing open her trap.

"We came to find you a husband." Rougé looked bewildered, calmed, interested. "But your presence is not required. It may take months to sift the candidates for the office, then months of negotiations, then the signing of the indentures, the contracts . . ."

"They say Wolsey is a fisher of men. He would think it an inordinate stroke of luck that the French should come to him with the business." That Renée had no intention of following through with this farce was of no import. She required entry into York Place. Haste-posthaste. She laid a hand on the marquis's silken sleeve. "Please, arrange it. I should very much like to visit with the cardinal at York Place—today, tonight, as soon as possible!"

Rougé stared at her hand. "I shall see what I can do."

Sir Walter, having tailed the French spies to the chapel doors, returned to the hectic gallery, wherefrom he had a vantage point of the chapel closet and of the entrance to the king's watching chamber. The richest woman in Christendom, Norfolk said. Daughter to the late King of France, sister-in-law to the present king, a duchess of two duchies, deflowered but not devoured.

Norfolk, a taciturn man, never gossiped unless it served his purposes. Therefore, Walter deciphered, his duke expected him to act upon the information in a way that would benefit his benefactor. The game Walter intended to play with the precious princess would be well worth the candle. Insinuating himself into her good books—and with any luck her bed—would repair his family's fortune. A predacious grin curled his lips. Pursuing her would hardly be a distasteful task. Notwithstanding her reputedly barbed tongue, Froward Renée was a tasty little treasure.

An officer of the Valois guard entered his vision. The man halted to survey the gallery, his breath coming swiftly. If he had to hazard a guess, Walter would say the princess had given her bodyguard the slip. With an amicable grin, Walter strolled up to the officer and said in French, "You shall find your royal charge at chapel, conferring with the French ambassador."

"I thank you, sir." There was a thick Italian accent to the officer's French. "Madame has no care for her safety and evades me to my great distress."

"Perhaps if you gave her the occasional slip, she would grow to appreciate your bucklering," Walter offered affably. He extended his hand. "Sir Walter Devereaux."

The officer shook it heartily. "Lieutenant Armado Baglioni."

"Baglioni? I know a baron by the name of Malatesta Baglioni, the lord of Spello."

A smile expanded on Armado's face. "Malatesta is my brother! You met?"

"Five years hence, when I fought in the League of Cambrai in Italy. Your much esteemed lord brother and I shared a few cups and a few whores." He refrained from mentioning that he had served as a man-at-arms, a poor mercenary, who could scarce afford his own armor. A brilliant idea struck him. He grinned in a man-to-man rapport. "How should you like to share a tankard of bad ale and a pair of liced but not poxed whores at the stews after midnight?"

Armado looked delighted. "*Con piacere!* I thank you for the invitation!"

"Splendid! I shall wait for you at the palace landing. Ah, there comes your princess." Walter touched his forehead and paced off before she glimpsed him. One at a time . . .

5

They come to see, they come to be seen
themselves.

—Ovid: *Ars Amatoria*

The opening feast of the annual festivities of the Order of the Garter was held with the great pomp and splendor King Henry was fabled for. The king's presence chamber, illuminated by a wealth of beeswax candles set in antique-style candelabras, wall brackets, and table candlesticks, was sumptuously ornamented with dewlaps of red buckram embroidered with Tudor roses and Spanish pomegranates spilling from the ceiling; its walls were richly hung with tapestries depicting knights, dragons, and ladies in grand scenes of chivalry and courtly love.

The long trestle tables, perpendicular to the high table reserved for Their Majesties and their entourage, were bedecked with Paris napery, herbs and flowers, lustrous plates, trenchers, bowls, spoons, goblets polished to a shine, manchet loaves wrapped in embroidered napkins, and gem-encrusted candlesticks. The air was spiced with fragrant aromas. A corpse of musicians fanfared the assembly to supper with a medley of notes played on flutes, trumpets, shawms, and tabors.

As the royal procession had yet to appear, the clinquant theater known as the court streamed into the hall in its finery. Most were men, but there were women interspersed among them as they clustered in select hives, speaking sotto voce and scrutinizing the rival camps. None of them paid attention to Michael as he sauntered inside, looking for the two conspirators and the mysterious spy, and in their indifference to anonymous and therefore insignificant life-forms such as him, they labored under the misconception that he must also be deaf and blind. They were mistaken.

Michael observed and listened with the alacrity of a predator on the hunt, catching snippets of intrigue, gossip, and flirtation unwittingly yet generously dispensed. He learned that the man to put one's purse on in the jousting tournament was last year's champion, the Undefeated Baron Monteagle; Dom Leonardo Spinelli, the papal nuncio, had lost a game of tennez to his friend and host, His Grace of Norfolk; His Grace of Buckingham had railed and misused himself in words with Cardinal Wolsey in the privy council and had been fomenting sedition against the lord chancellor ever since; Queen Katherine had remonstrated stridently with the king over the lewd theme of the midnight masque, but the king had stood pat, and well he ought to have, for the queen, should she care to preserve her dignity, would do well to avoid public rows in the future.

The last piquant crumb to fall into his ear as he prowled King Henry's ambry of information concerned a recently arrived French princess. Young blades wishing to rise high in the world discussed the value of her dowry in jewels, plate, demesnes, and farming land, hailing her a prize worthy of a prince. Ribalds keen on disporting themselves praised her beauty and wagered on the odds of bedding her. A corpulent dame, gossiping with her matronly friends, was making a star chamber case against the French princess's pernicious influence: "Now we are all French in eating, drinking, and apparel, and our young men, these fashion-mongers who attend so much on the new form, are all *pardonnez-moi*, *bons* and *mais oui*, French in vices and brags, afflicted with these strange flies, as if they can no longer sit at ease on the old bench. Fah!"

The courtiers, he noted, were somewhat licentious in their disposition: ladies kissed men on the lips in greeting, laughed at bawdy jokes, and tippled aplenty. A merry court, indeed.

Evidently the path from dismal obscurity to infamy or glory ran through this crowd. Michael frowned. For the nonce he was a nameless arriviste, skirting the fringes of society, but soon, once he foiled the attempt on the king's life with swiftness and élan, he would strike them with awe.

A troop of ushers sporting green badges of the household staff came to herd the courtiers to their designated seats, allotted according to rank, family connections, and closeness to the throne. Michael found himself standing like a maypole, or rather a clodpole, amid the fast-manned seats and glaringly being ignored. His gaze found Walter, the popinjay who had plowed into him in the yard. Brother and sister were sitting high up the middle table. As he scrutinized the fair pair, Michael's gaze collided with Walter's, who smiled maliciously and offered a mock salute.

Around them, all the seats were occupied and gusty with conversation. Feeling and looking like the gawky village idiot no one wanted at his table, Michael turned his back to the peacockish jackslave. He was confronted with the nasty Riggs, who condescended to crank a slight bow.

"Good-den. Master Devereaux, am I correct? How may I serve Your Worship?"

Michael choked down his fury and humiliation to rasp, "Pray point out my seat, good man, ere I commandeer the throne and explain to His Majesty that you seated me there."

Muttering, "Aye, great one!" under his breath, the sergeant led him to the last pair of vacant seats at the end of one of the rear tables, closest to the entry and farthest from the throne.

A seat to suit his quarters, Michael fumed inwardly, and slid onto the edge of the bench. A murmur, a snicker, and the odd sensation of having eyes upon him sped his gaze back to Walter in time to catch the conspiratorial nod bestowed on the sergeant. Michael gnashed his teeth, pretending not to have noticed. The venal Riggs was in league with the popinjay to play him for a fool. What a foul prank, billeting him in the dungeon of the undercroft and seating him at the foot of the banquet! An act of retaliation was in order, but he would have to become acquainted with the lay of the land first in order to come up with a foully contrived prank of his own by way of reprisal. For the nonce, he would have to sit at the edge and sleep in a warren.

"Hark, Stanley, Baron Monteagle! Be this not your place of last year?"

Michael saw a corpulent fellow cackling complacently with his close neighbors at the high end of the opposite table.

"Hark, Lovell! Be that not tomorrow's carcass all fattened up for its slaughter at the lists?"

Michael's head swerved in the opposite direction to find a bearded, burly fellow standing two paces inside the door, affecting a fearsome glower to disguise his discomfiture—albeit his riposte did earn him several sympathetic laughs—at finding his seat of last year usurped by this Lovell fellow. Michael was aware that the last vacant seat was the one beside his, but Stanley, awkwardly scanning the better tables for a place to sit, failed to spot it as he kept looking farther up, all the way to the great salt, cursing his gaucherie under his breath.

Commiserating, Michael called out to the man discreetly, "Sir, would this be your place?"

Stanley eyed the vacant spot with disdain, then with a disgruntled snort swaggered over, sat down, and stared morosely at the empty goblet set before him. As if on cue, an army of servitors stepped forth, brandishing flagons overflowing with wine, and filled everyone's cup to the rim.

"Do you also make food appear on plates?" Michael chuckled, reaching for his wine goblet.

Stanley's paw fastened around Michael's forearm. "We wait for the king's pleasure, codling. What hoa! What have you there?"

"A hand?" Michael suggested wryly, though he knew what had captured the man's eye: the gules peeking from under his sleeve, painted on his wrist in the shape of three red roundels and a red band that circled his wrist like a bracelet.

"Nay, your markings. What are they?"

"A birthmark," Michael hedged.

Astute eyes alight with humor met his. "Bless the fathers whose sons are born bearing their arms on the skin, and may Our Lord pity their adulterous wives and indiscreet mistresses."

"I surrender to your logic." Michael grinned. "In truth, I was marked upon birth."

"Why?" The bearded lord scowled in bewilderment.

"To keep me from getting lost, I imagine."

"Did you make a habit of getting lost?"

"I was found." Michael flashed him a sphinxlike smile.

"Why keep painting your skin, then?"

"The markings do not wash off."

Bushy brown eyebrows snapped together. "You do wash, do you not, as all good knights do, once a year to please the ladies?"

"I endeavor to." Michael laughed, recalling his testiness as a boy when the Earl of Tyrone's emphatic intolerance of rancid smells, above all in humans, sent him a-bathing daily before bed. He explained, "The dye was pricked into my skin with a needle. Hence, 'tis called pricking."

"Bless my black heart! And here I thought pricking meant something else entirely." A wink and a thick elbow in the ribs gave Michael a fair idea of what his neighbor referred to.

"It is an ancient Pict practice," Michael elaborated. "Old King Harold of Wessex had two on his chest, which ultimately served in identifying his mutilated body at the Battle of Hastings."

"You come prepared for the joust, I see. But harken, you may yet live, my prickled friend." Stanley guffawed at his own gibe. "Now tell me, was it painful?"

"Not as much as taking a Norman arrow in the eye, methinks."

Stanley chuckled. "I take it you are with the Devereaux brood, eh?"

Michael's startled gaze locked with Stanley's. "You know my name."

"I know your arms." Stanley indicated the mark on Michael's wrist.

With a negligent shrug, Michael replied, "I am a stray Devereaux."

"Then we shall have to bring you back into the Devereaux fold, runt."

"Your pardon, I neglected to properly introduce myself. Michael Devereaux is my name. I come to represent the Earl of Tyrone in the tournaments with the honor and flair befitting his august house. You are the Undefeated Baron Monteagle everyone is betting his purse on, eh?"

"Ah, the pleasure of notoriety! But you are wide of the mark, m'boy. I am Baron Monteagle to my tenants, Edward to my lady mother, Ned to my beauteous future bride, whoever the good Lord should deem her be, and Stanley to my mates, even the prickled ones."

Michael shook the proffered paw. "Undefeated, I'm honored to make your acquaintance."

"A fine device you have there, my spruce friend"—Stanley indicated the rampant bloodred eagle of rubies stamped in the scabbard of Michael's eating knife—"the lord of which this court has oft extolled but never entertained. You serve him? Why has he not come in the flesh?"

"The king's business keeps my lord in Ireland. I am here on his behalf, an ambassador."

"An ambassador, not a knight?"

"Alack, no." Michael grinned sheepishly, then sobered. "Not yet, anyhow."

"Not a knight? A strapping runt such as you? Saints, you are twice my inches, Devereaux! I was rather anticipating aggrandizing my reputation at your expense."

Michael appraised his newfound friend. Although Stanley was a good deal shorter in height, the muscled, barrel chest rivaled that of an ox. "I do intend to compete, under my lord's arms. So you see"—he gave a fulsome smile—"you may yet trounce me with a glad heart, and may the mud of your glory stick to my breastplate."

Chortling ebulliently, Stanley slapped Michael's shoulder fondly. "Save your glib tongue for the ladies, codling. Your poetry shan't sweeten me up for our engagement in the lists."

"It was worth a try." Michael's grin turned lopsided.

Stanley studied him soberly. "I suggest you bank that high-resolved gleam in your eye, runt, lest you tempt the hardy dogs of the jousts to shiver their lances on you."

"Would a bloodless, meek mien make me less of an appetizer? I am thinking not. They will know me for the unfledged challenger that I am, whether I cower or strut."

"True, but your inevitable defeat will hurt less if you prudently dampen your ardor."

"A goodly advice, I am sure."

"Aw, that wasn't a nettle! Hark, you did me a good turn beckoning me hither. I shall repay the courtesy. Two years I am undefeated. My Lord Lovell over there, all high-proud and merry"—his glower indicated the man who had baited him—"comes last at the tournament and reaches higher each year. The reason is . . ." He lowered his voice to a whisper. "Our king is a passionate jouster and despises defeat above all things. Hence, this time next year, the Undefeated shall be known as the Once Defeated and dining at the king's table. Savvy?"

"A shrewd strategy and very politick." Michael appreciated the hard-earned advice for what it was: his first significant lesson in court politics. "I thank you. I shall not forget your counsel."

An usher appeared in the doorway, thumping a gilded staff on the rushes-strewn floor and heralding at the top of his lungs, "His Royal Majesty, Henry Tudor, by the grace of God, King of England and France, Protector of the Faith, Defender of the Realm, and Lord of Ireland!"

The result was a thunder of wooden legs scraping the flagstones as everyone pushed to their feet and plunged into deep bows and curtsies.

King Henry VIII, magnificently dressed in gilt-embossed imperial purple with a heavy gold chain twinkling with gems slung across his wide shoulders and a crown set atop his reddish gold head, entered the great hall with his regal-looking, matronly Spanish queen on his arm.

"—and Her Royal Majesty, Queen Katherine of England!" the usher finished.

Leading a solemn procession of lords and ladies, splendidly clothed and lustrously jeweled, followed by pursuivants, pages, and footboys, the royal couple made its way to the high table.

Michael went stock-still as he recognized the treasonous Lord Ned walking behind the king, paired with a churchman in rich scarlet robes—doubtless the illustrious Cardinal Wolsey—and looking none too pleased. The Lady Anne his sister appeared in the queen's train, her curvaceous assets alluringly displayed in a red gown, and gliding next to her was the mysterious spy.

Dainty and petite, her head held regally high, she shimmered in a low-cut, waist-tight, pearl-dripping gown of nacre satin that set off her alabaster skin. Her ebony tresses, partially veiled by a stylish jeweled hood, glistened under the cresset lights. She floated swanlike among the geese in the queen's train like an otherworldly sylph in a dark wood. When her thick-lashed, purplish blue gaze cut to him unexpectedly, Michael felt a kick in his gut. She was exquisite.

His neighbor's wry observation anchored him in reality. "The vision you are hard ogling is Princess Renée de Valois of France, Duchess of Brittany and Chartres. Best couch your lance at the red-blooded prizes of this court. That one is much too lofty and blue for your blood."

A sweeping glance about him confirmed that Michael was not the only one agape; Renée de Valois looked so pearly pink white and deliciously pretty that every man in the chamber was stripping her bare. So this was the notorious princess of France. A delicate creature with a rapier for a tongue. He would have been hard put to believe it had he not caught her spying fearlessly in the cellar. She intrigued him, and she aroused him. Then the crux of the matter dawned on him: the French were now apprised of the conspiracy. Which way would the notorious weathervanes intervene, if at all? He was in need of information, and Stanley seemed as good a fount as any. Fixing his gaze on Anne, he affected a lecherous smile that Stanley, in his predilection for using bawdy tourney language, would describe as codding, and said, "Who is yonder poppy?"

"My Lady Anne Hastings, His Grace of Buckingham's lady sister."

Of course—Lord Ned was the Duke of Buckingham! His father, Harry Stafford, the second Duke of Buckingham, had backed Richard of Gloucester to the throne and then rebelled against him, thus opening the road to Henry Tudor, the late king. Jupiter's thunder, how had he missed that? Maybe because his mind had been soused with lavender and ambergris. . . .

"The Lady Anne," Stanley gossiped, "is newly restored from

dieting on piety at St. Mary's and with any luck all the lustier for her three years' deprivation. By comparison I hear the French princess is flint-hearted as her royal sire, the not-so-much-lamented King Louis the Twelfth, and the scourge of princes. Her affianced have all fled the snare, some by dying, others by running."

Michael was hard put to accept Stanley's word on this matter but kept the observation to himself. "King Louis's daughter?" A veritable princess of the blood, her kind was usually kept under lock and key until a connubial alliance was contracted with an heir to some throne.

"Aye. The king her father coaxed the pope to grant him a dispensation to put aside his first wife and then browbeat the lady's mother, then the Duchess of Brittany in her own right, into accepting his troth, just so he could add Brittany to his dominions. Queen Claude of France is my Lady Renée's sister, a docile creature, mind you. Certes, at that slippery court, a lady may either become a biddable crone or a—" Stanley clammed up, refusing to say more.

"Or a what?" Michael dogged, inordinately curious. "A jade?"

"Aw, who needs the poxed French when England bestows us with flirt-gills to spare?"

Renée de Valois did not look poxed. Still, Michael's mind was not on flirting. His crackpot plan to cozen up to Ned and get him pickled before midnight was unfeasible, ludicrous, and very dangerous, insomuch that it might turn the most puissant duke of the realm into a mortal enemy. He needed a new plan to obstruct the assassination plot, but his mind drew a blank. Two women, a former royal mistress and a French princess with murky concerns, and a formidable duke with an eye on the throne—what to do? As he chewed the cud of that, he wondered if he were mad to wade into this quagmire, but was he not already up to his neck in it? The little spy had seen him.

Their Majesties took their state at the great salt, then the prominent lords and ladies in their train. Obligingly, Stanley ran his memory along the faces filing onto the dais, as a pious widow going over her rosary beads, throwing in morsels and tidbits of gossip to spice up the litany.

King Henry, on his feet behind the middle of the high table, above the salt, his face visible to the whole view of the chamber, smiled broadly and raised his goblet, commanding silence. "Our noble friends! We welcome you to our annual meeting of our Most Noble Order of the Garter!"

A great cheer went up.

"In honor of St. George, the patron saint of England and of our Most Noble Order, we shall feast, joust, dance, and disport ourselves abundantly! We shall hunt and rejoice and make merry! But tonight"—he paused for effect—"we shall be even merrier!" Beaming at his enthusiastic audience, the king exclaimed, "Let us drink to St. George!"

Everyone hoisted sloshing goblets high in the air. "St. George!" And a deep draught later, a second toast ensued, everyone shouting, "The king!"

❧ 6 ❧

He that is warned afore is noght bygiled.

—J. Arderne: *Treatises of Fistula*

The bells rang the new hour in. Queen Katherine, having performed her duty as hostess, rose gracefully, bade the assemblage a blessed night, and retired with her Spanish ladies. In her wake, space was cleared for dancing, the musicians struck up a passamezzo, and bowls brimming with coins, cards, and dice were brought to the tables for those more inclined toward gambling.

An hour to midnight, Renée fidgeted. No word from Rougé. Mayhap she had pushed him too far, or he was unsuccessful in securing her audience with the Cardinal of York. She was not used to having to rely on other people in her little schemes—and she hated it!—and this was not some petty ploy to help her sire destroy dispatches from a Spanish spial guised as an ambassador or glean gossip from the King of Naples's mistress or steal the battle notes of the Great Captain Gonzalo de Córdoba or counterfeit the seal of the Lord Bishop of Tournai or any of the trifling assignments she had carried out for the Father of the People of France. The King of England was about to be assassinated—and she had to steal the Lord Chancellor of England's talisman.

How would she accomplish that? *Merciful Jesu, protect me, Holy Lady, precipitate my cause.* She murmured a few Aves, kneading the rosary beads stashed in her purse.

As the candles guttered and the shadows lengthened, she grew exceedingly anxious. If only her friend the Lady Mary were here to cheer her, distract her, squeeze her hand . . . Unfortunately His Grace of Suffolk had sent word that his best horse had thrown a shoe and that he and his new wife would be spending the night in the city and would arrive on the morrow. And where was the dratted Rougé? Relocating himself to Norfolk's demesne on the Strand? Hateful cretin. She had bested him today, a fact the marquis was unlikely to forgive or forget. If—Jesu forefend!—she failed in her mission, or if King Francis and Cardinal Medici grew tired of waiting for their prize, they would unleash their malcontent raptor on her, and then may God have mercy on her soul!

With the candles burning low, the hour felt ripe for cavorting, the forthcoming great romp creating a lascivious anticipatory ambiance. King Henry's decorous court was transforming into the rowdy brothel Buckingham had disparaged. The English, Renée mused, were worse than the unblushing French who made a national sport of indulging in carnal love. King Francis was wont to send for several women at a time and oftentimes invite his male companions to partake of the dalliance. The French were captivated by all things beautiful. Love was so esteemed among them that girls became the erotic fancies of noblewomen and boys of noblemen. Promiscuity was rife, but they depleted themselves privily and did not burst at the seams with distasteful ribaldry as the English did. Here riot and rumpus reigned. Like naughty children, they drank too much, groped, and importuned. The ladies kissed men, allowed themselves to be indecently mauled, roared with laughter, told lewd jests, diced and cussed like stable hands, frolicked boisterously, and taunted the men to catch them as they danced and gamboled around the softly lit chamber.

Renée, disgusted with the activity, broke her abstemious regime and reached for her full cup of hippocras. The warm, sweetly spiced wine soothed her high-strung nerves and aching wits.

A coterie of the queen's lingering gaggle, maids of honor, dropped on the bench beside her. They were agog about the novelty Sir William Cornish, the chief adviser of court entertainments, devised, a thing not seen in England afore. "Disguised after the manner of Italy!" tweeted Lady Dacre.

"Appareled in garments of silk with gold, with visors and caps of gold," peeped Lady Percy.

"The gentlemen will bear torches and will issue a warlike proclamation. . . ."

"We shall make a stand, and then the victors will desire the defeated to dance. . . ."

"I know the fashion of it," muttered some matron. "It is a thing most unseemly."

Renée's gaze slid yet again to the far corner of the chamber and locked with the turquoise eyes that had been watching her all evening. The fair stranger's identity remained a mystery, but the edge of the table seat was a testament unto itself. He was a nobody.

He smiled at her, as if saying: *Whether you like it or not, you and I are secret partners now, silent coconspirators, custodians of a great secret.*

"Who is that man staring at you?"

Renée found Lady Anne Hastings—whom she had taken pains to befriend this afternoon—at her elbow, her breath sour, her eyes overly bright, her bounteous cleavage bereft of tuckers. Renée could not fault her for overindulging. Were she in Anne's tight shoes, ordered to lure the King of England to his death, she would be drinking herself into a stupor.

Anne leaned her heavy bosom into Renée's shoulder, her eyes to the front. "He stares at us. Should we put on a spectacle for his benefit? I daresay he should be able to handle the two of us together, a golden-maned stallion like that. Come, let us walk arm in arm, see if he follows." Taking her arm, Anne squired Renée around the room. "Oh, look. Our admirer comes our way."

Renée was unsure whose admirer he was, if at all, and, as she had not yet fathomed him, it was imperative to keep him away from Anne. She steered her cloying companion in the direction of the most hectic gaming table. Anne needed to renew her acquaintance with King Henry for Buckingham's plot to succeed.

"He is stalking us, methinks," Anne updated excitedly. "Such a fine specimen of virility."

"He is pleasant to look at, I suppose," Renée acceded without looking at the man.

"Pleasant! Show me a woman who will say nay to a little dalliance with that and I will show you a ninny. Would you say he is as tall as our king?"

Renée cut her eyes to him fleetingly. "Taller." She instantly regretted her answer; Anne did not need encouragements in *that* direction tonight. "Mayhap not, definitely not as hefty." It was the truth. King Henry's fondness for feasting was manifesting, whereas the golden stranger was a towering artwork of brawn. . . . Holy Anne! She should not be admiring men while her true love wasted away in a cage. "I find him bland and uninspiring," she muttered meanly. *The uninspiring stuff that immortalized artists like Raphael,* her conscience scoffed.

"Bland!" Anne let out a throaty chuckle. "I should very much like to blend with that."

Renée decided to shift their conversation to a more conducive lane. "Who is the pretty lady putting her talons in the king?"

"Elizabeth—Bessie—Blount," Anne replied scathingly. "She certainly has him by the dice."

They stopped outside the ring of courtiers to watch the lady in question kiss the royal dice for luck. Not for the first time Renée wondered why queens were determined to be foolish. Her sister Claude was one example, but she had a dissolute swine for a husband and had to vie for his attention with Francis's recreant lady sister and a long procession of mistresses. Queen Katherine was married to a man who seemed to bear her affection as well as respect, and yet in her way she was alienating him. On second thought, Renée might also look the other way if married to such a man. How weary she was of self-absorbed, tyrannical epicures. She hated court life and longed for the peaceful simplicity of the country, married to a quiet man, whose greatest ambition was to create beauty, not accumulate castles. Yet she was not so naïve as to imagine that without the benefit of wealth and rank there could be freedom. As Duchess of Brittany she would attain the most liberty a woman could hope for. She would bear the rood of no one, save a remote king.

"Sister, come make a stand with me against great Midas here!" a man called with false levity from inside the girdle of courtiers besieging the king's gaming table. "Beauteous sister, I bid you come quick to my rescue! My losses are piling, and I have no Fortuna in my corner."

A surprisingly good ploy on Buckingham's part, Renée granted. Mistress Blount might very well lose her office of dice kisser. Sensing Anne's hesitation, Renée nudged her into the bevy of gallants, all deep in their cups and reeling with exuberance.

A jolly drunkard blocked their path. "Hark! Plato and Socrates walk into a tavern—"

"Aw, we have heard that one," someone exclaimed. "Refresh your arsenal, dear Compton, for your jokes are getting on in years!"

"And with the ladies!" Compton grabbed Anne by the waist to his friends' roaring delight. "Hullo, my darling lady! Kiss me quick, for you have been much missed."

"Take your greedy paws off me, you swine-drunk fool! You may put Plato and Socrates in a tavern, but you shan't put me." The newly pious Anne shoved him away, and he fell straight into the arms of his amused mates, who heaved him to an upright albeit wobbly posture.

"Stung by a honeybee!" Compton slurred jovially as he staggered before Anne.

"You unhappy honey bag!" someone jeered, eliciting guffaws among the tomboys.

"Lady Anne, your lord brother pleads for your lucky touch. Pray do not keep him waiting," a baritone voice called from the center of the hive. All at once, the swarm of courtiers parted like the Red Sea before Moses, creating a human corridor to the table. Clutching Renée's wrist—for courage—Anne came to stand beside Buckingham. The king lifted sparkling blue eyes and with the voice that had just spoken, exclaimed, "Lady Anne, we bid you welcome! My court has been disgarnished for lack of your beauty. And, my Lady Renée, *bon soir*!"

Renée sank into a supple curtsey beside Anne, sensing dozens of eyes perusing her with avid curiosity. She did not appreciate the sudden attention and so kept her eyes downcast.

"Your Grace is most kind," Anne murmured, her hand dampening around Renée's wrist.

From beneath her eyelashes, Renée saw the king take Anne's measures. "Come, Anne," he cajoled, "kiss my dice for luck. His Grace your brother may enjoy Mistress Blount's services."

Ribald laughter rippled, accompanied by unsubtle remarks when Mistress Blount refused to relinquish her post. "Have I not served His Grace well? Fortune favors him tonight."

All held their breaths, waiting to see who would prevail—the old mistress or the new one.

"Your Grace's dice seem well kissed," Anne remarked cattily, her resentful gaze bouncing between the king and Bessie, who stood her ground with daggers in her eyes.

The king smiled. Like all men, Renée thought, he enjoyed being fought over. He opened his mouth to speak. Buckingham cut him off. "Do as His Majesty says, Anne," he snapped tersely.

King Henry lost his cheer. Buckingham was a fool, Renée decided. Henry wasn't. The king contemplated the duke, then settled his gaze on Anne. "Well kissed though my dice may be, as king, I require a dutiful kiss from a Stafford set of lips." A direct hit. Buckingham reddened.

There were sharp intakes of breath among the spectators. Renée stifled her shocked laughter. No wonder Buckingham felt rabid. More than desiring obedience, King Henry wished to humble the arrogant duke. She waited for Anne's rejoinder, knowing what hers would be. Anne giggled. "Jesu, spare me of this plight! To please my beloved king, I must neglect my beloved brother!"

Renée groaned inwardly. The pie-goose! Lacking the wit to appreciate the fine subtleties of this treacherous game and the skill to play it withal, poor Anne had stupidly taken the king's words at face value and opened herself to attack. Someone was sure to pounce on her answer.

"Verily a plight that bears a weighty and serious brow," observed a gentleman at the table. Renée narrowed her eyes on the dark-haired lord. Earl Surrey, Norfolk's son. "The question that needs must be answered is whom my Lady Hastings loves more— her brother . . . or her king?"

Murmurs then silence gripped the air as the courtiers waited to hear how Anne would extract herself from this self-inflicted bind. Buckingham's hard gaze locked with Surrey's.

A clever trap, Renée acceded; the sort her father would delight in setting. A fool will fall, a wise man will keep the fool down and fell more fools with him, had been his motto. Certes, Buckingham could rescue Anne graciously, but his pride impeded him from admitting to coming second to Henry Tudor in anything, even if just for show. As for Henry, the alert glint in his eye attested to his disapproval of Surrey's ugly maneuver. Nevertheless, he was interested in hearing Anne's response—and in Buckingham's reaction to it.

Anne, bewildered by the strange undercurrents, dreaded opening her beak, her apprehensive gaze darting between the men at the table. Renée took pity on her and whispered a reply in her ear. She felt Anne squeeze her wrist in thanks before plastering a smile on her face and saying, "I love my brother as I love myself, but I would lay my life for my king, and there is your answer, my lord." She leaned over to rake the royal dice, presenting King Henry with an alluring view of her magnificent udders, pressed the dice to her wide lips, and then offered them back to the king with a curtsey. Pleased with her answer, King Henry shot the dice across the board and won. The spectators applauded.

"Our adored king is most fortunate to claim the love of a lucky lady, in dice as well as in her choice of friends." Surrey's gaze veered from Anne to Renée. Black eyes assessed her with cold deliberation. Thomas Howard was Rougé's English counterpart in looks and years, but she had a feeling he was colder and more dangerous for the backing of a powerful duke as his sire. Foiling his trap, whereby attracting his notice and enmity, had been unwise, or mayhap not. Anne was in the king's good graces once again and well on her way to becoming his partner for the masque.

Renée eased her wrist out of Anne's clasp and let the courtiers pushing to stand in the royal radiance spew her out. She refused to feel guilt or remorse over what she had helped precipitate. King Henry was no innocent. He ordered people's deaths; he lived in luxury at the expense of his poor, plague-ridden subjects; he was spoiled, vainglorious, and adulterous. He was king. Perhaps he did not deserve to die tonight, but such was reality. It was him or her.

She searched the room for Rougé. Her gaze collided with turquoise eyes. The fair stranger. As evidenced by his pleased expression, he had been watching her, waiting for her to notice him again. Leaning against the wall beside a bearded fellow, he pinioned her with a stare so direct her belly fluttered. There was no putting off this confrontation. She had to know who he was, what he was after, and whom he served. She started toward him at an easy pace, skirting the dancers. Anticipation lit his bright eyes; white teeth flashed in a smile between tanned cheeks. He pushed away from the wall. Of a sudden a man blocked her view of him. She stiffened. Norfolk's man!

"Sir Walter Devereaux, madame. At your service." The intruder bowed. "I have decided to be overbold and present myself as your most enchanted admirer, yours to command in all things."

Renée eyed him disdainfully. Gallophobic churl! Did Norfolk put him up to wooing her or was he serving his own interests? "Sir Walter." She bobbed politely and made to sidestep him.

Again the irksome importuner stepped into her path. "My lady, would you do me the honors of standing up with me at the midnight masque?"

She smiled coldly. "Sir, I challenge you to recognize me masked. *Au revoir!*"

He shifted again. "You shall discover, madame, that I rise most potently to every challenge."

Did he, now? The insolent knave! "And you shall discover, sir, that I snip overreaching vines like . . . that!" She snapped her fingers, making him flinch. With a smile and a flounce of skirts, she moved past him without breaking into a run and rammed into another obstacle: hard, large, and tall. She would have toppled back if strong hands hadn't caught her arms and set her aright.

The hands let go of her. "Your pardon, my lady."

Renée looked up into luminous eyes, reminiscent of the Mediterranean Sea, set in a striking, suntanned face. She lost her power of speech. He smelled wonderfully, Castilian soap, a whiff of bergamot musk, body heat. A patch of burnished skin on the side of his neck betwixt his white lawn collar and the silken filaments of gold hair enticed her eyes. She imagined pressing her lips there, learning the texture of—Jesu, mercy! What was the matter with her?

The spellbinder's features furrowed with concern. "Mayhap you should sit. You look faint." Gallantly he conducted her to a bench and knelt before her, handing her a cup of perry.

She accepted the drink, lowering her gaze lest he read her mind. "I thank you, sir."

"Was that man troubling you?"

"No more than others." Feeling sufficiently restored, she looked at him. "Who are you?"

He straightened and bowed with a hand across his heart. "Michael Devereaux, *enchanté.*"

"Another Devereaux?" She noted the likeness, but Michael was . . . She sipped her pear cider.

His expression shuttered. "I am unfamiliar with others who lay claim to my surname."

Renée ventured a direct look at him. "Why have you been staring at me?" It was a probe.

A soft smile curled his lips. "Two reasons. I daresay you can guess them, madame."

It pleased her that he found her appealing. "What was your business in the undercroft?"

Her straightforwardness wrenched an embarrassed laugh from him. "May I?" At her nod, he eased himself down on the bench. His eyes glittered as he gauged her humor. "Quid pro quo?"

"Tit for tat," she consented with a smilet, and realized to her shame that she was flirting.

"I was given lodging there and was looking for the stair to the upper level. Now you."

"Lodging in the undercroft? Surely not!" She wrinkled her nose in distaste, taking in his fine apparel, which lacked the exuberance of the courtly male fashion and yet exuded sophistication.

A vulnerable look came at her, swiftly banked—and she knew. "Your first visit to court? Did the usher swear all the better lodgings were taken and the inns overcrowded?"

"You have divined it, my lady."

"Renée." She offered her hand. As warm lips lightly touched her knuckles, startling pleasure blazed through her. She retrieved her seared limb. "You sleep there, with the wine and the rats?"

He gave an indifferent shrug. "I have not yet had the pleasure. I arrived today."

Renée read discomfiture in his eyes. Clearly someone had practiced on him, and he had not the savoir faire to rectify the situation. What an ignoramus he was, a boy in a man's body. How he would suffer at this court. Then again, the wounded cub one petted yesterday might turn into a mastiff and bite one's hand tomorrow. Notwithstanding his ingenuousness, she sensed strength and secrets. He had the appearance of a warrior angel, St. Michael slaying the Serpent. Her mind spun mischief. "I owe you a tat. I suggest you have a word with one of the White Sticks, the six officers of the court," she explained, ticking them off her fingers. "The lord steward, the lord chamberlain, the master of the horse, the vice chamberlain, the comptroller, and the treasurer. You may recognize them by the gold collars with the SS links, their badges of portcullises and roses, and their wands of office. They administer the palace. All requires their seal of approval. Whoever assigned you the inadequate quarters answers to one of them."

"Whom do you recommend I speak to?"

"Without doubt Earl Worcester, the lord chamberlain. The old bibber has had a run of bad luck at the gaming tables. I imagine he should appreciate a discreet contribution to his private treasury. A liberal sum will purchase a scolding and penalty for the usher who wronged you."

"Earl Worcester," he repeated, committing the name to memory.

"In future do not hesitate to press coins into hands. Greed makes the world go round. All is purchasable at court: a higher seat, a softer bed, a bowl of fruit . . ." A wealth of information.

A dazzling smile broke out on his tanned face, transforming him from handsome to gorgeous. "I am much obliged to you, madame. In truth, I had not thought . . . You must think me a noddy."

In truth, she did not like the direction of her thoughts. "Are we even?"

"Hardly. You are a princess, and I . . . your grateful student." He inclined his golden head. He was a gentleman, Renée realized. He knew she had tricked him with her answer and let it slide.

"There you are!" Anne materialized before them.

Michael shot to his feet and offered Anne a fluid bow. "My lady."

"Why did you leave the gaming table?" Renée demanded to know.

"Everyone is gone to dress for the masque." Her eyes devouring, Anne offered Michael her hand. "Good evening, sir. I do not believe I have seen you at court before."

"It is my first pilgrimage, my lady." He kissed her plump chilblained fingers.

She smiled provocatively. "Your first time . . . Are you prepared to lose your innocence?"

Renée felt nauseated. Michael chuckled. "Most heartily, beauteous lady."

"Anne." She glided closer to him, keeping her hand in his. "Who might you be, Viking?"

"Michael Devereaux, at your service." He honored her with a courteous tilt of his head.

"Are you come to plunder and ravish, Viking, or to joust and make merry?"

"I am come to do all four, madame."

Renée watched the interlude with grim annoyance. The horrid flirt had destroyed any chance of gleaning information from the man and was neglecting to do her part in her brother's plot. She stood. "Shall we go dress for the masque?"

"Anon, friend." Anne dismissed her as if Renée was a pesky fly and ran her fingertips over the sporran attached to Michael Devereaux's sword belt. "It seems I was mistaken. You are a Celtic warrior, not a Viking."

He laughed. "Mayhap a bit of both, a Norse-Gael."

Her fingertips continued playing with his sporran. "What do you carry inside your pouch?"

"Magic potions, my Lady Anne, to bespell the delightful ladies of the court and make them fall violently in love with me."

An inch to the left and Anne would be caressing the magic scepter, Renée fumed, disgusted with Anne's wanton, sabotaging flightiness. "Pray excuse us," she told Michael. "We would not want the battle to begin without us." She linked her arm with Anne's and dragged her away.

Armed with flowers, fruit, and sweets, Templar knights and Saracen ladies blasted at each other across the chamber, their ebullient laughter drowning out the accompanying music. Their identities effectively concealed with half masks and cowls, some of the participants, ladies and knights alike, jumped on the tables and were slinging their ammunition with ribald accuracy.

Renée could not recall laughing as heartily or indulging in such frivolity. For a few precious moments her worries dissolved, banished by mirth and mayhem. Regrettably the combatants ran out of sugared darts all too soon. The king's fool, presiding over the romp as Lord of Misrule, pronounced the ladies victors. With shrieks and bounds the Saracen sirens herded the vanquished Templar army to the center of the hall and ordered them to line up for a volta.

Sobering, Renée sought the king and Anne among the disguised. Anne's curvaceous figure was identifiable, but there were several knights who matched the king's physique. As the ladies chose partners, she saw Anne move toward one of the king's lookalikes. Was he the king? He was too lean, too tall . . . *Oh no!* The pie-goose would ruin everything! Certes that was what Anne wanted, to hoodwink her brother with impunity. *Would you say he is as tall as our king?* How could Renée have thought Anne a wantwit? She was the witless one. She should have read the signs—the interest, the aggressive flirting—and realized Anne was netting a scapegoat. After the deed was done and the victim was unmasked, Buckingham would be hard put to accuse Anne of trickery.

Disregarding the rules of decorum, Renée hurled herself at Anne's chosen dance partner. There was no mistaking his identity when eyes the color of the sea in Marseille touched hers. Then the heavy-lidded eyes slid toward Anne. *No! Choose me*, Renée implored silently, and in an act of despair took her boldness to a new zenith. She stepped closer to him and gripped his hand.

Michael's hand was large, gentle, and very warm. Transfixing her with the force of his gaze, he opened her palm to his kiss. Heat filled her belly, swirling, tumbling, doing strange things to her mind and body. Then, wordlessly, apologetically, he let go of her hand and took Anne's. No! Renée was in turmoil. She could not allow this to happen. She gripped his arm, rose on tiptoe, and whispered harshly in his ear, "Do not dance with her, you fool! He will kill you!"

"I know," he murmured, clouding her with his heady scent. He craned his head until their lips nearly touched. Her heart pounded. There was steel in his eyes. "Forewarned is forearmed."

Renée stumbled back in shock. He was rescuing the king. He was using Buckingham's trap to ensnare the traitor—and there was nothing, absolutely nothing she could do to stop him.

The musicians struck up a volta. A Templar knight whisked her to the dance. She performed the sinkapace perfunctorily, right, left, right, left, all the while chasing Anne and her partner with damning eyes. Her perfect opportunity was lost. She would have to start scheming afresh.

A murrain on them both!

On the fifth count, all the knights grabbed hold of their female partners' hip with one hand and the hard waistline edge of their busk with the other, closing the position for the spring, and Renée, feeling numb with defeat, put her hand on her partner's shoulder and presented him with her masked profile, as was the rule of the dance. The step before the leap was the most sensual of the volta, when words of love and desire were whispered. She felt her partner's humid breath on her temple, his lips almost touching; then he boosted her into the air and held her up with his hands, his thigh under her thighs. She stared down at him as he turned and slid her along the length of his body to the floor, and knew who he was: Sir Walter Devereaux, Norfolk's man.

Feminine laughter rang hard by, Bessie Blount delighting in her chosen dance partner, a tall, robust knight with broad shoulders and an authoritarian posture—King Henry.

The dancing continued with no end in sight. Tired and dismayed, barely able to stand on her aching feet, Renée saw no point in her waiting for the unmasking. Hence, when the dance ended, she thanked her partner and turned away from him, but his arm insinuated itself around her waist and drew her back up against his chest. "You owe me a kiss of peace," he murmured in her ear.

"Let go of me, sir."

"And let us part as enemies? I think not."

She saw a couple sneak out of the chamber—Anne and Michael—and felt the familiar tug of curiosity propelling her after them, but her dance partner was holding her put. *Better this way*, she thought. *I cannot be caught lurking.* As the couple vanished, so did her last drop of strength. Oh, it would have been so easy, if the fools had not decided to extemporize. She turned around in a swish of skirts and glared up at Sir Walter. "Make it brief." *Or you shall live to regret it.*

A gleam entered his brown eyes. Oh, he most definitely had plans for her. "Aye, madame." Placing a finger beneath her chin, he tilted her face up and touched his lips to hers. His kiss was adequately civil. "Do remember what I said, Princess. I am yours to command in all things."

With a humphy toss of her head, Renée took her leave of him and strode out of the room.

"Come away!" Anne dragged Michael by the hand along the dim hallway. He followed her tamely, aware that they were being followed. The bay behind the Venus tapestry, the Duke of Buckingham had said. When they reached it, Anne snatched back the arras and dragged him into the snug dark recess with her. Facing him, she curled her free hand around his covered nape and pulled his mouth down on hers. Their visorlike masks compressed as their kiss grew hotter, but he dared not unmask, not before his would-be assassin made his attempt. The assailant was close. Any moment now a blade would plunge into his back from behind the tapestry; that was the plan.

Abruptly Anne tore her mouth away. There was an edge of panic in her voice. "Leave!" she blurted urgently. "I beg you. Leave now!"

Michael went still. She had set him up and was now alerting

him to the danger. Her change of heart surprised him—but did not elate him half as much as the French princess's forewarning. She, too, had realized Anne's ploy and tried to talk him out of his heroic undertaking. For a brief moment he had been violently tempted to forget the plot and choose Renée instead. Ultimately his brain had made the selection, as Lord Tyrone was wont to say: "Dare to be wise and leave the rest to the gods." Yes, he was very wise. Disgustingly sensible. He deserved a trophy.

"Hush." Michael put a finger to Anne's lips when she grew hysterical, imploring him to flee. He sensed the assassin creeping closer to the tapestry. Excited and tense, the man—the duke—reeked of sweat. Michael heard his heavy breathing. He waited, keeping Anne's back to the wall inside the recess, his back exposed to the arras. The duke could not suspect his sister of betraying him. Michael needed to react to something—a noise, a movement—rather than anticipate the assault. His senses signaled that the duke was directly behind him. Tension sizzled through his taut body. He heard the soft rasp of a dagger sliding from its sheath. . . . He stepped out swiftly.

The masked assailant jolted and thrust. Steel flashed against Michael's abdomen. He caught the wrist wielding the blade and knocked the hand against his knee. As the dagger clanked to the floor, he grabbed the duke by the throat and sent him crashing against the opposite wall.

The guised Duke of Buckingham sank to the floor with grunts and invectives. Michael was already towering over him, the dagger in his hand. In the dying light of the gallery's cressets, his form loomed as a sinister hulking shadow. "Go off! Or I will hack you, my word upon't."

Groaning with pain, the duke looked up at him. "Who the pox are you?"

"Your worst incubus, if you do not remove yourself hence." He watched the duke push to his feet awkwardly and stumble out of sight. He sheathed the duke's dagger in his sword belt and returned to the dark alcove behind the wall-hanging. He found Anne juddering as a terrified rabbit caught in a huntsman's snare.

"Wh-what happened?" she asked in distress.

"A drunkard slinked behind me and tried to cut my purse. I chased him off."

"Th-that's all?" She tilted her head back, the white of her eyes visible in the shadows.

"Not a drop of blood was shed tonight. Be at ease, sweet Saracen."

Suddenly she threw her arms around his neck and kissed him, plunging her tongue into his mouth and rubbing her body against him. Her hand found his codpiece and kneaded him artfully. "Take me, take me," she implored, yanking her sleeve down to bare a generous white globe. She put his hand on her breast and wiggled her thighs against his groins. The lady was afire!

Her breast felt deliciously heavy and ripe. Not one to disappoint a lady in distress, especially one who had spent three years in pious chastity, Michael ran his thumb over the firm nipple. She cried out for more. His semiaroused cod grew taut and aching for fulfillment. Bowing his head to suck the hard nipple into his mouth, he grabbed fistfuls of her multilayered gown with both hands and bared her legs up to her waist. Her gasps and wiggles encouraged him to do his worst. He probed between her thighs to find the lips of her sex slick with her lust. Stroking her with one hand, he unlaced the points of his codpiece with the other. He was stiff as a pole. "Cling to my neck," he instructed. He hoisted her plump thighs, which instantly parted wide to accommodate him, and thrust into her, pressing her back to the wall. She smelled of civet and too much wine. She locked her legs around his waist as he pounded into her, working his cod into her moist depths with swift, forceful lunges. The air in the recess grew muggy with their labored breaths.

Their joining was rough and urgent, pure lust, naught more, and Anne seemed to relish their shameless savagery. As she bounced in a frenzied rhythm, her hips gyrating with increasing urgency, her mewing took on a higher pitch. Sweat coated his skin as he fought the inexorable urge to blow. She was hot and wet, and he was primed to take his pleasure. He shoved himself into her harder, faster, on the edge of endurance. He felt her tighten into a fist around him; then with a shrill cry she clenched spasmodically, her body shuddering on a wave of rapture. With a low growl, he surrendered to the roaring tension shooting up his spine, finding his release at last.

Renée strode rapidly to her apartment. She had failed, but what could she have done? The big ape was not to be swayed. And Anne—that qualmish trollop!—she outfoxed her. God's pity! Aware of the two armed guards shadowing her, Renée quickened her step. They were her guards, but she was not used to being watched over all the time. It was unsettling rather than comforting.

Two more Valois guards waited outside her palace apartment. Sentries. By King Francis's fiat, the bodyguard was to escort her everywhere, safeguard her residence, and assist her in all of her endeavors. They flung open the door to let her in. She bade all four a good night and entered her apartment. The privy chamber was disconcertingly gloomy, the fire on the hearth reduced to glowing embers. "Adele?" she called, bolting the door.

Out of the darkness a pair of strong hands grabbed her from behind, one swooped across her mouth as the other pinned her to a hard body. She could not move. She could not scream.

Michael eased Anne to her feet and laced his codpiece. She put her breast inside her bodice, pulled up her sleeve, and shook out the folds of her gown. "I have not been with a man in over three years," she whispered. "I enjoyed you very much."

"I enjoyed you." He smiled, noting that he and Anne had shed their masks. "Had we a bed, I would indulge further." The very idea of returning to sleep in the undercroft dismayed him.

"I have a great bed and an absent husband. . . ."

Michael grinned. "If this is an invitation, I heartily accept." He cupped her waist and melded their bodies together. "Though I warn you, you shan't get much sleep with me in your bed."

She gave a breathy laugh, a trifle jaded, but he did not mind. She took his hand. "Come, my young Norse-Gael warrior. Let us establish the extent of your vigor." She led him outside the alcove, her wary gaze scanning the hallway for people. There was no one in sight. Laughter rang from the royal apartment, mingling with music notes. The revelry would continue till dawn.

As if on muted accord, they traversed the passageways at a fast pace, watchful for passersby, disinclined to be seen together. So long as Buckingham never discovered the identity of the man Anne "mistook" for King Henry, the duke would not be able to retaliate against Michael or Anne.

A pair of nightwatchmen guarded the entrance to the wing where the king housed his noble guests. One of the guards turned his head in Michael and Anne's direction. Perdition! Michael cursed, realizing they had left the half masks in the alcove. He pulled her into his embrace and dragged her aside to lean against the shadowed wall, the sconce of which had been snuffed out.

"Wait here," he whispered, and tore back up the passageways. He collected the masks from the floor of the alcove and returned to her side within moments. His cowl had slipped off his head. He tied on his satin visor, pulled the cowl back up, and tugged it low over his eyes.

"Do you suppose he saw our faces?" Anne inquired worriedly.

"Let us proceed. The longer we delay, the more he is likely to remember us." Wrapping an arm about her and stooping to disguise his true height, he let her conduct him to her chamber.

Renée swallowed her panic, reached inside her inner sleeve, and gripped the hidden hilt of a tiny dirk. She slid it out smoothly, then stabbed the thigh pressed to hers. Her attacker cursed and released her. Her heart thudding, she unbolted the door, shouting for the guards. They burst in but instead of pouncing on her assailant stood gaping at his obscure form.

"Well done, madame," the interloper rasped, pressing a hand to his thigh.

Renée staggered back. "Sergeant Francesco! What are you at, sir? Who did you think I was? Jesu, you are bleeding! Where is Adele? She will dress your wound. Adele!"

Her tiring woman stepped out of the bedchamber, clucking her tongue disapprovingly. "He can clean his own muck," she muttered in thick Breton dialect, a mixture of Gaelic and French.

Renée's gaze bounced between Adele, the sergeant, and the guards. "What goes on here?"

"He"—Adele gestured at Sergeant Francesco—"thought it wise to put your new training to the test. He bade me douse the fire and stay out of sight in the bedchamber."

Renée leveled a glare at him. "Is this true, Sergeant? Did you ambush me on purpose?"

"Your pardon. I followed Lieutenant Armado's orders. He thought it prudent to practice."

Incredulity rounded her eyes. "At this hour of the night?"

"It is our responsibility to ensure you are well trained, which you are."

"Where is Lieutenant Armado?" When he did not volunteer an answer, she looked at the bloodstained silver dirk clutched in her fist. Her heart was still in palpitations, but her hand was steady as a rock. "Do sit down by the fire, Sergeant. I will tend to your wound. Your men may return to their post or . . . to bed." She had no idea what their routine was. She did not know all of their names yet. She only knew that when they were not stalking her, they were staying in one of the inns at the wharf. "Adele, fetch me clean wads of linen, hot water, and wine, if you please."

Snorting her displeasure, Adele turned on her heel and stalked back into the bedchamber.

"Pray forgive my assault and allow me to commend you on a most competent retaliation." The sergeant limped to the fireplace, threw a few logs in, sending sparks swirling up the flue, and sat on the long cushioned settle in front of the hearth. He was wiry and agile, stalwart, too.

Renée was fond of him. She sat on a stool to examine the cut she had inflicted on his thigh.

"The gash is not deep," he reassured her. "My costume's thick leather hose was designed to protect the muscle from a deep stabbing, and your dirk is quite small."

"Lieutenant Armado gave the dirk to me when we trained in France."

Adele returned with the items Renée had requested. She offered the sergeant a cup of wine, dropped clean strips of linen on the little table beside him, and set a kettle of water on the trivet in the fire. With another harrumph directed at the soldier, she cleaned

Renée's blood-smeared silver dirk and returned it to her mistress. "His blood will ruin your gown. I will bandage him."

"Thank you, Adele." Renée got up and moved to sit on the settle by the sergeant.

"We must speak in confidence," he said, eying Adele with misgiving.

"Bah!" said Adele.

Renée smiled. Since the fiasco in France, her old nurse refused to leave her mistress alone in the company of men. "Whatever you wish to discuss, Sergeant, you may do so in front of Adele."

"As you wish, madame." He saw her slide the thin silver dirk back inside her sleeve. "It is a clever little blade, easily concealed and wielded, as you have demonstrated. Ouch!" He flinched when Adele ripped open his hose and dabbed a wad of linen soaked in green ointment at the cut.

"The watercress will purify the proud flesh," Adele muttered in Breton.

Renée translated the phrase to the sergeant. "Madame," he said tentatively. "We are here to serve, protect, and abet you. We are bound by a sacred oath to accomplish this mission. It is our duty as well as a privilege. I understand my Lord Cardinal explained about our specialty."

"Yes, Cardinal Medici told me all about you. You are *deletoris*."

He nodded. "Perhaps Lieutenant Armado wanted to make a point tonight, with the exercise."

"What point might that be, that you can make sport of me in the middle of night, Sergeant?"

"No, madame. The point is that we are yours. We belong to you. We do what you say. We are your loyal bloodhounds. You give an order, and we jump. No questions, only obedience."

Renée gave an unnerved laugh. How slavish he sounded. Her thought must have showed, for he said, "We are well trained and educated. We hail from good families in Italy. We take pride in our office. We are soldiers in service of God. Employ us. That is what we are here for."

Not common men-at-arms. She took a life-threatening gamble.

"Cardinal Campeggio is in London. Did you know? Rougé informs me the good cardinal is calling for a crusade."

"No, madame. He safeguards the Ancient. Although he was the one who convinced the pope to appoint Wolsey papal legate, Campeggio does not trust his ambitious English colleague and remains in London to keep an eye on him at York Place, Cardinal Wolsey's palace upriver. He rarely comes to court and always travels with his *deletoris*."

Jesu mercy, she was a fool! What had she thought to accomplish by abetting Buckingham tonight? Supposing he had killed the king, what would she have done? Hailed a barge to York Place in the dead of night? Infiltrated the Lord Chancellor of England's bulwarked palace? Rummaged around for the Ancient? Thank God the plan had failed. Now that she thought upon it, Anne had done her a good service. She burned with curiosity to know what had transpired. Had Buckingham slain the wrong man? *Forewarned is forearmed*, Michael Devereaux had whispered.

He was not dead. Somehow he had thwarted the duke. He might not be well informed in the ways of the world, but he was clever. He had played into Anne's trap with all the innocence of a lamb, knowing precisely what he was about. He would not have let Anne lure out anyone else.

Now she must pray His Grace of Buckinghamshire would try again—and she would be ready next time. "Why do you serve Medici instead of Campeggio?"

"A long-standing political feud between Lieutenant Armado and Captain Luzio in charge of Campeggio's *deletoris*. We broke from them. We serve the next pope, madame. We serve you."

She decided to trust him. "Sergeant, send your best man to masquerade as a servant at York Place. We need to know the precise whereabouts of the Ancient. Is it interred in the undercroft? Is it locked away in the treasury chamber? Is it under the cardinal's bed? Under his hat?"

"Yes, madame!" Sergeant Francesco stood, his thigh poulticed, his expression laying bare his dedication. "I shall undertake this assignment myself and inform Lieutenant Armado."

His gusto was infectious. "Proceed with due caution, for I imagine this Captain Luzio cannot know you are in London, and with all speed, Sergeant. The opportune moment is ripening."

Fever hailed the dawn. His skin afire, his throat parched, his head hammering mercilessly, Michael tumbled out of Anne's bed and grabbed his sporran. The bottle inside it was empty. He cursed in Gaelic. He had drained it before the masque. How would he make it to the undercroft?

His condition was deteriorating. Most of the time, he felt strong and invigorated, but at dawn he was nothing, a slave to the dragon's blood. . . .

With immense effort, he pulled on his hose, boots, shirt, and doublet, strapped on his sword belt, and with a backward glance at the naked woman passed out amid tangled linen staggered for the door. Outside in the passageway the nightwatchmen were fast asleep, some on their feet, others sprawled on steps. Feeling faint, Michael negotiated the dim palace corridors with his eyes half closed, his skin dripping sweat, his heart galloping like a stampede of wild boar.

All of a sudden his hackles rose. Someone was following him. Was it the duke? He felt too ill to defend himself but drew his sword nonetheless and investigated the shadows.

Something stirred behind him. Michael span on his heel and squinted against the first sunray piercing the lozenges. Whoever had been stalking him was gone, wafted away. He swiped a hand over his damp face, gasping for air. Was he sickly delusional or had the danger been real?

Drawing on his last drop of strength, he trudged to the undercroft, swaying against the walls, panting. He nearly tumbled down the stone steps. Most of the torches had stubbed out. Dimness reigned, yet he kept on moving, navigating by instinct, by memory. He gave a hoarse shout of relief upon sighting the door to his lair. With shaky hands, he unlocked it and pushed inside. He dropped to his knees before the iron casket. Inserting the tiny key took an eternity. Finally the lid was open. He grabbed a bottle, unstoppered it, and swilled it to the dregs. *Bliss.*

Michael locked the casket, shoved it aside, and fell back on the truckle bed. He managed to pull off one boot and felt the brew's potent kick lull him to sleep. . . .

The door banged open against the wall, and a jovial voice exclaimed, "Rise and shine!"

Oh no. Michael groaned. He had forgotten to lock the door. "Go away . . ." he pleaded.

"A new day has dawned! The king would have a shot at a stag, and we go with him!"

"Methinks not . . ." Michael murmured, willing Stanley's noxiously jolly voice to fade away.

"How swiftly is duty forsaken when Hypnos and Morpheus beckon. . . ." Without warning, a pail of ice water hit Michael's face, shocking him into wakefulness.

Sputtering, he pulled off his second boot and flung it at Stanley. "Verily you are a fellow of wild and eccentric habits. Do you drown all your adversaries?"

The boot ricocheted back at him. "The hunt is up, the morn is bright and gay!" Stanley sang in his deep voice. "The fields are fragrant, and the woods are green! Comb your fair locks and look hearty, for there be no place for a shag-haired scruff at the king's hunting party!"

Michael squinted at the bearded man grinning at him. "Hunting? Let it be a shooting from a standing, or better yet, dispatch me now and be done. You are no friend of mine, Stanley."

"How misguided you are, runt. You shan't find a better companion at court. Now up, my somnolent friend. Time to show the King of England what Irish-bred upstarts are made of."

"I give Your Grace and Your Lordship good morrow."

"Ah, Sir Walter." As the hour was early, the Duke of Norfolk welcomed him in a housecoat and a homely biggen. His son Surrey was splendidly dressed for the hunt. "Some mead?"

"I thank Your Grace." Walter sauntered in, his muscles taut with exuberance over what he was about to relay. After squiring Lieutenant Armado Baglioni of Princess Renée's bodyguard in the Southwark stews all night, he returned to his chambers, washed off the stank of whores, stale ale, and contact with rank persons, dressed, and hurried to report. Awake since yesterday, he felt more alive than he had in a long time. "I have tidings Your Grace will find interesting, I trow."

"Sit with us." The duke indicated the X chair facing the cushioned settle before the fireplace.

"Your Grace, although I have yet to fathom the great secret concealed behind the evidence I have uncovered, I believe I have touched upon a vein in Cardinal Wolsey's schemes."

The ancient duke's left eye twitched—a good sign. "Go on."

Walter described how he had approached the officer in charge of safeguarding the princess and lured him to a night of revelry in the stews, how he had poured ale down Armado's gorge and encouraged him to lose money playing with false dice, and how he had returned him safe and sound to the palace. "He wears a pendant round his neck," he went on with barely contained glee. "A gold cross over black, with a Latin motto that says 'Soldiers in Service of God.'"

"Same as the insignia of Cardinal Campeggio's bodyguard," remarked Surrey.

"Precisely!" Walter exclaimed. "Very peculiar, methinks. The princess's guards are liveried in the blue colors of France with the golden fleur-de-lis. Also peculiar, as one would expect her bodyguard to display the field of ermine over white, the badge of the duchy of Brittany."

"This is perfectly understandable, considering she is come on a peace mission. Her embassy, headed by the French ambassador, the Marquis of Rougé, represents France."

"Why the gold cross over black, then? Soldiers of God, a secret papal army none has heard of arrives with an Italian cardinal calling for a crusade while at the same time a French princess on a dubious peace mission is bucklered by the same army, only in disguise."

"I wonder if Rougé knows aught about it," murmured the duke.

"We must determine how Wolsey fits into this fretwork of spies," Surrey told his sire.

"Shall I continue entertaining the dice-happy lieutenant?" Walter asked. He felt ebullient. Here he was, conspiring with the powerful Howards, sharing confidences.

"Bring me his pendant," the duke ordered. He stared at his son.

Surrey rose. "I am to hunt with the king this morning. Join me, Sir Walter."

Walter leaped to his feet. Hunting with the king! "Thank you, my lord. Your Grace."

For I felt myself drawn from my own image
And into a solitary wandering stag
From wood to wood quickly I am transformed
And still I flee the belling of my hounds.

—Petrarch: *Poem XXIII*

King Henry's hunting party, led by a pack of boisterous hounds, galloped across sprawling hills of green and through woods of beech in a triumph of bursting virility and equine muscle. The hunt had begun at daybreak, before the king rose. The Greenwich Park huntsmen had chosen a specific deer and positioned themselves with teams of dogs in a few strategic places around the hunting area. When the king's party arrived, the hart was roused and the chase began.

Horns blared ahead, informing the main hunting party of the progress of the deer. Glowing with the exuberance of the sport, King Henry brought his party to a standstill at the top of a knoll overlooking the lush hunting ground and shielded his eyes against the gray-white morning sun.

Michael, sluggish and brain-numb, drew rein alongside Stanley. The hounds, fresh and alert after a good night's sleep in the royal kennels, surrounded him thereupon, barking alarum like sergeants-at-arms berating a slothful straggler, drooling rosaries, and affrighting the horses.

The king, the archers of the royal bodyguard, and the noble huntsmen drew back to calm their jittery coursers. Michael flushed to the roots of his hair. He was isolated by the snarling dogs and the hound-boys striving to gentle them, aware of the derogatory glowers lobbed his way. Mortified, he brandished his hand swiftly like a sword over the hostile bloodhounds. *"Sede!"*

Astonishingly the fearsome dogs slumped on their haunches, yapping like penitent puppies, heads bowed meekly. Mentally wiping his brow, Michael nodded at the awestruck king and his men and stirred Archangel to Stanley's side, as a boy seeking refuge in his mum's kirtle.

"Well done, runt!" Stanley laughed heartily. "Next you shall teach the monstrous beasts how to tumble, dance, and balance cups on their brown noses. Ho there, my minion." He soothed his agitated horse as it shied away from Michael. "You do not care for hulking Irish trolls, do you? They have a penchant for inhabiting foul underground places, under bridges, under the palace . . ."

"Ha-ha. How did you know where to find me? I have yet to understand the geography of the depressing burrows, myself."

"I asked." Stanley kept soothing his restless mount. "Herne is a splendid hunter. Harry sits his brother, Hermes. The surest way to please our king is to give him a fine courser." *Or falcons*, Michael added silently. Stanley smiled at him. "So . . . did you lose a wager or something?"

"No," Michael growled; he was tired, irritable, and in no mood to be gulled.

Stanley could not help himself. "Then how come you are sleeping with the rodents?"

"Forsooth, I got it already. I should have bribed the confounded usher for better lodging. But how the deuce was I supposed to know the man was peddling when he insisted the best quarters have all been snatched by the early arrivance?"

"Hmm." Stanley scratched his beard gravely. "The bones to the latecomer, eh? I reckon His Grace of Suffolk who arrived early this morn with his wife the Lady Mary, our king's lady sister and the Dowager Queen of France, will be bedded down with the horses tonight." A grin broke out on his face. "Aw, do not give me that look! I shall burst into tears. Speaking to you this morn is like bear-baiting."

"So don't bait." Michael, his sleep-deprived brain lagging behind the conversation, recalled the illuminating advice dispensed to him last night, courtesy of Princess Renée de Valois. "Yes, well, I'm seeing Earl Worcester, one of the White Sticks, later today to discuss this business of my lodging. By dusk, I will have relocated to a softer, more salubrious bed, be at rest as to that."

"Ho-hoa! The youngling learns! Methinks a clever bird has been singing in your ear. Which one? The robin redbreast or the lily bluebird?"

"Bluebird." Blue-blooded, blue-eyed, blue-blazoned. She was never speaking to him again. She had wanted to dance with him, protect him, give him the kiss of peace, and he had spurned her—to be a plaguey hero! So he had frustrated the plot, confiscated the duke's dagger, but there were no laurels for this victor. None knew of his triumph, except Princess Renée. *Blockhead.*

"Why are you shaking your head?"

"Not why, at whom, myself. I am daft."

"Oh no." Stanley scowled. "I would not slobber after her, runt. Waste of time, bad business. Her king won't thank you. Nor will ours. She is a pretty painting to be admired from afar."

Michael felt something akin to unfledged contrariness well up in him. He felt querulous. He wanted to inform Stanley, growlingly, that he didn't give a toss who had sired her, that her being predestined to be sold at market like a broodmare to the highest bidding prince did not mean the lady knew not her mind and had no say in her choice of companions. She liked him. She was drawn to him. He knew it. He had sensed it the night before when he kissed her hand.

Lugubriously Stanley was right. He had no business tomcatting after a maidenly princess of France while duty-bound to serve his noble lord and fulfill his pledge of honor. He sighed. There were Annes and Cáits aplenty to alleviate any future discomforts the bluebird might rekindle. *Enthrall but do not love; be loved but do not be thralled.* Sound advice. Resist at the beginning, Ovid lectured. If one did not stamp out the disease of love at the start, one was lost. Oh, he was a fount of saws: *We always strive after what is forbidden and desire what is denied us.* Also Ovid.

Stanley's groan alerted Michael to the rider coming to join them. "Hastings, how now?"

That was all the invitation Sir George Hastings required to recount his hottest feats on the Welsh border in the service of his brother-in-law, Buckingham: hanging horse thieves, drubbing local dissenters, quelling sedition. What a dull, painful-to-be-around braggart, Michael grimaced. Anne's husband. No wonder she dallied. The man was a moldwarp, hairy and unnecessary.

It was King Henry who saved them from the affliction. "There!" The king pointed northeast to a lush hillock. The hart raised its shiny neck from a tussock of grass and stared at the looming riders. In the early light Michael saw its ingenuous brown eyes round in apprehension, could almost feel its heart accelerating its rhythm. Suddenly it took off. The king kneed his bay to a gallop. The hunting party flew after the king, fur-lined surcoats swelling in the wind, boisterous shouts letting whomever was watching know they were a hardy, savage gang of huntsmen, full of vim and vigor. The earth shook with the force of the hoofs tearing downhill, jumping over hedgerows of bracken, directed by the bloody-hunting dogs and the bray of bugles.

The hart fled at an astonishing speed, confounding the huntsmen scattered round the park, whereupon they communicated their confusion with horns. Doggedly in pursuit, the king's party chased the hart with bows in hand all the way to the stream, where the hart hounds lost the scent. The frustrated dogs leaped back and forth along the mossy bank, barking up a storm.

A flock of birds exploded into flight from the treetops as Michael reined in between Stanley and another fellow. King Henry addressed his head huntsman. "Why has my buck escaped?"

"I have never seen the like, sire," the huntsman mumbled apologetically. "Grew wings and vanished into thin air, it did. Something must have spooked it viciously, Your Majesty."

"See? I told you to wash," Stanley snickered.

The taunt glanced off Michael. His keen senses were picking up strange sounds: squirrels fleeing the nearby trees, rabbits diving into burrows, grasshoppers hopping off; a wholesale mad flight of animals. Before long, eerie silence surrounded the hunting party.

"You should have bloody well used toils to fence the buck in," said the fellow to Michael's right. Then he tossed Michael a man-to-man grin. "Incompetent addlepate."

Stanley leaned in, grinning. "I see your sportsmanship has grown rustic while you have been rusticating, Your Grace. We are here to shoot the buck, not let the dogs upon it."

The fellow snorted amusedly. "My Grace thanks you for sharing that morsel from your vast pantry of wisdom and perspicuity, but as you have shrewdly pointed out, Stanley, we are here to catch the buck in our cross-bolts, not fritter the day away sniffing after it like dogs."

"Little wonder the hapless creature decided its life should not be made sport of. Michael, I present my longtime brother in arms, disports, and taverns, Charles Brandon, His Grace the Duke of Suffolk. Charles, Michael Devereaux is the Earl of Tyrone's liege man and heir."

Suffolk turned aside in the creaky leather saddle to offer Michael his gloved hand. "Tyrone, eh? Never had the pleasure. Still fighting the blue-faced devils in Ireland?"

"More like keeping the peace, Your Grace." Michael gave the hand a strong squeeze.

"Like a big mouser, Tyrone keeps the mice down, eh?" Stanley put in.

Michael shrugged. He liked the Irish. They were valiant, good-natured people. "They are not exactly mice. . . ."

"Bloody savages," muttered Suffolk. "I trust my Lord Tyrone is grooming you to take over the governing of that island. I would not care to replace him. Say, is that a flask of Irish firewater tinkling in your pouch perchance?"

"*Uisce?*" Michael grinned. "No."

"Pity. Stanley, know you of any Irish taverns that serve the golden poison?"

"None that would serve Your Grace. You have been successfully banned from them all."

Suffolk smiled at Michael. "Heartening, is it not, to know one is successful at something?"

Michael smiled back. Charles Brandon, he recalled, was the son of a standard bearer, whose close friendship with King Henry yielded a dukedom and the hand in marriage of a princess.

The king was getting restless. He had already sent the huntsmen on foot to reconnoiter the woods beyond the stream, see if they could locate the fleeing hart.

"Why the delay?" Michael asked Stanley. "We could scout the grounds on horseback."

"Once the game escapes beyond the boundaries of Greenwich Park, we proceed with caution lest we kill the wrong buck. A blunder will result in embarrassment for Harry, as he'll be forced to pay compensation to the owner of the other buck, not to mention invalidate his prowess as a distinguished huntsman. Best be certain afore we proceed."

"I can tell you one thing for a certainty. The hart has crossed the stream. Did you not notice the animals of the forest fleeing? Look around. There is not a bird in sight. Some great predator is on the prowl. Nature is still, as if holding its breath, but only this side of the stream. Odd."

Wide yet shallow, the stream's cool waters rushed through amorphous boulders that caused rivulets and frothing. What sort of marauder would hesitate to cross water? On the opposite bank life thrived: rodents, crawlers, insects, and amphibians went about their business unperturbedly. As he regarded the lush vegetation beyond the stream, Michael glimpsed the regal hart, red-gold coat glistening with water, brown eyes wide and alert, hiding among the trees and spying on the hunting party. "There it is," he said softly, smiling. "In the leafy copse."

Stanley and Suffolk stared at Michael, then squinted at the area he pointed at. "You see it?"

"There. In front of us. See how vigilantly he observes our party?"

Stanley glanced at the king and lowered Michael's hand, murmuring, "Best be certain."

"I am. There is the buck. I see it." Were Stanley's eyes blind with the pin and web?

"If he says he sees it, we ought to let him lead us to it," Suffolk argued, and stepped his horse toward the king. "It appears we have a scout amongst us with a bloodhound's snout."

Stanley gave Michael a gimlet eye. "How can you tell it is the same buck?"

The question startled Michael into silence. *The scent.* Jupiter's thunder, he could not admit to picking out the scent of a specific hart. He was hard put to believe it himself. He just knew. "Irish methods," he hedged jokingly. "A trick I learned from the blue-deviled savages."

"So-ho! You have spotted my buck, have you?" King Henry drew close with Suffolk. "Well, where is it?" He surveyed the trees beyond the stream. "Point it to me."

"You had best be right," Stanley whispered to Michael's ears alone. He was not smiling.

"The buck hides in the thicket a hundred yards in front of Your Majesty," Michael said.

"Well, what do we wait for? Lead us to!" King Henry started crossing the stream.

Michael was waylaid by Stanley. His friend wanted to say something but changed his mind, shook his head, and followed the king into the stream. As soon as they emerged on the opposite bank, the same phenomenon occurred: a frantic migration of wildlife and no sign of the deer. Some of the king's gentlemen voiced their doubts. The king hung his eyes on Michael.

His confidence ebbing, Michael surveyed the area. Sure enough, the scent was strong. There was another telltale sign: rhythmic thudding. Hoofs or . . . heartbeats? His pulse remained calm and steady, whereas the unidentifiable thuds were frenetic, like a hammer hitting the anvil, faster and faster. "This way!" He spurred Archangel into the clustered birch trees, giving chase after the fleeing hart. The thudding grew stronger. King and party were hard behind him. They were forced to ride at a maddening sumpter pace to keep from getting prized out of the saddle by a twisted leafy bough or thick roots sticking out of the ground, while the agile, fleet-footed hart, unimpeded by such concerns, drew farther and farther away.

A league into the woods Michael began to rue his outspoken-ness. He could not see the hart; he was following it as a hound would, by scent, sound, and instinct. *I am gone mad*, he thought as he let his senses—or rather lack thereof—guide him onward. He should have stayed abed, or leastways heeded Stanley's warning. Taking the King of England on a wild hart chase to the next shire was probably not the brightest approach to curry favor with him. What a colossal gaucherie it would be should they be forced to turn back empty-handed. Mayhap he ought to call this off now in-stead of later and spare himself the greater embarrassment—

All of a sudden the hart halted, sweating, panting, slavering . . .

"Not far!" Michael cried over his shoulder, his confidence re-stored. Ignoring the leaves and offshoots swatting at his face, he rode faster for fear the hart would break into a dead run again.

The hart remained put; its scent grew stronger, as did the thud-ding. The hunting party with Michael at the lead was almost upon it. Its squeal of terror pierced the air. Birds flapped from their nests in distant treetops, soared into the sky, and circled high above their heads, screeching vociferously, as if alerting the animals to the formidable prowler invading their realm.

"There!" King Henry pointed at the ill-fated buck caught in a thicket by its majestic antlers.

The hunting party dismounted, crunching dry leaves and twigs under their boots. Awestruck, they approached the mythical golden creature with admiration in their eyes. In ancient times, the regal hart would be protected by the Melians, fierce nymphs that had germinated from drops of Uranus's blood, when his son Cronos castrated the Titan of the sky as retribution for imprisoning the children of the earth goddess Gaia in their mother's bowels, thus depriving them of sunlight for all eternity. King Henry drew his huntsman knife. Michael made the mistake of looking into the hart's fearful eyes as the king made the kill. All at once he felt his heart bursting, his lungs burning. Warm blood spilled to the ground. He stumbled off to hide behind a thick trunk. He was in agony. His eyes hurt. Bitter saliva filled his maw. What dementia was this? He could not count the times he had hunted in Ireland. Not once had he felt like this—his skin feverish, his senses raw, blood rushing thick and hot in his veins, as if he were about to faint. Only before dawn.

Michael leaned back against the rough-barked tree, got out the bottle stashed in his sporran, and bled it dry. *I must quit it*, he thought despairingly. *He conquers who conquers himself.*

The horns signed the mort of the deer, summoning the huntsmen to carry back the game. As Michael, his sanity restored, stepped from the brushwood, Stanley grabbed his shoulder. "How now, my brave-hearted! Where have you been gadding? Come. Harry requests you attend him."

Michael steeled himself for answering questions for which he had no answers. There was no credible explanation for the insanie afflicting him. Stanley said, "Your Grace, I present Michael Devereaux, my Lord Tyrone's man and legal heir, arrived yesterday from Ireland."

Michael knelt before the king, head bowed, heart thumping against his ribcage.

"Devereaux." King Henry's tone was pensive and amused. "Are you the one responsible for the new Irish birds prattling pompously like some Celtic parliament in my mews?"

The query coaxed laughter from the onlookers and a grin from Michael's grimly set mouth. "Aye, so please Your Grace. My most noble protector sends Your Majesty the Lord's blessing and pledges his love and ever-steadfast fealty."

"If your loquacious gifts share your talent for snagging prey, I daresay we shall see some superb hawking. Shan't we, gentlemen?" His comment was accepted with murmurs of consent. "Are you the son of Sir John Devereaux of Chartley of his second marriage?"

The murmurs took on a different note. "Aye, Your Grace," Michael confirmed, baffled.

"Begotten by an attainted traitor and raised by our most valiant loyalist, an interesting breed. My Lord Tyrone wrote us of your coming and alerted us to expect great feats from you."

Michael was dumbfounded. His sire a traitor? Surely not! *Your noble sire, who fought like a lion and died for his king at Blackheath during the Cornish rebellion, had sworn me to take his son, begotten off a second wife . . .* Why should his worthy lord tell him falsehoods?

He scanned the curious faces of the lords whose ranks he strove to infiltrate. Most of them had never met his father. He was relieved to note that the drone of speculation carried no venom. Only Walter the Peacock looked aghast. The king said, "My lords, we will judge this lion by his own claws. Rise, Devereaux. We are well pleased."

Renée was in high spirits. Her dear friend the Lady Mary had arrived shortly after Mass. Their reunion, sweeter for Mary's surprise, was a muddle of tears, laughter, and inquiries. Mary was happy, beautiful, radiant with love. She had two babies, Lord Henry and Lady Frances, and was expecting her third child. Two years Renée's senior, Mary was bright, headstrong, with gray eyes, a fiery mane, a Grecian profile, cool pallor, and regal height. From the moment they had fallen into each other's arms, she could not stop prating about her husband and the changes in her life. Renée, burdened by forbidden secrets, proved the perfect listener to the cheerful narration.

"Henry was furious. Knowing our hearts, he still made Charles swear he would not propose to me when he sent him to fetch me from France. When he learned of our nuptials, conducted in secret and haste and without royal consent, he flew into a rage, labeling Charles an overreaching traitor and opportunist and swore he would not see us again. Charles was his closest friend and I his cherished sister, and yet he was hard put to bless our union with the old men on the council clamoring for an execution or a lengthy imprisonment for my husband. Thanks to Wolsey's intervention with the council, Charles escaped the gibbet, and I was spared the heartache of mourning my dearest lord and of premature widowhood. Henry fined us heavily and banished us from court till the storm blew over and his wrath cooled."

"But you are restored to favor. That is wondrous!"

Mary's eyes shone. "All is well now. He was with us at Abingdon last month and was much content, for no man came to tell him of the death of any person from the plague, as they were wont daily. And how have you done since last we saw, Renée? You are very quiet."

Renée sighed. Mary was bound to hear of her indiscretion. She did not care for her friend to get the sordid version from strangers. So she told Mary about Raphael. Unbosoming herself to a sympathetic, trustworthy ear was a relief. They had become friends during a difficult period in both their lives. Renée had lost her mother to illness. Mary had just become the young bride of an old king in a foreign country. Discovering they had much in common had been their salvation. King Louis's death had liberated Renée of a despotic sire and Mary of an unwanted husband. The English Rose was free to marry her true love: Charles Brandon, the first Duke of Suffolk. Parting with Mary had been a wrench. She had grieved more over the separation from Mary than the death of her sire and inevitably drifted toward the Lady Marguerite, the fickle witch. Seeing Mary so blissful was a breath of fresh, blossom-scented air. Mary had achieved the impossible: she had married an upstart and gotten away with it. Her success and happiness instilled hope in Renée. If an English princess of the blood could do it, why not a French one?

"A painter?" Mary raised a reddish eyebrow when Renée finished her story. "Why not settle on a gentleman of noble parentage and of fair demesnes?"

"Bloodlines mean naught to me, and I am dowered aplenty. I have the duchy of Chartres and Brittany. As soon as my banishment is over, Raphael and I shall retire to the countryside and live contentedly, as you and Charles do."

"Come now, Renée. Be reasonable. Long-Nose will make your lover disappear and contract a marriage for you. I say choose a pleasing man from among the king my brother's friends and marry in secret, as I have done. Leastways you shall have a say in your future and be happy."

"I shall never be content with a man other than my beloved Raphael."

"Contentment is a relative term. The instant one gets one's heart's desire, one wants more. My darling lord loathes the country. He misses court life. He hungers for offices, for amusements, for wars. I plan improvements to Westhorpe Hall, our seat in Suffolk. He plans to raise a brick London residence on his ancestral lands by the Thames." She sighed. "And what of you, Renée? You are the perfect courtier, bred for power and intrigue. With your brain and application, would you be content growing vines and—"

"Apples, for cider and brandy, barley for sweet ale, buckwheat for galettes . . ." Closing her eyes, Renée could taste Breton butter crêpes filled with minced apples, cream, and black currant on her tongue, slicked back with a cup of lambig, the delectable Breton apple brandy.

Mary smiled. "So we have established that you will be content, but would your painter?"

"So long as we have paint."

As the gentlemen had gone hunting, Renée knew not whether Michael Devereaux had evaded Buckingham's dagger. However, as there was no talk of dead people behind the Venus tapestry, she assumed the golden impostor had been successful and hoped the duke would not lose heart.

With her improved humor came a longing to bask in the sun and a scheme was born withal. She ran her idea by Mary, who declared it a stroke of brilliance. Together they approached Queen Katherine and made a case in favor of dressing up to lie in wait for His Majesty's hunting party as the gentlemen returned from the hunt. What a delightful jest it would be, they said, should Diana the Huntress and her maidens surprise the hunting party with an al fresco midday repast on a lush patch of green in the park. The proposal was a winner, the queen matching exuberance with the silliest of the maids of honor, who, Renée thought, were very silly indeed.

Orders were given to the officers of the household. On the noon hour bell, the queen and her ladies, gowned in vivacious spring colors and accompanied by the disgarnished court deprived of the gallants out hunting with the king, set out to find the perfect locale for the ambush.

Dressed in a cerulean habit with a matching plumed hat, Renée spent the ride chatting with Mary, laughing with Wyatt, a poet and flatterer extraordinaire, and caroling with the damsels, all mounted on white palfreys. The queen, traveling in her pretty litter, chose a picturesque sward, and the cavalcade dismounted to prepare the surprise reception. Velvet carpets were unfurled, the queen's chair, padded with her tasseled cushion, was deposited at the center of the stage, pillows were scattered for the ladies to sit upon, boards were erected and covered with fine linen napery, rich plate, and delicacies brought from the queen's privy kitchen. Trunks from the wardrobe, stuffed with figurative trappings, were cracked open and mobbed, the party hastening to disguise themselves: Queen Katherine as Diana the Huntress with her golden bow and quiver of arrows, the ladies-in-waiting and the maids of honor as the goddess's nymphs, and the gentlemen, even the severe and ancient ones, masqueraded as creatures of the wild.

Renée found the scenery intoxicating: the welcome shade of trees, lively with birdsong, the rainbow of flowers in early bloom, perfuming the air, beckoning butterflies and buzzing bees. It seemed such a waste to sit and do nothing as they waited for the hunting party to fall upon them.

"Your Majesty." Renée curtsied to the queen. "I crave leave to gather flowers for wreaths—chaplets for us, garlands for the dishes."

The queen approved, whereupon half the party scattered to cull basketsful of honeysuckle, yellow cowslips, hawthorn, rosebriar, pansies, gorses, marigold, lavender, white daisies, laurels, lilies of the valley, blossoms, and herbs to garnish and perfume the spectacle.

Renée and Mary strolled together, chatting and gossiping. They hardly noticed their follower until they were overtaken near a bed of thistle. Lady Anne Hastings, dowdily appareled with her rosary in hand, all for the sake of currying favor with Queen Katherine, dipped diffidently. "My Lady Mary. My Lady Renée, I was hoping I might have a word with you. Privily."

Renée contemplated the sly chameleon. Jade by night, nun by day. She would have said nay with an illuminated *N* if not for the fact that Anne was Buckingham's sister and confidante and that maintaining the charade of friendship with Anne could lead to interesting discoveries, such as the how and when Buckingham would strike against the king again. "Mary?"

"Go off. Mind me not." Mary smiled, petting her invisibly pregnant belly. "I was about to suggest we return to the camp to rest awhile."

And so, Renée was left alone with Anne. They ambled side by side in silence.

"You are cross with me," Anne said.

"Cross? Why would I be cross?"

"You were kind to me last night. You rescued me from Surrey's trap, and I repaid you with a hurtful disservice. I apologize. I would very much like us to be friends. Please forgive me."

"What disservice?" Renée inquired with interest, suspicions buzzing in her head like bees.

"My husband, Sir George Hastings, arrived this morning. Have you met him?"

"I have not had the pleasure. Has he gone out hunting? Introduce us later, then."

Anne laughed bitterly. "You would not thank me for that pleasure."

"Oh?"

"Is it true, about the Italian painter?" At Renée's appalled expression, she plowed on. "Your pardon. That was rude. I merely ask because I felt . . . My name is also tainted with scandal." She plunged into an intimate account of the events that had gotten her packed off to St. Mary's three years before. She must have reckoned Renée had heard the gossip and hoped to establish a close rapport by unbosoming her disgrace. Renée was silent. "The fair Viking, you fancied him."

Renée was not used to being jolted twice in the space of a single conversation. The hen was outwitting the fox. Her curiosity whetted, she had to know what had transpired behind the Venus tapestry last night. With her cardsharp visor lowered, she said, "I never fancied him. Did you?"

Anne's complexion turned a bright red.

Oh. Renée felt something drop inside her. So that's what had happened behind the arras. Had the duke perceived the switch and abandoned his plan? Or had Michael wrestled with him?

Anne turned and gripped her hands. "Oh, Renée. I must see him again privily. I must! But with George at court, I cannot speak with another man, I cannot even look. After last time . . ."

Saints! Renée was truly and utterly shocked. Anne was asking her to play the bawd! Red-hot anger surged through her, twisting her into a knot of hostility. It made no sense. In France she had oftentimes played the covert pigeon between the dissolute members of the aristocracy. Lust was a great weakness, an asset, to be exploited in affairs of state, to her royal sire's advantage. It would be the perfect arrangement to learn of Buckingham's plans. Why was she hesitating? "I will help you!" she blurted out. "I have done it countless times in France. I master the game."

"Oh! You are a true confidante! A priceless friend!" Anne hugged her. Renée felt sick.

"The king! The king is coming!" The ecstatic exclamation was followed by a bray of bugles.

Renée and Anne dashed back to the campsite to take their place around the queen. When the hunting party reined in, the Huntress Diana was lounging leisurely in the shade, attended by her nymphs and animals of the forest, sipping wine and gobbling berries, with white palfreys grazing in the background. Renée watched the gallants swing off their shiny mounts and toss reins to grooms. She made out Buckingham, the king's six minions—Neville, Bryan, Carew, Compton, Norris, and Knevet—Earl Surrey, Sir Walter, faces she had yet to pin names to . . . Her gaze fell on the triplet at the back: Michael Devereaux, his bearded friend, and a dashing newcomer. The mystery of the latter's identity was solved when he strode off to Mary and kissed her soundly.

The king was delighted with the surprise. He rewarded his queen with doting that put roses in her cheeks and earned Renée a gold point for merit. She studied Mary and her debonair duke. They beamed together. Did she beam with Raphael? King Henry presented the hero of the hunt, extolling his Irish snout and methods. The Irish eyes locked with Renée's. She looked away.

Queen Katherine's ambush put the king in good cheer. Michael thought the mythical scene would have been more convincing without the dicing. But what did he know? The occupants of Olympus might have been avid gamblers, too. His mood was much improved. He had scored his first good point with the king without raising eyebrows.

The party sat down to dinner on the carpets. Chapleted nymphs with flowing sheer scarves surrounded the queen as luscious petals, tempting the eye. Renée, in cerulean, sat between Anne and another lady. He wanted to speak to her but did not know how to approach. She seemed so distant; she would not meet his gaze. He wanted to apologize, to whisper secrets, to steal a kiss of peace. As for Buckingham's dagger, secreted in his casket, there was not much he could do with it. He could not walk up to the king and say, "Your Majesty, the Duke of Buckingham is working to supplant you. Here is the dagger I wrested from his hand last night when he mistook me for you and tried to stab me." He had no powerful allies to corroborate the allegation, no mentor to consult. The dagger was unique and had a big *S* etched in the hilt but lacked the power of speech to admit it had played a part in a failed attempt on King Henry's life. Buckingham would learn Michael's identity and say his blade was stolen. His only recourse was to stay on the alert, in case Buckingham should try again, as Michael believed he would.

"Does the French court play games after al fresco feasts?" Wyatt asked Princess Renée.

The assembly, replete with venison and frumenty, leaned in to hear her response so that they could repeat it afterward to unlucky absentees and sound amazingly au fait, stylish, and French.

"Certes," she answered. "Many games."

Michael's mind hardly registered the games she listed; he was preoccupied with ogling her. Her skin was creamy, her hair dark, thick, and glossy, her neck a fragile stem; her pink lips were a perfect rosette, her teeth pearly and even. Her breasts, swelling above the jeweled bodice, were small and intriguing. He marveled that he should become aroused imagining how the pert things looked when his taste tended toward plump dukkys. Everything about her was confection-like, petite and dainty. She glowed with youth and vitality. She exuded fierceness and wit. Above all, he admired her eyes. Vivid, purplish blue, framed with dark eyelashes, the windows to her soul were flames, like the flower-de-luce, the armorial motif of the Valois royal family and of France.

Renée was the brightest jewel in Queen Katherine's entourage.

I could burn, he thought with foreboding, startled, besieged, heart pounding turbulently. *I could burn for this wisp of a woman.*

"What is your favorite game, Princess?"

"Cache-cache." She smiled, her eyes twinkling naughtily.

"Pray, teach us!" King Henry demanded.

"*Eh bien*"—Renée took a sip of wine, dampening her lips—"the ladies run and hide, and the gentlemen, wearing blindfolds, look for them. When a gentleman catches a lady, he guesses her identity. If he is correct, she bestows him with a kiss; if he is wrong, he must atone for his error with a gift. His gift could be a poem, a flower, a trinket—if he is generous—anything."

"I say!" Wyatt beamed. "Blind man's buff with a naughty French twist!"

The king looked fascinated. "If a gentleman is blindfolded, how will he catch the ladies?"

"Oh, we make bird sounds to lure him." Renée offered imitations of bird communication.

Michael's eyes were riveted on her mouth. The only thing keeping him from pouncing on it was his vow to be the one to kiss the rosebud lips at the end of the game. His body stiffened as he imagined her nipples in the shape of those lips, but he dared not stretch his imagination toward the petals between her thighs for fear he might embarrass himself.

"Do you get caught often, Lady Renée?" asked Wyatt.

Michael did not like the interest he perceived in the man's eyes.

"I always get caught!" Renée laughed. "And have plenty of gifts to show for it."

King Henry laughed. "Ladies, dare you venture into the greenwood with rascally fellows?" At the excited assents, he stood up. "What shall we use for blindfolds?" Before he completed the sentence, the nymphs were plucking off mufflers, scarves, tuckers, and stoles and dropping them in a colorful heap at his feet, loot to the conqueror. "Ladies, disperse!"

"All hid, all hid!" Wyatt clucked, as if herding chickens.

Giggling, chirping, and tweeting, the queen's maids of honor and youthful ladies-in-waiting scattered in all directions, dissolving into the shrubbery, taking cover behind bushes and trees.

Michael was not about to miss this for the world. He snatched a diaphanous cerulean scarf, redolent of ambergris and lavender, and took to the trees.

Renée clasped Mary's hand and ran into the wood, then went back and whisked Anne with them. She was not letting this woman out of her sight. A medley of silly twittering and hysterical giggles arose from the surrounding greenery. All the flower bushes were animated with birdsong.

"God's teeth, you have conjured a menagerie, Wyatt."

"That's my Charles," Mary whispered excitedly, and chirped in response.

"A dovecot," said the bearded fellow, Lord Stanley.

"Hen coop."

"Mews."

"A female privy council!"

"God protect us!" cried Sir Francis Bryan, eliciting masculine chuckles from the thicket.

"An apiary," said Michael Devereaux. "With three bees in the nearest skep, methinks."

"Glad will this honey-stalk be should you let me to your honey-comb, bee," berhymed Wyatt.

"And pump you full of honey-seeds," finished Compton.

"Pray, do not leave us, Your Grace," Wyatt pleaded with Suffolk when the duke drifted away from their group, "for I might grope Stanley by accident, and then what will become of me?"

"A holed honey-bag, for I will run you through, Wyatt. I swear I will," Stanley replied.

"Heartless rascal," Wyatt protested in a mock prissy tone.

Male laughter boomed. Anne squeaked at Michael. Mary darted to another tree, closer to her lord, and chirped sweetly. Suffolk stumbled toward her, his arms outstretched. Mary took a step back, softening her song. Observing them, Renée recognized their play for the courting ritual it was: she flirted, he responded, she retreated, he pursued, listening for hints. He caught her. She melted in his arms. "My canary," Charles murmured before he kissed his wife, still blindfolded.

Suddenly embarrassed for spying on them, Renée turned away, leaning back against a tree. She had had to scheme and apply herself so hard to get Raphael to notice her, really notice her, as a woman, and he had been so timid. She assumed it was her elevated station that daunted him, turning him into a skittish responder, never the aggressor. And yet here was Charles Brandon, grabbing and pawing his wife—Renée's English counterpart—with all the passion and mastery of a man in love. But then Suffolk was a soldier, whereas Raphael was an artist. His was not the type to conquer and plunder. He was reflective, gentle, and absentminded. He needed her to take care of him. Oh, how she wished she had not seen Mary with her ardent husband.

She opened her eyes to find Michael Devereaux lurking nearby. Jesu! He had her cerulean scarf tied around his head, a vivid contrast to his golden mane. As if he felt her eyes upon him, he advanced in her direction. Did he hear the rustle of skirts and expected her to tweet at him? Never! Let him find Anne and then let them find a secluded corner wherein to amuse themselves.

She spotted King Henry turning about helplessly as a chorus of squeaking females beckoned him from behind trees and bushes, gamboling around him, bubbling with laughter. He resembled a splendid sightless lion being baited by a flock of noisome ducks masquerading as butterflies, or he could be Aengus, Renée mused, the Celtic god of love, pestered by the four birds flying about his head, symbolizing kisses. Guffawing and calling to them, he was having a hard time deciding which he should seize upon. Predictably, Mistress Blount stumbled into his arms.

"Oh-hoa, my little nightingale!" exclaimed Lord Stanley as his muscular arms locked around a lanky young woman with light blond hair.

"You may never guess my name, sir, for we are not acquainted." The woman smiled at his half-covered face with what Renée recognized as budding interest.

"By all means, introduce yourself!" he suggested jovially, making the woman laugh.

"That is my sister you are fondling, sir!" a blindfolded Sir Walter Devereaux fumed hard by.

"I show your sister naught but courtesy, sir. Do not doubt it!" replied Stanley.

"Show her aught else, and you'll be wedded at sword point by suppertime," Wyatt gibed.

"There's my husband," Anne whispered dolefully, indicating the man wandering aimlessly, companionless, calling his wife's name insistently, for none of the "birds" would flirt with him. He looked awkward, lofty, and ridiculous. "He will expect me to sing to him."

"I thought you wanted to be caught by the Viking," Renée whispered back. She had already made up her mind to let Wyatt catch her, for he was harmless. She planned to wrest a witty poem from him. Annoyingly, the hulking hindrance, Michael Devereaux, was guarding the lane to her hideout like a rockfall or rather a tenacious cat stalking a songbird. Was he hunting for Anne?

"I cannot, not in the common gaze. But . . . might I beg a favor? Will you give him a message from me?"

Renée's ears prickled. "What is the message?"

"Tell him I would see him again." Without warning, Anne nudged Renée into the lane, into the fair giant's path, and dashed to her husband.

Michael waited for Renée's friends to flounce off or be caught before he made his move. Wyatt and the peacock were prowling after her. Hence, he planted himself between them and her. Not a moment passed when he was unaware of her whereabouts. While her fragrant scarf blindfolded his eyes silkily, his senses followed her bodily presence like a mariner navigating by the pole star, as he had stalked the hart in the thicket. He listened to her hushed conversation with Anne and as soon as she stepped into the lane he seized her wrist.

"I have you fast now." Michael smiled, pulling her closer. He slid his hands around her slim waist, embracing her sylphid body to his. She felt wonderful in his arms, lithe and delectable. He wanted to carry her to a magical wood, lay her on a bed of moss, peel off her clothing, feast his eyes on her beauty, scatter kisses on her quivering maidenly flesh, and make her mad with desire for him. A privilege he would never have. But he would have a kiss. "Will you not greet me that I may hear your voice and guess your name?"

"Twit." She felt rigid, the light musk of natural perspiration spicing the costly perfume she wore. Around them, birds in brocades and silks chatted with and giggled at their captors, whether because they wanted to be recognized and kissed or could not contain their exuberance.

"Sing a whole song for me, little wrenne, that I may hazard a guess." As Michael waited for a response, he felt her stiffening, tilting back, discouraging further contact. *She did not want him to kiss her.* Stung, he let go. He untied her scarf from his eyes and was struck dumb seeing how beautiful she was up close in the white light of day. Her face was alabaster smooth, delicate as a white orchid; her dark-lashed eyes were stunning amethysts. He met them squarely, unsmiling. "Once again you have outwitted me, madame."

Renée blinked up at him. "Why did you not try to guess my name?" she asked softly.

"I knew your name."

Annoyance erased any hint of vulnerability or shyness. Her gemlike eyes flared, becoming brilliantly hard in intensity. "You knew me but would not demand your reward?"

He was flummoxed. Did she want him to kiss her? "Name your pleasure."

She snatched her scarf from his fingers, hissing, "Go and be hanged!"

❧ 8 ❧

To accept a favor is to sell one's liberty.

—Publilius Syrus: *Sententiae*

"So you relocated to Norfolk's house and made no progress in arranging my audience with Cardinal Wolsey. . . ."

Pierre eyed the brat pacing in front of the fireplace in her privy chamber. She looked taut as a drawn bowstring. "Did you know we were distantly related through the queen your mother?"

Purple daggers cut him up. "What has that to do with anything? No, I did not know."

"Verily, I speak the truth. I am as Breton as you, dear lady. The lords of Rougé were and are legitimate descendants in male line of the Kings of Brittany, through Saint Salomon, Count of Rennes and Nantes and Duke of Brittany. Your noble grandsire, Francis, was my namesake."

"What do you want, Rougé?" the little wasp demanded tersely.

"The bulk of my estate is in the Loire-Inférieure around Nantes. Rich soil, especially in iron. But you knew that. What you may not know is that even my name, Rougé, is closely associated with Brittany, derived from the Latin *Rubiacus*, *the red place*, for the high iron composition of the land. I have always thought the Rougé red roses should look fine on a field of Breton ermine. What do you think, Princess?" He cautiously refrained from affixing the Valois golden fleur-de-lis on a sheet of blue to their future crest. Subtlety was everything; he did not want to alarm her. "Know you that red is the military color for excellence and fortitude? It is symbolic of ferocity, boldness, and nobility. And the rose is a symbol of hope and joy—"

"Your armorial history is not in the least interesting. I repeat, what do you want?"

"Why, I want what you want!"

"And what might that be?" She eyed him witheringly.

He wondered if she applied her authoritarian nature under the covers, too. He did not enjoy being ordered about, in or out of bed, and he found the idea of introducing the pretty shrew to the pleasures of total submission vastly titillating. He knew for a fact that her domineering sire had secretly collected silk whips and other stimulating apparatuses, and Pierre had a feeling that King Louis's youngest daughter had inherited all of her sire's visceral traits, not just his superlative intelligence and indomitable character. Renée's fragile beauty—the only thing she had inherited from her mother— was a trifling. He preferred his women fleshier and flashier and had not given Renée a second look before she stung him with her thorny tongue. Her brains and spirit would be additional boons she would be bringing to their union. Alas, these particular qualities also made her a difficult conquest. He had heard the gossip concerning her last broken betrothal, how she had circuitously spread rumors and counterrumors to convince her German prince that he had excellent chances of meeting the fate of Attila the Hun on their wedding night. Hence, he had to handle her with diplomacy, cunning, and care. He needed to convince her that in throwing her lot with his, she would be unifying the pieces of her mother's inheritance King Louis had scattered amongst his lords. Resolved to win her confidence, he assumed a wistful tone. "My lady wife, whom I married at the tender age of eight and ten, surrendered her soul to God ten years gone. Our boy, my heir, also died. I deposited their beloved bodies in the warm earth of Brittany and went to court to faithfully serve *Le Père du Peuple*, the king your father. I won many battles for His Majesty, collected his rewards, and drowned the quiet pain of my loss in the amusements of his splendid court. Now I find myself reflecting late at night on hearth and home. I am grown weary of court life. I long for peace, for quiet days with an adored wife and babes in the balmy shade of the verdant apple trees of Brittany." He tried gauging her reaction. *Nothing.*

For a fleeting moment Pierre lost his composure. He had been baring his soul to her, picking at and disturbing memories best left untouched, and she was unmoved. *My God*, he thought, *she has the ruthless single-mindedness of her father.* He marveled that her antipathy should arouse him as much as it chafed him raw. He had to tread on eggshells with her. "Our objective should be one and the same, to reunite Brittany and revive her ancient glory."

"Your dream is beautiful, I admit, but I am ordered by my king to find an English husband. I cannot go against my king's wishes, Pierre. Nor can you."

"We could wed in secret," he suggested softly. "We will make right by King Francis later."

Her laughter startled him. "Since leaving France, you have been discourteous, patronizing, aggressive, and useless." Her humor vanished. "I do not feel duly courted, Rougé."

His jaw was hanging open. He clenched it. "So you have thought about it?"

Her lips pouted. "The thought has crossed my mind, but your insulting behavior put me off the idea. Now I must write to my king and alert him to expect our failure in this expedition."

Merde, he thought. She had him pinned to the wall. To ingratiate himself with her, he would have to secure this audience with Cardinal Wolsey, which would lead to a husband that was not him. Kidnapping her would be an impossible task with the guards attached to her skirts. He had to think upon it. "I will arrange the audience." He flaunted his most charming smile. "But I give you fair warning, madame. I shall do my utmost to convince you to choose me."

"Rougé." She stopped him at the door. "I am beginning to like you better."

"Did you convey my message?" Anne asked in a whisper later that evening while the ladies entertained the queen in her presence chamber. The king had sent his musicians, and the maids of honor were practicing the dance they would perform for His Majesty when he arrived.

Renée would not dance; she would sing. Mary had been lauding her singing and lute playing to the queen, and now Queen Katherine, who had become fond of Renée, despite her Frenchness, was eager to hear her. Renée wished Mary had not spoken of her talent. She cared neither for the attention nor for the praise. She needed to think. Rougé had finally caught on. She would make the ideal bride for him. It made him more malleable, but she hadn't harnessed all of his ambition, for she had also given him a reason to keep her away from Wolsey. She could have persuaded him to return to reside close to court, but it suited her to be distanced from him. The marquis had but one purpose: to secure the audience. The game she played with him was tricky; the marriage card was not even fully played yet. She kept it for the worst occurrence—his finding out the truth about her presence in England.

"Well, have you?" Anne persisted.

Renée flushed. She had forgotten to tell Michael Devereaux that Anne wanted to see him, be with him, again. Something had gone awry when he caught her. It was a subtle thing. Tremors, heat. She had been unable to think except wonder if he would kiss her and fret over it.

Anne's tone turned accusatory. "You did not give him my message."

"I did," Renée lied in a soft voice, plucking the frets of her lute.

"Oh! You are a dear friend! What did he say?"

"He . . . he was flattered, naturally . . . transported . . . humbled."

"Does he wish to confer with me . . . privily?"

"Most certainly!" She thought quickly. "He is aware your lord husband is come to court and begs for time to arrange a rendezvous. His lodging in the undercroft is not fit to entertain—"

"You have been to his lodging?" Anne asked sharply.

"*Mais non!* I am repeating his message. He will give me the particulars for your tryst on the morrow." *Morbleu.* Supposing he did not care to commune with Anne again, what would she do?

"Good." Anne frowned darkly, rubbing her temples. "I thank you."

"What is it? You look ill."

"It is nothing." Anne twined her rosary round her chilblained fingers, her gaze lowered. "His Grace my brother is displeased with me. Such rows give me a megrim."

Snapping to attention, Renée draped an arm around Anne. "Poor friend . . . My tiring woman, Adele, works miracles with herbs. If you are in need of a cordial or . . . or a kind ear . . ."

Something, alertness, flickered in Anne's eyes. "Your tiring woman, she is a healer?"

"A gifted one." Letting go of Anne, Renée plucked gentle notes from her lute. "'Adele, take away my flux pains,' I beg her, and she does. 'Adele, I would be a fecund wife to the king my husband,' the queen my sister said, and Adele brewed fresh herbs from the garden, and the queen my sister had Louise and Charlotte, daughters of France, and this year Francis, the Dauphin of France." Her little song banished the darkness from Anne's eyes, bringing forth a smile. "See? My quiver of remedies is already at work, for I have coaxed a smile from you." If Buckingham was plotting, she needed to know the particulars. She had to ask Lieutenant Armado if Sergeant Francesco had reported back from York Place. She would have to deal with the dark horse called Michael Devereaux. He would need proper lodging. Had he spoken to Earl Worcester? So many variables . . . The trickiest part would be convincing Michael to strip Anne of the duke's secrets and report back to her. How would she accomplish that when he would not give her a kiss?

"Did he kiss you?"

Renée started. "No, he didn't recognize me." She frowned. He had recognized her but would not kiss her. Or perhaps he had changed his mind. God knew what went on in men's little brains.

"The king! The king! The king!" the sentries lining the passage to the queen's apartment echoed each other, and then the ladies panted excitedly, "The king!"

Those who were not standing jumped to their feet; the queen sat regally. King Henry strolled in with a gaggle of gallants. The ladies plunged into curtsies. "My lady." The king smiled at the queen. "I come to bid you a good evening." He lifted her proffered hand to his lips.

The musicians resumed playing. Renée surveyed the king's rowdy entourage for the pinions she must fit into the teeth of her cogwheel, the larger scheme of things. Rougé was absent, as was Norfolk, Surrey, and Sir Walter—what were they plotting? Buckingham was missing also. She knew what he was plotting, she only lacked detail. Suffolk, Compton, Neville, Wyatt, Bryan, Carew . . . all the king's cockerels were present. As they took over the chamber, mingling with the ladies, she recognized Michael's bearded companion, Lord Stanley. But where was Michael?

"I think you have an ardent but bashful doter," Mary whispered in her ear.

Renée pivoted, and there he was, leaning against the wall behind her. How had he gotten there without her notice? Michael's tall, golden head glowed atop lean muscularity molded in black velure with a gilt metal platelet belt riding his hips. He was always protecting his back, she noticed. It was less awkward than standing idly at the center of a room, uncertain whom one should speak to, what topics made for good conversation. He needed guidance.

The turquoise eyes were fixed upon her, oblivious of aught else. His attention made her feel self-conscious. She waited for him to approach her, but he merely nodded a polite greeting and remained where he was. The pox to him, she thought. She would have to go to him.

"Who is he?" Mary inquired. "I saw him at the hunt feast. *Bel homme, hein?*"

"Ask Suffolk about him. Surely he knows." Renée pasted a cool smile on her lips, lifted her chin, and went to him. "I give you good evening, sir." She dipped.

"Madame." Michael swept her a bow.

"Have you had a chance to speak to Earl Worcester about a change of quarters?"

"I—no." A sheepish grin shattered his sternness at last. "His Majesty held an archery contest after the queen and her ladies left the campsite. There was no time."

"How did you do, in the contest?"

He produced a silver rose from behind his back and held it out to her by the bloodred silk ribbon tied around its thorny stem. "I beg your pardon for my poor behavior in the woods."

Renée studied his face as she accepted the rose and jokingly brought its argent petals to her nose. "You won the prize."

"Not the one I wanted."

A sensual quiver streaked up her spine, tickled her neck, and tumbled into her belly. "Let us speak to Earl Worcester now." She threaded her arm through his and detached him from his wall.

Large as he was, Michael let her steer him. It thrilled her, to have the leading rein of a man who could snap her in two. He was passive but not graceless like Sir George Hastings, who towed his unhappy wife to a card table. King Henry took his state beside the queen. The maids of honor formed a circle to perform their dance. The gentlemen and the ladies, dicing and playing at cards, stopped to enjoy the performance. Except Anne Hastings, who was watching Michael and Renée.

They halted to observe the spectacle. "You do not dance?" Michael inquired quietly.

Renée shrugged. "Nor do I embroider. I am sans accomplishments. It is very sad."

He laughed. "You are gulling me."

The dance ended. Applause rang. Maria de Salinas helped the queen to her feet.

"The queen is unwell." Renée exchanged a laden look with Michael. Katherine of Aragon was thirty-three years old, six years the king's senior, had been pregnant four times, with but one surviving daughter, the two-year-old Princess Mary. Mayhap the queen was merely being careful. Renée would not be singing after all. She wondered if this was a good time to play the bawd and decided against it, for she must also lure Michael to a confidence. She wanted to hear about last night and to secure his collaboration. She guided him toward one of the card tables, indicating a blowsy lord. "Charles Somerset, Earl Worcester, is the king's third cousin on the Beaufort side of the royal family. Illegitimate," she whispered. "His sire was a commander in the Lancastrian faction in the old wars. He is also related to the Duke of Buckingham, is unto his third wife, Lord Dudley's sister, and was invested Knight of the Garter some twenty years gone."

"How long have you been at the English court?"

"Not long. A week."

His eyebrows lifted. "And already you are acquainted with everyone. Remarkable."

"Many attended my presentation to Their Majesties. Such formal receptions are routine when a foreign embassy comes to court. Earl Worcester regaled me with stories about his noble sire's military feats, about his wives, and about his own accomplishments and importance. You should make it your business to form as many alliances as possible and learn the personages—"

"Rank, family connections, and closeness to the throne, I know."

She smiled. "I was about to say vices, but you are correct. One should know everything." It occurred to her she knew naught about him. "Perhaps you ought to tell me about yourself, Master Devereaux, so that I may introduce you properly."

"Pray, call me Michael. As for my vices . . ." He grinned. "I shall introduce myself to Earl Worcester and surprise you." *Why are you helping me?* His blue eyes glimmered quizzically.

"I think the best tactic would be to join Earl Worcester's card game."

"Ah, but I do not play cards. Sans accomplishments, very sad."

Touché, she thought. "King Henry enjoys the game. It would benefit you to learn."

"I would need a tutor."

Or a tutoress, Renée thought, a seed of an idea germinating in her brain. She pointed out one of the young men laughing with the king. "You might wish to consult Sir Francis Bryan."

Michael followed her discreet chin gesture. "Stanley introduced us at the archery contest. Bryan's aim was astonishingly true despite his eye patch."

"He lost his eye in a joust, or mayhap while serving at sea aboard the *Margaret Bonaventure* five years hence. He told me, but I do not recall. Mind, he is a talented cardplayer as well as an able jouster. He excels at tennez, at playing bowls and shovel board. He is a versatile raconteur and poet. He tells stories and anecdotes with skill and wit and—"

"You are fond on this gentleman."

Renée cocked an eyebrow at his hard tone. She detested Bryan. He was a reptile. But it was none of Michael's concern. Moreover, the glint of jealousy she perceived in his eyes might serve her purposes well. "I am merely specifying the qualities of bonhomie King Henry appreciates in his companions. Bryan masters the art of preserving royal favor. He is always at King Henry's side, carrying out his offices as gentleman of the bedchamber, cupbearer, and master of the toils. He loves whom the king loves. He absorbs himself in matters that fascinate his king, such as the works of Erasmus, the meaning of celestial bodies, the nature and portent of comets . . ."

"Astrology and fortune-telling, eh?" Michael's grin was luminous. "Madame, I will astound you. By sheer coincidence, these subject matters happen to be my métier."

"Oh, really?" Renée appraised his devilish smile. "You tell fortunes?"

"Legendarily. For instance, I predict that you and I shall become fast friends."

She laughed. "Are you a rock gazer, a necromancer, or do you cast horoscopes?"

"I am an oneiromancer, madame. I foresee the future through the interpretation of dreams, and I prophesy that you shall have a dream of me."

He was hilarious. "That is not interpretive science—it is wishful thinking!"

"Ah, but my gift is unique. After you have this dream, come to me. We shall discuss it at length, and I will explain the hidden meaning."

Her peals of laughter began to draw eyes. She pressed a pomander to her nose, murmuring, "I might not be able to meet your price, sir. Surly such a goodly gift is not cheaply spent."

"Verily it is not," Michael replied sotto voce. "However, I—"

"Michael!" A bantam-sized gentleman with a tuft of white hair waddled toward them.

"Sir Ned!" Renée and Michael greeted the amiable threescore-year-old Sir Edward Poynings in chorus and blinked at each other. "You know him?" Again in unison. Michael grinned.

"I detect confusion in the ranks." Sir Ned waved a gnarled finger with a twinkle in his eye. "A man knows he is old when his travels make young minds ravel." He lifted Renée's knuckles to thin lips. "How now, my lovely? You are grown fair as the queen your mother. And you"—he shook Michael's large hand and made a jest of looking up and up—"I require a stool to speak to you, lad. How does my Lord Tyrone? Holding the reins of the Irish parliament, I trust?"

"The Irish are peaceful. My lord's reputation shakes respect out of them with little effort."

"You come from Ireland?" Renée gaped at Michael. He sounded so English she never would have guessed. Her astonishment multiplied as Sir Ned, with something akin to avuncular pride, told her how high Michael was in the esteem of the noble Earl of Tyrone, Lord Lieutenant of Ireland, and that he stood to inherit the earldom and doubtless the office, for none of the boastful cockerels in this chamber, not the stalwart military commanders of the realm, not Buckingham, not Norfolk, not Suffolk, cared to be pitted against that fearless, rebellious, savage nation of old, who feasted on the flesh and blood of their dead fathers, in the mythical land where time stood still and where the grazing was so succulent cattle burst if allowed to eat unchecked.

Renée found herself taking Michael's measures afresh. The dark horse, abashed at the praise heaped on him, averted his gaze from her scrutiny. "And how have you done since last we saw in Drogheda, Sir Ned?" he asked.

"Healthful, I thank you." The old man nodded resignedly.

"Sir Ned is His Majesty's comptroller." Renée jabbed a discreet, sharp elbow into Michael's side. "One of the six White Sticks of the household."

"You never told me you knew Queen Anne of France," Michael said, ignoring her cue.

Sir Ned grew wistful. "God save you, lad. You take me a long way back. My Lord Harry of Buckingham led us against King Richard the Third and lost his head rebelling. I flew to Brittany and sought refuge with the most gracious, enlightened Duchess Anne. Upon my arrival, she gave me a precious gem to light up my path." He produced a black-veined, red jasper pebble and rubbed it in a practiced, fond gesture. "She invited me to be her worthy guest. As God willed it, I struck a friendship with other English fugitives residing under Her Grace's roof. Jasper Tudor, our beloved king's great-uncle, was assembling an army against King Richard. Two years later, I sailed back with my Lord Henry Tudor, the future king of England, and fought with his grace as he wrested the throne from the last of the Yorkists." He stared at the jasper stone and offered it to Michael. "Here, lad. My path is good and set. God willing, my lady's stone will light up yours."

Michael was grateful for the gift. Renée decided they had wasted enough time on frivolities. Michael needed better accommodation for his tryst with Anne. She told Sir Ned how Michael had been played a blue trick upon by a servant of low morals. "Sir, I am confident you will agree such lodging is beneath my Lord Lieutenant of Ireland's right-hand man and heir and would have taken personal offense if the matter was not brought before you. The knave must be punished." She went on and on, pressing on his honor and duty, touching upon how the matter might shame His Majesty, whose hospitality and the magnificence of his court were the litany of the world.

Michael stood beside her, his eyes alight with humor and respect. *He is in awe of me*, Renée thought. He owed her and knew it. Soon she would have him eating from the palm of her hand.

Her oration drew a crowd. Everyone strained to hear Sir Ned uttering apologies and threats to the trickster and then promise to rectify the situation at once. Sir Lovell, the treasurer, another White Stick, vowed to discharge the man for his misconduct. The lord steward, George Talbot, Earl of Shrewsbury, whose motto was "Ready to Accomplish," was appalled to hear of a servant of the royal palace not of good honesty, gesture, behavior, and conversation, and declared that heads would roll at tomorrow's meeting of the Board of the Greencloth.

Every White Stick who joined the discussion Renée introduced to Michael. "Do you know the name of the usher?" she whispered in his ear, her lips caressing the whorls ever so slightly. Now, why did she do that? She met Michael's gaze. Surely he noticed. He must have noticed.

Michael gave no indication whether he did or not. "His name was Riggs."

King Henry, attracted by the uproar, demanded a prompt solution to the affair and the matter was resolved. Michael would relocate to proper chambers straightaway.

"I am in your debt," Michael said to Renée as they left the queen's presence chamber in the wake of a procession of White Sticks and intrigued followers. He bounced the jasper stone in his hand. The sideways smile he slid toward her would have melted brick. "Lithomancy?"

The queen her mother had always given a random stone to her visitors. Had Duchess Anne artfully influenced the course of history? Renée smiled. She was her mother's daughter after all.

"Are they true, the rumors concerning your charge and the Italian painter?"

Pierre's bloodshot eyes, heavy because of the firkin of wine he had put away, regarded his host, Thomas Howard, the Duke of Norfolk. He affected a smile to soften his response. "I cannot gossip about a daughter of France, *mon ami*. It would be treason."

Norfolk gestured to a manservant wearing his livery to refill their tankards, then sent him out of the privy chamber. "I understand. Allow me to tell you what I know, and then you may tell me what you know, and afterward we will never discuss this matter outside this room. Agreed?"

I am too fatigued and drunk to play at intrigues, Pierre thought. He should retire before he said something he might regret. Nevertheless, he could not bring himself to withdraw, not after Norfolk had so overtly insinuated he had intelligence concerning Pierre's shrewish charge. Ever since the idea of becoming the Duke of Brittany sprouted in his head, Pierre could think of little else and was starved for any piece of information pertaining to his future bride. "I am listening."

Norfolk's dark eyes glittered with purpose. "Several weeks hence the Cardinal of York came into possession of a reliquary, the contents of which are unknown, sent from Rome and delivered by Cardinal Campeggio, who shows no signs of homesickness to Wolsey's great vexation."

He is focused as a bloodhound, utterly sober, and I am sloshed, Pierre thought, instinct urging him to quit the conversation and retreat unscathed. "What has this to do with Madame?"

"Maybe nothing, maybe everything." Norfolk leaned forward. "The lieutenant in charge of her safety, my source tells me, is a former soldier of a mysterious papal guard."

"The guard that protects the Holy See is Swiss and is assembled of Switzers." Pierre started at his sibilant speech. He knew he ought to stuff a spigot in his mouth and just listen, and yet he heard himself say petulantly, "The lieutenant is Italian."

"I am not referring to the Swiss Guard but to a special army, secretive and small. Cardinal Campeggio is also protected by this army."

"Does this army have a designation?"

"They are called *deletoris.*"

"Destroyers?" Pierre moed. "Italians have such flair for the dramatics," he reasoned dryly. "I am sure this army is no more than a collection of carpet guards, furnished with sumptuous livery, sent to inflame King Henry's Christian chivalry and tempt him to defray an attack on the Turkish heretics. Pope Alexander the Sixth was wont to call for a crusade whenever his coffers were empty."

"My source informs me there is no crusade in the offing."

"Your source—or should I say Dom Leonardo?—is a bibber and a jay." Another intemperate houseguest of Norfolk's, the papal nuncio was conveniently absent, visiting his favorite fleshpot in the stews no doubt. "I see you are amassing your troops against the good Cardinal of York."

"I am a generous host."

Pierre grinned, thinking of the lustful chambermaid Norfolk assigned to service him nightly. He drank his cup to the dregs. Sotted though he was, he knew he would not have to do anything, except lie on his back and let her practice her fellatio skills on him.

She was improving nightly. "My dear Norfolk, you are generous with your wine, your servants, and with your friendship, but I have nothing of astounding import to divulge. I bid you good night." He pushed to his feet. The chamber swam before his eyes. He grabbed the back of the chair to keep from collapsing.

"You have overindulged tonight, my friend. We will resume this conversation tomorrow." Norfolk also stood. "Before I forget. This arrived for you earlier." He took out a sealed note from inside his jerkin and offered it to Rougé. The dried wax bore the Cardinal of York's insignia.

Pierre narrowed his bleary eyes on Norfolk. "What does it say?"

Norfolk affected an insulted look. "How should I know? The seal is unbroken."

Pierre knew Norfolk could have read the missive without breaking the seal. A lusty serving wench with access to one's chamber and a razor-sharp blade heated in fire would do the trick. Renée was right. He was a fool to have accepted Norfolk's hospitality. *She is cleverer than I*, he thought. A dangerous trait for a wife. Propping an elbow on the back of the X chair, he broke the seal and read the missive. "She will be pleased." He offered Norfolk the parchment.

Norfolk skimmed it and looked up at Pierre. "Supper to discuss possible bridegrooms?"

"My king shows great care for the queen his wife's relatives."

Norfolk gave him a gimlet eye. "Why not marry her yourself?"

Pierre smirked. "Indeed why not?"

"Is the gossip true?"

"Oh yes. The royal minx took a lover." A boil of Breton expletives burst in his head. He should not have said that. How had he allowed the words to come out of his mouth?

"A common painter, and yet your king bestows her with Brittany. I wonder."

"To sweeten the bargain."

"You see no connection between her lieutenant and Wolsey's unwanted houseguest?"

"The only connection I see is that Froward Renée has a predilection for Italian lovers."

"Perhaps you are right. Pray remember I am at your disposal

should you decide to claim the prize. The duchy of Brittany is a handsome dowry, wouldn't you say? I can help you get it."

"If I help you get the Cardinal of York."

"A fair trade. A rich churchman for a rich duchy."

Pierre smiled at Norfolk as they left the chamber together. "A very rich churchman."

"A very rich duchy."

A rich duchy, an appealing duchess, and a troth cup of poison in the connubial bedchamber, was Pierre's last thought before he tumbled into bed.

"Any word from our spy at York Place?" Renée asked Lieutenant Armado as they entered her apartment. Seeing the two of them enter, Adele clucked her tongue.

"Sergeant Francesco has yet to report. A note, even in cipher, is too dangerous."

"So we wait?"

"We wait."

"Our sand is running out. Make watch on York Place. I want to know who goes in and who comes out." She must have a strong word with Rougé on the morrow. "Lieutenant, find Master Michael Devereaux and bid him come to my chambers. He is one of the king's gentlemen."

"Very well, madame." He bowed and left

Renée removed her headdress. "Adele, get out the lambig and the cards."

"I do not like this," Adele muttered in Breton. "Too many men . . ."

"Pinions, Adele. Mere pinions."

A bottle was missing from his casket, but the lock was intact. Unease settled over Michael as he fingered the key hanging from his neck. He was always careful to return the empty bottles to the casket. There was no doubt in his mind that one was missing. He relocked the casket.

"My esteem for you is increasing by leaps and bounds," Stanley said from the doorway.

Michael cracked a satisfied grin. "The troll moves up, eh?" His toecap pushed the casket through bunches of mulberry twigs scattered under the bed to repel fleas. The soft bed he would be sleeping in tonight was furnished with five wool-stuffed mattresses and lawn bedcovering.

Stanley sauntered inside, his gaze taking in the pleasing, spacious chamber. The ceiling was dark caisson, the walls lined with timber paneling, the diamond panes in the mullioned windows stained with the king's coat of arms. Wainscot cupboards, a mountain of trunks, a saddlebag, and appurtenances occupied the inner wall. Two stools and a wood and bone table fronted the hearth. A wicker basket full of logs, a fire fork, and a shovel were tidily stacked there, but no fire burned in the fireside. "Tester bed, fresh matting, stool chamber to spare the unpleasantness of the public jakes. An agreeable space, although, having heard your protectress's speech, I wagered Suffolk five pounds sterling you would get the double lodging. But this is quite nice. I have the same."

"My protectress?" Michael smiled bemusedly. He wanted to masticate the subject of Renée of Valois from all angles and hear Stanley's observations.

"God's mercy, wipe that big smirk off your face, braggart. Yes, she has taken a shine to you. Anyone with eyes and ears in their heads could tell. The reason, however, eludes me."

Michael chuckled. He was equally puzzled and flattered, albeit afraid to make too much of her interest. The lady maneuvered in mysterious ways, one action at odds with the next. Cold-hot-burning wench. She shied away from his kiss in the woods and kissed his ear in the queen's presence chamber. Were she and Lady Anne Hastings rivals of sorts? He still did not know why Renée had followed Anne to the undercroft. Then Anne had interrupted his flirtation with Renée. Then Renée tried to stop him from dancing with Anne and this evening latched herself to his arm while Anne was watching. However, whereas Anne took what she wanted unapologetically, the maidenly princess seemed to want to play. "What do you make of it, Stanley? A nubile princess of France championing a new arriviste, does it not seem peculiar to you?"

"It depends. You caught her at the game today. Did you win a kiss?"

"I . . . failed to guess her name correctly."

"A gross error, to be sure." Stanley snickered. "Did you offer her a gift to compensate?"

"I gave her the silver rose. Do you recommend aught else?"

"A flower must be offered with a poem, or the lady might think you a witless gardener, said Sir Francis Bryan when I consulted him about Meg."

"Who is Meg?"

Stanley cocked his head to one side, eying Michael strangely. "The sweetest thing you ever saw, a lady aglow with a gentle heart and pleasing grace, the fairest Devereaux to be sure."

"The fairest Devereaux? What are you babbling about?"

"I am babbling about the lovely widow I am courting with marriage in mind. Her name is Mistress Margaret Clifford, sister to Sir Walter Devereaux, whom I believe you met at the hunt. She has Plantagenet blood on her maternal side and disgrace on her paternal one."

Michael blinked doltishly. "Sir Walter *Devereaux*? The popinjay? Norfolk's man?"

"Don't be an ass. She is your sister, her brother your brother. It is plain as a pikestaff."

"Stanley," Michael said quietly. "I have no sister. I have no brother."

"Your father, was he not Sir John Devereaux, son of Lord Walter Devereaux, Baron Ferrers of Chartley? He fought for King Richard the Third under Jock Howard, the first Duke of Norfolk, in the Battle of Bosworth field against Henry Tudor, our king's royal sire."

"Go on."

"Go on! Do you not know your own history?"

"Enlighten me. Please."

Stanley sighed and fidgeted with the haft of his dagger. "Your pardon. You said you were a stray Devereaux. I misconstrued. I . . . thought you had left over some ancient quarrel."

"My mother was Elizabeth Langham, the former queen's maid of honor. My father, Sir John Devereaux, took her for his second wife. She died shortly after she had me. My father fought for King Henry the Seventh and died during the Cornish rebellion."

"Your noble sire fought for the other side, Michael." Stanley's brown gaze was sympathetic. "His own sire died on Bosworth Field, and Sir John lost his patrimony to an act of attainder."

Michael fell silent. Then it was true. Tyrone had lied to him. "I have a brother and a sister."

Stanley smiled at his bemusement. "I imagine you do."

"Do you suppose you could arrange for me to meet Margaret? I do not know about Walter."

"Betwixt us, I distrust any man who is hand in glove with Norfolk. His Grace promised him a knighthood of the Garter at the end of the chapter, to quote Meg, and I am certain I do not care to know what Sir Walter accomplishes for the duke in return, to quote myself. But I am keeping an open mind as regards my future brother-in-marriage. By the by, Harry has given his consent to the marriage and Her Majesty has offered Meg a position among her ladies-in-waiting."

Michael grabbed Stanley's paw. "Congratulations—Stanley, we shall be brothers!"

"Aye, we shall!" Stanley opened his arms in mock sappiness. "Brother!"

They clapped each other's back and laughed heartily. "This calls for a drink."

Stanley yawned. "On the morrow. Off to bed I am. A great day to come and all that. Sleep tight and don't let the bed fleas bite."

"I promise to hug the mulberry twigs to my bosom."

At the door Stanley paused. "I shall ask Meg. She might like to have another brother."

"I thank you, Stanley. Verily, you are a splendid fellow and a worthy soon-to-be-brother."

Alone, Michael sat down by the cold hearth, tapping his boot-cap against the andirons. His sire had been a Yorkist. He had a brother and a sister. He was not alone in the world, after all.

Pippin walked in with an armful of all-night victuals he had pilfered from the kitchen. "Shall I start a fire now?" he inquired hopefully, unburdening his loot on the little table.

"No." The night was chilly, and yet Michael was hot, always hot, courtesy of the Sweat and the irreversible searing of his skin. Catching his manservant's frown of disappointment, he said, "You may go off, if you wish. Take Conn with you."

A glint of interest lit Pippin's eyes. "All night?"

"Here." He dropped a handful of silver coins into the eager hand, enough to sponsor a merry night with wenches. Pippin was out the door in a twink.

Michael's two-day exhaustion had transmuted into restive alertness. He did not know what to do with himself. The palace was relatively quiet. Some of the gentlemen had spoken of taking a barge to the southern bank of the city where there was no watch and no curfew, but he was not up for revelry, not unless it included a violet-eyed princess. He removed Buckingham's dagger from inside the breast of his jerkin and studied the superb craftsmanship by candlelight. Rubies formed the letter *S* for Stafford in the gold hilt. "What shall I do with you, my beauty?"

There was a knock on the door.

Michael sheathed the dagger in his clothes. "Come in."

An officer liveried in blue and gold fleur-de-lis materialized in the threshold. "Sir, my lady solicits your company," the man said in French. "Please, I will escort you."

Michael stood. "Your lady wishes to see me *now*?"

"Sub rosa, as you say in England. Confidential." The soldier smiled, but otherwise gave no indication as to the princess's purpose in summoning Michael to her chamber past midnight.

Michael tugged on his jerkin to conceal his physical enthusiasm. "Sub rosa, lead the way."

His absurd hope to find the royal confection waiting in silky nightclothes was dashed when the Italian officer opened the door to a brightly lit chamber. A draught of ambergris and lavender came at Michael's nose, suffusing his mind with sweet longing. Renée sat primly on a settle of blue velvet cushions decorated with gold tassels and fleurs-de-lis. She was fully gowned save for a headdress, and in its absence, a cascade of thick ebony locks framed her petite torso.

A heavyset old dame sat on a padded stool close to the blazing fireside, her needle flying in and out of what appeared to be a diaphanous white smock. Michael began to sweat.

Renée greeted him cheerfully, waving him in, as if his midnight visit were standard routine.

The absence of a great bed suggested that this was the privy chamber of a double lodging. True enough, he detected a closed door opposite the entrance. Grise matting scented with saffron and lavender carpeted the floor, supplemented with blue velvet foot clothes, also stitched with gold lilies. Candlelight flickered all around. An oaken table covered with felt took up half the space between the settle and the fireplace. A flagon, two cups, and an enameled box graced it.

Michael sketched a bow, unsure what to expect. Customarily love trysts were not conducted in the presence of one's servants. Renée patted the cushion beside her. "Come, sit by me."

She is playing with me, he thought grimly, and eased his much larger frame beside her. She caught his gaze, blinking. He sensed the air charging between them, as before a thunderstorm.

"Does your new residence please you?" Her voice was husky, tremulous of a sudden.

"Aye, madame. My chamber . . ." He craned his head, taking in the tasseled tapestries on the walls, the soft furs aired on a rack, a painted walnut cupboard, newfangled trunks, a golden clock and a lute exhibited in a case of bone, and the cushioned seat on the windowsill. "I thought my chamber lavish until I entered yours. That is extraordinary!" He pointed at the largest tapestry, done in the antique style rediscovered by the Florentine humanists.

"*Le Triomphe d'Amour*. The original painting is a mural in my bedchamber in Amboise, painted by Maestro Raphael di Perugia, a brilliant young artist on the rise at the French court."

The way she pronounced the painter's name, with soft, caressing syllables, made him say, "I thought Jean Clout was the brilliant French court painter."

Her eyes flashed. "Yes, he is the Lady Marguerite's protégé. Raphael is better."

Michael decided that he did not much like this Raphael. Wanting to impress her, he read the Latin inscription at the bottom of the tapestry:

"There, whatever I shall be, I shall always be called the Shade that belongs to thee: the might of Love crosses even the shores of Death."

He smiled at her, quoting a subsequent line he surprisingly remembered:

"There, even if in a troupe to greet me come all the lovely heroines whom the sack of Troy gave to the heroes of Greece, there is none of them, Cynthia, whose beauty will please me more than yours; and (so may the righteous permit) though the destiny of long old age detain you, still will your body be dear to mine tears."

"Bravo!" She daintily clapped her hands. "You like Roman poets?"

"I was brought up on Roman text, but, eh"—a smile twitched at the corners of his mouth—"Propertius is for starry-eyed maidens, as is your enchanting tapestry."

"You think it maudlin?" She studied the tapestry with a thoughtful pout.

"Look, his sword is broken, his wings are in tatters"—he gestured at the nude, soot-smeared fair angel kneeling before his earthly sweetheart—"and instead of fighting the wolves making a meal of his shredded wings, he weeps in a woman's lap. Romantic but hardly heroic."

"That is debatable. He forfeited his place in heaven, cast out his demons, and found peace in the arms of his beloved. His tears are the cleansing. His capitulation is the triumph of love."

"Pardon me for not subscribing to yon principle. I was reared to be a soldier. In my opinion, your effeminate angel has not the mettle to face his foes. This is . . . sentimental folderol."

"Folderol! You perceive his vulnerability as a flaw, but you are mistaken. Look at the slain men in the background. Look at the blood on his sword. He broke it because he was tired of war. Supposing he foreswore love for the glory of future battles, would he be happier? Do poets not teach us that the ultimate prize is love *and* glory, for without the former the latter is bitter?"

Michael perused Renée's flushed face, her sparkly eyes. The fire in the hearth burned hot as lust. His loins throbbed. "Why am I here?" he whispered. "For love . . . or glory?"

"For both." She filled the cups with wine and offered him one. "Breton apple brandy?"

Her practical manner stunned him. He watched her beyond the rim of his cup as they sipped, wondering what surprise the mercurial fey would deliver next. She set aside her brandy cup and opened the small box. Cards! She shuffled them in a flurry and set them in a neat square pile on the table. "I shall teach you how to play primero. It is King Henry's favorite card game, though he is a poor player and often loses fat purses. I will teach you all the tricks, how to gauge your opponents' hands and beat them, but you must always lose to the king. You understand?"

He nodded dazedly.

"Oh, and I have a message for you."

He waited, fascinated by the contrast between her curvy softness and her cerebral sharpness.

"My Lady Anne charged me to tell you that she would see you again. Alone."

Her message was so inappropriate he was dumbstruck. She knew about last night! "I see."

"Well, will you?"

"Your pardon?"

She sighed with impatience. "Have you a response for my Lady Anne?"

Anger struck him. There was a word for what she was doing. "Pray tell the Lady Anne that she has my highest regard and that I hope she remembers me in her prayers."

"That is it? You would not see her?" she demanded, put out.

"I will see Lady Hastings at public occasions and admire her from a distance," he rasped.

Renée's nostrils flared. "You had no qualms admiring her up close last night!"

So-ho. "Madame, since you have dispensed with formality, I will speak my mind, but it is to you alone that I say this: I have not come to court to gain a proficiency in extramarital intrigues and a reputation as a scoundrel and mischief-maker, but to distinguish myself as a sportsman and a worthy companion to His Majesty. My actions of last eve were congruent with my goals." He glanced at her maidservant's back and recaptured her gaze, transmitting his thoughts eloquently. *I shan't say more so long as another person is present.*

"Adele knows not a word in English," Renée clipped. "You may as well speak your mind."

"I believe I have communicated my standpoint unequivocally. Last night I was saving the king's life. Pursuing the lady further would be underhanded and dishonorable."

Understanding brightened her eyes. "What if I told you that the king is in mortal danger yet again and that your honor and skills are once more called upon to save the day?"

"Did Anne specifically tell you this?"

"Not in so many words, but I got the impression that her brother the duke is plotting again and thinks to use her as bait. What happened when you and Anne left the masque?"

"Why were you in the undercroft?"

"I was following her. She is my friend and has a penchant for getting into trouble. Please tell me what happened last night."

"Anne took me behind the Venus tapestry, where we waited for the duke to come at me with a dagger from behind. I turned around in time and stopped him."

"Did he see your face?"

"No. Nor did I see his but I recognized him."

"How did you stop him? Did you wound him?"

"I seized his dagger without inflicting any injury, then chased him off."

"How did you deal with Anne? Did you speak of the affair? What happened next?"

As her questions kept coming at him like cross-bolts, Michael studied her upturned face, the alert glint in her eyes. He could not very well tell her he had lifted Anne's skirts and plumbed her against the wall and then in her bed, several times till dawn. "I told Anne that a man tried to cut my purse and that I frightened him away. We did not discuss it further."

She searched his eyes. "There is more, but you will not tell me, will you?"

I could show you, he thought wryly. He sensed her awareness of him, her curiosity. If all she wanted were answers about last night, she could find an occasion to ask him in the public haunt of men at a decent hour. She did not have to offer to tutor him in primero to get those answers.

Something shrieked and fluttered outside the window. Renée jolted back against him, staring at the dark windowpanes. "What was that?"

His hands, clasping her shoulders, felt her quiver. "I do not know," he murmured against her scented hair. She was so soft and small and vulnerable. "Shall I investigate?"

Renée gripped one of his hands, nodding her head against his. "Please."

He left her at the settle gripping her tiring woman's chubby hand and went to the window. He pushed open the mullioned door and stuck his head outside. Darkness reigned. The cold night air was a balm to his fire-roasted skin and the desire simmering underneath. Mist hung heavy on the river. A distant bobbing light floated downstream. As he squinted at it, he discerned a lantern pinned to a pole on a boat. There were no passengers aboard the wherry except the waterman, who was humming a bawdy tune and counting his coins. All was quiet and unthreatening. Of a sudden an owl flew past him, jerking Michael back. Renée let out a squeal. "Is it a rook? A bat?"

"Neither." Michael stanched his laughter. "An owl. Naught to be alarmed about." He shooed away the nasty creature, closed the mullioned window door, and secured the latch.

"An owl?" She was deathly pale. Her tire-woman thrust the brandy cup into her trembling hands and urged her to drink it. Renée juddered. "I hate owls." She sipped the brandy.

Michael returned to her side, relishing his heroic moment. "Are you all right? Shall I leave?"

Soulfully she searched his eyes. "Will you help us? Anne will not tell me what Buckingham has planned. How can I protect her when she keeps mum?" Her fingers curled around his sleeve. "Please, Michael. Charm the details out of her, so that you and I may put our heads together and come up with a sound scheme to rescue both His Majesty and Anne from a terrible calamity."

The tangible fear he perceived in her touched him. He wanted to believe her, to help her, to save her, but something he could not quite put his finger on disturbed him. "Why did you try to stop me from saving the king last night?"

Her gaze dropped to her lap. "I was concerned for you."

He smiled. "Shall I show you the dagger I wrested from Buckingham?" At her eager nod, he extracted the dagger from inside his jerkin. "Handsome piece, is it not?"

With a feathery caress she took the dagger from his hand. "It bears his arms." She sought his eyes. "Have you considered taking it to the king?"

"Will he take my word over that of the first peer of the realm, should Buckingham decide to accuse me of stealing his dagger? I think not. Besides, Buckingham is not aware of my identity, and I should like to keep it that way."

"Yes, I see your point. I could ask the French ambassador the Marquis of Rougé to bring it before Cardinal Wolsey. That should give the matter more credence, do you not think?"

"Let me speak to Anne first." He took the dagger from her, sensing her fleeting reluctance to relinquish it. "I imagine she has appointed you our"—the unwholesome word *procurer* dangled on his tongue—"broker-between to keep Sir Hastings in the dark."

"I will be the negotiator for the sake of decorum and propriety, but I do so only because our mission is a noble one."

"My most proper and noble negotiator, do I wait for further instructions or am I to come up with an arrangement myself?"

"Anne left the matter to us."

He noticed the emphasis on *us*. "I shall think upon it and let you know."

"I have an idea. I will tell her to visit your apartment before supper tomorrow."

His jaw clenched. Next the shrewish malapert would inform

him that she would oversee his meeting with Anne, whom he absolutely did not care to entertain in his bedchamber. "My lady, I am perfectly capable of negotiating my own trysts!"

The old tire-woman threw him a bilious harrumph over her shoulder.

He narrowed his eyes on her. "I thought the old bag did not understand English."

"The old bag understands growling, sir," Renée snapped.

He stifled a curse. Somehow he had carelessly landed in her hot pan and was continuing his descent unto the burning coals below. "You called me Michael a moment ago."

"That was unseemly. Your pardon. I should not have spoken your baptismal name."

"But I gave you permission—" The fickle wench! *Virgins*, he thought uncharitably. "Is this"—he brandished his arm in an encompassing gesture—"this is seemly?"

"I asked you here to discuss serious affairs. As strange travelers going in the same direction may oft share a bed, so must we join forces to frustrate the traitorous duke's plans."

He felt his jaw slacken. Did her carefully chosen words harbor a sensual promise, or was she feeling sufficiently chaperoned to toy with him as a cat would with a leashed hound? Instinct told him that he was being handled. Her intermittent sweetness, albeit bubbling of a natural spring, was not bestowed lightly. She was incredibly shrewd. She suggested they joined forces, and yet he had the distinct impression that he was being kept in the dark. "So," he said. "No cards?"

The rosette smile she cast him as she collected the deck of illuminated cards was femininity at its most lethal.

"Tell me about your mistress. What is she like?"

Armado Baglioni, wobbly on his feet, his eyes bloodshot with too much drink, shot the dice across the filthy table at the Bell and the Cock. "Difficult."

Walter smirked. "You weigh your words as a miserly Jew counts his coins."

"*Porca miseria!*" Armado cursed when his dice throw fleeced him of his last borrowed doit. "Walter, lend me another angel. My luck is returning. I feel it!"

"Your . . . medallion is . . . intriguing."

Walter dithered. *"Ahhh! Bene, bene!"* Armado removed the chain from around his neck and tossed it on the table. "Give me an angel! This is pure gold!"

Walter fingered the gold-cross-over-black pendant. The tiny gold Latin motto at the bottom read *Soldiers in Service of God*. Norfolk would be pleased. "How did you come to be in the princess's employ? Do you serve her long? Do you also serve the King of France?"

Armado shrugged. "A former soldier of Rome must make a living somewhere."

"Easy living, if you can leave your post two nights in a row."

"Bah!" Armado slumped on his stool. "She is entertaining privately tonight."

Walter stemmed his resentment. "Does she, now? Who is the lucky devil?"

"A nobody. The fair, tall fellow from Ireland. Walter, two angels?"

Masking his sudden rage with false levity, Walter raked the chained pendant from the table. "How would you like me to settle all of your debts, *amico*?"

Seize the day; trust as little as possible
to the morrow.

—Horace: *Odes*

Black raptors barraged the casement, rapping, screeching, claw-ing at the stained glass panes. She was trussed as a chrysalis, her mouth stoppered, screaming but barely whimpering. All was black. She was—as always—on her own. No one would come to her rescue. A glimmer, a flame, pierced the darkness, husking, *Trust me, trust me . . .* She dared not, could not, must fight alone. Sunshine. Brittany. *Run!* Run and be saved . . . *Boom.* The windowpanes ex-ploded. The evil black birds were upon her, shadows, grabbing her, shaking her, uttering her name . . . Renée shrieked.

"Open your eyes, child."

With a start Renée sat up amid churned bedclothes, wide-awake yet disoriented, her cambric smock soaked in sweat at her back, at her neck. Adele's fleshy face, creased with concern, filled her vision. Heavy rain sheeted the pale daylight outside her win-dow. She sagged. *Thunderstorm.* Sweet Jesu, she was falling apart, and yet she had to ratch up the pressure and do what she must.

Little flames came to life in various corners of the chamber, their glows a welcome comfort.

"Drink this." A warm cup was thrust into her hands; a cool wet clout slapped unto her brow and stuck there. "Foul, miserable weather," Adele groused at the window. "Pah!"

"Thank you." Renée sipped the warm, spiced elderberry wine.

Fragments of her nightmare played before her eyes: the black birds, the beguiling flicker of gold, knowing she would have to surrender a fundamental piece of herself to survive. She stared at the window. Dismal weather. What to do with Michael and Anne? She should not have assisted him in obtaining finer quarters. Had she left well enough alone, she would have arranged a "chance meeting" in her rooms.

Michael was exciting, fair-looking, and dangerous. He had backbone. His mind was an array of operations, absorbing light-fast, implementing, sneaking up from behind, and couching it with charm. He had long, swift, clever fingers. He made her laugh and stole her scarf from inside her sleeve while she was noticing his dazzling smile. One learned a lot about a man playing primero. He remained a mystery. A wild card. Unfathomable. She did not trust him for a moment.

Renée pushed aside the bedclothes and ambled barefooted to the lectern. Two coffers were placed there. One contained her jewels, the other documents. Each had three argents embedded in the rim of the bottom box. She dragged one closer, touched the silver dots at a specific order, and the curved lid opened. Inside were rolls of vellum, clean parchments, an assortment of inkwells and quills, a pot of wax, a bag of sand, and her mother's ring: the Seal of Brittany.

"A year in a cloister would have done you a world of good," Adele muttered while placing clothing articles on the bed: a Rennes lawn smock, woven of gossamer-fine thread and spangled with gold fleurs-de-lis whose ruffled cuffs would peek from the gown at the wrists; a scarlet satin kirtle, petticoat, linen squares to stuff inside Renée's stiff bodice to create the de rigueur illusion of a spectacular bust; and a low-cut gown of shimmering ruby taffeta and black velure.

"I do not recall soliciting your opinion, old witch." Renée took out a square of parchment, dipped a quill in the inkpot, and formulated the note she would dispatch to Rougé.

Adele harrumphed. "A daughter of France does not scheme with strange men in her chamber well into the night," she lectured as she stuffed an ambergris and lavender pomander into a gilt-latticed black velvet purse adorned with ruby cabochons and gold tassels. She attached it to the matching silk girdle that would go round the waist. "Conspiring to steal from cardinals, training to fight like a man, bullying powerful lords, playing cards and giggling with nobodies . . . Pah!"

A direct hit. "You know what Long-Nose would have done to me had I refused—Soubise!"

"Your weakling of an artist is not much better. You need a strong man to take care of you," ranted her old nurse as she lovingly laid out a pair of perfumed kidskin gloves, slit at the fingers to reveal the rings worn underneath, scarlet stockings and wool hose to warm the calves, ribbon garters, and pewter hooks to keep the purfiled hems of the gown off the muddied floors.

"Raphael is artistic and gentle," Renée disputed, tickling her nose with the feather.

"A common poacher, he cannot appreciate the pearl that has fallen into his paint-blotted lap. He does not deserve you, child." At the neck of the gown, Adele spread out soft marten fur and a stylish French hood. In accordance with St. Paul's decree that women's hair must be covered—unbound hair, even for maidens, signified lack of discipline—English ladies wore somber, gable-pointed hoods with thick lappets and a heavy veil.

"Yes, he does!" Renée breathed emphatically, glaring at her smudged letter. She would have to copy it to a clean square of parchment.

"Stubborn girl! Same as my beloved queen your mother. You know I speak the truth. Your painter's blood is thin. He cannot give you the babes you long for, your *marmaille*, little boys and girls scampering along the banks of the Loire. A life with the painter will be fruitless. I read it in his skin, in the white of his eyes. Will you sacrifice your heart's desire for a minute fancy? You need a virile man whose blood is strong to plant babes in your fertile womb and enrich your life with children's laughter." The crescent-shaped hood joining the tricking on the bed was designed to be set back on the head to display some hair and adorned with gold billiments enameled with teardrop pearls and rubies dripping over the ears; its gauzy bongrace could be worn over loose hair or flipped over the face to protect the skin from sun. The pert hood suited Renée perfectly. She had no desire to confuse anyone into thinking her biddable.

"Your prattling distracts me from composing an important letter." She crossed out ill-chosen words. She needed an apt finishing line to put the fear of Long-Nose in Rougé. Her concentration was lost. Adele's diagnosis overcast the joyful future Renée fought for. Would she be content with a man she loved but no babes in her arms? "You may be mistaken."

"Have I ever been?"

Renée closed her eyes and gritted her teeth. How well Adele knew her. She adored children, loved playing with her tiny niece and nephew. If Adele reminded her not of Raphael's disability, Renée would soon forget, and all would be well again. Until Claude had another babe. "Pray let us speak no more of my situation. I am here, and I shall do my duty." She reread the letter.

"I need jewels."

"How many demonstrations will it take for you to commit the cipher to memory?"

"As many sermons as it will take for you to realize you are playing with fire." Adele burbled something in her ancient patois.

Renée glowered at her. "Did you just call me a little goose?"

"If the shoe fits!" Adele smacked together a pair of low-cut, square-toed black leather boots, fastened with red satin ribbons and gold buckles, and dropped them at the foot of the bed.

"Irksome old hag." Renée dragged over the second coffer and touched the argent knobs.

As soon as the lid burst open, like a scrofulous beggar, Adele mobbed the coffer of all its red and black jewels: gold rings inlaid with black sapphires and bloodred rubies; agate medallions enameled with cameos of Renée's parents; a ruby-rimmed brooch of black crystal engraved with the Porcupine, King Louis XII's emblem; another brooch of tiny jet stones depicting the Breton black ermine on a field of diamonds; matching bracelets and necklets with pendent gold fleurs-de-lis and marguerites linked with rubies, glossy white and black pearls, and sparkling jet; and lastly a rosary of flame opals, black amber, and garnets guarded with gold.

Renée rolled her eyes as Adele dropped everything into her folded apron. "Am I addressing the English Parliament this morn or attending my own coronation?" she asked tartly.

Adele snorted. "You are a princess of France, a duchess of great dominions. You must look the part. Familiarity breeds contempt, and you have been too familiar with certain insignificants of this court. Your appearance today must remind them of your elevated station and how swiftly their high-ceilinged heads may be cut off should they presume to overextend their necks further."

"God's pity!" Renée laughed. "You think I have taken a fancy to Michael Devereaux! Ha! I am playing with him."

Adele gave her a wry look. "Do not get too confident. He might start playing with you." She gave an awful imitation of the giggles that had spilled unchecked from Renée's lips last night.

Renée fumed. It had been the brandy's fault! "Here, warm the wax. I need to finish this."

"Elizabeth Langham did not have a boy. She died of pestilence three months after our father married her." Walter kept his voice low as he squired his sister into the Church of the Observant Friars at Greenwich. It was imperative to attend Mass with Their Majesties, notwithstanding the weather.

Meg frowned. "How do you explain the skin marking Stanley told me about? People do not needle dye into their skin for the pleasure of it. Moreover, the Devereaux coat of arms has been out of favor since King Richard lost the battle to Henry Tudor. Why go to the trouble of marking yourself as the son of an attainted, dead traitor? I say our father wanted him—"

"Sir John died the same year as his second wife. He had no time to raise a boy."

"You say Michael is an imposter, but you cannot ignore the physical likeness. He looks exactly like Father, only with blue eyes."

"I say he is an ill-begotten whoreson!" Walter seethed. "A trickster and an adventurer!"

Meg pursed her lips. "I liked him. I would meet him. I do not require your approval."

"Meg!" Walter exclaimed, shocked. "You would defy me on this?"

"You are full of hate, Walter. It is not a quality the king appreciates in the men of his circle."

"What do you know of the men in the king's circle?" he snarled. "And that Stanley fellow, I do not approve of him. You should look higher. Perhaps . . ."

"I am not minding you, Walter. I am not minding you."

Michael never missed Mass with Their Majesties' households in the Church of the Observant Friars. Like a skittish *marrano*, he was always on time, worshiping with solemnity and reverence befitting a bishop. While the people whose good opinion he sought sat on the front pews, he was mindful of those at the back: servants, who despite having lost all capacity for astonishment and indignation in their masters' and mistresses' service, still expected some fascinating sport from their betters. He could not afford to err. They burned pagans in England.

While his ignorance of Christian beliefs could light a woodpile beneath his heretical feet, the salvation of his flesh, if not of his soul, came in the form of three mercies: his fluency in Latin, a Bible he had pilfered, and the minutiae of the service explained to him by a priest in Ireland.

The three blessings served him well throughout the Confession of the Sins, whereupon came the reading of the biblical passage. The priest read: "And it came to pass after these things, that God did tempt Abraham, and said unto him, Abraham: and he said, Behold, here I am."

Michael was a trifle disappointed when the ensuing sermon centered on what man can do for God and not vice versa instead of on the story of the attempted sacrifice of Isaac. The concept of God asking His faithful servant to sacrifice his only son prickled Michael in deep, dark places. As a result, he lost interest, allowing his gaze to wander toward the bantam-sized confection sitting in the ladies' pews with the queen, willing her to look back at him. The miracle did not happen. Evidently, God, a discerner of hearts and minds, did not grant wishes to disbelievers.

This woman . . . she bewitched him! He liked it that she had a strong, sharp mind and a steady, forcible manner. Her delicate

beauty enchanted his eyes, and the scent of ambergris and lavender drifting from the kerchief tucked inside the breast of his jerkin
befuddled his senses altogether.

To keep from dozing off at the priest's benumbing drone—the
pretty shrew had kept him up half the night playing cards and
drinking apple brandy, scolding him most severely for missing
tricks—he tried to imagine her little breasts freed of their elaborate trappings. His musings made him physically uncomfortable,
so he pondered other things: her laughter. Whenever she caught
him staring and the silence betwixt them grew intense, he came
up with silly jests to make her laugh. He loved her laughter, peals
of sweetness, enticing bubbles that tickled all his soft spots. They
said women grew fond on men that made them laugh. He was
going to become court jester.

Desirous to make a good impression on the delectable intriguer's deity, Michael knelt as a true believer together with the
faithful as the priest, his back turned, attended the Tabernacle. He
remained on his knee during the transubstantiation and the blessing of the Host, and when the priest faced his flock, raised the
wafer for the Holy Spirit to possess it, and said, "The body of Christ!"
Michael replied wholeheartedly, "Amen!"

After the Holy Communion, the priest blessed the king, the
queen, their infant princess and future offspring, the realm, and offered a special blessing to the Knights Companion of the Order of
the Garter, summoning the Holy Spirit once again to steady their
fighting arms, to speed their destriers, and to protect them from
noyance in the forthcoming tournaments. He then called upon the
entire congregation to renounce Satan and his evil works and
cleave to the Lord Christ.

Taking his cues from the crowd and recalling the Irish priest's
lecture about God and Satan, Michael meekly rejected the Bad
and embraced the Good. Black and White, Darkness and Light,
with nothing in between, was a foreign concept to him. The Greek
and Roman scriptures his lord had pumped into his brain since
boyhood and the caldron of Celtic myth he had gulped from the
common folk in Tyrone celebrated the complex contradictions in
human nature. Religion was of the outside world, of ignorant vil-

lagers and distant countries. The Earl of Tyrone never discussed it, except to ascertain that Michael was sufficiently informed for his court adventure.

To conclude the service, the Children of the Chapel Royal, the dozen boys Master Cornish had handpicked from cathedral schools and church choirs, sang like angels; their voices, more divine than human, rose to the heavens, transporting the assembly to higher planes of spirituality. Their appeal must have fallen on favorable ears. Michael saw Renée's head crane slightly aside. A vivid, side-long flash of violet eyes came at him of a sudden. He winked—and she smiled.

King Henry's court had two remedies for atrocious weather: drinking and gambling. Renée, observing the card tables from her vantage point in the bay window, was proud to see her student applying her teachings to impoverish the courtiers and enrich the pleased king. The grace, charm, and wit with which he conducted himself were all his, though. Michael was a natural.

A blowsy woman stepped in to block her view. "May we speak privily?" Anne asked. Her eyes were red, she had dark circles underneath, and her voice quivered on the verge of tears.

Renée draped a sisterly arm around Anne's quaking shoulders and led her to her apartment. She sat with Anne on the cushioned settle by the fireside, looking saintly. "What is it?"

Anne's entire frame shook. "I—I need y-your help."

"Adele, mulled elderberry wine for my friend, if you please."

"You look grand this morn," Anne remarked, sniffing, as Adele removed a pot from a tripet set upon the hearth and filled a goblet with warm, scented wine. Anne's hands twisted in her lap.

"What is amiss, Anne? I will help you."

Anne shook her head wretchedly. "'Tis too awful to speak of."

Renée put the warm goblet in Anne's hands, encouraging her to sip. "You are safe here," she said soothingly. "Naught is as awful as it seems. A trifling imprisoned in our minds may take the shape of a bugbear, but once we speak of it, the devil is not as black as he is painted."

"Thank you." Anne hiccupped. She drained half the goblet and sought Renée's gaze, unshed tears trembling in her wide brown eyes. "Please do not judge me too harshly. The last three years I have done naught but worship Our Lady on my knees." Her knuckles whitened around the goblet. She drew a fortifying sip and blurted, "I am with child!" Then she burst out crying.

Renée was astonished, Anne's admission having caught her off guard. Her initial guess had been that either Buckingham or Anne or both had come under suspicion of conspiring to commit high treason. Now she felt unchristian envy tug at her. In contrast, Anne did not seem to consider a tuft-pated angel quickening in her womb auspicious tidings. Renée pulled a kerchief from her sleeve and dabbed at Anne's cheeks. "Why are you crying?" she asked gently, while she felt like crying herself. Her greatest wish of all might never come true.

Anne's puffy eyes etched with shame. She took the kerchief and blew her nose in it. "You would think so ill of me. I should not have come, but—merciful Mary!—I did not know what to do, whom to turn to, and you said your tiring woman"—she cast an inquisitive gaze at Adele—"performed miracles with herbs." She clutched Renée's hand to her bosom. "I am aware I ask a great deal of you, but I am desperate, truly desperate. If my husband should find out . . ."

Understanding dawned on Renée, but she asked anyway, "Was the child conceived"—she stopped herself from saying "in sin" and chose kinder words—"outside the connubial bed?"

Anne nodded, sobbing. "I must be rid of it. George and I share the same coloring. Both our children, Francis and William, have brown eyes and red-brownish hair. If the child I carry takes after his natural father"—she started wailing again—"my husband will kill it and lock me away in the cloister for good. I am lost, unless you help me. Last night you offered. I would not have come begging you to assist me in this horrid, ungodly business otherwise." Anne knew what she was asking could send her, Renée, and Adele to burn at the stake for practicing witchery.

"Verily an ugly bugbear," Renée hedged.

With a shuddering breath, Anne buried her face in Renée's lap.

Caterwauling inconsolably, she pleaded with God to put an end to her misery one way or the other. Her voice was muffled. "Th-the chaplain a-at St. Mary's, h-he caught me o-one day in an out-of-sight corner a-and—"

Renée was outraged. "A chaplain forced himself upon you?" Anne nodded. "When?"

Anne lifted her head. "The week before I left."

Less than a month, then. "Should you not wait two months to be sure?"

"I am sure!" Anne's tone was adamantine; her eyes were wild with fear. "A woman knows, a mother who has given birth to two children knows. I cannot wait! It must be done tonight!"

"Tonight?" Renée felt the chill of suspicion spread through her bones. She forced herself to sound reasonably concerned. "Can it not be done in a month? Sir George will never—"

"I beg you! Do not sentence me to prolonged suffering! It must be done *tonight*!"

The emphasis on the word *tonight* verified Renée's suspicion. Things were progressing too fast. Buckingham was moving against the king again! Where was Sergeant Francesco? "I shall consult Adele, with your permission." Upon Anne's nod, Renée said in quick Breton, "She lies. I do not believe it is her pregnancy she wishes to terminate but the queen's. It is part of the plot hatched by her brother. He is behind the dramatic interlude performed for our leisure."

Adele sniffed. "She dissembles well."

"She is full of falsehoods, but her distress is genuine. I trow the duke her brother is bringing pressure to bear on her. He is so desperate for the throne that he would assassinate the king and his unborn heir. While I cannot fathom his method, his solution is surprisingly ingenious, if horribly cold. I did not expect it from the man. Unfortunately tonight is much too soon." She was two vital pieces of information short to facilitate the assassination plot: one was the exact hiding place of the Ancient at York Place and the second was the time of her audience with Cardinal Wolsey. Where in perdition was Rougé? He should have received the note by now.

Adele worried a wart on her dewlapped chin. "Tell her I do not have all the ingredients at hand and that it would take a few days to collect the herbs and—"

"She will go elsewhere. I doubt not there are plenty of knowledgeable women depopulating the bathhouses in the stews, and I should not want the queen to come to any harm. We must take charge of the situation. Now I want you to look disconcerted by the sinful task you are given but not entirely dismayed. Nod your head in agreement and get out your mortar and pestle."

"If you agree to help her, the time constraint . . ."

Oh yes, she felt the sand of time spilling through her fingers without having to be reminded of it. Still, she had a whole day between now and tonight, time to come up with a contingency plan. She smiled reassuringly at Anne, whose gaze kept bouncing anxiously between Renée and Adele. Once more she wondered how simpleminded Anne truly was. There were times when she could swear Anne had the brains God gave a cow, and there were other times when Anne would unveil a thick vein of cunning worthy of a Roman courtesan. Renée would not underestimate her.

At the laden silence, Anne burst into fresh tears. "Very well," Renée said. "I will help you."

Anne clutched her hands. "How good you are to me! The nuns said constancy is tested by adversity and that a friend in need is a friend in deed. I feel blessed with your friendship."

"As do I. Now dry your eyes and finish your wine."

Her distress forgotten, Anne hung hopeful cow's eyes on Renée. "Did you perchance receive word from . . . our golden friend?"

Par dieu, Renée thought, disgusted. The lustful adulteress did not give up. No sooner would Anne be rid of one unwanted albeit imaginary babe, and she would be heavy with a real one. It was on the tip of her tongue to ask whether trysting with a man who was not her husband would be prudent under the circumstances—but that would sabotage her assignment.

At her silence, Anne plowed on, "Did he not express a desire to see me? I thought he might want me to pay him a visit at his new quarters."

"I spoke with him before he was bestowed in finer lodging. I will speak to him again."

"Oh, good." Anne clasped her hands together, her eyes shining.

Before they left the apartment, Renée halted and spoke to Adele. "I have it. Brew a harmless physic of lungwort, a mild purgative for the bowels but naught more. The queen must not lose the child. Nor suffer overly much. Have it ready by dinnertime. Should a note arrive from Rougé, send a page to me at once. I will be with the queen."

Tonight! Renée fidgeted on her perch at the tennez court. How would she manage to be at York Place tonight? She wanted to scream with frustration. The warp and the weft of her scheme were raveling again! Rougé was useless; Armado seemed to have lost focus; there was no word from Sergeant Francesco; and Anne was expecting a hemlock brew as well as the particulars for a love tryst with the dark horse Renée had needlessly taken into her confidence last night.

Whatever Buckingham was planning was scheduled for tonight. Michael could not find out. He would only disrupt the plot in his zeal to rescue his king and carry the day. So now, besides having to find her elusive scout and contrive a way to gain entry into York Place this evening, she would also have to play stave between the fallacious wanton and the fair fortune seeker.

The only certain factor in her life was the Goliath of a megrim expanding inside her head.

The ambiance in the indoor tennez court was painfully boisterous. Sweat and perfumes hung heavy in the air. Sports-minded gentlemen shouted odds and bets and cheered the players. King Henry partnered the Duke of Suffolk against Sir Francis Bryan and Sir William Compton. Mary stood up beside Renée and clapped elatedly as her beloved Charles scored a point.

Renée wanted to incinerate all of them. She could not leave. She had to keep Michael from Anne and lurk for Rougé, in case the cretin decided to grace the court with his odious presence. Closing her eyes, she prayed to Our Lady for help and guidance, appealed to St. Expeditus to do something about Francesco's procrastination, and begged St. Ubald to slay the monster pounding inside her head. A tap on her arm jumped her. Robin handed her a note. "For you, my lady."

Finally! She gave the youth a coin and unfolded the missive. It read:

> *Love hurts me with its craving,*
> *And madness sends me raving,*
> *A girl so tortures me.*

What the devil? She had expected a note from Rougé or Francesco—not a love poem, of all things! A burst of hysterical laughter bordering on tears escaped her lips. She covered her mouth with her gloved hand and went on reading the stupid thing:

> *I never tire of seeing*
> *That most enchanting being;*
> *I groan and cry my plea:*

Mockery blossomed into curiosity as to the poet's identity. She skipped the rest of the lines and read the signature at the bottom:

> *Written with the hand of him which I would were yours.*
> *Perdu (a soldier lost to a forlorn hope)*

Oh, this was too much—a secret doter! She never had one before. She felt . . . nonsensically flattered. The rest of the poem read:

> *Have pity on my wrongs,*
> *Lady who brought me pain,*
> *And make me whole again!*
> *To you my life belongs.*

Renée reread the poem several times. It was beautiful. It took her mind off her troubles. She looked around her, hunting for a telling grin or wink from a specific gentleman. She spotted the loathsome Sir Walter, who caught her gaze and beamed at her. Fah! She looked away. She did not want him to be Perdu. She continued her survey. Some of the gentlemen were intent on the tennez ball bandied back and forth; others seemed more inclined toward bandying flirtatious glances with the ladies. Servitors served wine and sweetmeats, and the company grew merrier by the minute. After the game, the court was to have dinner in the king's presence chamber, where they would make merry till midnight. There was little else to do with the inclement weather raging outside but drink, eat, play, and pander to the king, activities most courts excelled at.

Anne sat betwixt her husband, Sir George Hastings, and her brother the Duke of Buckingham amidst a gaggle of richly robed aristocrats whom Renée recognized as the exalted White Roses, the last of the House of York and other Plantagenet scions. Anne waved at her, the nuisance.

Renée kept looking. Having failed to spot a debonair smile fixed on her in a telling manner, she permitted her gaze to linger on the burnished blond head she had been deliberately ignoring since joining the queen's entourage. Michael Devereaux towered as a gorgeous lantern above the dark hats and hoods clustered together on the opposite side of the tennez court. Standing next to his bearded friend, he looked restive and ill-tempered, neither reciprocating Anne's importunate looks nor following the energetic tennez match taking place beneath his nose. His agitation was blatant as a gaudy coat of arms. He gave off the impression of a man in extreme agony.

Michael's abstractedly wandering gaze found her. Turquoise eyes focused. She read a silent question mark. Renée tensed, a flush of color playing traitor on her cheeks. Could he be—? She discarded the notion thereupon, recalling his disparagement of poetic love. Laurels were what he lusted after. Ambition was crawling all over him. He began shouldering a path out of the throng. She sucked in a breath. If he were making his way toward her, surely he was Perdu.

Michael did not even attempt to reach her. His destination was the great doors to her left.

Naturally, Renée decided to follow him.

* * *

Michael staggered out of the clustered, noisy tennez court with a thick sheen of sweat on his brow. The stench of cloying perfumes coating rank bodies, the brain-needling din, and the echo of the tennez ball bandied back and forth had reduced him to a jumble of sweaty, rattling, aching nerves. He was losing his sanity, for sure. His head was about to burst—and he thirsted for the dragon's blood with urgent desperation. Gritting his teeth, he slunk into an out-of-the-way corner and yanked the glass bottle out of his sporran. As he gulped it down, he sensed the industrious little spy tiptoeing toward his hiding spot. Did the woman never rest?

"Madame!" a male, French-accented voice rang with bitter irritation.

"Finally!" Michael's stalker snapped. "Your condemnation is growing apace, Rougé!"

Michael heard a gasp and a rustle of skirts and realized the spy had been physically grabbed.

"You lying schemer!" the Frenchman hissed. "You are not here for a husband! You—"

"Please remove your hand from the lady," Michael bit out with a tight, menacing smile. He would have loved to eavesdrop on their fascinating conversation but could not stomach the idea of her being mauled. The marquis's hand dropped. Dark eyes glared at Michael. A pair of Valois guards rushed forward with rattling scabbards. Renée looked relieved to see them. Michael ought to explain to the shrewcat that skulking about unprotected was a perilous endeavor.

Renée flashed him a grateful look and strode off, the guards and the marquis on her heels.

Pierre felt like a lapdog being led on a tight leash as he hastened after the deceitful witch, aptly gowned in scarlet and black and dripping jewels, her shadows in azure and gold following her. She was startlingly fleet-footed for such a tiny morsel. He had to lope to draw level with her.

"My audience?" she hissed softly, maintaining her brisk pace.

Pierre was deliberately silent. Served her right to sweat!

"If you tell me you have not heard from the cardinal, I shall pack you off to France, Rougé, with a letter of Bellerophon to King Francis in your pocket."

"Ah. The content, unbeknownst to its bearer, will urge the recipient to put me to death."

"I've tolerated your phlegmatic attitude long enough. When you choose to be unconstructive you become disruptive. This offense alone is punishable by death."

Rendered speechless by spleen, Pierre stared at her little neck and envisioned wringing it till the termagant's complexion matched the color of her eyes. Having come bearing good news, he now resolved to say nothing, just for spite. The violet flames scorched him. "I see you would fain suffer the disgrace of my personally informing the Lord Chancellor of England that His Most Christian Majesty has conscripted me into relieving you of your office." She snapped her fingers at her quietly skulking bodyguard. "Flag down a barge. We go to York Place."

Pierre caught her wrist in a manacle grip. "You would not dare!"

"But I would." Renée nodded at her guards. The sharp tip of a stiletto touched Pierre's neck.

He froze, belatedly realizing that the she-devil had outmaneuvered him again in leading him to her quarters, and now four of her stalwart Italian guards surrounded him. Tasting the pungent dish of defeat, he grudgingly drudged up the words to save his life. "Cardinal Wolsey has invited us to sup with him tomorrow evening."

Renée gestured to her guards to sheathe their weapons and walked inside her apartment.

Pierre followed with an oath. He wanted Brittany, fully aware that Renée would not make the sort of wife who fell in line the first time she felt the back of his hand across her cheek in a husbandly demonstration of authority. She would execute him. Nice and easy. He would never feel a thing. "Will you not congratulate me on my industry in securing the audience?" he asked.

She stood at the casement, watching rain sluicing the panes. "Congratulate you? I marvel that our king should assign me a slothful mouser instead of a tiger."

"Much as I enjoy being henpecked by you, you go too far, madame!"

"I disagree. I think henpecking improves you, Rougé."

"Have you an inkling of how difficult it is to obtain an audience with the holy tyrant?"

"I want you to advance my audience with him. I would see him this evening." She whirled to face him. "You want a page in my good books? Do it!"

In the grayish daylight, he at last discerned her pallor and the taut set of her shoulders. She was not pothering. She was angst-ridden. The load King Francis had placed upon her shoulders was a matter of life and death. Perversely he found himself applauding the brat's mettle. No one but a king would dare to scold him, threaten his honor, and point a knife to his neck in a single conversation. "Acquit me of making foolish judgments, madame. This English cardinal is drunk on power. King Henry's abdication of matters of state to his lord chancellor and handing him the Great Seal of England has made Wolsey *ipse rex*. That he is the beginning, middle, and end is the litany of the foreign ambassadors. Anyone seeking an audience with the king must first pay obeisance to his cardinal and kiss that hand. While King Henry has been hard at work acquiring the reputation for being the spring of all things frivolous and amusing in England, York Place has become the center of temporal power. Cardinal Wolsey has long since abandoned all pretense of couching his replies with phrases such as 'His Majesty will do so and so' or 'We shall do so and so' but openly and unabashedly says, 'I shall do so and so.' If I should dispatch a note begging to advance our interview, I would wager my lands, my chattels, and my stopped iron mine that his answer would be further deferment. Do you wish to jeopardize your mission by alienating him? Surely you are acquainted with the adage 'when a slave becomes king'?"

She was silent for a long count. "I could deal with a pet tiger, if he were true and constant. If you manage to advance the supper . . ." She faltered, pressing her hands to her temples.

"You are ill." He moved to offer a gallant arm. "Come sit on the settle."

Her head jerked up. "I shall see you tomorrow evening. Good day, Rougé."

His face hardened. He wanted to question her about the true reason she was in England but sensed that in her present humor she would call in her guards before revealing anything. Curbing his annoyance, he affected a laconic smile. "Adieu for now."

Tomorrow. Renée sank on the settle in front of the fire and rested her head in her propped-up hands. Whatever Buckingham had in mind would be carried out tonight; tomorrow would be too late. If not for the abysmal megrim trammeling her brain, she would have raked the marquis down until he cried mercy and acknowledged his ineptitude as an ambassador of France. A savvy diplomat would have anticipated the cardinal's response and known how to expedite matters. But Rougé, for all he thought himself giftedly cunning, was in effect a lazy parasite. How obsequious he was in his pursuit of her duchy. Did he really think he stood a chance?

Adele appeared before her. "This is for your head." She thrust a cup into Renée's hand. "And this"—she produced a vial of stone—"is for that lady."

Renée examined the plain vial, sealed with simple wax. None would be able to trace it back to her. "Bless you, Adele. I knew I could count on you, although I have grave doubts. . . ."

"Drink the cordial. It will dull the ache in your head. And if you decide to give the extract to the lady, tell her to use no more than three drops and to let it sit in wine for an hour beforehand."

"An hour?" Enlightenment struck. "If an hour . . . why not a day?" Renée subsided against the settle's back, sighing, the kernel of fear beginning to dissolve. "Oh, Adele. I am saved. I shall tell Anne the poison needs a day to ferment and that it will be ineffective before tomorrow evening. Surely the duke will not refuse to delay by a single day."

Adele grunted consent. "Your ploy is good. I believe it may work."

"One day . . ." She sipped her cordial. "Please tell the guards I would speak with Lieutenant Armado. Jesu, I am so tired. . . ." She closed her eyes. "Summon the lieutenant for me, Adele."

Forty winks later, the door opened and two pairs of boots marched inside her privy chamber.

"Madame."

Groaning inwardly, Renée sat up to find Lieutenant Armado and Sergeant Francesco before her, Armado in uniform, Francesco in a burgher's garb. "What news?" she demanded. "Pray let your tidings be favorable to our cause." Her headache had lessened, yet she felt unfocused.

Sergeant Francesco shuffled his feet. Renée's heart sank.

"Tell her your news," Lieutenant Armado urged his sergeant.

"Regrettably, my time at Your Place was insufficient to detect the Ancient's exact location. Cardinal Campeggio's *deletoris* are everywhere. I had to flee when one of them spotted me."

"You were recognized?" She knew this was disastrous—Cardinal Wolsey finding out about her *deletoris* was the end of her life—and yet her mind remained calm. Suspiciously calm.

"It was a near thing. I cannot be sure." Sergeant Francesco looked terribly upset. "Marcello, the soldier who may have seen me, was my mate in the academy. He did not get a good look, but I thought it prudent to leave before he investigated. Maybe he will say nothing to Captain Luzio, our"—he exchanged another awkward glance with the lieutenant—"former commander."

"Have you anything to report?" she asked hazily—almost giddily. She would kill Adele!

"The *deletoris* have taken over the watch of York Place. Hill, the captain of the guard, is up in arms. Every day brawls break out between the two camps. Cardinal Wolsey wants Cardinal Campeggio gone but dares not enforce it. The *deletoris* patrol the premises constantly, all hours of the day, as if the entire house is a vault. I tried to stay out of sight as I searched the place from top to bottom, at night as well as during the daytime. I found nothing."

"Where do the cardinals spend most of their time?" Renée demanded to know. Her head was no longer pounding, but she was finding it inordinately difficult to concentrate.

"In their private chambers, in chapel, and at table."

"Adele, do open the window. I need air. Sergeant, did you search these rooms?"

"As best I could. As I said, there were watchmen everywhere."

"You saw nothing? Nothing you wish to impart? Think carefully, Francesco. Any detail, no matter how small, may be significant."

Francesco clasped his hands behind his back, his brow furrowed. "Early this morning, I was ordered to broom the dirty rushes in the gallery outside the chapel. I heard the cardinals arguing inside. I nudged open the door and saw Cardinal Campeggio throw his arm around *La Pietà* and swear on the Holy Grail that he would not be leaving without 'it.' I took it to mean the Ancient."

"Pray continue . . . eh, what were they arguing about?"

"The brawling, it is getting worse. George Hill flogged one of the *deletoris*. A nasty one, this Hill. In retribution, Captain Luzio crucified Hill to the courtyard wall with arrows, shot straight through Hill's garments without touching skin." Francesco grinned at his lieutenant. "He was my trainer, madame, the captain, in Rome."

"This *Pietà*, tell me about it."

"La Madonna, a great white marble sculpture of Our Lady cradling Our Lord in Her loving arms. It is an excellent duplicate of Michelangelo's *Pietà* in Rome."

"The *Pietà* the French ambassador in the Holy See commissioned from Michelangelo for the accession of Pope Alexander the Sixth to the chair of St. Peter five and twenty years ago?"

"The very one!" Francesco announced. "A beautiful monument, a masterpiece!"

"So . . . Cardinal Campeggio had his arm around *La Pietà* when he told Cardinal Wolsey he would not be leaving without 'it . . .' This is our Ancient. *La Pietà*." She wanted to shout with glee and could not muster the exuberance. She noticed something. "Lieutenant Armado, where is your medallion?"

Armado flushed. "I left it in France, madame, as you advised."

She saw the sharp glance Sergeant Francesco shot his lieutenant. Armado was lying. Why?

Armado brightened up. "So we have located our prize!"

"It is our best guess," she said. "We shall find out soon enough. The audience is scheduled for tomorrow evening. The marquis and I are invited to sup at York Place. I suggest you borrow theatrical properties from the revel office to disguise yourself, Francesco. One last thing, make good watch on the marquis. Intersect his correspondence and bring it to me without delay."

"It will be done," the lieutenant promised.

Renée put a hand to her brow. There was something imperative she wished to tell them, but the detail was as elusive as a forgotten dream. "Remain on the alert this evening." If Buckingham proceeded with his plan for tonight, Cardinal Campeggio's guards would remove the Ancient from England. The logical destination would be France, but Renée would not wager her life upon it. "How many men in Captain Luzio's army?"

"Five to our one," Sergeant Francesco replied, sliding an uneasy glance at Armado.

"We must be vigilant, sirs. If they move the Ancient, our capturing it could only be achieved by stealth. . . ." She was not making any sense. She needed to think deeper on the problem, come up with a clever stratagem, but her head felt woolly and her sharp logic seemed to have abdicated. "Thank you. You may leave." She glared at Adele. "What did you put in the cordial, Breton hag? I cannot think!" She groaned as her tiring woman offered an impish, gap-toothed smile. "Oh, Adele. Do you not see that I cannot afford a single slip? If I do not have the reins of my mind, I have nothing. I am dead."

Impenitent, Adele took her by the arm and led her to the door. "The vial is in your purse. Give it to the lady and tell her not to use it before tomorrow even. I say your work for the day is done. Divert yourself. Mayhap you will sleep better tonight if your mind is not forever plotting."

"Do not be absurd. I have no guarantee that Anne will take the bait. The assassination may still take place tonight. Furthermore, I cannot allow her to speak privily with Michael."

"So . . . distract him. Giggle at him. Here is your excuse."

Renée stuck her tongue out at her. "Evil witch."

❧ 10 ❧

Either the man is mad or
he is writing poetry.

—Horace: *Satires*

With her assignment in abeyance and her brain staging a moratorium, Renée's onus lifted as if by magic, the yoking weight of the sky becoming a butterfly upon her shoulders. She found an occasion to give Anne the vial with the caveat that three drops would do but would be ineffective till tomorrow night and left Buckingham's sister to stew in her juices without a backward glance. Adele's witchy tonic had done more than dispel Renée's headache; it allayed her angst as well.

Trumpets, tabors, shawms, and pipes fanfared the court to the midday repast in the presence chamber. Archbishop Warham offered a Latin benediction. Each succulent dish delivered to the tables was accompanied with entertainment. A French minstrel sang a *chanson de geste*, an epic poem about a valiant hero, a shifty traitor, a beautiful Saracen princess, giants, and magic. There were the companies employed by the Revel Office: the King's Players, the Queen's Players, and the musical Children of the Chapel Royal, Sir Cornish's choristers who sang and danced.

Sweet allegorical subtleties, such as marchpane castles and St. George's fruit tarts slaying green sugary dragons, were served in between courses of lobsters, fawns in ginger, storks, geese in garlic, pheasants, calves' heads, porpoises, capons, woodcock in cinnamon, oxen, dolphins, and partridges, generously herbed and sauced.

Simpler confectionaries to grace the tables were sweet wafer biscuits stamped with the royal arms in gold, gingerbread, and quince
marmalade

As wine loosened the belts of sobriety, the company grew
louder, eager for merrymaking. A troupe of traveling Italian players, fished from a puddle in Smithfield Market, took the floor and
created misrule. The "misfits," widely known as *zanni* or *Santi Os-
tinati*, *Unruly Saints*, mounted a bawdy romp in the grand style of
Chaucer and the *Commedia dell'Arte*, an uproarious mockery of the
nobles, the clergy, and their servants. They portrayed the tight-
fisted Lord Pantalone and his wily manservant Harlequin, whose
interests never coincided with those of his master; Harlequin's
beloved Colombina, the witty-pretty soubrette of a lady in lust
with young Tristano, a handsome minstrel on the run from Capi-
tano, the bully whose bluster equaled his stupidity; the stuttering,
myopic Dottore, unlucky with the ladies and ever erroneous in his
diagnoses; the cunning humpback who squeaked because he could
not speak; the fearful knight, who fled from fights but dreamed of
becoming a fulcrum; the tavern keeper who fleeced his patrons
and watered their ale; and the snickering, plotting Scaramouch, a
cowardly villain duped by Harlequin and Colombina.

They tumbled, they quarreled, they emptied hidden bladders
on each other and the audience; they tried to sit in Norfolk's lap,
crashed into walls, dangled from the cressets, crawled under the
tables, peeked under hems, and poked at purses. They juggled
and clowned; they flashed garish, yard-long appendages from cod-
pieces and thwacked onlookers' bums, and vanished whence they
had come to the screaming delight of the court. King Henry, contrary to his habitual observance of clean speech in his courtiers and
his distaste for vulgar jests, collapsed in fits of rumbustious laughter and ordered Master Cornish to pay the mad ruffians right handsomely.

As the afternoon shadows elongated, the court caroused and in-
termingled. The braziers, the dancing, and the plethora of wine
and ale kept the party warm, notwithstanding the draughts and the
rain sheeting the panes. Renée had enough rosé in her to cheerfully acquiesce to singing and playing the lute for Her Majesty's

pleasure. She chose the love ballad of the poor English knight and his Spanish princess she had composed in advance before leaving France.

Her audience was riveted. Queen Katherine smiled tearfully when King Henry took her hand and kissed her fingertips. Wyatt dubbed Renée "the French nightingale" and sweet-talked her into performing a duet with him making up the lyrics and she the music as they went along.

Wyatt sang:

> *And wilt thou leave me thus?*
> *Say nay, say nay, for shame!*
> *To save thee from the blame*
> *Of all my grief and grame.*
> *And wilt thou leave me thus?*
> *Say nay! Say nay!*

Utterly besotted, Michael did not notice Stanley showing up at his side with a companion. He was absorbed in the beautiful song-bird sitting on a stool at the center of the room, glistening skirts spread like lush scarlet florets, dainty fingers plucking the lute. Her amethyst eyes flared at Wyatt's verse in mock outrage as she parried with waspishly amusing chorus lines:

> *Monsieur, your words are pretty*
> *How many heard this ditty?*
> *Begone ere I hit thee!*

Leaning against the wall to the side, Michael laughed together with the courtiers encircling her. Wyatt did not give up:

> *And wilt thou leave me thus,*
> *And have no more pity*
> *Of him that loveth thee?*
> *Hélas! Thy cruelty!*
> *And wilt thou leave me thus?*
> *Say nay! Say nay!*

The princess was seemingly unmoved, her eyelashes fluttering with the frets of the lute:

> *Monsieur, I do you pity*
> *Were all your loves unwitty?*
> *Take thyself off, rudesby!*

"Michael!"

He jolted, as if from a pleasing dream, recognized the willowy, fair widow on Stanley's arm, and lost his power of speech, the sentiment the woman stirred in him alien yet not unpleasant.

"Meg," said Stanley. "I present Master Michael Devereaux. Michael, meet Mistress Margaret Clifford, the late Sir John Devereaux's daughter."

There was no need to say "your sister." Michael knew, as seemingly Meg did. Her eyes were alight with excitement and warmth as she curtsied to his bow. Though they had met on the day of his arrival, this encounter bore a sense of occasion that was lost on neither of them.

"Meg is to be Her Majesty's new lady-in-waiting," Stanley filled up the bashful silence. "Her duties begin tomorrow. Michael, will you not congratulate Meg?"

At last Michael found his tongue. "Doubtless any congratulations are due to Her Majesty for adding a gem to her household. I am delighted to make your acquaintance, Mistress Clifford."

She smiled brightly. "Please call me Meg. May I call you Michael?"

"That would please me very much. Have you been to court long?"

"Not long. My, eh . . . our . . ." She cast an irritated glance at the peacock joining the princess's gaggle. "Walter sent for me when His Grace of Norfolk made him master of the horse." Smiling, she touched Michael's arm. "I should like to further our acquaintance and become friends. As for Walter, please be patient. Living in the shadow of an attainted father has not been easy for him."

"I understand." His smile was rueful. "I am happy you consented to converse with me."

"Consented?" Meg looked at her escort. "I plagued Stanley to introduce us!"

"She did." Stanley beamed at Meg. His friend, Michael discerned, was deeply in love. "As soon as I broached the subject, my shy lambkin transformed into a pesky bee." His beefy hand covered the dainty one she returned to his wrist with remarkable gentleness.

So this was how true love looked like, Michael marveled. "May I be the first to congratulate you, Baron Monteagle? I believe you are now truly Undefeated."

The tender smile exchanged between the pair was enviable. Stanley patted Meg's hand. "Not yet, but with God's good grace soon. Godgigoden, runt. We leave you to your"—he frowned at the lady commanding the majority of male interest in the chamber—"foolish endeavors." To Michael's ears alone, he muttered, "Aim higher and you will have reached the queen."

Meg lingered another moment, her amused, warm gaze darting between Michael and the lute player. "Methinks you have been shot through the heart with a love song."

Michael started. *The heart?* Surely not! Renée's dart had hit a mark farther down. *Enthrall but do not love. . . .*

"Keep at her." Meg grinned. "A woman's greatest ambition is to inspire love."

And every man's fancy lures him, Michael sighed. He was in trouble.

Indeed, as they retreated, his eyes sought Princess Renée. Her duet with Wyatt had made her the focal point of attention, a status she had avoided hereto. What had changed? And what could he do to set himself above her slobbering wooers? Ranging from the loftily titled adulterer to the adventurous green idolater, they all wanted her, every man jack of them. Lecherous jackals. He observed her ply her alert, glittering wit, punctuating each quip and jibe with an apt note on her lute, sending them roaring with laughter.

"Play us 'Light O'Love,' my lady!" Sir Francis Bryan begged with his fabled rake's charm.

Her attention was commandeered by a page with a note. She

snatched the folded parchment, pressing a coin into his hand. "Who gave you the note, Robin?"

He smiled with such devotion one would think she had bestowed her livery on him. "A gentleman's servant. In future I'll watch out for colors." He touched his nose, winking.

A pulse beat at her neck; her milky cheeks flushed. She excused herself from her panting slaves and ambled distractedly to the great iron candleholder in the corner, her eyes on the letter.

Curiosity spurred Michael's heels. He found himself at her back, hovering over her shoulder like a jealous shadow and reading her note with her:

> *Best of beauties fair,*
> *I languish in despair;*
> *Loose the bonds which stay me!*
> *Let all your coolness cease,*
> *And send me words of peace*
> *At once, before you slay me.*
> *I am restless like the roe;*
> *Though all men show me hate,*
> *My love shall not abate*
> *In spite of every foe.*

> *—Written with the hand of him who wishes you joy.*
> *Perdu (a soldier lost to a forlorn hope)*

Princess Renée let out a breathy chuckle. She liked the soppy words. Her reaction coaxed a smile from Michael. He could not resist saying, "A mystery lover, is it?"

She whirled around with a swish of silks and flared at him, "How dare you, monsieur! There is no dignity in skulking at a lady's back and prying into her private correspondence!"

Ye gods, she was fantastic! No peeping at him beneath curling lashes, no coquetry. Violet daggers cut out his heart and served it up to him spitted and bleeding. "Private?" he drawled. "I say secretive and craven. Your woeful soldier-in-love has not the backbone to expose himself."

"Master Devereaux, service to love is only possible for the noble heart. A peasant could never appreciate its delicacy."

A peasant! Her icy hauteur, stropped to draw blood, was kindling to the lust roaring in his veins. He gave a vulpine smile meant to infuriate. "Delicacy may not be my métier, madame, but acquainted as I am with the 'restlessness' of the male of the species, I assure you that your noble sufferer had naught noble in mind when he scribbled this trumpery."

She held up a hand, the other pressing the note to her bosom. "I pray you speak no more, for you only lay bare the embarrassing magnitude of your ignorance. Poetry is the fruit of the heart, not of one's"—her gaze dropped to his loins and she blinked rapidly to camouflage her gaffe—"armory. Love service to a noblewoman gains merit by the self-abnegation of the lover, or—"

He laughed. "Trust me when I tell you that the cogent argument which sends your lover into hiding is your exalted station, not some ill-conceived notion of poetic self-starvation, *Princess*."

"Or"—she leveled a reproachful glare at him for interposing—"gains merit by the loftiness of the lady's rank." She concluded her sermon with a prudish sniff.

"Light a candle of innocence at your rhymer's altar if it pacifies your chaste heart, my lady, but I would wager a great deal—"

"What would you wager?" Her violet eyes twinkled challengingly.

"We shall discuss that anon. I say that before long your languishing poetaster will insert a glib line suggesting you invite him to a nocturnal unmasking in your chambers."

"I should think not! My noble poet knows who I am, and therefore he will not conceive of suggesting anything of the sort." She pouted, then smiled in victorious defiance. "'Of safe lovemaking do I sing, and permitted secrecy, and in my verse shall be no wrongdoing.'"

"Ah, Publius Ovidius Naso. I did tell you that Roman wordsmiths were my forte, did I not?" He cleared his throat. "'She is chaste whom nobody has propositioned,'" he wryly quoted Ovid's famous line. "'All women can be caught; spread out your nets and you will catch them.'"

"Ha!" Renée blazed ferociously. "Your poetical repertorium is markedly selective. You only approve of rhymes that liken love to warfare. Now, if you read the *Romance of the Rose*—"

"Yes, let us discuss the *Le Roman de la Rose* for a moment. You might be able to shed some light on this confusing metaphor I have been struggling with."

The headstrong beauty gave an imitation of an imperious governess, clasping her hands and tilting her head to one side, lips pouting critically at her witless student. "By all means!" *Embarrass yourself further*, he read the unspoken thought.

Michael stanched a devilish grin. "Well, my conundrum, thus far unanswered, concerns the leading lady of the piece. In your learned opinion, why did the author settle on the name Rose? We all know the *rosa* to be a superior flower, which imagery encompasses love, grace, courage, beauty, mystery, innocence, devotion, purity, a manifold of the admirable qualities which exist in every daughter of Eve. Do you suppose the poet aimed for an allegory of nature? And if so, was the metaphor extended to the anatomy? The rose's hips, for instance, are the fleshy, edible fruit, and her petals—luscious, delicate, unfolding at a mere caress to bestow the nectar within . . ."

Her face turned beet red. "To the point, sir!" Aglow with discomfiture, she developed sudden interest in the biscuits, various fruit, Spanish paps, and marchpaned menagerie heaped on the gilt iron epergne that presided over the buffet like Dionysus, god of wine, vegetation, and ecstasy.

With a Scaramouch snicker, Michael stalked her as a hunter would his prey. "Hence my—"

A squirt of juice filled his left nostril. The little witch, nibbling on a ripe medlar, pealed with laughter. Michael offered her a napkin, then swiped the nectar beads off his upper lip and sucked his finger. "Hence my dilemma, madame. When the troubadour sings of his beauteous lady and of the feelings and desires she enkindles in him, it is unclear whether he should go through life repining in perpetual desire, conducting his vigor to higher ends, or strive to consummate—"

"It is quite clear to me," she bit out, "that the pure love the great poets speak of, the sort which binds the souls of two lovers with every feeling of delight, stems from the contemplation of the mind and the affection of the heart, as is permitted for those who wish to love purely."

He selected a pear and bounced it thoughtfully. "What of the kiss, the embrace with the nude lover, the final solace the poets promise us? The delights of the flesh which culminate in the final act of Venus? Ovid does not waffle about that. He comes straight to the point."

"Does he?" She snatched his pear. Mimicking his baritone, she declaimed, "'O youth, make war, and with the experience and authority of thy sire shalt thou conquer.'"

Michael splayed a hand over his heart, pitching his voice effeminately high, mimicked her, "'Nay, even she, whom you think cruel, will be kind. And as stolen love is pleasant to a man, so is it to a woman; the man dissembles badly: she conceals desire better.'" He gave a cockish grunt and quoted in his own deep voice, "'The mare always whinnies to the horn-footed steed.'"

Reckless amid a large company, Renée stared up with feisty bravado at her challenger. "Oh, you tempt me to baste you with retaliatory lines on other horned beasts and cuckoos!"

"'In us desire is weaker and not so frantic: the manly flame knows a lawful bound.'"

"'Corrupt her with promises, corrupt her with prayers!'" The angry words were tossed at him valiantly, accusatorily. "'Let the fish be held that is wounded from seizing the hook; once you assail her, press the attack, nor depart unless victorious.' That is what your Roman wordsmith preaches, and only God knows why he should demean women so, as to compare them to fish!"

Michael choked. Whether the virginal Amazon would appreciate a clarification or not, he doubted he would survive offering one. Meg was right. His attraction for her was more than skin-deep. Expostulating with Renée de Valois was erotic swordplay; her fierceness of spirit and witty mind ensorcelled him as no woman had done before her. Smiling at her vehemence, he raised his hands in surrender. "Pax, lady! Your tongue is like Don Álvaro's innovative *espada ropera*."

The refractory, truculent wench smirked archly at him. "Too sharp for you?"

"Nay, rapid, when . . . 'my task is to make love long endure.'" Hearing the notes of a volta, he offered his arm. "'When hearts are glad, Venus steals in with persuasive art.' Dance with me."

There was no hesitation in her expression. Nor in her gestures. Sustaining his gaze, she put her hand on his wrist and let him lead her to the other dancers. They danced in absolute silence, without breaking eye contact. Michael pressed his right hand to hers, then his left, and turned slowly to find her glittering gaze returning to his at the end of her twirl. It was magic. And when the sensual leap came, he took possession of her slender waist as he ached to possess the rest of her and hoisted her high. He turned with her, then let her slide back to the floor along his hard body. He repeated the arousing leap ad lib, willing the musicians to play on till cockcrow.

He craved her, body and mind, wanted her vulnerable, confused, ablaze, as he was, and if she should hurl such barbed insults at him during their lovemaking, as she had done this evening, her soft, lithe body would be all the more sore for his ardors the ensuing morning. Alas, he was deluding himself, as torturously as her forlorn poetaster, for no matter how persistent, how witty, how honeyed his seduction might be, Renée de Valois would be bestowed unsoiled on a king, and like her restless rhymer, Michael's lot would be to languish in despair.

When another dance ended, and all the pairs made their bows and curtsies, Renée tried to detach herself from him. "I am thirsty."

A full winecup miraculously appeared before her. Michael and Renée looked up in surprise.

"My lady," slobbered Sir Walter. "As always, I am yours to command in all things."

Michael envisioned restyling the peacock's face around his fist. They locked horns as Renée accepted the cup, Walter smirking, Michael gnashing his teeth. She sipped delicately, thirstily, and with a grateful exhalation returned the empty vessel to Walter. "You are most kind."

He offered his arm. "Would you care for a stroll?"

"I thank you, sir. Another time." She smiled at Sir Walter and to both men's astonishment curled her hand around Michael's arm.

Gloating, Michael touched his forelock. "Another time!" He grinned at the livid peacock and dragged Renée away. So long as she did not dispute it, she was his for the evening. They rested in a bay window and stared at the candlelit dancers. "You owe me a secret tryst," he whispered.

She stiffened. "I beg your pardon?"

He chuckled perceptively when he caught her telltale blush. Mayhap there was hope for this troubadour yet. He put his lips to her ear, speaking softly, "Have you forgotten your promise to match me with another lady? I say this pair of night-travelers-cum-dancers ought to leap into the shared bed and join forces to frustrate the traitorous duke's plans."

Michael derived brief satisfaction from discerning the shock that marred her brow before his true meaning sank in. "By the Saints, how you enjoy diddling with words!" she protested.

Diddling! He blinked at the sexual connotation. "Now who is playing?" he said, but the look in her eyes confirmed that her mastery of the English tongue did not extend to tavern language.

Across the candlelit floor, Anne stood with her bumptious male relatives, watching Michael and Renée with the keenness of a hissing cat. "Dance with me again," Renée husked.

What was she at now? Michael wondered. "You are supposed to be our procurator."

"Negotiator," Renée amended, swaying into the dance steps.

"Negotiator, procurator"—he fell into step with her—"you said you would arrange for me to meet with her privily so that I might winkle pertinent information out of her."

"After the hiatus," Renée breathed cryptically, twirling with the other female dance partners, the fingers of one hand clasping his. In keeping with the steps, she leaned into him, cutting her gaze up to his. Violet eyes gleamed with a mercurial heat that bamboozled him into forgetting aught else. "Tonight I would fain take pleasure in terpsichoring with you," she confessed softly.

Michael shut his eyes briefly against the sudden onrush of am-munition to his armory. What was it Stanley was wont to say? "God ha' mercy, lady."

Silhouetted by guttering candles, they were the last dancing pair on the presence chamber's floor when the king's liveried corpse of musicians played the closing note. The better part of the night had gone by without a hiccup from the queen's quarters, which allowed Renée to hope that tomorrow evening everything would fall into place. She had purposefully stayed up with the hard carousers to be within earshot of Her Majesty's rooms should aught betide the queen. Dawn was four hours away, but it seemed that Buckingham had swallowed the lie she had fed to Anne.

"May I have the pleasure of escorting you to your chambers, Princess?"

Acutely aware of her shambolic appearance after hours of merry-making, Renée assessed the golden gentleman at her side and marveled that he should look like an archangel come down to earth. Michael's sun-kissed complexion glowed with life. His breath was hippocras-sweet; his scent soapy; his hair slightly tousled. His garments had escaped all the smutches and spillages of the rich feasting and were wrinkleless. She felt like an effete jack-a-lent next to him.

Never before had she spent so many hours—wondrously amus-ing hours—in the company of one man, bandying word for word, thrust for thrust, step for step, a set of banter well played, for in France it would have been impossible as well as unseemly. The French court was more formal than the English, and, as a compan-ion to the Queen of France, her duties were many and varied. Here, because she was Rougé's ward, ostensibly answerable only to the ambassador, because she was a foreign, unconventional, newly minted duchess, and because no one had been told what her duties were exactly, they left her to her own devices. "I have an armed guard to escort me."

"I am offering you a social escort, madame," Michael said.

He surprised her. Her acquaintance with the male of the species predicted a suave attempt at seduction, especially after whiling away the entire evening and half the night with him. But as Michael smiled at her, affable and collected, his face betokened no untoward presumptuousness. There was goodness in his face, but what struck her deeper was the discovery that he genuinely respected her. Nonplussed, Renée put her hand on his proffered wrist, and together they left the royal apartments with Lieutenant Armado falling into step at a discreet distance behind them.

Peaceful amity ensconced them as they negotiated the taper-lit passages, the lulling quietude of the late hour disturbed by a startled snort of a nightwatchman jolted into wakefulness or lewd laughter muffled by a closed door. Deep within herself, however, Renée was aflutter. Michael's good opinion of her, unprejudiced by gossip, stroked her bruised dignity and brought about some unpleasant soul-searching. For years it stuck in her craw that the world should view her as little more than a precious, vapid blossom in the royal garden, something to be admired from afar and to be used in the game of kings. However, there was also security in being perceived as such. It made her wonder if flouting the general custom by taking a lover had been, in fact, an infantile act of rebellion, for why else should an adventurer's opinion matter so much? Her mutiny smacked of a bargain with the devil. In losing her maidenhead she might have gained a degree of freedom but had also forfeited something of great value, and it chafed her.

"Why of a sudden in the dumps, my lady marmoset?"

Renée slanted Michael a diffident look. "You think I look like a small monkey?"

"I think you are beautiful," he breathed. "So why so sour?"

She exhaled morosely. Sooner or later he would hear of her transgression. His high esteem would not last. "Do not be putting up a shrine for my honor and lighting candles at my altar."

He grinned. "Superstitious, are we, my lovely Gallic-Breton?"

She halted before her apartment. Had he understood her Gaelicking with Adele about him last night—to his face? Jesu, she hoped not. How embarrassing! "No, it is not that. I—" She liked that he perceived her as a precious, forbidden rosebud. It was a pleasant change from being disdained for a French wanton by the ladies and being ogled as a common pie by the gentlemen.

Michael shot Lieutenant Armado a look that sent the officer joining the other guards at the door and stirred her to a window embrasure several paces down the gallery, close enough so that their dark silhouettes would be visible but out of earshot of the guards.

His smooth maneuver was a pebble hurtled at the windowpane of her newfound faith in him. She complied out of brazen curiosity, perversely anticipating putting him in his wretched place. Expecting him to pounce, Renée was bemused yet again when he propped a beaked boot on the windowsill, leaned his forearm along the lintel, and contemplated the dark night reigning outside.

"I thank you for gracing me with your undivided attention for the evening," he whispered. "However, I cannot help feeling that you—*we*—have been avoiding a certain pressing matter. Last night you solicited my assistance in foiling a calamity. Now I get the impression that you have had a change of heart. May I ask why?"

Saints! Renée had doubly underestimated him. He was cleverer and more courteous than she had assumed. He had seen through her ploy to play the bolster between him and Anne and now wanted answers, not a tumble, not even a kiss. He still respected her, which was gratifying, but also suspected her of intriguing. Or was it her faith in him that he worried he had lost? Whatever reason she gave him would have to keep him away from Anne for one more day. Once she had the Ancient, Michael could play St. George to Buckingham's dragon and Diomedes to Anne's Cressida. The trouble was she had no ready justification. She had felt safe flirting with him in the royal apartment, but only a pied ninny would provoke a man in a darkened gallery and then set off the hue and cry when he tried something. Unfortunately she had no time to come up with the perfect answer to wheel his thoughts down the laneway of her choosing without whetting his masculine claws. She affected an insulted tone, flaring, "If dancing with me was such a chore, you should have relinquished me to Sir Walter! Good night, monsieur!" She stomped away.

Michael caught her arm before she fled to her apartment. Standing behind her, his clasp firm yet gentle, he fanned her temple with his breath. One shriek would summon the guards, but she could not speak. Nor could she move. His large frame at her back enveloped her in a blanket of delicious warmth. The ripples and eddies that had swum in her belly while they had been dancing together now coursed lower till she felt a sensual melting between her thighs. "Are you saying tonight was no pretense?" His rich voice caressed her. "You danced with me because you wanted to?"

Renée shut her eyes, her breathing seesawing. She dared not turn her head aside. If she did, they would kiss, she would be unable to resist, and she was honest enough with herself to admit that kissing Michael would be a voluntary act of infidelity to Raphael. *Morbleu.* How could she find this man so appealing to her senses when she was in love with another?

Michael emitted scorching heat. His voice was husky. "I wish you were not a princess."

"Please let me go," she begged softly. She was shaking.

Thereupon he released her. "As for our wager," he called good-naturedly at her fleeing back. "If your abashed minstrel turns out to be a red-blooded man like the rest of us poor mortals, I insist on being present at his unmasking!"

Having put a safe distance between them, she turned around to face him with a smile. "If I am right, and he turns out to be a timid young knight, then I shall insist *you* write me a poem!"

"Madame, you have a wager!" Michael flourished a dashing bow and strolled off, whistling the duet song she had composed with Wyatt earlier that evening like a cocksure Orlando.

Renée leaned in the open doorway of her apartment and watched his tall back disappear. She had two courtly doters: one poetic but in hiding, the other warlike and enchanting.

❧ 11 ❧

I hate and I love. Perhaps you ask why I
experience this. I do not know, but I feel
it happening and I am in torment.

—Catullus

Apageboy wearing the queen's arms on his tabard ambushed
Renée when she came out of Mass the next morning. "My
lady, a manservant bade me give this to you."

Renée grasped the folded missive with slightly trembling fingers. She read it at once:

> *Lady, my desire*
> *For you is all on fire*
> *To honor you when I may.*
> *Pity me, befriend me,*
> *For since to death you send me,*
> *I die before my day.*

"And . . . a gentleman by the name of Devereaux begs a word
with you," the page added.

Renée barely heard him. Her entire being was seduced by the
poem, lured to read on:

> *Believe my song, for I*
> *In perfect faith shall do*
> *All I have sworn to you*
> *Until the day I die.*

Written with the hand of him who admires you above all others.
        —Perdu (a soldier lost to a forlorn hope)

Renée felt . . . adored. Raphael used her as a Muse for paintings that were a need of his spirit, a gift for the world. Perdu's verses were secret, tender, for her eyes alone, and they inspired such languishing in her heart . . . Maybe her mystery poet was Wyatt. He was a proficient wordsmith. Most of the works enacted by the royal companies were doggerel or drearily pious. But this . . .

Lady, my desire
For you is all on fire

"He is waiting thitherward," the page boy interposed.

Renée followed his direction into a side corridor with contradictory sentiments. Not that she was averse to bidding Michael a good morrow, but the little sleep she had managed in the scarce hours between their parting and this morning's Mass had not replenished her with sufficient guile to walk the treacherous line between harvesting and crushing the fruits of last night's labors.

The gorgeous fortune seeker had already proven that he would not be easily manipulated. If she was cool, he would know her for a fraud, and she would have lost the only tenable bulwark available to her against Anne. Alternatively, if she was approachable, the situation might get sticky before her mission was accomplished. By his own admission, Michael was a red-blooded man. While he regarded her as a protected floral species, he might still try to steal closer snuffles.

But it was not Michael Devereaux who awaited her in the vacant, off-the-beaten-path corridor. "Madame." Sir Walter bowed. "Permit me to say how lovely this morning finds you."

"You are very gracious." She dipped, her hands intertwined with the rosary. She caught the beck he directed at the officer standing behind her, and when she turned, Lieutenant Armado was gone. What was the matter with that man? she fumed. He was supposed to protect her at all times. Last night he took a dismissal from Michael and now from Norfolk's henchman without seeking her approval. Well, they were going to have a serious chat before the day was over.

"Lady Renée." Sir Walter took her elbow. "I have arranged a special treat for you. As you are new to this country, I thought you would enjoy seeing the sites: Westminster, St. Paul's, and such. The Duke of Norfolk's splendid barge awaits us at the quayside to take us upriver into the heart of London. It is at our disposal for the entire day, with His Grace's blessing, naturally."

What a pest! "Monsieur, His Grace's generous hospitality has not gone unnoticed, I assure you," she clipped. "However, my French lungs are dreadfully susceptible to ague brought on by bad weather and it is raining pailfuls. Another time." She bobbed and turned to make her escape, wondering if Rougé had a hand in this. She sensed that he had a secret truck with Norfolk.

Steely fingers gripped her arm, not gently as Michael had delayed her last night, but hard as manacles. Without warning she was thrust back against the wall, both her arms pinioned.

"Why him and not me?" Walter growled at her, rage distorting his visage.

"*What?*" She stared at him, wide-eyed and half numb with shock.

"God knows I tried to befriend you, as a gentleman would a lady, but you still chose him!"

Pity me, befriend me. She shuddered at his word choice. Was he Perdu?

"Why?" Light brown eyes judged her acrimoniously. "Why the bastard and not me?"

"Are you mad? What in God's name are you talking about? Unhand me, sir! I am a daughter of France. *Nōlī mē tangere!* Or in plain English, take your filthy hands off of me!"

His face red as a cock's wattle, he released her left arm and clamped a hand over her mouth. "I know all about you, lusty princess. Or shall I call you Froward Renée, the wanton Valois who tumbles into bed with nobodies? Well, your pardon for my being green with ancestral honors, but let me assure *you*, cherrylips, that I am well endowed in body as well as in arms." He pressed his codpiece into her belly with gyrating motions of his hips. "I would swyve you right lustily, I would. What say you, Princess? One fast and hard up against the wall? I trow you will like it."

Sickened, Renée looked daggers at him. She knew precisely where she would love to plunge her hidden dirk, if only he freed her second hand to unsheathe it from her sleeve.

"Think you I know not about your Italian painter? Or that you let that baseborn arriviste styling himself Michael Devereaux poke you every night? Save for a dubious connection to the lord in charge of a godforsaken apology for a country, that tike has naught to commend him!" He removed his hand from her lips and silenced her protests with his mouth.

Fury rippled through her like a rolling bolt of thunder. Struggling to jerk her head aside, she also fought the rough fingers grasping her skirts with the only free hand she had at her disposal. Apart from her smock, she had naught between her honor and this brutish knave. Armado—God pity his deserter's soul!—had not taught her how to obstruct men from slaying her dignity.

Walter was clever enough to keep his thighs together to prevent her from kneeing him, but as he laved her lips with his disgusting saliva, rendering them slippery, she managed to jerk her head aside, screaming for help at the top of her lungs, before she was silenced again. Brutally.

As the rainstorm refused to abate, ruling out al fresco disports, King Henry was in a pother. With his having played tennez the previous morn, followed by troll-my-dames in the afternoon, Suffolk's suggestion to practice weight lifting and wrestling was accepted with good cheer.

"Why are you grinning? Are you ill?" Stanley inquired en route to the king's apartment.

Michael chuckled. "Is it a sin to grin in the morning?"

"Generally no, but your usual morning humor leaves a lot to be desired. I say this ailment calls for a learned opinion."

Michael's face ached from smiling all through the night. "Fetch me a witch and not a doctor, then, for I have been folly fallen and bespelled. Oh, Stanley, the gods shine on me today!"

"The gods are spitting large hailstones and you say sun kisses, hmm. I know it! An inflamed liver vein, a serious malady, to be sure. Forsake the mages and the quacks. A legionnaire of God is what we need, or better yet, a holy general—Archbishop Warham might be available."

Michael laughed. "Am I to be shriven for playing the fool to a goddess?"

Stanley's bushy brows snapped together, but he would not look at him, nor speak his mind.

"You think me mad as Ajax for lighting candles where I cannot worship."

"I think my thoughts would get me cudgeled, since I gave you good advice on the subject, which naturally you took care not to adopt—*what*?"

A scream brought Michael up short. *Help!* He took off as a bat out of hell, not giving a cuss if Stanley thought him unhinged. Renée was in trouble. He would recognize her voice anywhere. He moved like the wind, driven by the uncanny impulses that had launched him in pursuit of the hart. Before he knew it, he was darting past the vigilant yeomen of the guard, unimpeded, as if he were King Henry. Or as if he were invisible.

The scene he came upon in the out-of-the-way corridor stopped his heart. Walter had Renée pinioned to the wall with his weight and strength, one hand lifting her skirts, the other stoppering her mouth from screaming. Rage unlike anything Michael had ever experienced combusted in his veins, followed by pain in his eyes and mouth. He felt himself altering, pulsing, sharpening . . .

Renée's arms stretched out and locked behind Walter's back. Jealousy seared Michael. *She was embracing the jackslave?* His dismay was short-lived. A small blade slid out from inside her sleeve. Michael gripped Walter by the scruff of the neck, ripped him off her, and flung him in the air to crash against the opposite wall of the long corridor. Grunting, Walter collapsed on the floor, out cold. Michael felt murderous. That a half-blood of his should be infused with so foul a spirit rankled with him. He wanted to tear Walter's heart out with his fingers and squish it.

"Michael."

He sucked in a calming breath, waited a moment to regain his composure, and turned to face Renée. Her mouth was chafed red. Her pretty French hood sat crookedly atop her head. Her eyes were wide with shock. He thought his heart would break. He wanted to enfold her in his arms, rock her gently, tell her that she was safe, and vow that he would let no man hurt her ever again. Afterward, he would lecture her sternly on the perils involved in giving the slip to her guards. At the moment, though, he did not know how she would react to strong familiarity after narrowly escaping being taken by force by another man. With the utmost gentleness, he righted her hood and cupped her face. "Be not afeared. He is out for the counts. Are you hurt, marmoset?"

She glanced at the heap of crumpled tinsel littering the end of the corridor. "You tossed him so far . . . as though he were weightless." Purple fire branded him. "You are very strong."

Michael swallowed. Her tone was awestruck not accusatory, yet he felt as if he were being reweighed in her balance. The damned potion's gifts were as inexplicable as its weaknesses.

"I almost killed him," Renée whispered, rubbing her cheek into his hand like a kitten. Then she pulled herself together and removed his hands. "If you had not come along when you did, I would have stabbed his black heart." She sheathed her dirk and collected her rosary from the floor before Michael noticed it lay there. She put the beads and tiny silver cross inside her purse. One moment of frailty was all she allowed herself.

A grumble heralded Walter's regaining of consciousness. They watched the vermin, spitting mad and sporting a cut above one eye, charge at them. He yanked a glove out of his sword belt and tossed it vengefully in Michael's face. "Misbegotten whoreson!" He cast a gobbet of sputum at Michael's feet, his hand clasping the sword hilt at his side. "I am for you! Outside! *Now!*"

Renée grabbed Michael's arm to keep him from striding after Walter. "This is unnecessary. My guards . . . I will deal with him. There is no reason for you to draw on him."

Michael stared at her in disbelief. "No reason? Apart from the obvious one, do you think me so pigeon-livered that I would run from a challenge? I hit him, he demands satisfaction, and my honor obliges me to act upon it. Frankly, I look forward to snipping this peacock's tail feathers."

Her violet eyes flashed. "What do you mean the obvious reason? You are not within rights to defend my honor, sir! I will not permit—"

"Do not worry about me, marmoset." He peeled her hand from his arm and, smiling into her furious eyes, brought her knuckles to his lips with courtly grace. "Consider me your champion."

As he took off, he heard her swishing after him. "I am not worried about you, *imbécile*! And I do not accept you as my champion!"

Mercy Jesu, this was a disaster! Renée could not allow Michael to fight for her honor for so many reasons that her thoughts tumbled one over the other. For one, if Cardinal Wolsey had not heard of her past exploits yet, he was sure to hear of them now and might cancel her audience. Two, Anne might become jealous and cease to confide in her. Buckingham might change his plans and Renée would never know. Then there were King Henry and King Francis to consider. If word of Walter's assault reached France, her king would demand a royal English apology! She did not even want to contemplate the storm this could breed. Another person to consider was the queen. Katherine, a virtuous lady, would not like this one bit. Renée might be sent back . . . Ohhh!

And there was Michael. Kind, honorable, considerate Michael, who had rushed to her rescue and was about to risk his life defending her honor, a reputation he believed was lily white. She had seen how strong he was, and yet concern for his life put an irrational strain on her.

She had to stop this sword fight!

Renée ran into the Marquis de Rougé as she hurried after Michael. "Oh, blessed Jesu! Pierre, find the Duke of Norfolk and make him tether his man, Sir Walter. *Please!*"

Rougé was dumbfounded. "Almighty Christ, you *are* ill!"

She dug her fingernails in his arms. "Please, Pierre! This is a catastrophe! Sir Walter tried to force himself on me and Master

Michael Devereaux stopped him and now they are gone to fight over my honor and should King Henry or King Francis—"

Rougé cursed. "You little fool! I do not know what you are at, madame, but if war breaks out over your inability to bridle your hot-blooded lovers—"

"Damn you, Rougé!" she rasped, close to tears. "Act now, reproach me later!"

"This will cost you, Renée. I want to know precisely what your duty is. I will find Norfolk. You deal with the braggarts." He paced off, leaving her gasping for air, doubled over with fright.

Michael, sprawled in rain-beaten mud, bleeding to death from a fatal wound . . . Just not that!

Scudding rain battered Michael's face as he circled Walter with a drawn sword in the muddy courtyard, fully aware of the faces jostling for space in the traceried palace windows. His private business with the popinjay was turning into a circus, the gossipmongering court waiting to see which half brother would give the mortal stoccado to the other.

Sober-blooded, the thrashing rain having cooled his vicious temper and dampened his desire for satisfaction, Michael was having second thoughts about the skirmish. He was not anticipating killing or getting killed by the sibling he had just discovered that he had. But he had staked his honor, and should he eat humble pie now, Lord Tyrone's name would bear the brunt of it.

Stanley, having equipped the duelers with leather brigandines and bucklers, courtesy of his friend Sir Henry Marney, the Captain of the Guard, positioned himself as sentinel at the nearest doorway to prohibit any interference that might distract them or alter the equilibrium.

Sir Walter was well known at court. Hence, those with a predilection for betting put the odds in his favor. "I give you three to one," Michael heard one gentleman wager with another. After today, Michael vowed, the odds would tip considerably higher toward his own name.

Gauging his opponent's agility, strength, and skill, he teased

Walter with feints calculated to annoy. Walter launched an aggressive assault. Long steel blades clanged with metallic rancor. Michael parried the passado smoothly and fell back, light on his feet. Then he heard her, Renée, arguing with Stanley. "Let me through, sir! This stupid quarrel must be stopped!"

Michael made the mistake of glancing at her and nearly got his liver skewered. "Stanley, get her away from here!" he growled in the rainstorm as he blocked a barrage of heavy blows.

"My lady, I beseech you! Remain inside! Your presence distracts him!" Stanley urged.

"That is the point, Lord Stanley!" she scolded. "They must be distracted from killing each other. Do not let your friend be slain over a . . . a disagreement! Sir Walter will be penalized by his duke."

"Lady, this is a matter of honor between two English gentlemen. Rest assured that Michael appreciates your concern, but truly, madame, this concerns you not!"

Stanley was right, Michael thought. It was not about her. This was personal family business.

Renée did not relent. "It is you who does not understand, foolish man! He is fighting for my honor—which he has no business defending! Now I am ordering you to stop this scuffle! He will cause a diplomatic discord and get himself killed withal! Do you comprehend me, sirrah? Or do I march out there myself?"

Stanley's patience was diminishing. "Lady, I am warning you—"

Deflecting another strike, Michael grinned at Stanley's exasperated tone. It took all of his self-discipline not to look at the tug-of-war taking place hard by. Stanley had his hands full with *his* heart's desire, but he did not envy him in the least. The obstreperous wench had a tongue like a joiner's file and the temper of a Sicilian charger. He equally pitied and begrudged the man who would someday put her through her paces. Perdition, he wished he were that man. He wished she were not a princess. He wished he had never set eyes on her. . . .

"Please!" Renée altered her tone from shrewish to full of feminine woe. "You are his friend! Make him stand down! I cannot bear the thought of him getting killed. . . ."

"Lady, I doubt he will listen. Now, if you care aught for his health, I firmly insist you leave him be and find yourself a warm place in a casement wherefrom to observe the scuffle. *Quietly*."

Walter astutely maneuvered them so that his back was to Renée and Michael had a full view of her. The little idiot, Michael noticed, stood shivering behind Stanley, blue-lipped, pale. Her eyes sought his with such heartrending wretchedness that he almost threw down his sword.

Walter saw an opening to run his blade through Michael and met steel instead. Blows flew in a torrent of rasping sparks before they disengaged and resumed circling each other like tigers, mud sucking at their heels, each man keeping the other in his sight. From the corner of his eye, Michael saw Renée cross herself and latch on to Stanley's arm. A swything flash of silvery metal pierced his vision. He swerved fast, swinging his sword with impetus and élan to bring it upon his adversary with a *punto reverso*. The ground was slippery. He lost his footing, performed an ungainly somersault, and landed in a wet pothole with a bone-jarring punch to his backside.

Stanley coughed forcefully to mask his chortles. Renée clamped a hand over her mouth, her eyes platelets of anxiety. The glass windowpanes were plastered with mocking, jeering faces.

Splendid. Michael cursed. He could add buffoonery to his list of accomplishments. Maybe, if he hurried, he might overtake the Italian players and beg a clownish office amid their vagrant ranks. He had meant to trim the peacock's tail and gotten his own stubbed instead.

Walter loured over his sprawled form. "Muddy-mettled?" He smirked maliciously. "I should have guessed you would fight like a fop. Cry mercy and I will spare your sodden arse!"

Scurrilous thoughts filled Michael's head as his fingers flexed around the hilt of his sword.

"I do not think so." Walter's boot drowned the blade in the puddle. "I give you three winks to beg for quarter afore I dispatch your soul to bastards' hell." The sharp tip of his sword pricked Michael's throat, inflicting a scotch on an exposed patch of skin. "One . . ."

A drop of blood beaded. Rage lanced Michael. His mind became abnormally alacritous. His eyes stung. His vision sharpened.

The world began to move at a much slower pace around him, even the plump raindrops fell lazily before his eyes. Oh no. Not again. Not now! He shut his eyes tightly, willing the insanity to pass. . . .

"Two . . ."

In a fluid, swift motion, Michael seized the menacing blade with his gloved fist and lunged up, ramming the hilt into Walter's groin, sending him staggering backward. He flipped the sword in the air to gain a firm hent and forced his foe to plonk his rear down in the puddle and recline all the way back till his entire body lay in the thick sediment carpeting the flagstones. "Three."

Applause thudded in the entryway. "Huzzah!" Stanley clapped. "Good on you, runt!"

The spectators in the casements overlooking the courtyard were astounded. "Did you see? A fleet-winged fellow if I ever saw one! One moment on the ground and the next . . ."

Michael's gaze fixed on one person. Rainwater sluiced his face, soaking into his mud-caked apparel. He did not notice any of it—not the downpour, not the people, not his friend—only her. Renée's smile was tender and sad. He felt sad, too. To love her with his heart but never with his body was not a fate he accepted willingly. She knew as well as he did, probably better, that there was no future, only heartache beyond this moment and that therefore they must resist, forget . . .

He returned his attention to his trounced foe. As far as he was concerned, the unpleasantness with Walter was settled. Tearing him limb from limb would be unsportsmanlike, pointless. He was of a mind to give quarter and to establish a degree of brotherly rapport with the peacock. Mayhap if he scratched the offensive surface, he would find a more likeable fellow underneath. He tossed Walter's sword aside and offered his hand as a lever.

Walter ignored it. He looked at Michael, at Renée. He smirked, sniggered, and then threw his head back, guffawing. "Godsakes, you fancy-sick dupe!" He beat the squelchy ground with his gloved hand, mud splotching his face. "You have not plugged her yet, have you?"

Michael shot an apologetic glance at Renée. She had gone deathly white. He glowered at the fool. "Foulmouthed jack, are you mad? Must I cut out your tongue to check you?"

"Oh, 'tis too much!" Walter chortled, as gleeful as the devil signing up another soul. "The out-of-town dolt plays Sir Lancelot to a French whore and thinks he is lighting candles for the Virgin Mary!"

Michael's tone was a menacing growl. "I spared you now, lunatic, but I will not be merciful if you come near her again. Best keep your distance and a still tongue in your head withal. It is a hanging offense to assault a princess of France and publicly question her maidenly honor."

"Enough! I beg you, no more!" Walter pushed himself up. "It was worth tasting mud to see you make a butt of yourself. Let me enlighten you about your maidenly princess. . . ."

Renée pushed her way through the throng. Everyone was discussing the Devereaux brothers, their discovering each other after decades and settling old feuds. No mention of her name, thank God. But the damage with Michael was done. Walter was filling his ear with all the embellished gossip, the calumnies, and false tales the court had to offer about Froward Renée. Henceforward, the sole beacon of decency in this wretched place would think her a jay, a wild piece, so many unflattering things that would make him look upon her in contempt. . . . *The royal French whore.*

Renée could not bear it. She saw Rougé approach purposefully, Norfolk at his side. Neither one looked pleased. "What happened?" Rougé demanded to know.

"They both live, with nary a scratch on them," she said flatly.

"They fought already?"

"*Calmez vous,*" she retorted tersely. "The general belief among the gossipmongers is that the Devereaux bloods learned they were half siblings and felt the need to settle the old feud the way young hawks do." She looked at Norfolk, offering a semicurtsey. "Your Grace, I will thank you to teach your attendants better manners. I do not enjoy being accosted in remote corners. Needless to say, your discretion in this matter will be appreciated. No need to alert His Majesty. . . ." She hated being in his debt! If she thought for a moment that he would accept payment in gold, she would make Rougé pay through the nose, but she knew the duke's price would be steeper.

"Madame, please accept my sincerest apology. Rest assured my man will be dealt with. You have my personal pledge that his misconduct will not repeat itself." He bowed economically and went to put a halter on Walter. Alas the knave had had sufficient time to poison Michael's mind against her. She should not care so much, but—*morbleu!*—she did. She blinked back tears.

"So you have enjoyed your first diversion of the day," Rougé drawled scathingly, "watching two fools brawl over you. Would you care to enlighten me as to what I am to expect for supper? Will the Cardinal of York launch into song and dance to your piping, perchance?"

"I owe you nothing, Rougé! You were too late, useless as always, a burr under my saddle."

At that precise moment, soaked to the bone and plastered with mud, Michael walked into the gallery. He sauntered right past her, spared her not a glance, as if he had been stung by a gadfly and she were the cow that had attracted the insect, and only stopped when Anne dimpled into his path, simpering, waxing worshipful over his speed and strength, making play with her bodice.

Clearly, sentencing had already been given, Renée reflected sullenly, wishing the pox on his golden head. She could list a number of calamitous events worse than losing His Worship's high regard. Let him strut victorious before the strumpets of this court. The fig for him!

Then it dawned on her: her problems had just been compounded!

Renée looked around. Sir George Hastings was nowhere in sight to rein his hussy wife. "We will discuss the supper on the way over," she told Rougé, and set out to find Robin. Her hunt was successful, for he materialized before her shortly after, carrying a pottle of sack.

"My lady!" He greeted her with a grin and a careful bow.

"Robin, I need you to point out Master Michael Devereaux's

lodging for me," she whispered. "You must not tell anyone about it."

"I could do that, if madame will follow me."

Renée stiffened. She was aware of the shadow following her discreetly, shuffling his feet. He had materialized while she had been pleading with Lord Stanley to stop the fight. "Lieutenant Armado, please apply your stealth tactics to pilfering mustaches and such from the revel office for our supper engagement." Her tone was as pleasant as poisoned honey. "I will proceed alone."

"Very good, madame."

"Hold," she said, not turning. "Henceforward you take orders from no one but me." She slid a coin into Robin's hand. "Lead the way."

Scanning the gallery for officers of the household and espying not a one, Robin pocketed the shilling and motioned her to precede him. She flipped over the dark veil, shrouding her features. Passersby might lift a brow at her shading her complexion from a nonexistent indoor sun on a stormy day, but leastways she was unrecognizable. She prayed fortune was her friend, for she was taking a foolhardy gamble. A party of gallants swaggered past them, her presence in their wing garnering cursory glances but no commentary. Robin halted once the passage was clear. Smiling, he laid a finger along his nose in a gesture of confidentiality. "The door to your left."

Renée nodded her thanks, sent him on his way, and listened at the door. All was quiet. She tried the doorknob. *Click.* With silent thanks to St. Quentin, patron saint of locksmiths, she stole inside, closing the door. A snort froze her in place.

Renée cursed, no longer amazed that the light-heeled brigand had outrun her. She imagined him cocking a brow at her back, legs braced apart in a belligerent stance. She had not expected to find him here. She would have wagered a duchy that Anne had not let him off the hook so soon. Her plan had been to lie in wait unobtrusively and eavesdrop when they entered. Now she would have to justify her presence. She well imagined the slanderous fodder Walter had spilled into Michael's manger. Would Michael expect her to live up to her tarred reputation?

With misgiving, Renée turned around. The chamber was vacant. . . . No, it was not.

A manservant lay curled up on a truckle bed before the cold hearth, sleeping. She offered thanks to the patron saint of idle servants, whoever he was, and tiptoed inside.

Michael's soapy scent hung heavy in the air, conjuring up pulse-quickening moments of the previous night. Unlike her apartment, this was a single lodging, consisting of a bedchamber and a screened garderobe. Fine oaken trunks, saddles, and various manly appurtenances were stacked against the wall. There was no place to hide save on the bed with the bed hangings drawn. Out of the question. Michael might think she had come skulking into his bedchamber with the intention of practicing her seductive crafts on him. The imp in her was tempted to poke her nose into his personal belongings, sniff his clothes . . . Jesu! She was such a goosehead.

The door creaked on its hinges. Renée leaped into the garderobe, snapping shut the arras.

"Pippin." A sword belt hit the floor. "Dump your slothful carcass elsewhere."

The manservant responded in Irish Gaelic, muttering about mud and a bath. Renée winced, reddening. If she could understand that, then Michael had surely understood Adele's chatter.

Michael sent the manservant scurrying out the door with facetious insults that betrayed the comfortable lack of formality between master and servant. The door lock clicked.

"Now, my lady," Michael husked. "You may reveal your charms."

Renée went utterly still; her breath caught. How did he know—?

"With pleasure," responded a female voice, followed by a rustle of taffeta and damask.

Renée's eyes grew round as turrets. *Anne was here*. She stifled her irritation, applauded her cunning, and peered through the Flemish weave. By the time she attained focus, she saw Michael open his arms in mock surrender. "My lady, I am all yours. Mud, warts, and all."

A naked Anne stepped over a pile of female garments to unloop the buttons of his drenched doublet. She pushed it off his massive shoulders and began work on his shirt laces. "Castilian soap." She sniffed his neck, sending a jolt of annoyance through Renée. "Very pleasing."

White teeth gleamed against tanned cheeks. "I am made to please."

"I am inclined to agree." Anne divested him of the sopping lawn garment, leaving him bare-chested, with only his muddy leather hose and knee-high boots on.

Renée goggled. He was magnificent. His was not a stripling's anatomy, nor a puny artist's. Golden skin covered streaming muscularity achieved through years in the combat yard, perfectly proportioned and defined. He was lean, chiseled, and long. Great shoulders capped thickly roped arms and a powerfully hewn chest that tapered to a muscle-winged waist. Beneath the corded wall of his stomach, the hose codpiece jutted out like a proud pennon of virility.

Merely staring at the honed contours of his body stirred up such turbulence inside Renée that her own flesh blushed and heated. He was gorgeously lethal for her peace of mind; his patrician, high-boned features declared a Norman ancestry as proudly as the rest of him affirmed the Norse invasion into his bloodline.

Anne splayed greedy fingers over the brawny expanse of his chest. Renée's nose wrinkled in disdain. While she did not care to watch this, she was incapable of looking away. Anne put her hands around his neck and pulled his handsome head down for a kiss, but Michael removed her hands and danced her bed-ward. *No kiss for you, Anne*, Renée sniggered silently. At his nudge, Anne tumbled onto the mattress, bouncing, her udders quivering. She sent the toes of one foot to prod at his codpiece. "Will you take this off, or am I to be pleasured with wool stuffing?"

"The stuffing, lusty lady, is all mine." Michael unlaced the codpiece points and shoved his hose and slops to his knees. Renée's gasp nearly gave her away. The sight of his backside she might have handled, but as he stood facing her, treating her to a full frontal view of his lean hips, strong thighs, and the thick lance saluting from a tuft of dark gold curls, her eyes all but popped out of their sockets. That he was lovelier than a young god she had already noticed, but the part about his "stuffing" was not an idle boast. He was well endowed and prideful of his assets. Still as bronze, he let Anne appreciate his genitalia as if he were flaunting his heraldic *genealogia*.

Renée peeled her eyes off that ominous sword and sought his face, anticipating a vain smirk, but Michael's expression was hard, and he was staring directly at the arras. She recoiled as if hit with a mighty fist, his piercing gaze giving her the willies. Did he know she was there? She shut her eyes tightly, cursing herself for an idiot. Shame racked her. *Hoisted with her own petard.*

"Michael, I am waiting," Anne simpered. "I am here, not there."

Renée, mustering her frowardness, returned her eyes to the scarlet curtain. Michael hooked his hands beneath Anne's knees and yanked her bottom to the edge of the bed. Tall as the tester bed was, his great height forced him to shove pillows beneath Anne's fat bottom to position her for his onslaught. He braced her knees wide apart and surged into her, joining their bodies.

Renée watched him go about the business as if he cared not who was on the bed. No petting, no kissing. Anne's panting enthusiasm mystified her. The woman was mad with lust, like a man. She moaned and thrashed as Michael pumped his hips against her without breaking rhythm or a sweat, without looking at her, his blank gaze staring ahead, at the arras, or at nothing at all.

Renée felt sordid spying on them. She looked away, yet the sounds—hard, slapping thumbs, the bed rocking, Anne's spurring cries—were worse. This was her penance for having begun the rigmarole by inviting Michael to her apartment. Their carnality touched her on the raw. The love she knew was gentle and quiet. Nice. This was the sin of the flesh priests preached against. She felt . . . jealous. Michael was powerful, masculine, seductive. Staring at him alone excited her.

Anne gave a shuddering cry and lay spent. Renée saw Michael stiffen, every muscle in his body taut as a stretched rope. Glinting turquoise slits stared straight ahead. His jaw was clenched.

Renée couldn't breathe. A blaze swept through her like a dragon's breath. Shaking, tingling, she sank down on a stool, burying her glowing face in her hands. A cool and logical voice spoke inside her head: *Focus on the important things. The Ancient, Brittany, Raphael. Your life.*

Boots thudded on the floor. Leastways they were fast, Renée thought. The entire ordeal had lasted minutes. Evidently Satan appreciated velocity in his subjects. She waited for them to talk. She needed to know every detail of the plot Michael might coax out of Anne.

"I feel so sleepy." Anne yawned. "You and a sleepless night have worn me out, darling."

Darling! Renée pulled a face. The man had been remote and impersonal and already he was her darling sweetheart. *Come on, Michael*, Renée willed him. *Begin your interrogation.*

"Sleep. I will awake you, fear not."

"Mayhap for a little while. My husband is due back at court for supper."

Imprecating the stupid man for his unwarranted solicitude, Renée prepared for a long wait. Of a sudden the arras shifted, and Michael stepped in, nude as Adam save for white, skintight strossers for a fig leaf. Mortified, Renée leaped to her feet. *Sweet Jesu, make me disappear!*

"What the devil do you think you are at, skulking in here?" His tone of voice, his eyes, every line in his handsome face manifested the angry volcano raging inside him. His presence crowded her, besieged her. She felt small and petty. She shut her eyes, cringing inside.

"Look at me, damn you." The command fell like a thunderclap.

Renée forced her eyes open. Tall and angry, Michael loomed over her in the compact space. His blue eyes burned her. She was cornered. Her face grew hotter and redder. "I . . ."

"You are what—a manipulative, headstrong, devious, nosy, maddening witch?"

The salvo of insults killed her contrition. Her temper flared. She straightened her spine and looked him in the eye. "I was waiting for you. I . . . wanted to thank you for rescuing me."

"Do not play gormless with me. I know you are up to something." He lowered his voice to a whispery breath. "It concerns the conspiracy. You are spying for your king."

"I needed to know the details concerning you-know-what, to stop it," she returned quietly.

He looked stumped. "I would have told you. All you had to do was ask."

Renée studied his expression and knew he was telling the truth. "What gave me away?"

"Ambergris and lavender."

"You knew I was here all along?" she sputtered. "Why did you not toss me out?"

"You were spying. I gave you something to spy on. So?" He smiled mirthlessly. "How did I compare with the French court? I hear their painters' brushes—" Her hand flew at his face. He caught it. "Oh no, you do not strike me, little princess. This is the part where you apologize."

"Apologize! You imply that I am a whore! A despicable knave spews venom in your ear and you believe every word. For one wading in sin, you—"

"Sin! Let us discuss my sins, shall we?" He planted his hands on the wall behind her, caging her between his thick arms and his impressive near nakedness. His voice was deceptively soft. "What precisely are my sins, pray tell? Was I discourteous to you? Did I presume on our budding friendship? Did I abandon you in your hour of need to be mauled by a swine? Did I demonstrate a lack of concern when you took me into your confidence and told me that a certain person was to be murdered? Oh, I know. I neglected to kiss you twice—or was it thrice? Is that it, Froward Renée?" He leaned in till his mouth was a breath away from hers, taunting her. "I would not kiss you now if you begged me to."

Her heart beat madly. "Your vanity is beyond belief!" she hissed. "You are what—a hedge-born wencher, a nameless upstart? How dare you insult me? I am descendent from a king!"

"Who should have given you the bastinado, or leastways a good spanking before he passed on to his reward. You are gallingly temerarious, have a mind like an adder, willful to the point of self-destruction, and every haughty word that comes out of your mouth is a cannon-shot."

"I guess we do not like each other overly much. Do we?" She glared at him.

"Not at the moment, no." He did not pull back but glowered right back at her.

The air between them could boil a cauldron of water.

"Well, then." She stuck out her chin imperiously. "This would be a good time for me to take my leave." She knew when she was defeated. He would not let her listen to his talk with Anne.

He did not budge. His eyes made a study of her face. She felt exposed. "Why did you play *advocatus diaboli* when evidently you shared my views on the subject of love?" he asked.

"I did not. I maintain my opinion."

"I see. You make a distinction. There is love and then there is . . . pleasure. One has naught to do with the other."

She clenched her teeth, seething, embattled. "I did not say that!"

"Let me rephrase, then."

"No. I will not discuss this further with you."

His eyes clouded. "You are an extraordinary female, Renée de Valois."

She decided to try her luck. "May I stay while you speak with Anne?"

His lips twitched. "No, you may not."

Michael leaned back against the door to his chamber and breathed, forcing his temper to cool. His stupidity deserved a shrine in the temple of stupid people. She had been playing with him all along, was playing with him still—and he wanted her, still, worse than before.

Froward Renée. He had to grin at the sound of her epithet. How accurately it depicted her, a firecracker that would meet her enemies with a sharp dirk and be no man's fool. Renée confused, annoyed, and entranced him. She plucked at his heartstrings as if they were the frets of her lute. He admired her, and he resented her for grooming him into a pie-eyed Blondel make-believing that the lowborn esquire could inspire love in the chaste bosom of his princess. Oh, aye, he was liver-veined as fools came. She would scorn him without batting an eye. She would use him and then discard him as leftovers from last night's feast; he might become a dog's dinner for aught she cared. She would not give a jot or mind his loss. She would never think, *He made me laugh, he made me dew with warm desire, he was chivalrous and kind, mayhap he was worth keeping.*

When he inhaled her scent upon entering the chamber, his entire self snapped to attention. He had not meant to touch Anne, had a subtler tactic in mind. But the embers of last eve's lust, fueled by Walter's oration, caught fire at Renée's furtive presence. The final proof that she was, in fact, using him catapulted him into an unwanted battleground, with a woman he did not want. Just to make Renée jealous. *Blockhead.* His foul temper had made him behave like a green lad, not a man, not the heir of Tyrone. He felt sickened with himself. The pox to the witch!

The game was over, Michael determined vengefully. He had met his quota of tomfoolery for this one chapter. It was time to attend to important, pressing matters.

Michael sat on the bed beside the curled female form. "Open your eyes, Anne."

Her eyelids snapped open. She stared at him glassily.

He had no patience to waffle. He leaned over her menacingly. "His Grace your brother plots to assassinate King Henry. He will fail. You are embroiled in this web of treason. Speak, and I will untangle you."

"I do not know what you mean." Anne flipped the sheet aside invitingly.

Michael did not bother looking. She stirred not a modicum of sentiment in him, except pity, for she was trapped in a marriage not of her choosing and lacked the will to mold the clay of her life into something worth living. She floundered, snatching transitory gratification from men like him, like King Henry—who cared not a doit about her—paying the consequences, and letting her brother use her as a means to his end. In contrast, Renée . . . He regurgitated Walter's obloquious utterances and expelled most of them like bile. Malevolence cankered the man's soul, quenching any desire Michael entertained to form a brotherly bond with the man. Princess Renée de Valois might not be a virginal mouse, but neither was she the indiscriminating jade Walter portrayed. If she had been, Michael would have tasted her already. The direction of his thoughts angered him. With a peremptory growl, he commanded, "Tell me aught you know, every detail, now!"

Anne's eyes went stark with . . . nothing. *Vacant.* "Ned contracted a Spanish assassin to kill King Henry. The queen will lose her unborn child, and my brother will be king."

"How will the queen lose her babe?"

Moon-faced, Anne droned, "Tonight, after supper, I will drip poison in her cup, three drops, not kill the queen, only the unborn babe. The king will come. The assassin will lie in wait. . . ."

"How will the assassin gain entrance to the royal apartments?" *How will I?* Michael frowned. The entire level was paved with the highly trained yeomen of the guard. Then he remembered his morning feat, tearing off to help Renée. Anxiety had bestowed him with *talaria*, the winged gold sandals of a messenger of the gods. Could he repeat the performance?

"Disguised as a yeoman of the guard."

Suddenly disgusted with the sight of her, naked and witless on his bed, he drew back. Dusk misted the window. "You must dress now, Anne, and go to your quarters before your husband returns. You will keep quiet about this. Tell no one. We never spoke. Is that clear?"

"I must dress now and go to my quarters before my husband returns. Tell no one we spoke." Like a docile lamb, she rose from the bed, her expression vapid, and dressed methodically. Her peculiar, slavish compliance baffled and alarmed Michael. He went to pull the cowl of her frock low over her eyes, opened the door, inspected the passage, and when he saw no one, let her pass before him. He walked over to open a window and let in cool, fresh air.

Whatever had just transpired was completely beyond his purview.

"Attend me, Sir Walter."

Sir Walter Devereaux, washed and groomed to toady penitently, noted that Norfolk did not invite him to sit down. Presiding over rolls of vellum and an assortment of quills and inkpots, the duke shifted in his high-backed chair as if it were a bed of nettles. His splenetic tone was grittier than usual. "I come from a distinctly unpleasant audience with His Majesty. The king observed the scuffle. To say he was unimpressed with you would be an understatement."

"I will apologize to His Majesty for picking a quarrel at his court and pay my fine to the palace marshal."

"Your will apologize to me, sir! The King of England saw the gentleman I recommended for a knighthood of the Garter make a sublime ass of himself! To make matters worse, the French ambassador is outraged . . . assaulting a princess of France under the king's roof!" His fist hit the table, frightening an inkwell. "What in damnation were you thinking?"

Walter jumped. Had he been gracing the table, he would be doing a Scotch jig together with the rolls. Nothing in his duke's earlier attitude, when Norfolk found him begrimed, squelching in waterlogged boots, had foretold a rancorous scolding. "Your Grace, I—"

"Was I not plain as a pikestaff?" Norfolk roared, rage contorting his ripened face. "Did I not instruct you to woo her? Did you think to plant a brat under her kirtle to force her into a union with you? In which book does wooing translate to rape and defamation? What you do reflects on me and therefore you do solely *for* me. You do not labor in your affairs! *I* advance your interests. *I* secure your future. *I* promote your cause with the king. I tolerate your indelicacies so long as you are discreet and useful to me—but do not ever miscalculate the scope of my intelligence! If I did not make it my business to know all that betides this realm, I would not be Norfolk!"

Walter longingly eyed the flagon of malmsey wine on the counting table. He felt like an overgrown hedge cut down to bantam size. "I will keep my distance from the French princess for the duration of her stay in England."

The duke was apoplectic. "Am I hard of hearing? Did you say you would add insult to injury and cut her altogether?" He pushed to his feet, growling, "You will apologize to her, sirrah jack! You kiss her feet if you must, or I shall put my penny on another horse with the same name!"

The last bit got Walter's dander up; the slightest allusion to the bastard rubbed his fur in the opposite direction. "I will do so at once," he choked out.

Norfolk plunked himself down. "You will do so on the morrow. Tonight you will shadow her to the private supper Wolsey is holding in her honor and report everything back to me. If she wears a rose in her ear and sniffles on the river, I would know of it. Is that clear, boy?"

"Aye, Your Grace."

❧ 12 ❧

The hour flies, death looms.

—Persius

Renée fed the crumpled dispatch to the fire and watched, un-nerved, as the chryselephantine fleurs-de-lis were consumed by ravenous flames. The sight chilled her. If she failed to steal the Ancient soon, she would suffer the same fate as King Francis's missive to Rougé. Long-Nose and his holy banker were getting restless; they wanted the marquis to spy on *her*. Ha! She would not be undermined by Rougé. She turned to the mustached, wigged man awaiting her pleasure. "Your lieutenant has become a liability. He lies. He has a secret truck with Norfolk's despicable retainer. He endangers our assignment." *He needs to disappear.* "Your suggestions?"

Sergeant Francesco did not dillydally. "He lied about the medallion. He deserted his post today. He imperiled your person, madame. I know it all. My suggestion? Give the order."

Renée was impressed. Francesco was stalwart, a serious man, dedicated and true. Efficient. She could not flinch in this matter. It had to be done. Were they in France, she would discharge Lieutenant Armado. Here, he would simply defect to Campeggio and Wolsey's camp. "Do it."

"Before or after, madame?"

"After." She would not rack herself over the flames for this, not now, after, when she came before her Maker. *Surrender a funda-*

mental piece of her soul. She had felt it in her nightmare. A tremor lanced her when he left. King Louis's daughter, made of ice, a murderess. God pity her.

Icy wind and drizzle nipped Renée's face on the choppy river. Huddled in a cloak of sable, she beheld the cluster of lights beckoning them to the city of London with growing apprehension.

Tonight was the night. She would steal the Ancient and leave for France. Adele had secretly packed her belongings. Sergeant Francesco had his orders. A boat with five of her men waited to take her from York Place to Gravesend, a town downriver with a century-old royal grant to ferry travelers, where Cardinal Medici's three-sail caravel docked. The crossing to France would take longer from Gravesend than from Dover, but in choosing this route, they would circumnavigate the perilous London-Dover land road, particularly Blackheath, a highwaymen's haunt and the perfect site for an ambush. They would journey longer by water than by land, which was safer, considering their rivals for the Ancient.

"Why are your Italians in clownish disguises?" her companion queried derisively.

"I have changed my mind about the audience," Renée said.

"What?" Rougé exclaimed. "What insanie is this? Madame, if you would be guided by me—"

"I meant our prospective duties. I want you to conduct the negotiations for my nuptials. You were right. It would be unseemly for me, a mere woman, to be present while two great men such as you and His Eminence discussed my future. We shall sup in amity, and when the sweet wine is served, you shall embark on your speech but begin with a subtle coughing. I will then beg leave to worship at the cardinal's chapel while you decide on my future. Pray, do not look stunned, Monsieur le Marquis. I promise to pray for your soul and beg Our Lord to guide you."

"You claimed to have a personal message from King Francis. What is it?"

"Here." She pulled a sealed missive from her purse. "Deliver it to the cardinal yourself. It lists my entire dowry." She chuckled when he clutched the letter-patent as if it were a map to a hidden hoard. "Oh, Pierre, we both know this is all a sham. I will never wed an Englishman."

"How about an Irishman?"

She caught his dark, glimmering gaze. "Only if he wears a tartan and paints his face blue."

"So he means nothing to you?"

"Who?" The note she had written to Michael was destroyed by fire. She never meant to send it. She had penned it down to allay an unfathomable need to say good-bye. In a week's time she would be reunited with Raphael. Michael, as this venture, would seem no more than a dream.

"You know of whom I speak. You spend every evening in his company, in private and in the common gaze. He fought for you today. Is he a passing fancy? A big toy to ease discomforts?"

Renée kept her eyes straight ahead. The scene she had witnessed in Michael's chamber was forever burnt into her recollection. She would never forget the sight of his glorious nakedness: a beautiful masterpiece of God, an artwork to admire and remember in the best of sense, naught more. To the man inside she had said good-bye in the letter he would never read. It was enough. "He was not my lover, Rougé."

"Was? Is one of you leaving?" Rougé asked perspicaciously.

"I said 'was' because after today's fiasco I vowed to have no more dealings with him."

She felt his eyes on her profile. "He meant something to you."

It was a probe. She stared at him, half smiling. "Did he?"

"Ah, here we are!" Rougé mounted the private landing to York Place and offered a hand.

Torchbearers in livery waited to usher them to the palace. A servant with a staff of office in his hand said, "If it please Your Graces, the two great cardinals wait in the presence chamber."

Hoisting the train of her gown with one hand, Renée took the marquis's arm and picked her way over the puddled potholes and mud cakes dilapidating the path to the palace's entrance, her guards—one flaxen-haired, the other carrottop—following in her footsteps.

* * *

"Leaving England? Are you sure?" Sir Walter whispered.

"Heard the Frenchie say so with me own ears, sir. Told the wharfinger they'd be leaving on the twelfth-hour bell tonight and to expect two cartfuls of trunks, coffers, and furnishings."

"Godsakes, Martin. Lower your voice." Walter pulled his surcoat tighter about him, cursing Norfolk for conscripting him into playing the pond frog outside York Place with the hell-black welkin pissing on his head. As for the princess, good riddance! "Did you fetch me a jack of ale?"

The manservant unstrapped a leather flask from his belt. "Mulled wine."

"Warm!" Walter's eyes lit up. He drank the sweet brew to the dregs and wiped his lips on his cuff. "Did the Frenchie have Lombard looks? Dark hair, dark eyes?"

"Flaxen hair to the shoulders. I saw not the eyes."

"Fair? Surely you are mistaken." Was she taking the ill-begotten upstart with her?

"Nothing amiss with me eyes, Worship. Mayhap me ears . . . but me hawks serve me well."

Fair. Either Martin was mistaken or Walter was blessedly rid of the whoreson.

Suspiciously, there was only one guard on duty outside Renée's apartment. "I would speak with your mistress," Michael announced.

"Madame sups outside the palace this evening."

Michael intended to question the guard further, but the door opened, and Renée's tire-woman filled the doorway. Beyond her, Michael glimpsed stripped walls and trunks crowding the floor.

Adele's eyes rounded on Michael; whatever she meant to say to the guard died on her lips. She stepped back, closing the door, but Michael's foot and hand were already in the way.

"What is happening, Adele?" he asked in Gaelic as he entered forcefully, slamming the door in the startled guard's face. "She has left, hasn't she?" He surveyed the naked room with rising alarm. Peeled of gilt fleurs-de-lis, only her distinct fragrance clinging to the air like a forgotten lover evidenced Renée's ever inhabiting the space. A sense of loss choked Michael. "Where did she go? Back to France?"

The superior-looking dame pursed her lips, refusing to answer.

Michael took her shoulders and stared into her eyes. "Listen carefully, Adele. The queen's unborn babe is to be murdered tonight along with his sire. I can protect the king, but Renée is the only one of us who has access to Her Majesty. You would not want a wee thing to suffer and die for the benefit of a power-hungry nobleman, would you? Please tell me where I may find her."

"You cannot reach her," the old dame replied. "She is supping with the French ambassador at the Cardinal of York's palace this evening. She will not return before midnight."

"She will not return at all. Is that not the truth? Why is she leaving? Answer me, Adele!" He could not believe Renée had left him without saying good-bye, without a single word.

"Young man, you must forget her."

Michael swallowed, barely able to dredge up the words, "I cannot."

As she sniffed the air between them, terrible awareness flared in her eyes. "You are infected with a disease!" She pulled away from him. "If you love her, do not seek her out. Leave her be."

"What of the babe?" he asked wretchedly, gasping at the pain in his chest.

Adele gave him a gimlet eye. "The babe will live. The king will die."

Michael clutched the doorknob. "Not if I can help it."

Cardinal Wolsey did not believe them. Renée sensed his eyes shifting between her and the marquis, trying to gauge their true motive. She knew instinctively that like many princes of Holy Church he did not observe a life of celibacy. She also knew that he would never forfeit the secret location of the Ancient's vault, not even if she appeared in his bedchamber without a stitch of clothing on and tantalized him with a Saracen dance. Rougé was not helping. His dilatory oration about peaceful amity and open trade routes between their two nations was contrived and without substance. Cardinal Campeggio wolfed down his supper wordlessly, but with every chime of the hour bell, he raised his head to the officer materializing in the doorway and grunted his approval.

Renée prayed her men fared well in the hallway and that they would not be recognized by their former brothers-in-arms. Her stomach in knots, she forced herself to taste the opulent fare— nine courses of ingenious cookery served on gold platters while the sumptuary laws restricted a duke to seven courses—for fear of augmenting Wolsey's suspicions.

They dined in splendor, surrounded by rare tokens from foreign sovereigns and sumptuous tapestries; their feet touched Venetian damascene carpets. Cardinal Wolsey conducted himself as though he had been born to the wealth and entitlement of the Medici rather than to a butcher's shop, his fingers heavily bejeweled, his scarlet robes spilling lushly around him. Practicing at being pope, Renée speculated scathingly.

Her fears grew hourly. Her thoughts kept spinning back to the capable meddler she had left behind. Whether his loyalty was to himself or to King Henry, Michael Devereaux would do his utmost to disrupt Buckingham's plot. She wondered if Anne had unbosomed herself to him. Odds were she had not. The woman had a cunning vein. As the new king's lady sister, she would possess the power to tether the lovers of her choice, willing or not, to her adulterous bed. Renée tried to imagine Michael's reaction upon learning she had left England. Would the tidings slide off him like a loosened mantle or would he miss her? She could not deny that they had formed an interesting connection.

With the serving of sweetmeats and muscatel, Rougé began coughing. For a moment Renée assumed he had swallowed wrongly and considered sending a page to thwack his back. Then she caught his brow-wiggling glare and recalled her instruction. She stood. "Your Eminences, Your Excellency, with your permission I should like to retire to the chapel and offer my humble prayer to Our Lord and beg for His blessing of peace for our war-fraught countries."

Cardinal Wolsey motioned her to approach him. "Are you aware we are to discuss possible connubial matches for you among the English peerage?" he asked softly, studying her.

"Yes, Eminence. I shall pray to Our Lord to bestow you with His guidance."

He sent a pageboy to fetch his amanuensis before readdressing her. "Being friends with the Lady Mary, the Dowager Queen of France, you may have heard that Her Ladyship's marriage to His Grace of Suffolk began with dissent in the council. Many opposed the union on grounds of the recent ennoblement and insufficient lineage of the groom, but mine own conducive labors on the lovers' behalf concluded the affair to everyone's—chiefly His Majesty's—satisfaction."

At first Renée failed to construe his intention. Then it dawned on her: he would bestow her on a new man, someone of his choosing, possibly to offset the influence of the old nobility, his bitter enemies on the council. Fortified with two French duchies, even a nobody could become a powerful instrument in the cardinal's capable hands. "Lady Mary confided the particulars of the affair and expressed her joyous gratitude over Your Grace's generous intercession on her behalf."

"And will you dutifully accept our judgment in choosing your future husband?"

Did he have someone in mind? she wondered. Despite this being a pretense, it made for an interesting puzzle. "To entrust my future in Your Eminence's goodly hands is to entrust it in God's. I will humbly and gladly accept your decision on the subject, whatever it may be."

"Good, good." He was not through with her yet. A nervous-looking young scribe hurried to his side with an inkwell, quill, and parchment fastened to a board. "With Monsieur le Marquis's permission, Master Kent will take notes of our conversation." The cardinal leveled a do-not-think-to-swindle-me look on Rougé that would have made a moneylender proud. "Madame, before you leave us, pray list all of your hereditary titles for the record."

As a fellow intriguer, Renée had to applaud the butcher's son's cunning. Evidently he meant to barter her away with all the trimmings of a fat, stuffed, garlanded Christmas goose worthy of the king's table. She began to perspire in her finery, smelling the heat of the cardinal's oven. She stared at the twitchy Master Kent. "Renée de Valois, Daughter of France, Duchess of Brittany and Chartres, Countess of Nantes, Montfort, and Richmont, and Viscountess of Limoges."

The cardinal smacked his lips. He extended his ringed hand for her kiss, then signed the cross over her head in blessing. He snapped his fingers at the page boy. "Escort my lady to chapel."

The rainstorm kept many of His Majesty's noblemen in their town houses, which made for a quieter supper. Throughout the repast, Michael focused his hawklike attention on Anne. If he could stop her from poisoning the queen, Buckingham's entire stratagem would disintegrate, but then there would be no glory to pluck.

The babe will live. The king will die. What had the troublesome minx gotten herself into? Had Renée switched the poison Anne intended to use on the queen? If so, why did Adele believe the king would die? Was that the reason Renée had packed herself off and left the palace like a thief? He contemplated the wisdom in following her to France after performing his duties here and found none, but the conclusion did not stop him from fancying her reaction upon seeing him. Would she be glad or would she pretend they had never met?

Michael had to decide whether he believed Renée's tire-woman or not. Supposing Renée had meddled in the child's favor, why did Adele implicate herself and her mistress? The witch-dame had divined his illness; mayhap she divined other things, as well. *The babe will live.* While he was convinced Renée was not so heartless as to overlook the murdering of an innocent unborn babe, her standpoint regarding the babe's royal sire remained vague. By the gods, he worried about her. If anyone should discover Renée had knowledge of the conspiracy—

Queen Katherine took her leave of the assembly earlier than usual, her face waxen. Taking advantage of Stanley's distraction with the departing Meg, a lady-in-waiting in the queen's train, Michael slipped out of the presence chamber and followed the ladies along the gallery. Keeping to the dark, he shadowed them until his first obstacle presented itself. He could not get past the guards stationed outside the queen's private rooms, and even if he could, a stray male would stand out in the female realm existing beyond these doors like a fox in a hen coop.

Michael hid behind a window curtain, pushed the glass doors open, and stared outside. He observed the queen's progress by the candlelight flickering along the wing's lozenges. The entire level housed Their Majesties and their personal attendants. Two wings built around a square yard, their apartments connected in two places: the great stair, the only staircase open to outsiders coming to pay obeisance in the two royal watching chambers, and the private passage between their bedchambers. Respectively, each watching chamber opened to a presence chamber, then led to a privy chamber, to closets, galleries, more private rooms, and to the bedchamber beyond.

Somewhere across the inner courtyard the two wings connected. Michael wagered that that was where the Spanish assassin lay in wait. He would have chosen the same spot.

He stuck his head out the window and studied the masonry, looking for ledges to walk along and crevices to cling to. Guards patrolled the torchlit court below. If he slipped but failed to get himself killed in the fall, barbed pikes would take care of that. The thought of knocking out a guard and stealing his garb did cross his mind—but how would he explain the uniform once he disabled the assassin? The whole point of the dodgy undertaking was to make a name for himself as the crown's hero, not to be charged with high treason alongside the plotters.

Resigning himself to the rough task at hand, he clambered onto the windowsill and grabbed hold of the joist for balance. The cold drizzle and the darkness worked in his favor. Since rising from his sickbed at Castle Tyrone, he found his night vision improved greatly, doubtless thanks to the hell-broth he kept pouring down his gullet, and he could see every nook and cranny with cheerful clarity. When he reached the parallel casement and had to watch out for an inside audience as well, he decided to scale the wall to the roof, thinking it should be easier to run along top ground than to crawl as a diligent spider along vertical masonry.

He stretched out a scouting hand, located a small fissure his fingers could hold on to, and pulled himself upward. He repeated the movement several times, climbing at a snail's pace, his entire concentration on finding the next hand- and foothold. Suddenly the chinked stonework he gripped crumbled to dust in his fingers—and he dropped like a stone.

Armado and Francesco fell into step behind her as Renée followed her liveried guide. She marveled at the unrepentant display of riches paving the route to Cardinal Wolsey's chapel. In his capacity as Lord Chancellor responsible for the welfare *of* the people of England, the cardinal was raking a fortune *from* the people. York Place boasted a collection of gilt work, antiquities, and art pieces that put King Henry's Pleasure Palace to shame. Even the guards forming her wake, sophisticated Romans at home with grandeur, gasped in awe.

The chime of the hour bell notified Renée that supper at the palace ended and that the queen retired to her rooms. According to her calculations, they should have two hours to find the Ancient before a courier arrived to inform Cardinal Wolsey, Lord Keeper of the Great Seal, that his king had been slain; the disaffected nobles should be fast on the pigeon's heels.

Two hours to locate and smuggle the Ancient outside the palace before the pandemonium.

"This way, my lady." The page pushed open the chapel doors for her to pass through.

Ever the courtier, Renée had a smile and a coin for the servant. "Please make sure I am not disturbed." She watched him disappear round the corner and turned to her men. "One of you comes inside with me, the other plays lookout."

"I shall guard the door," Lieutenant Armado volunteered. "You go with madame, Sergeant. Mayhap you will remember something of import from your stay here. Go."

The door closed softly behind Renée and Sergeant Francesco. Candlelight illuminated dark oaken benches cushioned with scarlet velvet, frescoed walls depicting Christ, the Madonna, and a great number of saints. Lifting her eyes to the enormous white marble sculpture presiding over the candlelit altar, Renée was awestruck.

La Pietà was beautiful, the Blessed Virgin crying over the body of the Son of God held in Her arms. She and Francesco knelt and crossed themselves. As she did so, Renée surveyed the chamber beneath her eyelashes, ascertaining they were alone.

She pushed to her feet. "There must be a secret vault beneath the sculpture." She ran to the altar and felt the dais for hidden devices. Francesco mounted the dais to explore the sculpture. They investigated it thoroughly and came up with nothing. "We are overlooking something."

The door cracked open. "How goes?" Lieutenant Armado whispered.

"We cannot find the lever," Francesco answered.

"Search the chamber. It may be located anywhere. I will look outside." The door closed.

They continued their meticulous search without any results. "I say it is inside the sculpture." Francesco leaped onto the dais to reexamine the marble. "Cardinal Campeggio was embracing it fiercely when he vowed he would not leave without it. Mayhap it is the sculpture itself."

"We cannot carry around a mountain of marble, and I doubt the Secret Council encumbered Cardinal Campeggio with such a monument. No, it must be small enough to convey unnoticed."

"Madame, with all due respect, 'it' may be as big as a man."

"We could smuggle a man out without anyone noticing."

The door reopened. "Nothing outside," the lieutenant reported quietly. "Any news?"

"I am thinking we should try nudging the marble," Renée said. "I cannot move it myself, but the three of us might be able to do so."

The lieutenant joined them on the podium. They stood to one side, planting their feet on the ground, leaning their bodies against the cool slab of marble, and pushed.

A pennon pole protruding from the outer wall spared Michael from getting splashed over the muddy flagstones of the inner courtyard. He edged closer to the wall, fist after fist, feet dangling in the air, and smoothed his hand along the outer wall. His fingers latched on to a crevice. It did not seem deep enough to hold him, but his choices were limited. Flattened against the wall, he sought another crevice at knee level with his toecaps to hoist him upward. Once he found one, he started to scale the wall again, jabbing fingers into tiny cracks, spiderlike. The higher he climbed, the more amazed he became at his prowess. He was hanging on by the slightest toehold, by the tips of his fingers. At long last he reached the roof and crouched, looking for sentries. There was no one up here but him and birds' nests nestled in the gables. As he walked along the roof, he came upon a depression, wide and wet. He had to jump it. He took a few steps back to gain momentum and leaped, hurtling into the air, upward, higher, weightless . . . *Jupiter's thunder—he was flying!*

Michael glanced around him, beneath him, mystified. His body started sinking, softly. His feet touched the ground at a far greater distance than he had intended, hoped to jump.

What had just occurred, in the name of wonder?

Amazed beyond words, he tried it again, leaping from the ground, aiming straight up—and he was soaring again! Higher and higher, whooping in the drizzle, embracing the night with open arms, dropping his head back and laughing at the gray clouds and distantly winking stars.

At some point he began sinking. His feet touched the ground, kicked, and sent him upward again. Not a bird, but an outstanding hopper. Could he leap distances? he wondered.

A cry of agony pierced the night. *The queen!*

Michael stared across the chasm that was the inner court at the opposite wing of the palace. The queen was in travail, her ladies in panic. He should have been there, stalking the stalker. If he ran along the roof, he might be too late. The king would be sent for within moments.

Suddenly he knew he could make the jump. He felt alacritous, powerful, light-fast. "You are Hermes, wing-footed and nimble, you can do it." He chanted the words as a litany, his warm breath misting the air. He gauged the distance of the leap, moved backward to the rear edge of the roof, sucked in a lungful of air, and sprinted forward. *Faster, faster.* He kicked the rim of the roof and soared over the inner court, disallowing himself to fall into the chasm. . . .

He landed on his hands and one knee, head bent. He did it. He actually did it! There was no time for premature celebration, though. The queen was in agony—had Adele misled him?—and the king would come charging to her room any moment now. He lowered himself off the roof by its rim till he hung suspended, gently kicked open a window, and slunk inside a dark chamber.

Michael found himself in a small study chamber. Moving stealthily, he opened the door and peered at the darkened passageway. His ears were instantly assaulted with the female din coming from the queen's bedchamber. The scent of smoke told him someone had recently smothered the tapers in the wall sconces. The stench of an unwashed body filled his nostrils. A shadow stirred to his left. Two lifeless bodies lay on the floor. Dead guards. Beyond the closed doors to his left, voices shouted one after the other, "The king! The king! The king!" The doors burst open, and King Henry stormed in, his strapping form moving toward the queen's bedchamber.

The shadow stepped away from the wall, steel flashing in his hand. Michael did not hesitate. He lunged at the assassin, gripped the wrist wielding the dagger, and slammed it against the wall in front of the shocked King Henry. The assassin's rank sweat was strong in Michael's nostrils. Spanish expletives and spittle came at his face as he banged the dagger-clutching fist against the wall with brutal force, again and again. The fist refused to open and relinquish the hilt. Michael's grip tightened, pulverizing the wrist bones. The assassin howled in pain. His fingers went limp. The dagger clattered to the floor. Guards stampeded into the darkened corridor and surrounded the king. Outraged, the king bellowed for Norfolk and Marney, the Captain of the Guard.

Feeling triumphant, Michael meant to step back and let the yeomen take over when sharp pain exploded in his right side. He looked down and saw the assassin's gory fingers clutching another hilt, the blade of which was firmly embedded in Michael's liver. An ambidextrous assassin! The possibility never occurred to him. Pain throbbed and spread through his body, awakening rage. His eyes burned. It was happening again. Third time today. He gripped the bloody hand holding the stiletto to his liver and yanked the blade out. Blood gushed. His heartbeats slowed. He sensed the assassin's heart pumping blood to every organ in his malodorous body. With a hissing breath, Michael twisted the foreign hand upward and pushed the blood-smeared blade into the assassin's chest. The Spaniard twitched, struggled, whimpered. Petrified, he stared into Michael's eyes as the blade cut through the doublet and impaled his heart. His lips moved silently. The expression on his face as he breathed his last breath was one of sheer terror.

Everything blurred. Michael staggered back, pressing a hand to his side to stanch the flow of blood, and dropped to his knees, swaying; his head felt heavy. Vaguely he was aware of the royal bodyguard descending upon the scene like carrion crows on a fresh corpse. They pounced on the dead assassin sprawled on the floor, thinking to kill him all over again. They shielded their king from noyance. They grabbed Michael and pulled him away, shouting at his face, demanding to know who the pox he was and what he had been doing inside the secret chambers. Flames flared to life on the walls. The doors filled with shocked female and male spectators at both ends of the passageway, the queen's ladies and the king's gentlemen. The king demanded to see his wife and was escorted within a thick entourage of armed bodies, guards and nobles alike. A familiar voice shouted. "Put him down! He is not the assassin! He saved His Majesty's life!"

"God's teeth, Stanley, he is dying!" another familiar voice exclaimed hard by.

A cacophony of speculation arose on all sides.

"I am dying," Michael murmured to himself, surprised, his thoughts wandering haphazardly, his spirit weakening, sinking. *What did it mean to die?* "Little soul flitting away . . ."

"Michael!" Stanley's concerned face materialized before him.

"Fetch a surgeon, blockheads! He is innocent!" he shouted at the hovering guards. "Michael, what were you doing in there?"

Michael grinned sottishly as the world swam before his eyes. "You were saying about my liver? Not lily, is it?"

Stanley shoved something soft beneath his head. "Heated with too much wine, methinks. Now explain your whereabouts! Look at me! This is important! Did you lose your way?"

What little strength Michael possessed, it was ebbing rapidly. They thought him pickled, did they? A drunken hero—he liked the irony in that. "Aye, lost my way in a pottle of wine . . . and the man, the smelly guard with the knife. 'Pray, show me out, my good man,' I said. He took me up literally, see, thought to dispatch me to Hades with his fancy Spanish blade. Two dead guards on the floor . . ." He sagged, near finished. Death loomed . . . "I showed him—ha! Cutthroats in the royal palace, Stanley. The times we live in . . . Ahh, I am cold. It is sweet and honorable to die for my king. . . ." Darkness claimed him.

All their efforts were in vain! Lady Piety refused to give an inch! They stroked every inch of the monument. No hidden knobs, no lever. The sculpture refused to budge. The sand was running out. . . .

Overwhelmed with despair, Renée lifted her head at the sudden commotion in the hallway. "Armado, see what is afoot." She had not confided the conspiracy to them.

Francesco's perturbed gaze sped after the lieutenant. "Pray God they have not found the boat with our men. If Captain Luzio sees them, we are done."

"Shh," she said. "Do not invoke the devil."

Listening at the door, Lieutenant Armado returned his head inside. "There was an assassin at the king's palace, sent in to murder King Henry. Someone else died instead. Your Excellency!"

The door swung open all the way and a furious Rougé appeared. "What is going on in here? London is in turmoil, someone attempted to assassinate the King of England, and you prostrate yourself before Our Lady. We must return to the palace at once. The cardinal has already left."

"He did?" Renée inquired, hearing a hopeful ring in her head. Mayhap all was not lost. They could still get rid of the marquis and scour this house from top to bottom.

Rougé entered and shut the door behind him. "Listen to me, Renée. Whatever you are up to, you are putting yourself—and your men—in great peril. So far, their ridiculous disguises held, but Cardinal Campeggio is rallying his special guards. If they see you—"

Renée's spirit sank. The entire operation was a failure. She stood. "Fine. Let us depart."

As they hurried out the door, Cardinal Campeggio with two of his *deletoris* emerged in the corridor. The two parties almost collided. "Monsieur!" the cardinal cried.

"*Christus*," Sergeant Francesco whispered beside her, head bowed. "We are lost."

"Keep your eyes downcast, and we will walk out as we came in," she breathed quietly.

"Your Graces, I must beg you to take your leave," Cardinal Campeggio expressed in a tone of voice that was courteous but brooked no argument. "Disaster near struck England. My good brother the Cardinal of York bid me secure the grounds against outsiders. We must protect the Great Seal in case the ruthless authors of the treasonous act attempt to break in here and steal it. Please." He gestured for them to proceed.

Rougé led the way, everyone else perforce falling into step behind him.

The march to the dockage was the longest of Renée's life. She could not recall an instance in which breathing in the chilly night air and being assaulted with needling rain imbued her with a more profound sense of freedom and relief. They were safe—but they had failed. She had failed.

She would have to start plotting afresh. She would also have to do something about Rougé. The snake knew more than he had let her believe. How much more was he still concealing?

Sitting in the barge on their way back to the king's palace, Rougé observed, "You have yet to ask me who forfeited his life in exchange for the king's."

"Who?" Renée asked distractedly. She hoped the queen and her unborn babe fared well.

"Some drunk who lost his way and stumbled by accident into the royal study chamber."

"Some drunk?" she repeated, watching the murky riverbank float by, lamenting her failure. Suddenly it hit her. Her gaze veered to Rougé. "Does he have a name?"

A cruel smile peeled his lips from his teeth. "Michael Devereaux. Is he not your Irishman?"

❧ 13 ❧

Death is nothing to us,
And it concerns us not a scrap.

—Lucretius: *De Rerum Natura*

"He lives, Your Majesty, by a blessed miracle after mine learned opinion," affirmed Dr. Linacre, the king's chief physician and founder of the Royal College of Physicians. "At first his heart was still, but the flesh was alive. He twitched and thrashed like a wild animal, making feral sounds, and demanding his dragon, in delirium for loss of blood. Four men held him down as my learned colleague Sergeant Surgeon Vicary sealed and dressed his wound. I am inclined to think the amount of drink Master Devereaux had put away tonight sustained him through the tribulations of near death. Most baffling, sire, and marvelous, as Our Lord's miracles are wont to be."

The king's gaze was fixed on the wan, agonized figure occupying the bed. "Be it a marvel or a scientific discovery, Doctor, we trow it merits a new chapter in your informative book."

"Your Majesty is most gracious." The doctor bowed his head at the compliment.

Sergeant Surgeon Thomas Vicary, master of the newly formed Guild of Barber Surgeons, known as the king's leech, took his cue from his superior in medical importance and embarked on his account. "Your Majesty, I have cleansed, stitched, and poulticed his wound right properly. His skin, I observed, has remarkable healing powers. No sooner had I sealed the wound than he—" A discreet cough from his confrere nudged him back on course. "Alas, he is not out of the dark wood yet, Your Majesty. He has lost a firkin of blood. Fever and putrefaction are dire concerns. Blood poisoning may yet ripen. We shall be better informed on the morrow, Your Majesty."

"Thank you, good doctors. I read in your faces that you are content with his recovery thus far. Stanley, repeat Master Devereaux's heroic valediction once more," the king commanded.

"'It is sweet and honorable to die for my king . . .' sire."

"Sweet and honorable . . . My lords," the king addressed his entourage. "I commend Master Devereaux unto you with high regard and affection. This man placed our person before and above his own. With selfless disregard to his life, he launched himself at a naked blade meant for us, before our very eyes, demonstrating courage, loyalty, and enterprise. In foiling the most vicious attack on our God-anointed grace, he frustrated our enemies of their insidious design for our throne and secured himself an honorable place at our court for life. He is our fearless shield!"

As the courtiers murmured their solemn approval, the king looked at his chief physician and barber surgeon. "Keep him alive. He is dear to us. We shall expect an account of his recovery on the morrow." In a flurry of fur-lined velvet, he marched outside, half the court forming his wake.

Alive and suffering for it, Michael groaned at the inconceivable pain. Were he in Elysium, he would be knocking gilt goblets of nectar with the gods. The burning-prickling sensation in his side was insupportable, driving him insane. "Stanley," he gritted, summoning his friend from the circle of Their Graces of Suffolk and other concerned individuals. "The queen? The babe?"

"Both well, thank God. The good doctor attributes the pains to food poisoning. However, as no one else seems to be suffering any ill effects, including Her Majesty's taster, Norfolk believes the culprit is one of her close attendants and is interrogating her household."

"Stanley . . . do something for me." Michael grimaced, squeezing his eyelids shut. "Please—"

"Priest? You want to be shriven? But Dr. Linacre said—"

"No priest!" His injured side burned and throbbed with a pulse of its own. Besides the pain, his maw felt as though it had been scratched raw with pumice powder. He could barely speak. He needed his remedy, his potion. . . . "Send everyone out. Give me time . . . alone. Pippin!"

"Yes, master?" His manservant came to hover on his other side.

"I cannot breathe. . . ." He was burning up, tumbling in and out of lucidity. "Open a window. Keep everyone out . . . stand guard outside . . . till I call you back. Go. Now!"

"This is not the time to hide your grandam's pearls, runt. You need to be looked after."

"Do not argue . . . *please*. I—must—have—a—moment—alone," Michael enunciated gruelingly.

"As you wish." Grunting his disapproval, Stanley politely herded Their Graces of Suffolk, the good doctor, who required a bit of prodding, and other curious visitors out the door.

"I am closing the door, master!" Pippin announced before he retreated to the hallway.

A gust of cool air rushed in through the open window. Michael sucked deeply of it, resigned to the task at hand. He could not afford to delay, or he would surely die. He was on the edge.

The tight linen bandage hugging his midsection constrained his movements as he rolled onto his uninjured side with tremendous effort and anguish and reached under the bed for the casket. His forefinger barely touched the metal handle. Cursing viciously, he played with the ring till he managed to hook it, then dragged the casket along the floor. He collapsed on his stomach, panting and juddering. Perspiration dampened his skin. His eyelids sank with exhaustion. If only he had a confidant, someone he could entrust with his life, a helpmate . . . There was no one. Not even Pippin, who had been with him for years, would serve a master infected with the Sweat.

Assuring himself that the hard part was behind him, Michael yanked the leather thong from around his neck and with trembling fingers sought the casket's lock. Everything took forever: inserting the key, unlocking the bolt, opening the casket. He grabbed one of the glass bottles and lifted it to the bed. *Perdition.* It was empty. He replaced it in the casket and chose another. His second selection was a winner. He unsealed the bottle with his teeth and fastened his lips around the rim, tipping his head back. The first drop was divine, the second better, the third climactic. . . .

Sweet vitality rushed through Michael's veins. The good doctor, he reflected, lolling on his stomach, ought to provide the recipe for dragon's blood in his informed book in lieu of his inane observations. He returned the empty bottle to his dwindling hoard and ascertained that his two additional treasures, Buckingham's dagger and Tyrone's secret ring, were safely stashed inside the casket. Despite having promised his noble lord to never wear the ring at court, temptation drove him to slide it onto his forefinger and gaze at the draconian she-serpent. Strength, pride, and a profound sense of belonging washed over him, sentiments the Devereaux gules pricked in his wrist never inspired. He felt restored, invincible . . . He feared nothing—and nothing on this earth had the power to destroy him. He relinquished his natural sire to his older offspring and thanked the gods for the living parent he knew and admired, a valiant loyalist, a great man.

He locked the casket, shoved it under the bed, and retied the leather thong round his neck. He reclined on his back and let out a cathartic sigh. The drink dulled his pain and saturated his mind with blissful tranquility, the kind one enjoyed after a hard tumbling, only a hundred times better. Whether the morrow should find him breathing or lifeless, he had his moment of grace. *The king's fearless shield . . . is dear to us.* If only the little schemer were here to see him shine. He fancied laying his head in her soft, sweet-scented lap like her fallen angel, wearing her gentle fingers for laurels. He would never see her again. He cursed and cursed and cursed. . . .

Money bags impaired memories. Large trunks coming in and out of places were forgotten in a shiny wink. Renée was on pins and needles, back in the king's palace, tidying her effects while her despotic tire-woman oversaw the hanging of tapestries and the reassembling of the four-poster bed brought from France. Two hours past midnight, and the men were slaving for Adele without so much as a peep. They all knew that come morning every table, trunk, footcloth, cushion, and stool had to be exactly where it had been before. No one was to know of the near departure.

The Duke of Norfolk, Earl Marshal of England, aided by Sir Henry Marney, the Captain of the Guard, had begun questioning the queen's household. Had Anne been interviewed? Had she blabbed? The interviews would continue on the morrow. Would Renée be summoned?

Was Michael dead or alive?

The snippets of gossip Renée had plucked upon her return to the palace were contradictory. Some said he lived; others swore he had died. Renée thought him the bravest fool that ever lived. Jesu help her, she admired him for cajoling the details out of Anne and for his amazing heroics. She did not doubt that he had been sober.

Bone weary, rosary in hand, lips silently saying the Aves, the Gloria, and the Paternoster for his sake, she returned every ornament to its former place—and waited.

The guard she had sent to inquire after Michael returned. "What news?" she demanded.

"He lives. The king's doctor says it is a miracle. The king dubbed him 'my fearless shield.'"

Renée closed her eyes on an Ave Maria, thanked the Blessed Virgin for sparing the fool, and vowed to distribute alms and largesse to the poor people and the religious houses of London.

Adele snorted from the bedchamber. "I told you he lived."

Renée scowled. "I do not trust these English savants. Mayhap—"

"Leave him be. He does not require my concoctions. That one cannot die." She crossed her thumb and forefinger against Satan and returned to ordering her slaves about.

"Parochial old pest," Renée muttered after Adele's retreating back.

The guard coughed. "Madame, a page delivered this early this evening."

One would think that with all the excitement she would not be moved, but she was. Renée snatched the missive and went to the fire to read it:

> *As lily-white she goes,*
> *Complexioned like the rose,*
> *She robs me of my rest.*

Renée chuckled. How incongruent—and yet welcome—the silly poem was with all that had betided her tonight. A ray of light. Her mystery poet lit up her foul mood. She had been sorry to leave without ever finding out who Perdu was. Now she would have another chance at unveiling the shy rhymer. Not all was bleak in her world. She had made contact with Cardinal Wolsey. He was selecting a husband for her. Tomorrow she would ponder how to use that to her advantage. All she needed to do was keep her spirits up and avoid Anne. She read the rest:

> *Of girls discreet and wise*
> *She proudly bears the prize*
> *As loveliest and best.*
> *This lady lives in the west,*
> *The fairest of noble kind;*
> *And heaven man would find*
> *At nighttime as her guest!*

Perversely—and possibly because Adele had forced down another calming cordial down her throat upon her return—the last line made Renée giggle. Michael had predicted correctly. Her poet seemed to have mustered an ounce of red-bloodedness to trawl for a midnight invitation. But how could she invite him to be her guest if he concealed his identity? She read the signature:

> *Written with the hand of him whom you have deserted to his woe.*
> *Perdu (a soldier lost to a forlorn hope)*

Her nerves prickled. The poet knew she had left but not that she had returned. "Franco!" she delayed the guard from resuming his post outside her door. "Has anyone been sniffing around my apartment while I was gone?"

The guard frowned. "Yes, there was someone, a gentleman."

"What did he look like?"

"Do not play the goose," Adele scoffed in the doorway. "You know what he looked like."

Renée whipped toward her, still clutching the poem. "Was he here? You spoke to him?"

"Raphael is rotting in a French prison for you."

"I thought you disapproved of Raphael."

"Better him than the other one." Adele harrumphed.

Renée sank on the stool before the fire and reread the poem. "The rose." It had to be Michael. He was Perdu. And he had ridiculed her poet so. Oh, how she had defended him to his own ears! He must have had several good laughs at her expense. And still he kept sending her love poems.

An image of Michael with Anne came to haunt her. The night she had taught him primero, he had adamantly refused to see the woman. He had insisted that dallying with married ladies was not his métier. He did not give a fig for the strumpet. *I gave you something to spy on.*

He had been so angry. Hurt by her mistreadings. She had been playing with him. He knew. If only that knave Walter had kept a still tongue! Michael's deed had been retaliatory. Defending a lady's honor in a duel, a lady one believed was pure as snow, only to learn afterward that the entire court sang of her transgressions, was a bitter brew to swallow, particularly for a gentleman, which Michael clearly was, in sharp contrast to his half sibling.

Michael's insight into her nature was not entirely wide of the mark. She was pellucid to him. She liked him, and she knew he liked her. That was the trouble. She took out Raphael's portrait medal and gazed at it. She reread the poem. Truth versus fancy. Retaining clarity was a challenge when one was removed from one's natural life. There was a decision to be made here.

"Madame." The men emerged from the bedchamber. They looked effete. "All is in order."

Adele grunted approval. The apartment was satisfactorily put together again, as if she had never left. "I am most grateful for your help. God give you a good night."

"Come to bed, child."

"Not yet." With a heavy heart, Renée took her rosary, knelt on her hassock at the prie-dieu, and repeated the Aves, the Gloria, and the Paternoster for another soul. The man whose blood was on her hands. The expected knock came soon after the men had left. A cheerless Sergeant Francesco walked into her apartment. They stared at each other. It was done.

❧ 14 ❧

The empty-handed traveler will
sing in the presence of the robber.

—Juvenal

Michael opened his eyes to a hint of daylight. An imposing, corpulent man loured over him; the bloodred tint of his hat and gown proclaiming his willingness to die for his faith. Shrewd eyes perused him from tip to toe and rested on his face. Michael blinked as his slumberous brain identified his visitor with shocking clarity. Cardinal Wolsey, the man he most wished to impress. The cunning chancellor, determined to have his finger on the pulse of the kingdom, would not be circumvented by the earl marshal and the captain of the guard in their pursuit of intelligence.

"Your Eminence!" Michael elbowed himself up against the pillows, realized in amazement that no sensation of pain resulted, and groaned to camouflage his perplexity. "Pardon my . . ." *Receiving you in my Holland drawers and naught besides . . .* By the gods, there was no pain!

An alien servant settled an alien, high-backed chair beside the bed. The visitor made use of it. "Leave us." The command propelled the servant to grab the snoring Pippin by the scruff of his nightshirt collar and prod him out the door, protesting unintelligibly. As soon as they were alone, the cardinal demanded, "What were you doing outside Her Majesty's bedchamber last night?"

Michael was thankful that his wounded, bedraggled appearance lent him more credence than he deserved. "I do not rightly recall. With Your Grace's pardon, looking for the jakes, I believe."

"Your defense does not wash, sir! The guards would have stopped a drunkard!"

"With all due respect, Eminence, they did not stop the man who mistook my liver for his scabbard. Faithfully, I cannot account for my whereabouts. I do not know how I came to be at the place that I was. Should Your Grace beg me lead him thither, I would not know the way."

"Whom do you serve? Who was the man you have killed? What did you put in Her Majesty's physic? Out with it! Ere I stretch the truth out of you on the rack. . . ."

Michael felt dully besieged. "I would I had answers, Eminence! Alack, I have none to offer, save that I recall stumbling in the dark, fighting a fierce need to, eh, relieve myself, and this man came at me out of nowhere. When I asked for directions, he pointed the way to Hades."

The cardinal leaned back stolidly, hands laced. "Why did you come to court?"

Michael marshaled his scattering thoughts into battle lines. "To represent my noble protector at the tournaments, to heap honors and distinctions upon the house of Tyrone, and, eh, to make my worthy lord proud of his heir, Your Grace." A touch of diffidence could not hurt, he felt.

"Ambitious, are you? Some would call it a vice. I say ambition breeds greatness, with proper nourishing, that is. Think carefully. What can you tell me of the man who attacked you?"

Michael laid a gentle hand over the dressing hugging his mid-section. "He cursed in Spanish, stunk to high heavens, and was ambidextrous. That is all I remember, I swear before God."

"How did you overcome him with his blade in your liver?"

A sixth sense told Michael he was being measured for something other than a noose. Did the cardinal see something worth cultivating? As he had done with Suffolk? "A theological question, Your Eminence. Why would My Lord Christ spare this sinner? Has He a greater task for me in the offing? And to this I reply, Behold, here I am." He had been listening at Mass.

The cardinal's lips twitched to mask a smile. "And should I have a task for you?"

Michael met the narrow-prying eyes squarely, soberly. "Behold, here I am."

"It has come to my attention that on the day of your arrival an usher played a nasty trick on you, lodging you in the undercroft, and that thanks to a strong word from Lady Renée of France, you were bestowed in this fine chamber. Are you well acquainted with Her Grace?"

Not as well as he would have liked, and in view of her cruel abandonment, there was not much chance of his ever furthering the acquaintance. "I have had the pleasure of conversing and dancing with Her Grace on occasion. I found her to be a most charming and gracious princess."

"Another incident to have reached my ears was the matter of your quarrel with His Grace of Norfolk's master of the horse, one Sir Walter Devereaux, I believe."

"Sir Walter was offended at the discovery that we shared the same male parent. He called me out in hopes of dispatching the insult to our mutual sire." He caught the slight narrowing of the cardinal's eyes and knew his half-truth was noted. He rectified his error of judgment. "My coming upon him at an inopportune moment while he was forcefully importuning a certain lady of this court gave Sir Walter the excuse he was trawling for, Your Eminence." His confessing the entirety of it while sparing Renée of obloquy offered justification for his slip.

"His Majesty is pleased with you, dubs you 'his fearless shield.' I trow he has good reason to. I, myself, defer judgment. Incidentally, have you any designs on an office at court or do your aspirations amount to replacing your liege lord in good time as Lord Lieutenant of Ireland?"

"My aspiration, Your Eminence, is to serve my king and the great men who serve him."

"His Grace of Buckingham and my lord of Northumberland have high offices aplenty for the constant sword arm. They would offer good lordship to His Majesty's fearless shield."

Cardinal Wolsey knew who the authors of the crime were, Michael realized. Ergo, this was a damp finger in the air to determine where the wind of his loyalty was blowing. He contemplated unearthing the dagger he had expropriated from Buckingham. He could fib that he had wrenched it from the Spanish assassin in the heat of the scuffle and withal send Buckingham to the block in the cardinal's tumbrel, but would it be wise? He might inadvertently implicate Anne and through her Renée. Maybe, for the nonce, he should keep this card up his sleeve and see how the inquest progressed. His wearing the pelt of an ingénue seemed to allay the cardinal's suspicions. Why temper with success? "If that be the sole office available for a man of my talents, who is not propped by ancestry, I had as lief serve my king and my noble lord in Ireland, Your Grace."

The cardinal stood. Michael, for all intents and purposes his bed's prisoner, inclined his head respectfully. It was not until the great man and his chair had gone that he noticed the ring Tyrone had given him was missing from his forefinger. He had forgotten to remove it last night!

Pippin came in, ushering two men: Norfolk and Marney. Masking his agitation, Michael fell back against the pillows and answered their questions: how he entered the secret chambers, if he knew the man he killed, how he prevailed over a trained assassin in a drunken, injured state, and if he had knowledge of anyone desirous of harming the king's grace. He offered the same replies he had given the cardinal, putting false emphasis on the tenderness of his wound.

In contrast to Cardinal Wolsey, Norfolk and Marney took no special interest in him. His tale and his delicate condition seemed to hold well against their scrutiny. They grunted and nodded and left. They had not even bothered to sit down. He doubted they would question him further.

With a curse, he leaped out of bed and stripped it bare, thinking the ring might have fallen off. A striped black-and-white feather floated upward to tickle his nose. Michael snatched it from the air and studied its serrated edges: an owl again. Unless storks, the harbingers of happiness and prosperity, were giving lessons in transporting goods, he doubted an owl had pilfered his ring. He crushed the feather in his fist and rummaged around the heap of sheets, blankets, pillows, and coverlet. To his despair, the ring was not in his bedclothes. He searched the locked casket under the bed, the floor, the garderobe, the cupboard, the trunks. The ring was nowhere to be found.

"Pippin!" he bellowed, plucking his manservant from a gossip with fellow attendants in the hallway. "Has anyone besides you set foot in this chamber while I slept?"

"Not that I know of . . . Forsooth!" Pippin howled at the havoc Michael had wreaked.

"I have misplaced my lord's ring, Pippin. You must help me find it in this hodge-pudding."

Lines appeared in Pippin's brow as his attention shifted to his master. "Sir, your wound."

He did not feel a thing. "Bother that. Find the ring." He stepped into the stool chamber and secured the arras. After relieving himself, he sat down to inspect his wound. Something uncanny had bechanced him last night. He needed to get to the bottom of it. His heart pounded fiercely as he rolled off the thick linen strip hugging his midsection. Neither aches nor discomfort ensued. The linen wads, visible beneath the strip, sported a large blotch of dried blood that seemed to affix them to his side buckramlike. Ripping these off would hurt like the dickens and bring forth a gush of fresh blood. Was it necessary? He steeled himself with a deep breath and set the linen bale aside. To his astonishment, the wads fell off and with them the surgeon's embroidery!

Slack-jawed, Michael stared at the side the assassin had gored and churned into a quagmire with a dairymaid's delight and found no evidence of the night's misadventure. The wound had vanished without a trace! Save for dry bloodstains bedaubing his epidermis, the skin was smooth as a babe's. He poked at the flesh and felt the healthy resistance of muscle tissue. His left side was in the pink, too, no dry blood there. The wound had healed. *Unbelievable!* What sorcery was this? *Venēnum*: potion, poison, or witchcraft? His brain demurred at the fraudful travesty: Was he insane? Was his memory impaired? Was his grasp of the present utterly warped?

A whole new set of troubles landed on his shoulders like packed panniers on an ox. How the devil would he defend the desertion of his wound to the doctor and the leech should they insist upon changing his dressing? *Good sirs, I am bodily robust and frantic-mad in spirit. . . .*

A murrain on Donough O'Hickey! Were he in Ireland, he would hunt down the cackling dotant and whack the truth out of him with a sword. Dragon's blood, his arse! This was sorcery! No wonder the old man told him to keep mum about the potion. He could burn for this!

Putting his head between his knees, Michael attempted to navigate the maelstrom that was his mind. He had contracted the Sweat but lived. A Spanish butcher had demolished his liver, but the sturdy organ had recovered overnight. He was stronger, sharper, faster. He sensed bucks from leagues away, leaped like a giant grasshopper, was inordinately and uncomfortably sentient . . .

The king's fearless shield examined his healed side. Sorcery or not, he mused, why fall apart over a marvel of the universe? He would conceal his abnormalities from the eyes of the court, and upon his return to Ireland, he would hunt down the healer and unravel the mystery.

With this thought in mind, Michael retied the linen girdle, careful to stuff the bloodstained patches over the absent wound. He was so much closer to accomplishing his goals. True, he was here out of a sense of duty but also to test his mettle. He did not need a beautiful witch misruling his mind, his cod, and the stupid organ in between. He should thank the gods for her departure. His wise lord had strictly cautioned him against such distractions. Contrary to his stubble-deep, forgettable dalliance with Anne, cavorting with Renée would have been an act of out-and-out insubordination. His task done, Michael reentered his chamber. Tyrone's pagan ring had to be found, and the Right Reverend Cardinal of York had yet to be sufficiently impressed.

Thoughts of her failed enterprise, of the inquest, and mostly of Lieutenant Armado Baglioni had robbed Renée of sleep, but by sunup she had her weapons amassed, polished, and fit to be deployed. She would press the connubial matter with Cardinal Wolsey, as a means to gain access to the Ancient, and call on her bashful poetaster. She anticipated great sport at the encounter.

Most importantly, Renée decided to continue playing the game. Her heart was in France.

First thing, she had to make her obeisance to the poor queen and inquire after her well-being. She regretted assisting Buckingham and his traitorous allies in their plot. In her haste to return to Raphael, she had hurt Queen Katherine, acted on supposition instead of on definite information, blundered and floundered, and taken a stranger into her confidence. She would begin afresh. She would not rush the business. The Ancient had been safe in its vault in Rome for centuries. There was no reason to think it could be easily stolen, or Cardinal Medici would not have bought Brittany for her. The assignment called for delicate fingers as well as patience.

Sir Walter Devereaux ambushed her outside her apartment. "My lady, I come to apologize."

Stonelike, Renée instructed, "Sergeant, pray remove the excrement from my path." She did not break stride as two of her three guards dealt with the obnoxious pest. Sir Walter did not dare follow. "Sergeant Francesco, I would resume my training this afternoon. Yesterday that vermin held me in a position from which I could not extract myself. I do not care to be caught in a defenseless position ever again."

"Very good, madame. We shall begin with the position you were unfortunate to be caught in yesterday and work our way to harder clenches. May I also suggest shooting butt-shafts?"

"I place myself in your instructive hands."

Cheerful sunrays played cache-cache with Renée through the tiny multihued diamond panes lining the way to Her Majesty's apartment. She was shocked to find Lady Anne Hastings playing Cerberus to Queen Katherine's private chambers, only in reverse.

"I am sorry, Lady Norris," Anne apologized fulsomely. "Her Majesty's physicians attend on her at present. She cannot be disturbed. May I take your message?"

After Lady Norris tearfully communicated her regards and blessings, Renée sashayed forth, her courtier's visor of pleasantness in place. "Good morrow, Anne. How fares Her Majesty?"

Anne let out an affected sigh. "What an ordeal, Renée! I cannot tell you how worried we all were. His Majesty had tears in his eyes, can you imagine? I do not think I have ever seen him so. He has sworn to make a barefooted pilgrimage to the Priory of Our Lady of Walsingham to give thanks for Her Grace's recovery. And our poor, sweet queen! When the learned Señor de Vittoria and Señor de la Sá concurred that the horrific convulsions were the result of an upset stomach, she insisted on spending the night on her knees at her prie-dieu, clinging to the holy girdle of her name-saint, and sent the keeper of her privy purse to fill the coffers of St. Catherine's Hospital. Naturally Her Grace is exhausted this morning. How was your supper with the Cardinal of York?"

Renée did not recall discussing her plans with Anne. Then again, very little went unnoticed at court. She found Anne's sangfroid bloodcurdling, especially since Anne was the one who had poisoned the queen with the intention of killing the unborn heir and was aware by now that the "remedy" Renée had provided was semi-helpful. In keeping with the masquerade they seemed to be playing with each other, Renée inquired, "And how are you faring? I trust you are . . . better?"

Anne's swift smile was startlingly genuine. "Oh yes, indeed! You are a godsend."

"I am glad." Renée's lips twitched in an agony of a smile. Anne literally turned her stomach. How could Michael touch this woman? She hoped he had had a good bathing. In view of things, bringing up the matter of the inquest struck her as unwise. The less said the better. Anne was more dangerous than Renée had surmised. "I should very much like to visit with the queen, but I understand les señores are with her. Pray tell Her Majesty that I was terribly distressed to hear of her woeful ordeal and give thanks for her recovery. I shall return later today."

The doors opened, and animated Spanish poured out as the physicians took their leave.

Renée moved to enter, but Anne blocked her path. "Her Majesty cannot be disturbed!"

The alarm in Anne's eyes shattered Renée's latest assessment of her yet again. She wanted to snap at her, *Why would I blab to the queen? Did I not give you the vial, you idiotic hypocrite?* Mayhap Anne had a talent for pretense but she was not, after all, wondrously shrewd.

Sir Walter's fair sister, the widow Margaret Clifford, came out, a buck-basket full of dirty linen riding on her hip. She bobbed with a bright smile that reminded Renée of Michael. "My Lady Renée, would you like me to inquire if Her Majesty would receive you?"

Renée blinked in surprise. "Yes, I would. My thanks."

A moment later she was ushered inside, leaving an agitated Anne in her wake.

Dr. Linacre and Sergeant Surgeon Vicary brought a third colleague to inspect the patient. Dr. Chamber had qualified at Padua before serving King Henry's royal sire as physician and apothecary. The three savants, assisted by apprentices, hovered over Michael like carrion crows, poking and prodding his face and chest with cold instruments for talons, and, astonished at his healthful signs, muttered educated observations without opinion. In short, they learned nothing.

Then Vicary, the pragmatic leech, decided to inspect the wound. Espying the shining probe and the lancet, Michael cringed against the pillows, fluttering like a skittish virgin, swatting at the cold hands. "My good man!" he cried, smiling tightly. "I have spent an entire night growing back my pelt and replenishing my blood. Surely ripping the buckram wound open would damage my recovery if not overturn my condition, which would be a most lamentable mishap, for I have sworn to give funds for a score of lectureships at Oxford and Cambridge, as well as to the Royal College of Physicians, the Guild of Barber Surgeons, and to the Guild of Apothecaries, to further research into medical science. Gentlemen, I assure you that my manservant is skilled at changing dressings. As you see, I am improving by leaps and bounds. Let us not remonstrate with success. I trust His Majesty will be contented to hear of the miracle you have performed on my person."

The scholars conferred on the matter and agreed to let Pippin nousle his master. Michael breathed a sigh of relief when they left with the promise to return for a later inspection.

* * *

Availing himself of the fair weather, King Henry abandoned interior tedium for the delights of hawking. Michael heard the gallants strut off with the sullenness of a boy sent to bed without supper. Searching his chamber for Tyrone's ring to no avail further soured his mood.

By midmorning, Michael found little to cheer him up. Disgusted with his begrimed self, he ordered a luxurious bath and sent Pippin outside while he submerged in the cool, soapwort water, indulging in a long, quiet bucking. He saved the bloodstained linen patches for further use.

By noontime, the king returned. The merry party burst upon Michael with gusty exuberance, King Henry marching in with a score of gentlemen in tow, servitors carrying in flagons of wine and platters of viands on their heels, to find the patient abed, sporting a velure housecoat over Rennes lawn undergarments, and resting against a mountain of cushions like a dying pope minus the skullcap. "We are right glad to see you on the mend, Devereaux!" The king gestured for him to be at ease when Michael made a move to clamber from the bed into a formal bow. "Wait till you hear of our new merlins, goshawks, and peregrines—awe and terror, my fearless shield!"

"Thrills and chills!" Wyatt intoned, a nasal *secondo* to King Henry's baritone *primo*.

"My new Irish raptors took to the sky like a peleton of harpies!"

"English game shall never be the same!"

Grateful to Pippin for perspicaciously forewarning him of the royal visit, Michael listened to gory tales of Celtic talons and cunning Brit game. "If it please Your Grace, I should like to write to my noble lord of Your Majesty's delight with his modest gifts."

"Modest! Ha! Yes, do so! Make our most hearty recommendations to my Lord Tyrone, for we love him well. Mention that his generosity does not go unnoticed. My lord treasurer tells me I may fund new ships if I so deign to sell the birds, which I never will." Standing akimbo at the center of the room, fists planted on hips, King Henry perused his bedridden shield. "You have thrice pleased us now." He ticked Michael's feats on his fingers. "The hart, the hawks, the defense of our person . . ." He elapsed into silent deliberation. Michael hoped King Henry was considering bestowing him with a reward for his services. He was opting for a knighthood.

Female laughter interrupted the royal thought process. Several of the queen's ladies, Bessie Blount, Anne Hastings, Elizabeth Carew, Meg Clifford, and Her Grace of Suffolk among them, flounced into the crowded chamber and dropped into curtsies. "Her Majesty is in good health and sends Your Grace her greeting," they informed the king, while his fellow huntsmen, bursting with vim and vigor, took the ladies' arrival for a tucket on the bugle and a new chase commenced.

"We come to see the fearless shield," the gorgeous Elizabeth Carew told her brother, Sir Francis Bryan, in hushed tones. "Introduce us."

In the ensuing hour, Michael was treated to fawning, crooning, blatant invitations guised as flirtation, questions about his life in Ireland, his artistic tastes, and his interests, and held court as a slothful sultan. With the snug setting conspiring with the wine to render the mixed company merrier, by cockshut time, as the evening twilight painted the windowpanes a spectacular purple, everyone was soused and disposed for supper and the amorous disport of the bedchamber.

The party departed, leaving Stanley, Suffolk, and a flagon of Bordeaux behind. Michael was grateful for their company. They were splendid pewfellows, the best he ever had. Their lives did not depend on Lord Tyrone and their eyes did not glaze over at five-syllable words.

"You ought to be proud of yourself, runt." Stanley slurred his speech. He hoicked himself onto the bed, caught a spilth of wine on his jerkin, and took care to overhang his crossed ankles. "Two royal visits—Harry has done you a great honor, mind you!—and a flock of nursemaids jostling for your attention, eager to wait on you hand and foot. I daresay you have arrived."

"That used to be me once upon a time," Suffolk waxed nostalgic, refilling their winecups.

Stanley snorted. "You had wet nurses till you celebrated—what? Your thirtieth birthday?"

"My third wedding, the day I generously bequeathed my wet nurses unto you, Stanley."

"And the day I handfast myself to beauteous Meg, I shall confer them unto the runt here."

"He has plenty of his own. Give mine back."

"I will keep them for the nonce, if it please Your Grace, as I am not yet wedded."

Michael, not unsoused himself, placed his hand over his heart in mock gesture. "Gentlemen, your speech makes me shudder to the marrow. Why should you be inconstant when you are happily matched?"

"You have it backward." Suffolk's ironic tone told of connubial bliss taxed with sacrifice. "A man is constant afore he is made happy and desires to be inconstant a moment after."

"Hark, runt. Merry is the man who never marries!"

They drank to that.

"Where was Harry in a hurry to be off to? Spain?" Stanley inquired.

"Judging by the smile worn by Mistress Blount, I'd say Jericho." Suffolk looked at Michael. "This is not to be bruited abroad."

"Aw, Michael knows to be discreet. Harry keeps a house on the river Jordan near Chipping Ongar, Jericho Manor. And speaking of Spain, tell us about your clash with the assassin. Does your wound make you suffer much? I hear Marney has the stiletto what cut you."

Michael regaled them with specifics as best he could without shocking them to the marrow, the tale differing little from the one he had narrated to Wolsey, Norfolk, and Marney.

"I do not suppose you will feel fit to participate in the upcoming tournaments, eh?" Suffolk queried. "I should like to have a go at you. Not much sport to be had with Stanley."

"The devil!" Stanley spluttered.

There was a light rap on the door. Pickled Pippin rose from his truckle bed in the far corner and galumphed to investigate. At the draft of ambergris and lavender, Michael's heart stopped.

Suffolk, on his feet, sketched a dashing albeit unsteady bow. "My lady, how kind you are to call on our injured friend. The dear boy, having lost a firkin of lifeblood, has scarcely responded to our nursing." He sent Michael a wink of a onetime rakehell.

Stanley, noting the taut expression on Michael's face, joined Suffolk at the door. Still they lingered, winking, giving him an archer's two-finger gesture. Michael sent them a warning look of dismissal couched with a tight-lipped smile. "You are capital companions. Your never-failing cheer raises poor souls in affliction." When Renée turned her head, he mouthed, *Out!*

"Let us withdraw, Your Grace. I see her very presence infuses genuine balm into his blood."

The drunken wits shuffled out, bowing and flourishing fulsomely. "Adieu!"

"Au revoir!" Suffolk caught Pippin by the scruff of the neck and dragged him out, too.

Embarrassed by their transparent fooleries, Michael smiled apologetically, tense and elated. She was back. Why had she left?

Renée glided forward. A smile softened her moist, rosy lips; her violet gaze glimmered with untold secrets in the diminishing candlelight. "My eyes tell me you are in health."

His eyes—gliding over her, touching but not touching—wished they were hands. Had he not so much to conceal, he would do something rash. All his excellent new resolutions flew out the window at the sight of her. All he ever wanted in a woman—and much more than he imagined—coalesced and manifested in the vision before him. With a little more heart, he might be content with an easier conquest, but as the saying went: he whose game was the eagle took no heed of sparrows. The principle reins of his character were ambition, constancy, and pride—and he wanted Renée de Valois more than he ever wanted anything else in his life. "Please, sit."

A stool, dragged over by his visitors, stood hard by the bed. She ignored it. "I can only stay a moment." With a rustle of sarcenet she sank gracefully on the edge of the bed beside him. She sat ramrod straight, close enough to touch and yet leagues away. "My poetaster has mustered the courage to unmask himself. We are to meet in the queen's privy garden on the hour bell."

"*What?*" Michael vaulted from the pillows but remembered his "wound" and sank back with a grimace. There was much to be discussed between them, and yet . . . "I loudly protest, madame. As I recall, we had a wager. Was it not I who foretold that Minstrel Jack would toss in a probe in his subsequent magnum opus? Since he has, it seems fair that you should defer the event—wherein I have won the right to participate—to a time when I may accompany you."

The little pantry of mysteries and enticements bestowed him with a witchy quirk of her lips. "I never said he had put in a probe. Nor that he had written again."

Michael scowled. "How did you communicate with him, then? I find this suspect."

She shrugged phlegmatically. "His man spoke to my guard and—" She faltered at the chime of the hour bell. "Ooo! I must go!" She jumped to her feet and cringed in pain.

He was beside her in a heartbeat, his hand on her slender back. His voice was thick with concern. "What is it? Are you hurt? Did that jackslave Walter—?"

"No." She winced, kneading her kidneys. "I, eh, did this to myself. I ill-used a muscle."

Michael calmed. He tried not to grin. "Been training hard at the quintain, eh?"

"Do not tease! It hurts." She craned her head up to meet his gaze. "Shouldn't you be abed? Surely your injury hurts more than mine does."

He half turned her to stand with her back to him. "May I? I am not untried in muscle aches." At her curt nod, he replaced her hands and gently rolled his thumbs against the stiff knots in her lower back, eliciting groans of pleasure. She was so sweet to touch, to inhale, to hold close. He thought he would burst with longing. "Better?" he murmured as her head rolled back.

Her eyelashes sank languidly. She was potée in his hands. "Yes, do not cease. . . ."

Her sighs drove him crazy with desire. Hands on her waist, his thumbs plying the taut tissue, he put his lips to her hairline in the lightest of kisses. "Why did you leave and then come back?"

"How did you enter the secret royal chambers? I know you were sober—*Merciful Jesu*!" She gasped as his thumbs located the crux of her agony. "*Oui*, right there . . ."

Michael drew deep breaths. His loins were afire, hard and heavy with arousal. In the girdle of his hands, he held a tight, luscious sheath to be seduced and pleasured, and in it, the treasure in the cave, was the bubbly spring of life, the wit and spirit he thirsted for. Were he not nursing a false injury, he would make a fool of himself over her, for sure. "Your Adele told me that the babe would live and that the king would die. How did she know?"

She parried with another question, "Why did you ridicule my poet . . . Perdu?"

Undone as he was by the lissome vitality pulsating in his hands, tempting him, words spilled unbridled from his lips. "He is ridiculous, hiding behind his quill, and I should tell you he stole the verses. I recognized the one I saw. It's an old English ballade, has been sung for ages."

She stepped out of his hands to face him. "I am glad you are alive and well. I must go."

He caught her hand before she fled. "You must?"

Lambent eyes vanished beneath dark eyelashes. She ran a finger along the embossed lapel of his dressing robe, a seam away from touching the strip of skin peering through the V opening of his shirt, sweetly tormenting him. "I thought he was you, my Perdu."

"Did you want him to be me?"

Laughing at the desperate clownish look on his face, she freed her hand. "To bed with you! You must recoup your strength if you wish to participate in the tournaments."

Raddled with emotions, aching to kiss her, he whispered, "My bed is cold and lonely."

She would not meet his gaze. "Let me help you with the robe and put you to bed."

His voice turned gruff. "I sleep in the buff, marmoset."

She jolted back as if he had bitten her. "Perdu waits. God give you a good night."

Damnation. At that moment, he wished he were bloodily injured—and that he had never touched Anne. "Go, then. We must not keep old Perdu waiting."

* * *

The following morning she received another poem:

> *When blisses on this beauty pour,*
> *Of all this world I ask no more*
> *Than be alone with her and draw*
> *No word of strife.*
> *I blame a lovely woman for*
> *My woes in life.*

> *Written with the hand of him who worships you from the shade.*
> *Perdu (a soldier lost to a forlorn hope)*

Renée smiled. Last night, as they strove to cozen up answers out of each other, Michael had very nearly convinced her of his innocence. She left his lodging undecided. Now she wondered. But whether he was Perdu or not was unimportant; neither were the stirrings of desire she was wont to feel in his presence. She was more interested in his reasons for not exposing Buckingham, or Anne, or any of the people involved in the plot, directly or indirectly, herself included.

Michael knew enough to send her to the block. Still, he remained mum. What was the gorgeous seducer after? Renée wondered in the hurly-burly days of inquiries and suspicions that followed. Norfolk and Marney conducted the hunt for conspirators like hounds on a scavenge, doubling the guard, striding purposefully hither and yon, questioning all those who had access to the queen the night of the incident. None but the kitchen workforce had been exculpated, for the offenders had covered their tracks well, and no evidence had turned up against the guilty party.

The feast day of St. George, the patron saint of England and of the Most Noble Order of the Garter, was the day King Henry had been anointed King of England nine years ago and was celebrated as his official birthday. Preparations for the festive tournament and the banquet were well on the way. Stages were erected for pageants in the city's square. Knights of the shire, merchants, tinkers, and pardoners poured into London. Tents emblazoned with coats of arms were pitched on the green around the tiltyard. Odds and bets were the litany of the court, as well as its servants. King Henry, when he was not chasing pretty damsels from post to pillar, trained rigorously with his companions, reasserting the poise the attempt on his life had robbed him of.

It was difficult to plot and scheme with woodbine and springtime courtships perfuming the air. Renée made up for it with a strict regime. In the days following her failed undertaking, she trained in her chambers, attended on the bedridden queen, and dashed notes to Cardinal Wolsey, thanking him effusively for laboring in her business, in hopes of establishing a rapport with the puissant man. In the afternoons she practiced archery among the honeysuckle and lavender, and the medlar, pear, and apple trees in the orchard. She passed the evenings feasting and dancing in the royal apartments, mostly in the company of Their Graces of Suffolk, their good friend Lord Stanley, and, surprisingly, Mistress Meg Clifford, who was witty and charming and never once tried to impose a reconciliation with her older and unpalatable brother, Sir Walter.

Renée adroitly eluded Rougé, who hunted for her like a bad-tempered bailiff. She avoided Anne and visited Michael in the company of Their Graces of Suffolk, Lord Stanley, and Meg, who embraced the convalescing invalid as a true brother. Meg, secured of Stanley's affections, took to playing Cupid with a total lack of finesse. Renée gave the friendly meddler points for effort, never mind that her good intentions were misplaced.

The nettle that was her assignment chivvied her unremittingly, the fear of failure a bodkin that punctured holes in her confidence. A competent intriguer would play up to Cardinal Wolsey as well as to his enemies, chiefly the Duke of Norfolk. She would tame every man in her sphere, including the lustful king, avail herself of every pawn in the game. She would be ruthless, cold, and soulless. She would draw on their foibles like a leech, for they had weaknesses aplenty—for sexual pleasure, for love, for gold, for power, for pretty things, for attention, for glory. Each of them had his or her price.

Her price had been determined in France. What was her Achilles' heel?

As a result of the grueling training, her muscles were constantly stiff and sore. She required Adele's blessed nightly ministrations in the form of poultices and rough kneading of oils into her aching flesh. And every night, as she lay nude on her stomach to be plied, molded, and chastened for developing the body of a scullion, Raphael's portrait medallion clenched in her fist, she remembered Michael's thumbs in her back, his lips brushing her temple, his pleasing scent, his strong naked body, his blue eyes always seeking, probing, wanting, and knew she was in trouble.

❧ 15 ❧

Unequal in conflict with Achilles.

—Virgil: *Aeneid*

The eagerly anticipated St. George's Day Tournament opened with fanfares to the joy of the court and the sports-minded Londoners who flocked in droves to the sunny tiltyard in Greenwich to cheer and boo the star jousters of the realm. As the joust was considered the ultimate theater of chivalry, wherein contestants had to demonstrate courage, strength, a good eye, and an excellent sense of timing, with the threat of severe noyance hanging over their heads, acquitting oneself well in the lists was regarded almost as honorable and prestigious as attaining glory in battle.

The yard, garlanded with verdant wreaths of St. George's crosses interleaved with ladyblush roses, white and red as the Tudor rose, and topped with a flurry of lively pennons in honor of the king, his nobles, and all the Knights Companion of the Order of the Garter, was full to capacity, a condition that caused a measure of discomfort for the debonair throng but also encouraged jollity, flirting, and betting opportunities. The royal gallery was sumptuously hung with cloth of gold and purple velvet embroidered with *H*s and *K*s, Tudor roses and Spanish pomegranates.

The eager crowd, either occupying the royal gallery or the castellated towers reserved for the courtiers or the tiered platforms sitting the city's officials—the mayor, aldermen, officers of the shrievalty, and guildsmen leaders—or the common folk jostling for space at the rails and outside the stockades, watched agape as the grand procession entered the yard. First came the marshals of the joust on horseback, followed by footmen, drummers, and trumpeters in Tudor tabards; then came lords and knights in costly flaunts, mounted on richly caparisoned steeds, with their spruce pages marching behind; lastly, ushered by thirty gentlemen clothed in velure, silks, and satins, King Henry rode out to a standing ovation. The embodiment of majestic chivalry, the king personified St. George in cloth of gold with a raised pile, symbolic of Ascalon, the sword that had slain the dragon, his high-stepping jouster sporting a suit of engraved gilded armor. The king waved to his animated people and, as soon as the participants entered their names on the Tree of Chivalry, galloped to the scorers and added Henry Rex to the delight of the throng.

Queen Katherine, having recovered from her stomach pains if not altogether from her fright, held court in the royal gallery, beneath which sat the scorers who presided over the lists, attended by her ladies-in-waiting and maids of honor, their dresses slashed with gold lamé in costly trim.

Renée sat between Mary and Meg, gowned in blue and gold, the regal colors of the House of Valois, sapphires round her neck and pearls sprinkled along the gilt billiments of her azure hood, ebony locks flowing unveiled. She could scarcely breathe for the butterflies in her stomach as she waited for the courses to begin. Accustomed to tournaments thrown in the Burgundian style, she was nevertheless amazed at the sheer magnitude and grandeur of the affair. The English, she granted, might not boast as fine a collection of art and marble palaces as the French did, but they made up for it with glamorous entertainments. Her eyes perused the cavalcade for a golden head of hair—to her dismay she spotted Sir Walter Devereaux—but Michael, his bed's hostage, was not among them. Disappointment welled within her. She didn't know what vexed her more: that she should not see him tilt or that she had been secretly looking forward to watching him do so.

The court minstrel took the haut place and with a thick Welsh accent regaled the crowd with the history of the Most Noble Order of the Garter, founded in the year of Our Lord 1348 by the Grace of God and His Majesty Edward III, King of England and France and Lord of Ireland, as the highest order of chivalry. He declaimed the legend of the patron saint of the joust, perorating with the Hymn of St. George, to which the Children of the Chapel Royal caroled harmoniously:

> *"Liberator of captives and defender of the poor,*
> *Physician of the sick and champion of kings . . .*
> *O trophy-bearer and Great Martyr George,*
> *Intercede with Christ our God that our souls be saved!"*

As the procession cleared the field, the court fool trotted in on a garishly caparisoned nag and wrung great laughs from the throng when he insisted on adding his jester shield to the Tree of Chivalry and cudgeled the marshal and the herald into announcing him as "Fool to Rex." The diversion diffused the excited tension that seemed to grip spectators and participants alike.

On a festive bray of trumpets and a roll of the tabors, a fierce looking, red, green, and gold papier-mâché dragon with a scaled tail arrived on a pageant car, drawn by mock camels, decked out as an Eastern citadel with palm trees and with the crescent emblem of the infidel imprinted on flags and shields carried by "Eastern citizens." When the car stopped before the royal gallery, a torch was lit inconspicuously inside the citadel and the dragon wielded it as his flaming breath. The audience *whewed* with amazement, then, twigging the trick, whistled and clapped heartily.

"That's my Stanley," Meg whispered breathlessly to Renée. "Is he not ferocious?"

The "citizens" sounded their horns. A rowdy gang of "infidels"—the challengers—guised in black robes as Saracen warriors, mounted the field, waving lustrous falchions over their heads. In the spirit of the allegory, the crowd booed merrily as the "infidels" presented their shields to the queen, and the dragon, the undefeated champion of two years, craved leave to break spears.

Upon the subsequent fanfare, a company of riders stormed the tiltyard, attired as Greyfriars, cowls obscuring their eyes, heading a procession of walking "pilgrims" in brown robes, carrying Jacob's staffs in their hands and chanting psalms, as if they returned from the shrine of St. James at Compostela. The riders approached the grandstand to receive the queen's permission to accept the challenge. When she gave it, they threw off their habits to reveal that they were King Henry and his favorite jousters, Suffolk, Buckingham, Compton, Neville, Dorset, and others, armored cap-à-pie and guised as holy knights, white tabards splashed with a red cross—the pennon of St. George and of England—worn over suits of plate damascened in silver. The king's silvered suit, wrought by Flemish artisans, afforded the highest degree of agility and comfort; it was chased in gold with the legend of St. George slaying the dragon and with *H*s and *K*s engraved on the skirt hem. Cheers arose as Queen Katherine, feigning utter astonishment over the monks' identities, bestowed their leader with a handkerchief embroidered with her arms, the Spanish pomegranate.

A movement in the corner of her eye alerted Renée to the lone rider coming from the palace, flanked by two servants on foot, burdened with his expedients. The suit of armor protecting his strapping form was glossy black as a raven's plumage, ingenuously constructed to fit the man as a second pelt and thus allow exceptional flexibility. His black tabard was emblazoned at the front with a rampant red eagle. His golden head reflected the shimmer of the sun in stark contrast to his suit and the spirited black stallion armored and caparisoned in black and red Tyrone colors.

The sight of Michael, glowing with masculine beauty and vitality, set Renée's heart aflutter. As he drew near, she read raw determination in the finely boned planes of his suntanned face and strength of purpose in the strong jawline, but the turquoise eyes blazed with disquiet. Though his advent was lost on the crowd, the day had become a lot more interesting where she sat.

"Ho! Look who comes to grace us with his company," Meg announced in hushed tones, the impish lilt and the sidelong smile at Renée implying foreknowledge.

Aware that her cheeks were afire, Renée blithely remarked, "I cannot fathom what he hopes to gain with his theatrical tardiness. His Majesty may take offense. Not very politick."

"I think you are mistaken," said Mary. "Edward of Woodstock, the Black Prince of Wales, was wont to ride alone to a tournament in a black suit of armor so that none would recognize the royal heir to the throne and refuse to break lances with him. This is a statement. He wishes to rise high and does so with courage and flair. Look at his crest, a red eagle, suggestive of Leopold of Austria, Captor of Coeur de Lion. Adds spice to the affair. Harry would approve, wait and see."

Renée studied his imperial emblem, searching her memory for a reference.

"You know he has taken a massive shine to you. He is madly in love. Charles says Tyrone is king in Ireland and that Michael is to inherit his titles and the governing of that country withal. Why the scornful look, Renée? He may not be of royal blood, but he is a fair, clever, amiable fellow, and he is on the rise. You are fond on him. Why braze your heart against his advances? I say better castles in Ireland than a brush and canvas for a settlement, *ne c'est pas, chère amie?*"

Renée jerked her eyes to the fore. Could a notion be more absurd or irrelevant than that? She was not here to procure a husband; she had come to thieve a powerful weapon. She remembered the bit of frippery stinking up her purse. After her deftly dodging Anne for days, the pious hussy had overtaken her after Mass, unctuously pleading, "If he should approach you for a favor, pray tie this to the tip of his lance for good luck." The request conjured up a double entendre, painting an amusing risqué image in Renée's head. She clamped a hand over her mouth to stifle her giggles.

She really should be rid of that smelly thing, Renée thought. The negotiator had long since resigned her office. Besides, she would not be singling out a man of low birth, not even a knight, when London was observing her in hopes of raking up fodder on the French princess to bandy about in alehouses. Anne's belief that he should be so churlish as to overreach himself in Their Majesties' presence by making an overture to a princess of the blood was a slight to his honor. And the presumption of the woman! To think that the sole reason Michael might ask to wear her favor would be a secret gesture in his pursuit of Anne! Ha! Renée was well aware that although Michael continued to conceal Anne's role in the plot to assassinate the king because he was kind and generous, he did not even notice Anne's existence anymore, despite the heated looks Anne painfully lobbed his way. His cold indifference convinced Renée that Anne was unequivocally out of favor and that the odds he would ever take her up on her blatant offers were abysmal.

"So-ho, my fearless shield!" the king greeted the latecomer as he trotted to enter his name on the Tree. The king's address set off a buzz of speculation in the audience; every man jack wanted to know who the "fearless shield" was and by what means he had earned the king's affection.

Mary was right, Renée conceded. Michael's cunning in arriving late paid off.

"How now, Devereaux? Healed and sealed?" King Henry demanded to know. "Forsooth, we should not care for you to bleed to death for taking a blow to your injured side. We will be better served with you observing rather than tilting. What advises the good doctor?"

"Your Majesty's concern infuses genuine balm into his loving servant's blood." Michael inclined his head. "The good doctor has pronounced me fit to partake of my first tournament."

Compton, a hardy jouster, came to the fore. "A green plum, eh? Be advised, dislodging rings from a post and tilting at the quintain are worthy exercises, but a live opponent strikes back."

And withal, Renée thought, Compton demoted the "fearless shield" to a "green plum."

Buckingham said, "Certain you wish to go up against us? A hole in the side is a sweet butt."

The king's eyes narrowed irritably on the duke. "There is no doubt in our mind, Your Grace, that Master Devereaux's superior armor can withstand any spear." To Michael he said, "You will give my secretary the name of your craftsman, for I am of a mind to have one made for myself."

The courtiers sitting within earshot in the gallery and castellated towers followed the hostile exchange between the king and his premier peer with bloodthirsty interest. None dared to speak.

His keen gaze bouncing between the king and the duke, Michael's smile quickened. "If Your Majesty will permit me to bestow him with mine own, I shall be deeply honored, though I must caution him that it is hotter than Hades inside. I expect to leak out of it by the end of the day."

The king, his gallants, and the courtiers laughed, all except Buckingham, who gave Michael the Evil Eye. Renée's gaze locked with Michael's and she knew they were wondering the same thing: did the king know Buckingham authored the failed assault or was he merely suspicious?

As the onlookers clamored for gossip on the parvenu, tumid accounts of Michael's heroics spread like wildfire from the castellated towers to the tiers and to the common folk in the stands.

Meantime, poles with loops were being pegged into the ground for the ring contest, the purpose of which was to eliminate the hopeless competitors. Each participant had three opportunities to charge with his lance to dislodge a detachable ring from a post in order to continue to the contact jousting. The "trials" turned out to be diverting and lucrative, the betting ranging from scores of three to nil for every man. As the inexperienced participants rode out and disqualified themselves greenly, King Henry and his party indulged in ale at the trestle table positioned outside the royal pavilion at the edge of the lists and awaited their turn to display their superior skill in grand style.

Renée was delighted when Michael speared three out of three, a high score for a greenhorn. Usually she was unimpressed with swaggering sportsmen, but she found herself rooting for him as he breezed through the trials. Mary's speech buzzed in her head. Michael madly in love . . . She did not deny that she was flattered, but she loved Raphael. She was not a minute jack. Still, she marveled that she should find Michael so attractive. He embodied the three manly denominators she had shunned hitherto: shrewdness, ambition, cockishness. Michael wore these traits well.

Trumpets fanfared the marshal waving his white baton. "In the name of God and St. George, and by the grace of His Royal Majesty, Henry Tudor, King of England and France, Protector of the Faith,

Defender of the Realm, and Lord of Ireland—come forth to do battle!"

Renée, having heard of King Henry's legendary prowess in the disport he perceived as the single measure of courtly excellence, was surprised when he entered the gallery. She stood to curtsey as he took his state next to the queen and ventured a gracious nod at Cardinal Wolsey. She leaned toward Mary. "Will we not see the most illustrious jouster in England shiver lances?"

"To placate Her Majesty," Mary whispered. "She is with child. I give credit to Katherine. She has succeeded where none of the 'ancient fathers' on the council have tofore. Since his youth, they have been fretting that he might injure or God forbid kill himself. Only the queen his wife could convince him to sit out the first courses and take pleasure in observing his knights joust."

"Enceinte! Joyful tidings!" Renée whispered back. "As for safeguarding His Grace . . . Hmm. I imagine Her Majesty's delight is so great she allowed herself to be hoodwinked by a sly husband, for the truly perilous passes are run after the chaff is winnowed from the grain."

Mary sent her a look of enlightened agreement that turned to wry amusement. "Oh, Renée, you would have made an outstanding council member. Pity you were born female."

"Yes, that is what my royal sire was wont to say," Renée murmured peevishly.

Mary laced their arms together. "'Tis very pleasant, being a wife. You mustn't dread it so."

Renée shot her a startled look, her heart kicking violently. Mary had touched her on the raw. "You say that, after being married to my father?"

Mary's eyes twinkled naughtily. "Charles did not expire after shivering one lance."

Renée smiled tightly and accepted a cup of rosé from a server brandishing a tray laden with goblets and platters of sweetmeats. She had not tasted the passion Mary alluded to and that Anne had spent with Michael—and it unsettled her more than she cared to admit.

A roll of the tabors and a tucket on the trumpets silenced the chatty audience. The herald announced, "Master Thomas Knightly challenges Sir Francis Bryan *au plaisant*!"

Bryan circled the tiltyard and stopped in front of a buxom maid sitting in one of the towers. Blushing at the flattery, she nearly lost her wares bending over to tie her favor to his lance. Bryan reached the starting line and lowered his visor. His challenger took position across from him, at the opposite end of two parallel courses divided by a wooden palisade known as the lists.

The kerchief was down. The jousters stormed into the courses, shields raised, lances poised horizontally, dirt pellets flying from their horses' hoofs. The assembly waited with bated breath for the first imminent clash. . . . A collective cheer went up when Bryan prevailed over the younger man. Everyone applauded the winner as the loser rode off, dazedly oscillating in the saddle.

"Good show!" King Henry pounded his armrest and tossed a jeweled medal of St. George to his triumphant friend.

The next pair to take the field was Stanley and Lovell. Stanley rode up to Meg, offered her a chaplet of golden Mary-buds at the tip of his lance, and asked to wear her favor. Renée observed the exchange between the doters with a slight twinge of envy. Meg beamed with the joy of love, openly, effulgently. Meanwhile, the feckless gamblers wagered on the degree of damage Stanley would inflict on his adversary, for the outcome of the engagement was predictable.

Stanley proved to be merciful and only felled the brabbler to the crowd's delight.

Twoscore courses, each beginning with the blare of the herald's trumpets and concluding to the roar of applause from thousands of throats and with a medal to the winner, were run much to the effect Renée had foretold: the famed tilter, usually a gentleman from the king's closest circle, defeating the "hapless victim" and even prizing him out of the saddle.

The herald cried, "Master Michael Devereaux challenges Sir William Compton *au plaisant*!"

Meg clapped heartily, elbowing Renée to do the same, when

Michael arrived atop his black stallion. There was no denying the thrill Renée felt watching his golden head disappear inside the shiny black helm. Pippin, clad in red and black livery, offered the lance and shield.

Michael's face, squeezed inside the tight helmet, glistened with perspiration. His eyes were fixed on his foe, patiently waiting at the opposite starting line with his visor down. Michael's horse kicked up a cloud of dust, raring to go. His master dithered.

Something was not quite right, Renée realized. Michael seemed unsure of himself, almost . . . reluctant to engage. He refused to lower his visor and kept blowing out air. People began booing.

"Come on, sweet'eart! Don't be afeared!" someone jeered, eliciting laughter.

"Ten pounds say he turns tail," crowed Norfolk.

"Will he, nill he?" the king murmured. He glanced at Norfolk. "Twenty pounds."

Suddenly Michael turned aside, doubled over, and cast the accounts of his stomach onto the dirt. The crowd *eheued* with disgust. The king's minions, drinking ale at the trestle table outside the royal pavilion, exploded with rumbustious laughter. Pippin handed Michael a wet sweat clout to wipe his face. Moments later, Michael lowered his visor. The king raised his hand, giving the herald the signal to proceed. The tucket urged Michael to the starting line. The tabors thundered. He adjusted his grip on the lance. The din in the yard lessened to a whirr of expectation. . . .

The kerchief was down. As coiled springs let loose, the contestants lunged ahead at full tilt; shields raised, lances couched. Renée's eyes were riveted on Michael as, adroitly controlling his hot-blooded destrier, he pounded up the course, picking up speed. The competitors drew closer, mounted giants about to smash into each other. She held her breath, her fingers steepled against her mouth. She would not have traded places with these madmen for all the duchies in the world.

At the last moment Michael hefted his lance and—taking a hard blow to his injured side that splintered his rival's lance thus gaining the man points—struck Compton's helmet with fantastic precision and shattering force. Compton crashed into the dirt, trounced through and through.

"Hoa!" The crowd was on its feet, transported by the rare sight of a nobody unhorsing a star jouster of the realm on his first pass and with exemplary skill. It was the stuff of legends, the humble man slaying the dragon, and the crowd loved him for it.

As Michael reined at the opposite end, Compton, a lump of metal sprawled on his back, was revived by his attendants and helped to his feet. He had a stunned look about him as he staggered off the field, supported heavily by his servants. Tilting was a dangerous sport, everyone knew the risks involved, and according to every rule—and the presiding scorers—Michael had won fairly.

The king dispatched a page to inquire after his friend and another to summon Michael to the royal gallery. As Michael crossed the yard on his horse, a man stood up in the tiers and shouted, "The king's fearless shield!" Forthwith he was echoed by the masses, applauding vigorously.

Meg clapped madly, ribbing Renée blue. "Was he not spectacular?"

King Henry gossiped with his lords: "Knocked by a virgin. Compton will never live it down. He'll be sour-eyed and cursing his knocked pate for a week." The lords, feeling duty-bound to laugh at his every pleasantry, laughed with him. "That would be twenty pounds, Your Grace."

Norfolk acknowledged his loss humbly. "Verily, our wise and discerning sovereign stands in the radiance of the goddess Fortuna today and commands her wheel of fortune."

"True." The king eyed Michael with satisfaction as the latter approached, for more had been staked here than a purse. "My green plum, you distinguished yourself smashingly. Well done!" He flung him a jeweled medal of St. George, which Michael caught in his gauntlet.

"I thank Your Grace." Michael pushed back his visor, baring a sweaty face and a grin. He cut his eyes to Renée, then smiled at his sister. "I cannot recollect having a better time, Majesty."

The king raised his goblet. "Master Devereaux, we commend

you on your first victory and command you to preserve a good measure of the steel you sheathe in your vambrace for us!"

Renée lifted her winecup along with the nobles schooling their expressions to appear merry and with the jubilant crowd swinging their flasks and wondered if the green plum had an inkling of the number of powerful enemies he was accruing at the velocity of an avalanche: Norfolk, Buckingham, Compton, and the other gallants jealous of their position with the king. Being the king's fearless shield was not a badge easily worn. Whether he would end up buried underneath or skate smoothly onto safe grounds remained to be seen.

❧ 16 ❧

Mars that frights cities with his bloody
    spears,
And Venus that releases human fears,
Do both together in one temple shine.

—Claudian: *The Magnet*

Aware of the baleful glares from Compton's partisans and the smiles of the unfledged tilters, Michael relinquished Archangel to Conn's ministrations and dropped the helm, gauntlets, and medal into Pippin's arms. His hair was sweat-soaked and plastered to his scalp, his armored body was smoldering, and his heart still palpitated ferociously from his first challenge in the lists.

Michael could not fathom Lord Tyrone's purpose in equipping him with a black dickens of a harness. He envied every lighthearted fellow whistling past him in a sun-expelling silvered suit. He did not give a cuss that the plates were wrought from the very one his lord's Roman ancestor had donned and no doubt cursed during the conquest of Britannia many centuries ago. Black might serve in Ireland, where continuous precipitation was the norm and the sun rarely shone, but he was melting inside the infernal thing!

"Conn! Fetch me a pail of water!" Struggling to draw air into his constricted lungs, he ran a finger under the gorget and quickened his step toward his tent, Pippin on his heels. The scorching heat was but one of his torments. His head seemed to echo every stomping foot, clacking tongue, and thudding heart in the tiltyard; his ears were ringing; sharp odors of sweaty horseflesh and unwashed bodies assaulted his nostrils; his eyes hurt. He felt ill. *Thirsty*. Desperate for potion.

His tent was neither grand nor spacious as the royal pavilion, where the king entertained his minions and strapped on his armor, but it was cool, private, and stocked with the amenities he required. Alack, its thin canvas walls did not block out the horrendous din rising from the stands.

Liberated of his armor, Michael stepped outside, seized the sloshing pail from Conn's hands, and dumped its contents over his head. A sigh of relief tore from his lips as the water cooled his scalp, drenched his garments, and doused the fire licking at his pelt. He returned inside and dismissed his attendants. Playing the bully had become an unfortunate necessity since his injury. He grabbed one of the bottles forethoughtfully stashed in his trunk, dropped onto a stool, and slaked his unnatural thirst. Then he put his throbbing head between his knees in an attempt to shut out the chatting, laughing, shouting, and clapping that had taken residence inside his head.

"Sir Thomas Howard challenges Sir Edward Neville *a la guerre*!"

The racket quieted. *Precious peace.* He found it positively uncanny how despite the megrim, the heat, the nausea, and the prebattle bout of self-doubt—throwing up before the king and all of London was not his finest moment, but never mind—he had beaten an illustrious tilter with ease. Was the dragon's blood at work again? One moment it brought him to his knees and in the next lifted him up high. Maybe he was dying and the yoking potion merely prolonged his misery. . . .

Neville beat Howard. Cacophony ruled the yard. Michael moaned at the charivari besieging his mind again. Why the pox should a tame and cheerful throng put him in such a dismal state? He was hardened to riot and rumpus. The Irish were a fierce lot, and while they did not break out in open rebellion, he had ofttimes confronted sword-wielding, fire-shooting warriors with murder in their eyes and vengeance on their tongues. No insanity, then; well, not in his head, anyway.

"Sir Anthony Brown challenges Sir William Carey *au plaisant*!"

Blessed silence reigned again. The knights were tilting furiously, breaking scores of lances.

As the potion took effect, his hearing sharpened further, a thousand different smells came at his nose. *Enough!* He shut his eyes against the disruptions and breathed. *In, out. In, out. Quiet. Think of something else.* The outside world dissolved. Memories flooded his mind: a soft, clean bed, an enormous chamber, his, at the earl's castle, rose petals floating in a water ewer, fresh bread piled on a platter, mead in a pewter cup, shoes to perfectly fit his boy's feet—marvels!—grassy hills outside his window, a hawk shrieking as it cut the sky—

"How now, John-a-dreams, away with the small folk again? To arms, codling! You've been challenged." Standing inside his tent, arms akimbo, Stanley eyed him with fond sympathy. "Why the green face, green plum?"

"Worms-meat," Michael prevaricated.

"Begnawed by Doubt and Dread, eh? Noxious pair of worms. Take heart, runt. You have a commendable first victory to carry you aloft. I say, let no impediment steal your future glory."

Michael sniffed. "One man's mistake does not a champion make. Is that not so?"

"Hoa, there! I came to offer congratulations, not consolations. I confess I did not expect you to perform so well, but hark, I watched your progress. Few aim for the head, for it is a famously tricky strike, but you accomplished it brilliantly. Your aim was true. You put all your might into it and knocked Compton onto his thrasonical arse. Your instructor knew what he was about."

"Aye." Michael grimaced sardonically. "Kept me on an evil regimen of Irish mud."

A great hurrah went up in the yard. "That would be Suffolk killing a fop from the north."

Michael's humor brightened at the mention of his illustrious friend, Charles Brandon, the son of a standard-bearer who distinguished himself in sports and in battle, who clawed his way to greatness with courage and loyalty, and won the heart of the flame-haired princess Mary Tudor.

Stanley gave him a gimlet eye. "This look I know and do not like."

"What look?" Michael inquired with feigned innocence, pushing to his feet. "Pippin!"

"Your fatuity amazes me, but I shall say no more. People in general only ask advice not to follow it. If they do follow it, 'tis for the sake of having someone to blame for having given it."

"You have been wearing the grandam scowl for days. Speak your mind afore it coagulates." Michael spread arms and legs for Pippin to strap on the black armor pieces, steeling himself to be broiled again in the sun. Now that he finally got the trick of developing an internal sieve, the ruckus in the tiltyard did not torture him half as much as before. All he had to do was think of Ireland. He loved that place. He missed everything about it. The lush island was his true home.

"Renée de Valois is some emissary of her king. Her duties are shrouded in mist. Her name is tarred with scandal. She is a woman who will draw you into a snare wherein you will lose your head as well as your heart. She is pleasing, I will grant you that, but I do not trust her, and neither should you. There, you are enlightened. Now do what you will."

"Hoa. When you speak your mind . . ." He heard the stern warning. He did. But as Renée's sweet face surfaced before his eyes, the effect of Stanley's oration dissolved. "My sister, your affianced, disagrees with you. She happens to like Lady Renée a great deal."

"Meg sees the look on your face, how you glow when the Frenchwoman walks into a room, and her misguided . . . God's pity! No one will let you have her, Michael! She is far too lofty for your blood. *She* will never have you. She is on a tear for a man in France. S'blood! I knew you would not listen. Why do I bother?"

Michael's heart clenched. "She loves a man?" Thought-sick, he vengefully pushed the bitter revelation aside, storing it for future deliberations. He could not think about it now. It might cost him his life in the lists. *She loves a man. . . .* "Who is my challenger, Stanley?"

"Sir Walter Devereaux challenges Master Michael Devereaux *a la guerre*!"

The crowd was agog. The upcoming clash promised terrific sport with the fearless shield on the field, the risk of death looming, and with the fraternal rivalry spicing the dish. Stanley did not share in the enthusiasm. "He has declared war against you," he warned Michael as they reached the lists, Pippin following with Michael's muniments, the jousting instruments, and Conn with Archangel. "He has no sense of chivalry where you are concerned. He'll aim for your wound."

"As did your friend Compton?"

"Unlike Compton, Walter Devereaux cannot afford to lose to you. This is a personal matter. Your rising high in Harry's favor sticks in his craw. He has much at stake, primarily the Garter knighthood. He tells people that you are intriguing to steal it from him."

Michael saw his opponent mount his horse, both caparisoned in the damasked Devereaux colors pricked into his own wrist. "So he is out for my blood. What can I do?"

"Forfeit the challenge. Lovell does that every year. You will have plenty of opportunities to make up for the lost points later on. In the final tally no one will remember."

"Alas, I am not of Lovell's ilk." Michael swung into the saddle and looked up at the gallery where his heart's desire sat in regal indifference to lesser mortals such as him. Froward Renée might be too lofty for his blood, but her riches and bloodline did not interest him in the least. What made him shake inside were the forbidden feelings she stirred in him. *She loves a man.*

Renée draped an arm around his sister, her lips murmuring encouragements. Meg sat stiffly, hands clasped in her lap; she found his gaze and smiled worriedly. Her affection warmed unused places in Michael's heart. No one, not even his lord, ever worried over him. Meg did but would never forgive him if he harmed her older brother. He did not want to kill Walter. He did not want to be killed. And he had to win. A knighthood would lubricate his path to fulfilling his pledge to Tyrone. That alone incited him to defeat Walter at his own game.

Stanley wished him luck. Michael pulled on his helmet, his pulse accelerating, and accepted the shield and the armed lance from Pippin. He slammed shut his visor with the guard of the hilt and walked Archangel to the starting line. His breath came hot and swift inside the helmet; his heart pounded forcefully. The tabors summoned his attention. Sweat broke from his brow. His self-confidence was seesawing again. He could do this, he had to. . . .

The kerchief was down.

"God ha' mercy!" Meg screamed. She jumped from her seat and dashed out of the gallery. Renée saw her run across the field to see to her brother, lying in the sand, his cuisse loose at the thigh, blood seeping from an open flesh wound. At the edge of the lists, Michael raised his visor, staring grimly at Meg and Walter. The crowd hurrahed, chanting his epithet, importuning him for a once-round the tiltyard. He did not stir. Walter sat up, cussing venomously. Disgusted with his ineptitude, he pulled off his helmet and tossed it aside. Only then did Michael spur his horse into a victory gallop, his tall back straight in the saddle, fair hair brushing at black pauldrons. He drew rein before Their Majesties, took off his helmet, and inclined his head. "Your Majesties."

"The green plum has ripened," the king observed. He rewarded Michael with another medal and engaged him in a discussion on jousting tactics, sharing his own repertoire. They talked and laughed to the surprise of all beholders and to the disappointment of those who felt neglected. Not once did Michael look at Renée. Mary gave her the eyebrow. Renée shrugged dismissively.

A pole stretcher was brought for Walter's use, but he insisted on limping off the field.

"Walter, God bless you." Meg exhaled with relief. "I feared the worst."

"I am not so delicate as to parish from one felling," Walter grumbled, hobbling beside her, his arm draped across Martin's shoulders. His thigh burned. His bottom groaned. He felt routed, humiliated, full of murderous spleen. "I have a bone to pick with you, sister. I am betrayed, cast aside for a baseborn arriviste and his exalted new friends."

"That is not true. I love you better than anyone. But he is our brother—"

"Enough!" Walter muttered. "If you insist on consorting with the misbegotten rogue, I will send you back to Surrey."

Meg's chin came up mulishly. "You cannot send me away. I serve the queen, Walter. Only Her Majesty can dismiss me. Besides, I am to be married soon, I trow."

"Master Devereaux!" Jasper, Norfolk's faithful, ripened varlet, greeted him at the entrance to his tent. "His Grace bade me inquire after your health, sir."

Walter's spirit lifted at the compliment. "Pray thank His Grace for his kind attention and inform him that I expect to dance the volta with the prettiest damsels at tonight's feast."

"His Grace will be right pleased to hear of your rapid recovery, sir!" Jasper declared for the benefit of passersby, then in a gossipy tone added, "Poxed Imperial style, aiming low, then swinging at the head. Handsome pennon, shame on the tactics."

Walter was instantly intrigued. "Tell me more about this Imperial style."

With a cautious glance about him, Jasper murmured, "At the Battle of Bosworth Field, old King Henry, styled Harri Tudur at the time, prevailed over King Richard with a private army of French mercenaries, including a company of Imperial lancers. They tilted same as the new man."

"Fascinating." *A Spanish assassin murdered by an Imperialist spy.* He knew just the man to cook up a pie of worms for the false trickster: a power-hungry duke who thrived on distrust and manipulation, relished intrigue, and held a seat on the council. Oh, he would unravel the mystery that was Michael Devereaux, seducer of princesses, savior of kings, hero of the joust, and when he was done with him, only God might show mercy to the bastard's subversive rotten soul.

"The Most Honorable Thomas Grey, Marquess of Dorset, challenges Lord Edward Stanley, the "Twice Undefeated" Baron Monteagle, *au plaisant*!"

Sergeant Francesco held out a missive to Renée. "For you, madame."

She tore her eyes from the competitors and took the note. "Who gave it to you?"

"A stable hand."

"Oh." She had begun to wait for her poems with bated breath. The kerchief was down and the contestants were thundering toward each other, but her eyes were on the parchment. It read:

> *How shall a singer sweetly sing,*
> *Afflicted so with suffering?*
> *Dreadful death to me she'll bring*
> *Before my day.*
> *Bow low to her, that lovely thing*
> *With eyes of ~~grey~~ blue!*
> *Perdu*

With a pleased smile, Renée pressed the poem to her bosom. Involuntarily her eyes fell on the golden head watching the pass with Suffolk at the trestle table outside the king's pavilion. He had just sent the Earl of Essex, one of the finest tilters in the realm, flying like a disk.

Omnisciently Michael raised his eyes to her, and her pulse sped frenziedly.

Lances crashed. It was a tie. Stanley and Dorset had two more passes to run till one of them scored higher or capsized his opponent. The herald cried, "The contestants shall reengage!"

The audience hoorayed, thrilled to finally have their first rematch of the day.

For Renée, the tiltyard had become a blur. Only the man imprisoning her in his gaze existed.

"Perdu?" Mary leaned in. "Who is he?"

Renée jolted. The eye contact, the magic thread, was broken. "I don't know. It's a mystery."

"Charles used to jot me love verses. Not as fine as this, but then yours is taken from a known English ballade. Not that it matters. Another doter and obviously crazed with love. I wonder . . ."

Renée smiled. "I know about the stolen verses. Michael told me."

"Oh? You let him read your love letters?" Again the reddish eyebrow lifted wryly.

"It's a long tale." Renée folded the note carefully and tucked it in her purse.

The herald announced, "Sir Richard Jerningham challenges Sir John Neville *au plaisant*!"

As the knights continued to shiver spears like reeds, the proficient jousters, hardly missing a stroke, effectively sifted the competitors' ranks, tiring horses in rapid succession. The king grew restless, muttering about joining in. The announcement following a blast of trumpets stayed him: "His Grace the Duke of Buckingham challenges Master Michael Devereaux *a la guerre*!"

"The king my brother scowls," Mary whispered. "Buckingham does this every year. He will crush the star jouster of the day and Harry will never have a go at his fearless shield."

Renée also scowled. Michael seemed to be the marked bull everyone wanted to spear in the day's corrida. Buckingham might be ignorant of Michael's interference in his first attempt on the king's life, but he knew who was responsible—wittingly or otherwise—for foiling the second. A trickle of fear ran down her spine. "Is His Grace a competent jouster?" she asked Mary.

"As good as Robert Fleuranges de la Marck, le Duc de Bouillon."

That did not bode well. Robert was the best tilter in France, a capable military leader, and a companion of Long-Nose. She stared across the field at Michael, busy flirting with several ladies in the left tower. His mien was no longer tense; there was laughter in his eyes. She heard Queen Katherine say in Spanish-accented English, "He is handsome and courteous. I like him well."

The tabors put an end to Michael's courtship with the female multitude. The duke emerged on his bay charger, his eyes hard. Renée peered at Anne, wondering whom the slattern would root for: her lord brother or her former lover. Meantime, Michael mounted his horse and took his lance from Pippin, but instead of taking position at the lists, he trotted up the stands. Twigging his intent, women flourished colorful scarves, mufflers, and tuckers at him.

He rewarded them with brilliant smiles and waves galore and continued straight for the gallery.

The maids of honor giggled in anticipation; they had been doling out fripperies for the past hour, a sport Renée was oblivious of heretofore. Her common sense willed Michael to adhere to courtly protocol and bestow his attention on one of the maids, but when his lance halted at Lady Percy, disappointment needled her. She looked away, but the maids' regretful sighs summoned her eyes to the fore. She felt a kick in her chest when she found him perched atop his great horse in front of her, a devilish smile lurking in his blue eyes. The tip of his lance pointed at her heart.

"My lady, might I beg the honors to wear your favor today?"

Every gaze in the tiltyard was trained on her. Their Majesties said nothing. Were the rules of decorum different here than in France? Or was a French princess fair game in England? Michael regarded her expectantly, gravely. Her refusal would humiliate him. Were it any other contestant she might have considered saying nay. But he was her friend. She stepped up to the rail, unlaced a blue and gold trimming from her wrist, and tied it to his lance with a bright smile and a silent benediction. Eyes twinkling, Michael tilted in thanks. The crowd cheered. Anne sat back irately.

A blast of trumpets summoned the contestants to their respective positions. The king leaned forward in his seat. The kerchief was down, and the tilters hurtled into the lists, the earth shaking beneath their armored horses' hoofs. Buckingham hunched over his lance, couching it expertly, holding his shield close. Michael aimed low, arm steady, he and his destrier moving as one.

"God's wounds!" Suffolk and Stanley, standing outside the royal pavilion in suits of plate and drinking malmsey, grimaced when Buckingham, their pet villain of the joust, was upturned by a mighty blow to the helm and smashed into the ground in a clangor of expensive armor. A coterie of the duke's squires, varlets, and poursuivants rushed to attend him, as if he were a king.

"The fledgling has become a firedrake," Suffolk observed as, flushed with success, Michael raised his broken lance high to a "huzzah" of the bloody-minded throng. He kicked into a gallop round the tiltyard, under a rain of love-knotted handkerchiefs, basking in his moment of glory.

"Christ!" Stanley lost his jollity when the king vaulted from his throne, bellowing for his armor. The green plum's wielding an arm of steel over the king's toughest rival and reigning supreme in his new lists was a red flag in the bull's face. Stanley exchanged a look with Suffolk. While they empathized with Michael's driving need to make a name for himself at court, impress a beautiful princess, and win over the hearts of London, stealing Harry's thunder would gain him the opposite. The sun of their universe had to excel all others, shiver the most lances, and upturn his opponents. Worse, the spectators adopted a new pet name for the fair jouster, riding bareheaded to tilt before his princess, and were chanting in chorus, "Archangel! Archangel!" Disaster loomed. Stanley sighed. "I explained the rule to him. I pray he listened."

"But you cannot guarantee he will play by it."

"He doesn't take advice too well."

"Then we must stop him."

"He shan't harm the king, Charles."

"You know it, I know it, but Norfolk may disagree. Michael killed a man in Their Majesties private chambers. If the king's grace should come to harm today, by mere accident, mind you . . ."

"Say no more." Michael had accumulated a cupboardful of medals; it should suffice him.

"Go to the herald and challenge him forthwith. I will take the brunt of Harry's displeasure." Suffolk stayed Stanley with a look. "Take him out of the tournament. No tomfooleries. Go to!"

Stanley strode to the podium, pulled the herald down to a crouching position, and put a flea in the man's ear. "I challenge Master Michael Devereaux *a la guerre*. Announce me at once!"

Eyes wide with fright, the herald bobbed his head in consent. "Aye, my lord! Straightaway!"

Trumpets brayed. "Sir Edward Stanley challenges Master Michael Devereaux *a la guerre*!"

Michael's head swerved aside in shock, and he missed Renée's witty retort to his belittling timid poets who did not keep their appointments. He never imagined Stanley would issue him an unfriendly challenge. The king halted midway to his pavilion, growling angrily, but Suffolk was there to soothe any discontent. Michael looked at Renée. "I beg your pardon, duty calls."

"Yes, of course, go to. And may God protect you!" Renée called at his back.

He approached Pippin with a heavy heart. Meg had left with Walter without sparing him a glance. Stanley wished to spear him with iron. He donned his helmet perfunctorily and took the lance. There was neither joy nor fear in his heart. Only the bitter taste of loneliness.

Stanley appeared opposite him, visor down. Michael slammed shut his. The signal propelled them into battle. Michael's fingers tightened restlessly around the hilt of the lance as he pondered the appropriate strike between friends. Certainly not the head. He settled on the shield.

The kerchief was down, and he was thundering up the course, aiming . . .

The hammer blow to the helm took Michael by surprise. His head whipped back and forth like a pendulum, the thump ricocheting in his mind a hundred times over. The pieces of his foe's shield flew in his visor as he rode on to the finish line, impressing the crowd with his hardiness, but thought-sick with offense. Stanley won the pass in a manner that was by no means amicable, but rather the Twice Undefeated seemed determined to defend his championship at all cost.

Michael's helmet was badly dented. Pippin handed him a new one.

The herald cried, "The contestants shall reengage!"

A chant arose, coupled with rhythmic clapping and stomping, "Again! Again!"

Again . . . The ominous word reverberated in Michael's head like thunder, transporting him to a muddy field with rain thrashing, his body bruised, and Ferdinand shouting, "Blood from a stone."

Someone shoved a lance into his gauntleted hand. The trumpets played the tucket, hurtling him from his stupor back into battle. Sweat stung his eyes. Breathing laboriously through the thin bars of his visor, he blinked to clear his vision, yet in his mind's eye he saw a black fiend bearing down on him. *Your incompetent sunflower is not ready! He will never be ready!* Blood pounded against his temples. His heart battered his ribs. The muggy prison of his helmet suffocated him. He could not muster his focus for the bruit inside his head. . . .

Stanley's lance splintered against his breastplate. A shrill neigh cleared his mistful mind. He saw man and horse plunging headlong into the dirt and realized he had dealt a glancing blow to the galloping charger. Horrified, Michael dove onto his capped knees before Stanley. He took off his helmet and pushed back Stanley's visor. His friend's eyes were closed. "Stanley!"

The knight did not respond. Michael's initial relief at Stanley's escaping the crashing weight of his horse evaporated. His heart beat with terrible foreboding. *He had killed his best friend.* He felt Stanley's neck for a pulse. *Gramercy.* It was strong, but Stanley remained insensible. A circle of people blocked the sun: attendants, knights, lords. Michael looked at Suffolk, his throat choked. "Fetch a surgeon! He is alive but unresponsive." Suffolk vanished.

"He is coming to!" Stanley's manservant announced sanguinely.

"God's teeth!" Stanley groaned. He stared up at Michael. "A regimen of mud—or of brick?"

Beleaguered with question marks and remorse and unable to speak for the lump in his throat, Michael smiled stupidly at Stanley's irritation. He was so joyous that Stanley lived.

Stanley grimaced. "Thanks for the drubbing, mate. I suppose I ought to be thankful you hit my horse and not my head, or my brains would be pulped right here beside me. Pittikins! You have the devil's arm, runt." He shifted, gauging the firmness of his bones. "Help me sit up."

"He can sit!" someone shouted in the direction of the king.

Stanley draped an arm about Michael's neck. "Remember, codling," he whispered in his ear. "Once defeated—and make it believable!"

The brass trumpets produced an elaborate fanfare. The herald cried, "His Royal Majesty, Henry Tudor, King of England and of

France, Protector of the Faith, Defender of the Realm, and Lord of Ireland, has entered the lists!"

Mary got up to tie her favor to Suffolk's lance. "May God keep you, my lord husband."

Renée followed Michael with her gaze as he assisted Stanley to his tent, Stanley's arm flung across his shoulders. Steady, dependable shoulders. As everyone else, she marveled at Michael's superior strength and prowess. He was very strong, almost . . . supernaturally strong. Lady Percy, nursing an imaginary rejection, said, "He has the face of an angel and the rest of the devil."

A dark shadow commandeered Meg's vacant seat. "I have a proposition for you."

Renée stared at Norfolk's profile, thinking, *The devil hears when invoked.* "Your Grace."

Suffolk scored points off the king. Mary clapped with gusto. His eyes on the tilters, Norfolk leaned onto Renée's armrest. His voice was a breath of snow. "Help me engineer the cardinal's downfall and you shall have what you seek." He opened his fist to dangle a medallion on a gold chain: a gold cross over black. "Refuse, and Wolsey will know about your *deletoris*, madame."

Armado's medallion! Renée's head swam. Jesu, the man whose death she had ordered was reaching out from the grave. She had not tidied up the loose threads. *This is a probe,* she assured herself. *He knows not what I seek, or he would hunt for the Ancient himself without informing me.* Notwithstanding her feverishly spinning top, Renée gave her coolest, most diplomatic smile. "Your Grace is a powerful man, and as a rule I never quarrel with dukes." He was so powerful, he could pronounce her the author of the attack on the king, manufacture evidence, and execute her. Obviously he had lost confidence in his French houseguest and thought to encroach on her. He could do anything . . . unless she took shelter under the wing of the red dragon, Cardinal Wolsey, and apprised him of Norfolk's intentions. The cardinal ruled England. "How may I serve you?"

There was surprise in his voice. "You are an extraordinary young woman. I anticipated tears, denials." He paused, hesitating. "Were my son not married to Buckingham's daughter . . . or were I a younger man . . . We shall speak again. Soon. Good health, my lady." He got up and left.

Gramercy. She had foiled his surprise attack. Next time she would be ready for him. It was the first time in her life that she sent a silent thanks to her sly sire. His teachings had just saved her life. Armado and his damned medallion! She should have ripped it from his neck in France!

"What did he want?" Mary asked, but got distracted as the king and Suffolk reengaged.

Renée sank back against her seat. There was nothing she could do but wait . . . and stall.

King Henry beat Suffolk on the third pass to thunderous acclaim, reasserting his reputation as a magnificent jouster. The two friends laughed the whole time, bandying taunts and insults. After his engagement with Suffolk, the king went on to eliminate the remaining competitors in swift succession. All but one. The herald announced *à haute voix*, "For the final course, His Royal Majesty, Henry Tudor, King of England and of France, Protector of the Faith, Defender of the Realm, and Lord of Ireland, challenges Master Michael Devereaux *a la guerre*!"

Renée saw Michael dash out of Stanley's tent, his expression one of tense resignation. Once they were mounted and armed, he and the king rode to the queen and tilted courteously. Queen Katherine stepped to the handrail with a gracious smile. "Beloved husband, may God bless and keep you." She tied her favor to his lance. "Master Devereaux, you have amazed and delighted us with a spate of victories. For defeating last year's champion of this tournament, we award you with this prize." She hung a gold bracelet inlaid with sparkling tear-blue crystals on his lance.

The ebullient throng applauded the gesture; the women called out to Michael, offering their wrists as boughs for his prize. He thanked Her Majesty and proceeded carefully down the gallery.

"My Lady Renée!" Michael grinned dazzlingly.

Renée felt a surge of warmth sweep through her, melting the ice administered by Norfolk's chill breath. With a broad and grateful smile, she walked up to the handrail and accepted his gift. "I shall wear your prize with honor and pleasure, *mon petit ami*. Thank you."

Everyone clapped as she clasped the bracelet round her wrist. Trumpets called the jousters to the lists. The crowd was on its feet, shouting, "Long live the king!" and "God bless!"

Michael assumed his position and waited for the king's pleasure. The kerchief dropped. The combatants roared into the lists like lions, one silvery, the other black. The spectators watched with bated breath as the king charged at his fearless shield with dexterous ferocity.

Mary joined Renée at the handrail. "He worships you," she said.

Renée felt a jolt in her heart as the tilters exploded into each other with brutal force, splinters flying, metal plates clanging. A collective "Hoa!" swelled from the stands like surf in a storm.

Michael fell to the ground, the pointed steel head of the king's lance lodged in his heart.

A pall of silence gripped the tiltyard. A man yelled, "The king has slain his fearless shield!"

King Henry's head jerked at the couched condemnation. He reined in beside Michael's still form, pushed back his visor, and bellowed for a surgeon, whereupon bedlam ruled. People were shouting, "Devereaux is dead!" and "Bless His Majesty, King of the Joust!"

Michael's attendants came running with a pole stretcher, a barber surgeon on their heels. Courtiers swarmed to congratulate His Majesty. The trumpeters flourished fanfares. Flower petals sheeted the tiltyard. Renée was running, squeezing, elbowing, forging a path in the stampede of overscented sycophants. Her heart thudded brutally. *Michael, damn you. You cannot die—again.*

Renée saw Pippin and Conn burst through the canvas flap of the tent flying the red eagle over black, chased outside by the pain-thick growl, "And let no one get past you!"

Merciful Jesu, he lived! Jubilant with relief, offering an Ave Maria, she ran to the flap door.

An arm shot out to bar her. "Your pardon, my lady. None is to go in, master's orders."

Sergeant Francesco arrived at a run, his sword belt rattling against his thigh. He glowered at Michael's manservant. "Step aside, imbecile! Let madame through!"

"I will handle this." Renée turned to Pippin. "Is the surgeon with him?"

The manservant looked grim. "Won't come within a furlong of my master, not after the, eh, unintended blow Master Michael dealt him."

"*He hit the surgeon?*" Renée was horrified. "But he is well, yes?"

"He will die lest he receives treatment, but he declines most violently, my lady."

"By the saints! What is the matter with him? Let me pass, Pippin. I will speak to him."

The varlet looked pained. "But his orders—"

"A pox on his orders!" She flounced past him, snatching back the canvas flap door.

Michael's tent was cool and shadowy. She found him slumped against a large trunk on the carpeted floor, amid a clutter of black armor pieces, his face half turned from her. His begrimed fair hair was plastered to his scalp with sweat and gore. Dark blood oozed from a wide hole right above his heart—it was awful! The pointed steel head of His Majesty's lance had been wrenched from his chest and thrust aside. While his left arm lay limp in his lap, his right arm was hooked over the trunk's open lid. He grunted because he could not reach deep enough inside the trunk. He was exerting all his strength but was too weak to lift his body. Abruptly he stiffened, sniffing the air. With a jolt, he turned his entire back to her. "Get out! Leave me be!"

The ferocious growl halted her. "Michael. You are severely hurt. Your wound needs tending. You may die of loss of blood if it is not sealed properly. Please, let me send Pippin for a—"

"Go back!" he roared, hiding his face against the trunk. "Do not come near me!"

"My God, Michael, if you won't see a surgeon, let me help you, please!" she beseeched. His behavior was disconcerting. Refusing to back down, she picked her way toward him. "You need a strong hand pressed against the wound, to stop the blood flow—"

"Stay the pox away from me, Renée!" he shouted gutturally, and resumed rummaging around the trunk with greater urgency. His efforts were in vain. Imbued with compassion, she ignored his dismissal and came to him. He cringed like a frightened porcupine. "*No!* Leave! I beg you. . . ."

Renée was at a loss. His stubborn helplessness tugged at her heart. "God's mercy, why will you not look at me? Leastways tell me what you seek in the trunk. I will fish it out for you."

Sharp tremors racked his frame. Moments passed. "The glass bottle . . ." he blurted out at last.

She bent over the trunk to poke through jousting appurtenances. "I do not—"

"In the sporran!" he rasped, fighting to restrain his violent juddering.

"There!" She pulled the bottle out of the pouch and crouched beside him. "Here."

Gory fingers seized the bottle, but still his face was turned away. "Leave me now. *Go!*"

Her throat constricted. "I cannot leave you like this." She extended a shaky hand to touch him. He howled in anguish. He tilted his head back and quaffed from the bottle. His Adam's apple bobbed in his naked throat as he drank greedily, draining the brown vessel. With a groan of pure bliss, he fell back, sprawling on the ground, the bottle rolling from his fingers.

"Michael," Renée whispered, crouching beside him. She looked at the wound. A shout of terror ripped from her lips. She staggered back on her hands and heels and pushed to her feet. She clamped her hands over her mouth to stop the bile. Like an entity, the torn fleshly hole was mending, closing, before her very eyes. Michael stared at her, sadly—and her horror multiplied.

His eyes were eerie pools of quicksilver, luminescent as moonstones, exuding preternatural, petrifying power. His expression was grim, his voice mournful. "I asked you to stay away."

Christ Almighty! Renée retracted her steps to the canvas flap, nearly tripping in her haste to get out, whipped around, and fled the tent. He had fangs! Sharp, white, like a wolf's. . . .

Renée choked on a sob.

Michael was a vampire.

He was the covert vampire the Vespers had sent to court to steal the Ancient!

❧ 17 ❧

It is the heart that makes men eloquent.

—Quintilian: *Institutio Oratoria*

"Wolsey!" The lionlike greeting carried the insolent freedom of royal bloodlines. "Come in, come in! What news, my Lord Chancellor? How fare my lords and knights?"

One of the king's pageboys, a youth by the name of Boleyn, ushered Cardinal Wolsey inside the dressing chamber, past Penny the barber. With a solemn bow, Wolsey approached his young master. King Henry stood at the center of the chamber, bathed, shaved, and sweet-scented, as a quartet of fussy gentlemen dressed him ceremoniously in the vestments and accoutrements of the Order of the Garter for this evening's activities: the service at chapel and the ensuing feast in the presence chamber. "If I may comment on Your Majesty's appearance, among a thousand princes the King of England stands out the tallest, the brightest, and the most magnificent."

Pleased with the compliment, the king inspected his image in the long mirror supported by a fifth man. He wore a gilt embroidered dark blue jerkin over an argent doublet over a snowy shirt with ruffled sleeves; a scarlet hose accentuated his fine claves, whereof he was mightily proud; and a trunkhose with red silk peeking from slashed blue velvet puffed around his thighs.

"Your Majesty will be please to know that Lord Stanley's bones are undamaged and, in his own words, he shall hobble merrily to the feast. Sir William Compton"—the cardinal hushed when the king ordered his attendants to fetch the famed garter—"begs permission to wear an eye patch to cover his swollen black eye." *Courtesy of Michael Devereaux*, Wolsey snickered.

"Granted!" King Henry smiled. "We shall have two pirates, Bryan and Compton! It will add a rakish dash as well as a flare of menace to my court that I daresay Francis would be hard put to equal, and will certainly give the Venetian ambassador something to gossip about in his letters to his master, the Dodge." He planted his hands on the hunched shoulders of two grooms as a third placed his foot on a stool and a fourth dressed his calf with a gilt-buckled blue riband embossed with roses and the chrysochrous motto of the Order: *Accursed be a cowardly and covetous heart.*

The legends surrounding the birth of the motto were many and varied. Some said it was first uttered by King Edward III in reproof to the courtiers who laughed when his mistress, the Countess of Salisbury, lost her garter during a dance; the king picked up the garter and tied it to his leg, exclaiming: *Honi Soit Qui Mal y Pense. Evil be to him who evil thinks.* Others insisted King Edward derived it from the immortal poem *Sir Gawain and the Green Knight* or mayhap from the tale of King Richard Cœur de Lion who was inspired by St. George the Martyr to tie garters around the legs of his crusading knights in the Holy Land and won great battles. It was Wolsey's personal belief that the motto concerned a claim to the French throne, in pursuit of which King Edward had created the Order in the first place. Land was the Holy Grail of kings.

"Buckingham," he reported, "suffers of injuries caused by his fall, which may preclude his grace from attending the ceremony. I'm told he aches all over, predominantly in his tail, is beset with a dreadful megrim, wears a glowing crimson welt on his forehead the size of an apple, and is subjected to excruciating ripples of pain whenever he breathes or moves."

The king's eyes twinkled uncharitably. "Fit to bluster and cuss, I trow."

The cardinal gave a sighful nod. "He has taken a vicious tap to the helmet, Your Majesty."

"Come, now, Wolsey. We both know he has a bilious, boastful, high-minded nature, which makes him a most unpleasant companion. Maybe he will wear his welt with suitable humility." A concerned frown replaced his grin. "What of the fearless Master Devereaux. How fares he?"

"Yes, I was coming to that. It pleases me to report that by the grace of God, Master Devereaux has survived Your Majesty's lancing thanks to the thick padding he had judiciously inserted under the armor. His slight injury is skin deep, I am told, a bloody scratch that will leave no scarring."

"Good man!" The image in the mirror beamed as the attendants draped his brawny shoulders with the official blue velvet mantle. The Knights Companions' mantles would sport the heraldic shield of St. George's Cross set in a blue garter. The Sovereign of the Garter's badge sewn on the left shoulder was of the star of the Order. Over it, the attendants hung the collar—twelve Tudor roses set in blue garters, interspersed with twelve tasseled knots—made of thirty troy ounces of pure gold. Suspended from it was the Great George, a vividly enameled figure of St. George the Martyr on horseback slaying the dragon, the Order's insignia that the knights were allowed to wear only on St. George's Day and the feast days of the court. The king looked at his chancellor. "You will see to it that the whole realm knows he is unharmed and let it not be said that the King of England repays his loyal defenders with death."

"I have done so already, Your Majesty. The heralds presiding over the pageantries in the city squares shall announce Your Majesty champion of the joust and the healthful Master Michael Devereaux, the king's fearless shield, his runner-up of the joust. However, if I may suggest . . ."

"Yes?" urged the king as the last article of clothing was placed atop his golden head: a black velvet bonnet sporting a white ostrich plume and black heron feathers.

"I was thinking . . . perhaps Master Devereaux ought to be rewarded for his valiant defense of Your Majesty's life. . . . I interviewed him the morning after the incident, and what he told me I believed. I am convinced that when Earl Marshal and Captain Marney submit their final report, their findings will corroborate mine own: Master Devereaux, having overindulged at the supper, and being unacquainted with every passage in Your Majesty's grand palace, wandered in his confusion straight into the path of the skulking killer. Granted, I do not approve of excess in drinking. However, I shall be eternally grateful to him, for even in his deplorable condition, his natural reaction was to leap to Your Majesty's defense. In conclusion, I applaud his merit."

"As do I," said the king.

"As do Your Majesty's loving people, hence my reason for suggesting a reward. In honoring Master Devereaux, Your Majesty shall promote loyalty, gratitude, courage, the high principles of chivalry, and above all the people's affection for their sublime and generous prince. In elevating one fearless shield, Your Majesty will erect an entire nation of such shields. No foreign assassin will find a warm welcome to this country, and no inbred rotten apple will ever receive succor. Thusly, with God's help, I trust we shall disappoint our enemies of their intended purpose."

"Walk with me, Wolsey." They ambled to the privy chamber. The king snapped his fingers for wine and halted at a casement overlooking the Thames, out of earshot of his attendants. "I found good logic in your oration. I like your idea. What sort of reward do you have in mind?"

"A knighthood, Your Majesty, a mere honorary title, no fiefdom attached. Master Devereux stands to inherit his noble protector's title and estate, and during our chat, he assured me that—and I quote—his greatest aspiration is to serve his king and his noble lord in Ireland."

"A knighthood without a knight's fief. You believe it sufficient to inspire the entire realm? Bear in mind a purse of gold is what most people expect upon performing a service."

"Yes, I see Your Majesty's point. Then, if I may, let it be a knighthood of the Garter."

"The number of members cannot be allowed to grow out of twenty-four."

"Your Majesty has two vacancies to fill this year owing to the lamentable demise of the Earl of Shrewsbury and Waterford and

Duke Giuliani de Medici. One of the vacancies was promised *in potentiā* to Sir Walter Devereaux, the son of Sir John Devereaux, Baron Ferrers of Chartley."

"What is your recommendation?"

"If Your Majesty recalls, there was an act of attainder against Sir John after the Battle of Bosworth Field, which stripped him of all titles and estates. Now Sir Walter serves His Grace of Norfolk in the hopes of regaining his patrimony. His Grace spoke highly of Sir Walter. However, I advise against this nomination, for it has come to my attention that Sir Walter has recently disgraced himself with unbecoming conduct at court."

"Oh? What did he do?"

"Sir Walter tried to impose his attentions on Princess Renée of France by exerting physical force. Fortunately, Master Michael Devereaux happened to be walking nearby and instantly came to Her Grace's rescue. Another feat of gallantry, Your Majesty, attributed to the same man."

"Why was I not informed of this? Has she complained to you? She is King Francis's sister by marriage! Godsakes, if Francis hears of it, I shall be expected to convey a personal apology!"

"I believe Her Grace wishes to keep the matter quiet, and so far there has been no mention of the subject. I have questioned Master Michael Devereaux about the affair, and he responded with exemplary discretion, refusing to name the lady to whose rescue he had rushed."

"That was well done of him." The king rubbed his chin. "They are half brothers. . . ."

"Precisely." The cardinal let that thought simmer, then said quietly, "Your Majesty, after the night of the incident, I took it upon myself to investigate Michael Devereaux's affairs and learned that through a formal parliamentary process, Your Majesty's royal sire, may the Good Lord rest his soul, had nominated Master Michael Devereaux the legitimate heir of the Earl of Tyrone. It is my belief, sire, that in securing the transference of his title to Michael Devereaux, Lord Tyrone has demonstrated not only his love for the boy but also his great faith in him."

"Yes, he is a worthy companion."

"I trow Your Majesty will permit that betwixt the Devereaux, Michael is the most deserving man for a Garter knighthood. And there is another point in his favor. Lord Tyrone is a member of the Order, and his ancestor, Tyrone the Elder, was the very first Knight Companion of the Order, nominated by King Edward the Third himself. As for the process of nomination, the rules state that each member may nominate nine candidates, of whom three must have the rank of earl or higher, three the rank of baron or higher, and three the rank of knight or higher. The Sovereign may choose as many nominees as are necessary to fill vacancies. However, he is *not* obliged to choose those who received the most nominations, but, in fact, may elect his *own* candidate."

"Hmm. I am familiar with this rule," King Henry said. "You want him for the office, and I confess I do, too. However, there is another statute which requires that each member be a knight."

"I have thought on the problem and learned that the initial members were only knighted that same year. The statutes, while clear on every detail, have conspicuously overlooked this specific occurrence. I infer that they have left the matter to the consideration of the Sovereign."

"I agree." King Henry stirred. "Very well. I'll knight him and then nominate him a Knight Companion during the ceremony together with . . . who is my second candidate?"

"Thomas Dacre, Third Baron Dacre."

"See to it, Wolsey." King Henry smiled. "The more I think upon it, the more it pleases me. As always, you have provided your prince with a goodly advice."

The cardinal bowed. "I am Your Majesty's most humble servant."

"You knew!" Renée glowered at the old woman sitting on a stool, a distaff in her hand and her needle flying. Michael a vampire! Jesu! Overwrought, she paced before the fireplace. When Cardinal Medici had spoken of the hounds of hell she had not believed him. Not really. He said they had been decimated, hopefully extinct, but that none knew for sure. Dread and skepticism had trammeled her since. Half of her, the daughter of King Louis

XII, had deemed this business of fiends preying on human blood and a weapon capable of vanquishing them an old wives' tale embellished by Holy Church for the sole purpose of inciting fear to govern the people and the princes who accepted the fable as truth. He in possession of the Ancient would wield absolute power over nations, which explained the pains Cardinal Medici was taking to obtain it, as well as his premature gloating whilst sober. Her other half, the daughter of Anne of Brittany, who had glimpsed terror in the cardinal's eyes whilst in his cups and listened to hairy tales of bloodlust, savagery, and decimation, had felt the truth in his fear. Hence, her fear.

Now she knew. *By the saints!* Why did Michael have to be the covert thief the Vespers sent to steal the Ancient? "The whole time you knew what he was and didn't tell me! That one cannot die," she mimicked sulkily. "How could you withhold this information directly pertaining to my assignment, not to mention to my health, from me? I saw the fangs." Her voice quivered. "I saw those silvery devil's eyes, staring directly into my soul . . . God rot him!"

Adele cocked her head at her. "Are you infuriated or affrighted?"

"Infuriated! And affrighted. He is a vampire." She moaned wretchedly. "He feeds on blood." She resumed pacing. "But he eats, he drinks, he ambles in the sun like a cockerel on a morning parade. . . ."

"His immunity to the sun is baffling, I admit. Vampires cannot withstand sunlight on their skin. The sun turns them to ash. If they must move in the sun, they will cover themselves from head to toe. His eating and drinking acquits him of being a Vesper, and means that he was turned into a vampire recently," Adele said, shocking Renée with her hidden trove of knowledge.

Still as a stone, Renée asked, "How did you know?"

"Family lore, passed from mother to daughter," Adele admitted. "My mother was a healer, as her mother before her, and so forth, all the way back to Dame Adelaide, my namesake. She had a lover in her youth. His name was Emiliano. He was a young count. Their romance ended, and he left. When he returned threescore years later, she was on her deathbed. He was still a handsome young man. He told her the truth about himself and offered her the gift of eternity. Dame Adelaide refused, claimed she was weary of life. 'If only he spoke when I was young and pretty,' said she. 'Now I am too old, he is too late.' Do you have feelings for the vampire, child?"

She was a gallimaufry of feelings! "How did you divine that he was one?"

"He has been drinking blood. His skin stinks of it."

Renée was embarrassed. "I found his scent most pleasing."

"Sweet like berry wine with an earthly male musk?" Adele smiled, her sagacious, deep-set eyes reflecting the glow of the firelight. Renée nodded wretchedly. She sank onto a stool beside her nurse and rested her chin on her fists, morosely. "A heady fragrance, is it not? It is the blood he drinks. Do not berate yourself, child." Adele patted her. Renée descried concern in her nurse's eyes but also faith in her capabilities. "They are the devil's spawn, irresistible, strong, and robust, masterful with their love, lethal in their lust."

Chilly tremors meandered up Renée's spine. "Masterful with their love . . . Christ forefend!"

"They are natural enchanters, territorial and proprietary. These qualities are vital to their survival. Think upon it, lambkin, this vampire is very powerful—immune to sunlight!—and he cleaves to you most ardently. Such traits may be beneficial."

"I do not think he is utterly invulnerable to sunrays. He sweated buckets in his black armor, when everyone else strutted about in silvered suits. Certes! He is sensitive to silver!"

"And to fire, as all vampires are. Remember how his skin glistened when he visited?"

"He must have lost to the king on purpose. He trounced Lord Stanley, among others."

"A vampire at a joust . . . They had no chance of besting him. Bring me one of his bottles."

"I am sure they are well hidden. There were two in the sporran, one empty, the other full. He sucked it dry like a hardened tippler. He was in such pain hunting for the bottle in the trunk when he could have . . . ." She faltered, unable to complete the sentence.

"Pounced on your vein, fed on you, drank your blood . . . Why do you suppose he did not?"

Renée got up and paced again, gripping her hands together, as if in a prayer. "Oh, Adele! What do I do with him? Do I hand him over to the *deletoris*?" If she gave Michael up to Sergeant Francesco, he and his men would slay him. She did not want Michael slain.

"You must decide what is best. You were put in charge of this embassy for good reason."

Renée felt helpless and distraught, torn between fondness and terror. Instead of forcing her to leave the tent, Michael had chosen to trust her with his awful secret. He resisted her blood for reasons that were most perplexing and instilled dread in her heart just the same.

The members of England's highest, most coveted order of chivalry were ipso facto the most distinguished men in the realm, with the Holy Roman Emperor and the Archduke of Austria bringing the tally to twenty-four. Listed among them were: the dukes of Buckingham, Norfolk, Suffolk, and their heirs; the Marquess of Dorset; the earls of Northumberland, Worcester, Essex, Kent, Wiltshire, Shrewsbury, and Tyrone; and at least six barons, including Stanley.

And now Michael was joining their illustrious ranks.

Clothed in his noble lord's Garter apparel, Michael knelt before the King of England in the great watching chamber, with the entire court present, to be knighted Sir Michael Devereaux and Knight Companion of the Most Noble Order of the Garter in quick succession. Afterward, the Knights Companion would follow the Sovereign and the officers of the Garter—the prelate, the chancellor, the register, the garter principle king of arms, and the usher—in a procession on foot through the palace with the court following at a respectful distance, to the Church of the Observant Friars at Greenwich, where the Cardinal of York would conduct the Garter service.

The harbinger of his good fortune had been none other than Cardinal Wolsey, paying him a second personal visit in his chamber. Michael was informed in no uncertain terms that just as he owed his windfall to the cardinal, so his downfall might spring of the same fount, for fortune was made of glass: it shone but it also shattered. Thusly Michael became the cardinal's henchman, with the sense of achievement he imagined some Christian souls registered to serve the devil.

Sir Ned Poynings, the comptroller, held the office of the Garter Principle King of Arms. He was the first to offer congratulations as Michael walked into the guard room, supremely thrilled with the tidings. Sir Ned regretted that owing to lack of time he could not bestow Michael with his own armorial badges to display at the chapel and at the presence chamber during the feast. Michael acquitted the old boy of the malfunction and shook his hand animatedly.

"You shall kneel before the king with your head bowed as His Majesty speaks your merits, whereby you have earned the spur, and confers the title of knight unto you," Sir Ned explained. "You shall swear fealty to the king and realm. Thereafter we shall all proceed with due reverence to the chapel, where you will be called upon to deliver the *Benedicto Novi Militis* service. Do not look so grave, my boy. 'Tis a happy occasion! I shall be by your side every step of the way."

Oh, aye, happy, Michael thought, dazed. His head shot up. "What religious service?"

Sir Ned chuckled at his skittishness. "Rest you, dear boy. I shall provide you with a leaflet."

Michael relaxed.

Cardinal Wolsey aspersed Michael with holy water, citing the appropriate Latin benediction.

King Henry tapped Michael's shoulders with the ceremonial sword and grandly exclaimed, "Rise, Sir Michael Devereaux!"

The court clapped, Suffolk and Stanley with more gusto than others. Michael faced the company and flourished a bow. His eyes located Renée beside Her Grace of Suffolk. Her gaze did not flinch from his, but her expression was stolid and her complexion was pale. She feared him.

Singers, lute, flute, and organ players, masquerading as mythical creatures of the forest, with Dionysius Memo at the lead, greeted the returning knights and courtiers in the allée outside the church and ushered the court to supper. The presence chamber had been magically transformed into a pleasure garden, spring blossoms interwoven in espaliered walls, frankincense and myrrh perfuming the air, and lustrous gold tableware reflecting the soft glimmer of a thousand candles flickering timidly in garlanded sconces. With his generosity and splendor King Henry embodied the prefect prince, as depicted in Baldassare Castiglione's book *The Courtier*.

The Sovereign, officers, and Knights Companion of the Order supped above the salt. The high table opposite them sat Queen Katherine, her ladies, the knights' consorts, and one princess of France. Flanked by Stanley and Suffolk, his greatest supporters, and sitting seven seats down from the king, Michael regarded the woman who would not look at him and chewed the cud of the cardinal's warning, borrowed from one Publilius Syrus, an Assyrian slave who had earned his liberty from his Roman master by his wit and talent for composing maxims: *Fortūna vitrea est: tum cum splendet frangitur. Fortune is made of glass: when it shines, it shatters.*

For an ephemeral morning, he and Renée had shone together—and then they shattered.

Wolsey had corrupted the text to suit his purpose, as Michael suspected the cardinal dealt with all things. The true meaning was infinitely crueler: a dream shattered the instant it came true. Renée would never look at him again as she had today when he gave her his jousting prize. Why had he allowed her to discover his terrible ailment? If intimacy born out of need, and trust built on confidences, had been his objectives, then he had erred, for in accepting her help, he had given her the power to destroy him with a word. Getting skewered so close to the heart—by his design, no less, for he had loosened the straps of his left pauldron to ensure the king's victory—must have stultified his brain as well as his body. Closeness could not be imposed.

Tearing his focus away from her, Michael heard Norfolk and Dudley, the "old guard" of the Order, who had served as field commanders in their heyday, muttering on the contamination of their set by undeserving wild fellows that roar into court and thereupon become carpet knights by means of cheap heroics and blandishments. Meanwhile, Buckingham was inveighing against the rushed ennoblement of upstarts to Lord Essex, "He would give his fees, offices, and rewards to boys rather than noblemen!" Both men were wearing his lance's imprint on the forehead.

"Mind them not, Michael," Suffolk said sotto voce. "They said the same of me."

As was the usual custom, when Queen Katherine left the magical forest of guttering cressets, the night-rule became misrule, ribald and promiscuous. Aware of the turquoise eyes recording her every gesture, Renée decided to emulate Her Majesty's sound example. Doubtless even solar vampires were in essence night prowlers; after sunset, their powers increased tenfold, as did their bloodlust.

"Do not depart yet," Mary implored. "The company will be dull without you, and I dare not leave Charles to be devoured by the wantons."

Opposite them, His Grace of Suffolk was drinking and laughing with Stanley. Michael had curiously vanished. Abruptly the lights dimmed. Servers filed in, carrying large bowls with figs, currants, raisins, almonds, and candied plums floating in brandy.

"Snapdragons, how delightful! Now you must stay, Renée. It is tradition. We play the game on All Hallows' Mass, on Twelfth Night, and ofttimes on St. George's Day, to celebrate the saint's slaying the firedrake. And"—she smiled temptingly—"the person who snatches the most treats out of the brandy will meet their true love within a year."

"I have already found my true love," Renée replied.

"There is another tradition," a deep voice spoke over her shoulder as a server placed a bowl on the table in front of them. "One of the raisins contains a gold button. Whoever snaps what we call 'the lucky raisin' may claim a boon of their choosing from anyone in the room."

Renée pushed to her feet, her eyes widening in terror. She dared not leave the room now.

Mary smiled. "Good evening, Sir Michael. And, yes, you are quite right. Each bowl contains one lucky raisin." As she spoke, the servitor put a burning taper to the bowl, setting the brandy afire. Blue flames played across the numerous bowls in the dimness. Everyone began singing:

> *"Here he comes with flaming bowl,*
> *Don't he mean to take his toll,*
> *Snip! Snap! Dragon!*
> *With his blue and lapping tongue*
> *Many of you will be stung,*
> *Snip! Snap! Dragon!*
> *For he snaps at all that comes*
> *Snatching at his feast of plums,*
> *Snip! Snap! Dragon!"*

The company clapped and pounced on the bowls. Shrieks of delight ensued as the courtiers braved the flames to fish out the raisins and swallow them aflame. Mary swished off. *Sir* Michael remained at Renée's back. When she tried to flee, his left arm slid around her waist, staying her.

A flush of fever rendered her light-headed. "Let go of me," she breathed. "Or I'll scream."

"Scream," he taunted, his lips brushing her ear. She opened her mouth and caught a flaming raisin on her tongue. Chuckling, Michael popped one into his own mouth. "You look like a demon."

Eating the raisin before it scorched her maw, Renée craned her head aside and stared at his mouth, eerily aglow, fangs sheathed. He closed his mouth, extinguishing the snapdragon. The wantonness of the game was not lost on her. Michael's blue eyes glittered; his strong jaw, his lips, so close to hers, offered a staggering enticement. Yet the memory of the argent eyes and the sharp white fangs chilled her to the bone. *Fire and ice.* She feared and desired him all at once, and the alliance of these two sentiments, so contradictory, dwelling in the same body, constituted a strange, volatile, diabolical passion. She stirred in his embrace, desperate to escape him.

His hand flattened on her stomach, pressing her back to his torso, as his gaze focused on the blazing bowl. Lightning fast, he dipped his fingers in the flames and plucked out another raisin. He scraped the raisin's surface with his teeth and held out the gold button to her view.

Renée seethed. Omniscient as well as omnipotent, vampires were notorious tricksters, full of ropery. She saw Sir Francis Bryan, equally successful, claim a kiss from a giggling Lady Percy.

"I claim a boon," Michael whispered.

Frissons of thrill rasped her nerve-endings. "You shan't get a kiss from me."

Michael laughed huskily. "Alas, at the risk of forfeiting future kisses, I must decline your . . . is it the third or fourth offer? Ugh!" He chuckled as she jabbed an elbow in his side. "What sharp stems you have, my prickly sweetbriar, but I will not be daunted by your spikes. Nor will I settle for a kiss when I may claim the whole." He inhaled her perfumed neck. "The fragrant leaves, the lush roseate flowers." He brazenly traced her lips with his finger-tips and nearly got them bitten off. "And the fruity silken hips withal." He smoothed the open palms of his hands along the equiv-alent parts of her anatomy, sending ripples of erotic awareness to the sheath betwixt her thighs. "Such a prize is sure to prop up my knightly courage and steel my lance's point."

"Oh!" Renée bristled at the untoward speech. "You satyr!"

"Pax, lady. Know you not when I tease?" The buoyancy ebbed from his voice. He wrapped possessive arms about her waist, mold-ing her to him. "The boon I claim is a private audience."

Heretofore this vampire had behaved surprisingly mild-mannered, but the sunny weather had evolved into a storm. "I refuse."

"Fear me not, marmoset," he entreated against the whorls of her ear. "I am harmless."

"H-harmless?" Incredulous, she searched the vampire's hooded gaze for traces of mockery.

Turquoise eyes fringed with long eyelashes beheld her mo-rosely. "'I wish her well, she wills me woe, I am her friend, but she's my foe.' I am not pestiferous, Renée. We've become friends, have we not? I was your"—he smiled plaintively—"*bel ami*. Will you not give me a hearing?"

"*Petit ami*," she amended curtly.

"What is the difference?"

Headily aware of his appealing scent, of the contours of his muscled chest, thighs, and arms, and of the seductive warmth he emitted, she bit out, "The difference between night and day."

"What you saw is my cross to bear," he said, somewhat irritated. "May I know in what way I have offended you? I, who ever since I have known you, have lived at your feet like a slave?"

Good angels keep her! Her mind and body became an internecine war wherein fondness and carnal attraction belabored terror and superstition. *Masterful with their love, lethal in their lust.*

Then something flipped her perspective as if it were an hour-glass. Across the room, beyond leaping blue flames and wildly romping courtiers, she saw the Cardinal of York watching them. A devilish scheme sprouted in her brain, frightful in its ingenuity. Hitherto, she had approached her assignment in an extemporaneous manner and failed. But no more. She tilted her head aside, slanting Michael a provocative look. "State your case or unhand me. We begin to draw eyes."

Her compliance took him by surprise. "May I suggest a less public landscape?"

Renée placed her hands over the strong arms caging her. "I . . . dare not."

Michael's voice was thick with feeling. "Have you ever had a person come into your life whose company became a compulsion and whose confidence you craved above all others'?"

She shook her head, undone by the melting heat journeying low in her body.

"I have. Recently, in fact. She is a perspicacious little thing, contumacious to the extreme, has a stropped tongue, the curiosity of a cat." He grinned when her eyes flashed. "Did I mention she has a passionate spirit, enchanting eyes, wit galore, and a kind and generous heart?"

In spite of herself, his words touched her profoundly. "Go on."

"I made a mistake today. My noble protector taught me to conceal my shortcomings and put my fortes on display, but in a moment of weakness, I let her see something that gave her a nasty jolt. She saw me bleed, she saw me heal. She saw my face become deformed by illness."

"What illness?" *She had seen his fangs. She had seen his eyes transformed into quicksilver.*

He put his lips to her ear. "The sweating sickness, I had it before I came to court. The potion in the glass bottle is an Irish remedy called dragon's blood. It keeps the ill-effects at bay."

What in the name of the Holy Virgin was he prating about? Then it dawned on her: little falsehoods vampires told uninformed humans who had seen them in their monstrous form.

"In a nutshell, one word from her lips will burn me for practicing sorcery. She saved my life this morn. She holds my life in her hands still." Sustaining her gaze, he lifted her hand to his soft, warm lips. "What do you suppose she will do?"

Renée thought fast. "She will tell no one. Mistrust her not. She will protect your secret."

"Will she spurn me? Loathe me?"

"No."

"Do I repulse her now?"

"No." She ought to find him repelling, but she did not. "She is fond of you."

"I am not infectious, I guarantee it."

"That is . . . good to know." Notwithstanding the dim lights, the dancing, and the rollicking ambiance, they had been standing embraced together long enough. Renée extricated herself from his arms and faced him. Beyond Michael's shoulder, she saw Stanley and Suffolk drawing near. "As for your elevation to knighthood, I am well pleased and think you most deserving of the honor. Will you be returning to Ireland soon?" she asked politely. His answer was obvious.

"I think I shall stay awhile."

"Would you . . . seek an office with the cardinal? I hear he supported your titling."

"I confess such an office would be advantageous, but I must think upon it."

To become his confidante you must become his lover, intuition said. The notion startled her, excited her, softened her, equally thrilling and frightening. She was not ready! She applied her wit instead.

"You know how to win, Hannibal, but you do not know how to use your victory."

"Whatever do you mean by that?"

His mates were almost upon them. She whispered, "Play the trump card. Rise higher."

"Be specific," Michael prompted. "What would you have me do?"

"The duke's dagger," she hissed. "Good evening, Your Grace, Lord Stanley." She dipped.

"Gracious lady, we come to rescue you from the clutches of this newly minted blackguard."

"In faith, he was a blackguard afore he was minted," Stanley corrected the duke, planting his heavy paw on Michael's shoulder. "Aroint thee, Sir Knight! Let others play the field."

"For shame, Sir Knight, you have exercised your unlicensed monopoly long enough."

Renée smiled brightly. "Gentlemen, I thank you for the valiant rescue, albeit I am equally to blame for having kept Sir Knight from well-wishers and friends. I bid you three gallants a good night." She intended to find her guard and retire to the shelter of her bed, but sashayed off slowly, curious to hear what they might speak of her. What Michael would say of her.

"Good Lord, deliver me from such devils for mates! The lady was about to give me a kiss."

Renée sniffed. The vampire sensed her presence. The remark was meant for her benefit.

"You dream, Sir Knight. She fled and in her flight was swifter than a doe."

"If she did flee, which I naysay, your fire-breaths chased her off. By my snout, you left the maids all the poorer for snapdragons and true loves withal."

"Sobriety on the night of one's dubbing is a sin," cut in Sir Francis Bryan. "Carew and I are for a tipple at the Hart. What say you?"

Renée slinked off. Thoughts tumbled inside her head like acrobats. Heretofore she had been treading water; every hard plotted approach had come to naught. Finally—having discovered that Michael was the Vespers' scout—she had the key to accomplishing

her task. The sad jolt she had gotten might yet turn out to be providential. Her newfangled strategy was logical, perfect . . .

Cruel.

Her resolve weakened. He was her *petit ami*. She liked him so
much. *Of course you would like him, goosehead*, she chastised herself.
Vampires were made to be charming. She must not tremble with
fear before the trumpet. Nor play Medea to Michael's Jason, not
when the Golden Fleece was at last within reach. *I see the better
course of action and I approve of it, but I follow the worse course.* She
wanted to crawl into her bed and cry. She would have to be cruel.

✑ 18 ✑

A monster with many heads.

—Horace: *Epistles*

A whistle of the wind carried shouts, laughter, and beastly snarls. Flickering lights and the stench of putrid fish permeated the river mist hanging on the landing steps beneath the southern end of London Bridge. The odors, the sounds, the very feel of the place gave Michael the willies.

"Now I reckon why they call this place the stews," he observed, climbing from the bobbing boat onto the bankside. Stanley flicked the boatman his fare and followed Michael.

"Stanks and stoves, it is a fishpond sort of stew," quipped Francis Bryan.

"They serve it raw, they serve it hot, they serve it at table boiled in a pot," rhymed Wyatt, the sixth member to join their party. "Whence we call yonder fish place a fleshpot."

Laughing, they cut the mist toward the haze of torchlight foretokening the thoroughfare. At the foot of the bridge, a cluster of people—regular, secular, palliards, mercenaries, apprentices, hardened rogues, younkers, and doxies—crammed a row outside the Bear Tavern and the wine-selling White Horse Inn, shouting odds and bets at a bearbaiting, while harlots and pickers plied their trades, blatantly or furtively, among them. The arrival of Michael's party, albeit in simple apparel, did not go unnoticed. A harbor wench drew away from the crowd, puckered her rouged lips, and sashayed toward Stanley. She leaned into him. "How now, luv. Want a kiss?"

"For love?" he teased her.

"Four doits," she replied matter-of-factly.

"You cut me to the heart, sweetheart."

Grumbling at his miserliness, she shuffled off.

Michael pursued her. When he had what he wanted, he returned to his mates and tossed the stolen purse at Stanley. "Next time, watch the grubby hands, not the pretty dukkys."

"Faith! The purse was hid in a secret pocket of my cloak, and I never felt a thing!"

"Nor did she," observed Bryan, staring after the trull as she darted off to gloat over the loot she had unsuspectingly lost. "Quite the creative legerdemain, and as I recall you also tumble."

Michael's gaze clashed with Bryan's. The barb was meant to draw blood. Stanley slapped his shoulder fondly. "You must teach me this trick, runt. Sleight of hand may be useful at court."

Unsatisfied, Bryan fell into step beside them. "Here's a riddle for you. What would you call a prestidigitator who is also a consummate loser at cards—when playing with the king?"

For pity's sake, Michael simmered. Bryan was spoiling for it.

"There is more to you than meets the eye, Devereaux. You acquitted yourself extraordinarily well at the joust today, unhorsing Carew, Compton, and Stanley, among others less capable."

Michael, choosing to overlook the unsubtle accusation that he was a sharper, refrained from rejoining and thus inviting further scrutiny into his character, for he had already weighed the man in his balance. Bryan was a cunning, unprincipled, viciously witty scorpion who presumed much with the king and apostatized regularly to remain in favor. "I'm glad I could return your purse, Stanley, but this place is . . . foul and evil." He knew he sounded like a wide-eyed lad, but could not help it. His aversion to Southwark grew apace.

"A necessary evil," Suffolk philosophized, filling in the awkward silence. "Human laws are inadequate for prohibiting all evils, and the multitude is unable to keep chastity."

"You would know something about that, eh Brandon?" ragged Bryan.

"Hence," Suffolk continued his oration pointedly, "smaller evils are permitted so that greater ones such as lustful rioting of evil-disposed persons throughout the city can be avoided."

"Methinks Your Grace is primed for Parliament," Bryan, undaunted, summarized.

Crowding High Street and its crisscrossing rows and alleys, a plethora of taverns, victuals, brew houses, hostelries, bathhouses, brothels, bearbaiting and bullbaiting arenas jostled for space with shops of stockfishmongers, garlicmongers, and bakemongers. The hour was past midnight, and business thrived at the signs of the Lion, the Antelope, the Dragon, the Boar's Head, Fleur-de-Lys, the Cross Keys, the Barge, the Rose, the Castle, the Bell and the Cock, and the Unicorn. At Gropecunt Lane and Maydenlane, harlots issued lewd invitations from upper galleries of whitewashed wooden messuages. But there was more to Southwark than vulgar merrymaking.

King's Pike Garden's stew ponds lay cheek by jowl with the ominous Marshalsea and King's Bench Prison at Angel Place. In between, vagrants, cutpurses, counterfeit cranks, walking morts, cutthroats, beggars, and priggers of prancers, the mean denizens of the stews, littered the murky alleyways—streets so dark, so narrow, rats scurrying across, the stink of dirt, of rot, of poverty—and their insidious presence made Michael's flesh crawl along his neck. He detested this place.

His mates, men of breeding, palace dwellers, epicures, notwithstanding the gutters floating down the middle of the cobbled or earthen lanes, walked fast, keeping one hand on the haft of the sword strapped to the hip, rattling the scabbard at every drunken tinker, expecting at any moment to be cudgeled from behind, robbed, and slain. He could smell them sweating in spite of the cold.

The bastard sanctuaries, this place was called, because it lay beyond the reach of the mayor of London, outside the city's Charter, a place that did not exist, except to sate illicit needs of the lewd flesh, where the mighty played in plaguey holes together with the stews' mean livers, their night sport intensified by the hazard, the perils lurking in the shadows. The whole time, Michael was conscious of footsteps, stealthy, quick, to whom human life meant nothing, stalking them. As he turned abruptly, the footsteps stopped, but as he continued walking, the footsteps resumed.

Surprisingly there was no fear in his heart; acute repugnance had overflowed it yards behind. He wanted to quit this place and continue walking, on and on, until he submerged himself in a blue Irish lake rimmed by lush hills populated with shrieking falcons and wash away the sounds, smells, and sights of the Southwark stews, obliterate the place from his memory, and be clean.

"Bryan, ye gorgeous rogue, where 'ave ye been?" A brunette wench in her thirties, wearing rouge and little clothing, her mussed hair a tangle of curls and knots held with scarlet ribbons and garish clips, stepped out of the Hart, tugged her bodice low, planted hands on hips, and sashayed provocatively.

"Margery, ma belle!" Bryan grabbed her waist with one arm, squeezed her bottom with the other, and bussed her three-quarters naked boobies with lusty appreciation. "You look better than last I saw you, old girl. Come to think of it, you smell much better, too."

"Aw, do not be reminding me o' that!" She pushed at his chest, not so merry anymore.

With cruel delight, Bryan debilitated her with mauling, turning his captive into a hedgehog, and setting Michael's teeth on edge, a reaction the astute Bryan did not miss. "Devereaux, meet Mistress Margery Curson, the sauciest, hardiest, most incorrigible bawd in all of London! They charged her with the triple fustigations: fornication, adultery—or was it bawdry?—and harlotry. Her penance . . ." Laughing, he pushed Margery at Michael. "Tell the man, cherrylips!"

Michael caught the blowze's waist as she stumbled into him. Steadying her, he gained a look into eyes that harbored a toughened, cynical spirit, broken and put back together in a warped way many times early on in life, a product of this wretched place. He felt a hand slide into his surcoat, feeling him up for fancy knops to pluck. He clutched her wrist. "I am thinking not, darling."

Grunting at her failure, she raised her free hand to her confined one but rather than unhook his grip fingered the inside of his wrist. Her eyes narrowed into slits. "I know ye, blue eyes."

"Not unless you have been to Ireland." He opened his hand, and she staggered back.

"Tell him of your trial and penance, Marge!" Bryan prompted, relishing the altercation.

Snickering, Margery perambulated around Michael. "For the first offense, a respectable lady such as meself is taken from the prison in a striped hood an' 'olding a white wand to Aldgate, and thence, to be pilloried at the thew, where the cause is proclaimed. Then they parade 'er with minstrels like 'Er Majesty through Chepe and Newgate to Cokkeslane, to take up 'er abode."

Bryan spurred, "Tell him what you—"

"For the second offense," she adhered to her telling with a sharper voice, "whipping in the churchyard, flogging round the marketplace, cutting off hair, pillory, prison, and expulsion from London, from one o' the city gates. For the third offense"—she threw a smile at Bryan, warming to her coup de grâce—"excommunication by 'Oly Mother Church!"

Marge and Bryan burst out laughing, as if she had told a hilarious joke.

"Of course," Bryan clipped with a smile, "Margery owes her good fortune to me."

So that was the point of the spectacle, Michael deduced, to remind Mistress Curson who her lord and master was and what she owed him for his protection. The stews were the dung hill of the city, where lords, churchmen, merchants, diplomats, criminals, and whores drank together in poxed burrows, and what they said Marge heard and reported back to Bryan.

Cackling, Margery twined her arm with Bryan's. "Enow with yarn telling! Come inside and bring your lordly friends with ye, darlin'! Ale's on the 'ouse, the girls at haw price!"

Carew, Wyatt, and Suffolk followed Bryan and the hardened bawd. Stanley delayed behind with Michael, who felt—and must have looked—out of sorts. "Too prurient for you, codling?"

Michael yanked his sleeve over the red mark pricked into the inside of his wrist and with an affected grin slapped Stanley's arm. "Too prurient? Get me a hard drink and a harder harlot!"

They crossed the gateway into a curtilage smoky with burning torch-staves that surrounded a dwelling, stables, and a garden. The ground floor was divided into linked taprooms with stairs leading to the upper gallery bedchambers wherefrom contralto shrieks and baritone guffaws burst intermittently. The bawdy house was packed full of fellows: journeymen, apprentices, merchants, men-at-arms, knights Michael recognized from the joust, servants, rogues, and lower clergy, distinguishable by their comportment, speech, and the smells clinging to their apparels. They were drinking, dicing, growling, spitting, feeling up the serving wenches, and playing drinking games, such as draughts, nine men's morris, pitch penny, and ringing the bull, under the alert eyes of Mistress Curson's bandogs. The bovine-faced twins employed as hostlers brought Michael up short, shafts of eerie awareness needling him. Such strangeness.

Stanley's paw prodded him onward. They joined their mates at the table Margery cleared for them in her best taproom. The room was less crowded but just as stifling, stale, and filthy as the rest of the place. She stood betwixt Wyatt and Bryan and was slapping their groping hands with feigned annoyance. When Michael sat down, he felt her appraisal in many cold, unsettling ways.

"I've a fresh stock o' unpoxed Flemish Frowes fer ye, good gents, straight o' the ship!" the slattern announced. "Dairy sluts, skittish as kittens, just as ye like 'em! In Flanders they milked cows and held the suckling lambs." Smirking, she rocked an imaginary babe, a motion calculated to make her unbound breasts sway and bounce. "So I let 'em keep at wot they do best!"

The gentlemen laughed uproariously, licking their chops at the forthcoming flesh feast.

With judicious timing, six *frawes de Flaundres* brought tankards of watered-down ale to the table, smiling and tittering at the well-groomed gentlemen. Their eyes, Michael discerned, were already sottishly glazed from drink, a condition encouraged by the bawd to lubricate their thighs. Wyatt hooked his arms around the prettiest pair and herded them upstairs. Carew was fast behind him with two more and crowing, "We'll share the women, Wyatt! It will be amusing!"

One of the remaining *frowes* came to stand between Suffolk and Stanley, who eyed her with scrupled chagrin. Bryan snatched the last one, a girl of fourteen years or less, sat her in his lap, and stripped her to the waist. Large rosy nipples topped unripe breasts. Lust etched his visage.

Michael felt a stirring in his loins as an image of Renée posed like that in his lap flashed in his head. Bryan caught his gaze and snickered. Plucking at the girl's teats to make them jut, he cried, "Margery, our young friend here has a lonely look about him! Attend to him, ma belle!"

Margery resettled the plunging décolletage of her boneless, scarlet kirtle and fingered the glass lozenge mermaid rising and falling on a string between her breasts as her shrewd eyes rated Michael's susceptibility to her appeal. She circled the table and halted behind him. A wet tongue flicked at his earlobe. "Come upstairs with me, blue eyes," she husked. "I'll suck yer bone dry."

"I thank you for the lovely offer, Mistress Curson. Alack, a jousting injury prevents me—"

With a furtive peek at Bryan to ascertain the man was not paying attention, she murmured in Michael's ear, "'Ow 'bout ye pay me ta' keep me clapper still 'bout yer mum, bung boy?"

The last two words lit a firecracker in his head. Michael shoved to his feet and towered over her with supreme disdain in the set of his mouth. "What did you call me?"

"I remember ye, little sharper," she intoned triumphantly, quietly, so as not to be overheard by his tablemates. She sailed a hand over his torso, purring, "Aw, ye be all grown and lofty now, ta' fine fer 'onest goodies like ol' Marge 'ere, ey? But ye can't fool me, sweet'eart. I knew yer mum, see. Ellen the washer of the stews of the Whyt Cok, the prettiest nun on the stewesside. Shame wot 'appened to 'er."

Nauseating heat filled his belly. "You are mistaken, mistress. I have never frequented this foul stank before tonight, and my lady mother's name was not Ellen." It was Elizabeth Langham.

"Aye, blue-eyed Ellen and the golden gent wot fumbled up her kirtle and got 'er swelling under it. But do not be afeared, pretty darlin'. Ol' Marge can keep a secret, fer a goodly price."

"Old Marge would be wiser to keep a still clapper in her delusional head lest she offend her *lofty* patrons and get clapper-clawed tightly." He pushed past her and kept on shoving through the sweaty swarm until he felt the night air on his face. This place. He hated it.

Naught about the stews was familiar, except the stench. But the sinister feeling festering in the pit of Michael's stomach would not go away. He shut his eyes in an attempt to restore a sense of sanity. *Bung boy.* He should not be able to fathom London street words. How the pox did he?

"Suffolk and I are for the Cardinal's Hat," Stanley told his back. "Come, Sir Knight."

Wordlessly, Michael followed his mates to the street. Hooded faces sauntered past them: the occasional wench halting to proposition, drunkards singing off-key, suspicious-looking fellows sniffing for easy prey, shadows rooting around the rubbish that floated in the gutters, perches that had been left in disrepair for decades. They walked fast, rattling the swords riding their hips.

Michael dismissed the whore and her outlandish attempt at extortion from his thoughts and concentrated on important matters instead. He would have to watch Bryan; the king's minion had sniffed a poacher on his territory and did not welcome the competition. Tyrone's missing ring trammeled his mind; his inability to locate it in his room meant that someone had broken into his chamber while he slept and taken the pagan ring; what would he tell Lord Tyrone upon his return to Ireland? Then there was Renée—always Renée, who muddled up his priorities and encouraged procrastination—and her advice to him as regards Buckingham's dagger. Supposing she had had no hand in the conspiracy, how would he explain to Cardinal Wolsey his capture of the knife?

The hospice of the sign of the Cardinal's Hat was situated to the west of the Stratford nuns' estate on the bankside. Confused violence greeted their party of three at the foot of the Cardinal's Hat Alley: a scuffle between laics and liveried men-at-arms from the neighboring Marshalsea. Punches flew pellmell, blades flashed and scraped. Shouts pierced the dust-thick mist: "Upon 'em! Down with 'em!" Hysterical screams and weeping blared from inside the inn.

"No doubt the quarrel is over fullam," Stanley surmised. "I am of a mind to forgo what little amusement we might find here for a good night's sleep at the palace."

Suffolk snorted. "What a wretched deuce-ace we make—loitering about, two lovesick fools and one marriage-yoked graybeard—while Carew, Wyatt, and Bryan are tippling and tumbling."

Michael's attention was elsewhere. "The quarrel isn't over false dice. One of the harlots was gruesomely murdered, and the murderer is at large." Without consultation, he shouldered a path inside the hospice, his senses inordinately heightened, stimulated. Hard on the scent of blood and terror, he negotiated the hurly-burly taprooms and corridors, reached a flight of steps, and took them two at a time. Whatever pulled his bridle was as unfathomable as it was unstoppable.

Wailing whores and half-naked patrons formed the cortege of the dead whore as the hostlers, a one-eyed old man and a youth, carried her out of her chamber, wrapped in dirty bed linen.

"Oy! Out of the way, gent!"

"Let me see her!" Michael demanded urgently, demons breathing down his neck.

"Ye related to Mariona Wood?" the one-eyed hostler scoffed. "Rest ye, milord. Wot little trouble ye sowed in 'er belly, the angels took care o' it fer ye!"

Remembering Renée's advice, Michael held out a shilling. "Would this buy me a look?"

The hostler let go of the bundle, dropping it on the floor, and snatched the coin.

Michael knelt down beside her. He lifted the edge of the sheet and jumped back in shock.

Mariona Wood's neck had been ravaged by feral teeth. Fresh blood coated the bite marks. His senses reeled. The drouth slammed into him, violent, sickening, a ravenous howling beast in his veins, burning behind his eyes. The craving for dragon's blood had him by the throat!

Through the blinding fog of acute thirst, he saw Mariona Wood's visage alter into an angelic female. She opened bright blue eyes and gazed upon him with untold ruth, her sorrow a rondel cutting out his heart. "Michael . . ." she whispered. He growled in misery, frozen in place.

The ostler flapped the sheet over her face; then he and his helper lifted the shrouded body, and carried the blood-soaked bundle outside. Michael tramped after them with heavy feet.

Stanley and Suffolk met him at the threshold. "Let us go!" Stanley urged, but Michael could not move. As the hostlers dumped the body in a ditch, a tiny fair boy of four or five summers darted past them and leaped into the gutter to lie atop the shrouded corpse, crying despondently, his sobs heartrending. Michael didn't know how long the boy lay there. At some point, he scrambled out of the gutter, pulled the body up by the sheet to the potted road, and dragged her away from the stew house, every inch a labor, stopping at times to catch his breath.

Michael wanted to help him, but his body was affected by an inexplicable impairment of physical function. He felt utterly incapacitated, neither able to lift his arms nor speak. Frustration raged within him. Yet his lips could not give vent to his wrath. He could, just barely, plod after the boy and observe his struggle in towing his dead mother to a plot of ground strewn with crude wooden crosses, broken as the souls of those interred in the unconsecrated earth.

The little boy began digging a hole with his tiny hands, digging and crying. Intermittently he would stop and cling to his shrouded mother, sobbing desolately, then would resume digging.

By sunup the grave was deep enough to encompass a body. The boy rolled the chrysalis into the hole and followed inside, where he lay with his dead mother, grimy, cold, numb, and slept.

With a start, Michael lunged up. He sat in a large, soft bed, drenched in sweat. All was dark. He recognized his chamber at the king's palace. His heart beat savagely, his throat was parched. He reached underneath the bed and found the casket open, his key stuck in the lock. Vaguely he recalled returning to his chamber and draining one of the bottles. Now he ached for another.

As he emptied the bottle, dawn broke over the horizon, and the first sunray pierced his eyes. Unbearable pain surged up within him, ripping his heart, his soul, his very being to shreds like a pack of ravening bloodhounds attacking a repast of fleshy bones. The cruel truth hit him at last. "He was me!" he howled, shoving shaky fingers through sweat-soaked hair. *"The boy was me!"*

❧ 19 ❧

The cowl does not make the monk.

—a medieval Latin proverb

A bloodcurdling scream pierced the lulling quietude of dawn. Jolted from a wink against a pair of pillars, nightwatchmen Miles and Hensley sprang into action. Halberds tipped, hearts thudding rapidly, senses on the alert, they negotiated the smoky corridors of the grand wing where the king lodged his nobles, ready to tackle any interloper.

An open doorway, silted with dusky mist, beckoned them forth. Naught stirred as on muted accord the highly trained yeomen entered the apartment. The privy chamber was vacant. Yet the scent of death hung heavily in the air. A woman wailed hard by. Vigilantly, they crept into the yonder bedchamber. A maidservant stood in a puddle of spilt water, her back to them, a pewter pitcher rolling at her feet. She was trembling like a wobbly funeral effigy.

"My lady . . ." she sobbed raggedly.

Drawing up on either side of her, the watchmen stared aghast at the bed. There, sprawled on fine tangled linen, naked as a newborn, loose-limbed, russet curls fanned out on the pillow, eyes agape, and her lips parted in an expression of ghostlike delight, Lady Anne Hastings, His Grace of Buckingham's lady sister and King Harry's former mistress, lay lifeless.

"God preserve us. . . ." Miles signed the cross. He knew the maidservant as Nan, a passing fair girl in the service of Lady Hastings. Terror-stricken, she had fixed her gaze on the bed.

"Gray as a Greyfriar she is," Hensley observed. "See you a wound?"

Perversely aroused by the female beauty of the cadaver, Miles gazed absorbedly over plump breasts, the triangle of dark curls at the apex of the fleshy thighs, the loosely parted legs. "Nay, kissed by an angel she was. A pity, that. She was a lusty one."

"This be not the kiss of an angel, Miles." Hensley stepped forth and shifted a hank of russet curls off the lady's neck. Nan shrieked and dropped to her knees, crying, her face in her hands.

"Holy Mother of God!" Miles staggered back in fright, crossing his thumb and forefinger to ward off the Evil One. "She was fanged! Bitten and bled!"

"Aye, she was." Hensley swept the nude female body with a dark glance, then drew the sheet over the corpse, all the way up to cover the ugly bite mark and the lady's face.

"Do not touch, ye fool!" Miles cried. "She might be plagued!"

"Not plagued, merely dead. I reckon His Grace her brother needs be told."

"His mighty Grace won't thank you for telling him, I can tell you that." Miles grunted. "He'd charge us with murdering the poor lady. And even if the maid spake for our innocence, and all was well for us, the high-minded stock would find a reason to deliver us a blow for meddling."

"Sir Hastings, then."

"Sir Hastings left court yestermorning, afore the joust."

"His Eminence the Cardinal of York should find interest in the case of a noble lady bitten to death by a devil dog. I say there will be a pretty penny in it for us if we keep this nice and quiet." He looked at Miles. "What say you?"

Miles felt a light shudder. "Aye. 'Tis a good thing our watch ends. I should not care to come upon any devil dog or foulness lurking about these halls this curst morn. Let us be gone."

Grasping the sleeve of his livery, Nan stared at Miles through eyes pooling with tears. "Who will keep watch over my poor mistress? None must see her so."

"There's a coin for your troubles." Hensley patted her shoulder. "Bolt the door after us and let none inside afore your betters arrive."

"Good morrow, Your Eminence."

"Morrow is it?" Thomas Wolsey, Bishop and Cardinal of York, looked over his shoulder at the burgundy curtains drawn across the Thames fronting windows. A sliver of gray light winked at him through the fissure. He grimaced. His bones ached from keeping the night vigil behind the massive writing table, his ink-smeared fingers stiff from scribbling away. There was no rest for the Lord Chancellor of England. Always so much to be done. Removing his nightcap and keverchief, he eyed his diligent gentleman usher filling the doorway to his spacious apartment. "What is it, Master Cavendish? Bedbugs?"

"Nightwatchmen Miles and Hensley from His Majesty's guard are begging an audience."

"Send them away." Cardinal Wolsey dipped his quill in ink and continued writing his letter to His Holiness, Pope Leo X.

"They insist on reporting news of the utmost urgency and import from court, Eminence."

"They would not say what?"

"Their matter, it appears, is of some delicacy."

Wolsey exhaled. "Very well. Send them in." He reread the half-finished letter, but his focus was lost. A matter of delicacy at the king's palace at dawn did not bode well.

The hulky fellows came in, caps in hand. "Your Grace." They bowed.

"Well?" His gaze darted between their anxious faces, communicating his impatience.

"Your Eminence." One of them stepped forth, looking pale. "Lady Hastings was murdered. Her maidservant Nan found her an hour hence. Her screams brought us running from our post."

"Lady Anne Hastings, His Grace of Buckingham's lady sister?"

"Aye, Your Grace." The more brazen of the two guards lowered his voice. "Bitten by a devil dog, on the neck," he whispered, and got an elbow in the ribs from his disapproving crony.

The cardinal's blood congealed. He schooled his features to appear calm. "What have you done so far? Have you mentioned this to anyone?"

"No, Your Grace," the second yeoman replied. "We told the maidservant, Nan, to guard her lady and lock the door to anyone and hurried hither, as duty demands."

"Excellent thinking! Well done, men! Master Cavendish, pay these yeomen a shilling each and summon George Hill." Once the door closed, Wolsey crushed his missive to the pope, astir with fury. God protect him, his future was about to go up in smoke!

George Hill, the captain of the guard at York Place, came in and closed the door.

"Dispose of the two yeomen that left. Quietly. The shillings you will find on their carcasses are yours. Do not mention this to anyone. Wait! I shall need an armed escort on the hour bell."

George Hill bowed respectfully and hurried after the departing guards.

The cardinal hastened to his chamber to dress without delay. There was much to accomplish before Mass. He could not allow rumors to filter—or he would be lost.

As the yeomen promised, Cardinal Wolsey found the whey-faced servant zealously guarding her dead mistress with a teary eye and a dripping red nose. Recognizing his commanding voice, she cracked open the door and plunged to kiss the hem of his scarlet robe, bawling inarticulately.

"Has anyone entered Her Ladyship's chambers aside from you and the two nightwatchmen?"

Looking up from the floor, Nan shook her head. "None has entered, Eminence, not without treading on your humble servant—and that I would have noted."

"Was His Grace of Buckingham informed of his lady sister's passing?"

"No." Nan burst into tears. "My poor lady! Bitten by a savage dog!"

"A dog, you say?"

"A savage bloodhound, Your Grace!"

Wolsey narrowed his eyes. "A savage hound?"

"A monster!"

Dread immobilized him for a moment. "You saw it?"

"Heavens, no! Our Lady spared this God-fearing serving maid. I saw the vicious teeth marks left on my lady's neck." Nan fingered the thick vein pulsing between her ear and collar.

The cardinal sucked in a hissing breath. "I shall take care of everything, child. But you must promise me to be very discreet. Absolute silence is mandatory in this wretched business. Do you understand? Good. Now wait outside till I summon you. Your poor mistress was taken from us unshriven and therefore needs be blessed and offered to Our Lord with a benediction."

"Yes, Your Eminence."

Wolsey handed her to George Hill with a pointed look. "I will have need of her anon."

He locked the door, marched into the bedchamber, and threw the sheet aside. He stumbled back in fright. The bloody teeth mark on the neck, the frozen expression evidencing the bargain Anne had struck with the devil: in exchange for carnal delight, she had allowed her spirit to be stolen by a vampire. Cold sweat coated his skin. Even he, a prince of Holy Church, quavered at the sight of the devil's work. They were coming. The vampires. For the Ancient—for *him*!

Wolsey took out a kerchief and mopped his perspiring face. Self-preservation recommended he return the torch to Cardinal Campeggio and be done with this life-threatening legateship, but no. He would persevere unflinchingly. He would hang on to his good fortune till they pry it from his fingers. Campeggio and his *deletoris* could never learn of the vampiric presence at court or they would whisk the Ancient to his rival in France and rob Wolsey of his future as pope.

Lamentably without the *deletoris*, he was ill-equipped to hunt down a vampire. What to do? He could never allow Norfolk to conduct an inquest. None could be allowed to meddle in this. The bite mark on the neck was indicative. He would have to control the affair himself. He would somehow find evidence leading to someone else, a scapegoat, one of the king's minions working to undermine him. That was it! He would say that Anne was murdered by a secret paramour and instigate a manhunt. He would engage the entire court in the enterprise, lords and servants alike, get their tongues wagging, maybe even unearth a few secrets. Only it would seem odd that he, the lord chancellor, should take such an interest in the murder of a courtly lady. Ergo he would require an aide, someone devoted to him, a young knight beholden to him, eager to rise high . . .

With a renewed sense of purpose, he covered the corpse up with the sheet. A female arm slid off to dangle listlessly over the side of the bed. A tiny object dropped with a tinkle on the floor, span wildly, lost impetus, and settled. A gold ring! He picked it up. The alien emblem carved in the gold featured a serpentine dragon with female attributes. Anne must have snatched the ring from her murderer—the vampire.

A chilling thought struck Wolsey: could the fiend be roaming the court in a courtier's pelt, dining at the king's table, dicing and playing at cards, flirting with the ladies, jousting with the knights, mayhap even . . . sitting on the Privy Council?

He stared at the ring. His first clue. Was it Bryan? The whoreson was dissolute and wily as a serpent. His daring feats at sea under Admiral Thomas Howard in the *Margaret Bonaventure* were legendary—and, in Wolsey's mind, questionable. The knavish Carew was another entry in Wolsey's bad books and therefore suspect. After Wolsey had finally succeeded in sending him away from court, Carew had managed to coax a countermanding recall from the king. Compton, a third troublesome burr, was, according to Pace, sniffing after the Lady Anne of late.

As for the lady, soon after her marriage she became the king's mistress, was disgraced, and banished to the nunnery. Clearly her newfangled piety had been skin deep; she had returned to court a greater strumpet than ever. He chewed the cud of his plan and came to the conclusion that it was brilliant: the lover killed her. This was the pretext he needed to hunt down the loathsome minions. He would take two boars, mayhap more, in one alley.

Wolsey dropped the gold ring into the fringed purse on his belt and let in George Hill. "The mark on the neck, make it look like a stabbing." He closed the bedchamber and admitted the maid-servant into the privy chamber. "How long have you served Her Ladyship?"

"Not long, Eminence. My mum serves Her Grace of Buckingham at Penshurst Place."

Nan's allegiance to the Stafford household made her a danger to him, but that, too, could be taken care of. "Child, I entrust you with a sacred labor. You will wash away the blood and dress your mistress as befitting her station and piety. Veil her disgrace. Burn the sheets. Put the rosary in her hands. When you are done, I will send you to your mother with an escort and funds, and you shall never speak of what you know. Do you understand?"

"Yes, Eminence." She nodded obediently.

George Hill materialized in the bedchamber doorway and gave a brisk nod.

"I leave you to your toils, my child." With a blessing, the cardinal sent Nan to dress her dead mistress. To George Hill, he said, "I am to Pace. Let none inside till I return."

"You deny my grief its due vengeance? I am Lord High Constable! Dare you outpeer me?"

Norfolk withstood Buckingham's vehement attack with affected gravity. "Your Grace's grief is great, and he has my heartfelt sympathy. I ask not to usurp his office but to serve him well in his time of condolement, as I have served England for a period of no less than threescore years, and as earl marshal these past nine years, faithfully and diligently. I hereby pledge mine own application and experience, which, in such dire, regretful matters, is extensive, to yield justice."

Pace, Wolsey's trusted ally in the council, interposed, "Your Majesty, if I may, I should like to tender my sincere condolences over the hurtful demise of His Grace the Duke of Buckingham's lady sister and second his just demand to head this investigation, for I believe that His Grace the Duke of Norfolk's praiseworthy application and experience must not be diverted from conjuring up the sinister authors of the Spanish conspiracy against His

Majesty. And as I have touched upon the subject"—Pace faced Norfolk—"how speeds Your Grace with that investigation?"

Standing at the king's right side and avidly following the debate whereupon his future balanced precariously, Wolsey mentally applauded his ally. The time to act was ripe. He leaned to whisper in the king's ear, "If it please Your Grace, mayhap an independent party is called for, a gentleman unaffiliated with either faction, impartial to the outcome of the inquest. Were His Majesty to elect such a man, he would achieve the following goals . . ."

"Go on." King Henry hushed his bickering councilors with a waving gesture.

"Clearly this debate will go on, unresolved, until Your Majesty will be called upon to choose sides," Wolsey whispered. "Which would put Your Majesty in a . . . an awkward position, at best."

"Yes, yes?" His young sovereign shifted impatiently, eager to be off playing.

"I fear a nonneutral party in charge of such a serious and delicate matter might be tempted to . . . nay, blinded," Wolsey quickly amended, "by either grief or . . . other concerns to mete out punishment hastily, imprudently, and—God forbid—unjustly, merely to satisfy these concerns."

"Pray, speak plainly," the king muttered. "What concerns?"

"Political and feudal concerns, Your Majesty. A murder charge is an effective weapon to wield. It has slain the mighty as well as the innocent, may the good Lord keep their souls."

The king's narrow-eyed gaze darted betwixt Buckingham and Norfolk. "We see your point."

"To ensure the sword of justice strikes down the offender and not those who offend Their Graces, Your Majesty may elect to oversee the inquest in a manner that would not rob the realm of its overtaxed monarch. An eagle does not catch flies. Which is why a sieve will come in handy."

"Godsakes, Wolsey. *Ignōtum per ignōtius.* 'What is Magnasia, I yow preye?' What sieve? Your explanation is harder to comprehend than what it is meant to explain."

"A promising and amenable young sieve, a Knight Companion,

whose honor and loyalty is above reproach, a man not too lofty in consequence, eager to please none but His Majesty, a man who can be trusted, molded, and . . . controlled."

"An investigator of our choosing . . ." The king gave a pleased grunt. "Suffolk!"

Wolsey gritted his teeth as the Duke of Suffolk raised his head. He hastily murmured to the king, "His Grace of Suffolk is far too exalted to serve as a sieve, Majesty. Might I suggest . . ."

The king shot him an annoyed look. "By all means, suggest!"

"Sir Michael Devereaux, Your Majesty's fearless shield, a chivalrous rescuer of princesses, an extraordinary jouster, a gentleman of impeccable breeding and principles, whose devotion to his king is absolute."

"Sir Michael Devereaux?" The king knitted his brow in thought. "An interesting choice."

"I have every reason to believe that he will make an excellent investigator, Your Majesty. His selflessness, constancy, intellect, and integrity have been established manifoldly."

"Very well. See to it. Find the culprit and put this to rest." He stood. "Your Grace, we deeply mourn the loss of your lady sister. Noble members of the council, we entrust the serious matter of finding the Lady Anne's killer to our lord chancellor and the investigator of our choosing, Sir Michael Devereaux." He stepped from the throne. "My Lord Norfolk, a word."

Rejoicing in his triumph, Wolsey watched his king pace off with the duke. The particulars of their exchange were known to him: the expulsion of Sir Walter Devereaux from court. One more triumph he claimed over Norfolk. With a sense of achievement, he left the hectic Privy Council chamber. He knew what they said behind his back—*ipse rex*, a cardinal who was not cardinal but king—and they were not mistaken. He had managed quite a feat this morning. Lady Anne lay spotless, attired, and veiled in her chamber, the servant Nan was gone from court, the ship had sailed with his hand on the tiller. The wheels and cogs of his so-called inquest set in motion, now to the business of conscripting Sir Michael Devereaux into finding Lady Anne's secret lover.

The minions would be an excellent place for his appointed bloodhound to begin his hunt.

Michael found Renée in the queen's privy garden, taking air in Her Majesty's entourage. The instant she spotted him, she snuck away and joined him for a stroll in the allée.

"I was thinking about you." She cut him a sideways glance when they had been ambling for a while without a destination in mind. Their entire liaison was conducted much the same way.

"You were?" While her proximity soothed him, his mind was leagues away. He recalled his bout of crazed thirst upon seeing the bite mark on the whore Mariona Wood's neck. He had kept the drouth at bay long enough to return to Greenwich Palace with Stanley and Suffolk, plunder his casket of potion, and fall asleep. The rest had been a nightmare, unlocking a hidden, muddled memory of a poor disgraced mother and a past in the stews. A past he could neither reconcile with the life of comfort and stability he had known at Castle Tyrone nor put out of his mind.

"I was wondering if you have given thought to my suggestion of last eve."

"Buckingham's dagger." He exhaled. She was anything if not tenacious.

"Yes, I have given the matter considerable thought myself. Admitting to how you obtained it in reality might be somewhat awkward, which is why I came up with an alternate explanation."

"I took it away from the assassin before I killed him, and when I discovered the origin of the dagger, I did not dare come forward for fear of the duke's retribution. However, I cannot in good conscience remain silent any longer. The king's enemies must be brought to justice."

Surprise and respect beamed at him. "Yes, exactly!"

"The gormless ignoramus astounds." He halted, his hands on her slender arms. "I will only do so if you swear to me that you had naught to do with poisoning the queen, Renée."

"Why would you think—?"

"That is not an answer."

"I swear it," she vowed with heartfelt sincerity, the little deceiver.

"What do you benefit from my currying favor with the cardinal?"

She hid her irritation well. "One would think you would be more appreciative of the morsels of advice on courtly stuff I have kindly dispensed to you since the day of your arrival."

"I am. Which makes me wonder . . . " He tugged her closer.

Apprehension and arousal clashed brightly in her eyes. "Michael—"

"Hush." His heart thudded in anticipation. "I'm going to kiss you, Renée, because the longer I withhold the hotter we seem to burn and therefore . . . the more we are in danger of—"

"Withhold, I pray you!" She fluttered in his arms like a skittish owlet but did not try to elude his light grip. She was vacillating, tempted but afraid, as he was. And he knew the reason why.

"I fear the worst, madame." He stared at the tremulous rosette mouth, starving for a taste of her, of the honey her body distilled to taunt and lure him with. "This . . . enticing tension between us, if we do not temper the little flames with a little kiss . . ."

"Michael, no . . ."

Despite her rising trepidation, her body softened helplessly when he enfolded her closer. His face connected with her cool cheek and a soft stray curl. Her silkiness and the wafting perfume of her womanly dew drove him out of his head. "Cruel desire, shall I tell you what will betide us the day you fall into my arms? And that day will come, marmoset, as the stars are ever burning." He closed his eyes and caressed her ear with his hungry lips. "Desire will emulate fire."

"Sir Michael!"

With an oath, Michael let Renée go and leveled an incinerating gaze at Pippin. "What is it?"

"His Eminence of York requests you attend him, sir. He is with the king's secretary."

Michael locked eyes with Renée, then set off for the royal secretary's counting chamber.

* * *

"Murdered?" Michael's gaze bounced between Wolsey and Pace. "By whom?"

"That is what you have been assigned to determine." The cardinal handed him a parchment bearing the royal seal. "Your letter of appointment."

Sorrow over Anne's misfortune and glee at his good fortune were two horses pulling him in different directions, distracting his mind as his eyes went over the contents of the vellum.

The cardinal put a hand on his back and walked him to the bay window. He spoke with quiet dignity. "The Lady Anne was found dead in her bedchamber at cockcrow, stabbed in the neck, with manifold clues indicating she had indulged in a night of dalliance. The man cannot be her husband, for Sir George Hastings left for Wales yesterday. Now, I happen to know that Lady Anne had recently formed an amorous attachment with a gentleman of the court, a man with whom she conducted secret illicit trysts. You will be looking for a depraved, devious, ruthless individual, who has taken great pains to conceal his adulterous relations with her."

Michael stared at the cardinal. *He was that lover.* "Sir George Hastings may have found out and sent someone to kill her. Jealousy, indignation, vindictiveness are all powerful motives."

Stolidly Wolsey replied, "He has not the brains for it. We are looking for someone else." He dug out a ring from his purse. "When I examined the lady this morning, this fell out of her fist."

Michael's heart gave a violent lurch. His ring! Tyrone's missing ring!

The formidable cardinal watched him like a hawk. "A most uncommon motif, wouldn't you say? A gift from her lover, or mayhap her killer, or possibly from both, as I suspect the two men are one and the same. Of course the origin of the ring will be investigated by my librarian."

Perspiration coated Michael's skin. How long before Wolsey linked his new investigator to the ring? Whoever killed Anne had set him up to take the blame for it. He forced himself to breathe and thought back to the morning the ring had disappeared. He had been roused by—

The cardinal sheathed the ring in his purse. "Every retainer with access to the lady's lodging is being questioned as we speak. Your task is to make inquiries with the members of the court. Question every man and woman who has had dealings with the Lady Anne. Begin with Bryan and Carew." He walked him back toward Pace. "But do so with diplomacy, for albeit men of questionable habits, they are the king's gallants, and we should not care to offend His Grace. Speak with Her Majesty's women. They are founts of gossip."

Michael was beginning to see a pattern here, but that observation was better stored away. He could barely dredge up his next words. "Stabbing a lady in the neck strikes me as a most peculiar method of killing. Mayhap we ought to be looking for an enemy of the lady in lieu of a lover."

The cardinal's face twitched with irony. "At court, your friends and enemies can be one and the same. Now, you will report to me alone. I should warn you, Buckingham and Norfolk are unhappy with His Majesty's choice of investigator, chiefly because I suggested you for the office. You are to speak of this inquest with neither one of them nor anyone else. Am I clear?"

"Yes, Your Grace." His temples throbbed. The stonework of his universe was disintegrating piece by wretched piece. The thought of filching the ring from the cardinal's purse crossed his mind, but then Wolsey would know who had taken it and would have found his "murderer."

"Summonses have already been issued for the six gentlemen on this catalog." Pace handed him another square of vellum and a key dangling from a red velvet ribbon. Michael skimmed the names: Bryan, Carew, Compton, Norris, Neville, Knevet. "Sir Ned Poynings the comptroller has made his counting chamber available for you. Sir Henry Marney the captain of the guard has assigned you two yeomen of the guard to be at your beck and call.

"Every scrap of information you will obtain, however insubstantial, must reach me at once," Cardinal Wolsey directed. "No exceptions. You are in effect working for me and under me, and I alone report to the king. If you cannot reach me, Pace will direct you."

"I understand perfectly."

"Excellent. That is all for now."

"I should like leave to examine the deceased, Your Grace."

"You may pay your respects with the court. Good day and may God speed you."

"Your Grace." Sir Francis Bryan overtook Buckingham outside the Church of the Observant Friars, where the Lady Anne lay in state like a shrine whereto the court made pilgrimages to pay their last respects before she was taken to be buried at Thornbury. "Pray, allow me to tender my deepest condolences over the untimely demise of your lady sister. A most distressing tragedy, and what a terrible loss of a grand and pious lady. This court shall mourn her for years to come."

Without breaking stride, the duke gave a curt nod.

Bryan pressed on. "Does the appointed investigator meet with Your Grace's approval?"

"What business is it of yours, Bryan?"

"I only ask because I have reason to believe he may not be the man he claims to be."

The duke slowed his pace. "Go on."

"Last night I learned from a reliable source . . ."

"Here's something interesting for your view." The Marquis de Rougé handed Renée an open missive. "Maestro Raphael di Perugia confessed: there has been no coitus. An innocent flirtation and a naughty painting in the nude, but naught remotely lethal to Her Highness's maidenhead. She is once again *virgo intacta*, with Cardinal Medici's seal of approval. Congratulations, madame."

"This letter was addressed to me!" Renée hissed.

"Madame is not the only one who thinks to thieve letters. And now, with her virtue restored, her name exonerated of carnal sin, and with the ample dowry and annuity from her considerable properties in Brittany and Chartres, claimants to her hand are springing up all over the continent, the spearhead being Ercole d'Este, eldest son to Duca Alfonso d'Este and Duchessa Lucrezia whose beauty, incidentally, was also immortalized in a *nudo*. Madame has much to rejoice over."

Renée skimmed the contents several times and found no mention of Raphael's fate. Jesu, she prayed they had not harmed him. If they had, by the saints, she would return to France with the Ancient and a vampire besides and then God have mercy on King Francis and his holy banker.

"Naturally I shall inform the good Cardinal of York that the ante is up and anything less than a duke will not bear scrutiny. With Princess Mary Tudor offered to the Dauphin, we should—"

"You will say nothing." Renée stuffed the letter in her purse to burn later. She knew whom the cardinal contemplated for the position of her husband—and that suited her immediate plans perfectly. "Let the cardinal do what he does best and stay out of his way."

Rougé stiffened, mulling this over. Renée wondered how long it would take him to twig that so long as they were keeping a card up their sleeve in dealing with Cardinal Wolsey, Rougé, too, had a place in the race for Brittany and Chartres. He grunted, looking pleased. "A wise decision."

"I am glad you concur." *Cretin.*

"Banished from court?" Walter exclaimed with horror. "Why?"

"Your misconduct with the Lady Renée has reached His Majesty's ears," Norfolk replied in clipped tones. "Needless to say, he was outraged. If King Francis got wind of your assault on Her Grace's person, King Henry would be expected to tender his personal apology."

Walter gnashed his teeth. *That whore!* "Did she make a complaint?"

"The matter was effectively hushed. Nevertheless, the king found your conduct offensive to His Grace as well as her and wishes you gone from his court. 'As a knight, a gentleman, and a king,' he said to me, 'I neither condone rape nor countenance coarse speech, lewd behavior, and disrespect for women, above all the ladies of my court.'"

Walter felt ill. Years of fighting for his patrimony gone to waste because of that whoreson styling himself Sir Michael Devereaux and his French harlot! "Before I take my leave, I have vital information to relay to Your Grace. It has come to my attention that His Majesty's 'new shield' may be a cipherer, a spial, and an assassin in the employ of Emperor Maximilian. . . ."

They ambushed him in the meanly lit passage leading to the comptroller's office.

"We hear you are looking for us, Devereaux!" a voice, possibly Compton's, taunted him from behind a pillar, and was answered by its echo as well as resounding snickers from every direction.

Michael was surrounded. His alert escorts put gloved hands to sword hilts, but he waved the yeomen back and continued walking alone. Footsteps accompanied him behind flanking pillars, ricocheting from the masonry. They stalked him like a hunting party of stealthy wolves.

"We thought to make it easier on you, cardinal's boy!" another voice, Carew's, resonated.

Through the swirling smoke of the sporadic torch, Michael smelled their sweat.

"Put your questions to us! What does the Right Reverend Cardinal of York wish to know?"

Knevet, Michael deduced. Maybe Wolsey was not off the mark after all. These men were a tight circle. If one of them erred, they would close ranks about him, and if a stranger were to eat into their pie, they would chase him off their territory, or eliminate him in cold, ruthless ways. One thing he was sure of: whoever had stolen his ring murdered Anne. "Why the post and pillar, gentlemen? I have no quarrel with you. Show your faces, and we shall talk without discord."

"How can there be aught but discord when the lord chancellor would have none but us for the killing of the Lady Anne and sends his boy to settle his own grievances?" asked Norris.

"Who is to say we trapped not the real villain and saw occasion to avenge the lady?" Neville addressed his invisible accomplices like a lawyer arguing his case before a jury.

"I reckon five," Michael said, knowing exactly who hid behind which pillar. "Where is your sixth consort, Sir Francis Bryan? I should like a word with him first."

"You boasted much courage in dismissing your protectors!" Compton sneered.

Michael moved swiftly. He had Compton by his throat, pressed against the wall, toes barely scraping the ground, before the man could squeak to his mates for help. "Where is Bryan?"

Pattering feet converged on him. Swords hissed out of scabbards and pointed at his back.

"Turn and draw!" barked Norris.

"Put steel behind your vaunt!" spurred Knevet.

"Sheathe your blades, or I'll snap his neck as I would a Christmas turkey's," Michael warned.

"Sir Francis Bryan is on the road to Ireland, sent by Their Graces of Buckingham and Norfolk to investigate your shady past, cardinal's boy!" snarled Carew.

What? Michael flung Compton at his cronies and drew his sword. "I am for you, gentlemen. You may reason your dispute with me now, or else depart, for I have other ladies to speak to besides you lot, and I trow they should display more backbone than to cluster in a quintet."

Compton, recovering his stance, plucked his sword out of his pilcher and made his passado. Michael parried fluidly and launched a counterattack, dealing blows with such force that sparks flew out of their scuffing blades. By force and swiftness, Michael had Compton at a considerable disadvantage, as Ferdinand was wont to have him. He sent Compton's sword clanging onto the flagstones, forced the man to his knees at sword point, and rasped at the advancing four, "Forbear your outrage, gentlemen. Or I shall put a second patch on your fellow's face!"

"Convey this message to your master, hound," Carew gnarled. "Tell His Eminence that if he wishes to establish his own kind of justice, let it be so, but God is higher."

To his surprise, the quintet gave ground. His sword slid into its sheath sibilantly as he set off to find Dr. Linacre. Establishing the gallants' whereabouts at the time of Anne's death was a priority, but to determine that, he first needed to know exactly when, where, and how she died.

Bryan was his prime suspect. He would not put it past the spin-

ner to slaughter the lady and then find occasion to conveniently remove himself from court.

Walter Devereaux had one stop to make before he set out with
Francis Bryan to Ireland on a combined venture devised by two
old enemies, Buckingham and Norfolk, who, unprecedentedly,
joined forces to knock over the cardinal's new henchman and rising new star of the court.

The French whore demolished what had taken him years to
build on the wreckage left by his sire. She would not get off scot-
free if he had aught to say about it, which he did, plenty.

Norfolk had impounded Armado's medallion from Walter and
now meant to use it to coerce the trull into an alliance against
Wolsey. But Walter had another use in mind for the medallion. He
did not need the actual trinket to destroy the slut. A description of
the gold cross over black would suffice. He had an inkling the cardinal would be most appreciative of the information. Not only
would Wolsey move against the Frenchwoman with the brutal efficiency the chancellor was notorious for, but Walter might find a position waiting for him with the cardinal upon his return.

With Michael Devereaux and Renée de Valois out of the way,
Walter would reinstate himself at court and hopefully with Bryan's
assistance reassert himself with the king.

Conveniently, Dr. Linacre, chief physician to the king, was a
resident of the court. Michael tracked him down in the gallery
conversing with Sir Thomas More. Michael had not yet made the
acquaintance of More—King Henry's favored counselor, an under-
sheriff of London, an erudite lawyer highly regarded by everyone,
including Wolsey—and hesitated to disrupt the scholars' exchange
by interposing an incongruous query.

Astute finesse was called for. "Sirs." He bowed to them both.
"Pray, pardon the interruption. I seek an academic opinion on a
murder the king has appointed me to investigate." It cheered him
to note that their curiosity was piqued. "Surely the victim's identity is known to you."

Dr. Linacre, who considered Michael a medical achievement

and a scientific marvel that supplemented his repertorium, was delighted to be consulted on a pertinent case and introduced Michael to More. As Michael shook the lawyer's hand, who instantly offered his services as an expert on the law, a waft of dragon's blood tickled his nose and he felt his mouth watering. With effort, he presented his question—if it was possible to determine a human being's precise time of death—and was treated to an animated lecture on rigor mortis, a state that lasted betwixt three and seventy-two hours subsequent to the time of death. Ergo, one would have to ply a fist open to extract a ring from it. Either Anne had been dead for less than three hours when the cardinal had examined her early that morning or the cardinal had the ring in his possession before that, which made him the ring's thief. Three hours meant she had been killed a short time before dawn.

"If I may snatch a laurel leaf . . ." said a riveted More once Michael thanked the doctor. "The foremost question an investigator must ask when considering potential murder suspects is this: *cui prodest?* Who benefited or stands to benefit most by the murder?"

Michael thanked More, secured permission to consult him further should legal riddles arise, and took his leave. *Cui prodest*, indeed? Who stood to benefit by his destruction? He studied his hands. He had three rings: his signet ring bearing his initials; another gold ring limning the arms of Dungannon; and a gold thumb-ring crowned with an armorial medallion of the red eagle over black. If someone sought to embroil him in Anne's murder, why steal the one ring none had seen him wear at court, a secret ring, etched with a pagan motif?

Time was the enemy. With every grain of sand slipping through the hourglass, the cardinal was getting closer to learning the origin of the ring. Once it were identified as Tyrone's, the hunt would be up, the hart snared. By a chilling twist of fate, Michael had become the pursuer as well as the pursued, the huntsman and the prey, in a deadly, fast-paced game he had no control over. And there was only one person he could trust to assist him in his quest for enlightenment.

* * *

"Come, my enchanting bag of tricks, I have need of you." Materializing behind her, Michael took Renée's slender arm and steered her away from the crowd of elegant mourners amassing outside the Church of the Observant Friars.

"You are doing well enough on your own," Renée muttered peevishly. "Seeing how thick you are with the Lord Chancellor of England, I daresay you were graduated from my Sapientia."

"Why so sour?" His pretty schemer was angry with him. A shaft of light struck hope in his breast. He quirked a grin. "Is it because I, eh, am turning out to be a damp squib?"

She iced him with a sideways glance. "Stabbed in the neck? By your successor, I presume?"

A direct hit. "Did I say bag of tricks? I meant quillets." At least she was good enough to use the conspiratorial tone they seemed to be perfecting. "Is there a question you wish to ask me?"

"Would you tell me the truth if there was one?"

His eyes warmed on her face. Distrust positively became her. "Marmoset, I would not dream of dallying without your supervision."

Stanley stepped into their path. "Did you hear? Sir Francis Bryan and Sir Walter Devereaux are gone to Ireland, emissaries of Their Graces of Buckingham and Norfolk."

"Walter, too? Let them sample the hospitality of the people of that country. If they do not speed back blue-deviled, my Lord Tyrone will make tumblers of them." *If he were alive. . . .* He had to be, Michael hoped; otherwise news would have reached him, informing him he was the new earl. Which he wanted to be—looking at Renée, more than ever—but not yet. . . .

"If you are at ease, I am at ease," Stanley replied. "I congratulate you on your new office, by the by. Henceforward I shall palm off all my noisome petitioners unto you."

"Only the pretty ones." Michael winked and was stunned by a flash of violet eyes. What was that? A token of jealousy from the flint-hearted voyeuse? Praise be to the gods!

"How fare you? Better now?" inquired his concerned friend. "Oh, I should tell you that I have gained a bedfellow. His Grace was not welcomed with open arms early this morn."

Michael stiffened at the allusion to his dismal condition on their return from the stews. "Ten pounds say he retakes the castle by midnight." The distraction worked. Stanley put his money on the next night and whistled off. Michael sailed his fingers down Renée's lissome arm and laced them with her reluctant ones. He leaned aside to tickle her earlobe with his nose. "Acquit me of wantoning where I should not. You know I have eyes only for you."

"Oh? Did you leave your eyes in a jewel casket last night when you took a boat to the stews with your faithless friends?"

"A unified front, is it?" Her jealousy pleased him; it blew away the dark clouds hanging over his head and let the sun shine upon him again. "Tell your friend to raise the portcullis. She has a husband who is true, dull, and tame as a sumpter."

She fixed him with an intrigued gaze. "Would you be true, dull, and tame as a husband?"

"A pusillanimous, henpecked, worshipful, starry-eyed meacock."

A curl of lip satisfied him that they were friends again and he exonerated of false charges.

"What would you have me do?" Renée whispered as he ushered her inside the dim church. Hushed sobs, coughs, and Latin murmurings shook the silence of the hallowed space as Anne's relatives, acquaintances, and people who had never spoken to her came to bewail her passing. She lay in state on a black bier and a hearse decorated with Stafford emblems.

"Swoon. Convincingly. I must have an unsupervised moment to examine the dead lady."

"What, now?"

"Wait till I am standing beside the bier."

"Michael." She hung on to his sleeve, waylaying him. His entire self stood to attention at her informal gesture. "Stanley inquired after your health. Does he . . . ?"

"No." He closed the space between them, staring at her. "Only you know."

"And"—her perturbed gaze swept their hallowed milieu—"how fare you now?"

Jealous and concerned. He was rising in favor. "Now that I think upon it, I may have an ache that needs soothing." He smiled at her glower. "Wait a moment and swoon."

The first thing he noticed about Anne's still body was the pellucid quality to the skin tone, neither bluish nor sallow. There was an odd smell about her. *Desire. Fear. Emptiness.*

Renée's timing was perfect. From the corner of his eye, Michael saw her drift faintly toward the nearest pew and collapse in the middle of the aisle with a flounce of skirts and a dainty gasp. As every person in the church ran to revive the princess, he peeled down the neckerchief veiling Anne's neck. Scrubbed of blood, the puncture was gruesome, not a mere stab but a burrow. Suddenly he knew why the skin was translucent. Anne's blood had been drained. Two women murdered in the same fashion, bitten at exactly the same spot, on the same night—a coincidence?

Michael tugged the neckerchief back in place and hurried to offer gentlemanly succor to his abettor. Not that she lacked attendants, mostly of the lecherous kind, he noted with irritation. A trifle forceful, he shouldered a path to her side and took over the squiring of the expert fainter.

Simulating a misstep, Renée gripped his arm. "How was I?" she murmured between them.

"Incomparable! Remind me to hire you out for next Samhain Night."

"So what have we learned?"

"Later, *á mhúirnín.* My thanks." He squeezed her elbow, for it was the only organ he could fondle in the common gaze without offending her virtue, and relinquished his frail lamb to the care of Her Grace of Suffolk. Remaining behind in the courtyard, he watched her being escorted away by her royal nurse with a score of slavering wolves forming her wake. She was a woman for a lifetime, a helpmate, he thought, admiring her courage and skill at dissimulation. A puff of sweet-smelling stink came at him. He found the French ambassador at his side.

"Do not think to acquire the Breton mare by the foal you foisted on her! And know this, when you play Perotto to her Lucrezia, prepare to suffer the fate of the lyrical lover!"

Wondering what had stung the marquis, Michael watched him

pace off in a pother. Ah, Renée's fainting spell. As if his cup was not overflowing already, earning the wrath of the King of France over a saddle-pack babe he had purportedly fecundated without once tasting the goods would—without question—crown him the most asinine wretch in Christendom.

At sunset, tired and troubled, Michael found himself clomping along the passage leading to Renée's apartment. He had no business with her, except a longing to put his head in her lap and unburden his soul. To his despair he was not wiser now than he had been earlier, even after hours of talking to the queen's women, to the courtiers with living quarters at the palace, to the yeomen of the guard, and to Cardinal Wolsey, who demanded an account of Michael's findings before he retired to his abode upriver. The pertinent whereabouts of four of the six gentlemen on Pace's list had been established, whereby acquitting them of the crime. Bryan and Carew were bereft of vindication. No one, not even Wyatt, knew when they had plodded back from the night revelry at the stews, which did not mean they had not returned before dawn. Michael had already made up his mind to revisit that place for reasons of his own. He would go to the Hart and have a chat with the bawd and her mean tenants. The reason he could not clock Bryan and Carew's return to court was in and of itself a matter that bore further scrutiny. The two nightwatchmen who at the time of Anne's murder had been on duty in the section of the palace where the Hastingses resided had vanished into thin air. No one had seen or heard from them since they had signed off after dawn that morning. Michael doubted not that their disappearance was connected to the crime. Tracing their following movements would not be an easy feat, but that was for the morrow.

The palace was a tad quieter with the festivities of the annual chapter concluded. The court supped with Their Majesties. As Renée failed to make an appearance, Michael left to seek her out.

The inauspicious absence of Valois guards outside her apartment gave Michael a hard jolt. He stared at the door in shock, refusing to register the fact that she had left him, again, without a word. Had the French marquis whisked her back to France? With so much of her dealings at the English court shrouded in mist, there was no way he could fathom why and where she had gone.

Rage and dejection overwhelmed him. To hell with her! Curse her! Curse everything! How could she leave him, in the name of wonder, without a single word? He was mad for her, and he knew she had feelings for him, too; he sensed her desire for him every time he was near her. He balled his fists, desperate to hit something, someone, anything to rip this torment from his heart.

Someone moved inside the apartment. Adele! Michael aimed his fist at the door just as it opened. The old dame gave a cry of relief. "She is gone! They took her! I looked for you—"

Michael's heart lurched. "Stop your bawling, woman, and tell me who took her and where!"

With an anxious glance at the taper-lit corridor, Adele dragged him inside the privy chamber of the apartment and shut the door. "The cardinal's men," she sniffed. "They came before supper with an arrest warrant for my lady as well as her guards."

"What? *Why?*" For collaborating with the queen's poisoners, he was certain of it.

"On suspicion of spying for the King of France. They took her to the Tower."

"I'll get her back."

"Bless you! I knew you would!"

"I'll go to the cardinal and—"

"No!" She grasped fistfuls of his jerkin. "Get her out of the Tower first, explain later. Use your powers, I beseech you! Break down the doors and get her out! You are the only one who can." She started wailing again. "My poor child, she is afraid of closed places. Please!"

Michael patted the old woman's back as she drowned his clothing in tears. "I'll get her out." Even if it cost him everything: his position at court, his pledge to Tyrone, his very life . . .

His promise instantly restored the old Breton. She smiled tearfully. "Bless you! Bless you!"

"Mistress, I vow to do my humanly damnedest, but I am not all-powerful."

"Pah!" she said. "Tell that to the small folk."

❧ 20 ❧

By night we drift abroad,
Night frees imprisoned shades,
And even Cerberus casts aside
His chains—and strays.

—Propertius: *Elegies*

They would execute her. She had played the game and lost. Who had betrayed her?

Her bravery at low ebb, Renée paced the small, dank stone cell, rubbing her arms against the chill, against the darkness closing in on her. A moldering palliasse on the floor, reeking of urine and feces, provided shelter to a family of red-eyed rodents. Her skin crawled. She went to stand beneath the barred window. The top of her head barely cleared the ledge. All she saw through the rusty grille was a patch of dark blue night. Staring at it longingly, she shivered and sucked night air into her lungs in attempt to banish the fetid odors and stanch the rising panic. Mercy, Jesu!

Renée hugged herself, scared of the dawn. How would they kill her? The penalty for women who committed high treason was to be burnt at the stake. They would manacle her by the ankles to iron rings set in a wooden floor of a tumbrel and drag her through London to be spattered with rotten fish, piss, and excrement on the way to the place of execution. They would pile sticks and faggots around her bare feet. Her skin would peel off from the calves to the thighs to her arms, breasts, and face. She would die in agony, screaming for mercy, within a flaming inferno.

Only the king could commute the penalty to a beheading. But

who would speak for her? Not King Francis. He would wash his hands of her, would renounce her as his instrument as well as a sister-in-law. Once again she was alone in her strife, nobody to turn to for help, none who would come to her rescue. Appealing to her mother's confessor would be a waste of time, for Cardinal Medici would thwart any help from that quarter; he would sleep better at night with her dead and his secrets burnt to ashes with her. Writing to her sister would be just as useless. Claude had retired into apathy years ago. Would she even grieve the demise of her only sister? Raphael's image flitted through her mind. Would her helpless artist rot in prison forever? It occurred to her that he might not be incarcerated anymore. How was he rewarded for signing that confession? It was silly and uncharitable of her, but the idea of him free to enjoy the patronage of wealthy ladies at the French court nettled Renée. How long would he mourn her loss and how soon would he find solace in the arms of another woman? As she listed the people she knew, the fabric of her life, she realized that the only person in the world whose heart would break over her death would be Adele. Her poor, constant Adele; leastways she would be spared the ignominy of begging for alms in her dotage, for Renée had set up a pension for Adele before leaving France, a necessary provision considering her assignment. Mayhap she ought to appeal to Their Graces of Suffolk. . . .

What was she thinking? She would never be granted quill and parchment. Now that he knew why she was in England, Cardinal Wolsey would keep her isolated till the moment of execution, or he might do away with her quietly, send an assassin to her cell, or poison her. Sure enough, if the cardinal lacked evidence to try her, he might keep her locked away in here for years till she died of lung rot or wasted away. Her mind conjured an image of herself as a gaunt, mad, grimy old woman, cringing in the corner on the rat-infested pallet, her hair all white and tangled.

No! She refused to die like that, or burn. If she must die, let it be by her hand, by her design! She withdrew the tiny silver dirk from inside her sleeve, grateful for the stupidity of the male of the species. For all their bluster, none of the cardinal's henchmen or the guards at the Tower thought to search her person for hidden weapons. Morbidly she caressed the shiny blade with her fingertips, testing its sharpness. Fear iced her veins at what she must do.

She was so afraid, quaking with terror, dampened with cold sweat. *Jesu, have mercy on me!*

Her cri de coeur was answered by a resounding crash of a strong-tempered door, the yeomen warders running and shouting, scabbards rattling, clouts, grunts, and a familiar voice growling, "You will release her into my custody this instant, or, by God, His Eminence will hear of it!"

Michael! Gramercy!

Astonishment gave way to dreamlike exaltation. It rushed through her frozen limbs, thawing the ice, heating her to the core. A vampire charging to her rescue—who could withstand him?

A heart-wrenched cry of relief tore from her throat with bubbles of hysterical laughter. Tears flooded her eyes. She sheathed her blade as the pandemonium swept through the bloody Tower. She heard the winded Sir William Kingston, the constable of the Tower, make a stand. "Sir, you cannot blow in here in a violent storm, claiming a prisoner without a written discharge!"

"I am chief investigator in this case, appointed by His Majesty, answerable only to the lord chancellor." Michael sounded terrifyingly authoritative as he marched up the passage, drawing nearer with every thunderous syllable. "Now unlock this door ere I break it down also!"

A chatelaine of keys jingled nervously outside her door. With a clang, the iron lock gave in, and the door to her cell was thrust open. Through the blur of flowing tears, tears she had not shed since the cardinal's henchmen had come to arrest her, she saw a golden head duck beneath the lintel and fearlessly enter. As he straightened his broad shoulders, the perennial masculine beauty of his features sharpened into an alternating web of rage, concern, relief to find her intact, and tenderness as their gazes touched. "Marmoset." Michael took her face in his large, gentle hands, his thumbs smudging the drops spilling from her eyes. "Are you in health?"

When she nodded, unable to speak for the riotous emotions choking her, he shrugged off his heavy cloak and wrapped her in broadcloth folds that carried his distinctive musk and body heat, draping his otherworldly armor over her, his pall of strength. Her knight in black armor.

"Let us go." He slung a protective arm about her and stirred her out the door.

Standing outside her cell, the constable of the Tower looked docile as a moonstruck lamb, becharmed into servility by the omnipotent vampire ushering Renée to freedom. He would not be alarming troops or blabbing on them to the Cardinal of York tonight. That was for sure.

By contrast, his warders, abused but unspelled, one nursing a punched eye, another hugging his ribs, and a third rubbing a neck with a hand imprint on it, eyed Michael with extreme awe as they escorted him and Renée outside the torchlit fortress and to the yonder river gate, glad to be rid of both nuisances. *She was safe.* At the Tower wharf, as cold mist blew freely in her face, the tension suddenly left her body and her knees folded beneath her.

Michael scooped her up in a fluid motion and carried her in his arms into the waiting barge. He sat down with her cradled in his lap—clinging to his shoulders, her face hidden in the crook of his neck—tucked his cloak carefully about her, and gave the waterman directions.

Ensconced in a cocoon of heady male warmth and strength, swaying with the gentle motion of the boat, she suddenly realized that her newfound sanctuary—incredibly, the arms of a vampire—was the safest place in the world. She could not imagine a doughtier champion. His expression of unflinching indomitability upon striding into her prison cell was a memory she would cherish to her dying breath. She felt infinitely grateful to Michael for winkling her out of that horrid place. She marveled that he should care so deeply for her to imperil his position with the cardinal and the king and possibly his secret purpose. But who was her savior? The handsome, stouthearted, intelligent man she had come to consider a fond ally or the supreme monster that he was in the flesh? Without the latter, could the former have saved her?

With a shuddering breath, she pushed thoughts aside. A lull of absolute safety descended on her. A feeling so strange, so sweetly seductive, it lifted millstones from her heart and demolished inner barriers. She nestled closer to the patch of hot burnished skin and warm muscle betwixt the camlet collar and golden hair, deeply inhaling the rich textures of his scent and the glowing heat he emanated, sensing tendrils of desire swirling between her thighs. Her lips grew adventurous, butterflies upon his velvety neck, navigating by feel, by the need welling up in her, the longing that had become her bedfellow. Whether in response to her call or venturing a quest all its own, the smooth-shaven jaw angled. Their lips met midway, touching, caressing, kissing, tasting . . .

The joining was sublime. Michael's mouth, his taste, his tongue, she could not get enough of him. She was lost, bespelled by this formidable warlock, sinking into a pool in a wild wood. The ache was sweet—the balm was sweeter. Sheltering arms fastened about her, drawing her closer against a muscled torso, cradling her head. Michael's kisses were achingly tender and slow, lazy and playful. Yet as he felt the fever rise in her, his loving grew hotter, deeper, plundering.

He made her throb, writhe, and melt for him. He fed the conflagration sweeping through her veins. He was inside her, around her, nothing existed but him. And she wanted more, more . . .

At the boatman's sniggers, Michael tore his mouth from hers, his head jerking up. "Mind the river!" He glared the man into apologetic submission, then held her cheek in his warm palm. His face hovered over hers; his eyes were dilated with desire and with something else. "Renée—"

"No. Do not say anything." Tentatively, her fingertips outlined his lips, his chin, his strong jaw. He was so beautiful, he made her heart hurt. She threaded her fingers through the thick mass of gilt spun filaments and drew his head closer, meshing their lips, teasing him with her tongue, exploring, savoring him. She could kiss him for hours, for days, and not have enough.

His prophecy was manifesting: *desire emulated fire*. With every kiss, the pull between them grew stronger, the flames brighter. She wanted him with a terrible ache that knew no bounds, and he, harboring a savageness in the blood, reciprocated and fueled this volatile, terrifying passion.

Renée nearly cried at the abrupt deprivation of his mouth when the boat docked at the palace landing and Michael broke their kiss to pay the waterman. She draped her arms around the broad stretch of his shoulders and returned her face to the soothing curvature at the side of his neck.

Michael chuckled at her self-indulgence. "Did we leave your dainty feet at the Tower, Lady Marmoset? If so, permit me to bear the brunt of this oversight." She concealed her smile in his neck as he lifted her in his arms and chivalrously carried her inside like a balled kitten.

The palace was aglow with tapers. A lively composition, played with hurdy-gurdies, viols, rebecs, and all manner of instrument blared from the royal apartments, crowned with a descant of singing voices. Neither plots nor murders could subdue King Henry's love of music or curtail his appetite for revelry. Heads turned as Michael negotiated the passages with his bundle, but for aught Renée cared, the court could prattle about her to every gossipy ink-bespotted ambassador, who would elaborate on the spectacle to the benefit of the scandalmongering courts of Europe.

Only she knew how fleeting her reprieve was and that once they reached her apartment, the magic would disperse, and she would have to rake her brains for a ploy to free her *deletoris* from imprisonment and snatch the Ancient before the cardinal got wind of her escape.

Adele clapped her hands when she saw her in the doorway. "Oh, bless you! Bless you!" She patted Michael's back, ushering him into the bedchamber. "You are an angel, a guardian angel!"

Chuckling, Renée suspected Michael would have been bussed heartily if not for his armful.

Legions of beeswax candles were alive with light on gilt silver prickets. The azure-and-gold-caparisoned bed was turned down for the night. A wooden bathtub lined with sheets stood amid carpets and furs at the center of the chamber, half filled with scented water. A platter heaped with sweet cakes and a tankard of apple brandy and goblets graced a small table at the settle.

Michael looked at Adele. "Mistress, your anticipatory preparations are equal parts flattering and terrifying. I dread to imagine my fate had I failed to bring back your princess."

"Pah!" Her hand fluttered dismissively. "Put her there."

It amused Renée to hear them speak a medley of Breton and Irish Gaelic, like mates.

Michael lowered Renée to the settle before the fire, where a huge pot of water was heating. She clung to his neck with a beseeching look. "Do not leave me," she whispered. "Stay."

"I had no intention of leaving." He sat down with her. "Adele, pack a portmanteau for your lady and yourself, expedients only." He stared at Renée. "You are absconding England tonight."

"What?" By all the saints!

"I will take you to Dover."

Renée blinked at him in distress. She needed him to steal the Ancient for her—tonight! Scheming furiously, she said, "Will you come with me to France? You are now in as much peril in England as I am. In rescuing me, you have intertwined your fate with mine own. Michael"—she gripped his hand, laced her fingers through his, and held it to her bosom—"the cardinal will be furious at what you have done. He will punish you most severely."

He lifted their entwined hands and kissed her fingertips. "Do not concern yourself with my welfare. I will survive his heavy weather. He needs my help in ridding himself of his enemies in the king's closest circle. If my efforts bear fruit, he might overlook my heroics. Leave everything behind but some clothes for the voyage and jewelry. And if you have been spying, Renée, I strongly suggest you burn whatever you have put down in writing. Do not sew notes into hems, because if he catches up with you, I might not be around to protect you."

She played along. "Must we leave right now? I have prison stench all over me."

White teeth flashed between tanned cheeks. "I smell naught but sweetness and flowers, but if you so wish, my delicate fey, we may leave after Adele scrubs and fusses over you."

Jesu, mercy, Renée thought, befuddled; if he got any handsomer or kinder, her mind would cease functioning altogether.

He hoisted her legs onto his knees, collected the muddy hem of her gown to her ankles, and removed the ruined cream leather slippers from her feet. Long fingers clasped her anklebones, as if measuring her for boot cuffs, and began kneading her sore soles with the utmost care. "Do you really want me to come with you to France?" he asked quietly, his eyes on her feet.

Renée studied his strong patrician profile. "My caravel docks at Gravesend. It should take us an hour to reach it on the river. By morning we will be in the Channel." She leaned in, running her hand up his sleeve, appreciating the roped power sheathed in the rich material of the doublet, basking in his irresistible scent. She chose her carrot sensibly but couched her offer with feeling. "Come with me, *Michel*. You will take the French court by storm. I guarantee it."

Stark hunger stared back at her. "I want to . . . I do . . . but I cannot. Not yet. There are two things I must perforce do before I am free to join you in France, if you truly want me there."

Her heart pounded excitedly. Finally she was getting somewhere. "What are those things?"

"You have private matters, do you not? Spying for your king, for instance."

"I was not spying! Let the cardinal produce evidence to support his allegation!" She knew Wolsey would fain cut off his hand than unveil the Ancient. "Michael"—she touched his rugged cheek—"you trusted me with your other secret, the ailment. Can you not trust me with the rest?"

With a swift glance at the tire-woman, humming and rummaging around the trunks, he stole a languorous kiss from Renée's lips. When his head lifted, her mind was hazy with sensual fancies, her body a glowing beacon. "There are queries pertaining to the murder and to mine own private affairs to which I would have answers, and I must retrieve a certain property that belongs to me."

Excitement gripped her. "I could help you recover your property!" she breathed, staring at his mouth, her fingers tangling in the silken hair that brushed the warm velvet of his nape.

Of a sudden he laughed, and Renée was struck by how fascinatingly vibrant he was and how devastatingly, lethally desirable. "Sweetheart, you are the last person in London who could help me in this," said the gorgeous tergiversator. "But I thank you for offering your services."

Jesu, she was falling, when she was the one supposed to be seducing him into falling in line. He was dangerous, more to her well-being than to that of any guardsman who happed in his way, because, notwithstanding his ruthless vampire charms, she liked the man he was far too much. "Why can't I help you? Did you not say I was a quiver of tricks and quillets?"

He chuckled deep in his throat. "I said bagful, but I admit you are delightfully a-quiver, my sharp-tongued shrew, and I should love to tinker with every subtlety and firecracker." She did not miss the quip. "However, you cannot help because the cardinal has my property."

Impatience encumbered her breathing. "Can you not retrieve it tonight?"

"Break into York Place when I know not where my property is stashed? I am thinking not. Besides, I told you there were—"

"Questions that need must be answered." A subtler tactic was required here—but what? Her intractable vampire was of a mind that the time was not ripe for him to snatch his prize. "I won't leave without you. Tomorrow, I'll throw myself at the queen's mercy and solicit her protection." A tenuous solution, at best. The amity she had painstakingly established with the Spanish queen could fragment if Renée were believed to be a French spy, but it might purchase a few days.

Her golden buckler pondered that. "Very well. If you wish to stay in England with the queen's blessing, I will protect you, but you must stay close to me—"

Her head dropped on his shoulder. She was falling, falling . . .

Adele appeared. "Would you be a dear and help this old woman with the hot pot?"

Michael eyed the cheerful blaze with mistrust but was too mannerly to refuse. "Certainly."

Coming to her feet, Renée watched him hoist the giant cauldron as if it were weightless and empty it into the half-filled bathtub. Task done, he returned to her and took her hands in his, eyes glinting, wanting, imploring. His voice was a raspy whisper. "Shall I wait?"

Saints preserve her, she wanted him to stay, she was afraid he would, she was so confused. . . .

"Time to wash!" Adele announced. She shooed Michael out the door, latched it, and then descended on Renée. "Goosehead," she mouthed soundlessly. "He will devour you."

"I know."

The scrubbing and fussing went on forever. Michael paced Renée's privy chamber, fighting to block out the scents and sounds of aromatic oily droplets trickling from nude limbs and failing. Scorching fancies misted his brain. No woman ever had him this crazed, dazed, spellcast.

Much as he was tempted to, he could not travel to France with her. Not tonight. He had too many unfinished dealings in London: Tyrone's ring; the mysteries of his nightmare; the nameless enemy stalking him; his pledge to the dying earl. He had to return to the stews to investigate his incubus and the whereabouts of Bryan and Crew at the time of Anne's murder, then snatch a few winks and confront the cardinal over his Sir Lancelot performance. Bringing a sleep-deprived brain into battle was the top of foolhardiness. But he could not make his feet leave her apartment.

The highborn enchantress submerging in Venetian bath essence in the adjacent chamber had come so close to granting him privileges to her sweet body tonight, he could taste it. Though his acquaintance with her mercurial nature warned him not to anticipate the natural consummation of what she had instigated on the river, he stayed, hoping, craving, his blood simmering. . . .

At the next hour bell, two hours before midnight, Adele opened the connecting door. "He is still here," she informed her lady, and eyed Michael fearsomely, eyes narrowed. "If you hurt her," the old besom-rider warned with an affected gravelly voice, "I will poison your blood, stake you through the heart, cut off your head, and burn you to ashes."

His jaw slackened. "Really?" Amused but not entirely unfazed by the preposterous threat, he skirted the old dame. "I thought we were mates, Adele." His speaking Gaelic did not mollify her this time. At the door he halted, eyes downcast, and whispered self-consciously, "How can I harm your lady when I adore her beyond the entire world?"

"Pah," Adele said, but her eyes grew sympathetic in the midst of a terrifying scowl.

Inside the perfumed bedchamber, candlelight flickered like starlight. He found his winsome quarry sitting on a three-legged stool by the fireplace, head hung askew to dry damp ebony locks, and toasting pretty little toes close to the firedogs. Her face was scrubbed to a rosy patina, body buttoned tightly into a peignoir of sapphire broadcloth stitched with gilt fleurs-de-lis, the snowy hem of her smock covering her graceful anklebones. The fire in the hearth blazed as ruthlessly as the lust raging in him. His heart drummed as the rest of him armed for a chevauchée. Whichever retreat tactic she might devise, he had auxiliaries lined up and a card of ten up his sleeve.

Renée smiled at him. He closed the door and ambled to her, his gaze drawn to the swanlike neck. "How fare you?" He knelt before her and smoothed his hand along the graceful, silky slope of her neck, caressing her, inhaling her flowery fragrance, imagining his hands on her body.

She stiffened at the caress but did not demur. In all fairness, she had done the same to him. He was entitled. Tit for tat. But when his hand curled on her nape and pulled her closer for a kiss, she captured his face between her hands. "Have you come to claim your reward, *bel homme*?"

"Does *bel homme* rank between *petit ami* and *bel ami* on the French endearments scale?"

"*Bel homme* means handsome man and *petit ami* is a close friend. You are both to me."

His voice sounded pathetically gruff and needy. "I would be so much more to you, Renée." He watched her as, without a word, she took out an open letter from her pocket and handed it to him. He masked his insecurity with glib humor. "Our indefatigable rhymer strikes again, eh?"

"It arrived today. Read it."

Her flat tone of voice boded ill. The royal French seal gave him the willies. He unfolded the letter and skipped the formal flourishes. The vicious blow caught him in the gut. He stared at her. "You cannot possibly marry that Italian duke's son."

"Why not?"

Perdition take her, she was going to make him say it. "Because you and I—" He faltered.

She blinked at him, a vision of innocence and calm. "What, Michael? What are we?"

It was her fault that he could not breathe. In a few days she had shaken all of his convictions. If he were not mistaken, some form of torture and manipulation was being deftly applied here—but for what purpose? He crushed the letter in his fist and fed it to the fire. "Do you think I give a toss whether or not you've partaken of the tournaments of the bedchamber?"

Abruptly she stood and faced the burning logs. The stratagem she had plotted must have gone awry. "My virtue or lack thereof is not a mutually agreeable topic."

Michael came up behind her and slid his arms around her waist. "Your king may have every prince in the world, from Catai to Hispaniola, queued up for your hand, but it will not make a plaguy difference. Do you know why?" He felt a tremor jolt her. He put his lips to the whorls of her ear. "Because you are falling in love with me, as I have fallen in love with you."

Another shiver shook her frame. "Do you honestly believe my future is mine own to chart?"

"I believe all is possible. Look at your friend Mary. She and Suffolk charted the Silk Route for us. All we need do is navigate by the conjugation of their planets." He scattered soft kisses on her cheek. "Do you know the moon is swifter in her course than any other planet?"

"Do you know the tale about the wrenne and the eagle?"

"I love a good tale." He breathed her in, undone by her allurements. He had never felt like this before, dazzled and enticed, ferociously protective, madly possessive. *Open and helpless.*

"Well, there was once a little wrenne who was unjustly caged by an evil raven. A great eagle came to her rescue and freed her from her barred prison. He was kind and debonair. She thought his feelings were true and tender. So she asked him to fly away with her across the sea to a safe land. But the eagle refused to come. All he wanted was a warm nest for that one night."

"The wrenne mistook him. The eagle wanted a warm nest for that night and the next night and every night thereafter, but before he could fly away with her, he had to overcome the raven."

"Michael—"

"Do you recall our wager?" he said against her scented hair. "Omittance is not quittance."

"The poet has not come forward."

"Maybe he has. . . . Shall I tell you the rest of the ballad?" He smiled when her face swerved up to seek his gaze, her eyes large, keen, and hopeful. Softly he recited:

> *"Yes, listen while my tale I tell.*
> *I burn, distracted in a spell:*
> *There is no hotter flame in hell*
> *Than lover's fire*
> *When secret lover dare not tell*
> *His strong desire."*

Tears suffused her violet eyes as she timidly smiled up at him. "He was you."

"He was me." He dipped his head and tasted her rosy kiss-comfits.

The beautiful sylph liquefied in his embrace. "I wanted him to be you." Her voice was a soft sigh in between mellifluous kisses. "I will never forget your kindness to me. I was afraid I would be locked in that foul prison for years, or . . . worse. You are my guardian angel, my champion."

Her admission set his heart aglow. He kissed her deeply, hungrily. Her satiny tongue burned upon his. Her taste intoxicated him, gillysop in brandy, flaming snapdragon. He was starving for her, for every delicious nook and cranny in her mouth and body. He could eat her up from tip to toe and still be famished for more. He loved her as he never imagined he could ever love anyone. He would die a thousand deaths for her and strut to every execution with a daft grin on his face. Never would he relinquish her to a grand duke or a prodigious artist. She was his.

"Why the masquerade? Why send me beautiful love verses and ridicule the effort?"

How could he explain? Until she had kissed him on the river, two men had been warring inside him: the fatuous dreamer and the cynical coward. "All men are craven heretics in love."

Renée's head fell back against his shoulder with a sigh of surrender. "Michael . . ."

His fingers unhooked the pearl buttons beneath her chin. He loosened the peignoir from her shoulders, unveiling her diaphanous smock. His hands, desperate to fondle, pleasure, and possess every enchanting curve, roamed the supple dips and hills swathed with gossamer linen. He slid a hand over her *mons veneris* as his other hand reverently cupped a small, delectably pert breast, tipped with a long nipple, demanding to be licked, suckled, and pleasured. He tweaked the tip gently, elongating and puckering it, and felt her catch her breath. "You like that?"

Her breathing grew strenuous. Her dark eyelashes swept over her eyes like feathers.

He pulled the ribbon of the smock, eased his hand inside, and groaned at the feel and heft of her breast, perfectly round and soft. With the utmost gentleness he teased the divine nipple while rubbing the cleft between her thighs. As he sensed the fine material of her smock dampen at his touch, a jolt of blinding need nearly made him climax in his slops. Her heat and moistness jarred him, shook him. The heady scent of her desire obliterated his mind. She was wet and ready for him. He groaned in torment. "Say you want me, Renée. I desire you beyond reason."

Her lips parted on a gasp as her head rolled back, her throat a milky white arch, beckoning kisses. Her body pulsed in his arms, but she would not give him the words he repined to hear.

Undeterred, he smoothed the sleeves of her smock down her slender arms, baring gleaming white shoulders. He growled deep in his throat at the stab of lust that pierced him when the filmy cloth snagged on the stiffly jutting nipples. It was the most arresting, gorgeous, arousing thing he had seen in his life. Delicately his fingers unhooked the smock and sent it floating to her feet.

He sucked in a hissing breath when the entire length of her beauty was revealed to him. The firelight delineated every flawless rise and shadowy dale. Her loveliness stunned him, mystified him, invoking every lyrical verse and tune stored unused in his brain. The pink paps, proud peaks of pearly curved breasts, inspired a ballad all their own. Her belly, dotted with a pretty button, sloped slickly beneath his hand and flared into graceful hips. His heart thumping madly, his hand slid into the nest of dark curls hiding the rose of her sex and gently parted the moist folds.

Renée cried out in excitement and protest at the invasion. She clutched his wrist and stared up at him, fretful and bewildered, fear and desire warring in her eyes. "This is too intimate."

"Too intimate? Marmoset, we have barely begun." He clung to self-discipline as the satiny florets bedewed his fingertips, as her natural feminine scent hazed his feverish mind. Her virginal skittishness surprised him. This was not the reaction of a wanton loved and tried in the ribald trouneys of the French court. Was she chaste, as the letter implied, or had she been sadly initiated by a selfish dullard ignorant in the fine workings of the female anatomy?

"Oh!" She whimpered, wiggling. "Michael, I—"

"Let me touch you," he whispered as his light fingers probed deeper, stroking the petal-soft corolla of her sex. He teased the lubricious rose leaves, wanting to bury his face there and lap up the succulent fruit like a famished beggar. He felt taut as a drawn bowstring, at knifepoint. His cod, leaking profusely in his slops, responded to the beacons her body lit as to a trumpet to arms. "I'm dying for it. I can smell your excitement, how luscious you are down there, my *rosa*. I know what I am about. Trust me. I'll make it good for you."

"You did not do this to Anne," Renée admonished petulantly.

Michael exhaled haggardly. The patron saint of overeager lovers must have heard his plight. Her remark doused his ardor somewhat, helping him restore a semblance of self-control, but also slew his good humor. "If you wish to unman me, you are going the right way about it."

"You desired her," she said flatly. "Do not pretend otherwise."

He regarded her with irritation but at the same time understood her misgivings, considering she had watched him bed another woman—to his supreme regret. "You crave insight into the cogs and wheels of the male mechanism? Prepare yourself for disenchantment, my love. It takes very little effort to crank our crude device—a look, a pat, a shapely shadow, a patch of skin—but it takes a great deal more to make us love-shaked, or worse, lovesick."

"What is the difference?"

"Love-shaked is shaken with lustful fever, lovesick is languishing with amorous desire, and you have love-wounded me with every bolt of Cupid's quiver. I amuse you?" The shrew-minx was smiling. "Then I'll be bolder. Sith I espied you in the undercroft, you . . ." He caught himself.

"Go on. Astound me with your revelation. Since you saw me . . ." She bestowed him with a sultry look of a budding temptress seeking assurance of her desirability, enticing disclosure.

He prayed for guidance. Telling her that Anne had been a vessel to tup when thoughts of her had teased his cod would be uncouth and insulting to her royally genteel sensibilities. How to couch the principle of the matter with finesse and appease her withal? "From the moment I saw you, knowing I could not have you, I still wanted no one else," he confessed. "And whether you were safely tucked away or taunting me with your witchy eyes, you provided the inspiration."

"Oh." She licked her lips against the smilet itching to blossom.

"Now may we proceed with the labor of love?" he murmured against her mouth as he kissed her sensually, seeking to overcome her defenses. The passionate wrenne from the river returned, swaying and sighing erotically in his arms, challenging his restraint, inciting him to plunder the treasures of her radiant city. He felt like a pauper invited to feast at the king's table, the imagery not altogether far-fetched if he were the stew-side urchin who had buried his ill-used mother. He was awestruck and humbled by his good fortune. A princess of the blood, descended directly from a king, made for another king, and she was all his to love and enjoy. He would pleasure her so thoroughly, bind her to him with silk jesses, that she would never flit away from him.

"Touch me," crooned the sylphyd siren. A psaltery of ivory, wreathed with black silk tresses and pink gillyflowers, she nestled trustingly in his embrace, her delicious pointy tongue parrying and thrusting in his mouth. Unable to withstand her appeal, he thrummed her delicate frets with his fingers, one hand on her firm breast, elongating and rolling the withy nipple, another between her heavenly thighs, unfurling the soft petals, spreading the nectar, and petting the succulent burrow.

He wrenched a telling cry from her lips when he touched upon the sensitive, swollen stigma of the rose. He began circling it slowly, deliberately, absorbedly, making her pulsate and moan. Realizing he could make her crest like this was not helping matters in his nether regions. "Say you want me. I can give you so much pleasure, make you fly in my arms, I swear."

Renée was lost to her own exquisite torment, gasping and pulsing. "This is . . . this is . . . ." Her breathless voice betrayed how vulnerable, aroused, and bewildered she felt. She arched her spine to serve up her sensitized breast to his loving hand, swiveled her pelvis to pleasure herself with his untiring fingers, and tantalizingly wriggled her curvaceous bottom to his burning loins. Her body vibrated, low cries of agony spilling from her lips. "I have never . . . I cannot withstand it!"

"You will, and you'll love it." He played with her nimbly, patiently, making tiny forays and sorties, applying all the skill at his disposal to render her dizzy with sensations. "Beautiful, pure fire," he breathed as he sensed the tension swell inside her. He rubbed the seat of her delight with increasing pressure to catapult her into a climax. "Let the ripples grow and cast you ashore."

"Michael, I cry you mercy!" she whimpered, straining for release, her body trembling.

He caught her about the waist with one arm when her legs sagged. "Do you want more?"

"*Yes* . . ." Her cries grew throatier, needier, her movements jerkier. Her talons used his arm as anchor for the storm rapidly gathering momentum inside her. Pressing his thumb to her Venus sweetness, he shoved two fingers inside her molten, tight tunnel, stroking deeply.

With a cry of wonder, she flared like a balefire, clenching spasmodically around his fingers, drenching them, juddering uncontrollably in his embrace. On and on it went. He was awestruck. The royal confection had come apart in his hand.

With a sigh, Renée uncoiled, her soft body quivery and liquefied. He lifted her into his arms, carried her to the great bed, and laid her on the cool sheets and the voluptuous silken cushions.

He was awash with sweat, his undergarments soaked, his heart basting his ribcage, his cod impossibly hard and aching. He beheld her serene face and limp body. She was a petite goddess, lithe perfection made for a man's pleasure. "I made you crest in passion for the first time."

Renée's eyelashes fluttered open. Deep color stained her cheeks. She gave a curt nod.

"A foretaste of things to come." Smiling cockishly, he began stripping with swift efficiency. The Bordeaux jerkin, the gilt-trimmed black velvet doublet, and the camlet shirt hit the floor one after the other. Enjoying her eyes on him, gliding and caressing with patent appreciation, he set his fingers to unlacing the points of his hose. "Only think, so far we have cruised along the coastline. Wait till we sail into the deep waters. You may meet a sea monster there."

Unexpected fear leaped into her eyes. She sat upright. "What monster? Bloodthirsty?"

Michael cursed his foolery. He had taken the codding metaphor too far. "Rest you. I meant it figuratively, a jest for you to catch and bandy back with a saucy quip." Shaking with a rampant need to lose himself in her lush body, he shoved the hose and slops to his feet.

"You are beautiful," she said. *A golden stallion.* The whisper came at his mind like a sylvan spirit but the voice was Renée's.

"What did you say?" He chuckled when her gaze fixed on his cod. The eager fellow swelled at the compliment of having a stunning princess bestow her amazed appreciation.

"I . . ." She blushed, looking up. "I said you were beautiful."

"I meant the other thing."

"What other thing?"

I am pitiful. He was so starved for words of affection from her that his mind shoveled imagined praises onto his alms dish.

Smiling, she fell back on the pillows. "Are you waiting for a chryselephantine invitation?"

He grinned sheepishly. "Maybe."

"Then you may grow a gray beard while you wait." She reached for the sheet and blanket to cover her nude loveliness.

Michael leaped on the bed and caught her hands before she disappeared beneath the covers. Bestriding her hips, he pinned her fists down on either side of her head and leaned in to kiss her. "You sly witch," he murmured against her honeyed mouth. "You would make a pirate of me."

"A pirate?" She arched seductively, scraping his chest with her gorgeous nipples, and licked inside his mouth with brazen hunger.

Michael groaned in frustration, madly aware of the lusciously aroused nest of spices trapped between his thighs. The hard length of his cod burned upon the softness of her belly, eager to be sheathed in hot, fluid, fragrant depths, almost desperate enough to plunder her vessel without a formal or leastways a verbal invitation. Luckily, he had a few sly tricks of his own to extract one withal. "Aye, a pirate who pillages and conquers. Is that what you want me to be?" Taking her wrists in one hand, he pinned them above her head and lashed at one erect pap with his tongue.

With little cries of delightful distress, she writhed beneath him as his tongue swirled round the tips of her breasts with preciseness calculated to drive her crazy with need for fulfillment. He laughed when the wild mare tried to unhorse him and penalized her nipples with hard sucking. But as her plump breasts seduced him to love them generously, his mouth wet and insatiable, she yielded to his ministrations with a happy sigh of pleasure, wiggling helplessly, offering her graceful, silken body to his worshipful mouth.

Michael wanted her feverish, demanding, and desperate, as he was. He released her hands and moved lower, paying no attention to her agitated protests or to the fingers pulling his hair, and forced her knees apart. The sight and scent of the rose of her sex dizzied him, drove him mindless with lust. His hands slid along the graceful slopes of her calves and clasped her ankles, once again marveling that his fingers should easily span the slim bones. He folded her legs up, opening her fully to his view, and breathed in. She was a delightful luxury, a nonpareil, a spicery of carnal pleasures, rosy and glistening with the dew the minstrels sang of and lovers thirsted for.

"Michael, you are a depraved, licentious madman!" Renée kicked her legs down and tried to behead him by clamping her thighs together, or leastways give him a tonsure with her fingers.

His heart pounding, his brain drunk on her flowery, rich, spicy scent, he did what any quick-witted man would do to keep from becoming baldpated. He pressed his mouth to her silky petals and licked her. Her startled cry of pleasure vaguely penetrated the mist of perfumes and flavors besieging his senses. He was lost, soused in sultry divinity, lapping the nectar of her sex as if he had never had a woman in his life. He felt like a god in tasting her desire. He wanted to live in this secret royal confectionary, master it, put up walls around it, and possess it by law.

The fingers in his hair loosened their grip as she softened under his velvety, stroking tongue. Her lithe body undulated in a rapturous, sensual, eager dance, her busy mind at long last hushed, caught in a tempest, straining toward the shimmering crest she had discovered earlier in his arms. He gave it all to her, his enthrallment with her vivacious spirit, her sharp wit, and her beautiful, delicious body inspiring, guiding, and bestowing him with the skill of a journeyman in the art of love. He anchored her in the storm as he pushed her higher, sucking the sweetness of her Venus.

Renée cried in torment, arching, thrashing, spreading her knees wider, her fingers clenching and unclenching in his hair. She was getting close. He thought he would go mad. Every moment was torture. His hips pulsed with unbearable impatience, grinding his eager cod into the bed. He was violently tempted to mount her now and pound into her flushed depths in furious abandon, but he was for the Holy Grail: her absolute love, trust, and adoration, every night hereafter . . .

Now, Renée. Now! his ravenous mind willed her.

*   *   *

With a cry, Renée peaked and shattered in long, fluid, intensely satisfying ripples. The night enveloped her in dark, glittering, smooth magic. The candles round the bed sputtered as one glorious crest chased another. She was Venus reveling in the sensual recklessness of her free nature, awakened by a lover whose skill reduced her to a limp, wobbly, luminous mass saturated with blissful contentment. Eyes closed, she lay very still, enjoying the sensations gliding through her body, the waves spreading and ebbing, dispersing into mist along her midnight shore.

The scorching weight pushing upward to cover her frame made her eyes open. Suspended on his forearms, Michael reclined between her thighs, blue eyes ablaze, rapacious desire imbruting his striking features, breath coming swift and insistent. His suntanned skin was coated with a fine sheen of perspiration; his godlike muscular body roped to stanch the tension vibrating through him. He was wondrous, fierce. She was utterly absorbed in him. No other thought existed.

"Take me," he begged urgently. The blunt head of his hot lance was couched at the ravished cleft in her armor, but he withheld his sortie. "Take me to you, Renée. . . ."

Moved by the desperate need she read in his face, she felt exulted eagerness surging through her. She wrapped herself around him like moonseed, caressing his sculpted velvety shoulders, broad back, hands sliding up his neck, her hips rolling in invitation. "Yes. I want you. Michael. *I want you.*"

With a grateful groan, Michael pushed himself into her. She anticipated discomfort, but as he forged his way with delicious ease, a prolonged, heavy, pleasurable stroke, blazing sweetness, memories of past experiences and worries of physical incompatibility melted away in the river of fire she had become. A growl of triumph ripped from his throat, as if he were crowned a king, the supreme ruler of her little country. He pulled out and plunged again, intensifying the pleasure eddying between her thighs. She welcomed the aggressive assault with unreclaimed hunger, her body emulating the furious, rhythmic motion he set with his hips. *She loved it. She wanted more.*

"You love it." His voice was as sure, strong, and masterful as his supernatural powers. "I see it in your eyes, purple gemstones, full of amazement." Gathering force like a destrier storming an opponent, thundering toward the inexorable clash, he gave her everything she craved and more.

She was so aroused she thought she would die. "You have struck me into amazement," she confessed breathlessly. Overwhelmed by a rush of delightful sensations, she flowed beneath him, holding him, the daughter of Louis XII, aching to let this vampire master and pleasure her body.

"Open wider," Michael implored gruffly, as if in pain. "Take all of me." He shoved his arms beneath her, allowing no space between their sweat-sleek bodies.

Dutifully Renée spread her thighs farther apart and lifted her hips to his rocking body. She cried out at the thick intrusion and fell helplessly into the glimmering abyss, her insides pulsing, bright sparks of pleasure spiraling and coalescing into a continuous overflow of satisfaction.

Michael gasped as the tight embrace of her femininity yielded with honeyed contractions, melting to receive more of him. He never broke rhythm, taking her with a passion as raw and potent as the human blood he fed on. His deep, strong possession dragged her back into the fiery maelstrom, a great pulling ascent toward the explosive pinnacle. She watched him with delirious eyes and held on to his sleek shoulders for dear life as he drove heavily into her glistening body, thrusting as far as he could go. Every foray was a jolt of exquisite pleasure, a shock of profound sensual awareness. His blue eyes burned into hers, commanding a connection with her spirit, invading her soul, as forcefully and unerringly as he invaded her body. He stroked and seduced all her secret places, his arcane powers permeating and taking over. The primal desire etched into his face exhilarated and terrified her all at once, for while his love poured into her, crashing like surf against her sealed heart, she wondered if the bloodthirsty, silver-eyed monster kept in irons within him was rattling its chains, demanding to be unleashed.

She was not immune to the stark vulnerability she perceived in him, though. His yearning to be loved tugged and clawed at her heart. She sank her fingers in his silky, golden hair, and of a sudden they were kissing, frenziedly, desperately, like two people possessed, hurtling toward a volcanic eruption. Her exultant cry of release blended with his shout of surrender as he pumped his hips, prolonging her rapturous spasms, and spurted into the convulsing depths of her body.

Slowing down, Michael emptied himself inside her with hissing groans of exquisite pleasure and sprawled atop her, hefty, sweaty, and hot, his breaths sawing harshly. As her languid spirit floated back from heaven to earth like stardust, she was astonished to find herself wrapped round him in a clinging, oversentimental fashion. Startled, she instantly loosened her hold.

Michael's voice was muffled and lighthearted as he recited:

> *"I wish I were a throstle-cock,*
> *A bunting or a laverock,*
> *Sweet birds of the air!*
> *Between her kirtle and her smock*
> *I'd hide, I swear."*

Something pulled at her chest, a feeling, a seductive ache, deafening thunders, dangerous.

He bestirred himself, pushing up and bracing his weight on his forearms so he could look at her face. Alarm flashed in his eyes. "Marmoset, why the tears? Did I hurt you?"

"No." She turned her cheek to the pillow, shutting her eyes tightly against the hot moisture spilling unbidden. She had given her maidenhead in a night of love that had begun with shining promise and ended with soreness between her legs and a dull ache in her heart. Still she clung to Raphael's pale, lean body, desirous of words of love and comfort to defuse the damp squib, and he stuttered an apology, saying that his art was beauty, not words. He loved her, she knew he did, but his first mistress was his art, whereas Michael percieved her as his canvas. There was more love in one stroke of his brush than in all the globules of paint she had collected from Raphael.

Soft, warm lips kissed her wet cheek. "You must be exhausted, honeymouse. Do you want me to leave you alone?"

No! "You may stay." Her hands slid along the taut muscles of his spine. He was still wedged deep inside her and seemed content to remain where he was. But he was cumbersome. Her pelvis was stuck in an uncomfortable position, curved against the bed. She re-arranged herself beneath him, and to her astonishment, he swelled inside her body. With a cockish grin, he began rocking smoothly against her, gliding in and out. Her belly fluttered as the delicious heat reemerged.

"Should I stop?" he murmured. He continued moving inside her, rhythmically, intimately, kissing her, his mouth adoring. "It is I who is struck with amazement. It feels like heaven inside you. Beauty and flowers and celestial fire . . . I am in thrall, Lady Áine, yours to command."

Renée closed her eyes and swayed with him, her hands on his lower back and gliding lower on their own volition. It felt like heaven having *him* inside *her*. Even his breathing excited her. Gentle tongues of fire licked the glowing embers in the hearth. The bed was shadowy and warm, surrounded by flickering stars. She felt transported, unchained from the humdrum, ensconced in another realm where magic and peril interweaved seamlessly, as she and Michael did.

He held her gaze as they undulated as one in a trancelike, lazy rhythm. "Do I please you?"

"You please me well, *bel ami*." She framed his handsome face with her hands. "My lover."

"I knew what it meant." Twinkling turquoise eyes smiled upon her face. "Now what are the French endearments for husband and father?" He dipped his head and licked her nipple.

Renée gasped, her enchantment with him intensifying. God's truth, she must be ensorcelled. This vampire spoke of sharing a bed for a lifetime and siring babes, and her body, playing traitor, became purest fire. Pleasurable tingles moistened her further as his tongue lashed at her nipple.

"You put a spell on me," he whispered with a note of wonder. "I could pleasure you all night long. Readily." To give credence to his words, he surged all the way, thickening, hardening. Her breath caught as sparks of pleasure flared through her, nearly tumbling her into ecstasy.

"Turn around," he said, lifting and pulling himself out of her. She flipped onto her stomach, biddable and unarmed, a wanton shade of herself. Hot anticipation glowed between her legs.

He stroked her derrière, his hands warm and exciting; then his fingers traced her cleft until they reached the opening of her sex, where they fluttered deliciously. He nudged her thighs wide open and lay atop her trembling frame. His hard penis prodded her feminine cleft as his hand slid around and beneath her to tease her lightly. Slippery and needful, she welcomed the marvelously thick penetration with whimpers of excitement, undulating and straining against him.

"You like this position?" His tone thrummed her senses like a bass string while he rolled his sensual thumb around the seat of her delight, filling her with voluptuous, unrestrained pleasure.

"This is wondrous," she panted, clutching the pillow. Her eager body clenched around him, reveling in the friction, grasping for the sparkly pinnacle. Consuming pleasure swelled within her. Her entire being concentrated on the heat increasing between her legs.

"Tell me what you want, sweeting." His fingers petted and coaxed her with gentle mastery as he pleasured his and her bodies, thrusting in and out persistently. "Shall I go deeper? Harder?"

"Yes," she panted, unbearably close to ecstasy and yet an eternity away.

Michael hoicked her onto her knees. Holding her hips, he surged into her, fierce and furious, asserting his compelling domination. Pleasure speared her, rippling and intensifying. She cried out her joyous relief, jerking and shuddering in sweet oblivion. Then another swell of clenching arousal rushed through her, a cannonball, rolling like thunder. It was Michael. She felt him. Her body tightened into an aching fist. . . . An overwhelming hot burst of enjoyment hit her as he let go with a hoarse growl, pounding hard and fast, lost to the wrenching climax ripping through him.

He collapsed on his back next to her, his chest rising and falling with his harsh breathing, his skin a dark glistening gold. "You please me, sweet-and-twenty. How well you please me."

Lying on her stomach, arms folded beneath her, Renée returned his smile. She was utterly in awe of him. The vampire she must betray opened his arm in invitation. She nestled up against him and put her head on his left shoulder. Holy Deodatus! Only yesterday he had had a hole in it, blood gushing out. Now the skin was seamlessly healed, unscarred. She touched the area of the absent wound with her fingertips. "How long have you had this . . . disease?"

"Not long. Several weeks. The first week was agony, but then it went away."

"And the fluid you drink from the glass bottle? Does it sustain you?"

"The dragon's blood doesn't sustain me. It's curative. It keeps the disease at bay."

Did he expect her to believe this? "If you have discovered the spring of life, you have a duty to share it with the world." Why was she goading him? Best leave matters unsaid.

"This potion, this sorcery"—he spat the word out like a curse— "is not the spring of life but a yoke around my neck. Every day before sunup, I wake up to a fever spell and suffocating thirst."

"You were injured at midday."

"The potion's remedial qualities also mend wounds."

"Does it really? How intriguing. Aught else?"

"I think my strength has doubled, and there are other things. I can leap to great heights."

Doubled! Vampires possessed the strength of a score of men. His feigned ignorance baffled her. "Is your hearing improved? Your sense of smell? Your eyesight?"

"There's the rub. I hear everything. I smell everything. And I tell you, it's a poxy nuisance." He exhaled, exasperated. "How did you guess?"

"Adele explained to me. She is . . . a healer. How does one get infected?"

"The Irish healer who bestowed me with the potion claimed I

had consumed bad blood. Do not ask me how, for I am in the dark on the matter."

Was he in earnest? "You said you were not pestilential. Can you infect others?"

"My blood is infectious, hence I would not let you touch me in the tent when I was bleeding. You must never come in contact with it."

The underlined promise not to turn her into his kind assuaged her greatest fear of him. She allowed herself to calm down. Her hand caressed his torso, her fingers moving over his chest like butterflies, circling his nipples, tracing the impressive grid of muscle on his stomach. *Her golden stallion of fable.* His sun-kissed skin was smooth as a babe's and feverish. "You are burning hot."

"Always. Courtesy of the Sweat. Besides, your chamber is a furnace and making love to you is akin to dipping in a volcano." The stack of eight woolen mattresses bounced as he left the bed. She watched him saunter across the chamber. Confident of his fine body, he made no pretense of modesty as he went to the window and threw the lozenged door open, letting in frosty drafts.

Shaking, she slid under the covers. "Do you mind?" she asked his chiseled backside.

He tossed her a grin over his shoulder. "Do you expect Smulkin to drop in unannounced?"

"No, Hobbididance and Frateretto, happier demons, with their entire nightly entourage of bats, owls, rooks, woodpeckers, and every night critter skulking out there. I am cold!"

With a wry grin, he closed the door and leaned back against it. His humor was short-lived. "I did not always resemble a roasted boar." He seemed distressed, as one who did not know what to make of himself. . . . Pendants of light flashed in her head. She regurgitated each word and nuance of their conversation. *Was it possible?*

"Do you mind if I avail myself of your bathwater?"

"The water has cooled," she replied distractedly. "And there's prison filth floating in it."

"I like cool, and your filth I do not mind."

As he submerged himself in her soapy bathwater, she marveled that she should be permitting such intimacy. Indeed the thought of any other man bathing for her view, in her used water, in her bedchamber made her cringe. Michael made it feel like the most natural thing in the world. Possibly because her body still hummed with the sinfully carnal pleasure he had given her.

The night was turning out to be one of revelations.

Inconceivable as it might be, she was beginning to suspect he had no idea he was a vampire. Whoever turned him had told him aught but outlandish falsehoods. Either that or she was being hoodwinked by a trickster who deserved a stake through his heart. But supposing she was right, why should his Vesper overlord send him to retrieve the Ancient and keep him in the dark? Was he, like her, a pawn in someone else's game? *Whatever madness possesses kings, it is ordinary Achaeans who get hurt.* Suddenly it dawned on her what tremendous power she held over him. An uninformed vampire in love with her—the possibilities were endless! Certes, she would have to be very shrewd and gentle with him. One false move and the beast would turn on her. Even if she forgot he was a vampire and treated him as Michael, the man she had come to like so much, she would still be holding a wolf by the ears.

Michael's face emerged from the water with a serene smile. "That was heavenly."

"How do you intend to retrieve your property from the cardinal?"

"I haven't the foggiest."

"Do you know where it is kept . . . exactly?"

"No." He stood, water splashing at his calves and sluicing from his body.

The sight of such glorious male nakedness awash in firelight robbed her mind of thought. He was magnificent, ominous, and beautiful, a golden archangel. She was utterly smitten with him—the poetic secret lover, the intriguer, the fearless soldier, the vampire. So many facets of the same man, and yet so much of him still lay in the shade, a mystery.

As he wrenched water from his hair, his lambent blue gaze descried the approval in her eyes. His grin turned sultry, predatory. He was primed for lovemaking—again!—and made no effort to conceal his condition. She left the bed to fetch him a clean linen towel. He stepped out of the bathtub and towered over her. A challenging glint entered his eyes. "Dry me," he said huskily.

That the lily-white princess enjoyed his body to the extreme was a sop to Michael's vanity. However, the days when her pure lustful capitulation would have put a swagger in his gait were sand through his hourglass. In his campaign to seduce her body, his heart had been captured, and now, a prisoner in her stronghold, he must take the tower of her heart with subtler means.

The problem was he felt . . . unworthy. She was perfect, regal. Her inky locks cascaded to her shapely hips like a luxurious fur cloak; her pert breasts swayed tantalizingly, seducing his eyes; her eyes were the color of royal purple. Godsakes, Renée was the late King of France's daughter! And he . . . He had been unable to blot out the stench of the stews. Nor the vivid details of his nightmare. And he was sick. She would be better off avoiding him like a plague-ridden village.

Alas, self-abnegation was against his nature. He coveted her with a hunger that transcended aught else. Whatever she needed him to be or do to deserve her, he would accomplish it.

He watched her as she dabbed the linen napkin at every diamond drop clinging to his skin, petting and looking him over with enkindling fascination. She crouched before him to towel his legs, her moist mouth on a horizontal plane with his pole-hard cod. Dark lashes shyly lifted and curious violet eyes studied the length of him. Fire and brimstone! If she applied her mouth to him, the last vestiges of self-restraint would desert him, and she would find herself on her back again, being ridden by a rampant bull, lost to his driving needs, with no care for her pleasure.

"Do not . . ." he implored throatily while his violently aroused body wished she would. What poxy spell had the fey minx cast upon him that he should not be sated? Another scientific marvel deserving of a chapter in Dr. Linacre's educative book, no doubt.

"Do not what?" asked the intrigued sorceress, her whispery breath caressing his cod into an impossibly febrile erection. With the same maddening absorption she applied to the rest of him, she lightly touched the napkin to his stones, then wrapped it around his cod and squeezed her fist around him, as if to soak up the water. A shaft of blazing stimulation ripped through him, making him flinch. In an evanescent moment of clarity, he caught her arms and drew her up.

"No, Renée. If you . . . tease me, I will . . ."

"Do what?" She cocked a daring eyebrow. Clearly his princess had shed her skittishness and grown an appetite for their bed sport. The observation pleased him, considering his prodigious staying power, which he attributed strictly to her effect on him. Regrettably he still had to return to the stews tonight and he wanted their last moments together to be memorable. He took her hand and led her back to bed.

They lay down face-to-face in absolute silence. "What o'clock is it?" she finally asked.

"Does it matter?"

"Do you—would you stay the night with me?"

He would have hooted with elation if he did not think it was her fear of the cardinal issuing the invitation. "I wish I could. I have business in Southwark pertaining to the investigation. Be at ease. No one will come for you tonight, marmoset. You are safe."

"You need to go now?" A wrinkle of chagrin linked her eyebrows. She did not want him to leave. Her hands began roaming, exploring, caressing him, featherlight. "You want me again."

"Renée, if my duty were not pressing—and yes, I do need to depart anon—you would have to boot me from your bed." He noticed the silk cord binding the luxurious bed hangings to the post. Mischief possessed him. He pulled the cord, releasing the drape, and gathered her into his embrace. Lacing his right hand with hers, he wound the cord around their wrists.

She snuggled into the nook of his arms with renewed hope. "What are you doing?"

"Handfasting us. It is an ancient Celtic custom between lovers. Every year at Lammastide, the first day of August, the Irish mark the beginning of the harvest season and the ripening of first fruit with a festival. Families come together and hold market fares, games, horse races, and spectacles, and on the last eve of the festival, young men and women that have formed amorous attachments can be handbound with a ribbon in a ceremony presided over by a bard, whereby they pledge their love and devotion to each other for a twelvemonth and a day until the next *Lughnasadh*. After the celebration, they go off to live together."

"For a year and a day?" Renée sought his gaze. "And afterward? Do they part company?"

"Only if they want to. They may renew their vows for another twelvemonth and a day—or forever, or even have a priest bless their union, although Holy Church has long since given up preaching against the old custom and recognizes the validity of the troth regardless."

"What? Like a marriage?"

"Not like," he said softly. "It is a marriage. It does not even require witnesses to be valid."

"Michael." She glared at their tethered wrists. "What have you done?"

He grinned sheepishly. "I married us, for a year and a day. Shall I speak my vow? I, Michael Devereaux, take thee, Renée de Valois, to my espoused wife and thereto plight thee my troth—"

His right hand jerked up as she silenced him with her fingers. "Not another word from you, scoundrel. Now untie us."

"You reject our marriage on our wedding night?" he baited her with a crestfallen expression, and laughed when she attacked the tied cord with her teeth and fingernails. "Do not sever us so shrewishly, *á mhúirnín*. Besides, 'tis done. We are handbound for a twelvemonth and a day."

Her tugging grew frantic. "You cannot prove it! And I never spoke my troth!"

"Rest you, shrew-witch." Hugging her waist, he rolled them aside and rested his chin in the crook of her neck while she worked furiously at untying the cord. The shadows enveloped them closer as the flaming candle wicks drowned in hot wax one after the other. "You need not worry, marmoset. Handfasting is difficult to prove without witnesses . . . albeit not impossible." He laid his left hand on her belly and rubbed her gently, wondering if they had created a babe tonight.

"Ohhh! You—you devil!" She pulled on both ends of the twisted cord and only succeeded in tightening the intricate knots he had fashioned. "I need a dagger. Surely you carry one!"

"Oh no!" He laughed. "I do not think I trust you with a dagger at the moment, for you may play honeybee and sting me."

"But then I would die. . . . A honeybee has but one sting, at the cost of her life." Dolefully she stared at their bound hands. "Is it true? You are not gulling me? We are married?"

"Only if we wish to be. I would never impose myself on you."

He felt her spinning top mulling this over. "Supposing we wish to be, will this knot suffice?"

"Ideally, yes. But you are blue-blooded, my love, and your king may hire the pope to declare our union sinful and therefore void."

"Do you . . ." She let out a shaky sigh. "Michael, are you saying you wish to marry me?"

"Not so sharp-witted, after all. Yes, my shrewish delight." He rubbed his cheek against hers. "I want to wed you and constantly bed you. I am mad for you. Will you have me?"

"You do not trust me."

"Not trust you! However do you mean? I trust you with my heart, with my woeful secret . . ."

"You do not trust me with your other secrets. You are slippery and equivocal—"

"Slippery, madame?" He slipped his fingers between her legs. She was soft and lubricious as he knew she would be. One thing she could never hide from him was the scent of her desire.

Nor her annoyance with his method of distracting her. "Michael, you are proving my point."

"How so? I am doing your bidding, like a dutiful servant. Let me pleasure you one last time, my darling lady, and I promise I shall bestow you with a full confession on the morrow."

Her bottom wiggled temptingly against his burning cod as he pushed a finger inside her. Little gasps of enthusiasm welcomed his caress. She was a lustful shrewcat. He felt her moisten and clench around his finger as he stroked her patiently, priming her body for his incursion. He delayed until she trembled and panted for him to take her. He removed his hand and cupped her breast, gently squeezing and plucking at her nipple, as his turgid cod slid between the lips of her sex, seeking entrance, nudging against the wet folds. Passion rushed through him.

The first shallow thrust jarred him with raw excitement. He buried his face in her silky neck, where her scent was so sweet it made him salivate, and pushed deeper with teasing prods.

"More. I need you." She pulsed restlessly against him. She covered the hand he kept on her breast with hers and moaned softly. Giving in to her pleas, he sheathed himself slowly inside her. He was rewarded with a hot surge of juices that enabled him to push a trifle deeper, his mouth on her delectable neck, biting tenderly. His pulse sped. He was sweating, shaking. He licked her throbbing conduit of life. Her heady scent made his teeth hurt and his eyes smolder.

She vibrated with need, her blood pounding, hot and thick. He felt it rush through her body, humming to him. *He wanted to taste it.* Irrational fear debilitated him. His throat felt raw.

"Michael?" Renée craned her head aside to look at him and screamed in horror.

❧ 21 ❧

The greatest care is due to the young.

—Juvenal: xiv.47

Michael stared at the sign of the Hart, the bawdy house administered by Margery Curson. He had no recollection of how he had come to be standing outside. One moment he was slashing the cord that bound his wrist with Renée's and the next he was in the stygian stews, meandering through the fetid footpaths like a demon, an escapee from Bedlam, a wounded beast, burning all over, lunatic. The canker maturing inside him was transforming him into a savage being of the underworld, vile, pernicious, and a thousand other profanities. He was turning into a monster.

Wrath at the obscure hand of fate that had struck at him—when, how, and why he did not know—was undermined by despair, fat and black, filtering into his soul like torch smoke. What did Renée make of him now? Had he lost her? *Damnation to all eternity!* How could he thirst for her blood when he loved her so? Every portent he had shut his eyes to returned to haunt him.

He was the peril the animals of the forest fled from.

The worst to affright now lives within. . . .

Michael wondered if he were mad to imagine himself a pawn in a universal conspiracy. It was time he wrenched back the leading rein of his life, and his quest for enlightenment had to begin at the bottom. Hence, the Hart.

He found Mistress Margery Curson in the main taproom, hosting a table of dicing Spaniards who were roaring a scurrilous song in their melodious tongue and drinking heavily. She flinched when she saw him bearing down on her. She snapped her fingers, sending the bovine-faced twins in charge of upholding the peace and disciplining ill-behaved revelers to block his path.

As his gaze shifted between the burly hostlers, the peculiar sense of recognition returned, as if time had reversed itself. "I have business with the goodwoman of this house. Stand down."

"W-wot b-business m-might tat-tat be, gent?" stammered the tyke to his right.

The stutter splashed a bucketful of cold memories in Michael's face. He saw younger faces, equally malevolent, little bullies pounding him with their fists, beating his face to a bloody pulp, kicking him when he was down. Once upon a time, in another life. "Which one of you is Roger?"

"Who wants to know?" demanded the mongrel to his left.

"I do." With a tight smile, Michael seized the man's throat and lifted him up in the air.

Half the room stopped whatever they were doing to gawk.

"Remember me, Roger? Look at my wrist." Michael showed the man the red gules pricked in his skin. Roger's eyes rounded in recognition. He choked and sputtered.

A mighty fist flew at Michael's ribs from the tyke to the right. Keeping Roger off the floor, Michael caught and snapped the beefy paw hard, breaking bone.

He finally got the entire room's attention. A spurt of stew-side curses came at Michael like pus jutting from a lanced boil as the more villainous-looking customers rounded on him. He did not even blink. He collared the tyke's windpipe and raised him high to face his reddening sibling. His mean audience recoiled at the show of superior strength. Sheer curiosity gave all pause.

"Is this not cozy?" Michael smirked at his choking fish baits. "Just like old times."

"Wot d'ye want?" Margery Curson appeared before him; her agitated stare bounced between the hostlers wiggling like plump, red-faced worms in Michael's manacling fists.

Michael looked at her. "I will pay."

She gave a resentful nod that sent her bandogs crashing to the floor, gasping for air, rubbing their fingerprinted gullets, and with a flounce of malodorous skirts, tramped to the stairway.

"Stay." Michael snapped his fingers at the subdued doorkeepers and followed her upstairs.

Shabby arras screened side rooms busy with grunts-inducing activity. Girls in various stages of dishabille eyed him coyly as he traversed the gallery in Margery's footsteps. The bawd barked at the girls to return downstairs straightaway and ushered him into the chamber at the far end, the only one with a door. She touched her taper to candle stubs, throwing the cluttered chamber into stark relief.

Furnished with an ancient four-poster complete with moldy bed curtains, chests, stools, and a table stacked with trinkets, dirty articles of female clothing, wooden cups, a tankard of ale, and a stained looking glass, Margery's private realm was—he surmised— what passed for luxury in this dismal haunt. Gaudy kirtles over-flowed an open trunk; smelly underlinen and stockings, muddy boots, and putrescent toadstools carpeted the floorboards. The air reeked of sweat, urine, stale rosewater, and mildew. It was a steep drop from a princess's bed. The place was revolting.

The slattern slouched on the window ledge and propped up a booted foot to show calf. "Ye want to know 'bout yer mum?" At his nod, she extended her open palm. "Two angel nobles."

He handed her a gold coin stamped with St. Michael slaying the dragon. "Here's one. Start talking." He kicked the door shut, leaned back against it, and folded his arms across his chest.

"Ellen wos 'er name. She wos a Stratford nun." She extended her hand again.

"I can *make* you talk, mistress," Michael warned. "You shall have your second angel—after I hear what I need to know!"

Petulantly, she muttered, "Ellen wos a washer of the Whyt Cok, a pretty piece o' piety. I wos a girl at the Cok. She'd wash me linen fer how price. Told me she came from a merchant family of five daugh'ers, Butler was the name, methinks. She was last, see, so they gave 'er to God, but He must not ha' liked the offerin', fer He sent 'er yer da."

"What do you know about my father?"

"Aw, ye have a clean speech on ye, blue-eyes." She gave a gap-toothed grin. "Ye should ha' heard yerself then, when ye were runnin' with the bung boys, pickin' purses and such."

"Your twin bulls, I knew them then, did I not?"

"Aye, they 'ad years and inches on ye, and they did not have Ellen fer a mum. Their da beat them somethin' fierce and put them a-working fer 'im, beggin', pickin', and stealin'."

A flash of recall stunned Michael: a darkened house hard by London Bridge, boys waiting round the corner of the laneway, urging him to knock on the door, a queasy feeling in the pit of his stomach, reluctance, when a bearded man with kind, surprised eyes answered the door.

"Yer da, a right fair gent he wos, lordly. Fought with Duke Jock and the Yorkists. Pity fer 'im, Tudor won the battle. Lost all 'is lofty titles and came to drown his sorrows at the Cok. There he met Ellen. Poor girl." She crossed herself, belying her heathenish proclamations of last night. This old whore might disdain Holy Church but she believed in God.

Unlike him. "Did my father rape Ellen?" Such a sweet and gentle name, he mused sadly.

Margery gave him an appreciative once-over, smacking her lips. "He didna 'ave to. Ellen wos in love. He took 'er to his 'ouse on Thames Street, their nest o' love. Then he went and got himself killed in a brawl, and Ellen got ye. She found work as a servant with the garlicmonger, but when 'er belly swelled, the fishwife booted 'er out, thought it wos the work of 'er 'usband."

"Why did Ellen not return to the nuns? Or to the Butlers?"

Margery spat. "They wouldna have 'er, that's why. No pardon from the pardoners for pious Ellen. She wanted to keep and nousle ye, blue-eyes. She came to live at the Cok, washin', cleanin', but when ye came, she was in bed fer weeks, and ol' Sande, he let 'er keep abed, see. After, he brought in action against 'er in the court o' the bishop of Winchester to get a judgment fer rent money she could never pay. It was prison fer Ellen or working fer Sande on 'er back."

Michael had a football wedged in his throat. He remembered a house of ribaldry and terror, getting the boot if he tarried in carrying tynes of water for baths, laundry, and horses. The dirty bodies, stinking rooms, and vacant eyes of women, he remembered. "How did she die?"

"A babe. They had to cut it out o' 'er. Poor pretty Ellen. God wanted 'er at last."

Terrible images flashed before his eyes: his mother in travail, lying in a pool of gore, knees spread, spewing a bloody pulp from between her legs. He remembered peeping in from the entry, frozen in shock. Her blue eyes found him. She dragged the blood-soaked sheet over her thighs and bade him come closer. She smiled tenderly, but he had already seen too much, had heard her screams and read the pain in her eyes—like the nightmare. He edged forward. He was very afraid. She raised her hand to his face. It felt soft, cool, and limp against his cheek.

"What is your name?" Her voice was the sweetest, gentlest whisper.

"Michael Dev . . . Devewow."

"Very good, my darling." His mum rewarded him with her brightest smile, her cool hand on his small nape. She was so beautiful and sad and tired. "Who was your noble sire?"

He held up his hand, displaying the design pricked into the skin on the inside of his wrist.

"How clever you are, my sweet angel," she praised him. "You are Michael Devereaux. Your noble sire was Sir John Devereaux. He fought bravely in the Battle of Bosworth Field with your noble grandsire, Baron Ferrers of Chartley, who died on the battlefield."

"Mama . . ." He needed to throw himself into her arms, but her loving fingers stayed him.

"How old are you, my valiant Michael Devereaux?"

Tears flooded his eyes. He splayed his fingers. "Five."

"How old will you be when the summer comes, sweet angel mine?" She bestowed him with a cheerful smile to distract him from the tears spilling from her eyes.

He was no noddy. What was amiss with his mum? "Six. Why are you sad, Mama?"

*"And when the summer comes again, how old will you be then?" she
urged. She knuckled a stream of tears from his cheek. She was trying very
hard to smile for him—why? Why?*

*He was cold and afeared. He burst out crying and at once felt ashamed.
He buried his head in her bosom, seeking comfort for the suffocating ache in
his chest. "Mama, do not go. . . ."*

*Her feeble arm came around his small frame. "Hush, my darling. You
are a good boy. You are my strong, kind knight. You are very wise and
good. You will survive. You must survive. . . ."*

*Something dreadful was occurring. Her arm fell from him. He lifted his
eyes to look at her. "Do not sleep, Mama," he pleaded with all his might.
"I'll be valiant and good and strong."*

*"You are, my sweet beloved, my son." Her smile fell; her eyes grew dark,
not seeing him. "Michael, I shall love you for all eternity, remember. Be
strong, my valiant knight, my dragon slayer, my angel, my champion . . ."*

*He didn't know what this word meant. But it was a good word, the best
word. He liked it a lot when she said it to him. He threw his arms around
her neck. She was not moving anymore.*

Michael could not breathe. In his mind's eye, he saw the bundle
of gory sheet that was his mum thrown into the open ditch, and
him darting after them and flinging himself on her covered, still
form. The rest was as he had dreamt it, lying atop her past nightfall, then dragging her out to the hill. Cross Bones, the cemetery
was called. After that his mind went blank.

"Tears, blue-eyes?" Marge's craggy face epitomized the stews,
hardship and scorn meshed into apathy. "I can cheer ye plenty."
She raised her skirts to her crotch, flaunting her goodies.

Bile rose in Michael's throat. He clamped a hand over his mouth,
looking away, willing the nausea to pass. No wonder he reacted as
he did to this place. The memories! He gasped for air.

The bawd entered his vision, coming to pour herself a cup of ale
at the table. "Where did ye go, all them years agone? Roger said
this great lord cut up his da and took ye."

He nodded, finally able to speak. "I was taken to Ireland."

She cast him an opaque glance. "Fine country, eh? Me da was
from Connacht."

"Margery, how would you like to go home with a purse of gold?"

A sharp look came at him. "What d'ye want now?"

"Sir Francis Bryan and Sir Nicholas Carew, when did they leave here last night?" No sooner did he utter the name Bryan than she was shaking her head in adamant refusal. Panic etched her eyes. Michael moved closer. "A heavy purse of gold, Marge. You can be on a ship for Connacht on the morrow. A new life, a cottage by the sea, never needing to work again, people who know naught of your past. Bryan will never know, as he has quit town today on business."

"How much?" she blurted out on a spurt of courage.

"You tell me, sweetheart."

"A hundred pounds!" she ventured insolently.

"Fifty." He would readily pay a hundred, but it would breed discontent, for she would later think she could have gotten more. "Be at Greenwich Wharf on the tenth hour bell on the morrow. My man will wait with the money bag. Now, when did Bryan and Carew leave the Hart?"

She dithered.

"Trust me, Marge. I will not fail you, upon my soul. I shall give you some coins now and the amount we agreed upon tomorrow."

She swallowed, shaking visibly. "Cockcrow," she whispered. "They left at sunup."

They were not the murderers! If none of the conveniently suspect minions of the king were guilty of Anne's murder, who was? Once again his thoughts veered toward Cardinal Wolsey and his missing ring. He found the lord chancellor's personal involvement in the matter disturbing. What was he missing? "You have naught to fear. This information will not set them on you." He dropped a handful of coins on her table. "Be at the wharf on the tenth hour bell."

"Why?" The aging whore—pockmarked, fierce, and scarred as an alley cat—gripped his arm. "Why sweep down like a fair angel and salvage me from the stinking street?" she growled at him, as if he were the angel of death, coming to claim her prematurely. Her eyes were stormy.

"Because"—Michael smiled wistfully—"a kind man did the same for me. May your God keep you, Margaret Curson."

"Wait!" The grimy, calloused fingers tightened on his sleeve. "Wot do they call ye now?"

"Sir Michael Devereaux."

Marge smiled. "A knight, eh? She always dreamt ye'd become a knight, like yer da."

"I know." Michael smiled sadly. He left her with huge tears trembling in both their eyes.

Michael, embattled by the demons of his past and of his present, departed the Hart with no intention of ever setting foot in the place again and took to the dark lane. Flashes of memory of a long-forgotten past cut through images of Renée's beautiful body, responding to him in passion. Margery's account had shifted aside the arras his mind had unfurled over the dismal facts of his early years in the cesspit of London. He remembered scraps: his palliasse on the floor, his mum gathering him in her arms at dawn, humming him softly back to sleep. He remembered running with the boys in the street, skulking, picking purses, darting into potholes to split the loot. They were pickers, bung boys, a band of tiny guttersnipes, managed by the twin bullies who, in turn, carried the lion's share of their pickings to their vicious father. No wonder he was quick-fingered and quick to glimpse the doxy pilfering Stanley's purse, Michael thought. And no wonder he had felt disgust but no fear. When he was a boy, the murky footpaths, the perfidious shadows, the putrid ditches overflowing with filth and detritus, were his domain; where his knee-high leather boots now treaded with contempt, he had once crawled on hands and knees, scavenging for oddments that had fallen from tinsel pockets.

How he had earned Lord Tyrone's good lordship was a mystery. Had his sire sworn the earl to care for his ill-begotten son should aught befall him? Michael scoured his memory for minutes of his earliest encounter with the earl—nothing. His last recall of his days in the stews was of him lying with his mother in her uncovered grave. Likewise, there was a gap between his visiting the earl in the eyrie and wakening fevered, a lapse between his seeing Mariona Wood's ravaged neck and the rousing nightmare, and another between his slavering over Renée's sweet-scented, throbbing life-conduit—her terrified shrieks still rang in his head—and finding himself outside the Hart. Damnation! His pestilent memory had more holes than a pauper's stocking.

Two women butchered on the same night, both while he was hard by, both linked to him—the whore indirectly through his past and Anne through an all too recent carnal association—both punctured in the neck, Anne drained of blood and in possession of his ring . . .

Every piece of evidence pointed at him: the flashing fangs, the unholy thirst, the stews, the ring. The killer, his shadow foe, knew of his past and of his malady; the clues were coming at him from every direction, homing in like darts from Sagittarius the Archer's bowstring.

The killer, Michael concluded, suffered of the same disease. The answers, he felt, were at hand, in the stews, in his head, tangled, locked away. He must think. He must remember more. Must connect the past to the present. The link was the key.

Michael returned to the Cardinal's Hat Alley to look for Mariona Wood's shrouded body in the gutter where she had been dumped the night before. The corpse was gone.

A pack of filthy little urchins sprang from a hovel and hurtled past him, one bumping into him on purpose. Michael swung around and streaked after them, past them . . .

He waited for them at the foot of the alley. With childish shrieks, the boys skidded to a halt, goggled, and shinnied back. He waited for them at the opposite end of the lane again, his smile shocking them into a standstill. They threw agitated looks past their shoulders, contemplating another mad dash for the end of the alley, wondering if he would overtake them a third time, but then decided he had them hemmed in. He held out his hand. "My purse, gentlemen."

The only boy in the quintet with inches taller than Michael's sword belt took a single step forward and pulled the purse out from inside a threadbare shirt. He offered it back to Michael with a servile bow. "Yer pardon, milord. Methinks Yer Lordship dropped this."

Michael smiled. Taking the purse, he dug out a handful of glittering coins and watched their faces transfix with longing. They were bony rats, their eyes huge in smudged faces, the whites of their eyeballs gleaming in the moonlight. "How should you like to earn these by lawful means?"

The tiniest boy, his sooty face roofed by flaxen thatching, stepped to the fore, arms akimbo, to make a stand. "Wot sort 'o means, milord?" he queried businesslike. "Yer Lordship wants to poke a fish? Lots o' divers in the 'at. We're fer men's work, sir. We ain't no fleshies."

Michael flinched. Staring at the boy, a futureless bastard of the bastard sanctuaries, was akin to seeing his own past reflection in a magic looking glass. "All I seek is information, my young friend. Last night a woman was killed at the Hat. Mariona Wood. You knew her?" All five boys nodded. "Last night I saw the hostlers dump her body in the gutter. She was wrapped in a sheet. Now the bundle is gone. Can you tell me what befell her soul-deserted body since?"

"The nuns took 'er to Cross Bones."

"The cemetery." His mother's resting place. "Will you take me there?" He flipped each boy a coin, chinking the rest in his fist to let them know there were more to be earned.

"Come with us," the tiny boy said sternly. "We'll show ye, milord."

Falling into step among the boys, Michael grinned down at the runt of the pack, the valiant scamp. "What is your name?"

"Christopher Rivers, after the saint wot saved the boy on the river." The boy puffed out his little chest like a pigeon. "Me pa wos a boatman."

"Was?"

The boy shrugged his bantam shoulders. "Tumbled into the river a night he wos a-tipplin'."

Michael rested his hand on the boy's shoulder. "And your mother?"

Another shrug. "Dunno." He looked up at Michael. "Will ye teach me, milord? To move like ye, like a dagger? *Zoom, zoom.*" He gestured with his hands, grinning childlike.

He is just a baby, Michael thought, saddened beyond belief. *That was me?* His poor mother, Ellen Butler. Seduced and abandoned with a child in her belly, bereft of means of sustenance. Clearly Southwark was beyond the reach of the Christian God as well as the aldermen of the city. What struck him as ironic was that Lord Tyrone, his savior, did not believe in Jesu, and therefore could not have been His henchman. "I—I do not rightly know how I do that, move with speed," he admitted apologetically, expecting to descry soulful disappointment in the boy's countenance. But when a look of blank acceptance came at him, he felt his heart breaking. Christopher Rivers expected absolutely nothing from life. Squeezing his bony shoulder, Michael offered, "I could teach you something else, though. How about . . . riding a horse? Would you like that?"

The boy's eyes lit up like cressets. "A horse, milord? A great black charger? Like a knight?"

"Certainly. I have a horse just like that, great and black. His name is Archangel."

"Where is he now?" asked another boy, blinking diffidently.

Apparently they were all listening keenly. "At Greenwich Palace, asleep in the stables."

"Does he bite 'ands wot feed him?" inquired a third guttersnipe.

"I should think not. Archangel likes little boys who feed him carrots. What is your name?"

"Thomas."

"Peter."

"Well then, Christopher, Thomas, and Peter, how about I come round with Archangel one morning and teach you how to feed, pet, and sit upon him, hmm?"

"Could ye teach us, too?" asked a fourth, with the taller boy hanging over his shoulder.

"Yes, of course. It will be my pleasure. What are your names?"

"I am Henry," said the older one. "And this one 'ere is Robert, me brother."

"Henry, Robert." His gaze swept over the five heads, some capped. "My name is Michael. I am pleased to make your acquaintance." He offered a courtly bow. It seemed imperative to show them courtesy, prove that there was more to the world than poverty, abuse, and neglect.

"Are you a knight?" Henry and Robert ventured in unison.

He grinned. "Yes, I am. King Henry knighted me yestereve, on St. George's Day."

The boys gasped in awe. "Did ye slay a firedrake?" asked Peter.

Michael laughed. "Not yet, but I hope to, very soon."

"We could 'elp, milord! We're sharp marksmen." Henry picked up a pebble and slung it at a gloomy domicile backed onto a tavern hard by London Bridge. At once his four mates followed suit, and a barrage of pebbles clanged against metal grilles screening wooden shutters. The much-abused brick house, Michael noted, was potted and smeared with feces. Another firecracker went off in his beclouded memory: a kind bearded man standing in the doorway. The pebble attack did not go unnoticed. Growls rose inside the house, and of a sudden the shutters were pulled in.

Michael's escorts raised their hackles and vanished in a patter of mischievous little feet.

The bearded man from Michael's memory materialized behind the grille. "Good-for-nothing scoundrels," he muttered angrily, then shook his fist at the cloud of dust. "Be off with you, little demons! Do not be coming back here, you hear! Let an old man rest his bones in peace!"

Standing beneath the window, Michael stared at the man with fascination. He was older, the beard grayer, the hair sprouting from beneath the nightcap thinner, the Spanish accent fainter, but Michael knew him well. "Sir," he called. "I apologize for my little friends' deficient manners. If the stones impaired your shutters, please allow me to defray the damage."

"Ugh!" The old man waved his hand dismissively. "This old house has taken more missiles than Agincourt and is still standing on its old bones, like its master." He cackled wryly. "It was right kind of you to offer recompense for their folly but unnecessary. Godgigoden, sir."

"Sir!" Michael called out as the old man closed the shutters. "Pray forgive the imposition on your nightly rest, but . . . Sir, we have known each other at one time, one score years since, and I was hoping you might be kind enough to answer a few questions for me."

The man gave Michael a gimlet eye. "Your name, sir?"

"Michael Devereaux. My mother was Ellen Butler of the Whyt Cok."

The man clapped his hands together, a sibilant exclamation in a foreign tongue escaping his lips. "I—I believed you dead," he uttered with feeling. "Come, come to the door." The shutters closed squeakily. A moment later the front door opened a notch. "Are the miscreants out there?"

"Yes." Michael stepped to the door. "They are hiding to my left. Come and apologize!"

"Noooo!" came the timorous response on the wind.

The old man gave a heavy sigh. "Alas, misdread is a conception of the mind that once sowed cannot be uprooted. Come in, come in. They will wait for you, I fear me. Little wretches."

"No trebuchetting, good knights!" Michael informed the night air before he stepped over the threshold of the glum pigmy house. He was welcomed by musty shadows created by the single lit tallow candle shifting around with the old man. Scrolls, tally sticks, ledgers, registers, ready-cut parchment, ink-spotted wads of linen, wooden platters with remains of supper, cups, a trencher, stubby candles, and a plethora of inkpots and quills littered a table flanked by chests serving as benches. Honeycomb shelves stuffed with rolls covered the walls. The entire ground level of the house resembled an eremitical counting room. The old man, wearing a houppelande, waddled to the table and filled cups with what Michael presumed was ale. "May I ask as to your occupation, sir? You are not a verger, are you? A comptroller for the Bishop of Winchester?"

Laughter that soon became coughing came as a response. "I am a comptroller of sorts."

"It is a secret, then." Michael sipped the drink. Not ale but wine, rich and sweet. Costly.

The old man sat himself on the cushioned chest and invited Michael to sit across from him. Shifting his scabbarded sword aside, Michael eased himself down. "I do not recall your name."

"Abraham Wiseman. I make accounts and supervise financial affairs for several upstanding gold and silver merchants on London Bridge. My instruments as you can see"—he indicated the untidiness on the baize cloth coating most of the table—"are quills and parchment. However, the good folk of this parish presume that taking stock of precious metals equates to hoarding treasure of mine own. Hence the iron bars. But enough of that. I am anxious to hear your tale. The last I saw of you, well, it was a nasty business that night." He refilled their cups, his hand shaking.

"Sir, I beseech you to tell me aught you might recall. I have no recollection of my days here. I have spent the last score years of my life in the house of the Earl of Tyrone, Lord Lieutenant of Ireland. I am anxious to know my roots. I had a dream wherein me"— hell's pains, he was about to say me mum; his memory was clearing all right—"my mother dies and is tossed into a gutter. In my dream, I should say nightmare, I cart her to Cross Bones, dig a grave, and then deposit her and myself in it. This nightmare induced me hither in search of truth."

"You lay in the cold grave for three days, methinks. I found you on a Saturday morn, the day I go to Cross Bones to visit my dearly departed wife and son. You were as pale and cold as snow. I thought surely you were dead. Then I saw the thin vapor of your breath and the slight heaving of your chest. I went down and got you. I carried you hither and nursed you to health. I began to apprentice you as a clerk. You had a sharp wit and a hunger for learning. You absorbed numbers with pleasing speed. Naturally, after two moons, I surmised that you were content."

"I was!" exclaimed Michael, images streaking before his eyes. "We had broth for supper and you taught me the letters of my name!" He beamed. "Then you drew serif lines on the *M*." He recalled other things, too: his mates coming to alarm him, saying he would be punished with eternal damnation, for Mad Abraham Wiseman was a heretical sinner and despoiler of souls.

"Yes, as I said, you showed great promise. I was content. Sith I lost my wife and son to the plague, I was alone. I was glad for the company. Then, one evening, I returned to find you gone. You were back with the little pickers, under the thumb of Roger Vise, a nefarious cutthroat if I ever saw one, and his rabid sons. They bade you knock on my door one night, crying for help, and designed to break in to steal the imaginary treasure trove."

"Yes." Michael recalled his shame, the queasiness, the misgivings, the fear of Roger Vise and his bovine-faced offspring.

"You knocked on the door, but when I answered, you shouted, 'Danger upon you! Retreat! Retreat!' Which I did with all speed. From the window upstairs I watched Roger Vise and his sons give you a drubbing from hell." He did not look at Michael as he spoke. "To my shame, I did not lift a finger to safeguard you. I was afeared, an old man such as I going up against Roger Vise. He would have slit my throat for sure. . . ." His age-worn voice shook. "God help me! I knew then why my wife and son had been taken from me. A man who lets a little boy take punishment meant for him is unworthy of family." Abraham shielded his eyes with a quivering hand.

Michael regarded the old man without condemnation. Poor Abraham needed his absolution. "What could you have done, sir?" he said soothingly, his tone light. "Brained Roger Vise with an inkpot, or mayhap stabbed him with a quill? You did well to conceal yourself, sir. I was saved. I awakened in Ireland. I do not recall how. I was hoping you might be able to inform me."

"Alas, I know naught. Did your lord not recount the events that had led him to find you?"

"I believe he thought to spare my feelings. I knew not I was of the stews until the dream." The Earl of Tyrone had told him that his sire, Sir John Devereaux, having lost his first wife, Cecily Bourchier, had taken a second wife, Elizabeth Langham, who died giving birth to him soon after, and that his sire, Sir John, perished in battle during the Cornish rebellion some four years later.

Abraham's melancholy was tangible. Michael patted the veined hand soothingly. "Sir, you did save my life, never forget, for which I am much beholden to you. Had I not been a fool to listen to the boys' defamation of your good character . . ."

Abraham's eyes came up watery. "Did they tell you I had a tail and horns?"

"Fooleries not worth mentioning."

Tears slid from Abraham's mournful eyes. "If I were the devil, would I have let my brother and his family and his wife's family be burned for heretics in Spain? I swear to you on the souls of my beloved kinsmen, may the good Lord rest them, that I am innocent of such charges."

Kinsmen burned in Spain? Unspoken, the truth came to him. "You are a Jew."

Old dread flickered to life in Abraham's eyes. "I am a good Christian man."

Since King Edward Longshanks had expelled the Jews from his kingdom over two centuries before, the nomadic people had dared not set foot in England, until . . . "The Edit of Expulsion, issued by Ferdinand and Isabella of Spain."

"They were burning heretics in Spain long before that." Abraham sighed.

Michael covered the aged hand with his. The bastard sanctuaries for the downtrodden. He thought of his illness, his aversion to fire, his sharp senses, his supernatural strength, the strange mental dominance he wielded over Anne and Sir William Kingston, the Constable of the Tower, a score of inhuman physical abilities, the healing powers, the elongating teeth, sheathed now, the thirst for the dragon's blood, for Renée's blood . . . How had this bechanced him? Why? When? No explanation, no recollection, only questions trammeled his foggy mind. He felt lost as a child wandering the mist, hopeless and forlorn. The love of his life thought him a fiend. If he must forswear her for lack of vindication, what was there to hope for, to live for?

"Who is like God? I taught you how to write your name in English, but I never told you its ancient meaning. There is great strength in you, Michael. I sense it. Whereas I—"

Tendrils of awareness, like ether, pervaded Michael's mind. He felt Abraham's black grief spreading within his ripened body, gnawing at the last drops of life force. Abraham was dying.

"I am dying," murmured the old man. "There is a growth inside me. I am right glad you came tonight, for I know now it is God's will that I should bequeath my moveables unto you."

"Abraham, I would rather you lived. I shall speak to the king's doctor. . . ."

"No, dear boy. My fate is sealed. 'Naked came I out of my mother's womb, and naked shall I return thither: the Lord gave, and the

Lord hath taken away; blessed be the name of the Lord.' I have no kinsmen. The Philistines out there will descend upon my corpse like carrion crows. To save a soul is to save a world. Let me die knowing I have enriched yours." A glint of mischief lit Abraham's eyes. "You see, my boy, I lied about the treasure."

The rascals, as Abraham had predicted, waited for Michael in the alley, sprawled against the wall of the fishmonger's closed shop. "Cross Bones, milord?" queried Christopher with a yawn.

"To bed with you," Michael berated fondly. "Cockcrow in an hour." And he was no closer to finding salvation than he had been earlier. If he failed to apprehend the monster stalking him, the storm Cardinal Wolsey was breeding up would drag him to the abyss of lost dreams.

Between Scylla and Charybdis . . .

"Cross Bones!" The quintet closed round him like a royal body-guard. For the boys, Michael realized, this was a grand adventure to regurgitate and embellish upon in the days to come. He hoisted Christopher onto his shoulders and ambled among the other four mischief makers.

The cemetery was as he had pictured it in his dream. No stone tablets to commemorate the dead. Sticks and stones marked the graves of the former denizens of the sanctuary of lost souls. He left his tiny mates outside the graveyard boundary and picked his way toward the grave he had dug in his dream. Weary and dispirited, he knelt beside the spot and was surprised to find a wooden cross etched with the name Ellen lying on the damp earth. Did the nuns visit her grave? He set it aright, the old ache weighing his chest. His mother's valediction haunted him: *You will survive. You must survive.* . . . In dying, his mum had commanded him to live. He rubbed his pricked wrist, her gift to him, to illuminate his path. A strand of the blue-and-gold silk cord from Renée's bed hangings was still attached to his wrist. He removed it carefully and tied it around his mother's wooden cross.

Help me, his soul cried out to his poor mum. *Help me get her back.* . . .

A bloodcurdling scream of a child in distress pierced the mist riming the cemetery. Michael vaulted thitherward, darting past the graves, cutting through the fog. The stench of decay hit his nostrils before he saw the willowy figure in a linen underkirtle hunched over a boy. There was no sign of the other four. The phantasma sensed his approach and lifted her head from Christopher's neck: Mariona Wood! She was alive! Or mayhap not. Her eyes were silver moons; fresh blood dripped from sharp fangs. Michael staggered. Was this what Renée had seen in her bed tonight?

The sight of Christopher's bloodily bitten neck rallied Michael. "Leave the boy alone!" He shoved the bloodthirsty whore aside, inadvertently sending her flying a good ten paces in the air to land on her back. He scooped the limp boy in his arms. "Christopher, are you in pain?"

Thankfully, the boy was alive and well. Blinking, he shook his head. "Me mates ran."

Michael felt himself destroyed at the cruelty inflicted on such a vulnerable, tiny person. Yet he had no time to tend to the boy, for the whore had risen from the ground and was swooping down on them. Michael set Christopher down and confronted her. "Who did this to you?"

Screaming in rage, she rammed into him, and they toppled to the ground. Any gentlemanly disinclination on his part to do battle with a female vanished when her claws raked his face and drew blood. Like Actaeon, he felt himself withdrawing from his own image, transmuting into the creature Renée had shrieked at, lost inside a beast, driven by bloodlust and sharply honed senses. They wrestled pellmell, rolling atop the graves, lashing at each other with unrestrained violence. They broke off and leaped to their feet to circle each other predatorily, communing by heightened awareness. They crashed into each other again and again, dealing lethal blows that would have sent Achilles to his gods. Anyone observing from the side would have thought them demons for their leaps and flights in the mist, the flashing strokes and kicks, and the savage snarls and growls emerging from inhuman depths. Theirs was not the fine dance of thrust and parry but a battle without steps and rules, fueled by brutality, urges, and survival instincts.

Michael gained the upper hand, a victory determined by gender, for his ferocious adversary was vicious as well as strong, but female nonetheless. Restraining her from the back, he rasped, "Who did this to you? Tell me!"

"A nobleman!" she screeched.

Michael meant to ask for details of this nobleman's person when the drouth came upon him. Shaking fitfully, eyes rolling into the back of his head, he lost the internecine war to the savagery raging within him. His fangs came down on the exposed neck, broke the skin straight to the vein, and latched on as hot, thick blood rushed forth, flooding his maw. He sucked hard, greedy for the palliative sensation the dragon's blood always infused in him. But this woman was no dragon, and her life fluid lacked the richness of the brew he was accustomed to. His thirst sufficiently slaked, he let go of her, stumbling back, appalled at his perversity, and wiped his mouth. At that exact moment the first sunray broke on the horizon. Her scream was the most horrific sound he had ever heard. Frozen to the spot, he watched the sun burn her to a cinder. Her body turned to ash. The gray-white powder drifted to the ground, settling in a heap.

Tiny cold fingers coiled around his hand. "Wos she a drake?"

Michael looked down at the blue eyes shining with wonder and astonishment in a sooty face. "No, she was a . . . harpy, but it must remain a secret between the two of us, all right?"

Christopher nodded. "Aye, milord. A secret. Between the two of us."

Michael knelt beside him and wrapped his arm around the diminutive waist. "Christopher, how would you like to come and live with me? I will be your father, and you will be my son."

The blue eyes grew huge as cartwheels. "In the king's palace?"

"For the nonce, yes. Afterward I shall take you with me wherever I go."

The smile that broke out on the little smudged face would have melted the heart of a dragon.

22

Do not yield to misfortunes
But advance the more boldly
against them.

—Virgil: *Aeneid*

Renée, shaken but unbitten, set out for morning Mass for the
first time without guards at her back. She ambled along the
corridor like a blind person, holding on to a dependable, hefty arm.
By the good grace of Our Lady she still had Adele for companion-
ship, chaperoning, and comfort; otherwise she would have been
utterly alone. Jesu, she was so miserable.

Michael. Her brain whispered his name like a chant, over and
over, as flashes of recall mixed and swirled before her eyes: his imposing entry into her prison cell, his strong body holding her close,
his hands protecting, caressing, his kisses, his lovemaking, nestling
in his arms . . . then the silvery eyes, the fangs, the ungodly monster slobbering over her neck . . . *Jesu, pity!*

Adele, responding to the strangled sob, patted her cold hand.
"Hush, child. All will be well."

Yes, Renée assured herself. All would be well. She would offer
solemn thanks to St. Amable of Auvergne for preserving her neck,
to St. Épipode, patron saint of victims of betrayal, for his gift of a
savior when she had most needed one, and pray to St. Jude the
Apostle, patron saint of lost causes and desperate situations, for
guidance. Afterward she would beg a private audience with Queen
Katherine and throw herself at Her Majesty's mercy.

"Renée!"

The deep commanding voice jerked her chin up. She saw Michael stride purposefully down the passageway, bawling toward her. She jumped back, clinging to Adele's arm, crossing herself. Her body felt chilled, aquiver, fire licking at her insides. She was elated and petrified all at once.

His candid expression shuttered upon glimpsing her parochial gesture; hurt etched his eyes. His thoughts and emotions pulsated to her: *I am no monster.* Not in character, she thought, just in the flesh. He was a vampire. He needed human blood to subsist. He hungered for hers.

"There is not much time," he said, reaching her. "I have been summoned to York Place. But I promised you a full confession on the morrow. Will you grant me a hearing?"

She stared at him in distress, fluctuating between the overwhelming need to fling herself into his sheltering arms and the equally frantic impulse to run and hide from the fangs and the eyes.

"Please," he whispered. His gaze bored into hers. "Hold Adele's hand if you must. I do not mind. I merely want to talk, to explain. A moment of your time."

"This is becoming a tradition." With her heart beating violently, she headed back to her door and unlocked it. The sun-washed windowpanes beckoned her like divine balm. Michael let Adele enter, followed her inside, and closed the door. Renée splayed her hands on the warmed tinctured glass and stared out at a distant hillock as her mind tracked the vampire advancing behind her.

"I am sorry," he whispered, moving close enough to rekindle the desire of last night but not too close to affright. "You are the faith of my heart, Renée, the last person in the world I would ever harm. I had as lief die a thousand deaths before I give you occasion to fear me."

Renée shut her eyes, tears occluding her throat. "You did not harm me."

He stepped closer, his tone remorseful. "I affrayed you, and for that I am deeply, genuinely sorry." He extended his hand to her view, holding out a nosegay of purple heartsease.

"Pansies, for *pensée*, for thought," she whispered with feeling. "What am I to think upon?"

"Pansies are also called *love-in-idleness*." His breath, redolent of Our Lady's mint, brushed her ear. "My enchanting myth goddess, I would love you idly, sweetly until the end of my life."

She pivoted to face him. His handsome face was open and sincere, his blue eyes red-rimmed with fatigue. He was soberly groomed, golden hair damp from a recent bath, athletic frame cast in a snug charcoal-gray apparel made of soft leather, without silver thread to lessen its austerity. His appealing mouth was set in a grim line. She detected not a hint of the vampire in him.

"Last night you were Aphrodite bestowing pleasingness upon a worshiper. Loving you was . . . grace." He took her hands, looking at her with the eyes of his soul. Yearning and despair, hidden savagery, and a dying glimmer of innocence. He bowed his head and kissed her fingers with reverent gentleness. "Will you absolve me of wrongdoing?"

Renée could not speak. What horses of willpower had bridled his bloodlust last night? And how long before the harness broke? They were futureless as Actaeon and Artemis. She was not Aphrodite, but a huntress morelike, for she must use him and then set the hounds upon him, and if her guards remained in prison, it would fall unto her to impale his heart with a silver dirk.

Misconstruing her silence, misery creased his face. "There are things I must say to you and things I need must beg of you. My illness . . . is not what I believed." He turned away to prowl her privy chamber like a caged lion. "It was not the sweating sickness I unwittingly contracted in Ireland, but a foul and evil curse. I am not myself. The cardinal holds the proof wherewith to condemn me for the murdering of Anne, whereof I am blameless, though he has not yet—or so I trust—woven all the colorful clues into a tapestry. My sand in his hourglass is sparse, methinks."

"What is this proof?"

"A ring, given to me by my Lord Tyrone, the property I told you about. If Cardinal Wolsey traces its origin to my lord, I will be blamed for the murder. Wolsey found the ring clutched in Anne's fist."

"Did you give it to her?"

"No!" He stopped to stare at her, stark solemnity furrowing his features. "It was stolen from me the night I got injured stopping the assassin. I wore it to bed and when I awoke the next day it was gone from my finger and the cardinal was hovering over my sleepy form."

"Do you suppose he stole it?"

"And then claimed to have found it on Anne's body? It is possible. But why single me out for elevation only to cut me down shortly thereafter? It is senseless! Stealing Bryan's signet ring would have made a deal of sense, for that could further Wolsey's cause, would you not agree?"

Did the cardinal suspect Michael of being a vampire? Was he contriving to eliminate him by legal means? "No, you are correct. It is senseless." For one did not catch a vampire with a halter.

"Yesterday I was given a list of his leading suspects." He dug into the breast of his doublet and handed her a folded parchment. True enough, it listed the king's favorite sextet, which made them the cardinal's natural adversaries and therefore convenient scapegoats. "In the course of my investigation, I learned that four of them lacked opportunity. I suspected Bryan and Carew. So last night, when I left you, I returned to the stews in pursuit of evidence against them. Instead I found an exculpating witness who vouchsafed their whereabouts at the time of Anne's murder."

"And the cardinal has your ring," Renée encapsulated pensively. "Describe it to me."

He exhaled. "Gold with a pagan motif. A serpent with the head and breasts of a woman and the wings of a dragon. My Lord Tyrone explicitly warned me against donning it at court."

"Why give it to you for the journey, then?"

"A talisman . . . Hell's pains, Renée, I cannot fathom what bedevils me! I am at my wits' end. This business is wearing me ragged. My eyes feel gritty." He ground the heels of his hands against his eyes.

Renée took a step toward him. "You need sleep."

"I need answers!" He shoved his hands through his hair, tousling it. "And there's more—"

"I, too, have a question, Michael. Yesterday you asked me to swoon at the church so that you could examine Anne. What were your findings?"

"Yes, I was coming to that. The night of the snapdragons, I left for the stews with Stanley and Suffolk, remember? It earned me your housewifely scolding, honeymouse. You recall?"

"I did not scold—"

The wistful smile he bestowed on her was a flash of sunshine in his somber face. "Yes, you did, you shrewcat, but we'll discuss that at a future hearing, if I get to have a future." Foreboding darkened his expression. "As I was saying, we were loafing at the stanks, pitifully trying to prove we were splendid rogues and not the meacocks we have become, when we came upon a brawl at the Cardinal's Hat Inn. A mean diver, a whore, had been murdered there and the burghers were aflutter, for the killer was on the loose, and, as I later discovered, on the rampage."

"The same individual returned to the palace and killed Anne."

"Quick-witted, as always." He halted before her, looking grim. "I noticed that some creative camouflaging had been applied to my Lady Hastings's lethal wound with a poker or some other sharp instrument. In effect, both she and the whore from the Hat were bitten on the neck."

"Christ forefend." Renée signed the cross and moved back against the window, instinctively putting distance between them. She stared at him in petrifaction, her angst resurfacing.

His eyes were seas of sadness. Quietly, wretchedly, pleadingly, he said, "It was not me."

"Who, then?" she gasped.

Angst, frustration, and wanhope thickened his voice. "The man we have been discussing, Renée, the one who stole my ring!"

"Another like you?"

"Another like me," he conceded glumly. "But hark, another odd hap. While at the stews, I was attacked before dawn, by the whore that had been bitten to death the night before last."

"You mean, you were attacked on your second venture there, early this morning?"

"Yes, by the dead whore. Renée, I had seen her corpse with mine own eyes. She had been lifeless. But then early this morn, before sunrise, this living-dead pounced on a little ragamuffin, this boy I befriended. I dashed to his rescue and fought her. Oh, she was vicious. Her eyes—"

"Moonstones." *Like yours.*

Silence fell between them.

Tears glimmered in his eyes. His voice was a bleak whisper. "I am curst." He dropped to his knees before her, flung his arms about her thighs, and buried his face in her murrey silk gown, like a sinner seizing the horns of the altar in a cry for sanctuary and salvation for his soul.

Renée stared at the fair head hiding in her skirts, not a sinner but a frightened boy, a pawn in the game of kings. She wanted to run her fingers soothingly through the silken strands, but was afraid that once she did . . . Her head fell back as she fought to stem the tears. Raphael's tapestry *Le Triomphe d'Amour* filled her blurry vision. The wing-torn, fallen angel sprawled in the lap of his earthly sweetheart was golden, like Michael. The girl resembled her. She recalled how they had remonstrated over the meaning . . . and now life imitated art. Her heart overflowed. She could not stopper the compassion pushing her to her knees. She gathered Michael into her arms, kissed his teary face, and created gentle furrows in his soft mane. She could never slay him. *Never.*

Michael burrowed against her, embracing tightly, his face in her neck.

"Did you foil the devil, *mon bel ami?*"

"Yes and no," came the muffled response. "The sun did."

"But you lived." Not a Vesper, a . . . *sunflower.*

His head jerked up, his eyes piercing blue. "What did you say?"

Jesu, she had given herself away! "I said you lived. She died. You lived. How did she die?"

"The sun burned her. Like a paintbrush, the first sunray incinerated her, blotted her out, and the ash drifted to the ground. But before she died, she told me a nobleman had done that to her. I think he is the same man who stole my ring and murdered Anne. This man wants me destroyed."

She searched his eyes. "You know who he is."

Michael rose to his full and very startling height, lifting her with him. His sense of purpose was restored; once again he exuded indomitable strength. "Give me the kiss of peace, my heart."

Spellbound by his abrupt transformation, she put her hands and the nosegay on his velvety nape and drew his head down. In his kiss, the tender intoxication of his mouth, she found truth, a terrible truth that set her heart atremble.

All too soon, Michael severed their mouths with a groan of reluctance. "The cardinal waits. May I borrow your Adele for the day?"

She cocked an eyebrow. "Am I insufficient that you should lust after my maidservant?"

His grin was dazzling, roguish. "Do not tempt me, witch. I respond to baiting most ardently and with a drawn sword."

Her body went up in flames. She wanted him again. "Come back tonight and I will tell you about the Vicomtesse de Limoges's *Salon de Sappho.*" Holy Anne, she was insane!

"You watched?" he asked, heat suffusing his eyes. At her nod, his hands skimmed her flanks with proprietary strength and melded their bodies. "I will expect you to narrate the minutiae, love goddess, as I worship slavishly upon your altar, when the stars come out tonight."

She tingled. Collecting her thoughts was an effort. "What need have you of Adele?"

He let go of her to include Adele in their conversation. He explained in Gaelic, "I have a boy in my chamber, not older than four or five. He is a little picker and a gutter brat. My man, Pippin, cleansed and put him to bed, but now I must send Pippin on an errand, and my groom, Conn, is off purchasing proper clothing for the boy in the city. His rags were crawling with lice and had to be burned. I am expected at the cardinal's and have no one to watch over him. He needs ten eyes upon him. He is a rapscallion and might devise to go on a tour of the palace, and I fear for him. The guardsmen will boot him back into the gutter and . . . Why the tears, marmoset?"

Renée wiped her cheeks on her sleeve. "Is he the boy you rescued from the . . . woman?"

Michael's tone was apologetic. "I had not the heart to leave him there. He is parentless and, well, I thought I'd give him a home with me. I did not abduct him. I offered, and he said yes." To Adele he said, "He'll have a mighty hunger on him when he awakes. Pippin will bring pasties."

"How kind you are. Of course you may have Adele." Renée slid her arms around his waist, hugging him, pressing her cheek to the loving heart she was duty-bound to cross, while her mind frantically warned against the perils involved in adoring him. "What is the boy's name?"

"Christopher." He embraced her close, kissing the top of her head. "You are to the queen?"

She nodded.

"Renée, if aught should befall me—"

"No! Don't say it." She covered his lips with her fingertips. "It is bad luck."

His long fingers circled her wrist as he kissed the palm of her hand. "Marmoset, if you sense danger, if you are afraid that Wolsey means to clap you in the Tower again, and you cannot reach me, preempt him—seek sanctuary at Westminster Abbey. Promise me?"

She rose on tiptoe and kissed him softly. "I promise."

Jesu mercy, another vampire! Renée was late for Mass. The court was at chapel, and by the sound of it, dispatching last requests to God. Why did Michael tarry to steal the Ancient? Was he not entrusted with the duty? And who was this other one working to undermine him? Did they serve feuding Vesper lords? Michael was honest-hearted—but the other one, killing helpless women for sport . . . Understanding dawned—they were reconnoitering! Neither one knew the exact whereabouts of the Ancient. Oh, this was the stuff of nightmares!

"I give you good day, my lady."

Robin. He looked terribly morose. "Is aught amiss?" she asked. He was her little friend as well as ferret.

On a burst of misery, Robin spewed, "Oh, my lady, 'tis my girl, Nan, maidservant to the late Lady Hastings, God rest her soul. She was taken from court yesterday by my lord chancellor!"

Renée grabbed his sleeve with a hiss of warning, her swift gaze ensuring that they were alone, and towed him from the gallery into a hidden alcove. "Jesu pity, Robin! You do not speak of the cardinal aloud. Tell me everything you know. This may mean life and death to your little friend." If only she had known beforehand that Robin's sweetheart was Anne's maidservant . . .

Robin's face contorted with distress, but his wits quickly recovered. He was a bright youth. He knew the game of court intrigue well enough. Breathlessly he whispered, "Yestermorning, afore my Lady Anne Hastings's demise was bruited abroad, I saw two men-at-arms of my lord cardinal's badge escort my girl Nan from the palace. By the look in her eye, I knew her to be much frayed. I followed them to the stables and saw them ride out with Nan perched with the smaller man. She had her cote on but no cloak-bag for personal effects. I thought surely she would come back that very day, and when she did not, I asked my lady Hastings's tiring woman, la demoiselle Antony, where my girl Nan had gone, and Antony said she did not know, that my girl Nan was an ungrateful wretch for disappearing thusly and my lord of Buckingham was in a pother looking to question the girl about his lady sister's death. I did not want to be questioned, so I kept mum. I tell you now, my lady, for I know you to be true and wise. What is to be done? Do I go to my Lord Buckingham and tell His Grace that his lady sister's little maid was abducted by the cardinal? Methinks a still tongue is better than no tongue, if you see my meaning."

"Oh, Robin." How could she tell him that he might never see his girl again? "Your friend Nan, do her duties include rousing Her Ladyship for Mass?"

Robin's hazel eyes darkened with apprehension. "She found her, didn't she? Nan found Her Ladyship dead in her bedchamber. And they took her away to . . . to . . ."

"We do not know that." Renée calmed him with logic. "A dead lady and a dead maidservant would raise too many questions. You said her escorts wore the cardinal's badge. If the lord chancellor had a pernicious end in mind for the girl, he would send plain villains. It is my belief she was taken for the nonce to keep matters quiet. If I were you, I would tell not a soul. These great lords will crush you between them. I shall see if aught can be done to locate your girl, but you must promise to leave the matter to me and say not a word to anyone."

He nodded keenly. "I promise. I thank you, my lady. I knew I could trust you."

"Return to your post, and no sulking. You do not care to alert anyone."

Why would the Lord Chancellor of England dispose of the star witness in this murder case, tamper with the bite on Anne's neck to make it resemble a stab, and then assume responsibility for the investigation? Renée puzzled when Robin left the nook. Because Cardinal Wolsey knew that Anne had been murdered by a vampire and thought to conceal it . . . from whom? From the person with authority to remove the Ancient from his safekeeping—Cardinal Campeggio! If the Italian cardinal found out the vampires were closing in, he would whisk the Ancient to . . . To France! Yes, definitely to France. Oh, this was easy! She would dispatch Campeggio a note forthwith and return victorious to France with him and the Ancient!

There was only one little wrinkle: Michael.

A sunflower! Michael's mind was spinning widdershins. *Cui prodest?*

O'Hickey said that he had been poisoned. Michael had not considered it then, but now—and there was no comfort to be found where his thoughts carried him—the logic was sharp and cold.

The lightless fire, which in embers hides, lurks to aspire.

"His Eminence will see you now."

Michael was ushered through eight magnificent rooms, heavily ornamented, until he reached the audience chamber. Majestically done in scarlet damask woven with gilt tread, the walls were adorned with murals and tapestries depicting the protagonists of the Christian faith, the caisson ceiling limned with gold, the floor covered with carpets. Beautiful instruments, gifts from foreign monarchs, were displayed on tables and in cupboards: jeweled hanaps, gold plates, framed maps, silver astrolabes, Venetian vases, globes, marble putti, gilt metal clocks, sumptuously decorative and engraved with arms and mottos, cast-iron firedogs, plates for candles dipped in bronze, silver brackets supporting wainscot bowls, and legions of gilt iron candlesticks in all shapes and sizes. The good cardinal, Michael mused, was growing cheerfully rich on the proceeds of his labors.

"Your Grace." Michael made his obeisance and waited for the cardinal's pleasure, grateful that patience was one of his stronger suits, as he had already been kept waiting for over an hour.

Pacing calmly by the northwestern casement overlooking the bustling city, hands clasped at his back, Cardinal Wolsey kept his eyes on the view. "I am relieving you of your post."

Michael clotted. "I should like to offer an account of my findings, if I may."

"Have you uncovered evidence against the men on your list?"

"Alas, there are witnesses placing each and every one of them outside the Lady Hastings's lodging the night of the murder." Not exactly true, as Margery Curson, Bryan and Carew's alibi, was on a ship for Connacht, but never mind, Michael thought. He was not for hanging innocent men, however disagreeable they might be. "As for last eve, I should like to clarify, if I may—"

"That won't be necessary. You have formed an attachment for the lady and dashed to her rescue. I rather hoped you would. Does the princess of France reciprocate the affection?"

Michael drew in a lungful of air, then let it out slowly. "I believe she does, Eminence."

"Good. You shall escort her back to France."

Michael's jaw dropped, his heart bouncing with alacrity.

"But you will not reach France."

An icy fist smothered his eagerness. He clenched his jaw. "Dispose of the lady?"

"No, you fool!" The red-robed cardinal swiveled to face him. "Must I put it in plain words so that you will understand? I want you to abduct her. Marry her in secret. Keep low for a while, and when she is enceinte, visibly swelling under the girdle, return hither. I shall smooth matters with my lord king and with His Majesty of France, and find good office for you."

Were he not flabbergasted, Michael would roar with laughter. Abduct Renée! She would kill him! Or mayhap she would not.

The notion had great appeal, to be sure. It would also serve the cardinal's ambition. The duchies of Brittany and Chartres would boost Michael to the highest echelons of European nobility, all the way to scrape royalty—for in the case of wholesale deaths in the Valois family, Renée's offspring would inherit a claim to the French throne—and withal would come sufficient power and influence to put him on the council as the cardinal's creature.

"You balk," observed the red fox. "Do not tell me you have a wife tucked away in Ireland."

"No, Your Grace. If I seem hesitant, 'tis only because I"—he smiled—"am amazed."

A sly grin formed on the clerical face. "You like my idea."

"Well, the lady is manifoldly endowed, in body and spirit, as well as in titles and land."

"I'll take your word on it, as you have spent the night in her chamber. Yes, I know all."

Michael nearly plopped down cross-legged on the carpet. Elope with Renée! Oh, he would have a shrew-witch on his hands the first week, but afterward . . . Yes, the idea had tremendous merit. Except that he had yet to fulfill his pledge to Tyrone. The thought was a sobering one.

Confusion in the hallway stole the cardinal's attention. The door burst open and another scarlet-attired prince of Holy Church waddled in, leaving his armed escorts at the door. "Brother Wolsey, I have grievous matters to address with you," the bearded cardinal said in Latin.

Wolsey's face turned ashen. "Wait here!" he ordered Michael, and flounced into the adjacent chamber with his colleague in his wake. The connecting door slammed shut; then another door was tightly closed, but the cardinal's voice rang loud and clear. "What business is so urgent as to interrupt serious matters of state? Another quarrel between your yeomen and mine?"

"Dear brother, I assure you this matter transcends the governing of England. I hereby relieve you of your office as legate and am preparing to relocate the Ancient to France."

Heavy silence lay beyond the closed doors. Suddenly Cardinal

Wolsey shouted, "You are forgetting, *Fra Campeius*, that you are in *my* house, wherein I am lord and master! You may have the authority but not the wherewithal to relieve me of anything!"

In "house" Michael reckoned Cardinal Wolsey meant England.

"You dare defy the edicts of the Holy Father?" rasped Campeggio.

"I demand to know the reason I am being so discourteously removed from an office I keep with diligence and solemnity!"

"You have been diligently covering up evidence that unequivocally indicates the Ancient is no longer safe on English soil. The lady that was murdered in the palace—I know what killed her. I pray you, brother, do not let ambition cloud your judgment. If the Vespers have not yet snatched the Ancient, it is because they have yet to discover its exact location. It is only a matter of time before the nefarious omniscents pick up the scent. Are you so vainglorious as to imperil the whole of mankind? As legate, you must look beyond the privileges of office. You must exercise prudence with the utmost humility. You must put the good Christian souls of this earth before personal gain. Our greatest weapon is secrecy. My small army cannot withstand a full-scale attack of legions of Vespers. I pray you, listen to reason, to your own conscience!"

Wolsey chose to ignore the sensible expostulations and instead responded astringently to the sermonic attack on his character. Meanwhile, the officers left at the door ambled inside. They nodded at Michael and, conversing in Italian, sniffed around for wine to slake their thirst. They wore black, with snowy sleeves bursting out of gilt-trimmed slashes, golden knops running in militant rows down their doublets, a badge displaying a gold crucifix over back sewn across the heart. Suave as courtiers, they were, in bearing as well as in speech. The cardinals continued to remonstrate vociferously beyond the doors, but the Italian soldiers seemed oblivious of the battle of wits taking place two chambers yonder. Michael was astonished. They did not hear a thing!

"Brother Campeggio, has it not occurred to you that the Vespers are deliberately attempting to alarm us? For the nonce, the Ancient is protected in a strong-tempered vault of pure sterling and stone, but once removed, it will be exposed to the insidious elements lurking at large."

"Hence, we must take measures to ensure its safe passage to France. I suggest we join forces to ensnare and exterminate the Vespers. And, as proof of my goodwill, I give you my word that when I'm assured the Ancient is safe, I'll reconsider my decision to relocate it. Are we agreed?"

"Give me the kiss of peace, brother."

"Oh," someone gasped at the door. "I was told that His Eminence . . ."

Michael turned to find a scrawny clerk fidgeting at the door. In his hands he held an inkwell, quill, and vellum pinned to a wooden board. His agitation was causing a small object to rattle on the board. *It was his ring!* Michael moved forward and crowded the man out the door. "Sir." He threw an amicable arm around the clerk's puny shoulders. "Seek you my lord cardinal?"

The clerk staggered alongside him down the passage. "Y-yes! I was told I might find—"

"His Eminence is in conference. I do not expect him to emerge any time soon." He eyed the ring and the little man. "Who are you?"

"M-Master Kent, my lord, His Eminence's amanuensis."

"Surely not! I took you to be his chief secretary."

Master Kent bowed his head in diffidence. "I—I am also h-his librarian."

"Verily? I'm honored. Sir Michael Devereaux, a pleasure!" He clapped the scribe's shoulder, hoping to jolt the ring off the board, but little Kent was alert. He snatched the ring to safeguard it in his ink-stained fist. Michael tried a different approach. "I was hoping to have a look at my lord cardinal's library. I hear it is richly stacked and superbly organized." He broke off to eavesdrop on the cardinals. Obligingly they were discussing the animosity between their retainers and how to enforce love between the rival camps. "Master Kent, would you grant me a tour of His Grace's library? Mayhap you will be good enough to suggest a pleasing verse I might declaim to the fair ladies of the court, some love-line to sweeten them up toward me. I promise to give due credit by mentioning your name, Master Kent."

"Philip Kent, sir." The scribe produced a little smile. "This way, if you please!"

The library at York Place was impressive but not nearly as extensive and diversified as Lord Tyrone's, which boasted scrolls from Ptolemy's library in Alexandria, from Jerusalem, from the Roman Republic, from the Rome of Caesars, and from the recently fallen Byzantium.

"I am interrupting your work." Michael indicated the open tome on the scribe's lectern, a gilt-embossed, leather-bound volume, many of its letterheads illuminated. Not a printed book but handmade by monks and very old.

"Oh, that is quite all right. My research is done." Kent put aside his instruments and the ring and set about to carefully close the tome and fasten its gilded clasps.

Done! Startled, Michael snatched the ring off the table. He could slip it into his sporran and walk away, but Kent would know. Moreover, he needed to know what the industrious scribe had learned. He inspected his lord's ring, as if he had never seen it before. "A pretty trinket. Yours?"

"Were I that fortunate!" Kent chuckled and tried to recover the ring. Michael turned away, making a pretend study of it by the light pouring through the nearest window. "Sir, I beg you!"

"Is this the ring my lord cardinal told you to research?"

"How did you know?"

"Oh yes. I see it is. So what have you learned? To whom does it belong?"

The scribe's brow began to glisten. "Sir Michael, I am hardly—"

"You may tell me. I am chief investigator, chosen by my lord cardinal and appointed by His Majesty." When he saw Kent hesitate, he turned the full force of his willpower upon the scribe. Capturing the beady gaze, he rasped commandingly, "Tell me what you know about this ring."

Suddenly lamb-eyed, Kent droned, "There is an inscription on the inside. Charlemagne."

"Charlemagne!" Michael examined the inner curve of the gold ring and found that Kent spoke the truth. The inscription KAROLVS IMP AVG was etched in Latin letters.

"That is how I traced the design."

"To the King of the Franks?" Michael inquired, astonished.

"To the Counts of Tyrol."

Renée, holding the nosegay of pansies to her face, distractedly observed the king, the queen, and their court play at quoits on the lawn. The deed was done. The pigeon she had sent to York Place returned an auspicious greeting from Cardinal Campeggio. She was to stand by till further notice, and yes, he would convey her to France. Now she worried this might not be enough. Cardinal Wolsey, the crafty jackal, was full of tricks and saws as well as the most powerful man in England. Who knew what was broiling at York Place? Two cardinals, *deletoris*, the Ancient, and a vampire. She needed her own assurance. The answer came from the most unlikely source.

"Madame." Norfolk and his black-eyed son, Surrey, eclipsed the sun. "Would you join us on a stroll to the fountain? I shall point out every flower species en route."

Glad she had deferred going to the queen, Renée took the duke's arm. As their party of three ambled along the pebbled path, the two lords gesticulated fulsomely and spoke the name of every blooming bud. Until they were out of earshot. "Madame, I shall come straight to the point. I have reason to suspect Wolsey receives a pension from King Francis and I would have proof."

Renée's silence seemed to upset the duke's tactic, for his voice grew edgier. "Madame, must I remind you I hold in my possession a trinket you wish secreted?"

"I remember, Your Grace. Pray, continue."

"Continue? Madame, I believe I was rather to the point. I want proof of Cardinal Wolsey's underhanded dealings with your king, and you will provide it!"

"No, I do not think that I will. You see, this is one nest of hornets I would fain avoid."

"But . . . but . . . madame!" the duke sputtered.

His dark shadow of a son came to his aid. "I fear me Her Highness is content with the nest of hornets she has brought with her. Mayhap we should jolt it, see how well she enjoys the buzz. . . ."

Clearly they were not accountable for her incarceration in the

Tower. So who was? She had to stir her eggshell boat very carefully, disclose very little information. "My lord cardinal knows about the medallion. Yesterday he arrested my bodyguard. Your coin was spent by another."

Disarmed, the Howards looked stumped and thwarted.

"But," Renée went on stolidly, "I should like my guards released and have a shiny coin, freshly minted, to barter with. I trow it will purchase a great deal of mischief for your cardinal."

"*We* shall determine the value of your currency, madame!" snapped Earl Surrey.

"My lords, I do not seek to trifle with you. I am anxious to leave England and have need of my escort. Whatever trouble befalls the cardinal is your business. I want no part of it. I do want my guardsmen released from the Marshalsea by nightfall. I believe the prison falls under your shrievalty, Earl Marshall. If we are agreed, I shall pay half a coin now and the second half upon delivery of goods. I give you my solemn vow to keep my end of this bargain."

"Foh! I thought English fishwives were tough bargainers!" The Howards exchanged looks. An entire conversation seemed to be taking place before her eyes. Norfolk frowned at her. "On the rood, madame, I shall release your guardsmen. What is it you know?"

"Your cardinal made a person disappear from court."

"What person? What do you mean? Be specific," demanded Surrey.

She gave it a moment's thought, not caring to reveal her hand too soon. "This person, whose identity I shall disclose once my guards are freed, knows something the cardinal had as lief no one else knew. Surely Your Grace will agree this matter deserves a weighty brow, *n'est ce pas?*" She calculated that by the time Norfolk discovered what bechanced Robin's little friend, mayhap even rescue the poor girl, she would be far away and in possession of the Ancient.

"It certainly does," muttered the duke. "Madame, we shall speak again before nightfall."

23

Who will guard the guardians themselves?

—Juvenal

Michael listened with the cringing sensation of a long fingernail scratching down his back as Kent narrated the history of a line of counts that had become extinct two hundred and fifty years ago. "In the first century before Our Lord Christ, this region on the borders of the Empire, Italy, and the Swiss, became *Regio X* of the Roman Empire under Augustus Caesar. It was conquered by the Goths, the Bavarii, Charlemagne, King of the Franks, and became the bishopric of Trento. Over time, the counts residing in Castle Tyrol near Merano took control of the region and made Merano the capital of their county. They expanded their conquests, becoming dukes of Carinthia and of Bavaria and wielded tremendous power in that part of the world. When the lay investiture controversy broke between the Empire and Holy Church over the right to appoint the pope, and the Gregorian Reformers founded the College of Cardinals, the Emperor Henry the Fourth contracted the counts' military support and declared war against Pope Gregory with the words *I, Henry, king by the grace of God, with all of my bishops, say to you, come down, come down, and be damned throughout the ages.* For centuries the wars raged on between the papal Guelphs and the imperial Guibellines, disrupting the balance of power on the Continent. Finally, in the year of Our Lord 1330, sickened of wars, Emperor Henry the Seventh and Pope Benedict the Seventh brought peace to the region. The counts lost their dukedoms and mysteriously disappeared thereafter."

Michael recalled that in 1330, his lord's illustrious ancestor, Tyrone the Elder, joined a loyal set of knights in support of young King Edward III's coup against Roger de Mortimer, the Earl of March, and fought to consolidate Edward's power as the de facto ruler of England. Tyrone the Elder became the first earl of Tyrone and was vested First Knight Companion of the Order of the Garter with hereditary rights to bequeath to his heirs. Did the Count of Tyrol become the Earl of Tyrone? He studied the red eagle over black emblazing his gold thumb-ring. His lord ascribed the eagle to his Roman ancestors, but the empire's insignia was also a Roman eagle.

"Show me the Counts of Tyrol's coat of arms."

The docile librarian, floating as if in a dream, unclasped the book and reopened it with care.

Jupiter's thunder! The emblems matched, both of them: the gilt-taloned red eagle over black *and* the she-serpent, two emblems of the same family! Clearly the counts did not vanish off the face of the earth. Their last descendant relocated to England, where he reestablished himself as Tyrone the Elder, King Edward III's prominent follower. And if he could make the connection, Michael realized, so would the cardinal. Wolsey would know the ring was Michael's.

He closed the book, ripped the report from the board, and stowed it inside the breast of his jerkin. "Listen carefully," he told the befuddled scribe, "you will begin your research anew. You will remember neither our chat nor the inscription inside the ring. You will remain here and say naught to anyone." He stared at the ring, itching to take it.

His thoughts were interrupted by the distant yet clear voice of Cardinal Wolsey ordering his secretary to send in Captain Luzio and Lieutenant Uberti of Cardinal Campeggio's bodyguard, Captain Hill and Lieutenant Wat of the yeomen of the guard at York Place—and himself.

Michael was forced to make a quick decision. He considered the spellcast scribe, wondering how long the effect of this strangeness would last and if Kent's memory would return in full. His cursed powers left a lot to be desired, chiefly guidance. If he took the ring, Kent might blab on him or be accused of stealing it himself, and the cardinal might order every person in the palace searched. Hence, he must forget the ring for the nonce, for Kent's sake and his own.

Leaving the ring with the woolgathering amanuensis, he returned to the presence chamber and followed the fainéant Italian officers and the scurvy Englishmen into the cardinal's sanctum sanctorum, his private chapel. The scarlet princes stood at the altar like monuments. The Italians and the English soldiers took position across from their respective masters. Michael filled in the gap like a rung. Mistrust and animosity thickened the air between the two camps.

The cardinals opened the gathering with a sermon on the merits of tolerance, collaboration, and unity in times of strife, first in English, then in Italian. Michael's eyelids grew heavy as he wondered why he was being subjected to this tedium. To divert and enliven his drowsy mind, he imagined sneaking back to the king's palace and crawling into bed with Renée. She had forgiven him. She had taken him back. Did she love him? Or was she still secretly languishing for her stupid painter? Wolsey's subsequent phrase snapped his sleep-deprived brain into full alertness.

"Good fellows," he said grimly. "We have summoned you hither to partake of confidences that surpass the purview of laymen, and that we, humble envoys of Our Lord Christ, are sworn to protect and conceal at all cost. The devil, good fellows, is among us." He unveiled a silver plate. On it rested a white bulb of ail and a silver knife. He broke the crisply skinned bulb into cloves and cut each with the knife. The bursting stink of garlic upturned Michael's stomach. The knife twitched in the cardinal's hand, inflicting a cut on his finger. Blood emerged.

Michael reeled, like a bloodhound sniffing wounded game; the instinct to pounce for the kill was all-consuming.

Cardinal Wolsey squeezed his finger, dripping blood over the smelly cloves. "Good fellows, I will have your vow of secrecy and allegiance."

Through the monstrous havoc of craving and revulsion, Michael saw the Italian officers pick a bleeding clove from the platter each and consume it without ado. The English yeomen, less composed, dutifully followed suit. It was Michael's turn; they were all watching him.

The ingenious purpose of this trial dawned on him with sickening clarity. The cardinals, the Italian officers, they knew *what* he was, if they had not fathomed him already. Sweat covered his skin as he fought to conceal his supreme tribulation. The foul-smelling garlic and drops of blood plopping from the cardinal's finger onto the silver platter rendered him insane. Swallowing bitter saliva, he clamped down hard on the feral forces tearing him apart, and put a clove in his mouth. It took an unuttered battle cry to force it down his throat. His stomach heaved. Heat-oppressed, he almost vomited there and then. His eyes burned, his teeth . . . *He was turning into that thing!*

He shut his eyes, curses tingling on his garlic-charred tongue; his stomach churned like the bowels of Vesuvius moments before the livid mountain obliterated Pompeii and Herculaneum. Had they poisoned him? The painful sensation spread throughout his body, enfeebling, burning. If he could only excuse himself for an instant and cure this affliction with a gulp of his potion . . . but they would know! They would burn him! A silent cry reverberated in his tormented body—and just like that the suffering ebbed. He sensed the presence of an invisible, powerful, palliative ally in the cardinal's demesne, a mystical, calming force that repelled the nasty spell.

"Is something amiss, Sir Michael?" Cardinal Wolsey inquired tersely. "You look ill."

Gasping, Michael forced his eyes to open. He gave a painful smile. "Heartburn."

To his relief, the yeomen, Hill and Wat, belched in agreement, and only the Italians smirked at the English bumbkins' inability to take nourishment more savory than beer, bread, and beef.

Satisfied with the result of the trial, Cardinal Campeggio decanted wine into silver goblets. As the other fellows and the cardinals raised a goblet each, Michael realized his troubles were far from over, for he well remembered the sting of the silver rose he had won in the archery contest. Steeling himself for the inescapable blister, he lifted the last goblet and exhaled blissfully when his fingers touched cool pewter. Cardinal Wolsey murmured benediction, and they drank deeply. The muscadelle was no treacle but it doused the lethal garlic fumes and soothed the gripes.

Cardinal Wolsey dipped his fingers in a silver bowl of water, touched his wet fingers to his forehead, his heart, and to each shoulder, then put his hand on the open Gospels and with quiet ceremony said, "I, Thomas Cardinal Wolsey, Lord Chancellor of England, by Christ's blessed body, renounce Satan and all who serve, worship, and cleave to him and solemnly vow to protect the faithful against the power of these demonic and most vampiric spirits. Amen."

Campeggio followed suit, then the soldiers and the yeomen. Again Michael was the last in line. He placed his hand on the Gospels and repeated Cardinal Wolsey's oath.

"Good fellows, before I speak of menaces and maledictions, criminals of the underworld, *malum in sē et arcāna imperiī*, I must caution you against prattling, for the secrets of the Empire are our last bulwark against Evil itself, which now walks among us. Unbridled tongues will be cut out, treasonous minds will be put in pincers, and informed ears will burn. You have been warned. Should you disappoint us, your bodies will answer for your faithless spirits and your souls be lost to eternal damnation."

The Englishmen, of simple stock, were duly affrighted, Michael noted, whereas the Italians simply nodded as their master translated the threat. This was no news to them, it seemed.

"Two days hence, a lady was murdered in His Majesty's palace. Her killer"—Wolsey's voice dropped to a faint, tremulous whisper, as if by speaking, he was conjuring evil—"was a vampire."

Michael blinked owlishly. A vampire, what the pox was that?

"A creature foul and pernicious, maleficent and pestilent, a murrain on mankind, so ancient that none knows whence it had spawned save that it has stalked in blood and staled the earth with wickedness sith before Christ Our Lord. This fiend in the shape of man feeds on mortal blood, spreads death and plague wherever it roams, and has the ability to imbrute and bethrall, with trickery, incantations, and savagery, the sons of Adam and the daughters of Eve."

Michael, his mouth wide open, hastened to emulate the others in crossing himself.

"Centuries agone, the Empire and Holy Church marshaled a great army against the demons and dealt them a fatal blow. For two hundred and fifty years they were thought gone, obliterated, razed to the ground. Now they have resurfaced in London. They are shade, immortal night men, shape-shifters, charmers in disguise, masterful and devious, bloodthirsty monsters of supreme powers. Evil incarnate. They may appear in various forms, as men, as raptors, as wolves, as unbeknownst beasts, as smoke. They must be rounded with crosses, with holy water, and put to the torch, for, like lice, they cannot survive fire, silver, or garlic, and above all— sunlight."

"H-how do they infect men?" asked Lieutenant Wat.

"With their blood. They bite their victim, drain him of lifeblood, and before his soul departs the body, drip their own poisonous fluid between his dying lips. The victim will resurrect as an immortal in the image of his abominable maker, a vassal to his Vesper overlord."

"Vespers or vampires?" Michael asked, chilled and benumbed, his heart sinking. Surely he misconstrued his condition, for he had not been bitten and had no recollection of confronting this creature. Sunlight hurt him not. Nor did holy water or any religious artifact for that matter. Silver scorched but did not kill him, and, as the cardinal's trial had proven, he could withstand garlic. Still, his new powers, the bloodlust . . . no defense to any of that. Oh, he was damned—but how?

The cardinal's secretary rapped on the door and stuck his head in. "Eminence, a messenger comes from court with some evidence pertaining to—" A commanding hand gesture summoned him inside. He handed his master a small traveling box and quitted the chapel. All eyes riveted to Wolsey's hands as he removed a canvas-swathed parcel from the box. Michael nearly jacked out of his skin. The contents—the so-called evidence—was a brown glass bottle. His missing bottle!

Wolsey pulled out the bung and sniffed the lip. Grimacing, he offered it to Campeggio. To Michael it seemed he knew not what to make of it. The latter was more pedantic in his study. He perused the bottle for distinguishing marks, sniffed its rim, and upturned it over the white napkin his colleague had used to clean his cut. A thick globule took forever to plop out. As it expanded to a burgundy stain, so dark in color it might be mistaken for black, Campeggio crossed himself and handed the napkin to Captain Luzio. Michael's smattering of Italian confirmed the worst.

"Vesper blood." Captain Luzio's tone was grim; he had gone deathly white. "I thought them destroyed. I hoped we were dealing with rogue vampires, refugees of the Decimation. This is . . ."

Michael was beside himself. His mind, a welter of frightful inferences, emanated terror. The Earl of Tyrone's ring, O'Hickey's potion, Ferdinand's hatred, the purport of Kent's academic investigation, and the facts he had learned in this chamber drew a diabolical picture. The counts of Tyrol and the earls of Tyrone shared the same devices; Holy Church and the empire's joint persecution of vampires had taken place the same year his lord's ancestor, Tyrone the Elder, backed King Edward III in his fight to reclaim his rightful throne. The point in time, the events, everything seemed to conspire against the lord who had fished him from the stews and given him a home, his mentor who had reared him with care and attention and groomed him to be his heir. In his mind's eye he saw his lord's magnificent collection of arms and ancient manuscripts in the grand library. He remembered his lord teaching him how to mount and dismount a horse without using the stirrup when he was a boy, how to grab the mane of a galloping destrier and jump into the saddle in full armor as a youth, and how to wield every weapon from that wall. He could hear the earl emphasizing the importance of cleanliness, of practicing his body regularly, of eye and arm coordination in fighting, of broadening his horizons, of using his mind. He remembered the generous praises lavished on him when he displayed courage or sustained blows in combat and the perpetual drumming of knowledge, lore of lost civilizations, into his head . . . The possibility that his beloved lord was a vampire—and that he had turned him into one—devastated Michael.

Cardinal Wolsey rang for his secretary. "I want to know who found this and where."

Michael's head came up. The noose was tightening around his neck.

"The messenger had no information. . . . I'll dispatch him with a note for Pace, Eminence."

"Mind that. I shall go myself." He conferred with Campeggio in hushed tones, then fixed his hard gaze on Michael. "Sir, I charge you, find this demon tonight. If it is not annihilated at once, it will increase in numbers until no one is safe. You are leader of this mission. Captain Luzio will demonstrate the special methods used to destroy vampires, and you will put it to my men in plain English. By nightfall, my men must be properly trained to battle vampires. You will accompany Captain Luzio's army of vampire destroyers to court and begin your hunt. Remember, discretion is of the essence. Do your utmost to avoid spreading panic and mayhem."

Cardinal Campeggio translated his host's dictate to his officers. Cardinal Wolsey motioned Michael aside. "As for our earlier chat, we shall revisit the matter once this threat is eliminated. Be informed, my guards and the cardinal's are at each other's throats. I expect you to mitigate disputes and bring them to heel. Heretofore, I have been much impressed with your talents. Take care of this business for me, and I shall reward you handsomely, Michael. I shall lift you higher than Suffolk, and together we will crush Buckingham, Norfolk, and their ilk. Doddy pates, rain-beaten beggars, whoresons, and ruffians, green with ribands and laurels, they think they are better than us, but we shall show them, eh? The mind carries a man a lot farther than might."

Interesting, Michael thought. It was his lord's motto as well. He kissed the cardinal's ring. "I am Your Grace's most humble servant."

"What is the difference between vampires and Vespers?" Michael asked.

Captain Luzio unlocked the door to the armory and stepped back to let his men carry out the chests of weaponry and ammunition to the training yard. "Vespers are pureblooded leeches, the spawn of an unholy union between female demons and human men. Vampires are common men infected with Vesper blood. Most vampires serve a Vesper lord, unless they are rogues."

"Female demons?" Michael thought of Tyrone's ring.

"Seductive, malevolent night shades that visit men in their sleep and tempt them to engage in coitus. The ancients worshiped them as goddesses of carnal love, fertility, and war, the divine personification of the planet Venus. We, Christian men, perceive them as the devil's courtesans. There were Anath, Ishtar, Inanna, Asherah, Lamashtu, Astarte, Lamia, Atargatis, Naamah, Isis, Karina, Pizna, and their queen of the night, Lilith, who was created directly from Satan." He crossed himself, hissing, "*Lilith, abitu, abizu, hakash, avers hikpodu, ayalu, matrota . . .*"

Michael, fast to cross himself whenever others did, was amused. "Hoa! Was that a curse?"

"A potent exorcisory chant that strips she-demons of their powers for the moments it should take you to make your escape. You had better memorize it, Sir Michael, just in case . . ."

"In case what?" The events of the last days made Michael put all skepticism aside.

"In case they are not all destroyed, as the scriptures tell us, although I trust that they are."

His mind was still on the ring, seeking answers. "Which shape did they take?"

"Fish, doves, young girls, the wind, and the storm. A discerning eye could tell them apart by their radiant starlike halo. They had a vicious carnal appetite, treated their lovers cruelly, and fed on children's blood. They lay with common men at night and gave birth to blood-sucking babes, the Vespers. The scriptures warn us, 'Woe to him whom they honor!' They enslaved their lovers with their black art, turned them into wretched beasts, and stole their vigor, so that they fell into traps laid by men and were either slain, tortured to death, or domesticated as pets and slaves. The worst evil"— the captain grimaced—"their lovers would castrate themselves in honor of their demonic mistresses. This is legend, but we know for a fact that vampires cannot propagate."

"But they can infect common men with their blood."

"Vespers and lesser vampires alike. Their victims become shades of the night."

"How did they disappear from the world, the she-demons?"

"God was furious with Lilith and her spirits for contaminating the world with their offspring, the plagues of humankind, and for despoiling God's heavenly creatures. He accused, 'Thou hast loved the lion-mettled man, mighty in strength, and thou hast dug for him seven and seven pits! Thou hast loved the steed man, proud in battle, and destined him for the halter, the goad, and the whip.' He killed the evil harlots, except for Lilith, who ran into the wilderness in despair. She fell into the sea, took the shape of a dragon, and hid on the bottom. God sent the Archangel Michael, the good angel of death and the field commander of the Army of God, to slay the she-dragon with his sword. The darkness on the floor of the sea blinded her, and she did not see the angel approaching. He struck her with his sword of light, and she turned to ash."

Ash! "So it was St. Michael who slew the dragon, not St. George."

"Each country has its own tales, like the *chansons de geste*. There is the Matter of Rome, the Matter of France, and the Matter of Britain. The ancients believed that the she-demons lived in the city of Ascalon. Hence, the sword." He gave Michael a gimlet eye. "You do not look afraid."

"On the contrary, Captain Luzio. I am terrified." His predawn clash with the demon-whore planted serious doubts in his mind concerning the soldiers' ability to fend off such fiends.

"Come, we shall practice in the yard. Our bow is not the long-bow you are accustomed to, but shorter and rounder."

Michael pulled on his gloves as he fell into step with him. "Like the Mongol bow? Shorter distances, higher velocity."

"Yes." The captain looked impressed. "I see you are knowledge-able in world weaponry."

Michael shrugged. The more he learned, the more probable his protector's secret became. He felt morose and betrayed. The captain's men, called *deletoris*, were teaching the ignorant English yeo-men how to use the Mongol bow. The language barrier put everyone in a pother.

Exasperated with the men, Captain Luzio threw his hands in

the air. "The Tower of Babylon had better odds of getting built! Sir Michele, I think you had better translate my instructions."

Michael imposed silence. "Master Hill, have you impressed upon your men the importance of secrecy, duty, and obedience?"

George Hill was white as a sheet. "Aye, sir. We serve our cardinal—and you."

"Good. Men," Michael called out. "We are to war with dangerous creatures, omnipotent and omniscient, that move with great speed. If we wish to survive and prevail over our foes, we will be wise to heed the Italian soldiers' advice, avail ourselves of their expertise, and become skilled at their methods." He let his words sink in and turned to Captain Luzio. "Go on. I will translate."

The captain cleared his throat. "We use short, thin darts with pointed steel heads dipped in silver. When the tip penetrates our enemy's flesh, the silver will dissolve in the blood and poison it. We must then use our swords to sever the head from the body and, if possible, set fire to the remains. In battle, there might not be time to perform all three steps. However, the silver will most likely destroy a weaker enemy and incapacitate a strong one."

Michael translated and asked the captain, "What determines a vampire's strength?"

"The vampire's sire. Pureblooded Vespers are resistant to silver. It hurts them no more than a scratch. A common man turned vampire may become gravely ill or be destroyed. If his sire was a Vesper he should have better chances of survival than if he was turned by a mongrel. The rule that applies to human nobility works in reverse; the longer the pedigree, the lesser the vampire."

Michael reasoned that he must have been turned by a strong one, for he survived the scratch of the silver rose. "I do not think the yeomen should be informed on this particular point. Please explain in your words why we use the short bow and I will translate."

"Our enemies move light-fast. Some have the ability to transport themselves from one place to another by sheer brainpower."

Michael started. "Wait! What do you mean by that?"

"Vespers and strong vampires are capable of dematerializing at one point and assembling at another. In Rome one moment and"— he snapped his fingers—"in London the next. But there is an impediment. They need a direct link to the place they wish to go to. A gold trinket."

Upon his soul! "Like a ring?"

"A ring, a pendant, a necklace, so long as it is made of gold."

Michael stanched a howl of bitter rage. What a pawn he was! His lord could be in London any moment now thanks to the ring. He had to steal it from Kent—and destroy it!

"About the bow," the captain went on, urging Michael to interpret his oration. "Our enemies are swift as lightning. Therefore our weapon must be easy to manage, easier than the longbow, and the dart must pierce the air with great speed. The longbow shoots to greater distances, but it is useless when your opponent may be at half distance by the time you release the dart. Always aim for the heart. A wooden stick through the heart will incapacitate if not kill our enemy. And when wielding a sword against the creature, victory can only be achieved with a decapitation."

The following hours were spent training gruelingly in the yard.

"Are there no female vampires?" Michael asked the captain as they practiced sword-fight.

"Certes, a vampire can infect a woman as well as a man, but there have never been female Vespers. The goddesses of the night produced male offspring."

"I conclude that neither vampires nor Vespers can produce young."

The captain hesitated. "A Vesper might be able to beget a child off a common woman. . . ."

Michael parried a blow and moved back. "What are you not telling me, Captain?" Suspicion gnawed at him. "My lord cardinal said the Vespers had all been obliterated, and yet you speak of them with supreme authority for one who has neither encountered nor engaged in battle with the fiends? Do not tell me you are the clerkish sort, Luzio." Michael grinned in a soldier-to-soldier-rapport, hoping to lure the man into a confidence. "I recognize field experience when I see it."

Captain Luzio beckoned him aside. "This is strictly between us. No one can know, not even your master, the Cardinal of York."

"I swear on the body of Christ."

"We know of one Vesper that survived the Decimation, an Italian count, five centuries old."

Michael's hackles rose. "Where is he, do you know?"

"In Rome. He is our captive, has been for three centuries. Count Emiliano. He was captured during the wars of the Guelphs and the Guibellines on a battlefield outside Sienna, fighting for the emperor, as all the vampires did, under the Count of Tyrol, a puissant Vesper lord. We keep him in a subterranean chamber of silver walls, nude, of course. His rings and clothes had to be burned and buried afar to prevent his brethren—if any of them survived the Decimation and are lurking abroad—from reaching him. We feed him rats' blood spiced with silver powder to render him docile and weak lest he turn into smoke and disperse through the grille of his cell door."

Michael's gullet constricted. "Underground, naked, for three hundred years . . ."

The captain smirked. "The beast has gone mad. He lies on the floor and speaks to the ceiling in ten odd languages, or he reclines in absolute stillness for weeks. Three hundred years and he looks no more than five and twenty years old. His sire was an ancient Vesper, he tells us. His mother was an Egyptian courtesan. He speaks to both of them often. A pitiable creature."

Michael felt ants on his skin, bile in his belly. This could be his fate. "I must say it sounds cruel to me. No light, no air, no clothing, no company . . . You keep a living creature in a grave."

"Do not be mistaken, he is a living dead. A man is made of three things: his soul, his spirit, and his flesh. The spirit is in the blood and connects the soul to the body. Since Vespers are the progeny of man and demon, their blood lacks the capacity to connect their soul with their flesh. No spirit." He snickered. "They need human blood to live. Emiliano likes the cold. All vampires do. He cannot suffocate to death, but sunlight and fire will raze him. We do not want him to kill himself. Although, lunatic that he is, he never once tried. He claims that he has survived our great-great-sires and will survive our great-great-grandchildren and that one day he will be free and we will be dust. Of course he is wrong. He is not immortal."

"Not immortal? But Cardinal Wolsey said—"

"His Eminence was wrong. They do perish, after many centuries, mayhap millennia."

"You admire them, don't you?"

"Imagine possessing the strength of a hundred men, your senses are sharper than a lion's, you heal instantly, merge with shadows, move like a dart, climb on walls, jump from towers and remain unscathed, able to metamorphose into the form of an owl or a wolf or into the very mist, live for centuries, forever young . . ."

Owls. Plaguey wonderful, Michael thought. He had had a vampire visitor in his bedchamber. And Renée! His heart stopped. The vampire knew about her, knew how insanely he adored her. . . .

The sun was setting when Renée received Norfolk's note. She was to meet him outside the Church of the Observant Friars. Oh, how she wished Michael were here to accompany her. She should not come to depend on him, but his strength was so seductive. Naught could hurt her in his presence—except the beast lurking inside him.

Adele wrapped her in a fur cloak and insisted on coming along. Renée did not argue. There was still no word from York Place. No George Hill coming to arrest her. And no Michael.

Renée let out a cry of delight when she spotted her *deletoris*, crumpled and dirty, sitting on the church steps. "Your grace, my lord." She curtsied to the Howards. "I thank you."

"Madame, you owe me a name," Norfolk said.

"Yes." She spoke in low tones. "The person who discovered my Lady Anne Hastings's body was her maidservant, a girl by the name of Nan. Nan must have been the one who called the two yeomen of the guard. I imagine they went to Wolsey, hoping to be well paid for the information. They were not heard of since. The cardinal is the one who alerted the court to Anne's passing."

"And this girl, Nan?"

"That same morning I saw two of the cardinal's yeomen, men in livery wearing his badge, towing Nan away. They mounted horses and left the palace grounds forthwith. None has seen her since. His Grace of Buckingham is in a pother looking to question the girl about his lady sister's death. But Nan is gone. I ask you, my lords, why should the Lord Chancellor of England make a primary witness disappear and then snatch the investigation from the hands of Earl Marshal?"

"Who happens to be me," the old duke said grimly. "My Lady Renée, there is no end to your accomplishments. I wish you would reconsider staying in England. I will be a powerful friend. I promise you that you shall never set foot in the Tower again."

So he had found out. They exchanged a smile of understanding. "Your Grace will have an equal friend in France, mistrust it not."

"When do you leave? I will provide you with an armed escort to Dover."

"Your Grace is most generous. I have my escort now." She smiled sweetly. "On the morrow, I will make arrangements to leave within the week. Please, Lord Rougé does not know—"

"Your secret is safe with us." Norfolk took her hand. A chain and pendant were pressed into her palm. "God keep you, Princess."

Watching the Howards pace off, Renée put Armado's pendant in her purse. The last thread. *Rest in peace, Armado*. She gave a silent prayer for his soul and begged his forgiveness. When she opened her eyes, Sergeant Francesco stood smiling before her. "Madame, we are grateful."

She returned his smile. "You are my *deletoris, n'est ce pas?*"

"Your most loyal *deletoris*."

She investigated their surroundings, prayed there were no vampires lurking within earshot, and whispered, "We are leaving tonight. Choose two men to escort Adele to Gravesend. The rest of you, surround York Place and stay out of sight. I will meet you there at midnight."

"You have a plan, madame, to snatch the Ancient?"

"I do." A plan that chilled her to the bone.

On principle, the *deletoris* refused to entrust the safeguarding of the cardinals' residence in the hands of the fumbling riffraff, were Captain Luzio's exact words. Playing mediator, Michael decreed that half of each force would stay and the other half accompany him to the king's palace. George Hill would remain in York Place as the officer in charge. Captain Luzio would lead their motley force to court, where they would sprinkle holy water and hunt down vampires discreetly.

Wolsey's plan was entirely flawed. Whatever the vampires were after was secreted here in York Place. Michael's every instinct told him they were close. He kept mum, though. Renée was at court, and her safety came before aught else. He would not be able to breathe until he installed her, clawing and cursing him to all damnation, in Westminster Abbey.

Captain Luzio ordered their small force to file down to the river gate and board the barges, then excused himself sheepishly and sprinted toward the jakes. It was the opportunity Michael had been waiting for. He stole inside the cardinal's palace and headed swiftly for the library. The ring had to be destroyed. He did not yet know what he would do with the little scribe. Trussing him up and locking him in a closet seemed to be Michael's best option outside of murdering the brainy lad in cold blood, which he could never do. He raced through the ornate passages, slinked inside the library, and skidded to a halt at the sight that greeted him.

Philip Kent's lifeless head rested facedown on the open tome, a gory bite marring his neck.

The ring—Michael knew—was gone.

Someone gave a shout of dismay. Michael whipped around and saw a house servant cringing against the door frame. The man goggled at him with fear and accusation.

Michael cursed. "Do you see a bloody weapon in my hands?" he growled, raising his hands.

The servant shook his head frantically, edging back. Michael waited, and the instant the man turned his head toward the passageway, he pulled off his signet ring, the one bearing his initials, and tossed it into the corner of the library floor. He pushed past the servant, flashed toward the boat landing, and hopped into one of the barges before the servant alarmed the household.

They took off thereupon.

24

Gentle in manner, resolute in deed.

—Anonymous

Halberds stopped them outside the king's palace. The officer in charge told Michael that Sir Henry Marney must issue a directive to permit a body of foreign men-at-arms at court and that no such order had been given as to these men. "You may go in, Sir Michael. They may not."

Michael explained the matter to Captain Luzio. "While I am obtaining the watchword from the Captain of the Guard, I suggest you begin your duties by purifying the surrounding area."

"Very good. We will asperse the entryways and the walls, then close in on the killer."

Michael hurried inside. He had expected the ever-efficient Cardinal Wolsey to procure them access. Something was amiss. As he negotiated the passageways, turning corners with all speed, he heard a man say, "The gentleman was tall and fair, sir. They were in costumes, masked, and it was dark. I did not get a good look at his face. I may recognize him upon sight, sir."

Michael slammed back against the wall. The yeoman speaking with Sir Henry Marney and his officers round the corner was the guard who had spotted him and Anne sneaking off the night of the masque. *Damn. Damn. Damn.* How now?

The court was at supper in the king's presence chamber. He had to get through this corridor to reach Renée. He looked around and upward. The beams! Captain Luzio said vampires could crawl on walls. He had to try, he had naught to lose. Using his arms to gain momentum, he bent his knees and jumped. His entire body clung to the beamed ceiling. He felt disoriented, stunned. He glanced down, got his bearing, and started moving quietly along the ceiling, as if he were crawling on the floor. He held his breath as he crept over the heads of Sir Marney's party, praying to whichever deity was listening to keep their eyes lowered. His luck stood.

The instant he spotted a vacant nook, Michael dropped to the ground and dashed toward the guard room. He caught a servitor by the scruff of the neck and gave him a message for Renée. He paced outside, his nerves prickling, the muscles across his stomach tight as ropes and keeping him from breathing. If aught had befallen Renée . . .

His heart's keeper came rushing through the door in a flurry of skirts. "What news?"

Michael caught her about the waist, dragged her aside, and kissed her passionately, fiercely. "I love you," he breathed. "I want you to know this, whatever bechances me."

She touched his cheek. "Michael, you are frightening me. What ills do you foresee?"

"I will explain later." He clasped her hand and started in the opposite direction from where he had nearly collided with the one witness who could misidentify him as Anne's murderer. "I must take you, Adele, my servants, and Christopher away from here. I am being followed. Anne's killer has struck again at York Place, killed the cardinal's librarian to get my ring. A servant saw me a moment after I discovered the body. And Sir Marney has found a guard who had seen me with Anne the night of the masque."

"Wait!" She tugged on his hand. "Where are you taking me?"

Michael halted to look back at her. "To your apartment, to get Adele."

"Let us get the boy. Adele will be fine."

He blinked in disbelief. "You would leave Adele behind?"

"You say there are killers and witnesses after you. You are in far graver danger, Michael. Let us get the boy. He is helpless without you. Adele will know to go to the French ambassador."

She was right. He changed direction for his lodging. Mayhem greeted them. His servants, Conn and Pippin, were kicking a bloated leather bladder around the chamber; Christopher, pink-cheeked and properly clothed, was bouncing on the bed, shrieking merrily. Michael and Renée's entry cast a pall of silence. The boy crashed on his bum, uncertainty clouding his eyes.

"Pippin, Conn. You are to escort my Lady Renée and Christopher to Westminster Abbey." Michael flung his purse at his manservant. "Go there now and do not set foot outside until I come for you. If you do not hear from me within a week, take my lady to the French ambassador and sail back to Ireland." It was his home, their home. No harm would come to them there.

"I am coming with you," Renée stated softly, entwining her arm with his like a vine.

"Aye, me, too!" Christopher leaped from the bed and rammed into Michael.

Michael tousled the boy's fair hair and smiled at Renée. They were the family he ached for. "You will not be safe with me," he whispered to her in Gaelic, not wanting to alarm the boy. The odds that he might die tonight or, worse, lose his freedom for centuries were adversely high.

Tears glistened her violet eyes. "Will I ever see you again?"

"I cannot promise. . . ." *Damnation.* This was agony. They were saying good-bye.

"Where will you go?"

"Back to York Place."

"Why?"

"Whatever the killer wants is there. He'll keep on murdering innocent people until I obtain it for him."

Renée leaned into him, her eyes pleading. "Take me with you. I can help. I have been there."

The desire to keep her with him, to know where she was at all times, was a mallet chipping away at his good intentions. "Please, honeymouse." He swallowed the rock in his throat. "Go with the boy to the cathedral. There are bad things abroad. I may not be able to protect you."

She pulled his head down to hers and gave him a sultry kiss. "Two are better than one."

Michael cursed himself for being ten kinds of fool. She would distract him, slow him down, burden his mind with constant worrying. The walls were closing in. "Pippin, toss essentials into a cloak-bag. We leave now." He knelt before Christopher and put his hands on the boy's pint-sized shoulders. "I am to fight a dragon. I charge you with the duty to buckler Pippin and Conn. They are not knights, like us. Will you safeguard them for me till I come get you?"

The boy's eyes etched with fear. "Ye'll come back, aye? Ye won't fall into the river?"

"I can swim like a dogfish." Michael winked. He gathered the boy into his arms and gave him a tight squeeze. He liked being a father, and he would absolutely love being a husband, if only . . . He looked up at Renée, wistfully imagining her petite figure with a big belly beneath the kirtle. "Lady mine, are you determined to risk your beautiful neck in my crazed adventures?"

"Yes, my dearest knight, without a moment's hesitation."

"Sir, there is a . . . a company of men-at-arms outside the palace gates insisting on searching the grounds for . . . for . . ."

"What? Speak up, Merton!" Marney grunted.

Sergeant Merton lowered his voice to a hesitant whisper. "Evil spirits."

The courtiers flanking Sir Marney along the supper table roared with laughter.

"Why bother us over a company of crazed brigands?" demanded Norfolk.

"Well, the matter is, they are not brigands, Your Grace. They are liveried soldiers who claim to serve His Eminence."

Marney slapped a hand over his forehead. "God's teeth, I forget! Yes, let them in."

"Hold on," Norfolk said quietly. "Who are these men?"

"Half the men are of my Lord Chancellor's retinue, and the other half are Soldiers in Service of God in my Lord Cardinal Campeggio's retinue from Rome."

With a pointed look at his son, Earl Surrey, Norfolk pushed to his aching feet. The time had come to enlighten His Majesty.

"Evil spirits?" The King of England chuckled as he swept the dismal faces standing before him in a semicircle in the council chamber. "Are you all gone mad? Secret Soldiers of God, my Lord Norfolk? Blood-sucking demons, my esteemed Cardinal Campeggio? Fetch John Skeleton! We shall have him jot your tales down on parchment and bring players to perform an interlude!"

"Worthy king, if I may explain," Cardinal Campeggio implored urgently.

"Yes, speak, by all means. I have not heard a good fable in a while . . . but mind," he warned, "if this be a trick to lure us into a campaign against the Turks, we shall be most displeased."

Cardinal Wolsey, irked that he had not had the foresight to truss Campeggio's flapping beak, interjected, "Your Majesty, I have reason to believe that the unknown evildoers plotting against Your Grace may strike again. There is another assassin at court. In the course of his investigation, Sir Michael Devereaux has learned that my Lady Anne Hastings, His Grace of Buckingham's poor lady sister, had made the acquaintance of a mysterious man and become his mistress. The astute lady soon uncovered his evil intent and was brutally slain before she could forewarn Your Grace."

"The devil!" roared the Duke of Buckingham. "Anne was involved in no plot whatsoever!"

Wolsey scrutinized the blowsy duke. "I did not imply that my poor Lady Anne was a part to a plot, merely that she had exposed one and was silenced for it." Good God, he thought. It was Buckingham who had hired the Spanish assassin. Alas, he could not bring charges against the Lord Steward of England without proof. Norfolk, the stiff noddle, had unearthed not a single scrap of evidence and together with Marney seemed to have given up on ever finding any. Of a sudden his own lies sank in. Buckingham, the failed assassination, the dead sister, the Ancient—there was an obvious connection here, and yet it eluded him like a distant childhood memory.

"Our dear Lord Chancellor," the king summoned his attention.

"Your findings are of interest to us, but you have yet to justify the cause for a search of our palace by a secret papal army and clarify why you are convinced our person is being threatened by evil spirits."

He could not avoid this, much as he tried; his carefully structured falsehoods were tumbling down. Wolsey could only pray that his loquacious colleague would keep mum about the Ancient. "Your Majesty." He knelt before his king. "The assassin sent to harm Your Grace is a vampire."

The palace was in a ferment when Michael, Renée, the servants, and the boy came out of the chamber. The *deletoris* and their newly recruited English auxiliaries were everywhere, sprinkling holy water, depositing wooden crosses in entryways, painting red crosses on courtyard walls, and chanting exorcismal gabble. A mass departure was under way, courtiers stampeding toward the entrances, servants lugging appurtenances, muttering about evil spirits and foreign armies.

"Their Majesties are going on progress," Renée reckoned aloud. "The court would not dare leave without them."

Michael tugged on her hand. "We need to make haste . . . unless . . ."

She met his anxious eyes. "Unless?"

"You would rather go with the queen. You will be safer, Renée."

"Hush." She yanked on his hand. "I do not intend to separate from you for a moment."

He gave a half grin. "I will hold you to that." He lifted Christopher onto his shoulders and towed her after him, his servants following behind. They pushed through crowded passageways, moving speedily, free of trunks. Michael brought them to a sudden halt. "Damnation, I thought I had that varmint dismissed! Pippin, take the boy and go on without us!" He transferred the boy to Conn's shoulders, gave them a nudge to be on their way, and whisked Renée into a side corridor.

"What did you see?" she gasped, striding with remarkable briskness beside him.

"Riggs."

"The nasty usher? Why are we escaping him?"

"One of my potion bottles was found this morning. I just spotted him speaking to one of the cardinal's yeomen. I do not think it is a coincidence. We must get out of here!"

"There he is!" someone shouted. Renée saw one of the guards pointing at them—at Michael. "That is the man I saw with my Lady Anne the night of the masque! Arrest him!"

Her arm nearly came off her body. Michael pulled her in the opposite direction, moving like the wind, cursing under his breath. "Damn it, Renée! You should have gone with Pippin!"

"You are leading us back to the great stair! We cannot get out from the second level!"

"We will leave through the kitchen stairs, or jump out a window, if need be. I told you this would be dangerous. You may still join the queen's entourage if you are afraid."

"I am not afraid for myself, you idiot!" Her breath was knocked out of her when he swept her into his arms and flashed up the great stairwell leading to the royal gallery.

He set her on her feet with a kiss. "Why can you not admit that you love me?"

"And if I admit it, will it solve all your troubles?"

"No, but it will help." He gripped her hand and drew her alongside him.

The gallery, lined with the giant yeomen of the guard, was empty of courtiers. "Stop them!" Sir Marney shouted, striding out of the guard room. The guards moved in to immure Michael and Renée in a circle. More people emerged from the royal apartment: the two cardinals, Norfolk, Surrey, Buckingham, lords of the council, and lastly King Henry in a loop of bodyguards.

"Is this the man you saw in my library?" Wolsey asked the servant at his side.

"Yes, Eminence! He killed Master Kent! I saw the bloody bite mark on Master Kent's neck, and Sir Michael raised his hands and said . . ."

Michael cursed. He could not take on an entire legion of the most highly trained soldiers in the land. "I am doomed," he muttered to Renée. "Run to them, say I dragged you against—"

"*You* are the vampire?" Cardinal Wolsey exclaimed in disbelief.

Jupiter's thunder, he was! "I am not the killer!" Michael vowed heatedly, his gaze skimming the appalled faces and coming to rest on the king. "Your Majesty, there is another one! He killed my Lady Anne and Master Kent! I am trying to find him and stop him from hurt—"

"Arrest him!" shouted Marney. Swords rasped out of the yeomens' scabbards. Buckingham and Surrey drew theirs. Cardinal Campeggio lifted the jeweled cross dangling on a chain around his neck and loudly declaimed an exorcisory Latin chant.

Michael's heart beat savagely. They would not listen. They would burn him or . . . incarcerate him underground for centuries. His eyes began to hurt, his teeth elongated. He was transforming into the *thing*. Still gripping Renée's hand, he spun in a circle, looking for fissures in the noose of armed bodies tightening about them. He snarled at the yeomen, baring his fangs, flashing his eyes, growling with viciousness calculated to jolt everyone back. The royal bodyguard closed ranks around the king and tried to usher him inside the apartment, but King Henry would not budge. He was entranced. They all stared at Michael as if he were the devil. Except Renée.

"Release the princess and surrender your arms, beast!" demanded the Duke of Norfolk.

Immediately Michael loosened his grip on Renée's hand. There was no point in dragging her under with him. To his astonishment, her fingernails bit into his hand, refusing to let go. "Get us out of here, Michael," she hissed fiercely in Gaelic. "Do it!"

Her fearless constancy anchored him, for the good and the bad. He could not break through the guards' dense ranks with her adhered to his side, but her stalwart presence inspired clarity. There might be a way out. It was insane, mind-boggling, but then so was his situation. His signet ring lay on the library floor at York Place. Could he do it, transfer them there by pure willpower? He might not be able to take Renée with him, but she would be safer with the king. . . .

The yeomen slowly advanced in on him, sweating fear, wariness impeding their movement.

Michael squeezed Renée's hand. "Look at me," he pleaded. "See what I am. Moonstones for eyes, fangs for teeth, a monster from hell . . . If I take you with me . . ."

Violet gems flashed, not with fear—with fury and irritation. "Fine! You need must hear it? I love you! There! Now get us out of here, Michael! *Move!*"

Michael yanked her into a tight embrace, closed his eyes, and pictured his signet ring.

A gust of air ruffled his hair. He opened his eyes. They were in the library at York Place.

He did it! Renée was stupefied, disoriented, ebullient! Jesu help her, this was heresy—and yet she was so pleased! "Michael." She beamed at him. "You are wondrous!"

He found his signet ring on the floor and slid it on his finger. His eyes resumed their natural color. There was no joy in the turquoise depths. "Monstrous, more like." He glanced behind him. "They removed poor Kent's body."

Renée took in their surroundings. "This library is beyond belief!"

"Hush. The place is crawling with men-at-arms." He laced their hands together and peeked outside, looking right and left. The passage was empty. He pulled her into the vacant corridor.

"What is your plan?" she whispered at his shoulder.

"I will find what the killer wants, lure him to a confrontation somewhere, and kill him."

"What are we looking for?"

"I do not rightly know," he returned in a low voice. "I will know it when I sense it."

"If it is something of great value, then it may be either at chapel or in Wolsey's apartment."

He crept onward, snuffing out wall sconces and keeping to the shadows. "Why at chapel?"

She chose her words with great care. "It is where he installed the pope's gift, *La Pietà*."

"Is it a gigantic marble statue of a woman cradling a dead man?"

"That is blasphemy," she scolded softly. "You are speaking of Our Lady and Our Lord."

"Your pardon."

"Well, do you suppose it might be what the killer wants?"

"I cannot see how, unless he is a mad collector of religious art. Still, it would take dozens of men with wheeled boards to convey it . . ."

Morbleu, Renée thought, and blanked her mind for fear he could read it.

"I suppose it cannot hurt to inspect it, though, as I have no idea what I am looking for."

Renée heaved a quiet sigh of relief, crossed her thumb and forefinger, and tiptoed after him. Strange that she should feel perfectly at ease with him. The heat of his gentle hand, his seductive scent, his strong presence . . . Without warning Michael turned around and kissed her. Holy Anne! "Will you stop that?" she gasped against his mouth, cupping and stroking his neck.

Michael grinned. "Stop what—kissing or divining voluptuous thoughts?"

"Both. We have little time. I am certain the cardinals are on their way with an army."

"Less than an hour, then. Come along, my quiver of concupiscence. The passage is clear."

They had to freeze occasionally as servants or guards walked by. Michael was getting better at employing his preternatural senses, Renée noticed. "Do you suppose the killer is here?"

"I do not think so. Ofttimes I get an alarming tingle. I believe that is when he is near."

"But you do not know for certain?"

"No. Here we are." He put his ear to the chapel door, then pushed it. The plush chamber was dim and quiet. Tiny flames flickered on a circle of silver candlesticks, illuminating Lady Piety.

They stood gazing at the magnificent sculpture with awe. "Michelangelo," Renée whispered.

"His original work?" Michael echoed her breathy voice, as if he, too, felt that speaking aloud would sinfully take away from the glory and sanctity of the piece.

"A replica."

"This is godly—what men are capable of creating. It is as perfect as nature." He sighed. "So what do I do with it? Shatter it to pieces and look inside?"

Good God! He was brilliant. "What do your senses tell you?"

"This is it." There was a haunted look about him. "It . . . it hums to me."

"Mayhap the thing you seek is trapped—"

"Aye, in the body of Christ." He let go of her hand and took the steps leading to the dais. He circled the monument, admiring every marble fold from top to bottom. "I will surely burn for destroying such a marvel, if not in a man-made woodpile, your God will punish me."

"My God?" Their gazes locked in silence. "Jesu, Michael. Do not tell me you . . ." Of course! She should have realized it! No wonder he did not recoil from the Cross—he was godless!

"Look away."

"Why?"

He scowled darkly. "I do not want you to see me smash your God."

His thoughtfulness moved her. Godless, he was, but not irreverent. "I . . . Are you absolutely convinced that what you seek is inside the statue?"

"I have to do it, Renée. I am sorry."

Renée recalled the new spiritual ideas she had heard whispered in Lady Marguerite's salon, the New Parnassus, the heretical concepts of a German monk defying his archbishop. *Why does the pope, whose wealth today is greater than the wealth of the richest Crassus, build the basilica of St. Peter with the money of poor believers rather than with his own money?* "This is not God but a block of beautifully chiseled marble." She turned her back to him. She tried not to think— should he read her mind—of how low she had sunk and would still go to regain her life and win her freedom. Then again, so would Michael. He would go to any length to please his overlord. . . .

Crash.

Her whole body cringed. Tears rushed to her eyes. She clasped her hands tightly in a prayer, her eyes shut. *Forgive me, Father, for I have sinned and sinned and need must sin again. . . .*

"Ouch! The thing burned me," Michael grunted. Renée whipped around and dashed up the steps. Michael removed his surcoat and handed it to her. "You take it out. The thing hates me."

Merciful Christ! He had put his fist into the marble. With a shaky heart, she put a trembling hand in the hollow belly of the statue and gently removed an exquisitely chiseled box of silver. Rivers of tears spilled from her eyes and washed her cheeks as she wrapped the box in Michael's surcoat. She stared at him in misery. "I think . . . you will not burn alone in your woodpile."

"Renée, we must go. They are coming." He lifted her against him with one arm, thrust the wrapped box between them, and dashed outside. She clung to his neck, clutching the parcel. This was madness! They were both mad! She dared not open her eyes. She was scared and ashamed.

Michael whished through the passageways like a clever arrow, shifting, cutting corners, and vaulting. When she felt cool air on her face, Renée opened her eyes—and squeaked. They were soaring skylark-high into the night, hurdling past the thick, tall wall that enclosed the compound. Michael kept moving at an incredible speed, his feet scarcely touching the ground. . . .

Saints! Her *deletoris*! "Michael, stop! I feel sick."

Thereupon he slowed and touched ground. They were in the orchard northeast to the palace, sheltered by a cluster of poprin pear trees. He set her on her feet carefully. "Marmoset?"

She turned aside, embracing the Ancient to her bosom, and retched, disgusted with herself, with what they had done, with what she had yet to do. . . . *Oh, mercy!*

A gust of wind ruffled the leaves in the trees. Michael pulled Renée into the nook of his arm.

Raspy laughter heralded the dark-haired stranger who materialized before them. "Well done, sunflower." The stranger, a large Englishman, clapped his gloved hands together, creating a thud. "Such competence . . ."

* * *

Michael, having anticipated the encounter, pushed Renée behind him and drew his sword.

Ferdinand's eyes shone with the eerie silvery light. "Tonight we shall fight as equals. I have waited years to dispense with you, foundling." He stared at Renée sharply and snarled, "Sit!"

Renée plonked on the ground like a puppet whose strings had been snipped. Her head wilted to the side. The parcel dropped in her lap. Michael's heart lurched. He dove to his knees beside her and cupped her cheeks. She blinked at him owlishly. She was moonstruck.

Michael choked. "How long will she stay like this?" he asked Ferdinand, the thought of her remaining like this forever gutting him.

"As long as it pleases me, fool! You fell in love with her, against my lord's command. It was your error. But see, I was merciful. I could have killed her instead of the other bitch."

Michael was on his feet, flexing his fingers on the sword hilt. Rage licked at his insides. He welcomed, stoked, and nourished it, until his eyes burned. He bared his fangs with a feral growl. "Equals, eh? Vampires." No wonder he could never fell the black-hearted nuisance.

Ferdinand's laughter grated on his ears. "You have me to thank for your transformation. My lord wanted to spare you. I proved to him that you could never fulfill your duty as a man."

"My duty was to rise high at court, win a page in the cardinal's good books, and rise higher! My duty was to bring honor and glory to my Lord Tyrone!"

"Your duty was to steal the Ancient!"

Yes, he knew that; the command pulsated at the back of his mind like a heartbeat, a megrim, though he did not recall being given the order. "Why did he not send you to steal it? What great weakness do you possess that made me the preferable candidate for this . . . duty?"

"Curse you!" Ferdinand roared savagely. "I have no weaknesses!"

"Really? So why did you not steal the box? You have been inside the cardinal's palace. You killed the scribe. Surely you sensed the thing was secreted in the statue."

"I knew precisely where it was!" Ferdinand roared with palpable frustration.

"Certes, you lured me to it but could not take it yourself. Why?" Suddenly he knew. "No weaknesses, eh? Then you will not mind if I do this?" He unsheathed his dagger and crossed it with his sword. Ferdinand flinched, as if Michael had struck him. "Well, well." Michael laughed triumphantly. "A former Christian soul lost to the devil. How long have you been a vampire?"

"Sith my lord came to the court of Mortimer and the bitch queen!"

"Count Tyrol, Tyrone the Elder, and my Lord Tyrone are one and the same. True?"

"Aye. Count Tyrol took a shine to young King Edward and rallied an undefeatable army to wrest back the throne of England from the usurper Mortimer and his harlot queen, the king's lady mother. King Edward won his crown and gave my lord the deputy of Ireland providing he took his army with him. My lord thought it a good jest to assume a title reminiscent of his own and an entire island withal."

"What happened to this army of vampires?"

"You have ridden out with this army countless times, fool!"

It got worse and worse. "Sir John? Sir Henry? All of them vampires? O'Hickey?"

"Aye, O'Hickey, too. Only the serfs are common mortals."

"Did you turn me?"

Ferdinand gave a bitter laugh. "My lord turned you with his blood. Vesper blood."

"Dragon's blood." *I have given you the best of mine, my knowledge, my strength* . . . "Why the bottles? Why the charade? Why did he not tell me what he was, what I had become?"

"Enough with the questions! You have served your purpose!" Ferdinand swung his sword light-fast. Michael barely had time to block it. Their blades clashed with such force that sparks of fire sprang out of the rasping steel shafts. Pain jarred Michael's wrist and shot up his arm. Before he recovered, a second blow came at him, faster, mightier, shoving him down to his knee. He had to drop his dagger to strengthen his hent on the hilt with both hands. Ferdinand kept swinging his sword again and again, dealing Michael a punishment from hell. *He is stronger.* . . .

"Not equals after all," Ferdinand rasped snidely. He vanished.

A whish of air at his back alerted Michael to the blade about to hack him in half. He spun and blocked. Lightning strikes flew at him from all directions. His sides, his head, and his back were exposed to the giant raptor whishing around him, coming at him from the sky, whamming birds from treetops. They clashed all over the orchard, whizzing like shadows, cutting the air. It was impossible to anticipate whence the next strike would come.

Michael fought on the defensive, his survival uncertain. *I am a vampire*, he thought. *Why am I fighting like a man?* This was combat without rules. He needed to adjust fast or his head would be cut off. Instincts and senses he had not yet gotten the hang of kicked in gradually. He forced himself to see, to smell, to use his brainpower. *Brains carry a man farther than might.* . . .

Ferdinand's weakness! It was his only chance. He crisscrossed through the orchard, drawing Ferdinand away from Renée, then retracted his steps and grabbed her purse. He found her rosary with the silver cross. Ferdinand came at him from the sky. Michael feinted, rolled on the ground, leaped into the air, and slashed Ferdinand's arm with the silver cross. The giant growled in pain. He collapsed on the ground. Michael stared down at him. "Beg for mercy, you rotten offal!"

"Curse you!" Ferdinand clutched his bleeding arm. "You poisoned me, filthy street bastard!"

"You should have begged." Michael thrust the tiny cross into Ferdinand's heart and watched with satisfaction as the bane of his existence turned gray as ash, then dissolved into powder.

A wink of gold caught his eye: Tyrone's ring. He dug it from the ash, slid it on his finger, and hurried to Renée. As if awakened from a dream, she shook her head, moaning. Ferdinand's death had freed her from the stupor. He lifted her gently to her feet and cradled her in his arms.

"Who was that man?" she demanded to know. "Was he the killer? Tell me you killed him!"

Michael smiled at his beautiful shrew. "It was a close shave, but we are home free, my love. Sir Ferdinand was my Lord Tyrone's captain of the guard in Ireland. He was a brutish imbecile in spirit and a vampire in the flesh. I vanquished him with your rosary."

"Oh!" She smiled brightly. "How clever you are!" She took the dusty beads from his fingers.

"It is ash," he said grimly. "The fate reserved for monsters like me."

"You are not a monster." She wrapped herself around him, resting her head against his heart.

"Honeymouse." He stroked her taut back. She shivered with cold. His senses alerted him to the men slinking into the orchard on foot. "Renée, we must go. They are coming."

She looked up at him fretfully. Her heartbeat was frenetic. She was crying. "Kiss me. . . ."

She loved him. How could he not indulge her, despite the imminent danger? One moment of bliss. He slanted his mouth on hers and groaned with pleasure at her passionate response. Desire, sweetness, pure abandon, urgent desperation . . . He was lost. She had him forever.

"I am sorry," Renée whispered despondently, her lips salty with tears. "I am so sorry. . . ."

Fire exploded in his side! Sharp pain. Overwhelming agony. His eyesight dimmed. . . .

"Do not hate me. . . ."

"Hate you?" he gasped bleakly, mystified, hurting, sightless. "I love you. . . ."

Darkness claimed him.

❧ 25 ❧

The drop wears away the stone.

—Ovid: *Ex Ponto*

Renée dared not take her eyes off her captive. He was coming to. Millstones lifted from her chest. Michael was strong. He survived the stab to the kidney and the silver poisoning. Her *deletoris*, sworn to serve with blind obedience, had carried him to the barge and whence to the caravel with supreme gentleness under her watchful eye. He was *her* prisoner, no one else's. Once she delivered the Ancient to Cardinal Medici and Long-Nose, she would set Michael free.

The little ship lurched as the river Thames flowed into the Channel. She braced her booted feet apart on the creaking floorboards, steeling herself for the inevitable confrontation when his wits recovered. Dawn was an hour away, but daylight would not enfeeble this particular vampire. He would awaken a firedrake, duped, betrayed, strapped to a bed, his sublime fury and bloodlust directed exclusively at her. The crossing to France would be a long week. *Jesu help her.*

The candlelight winking from the iron bracket pinned to the beams gilded the muscled limbs stretching to the four corners of the bed. Michael's very presence, albeit insentient, mocked her. Never again would she know the joy of his friendship, the safe haven of his embrace, the sensual delights he stirred in her, the secret pleasures of his body . . . She had destroyed a precious thing.

Was it worth it? Had she done the right thing? *In a just cause it is right to be confident*, said the great Sophocles. Better Cardinal Medici have the Ancient than a Vesper overlord.

Michael groaned. His eyelids flickered as he struggled to wake up. He shifted but could not alter his spread-eagled position. He blinked at the ceiling, frowned, looked around.

Renée was silent, rigid, her back to the door, the silver dirk clutched in her fist. She held her breath, waiting for him to notice her—and curse her to all eternity.

Tension gripped her stomach when the turquoise eyes homed in on her like bolts. "Renée . . ." His voice was hoarse, serrated. "What . . . what?" He could not speak, and she could not answer. With effort, he raised his head to inspect the length of him. He was barefoot, unarmed, wearing his shirt and slops, and fettered by the wrists and ankles to the bedposts. "I—I am in irons?"

"Silver."

An incredulous expression snapped across his handsome face. "You did this to me?"

It took every drop of courage not to look away. Averting one's gaze was a sign of weakness, of remorse. She could not afford to show him either. She took pity on his straining neck and went over to put another cushion beneath his head. "Do you want some wine?"

She recoiled in fright when he rattled his chains. "Damnation, you shrew! Unchain me!" He howled in torment as the silver cuffs grazed his wrists and ankles.

"It is best if you do not move," she proposed pragmatically. "The silver is not iron but it will burn your flesh and might render you unconscious again."

"You poisoned and shackled me?" His shock redoubled. "How long have you known?"

His accusatory tone shoved the knife she had plunged into herself an inch deeper. She felt ice-cold, deadened inside. It would be easy—a relief—to set him loose now, but then she would have achieved nothing. He would disappear with the Ancient and carry it to his Vesper lord.

Her guilt-ridden expression extinguished the last spark of innocence in his eyes. "The joust. You fathomed what I was from the start. You knew the cause of my plaguey ailment—and you said not a word!" Betrayal. Rage. A river of hurt so deep and wide stared back at her she almost drowned in her self-inflicted misery. His Adam's apple bulged in his naked throat. "Cruel."

Unable to withstand the ugly reflection of her in the damning eyes, she turned away. *Cruel.* He had summed her up with a single word, and it hurt—because he was right. Cruel Renée, no longer froward, just soulless. Cold and heartless. But the tears limning her cheeks were warm. She sought refuge in the night reigning beyond the porthole. She hated herself at that moment.

"Your disguise." Michael's voice drifted to her. "I hate to ruin it for you, honeymouse, but it falls wide of the mark. The black leather hose does too good a service displaying the curvaceous delights of your backside. No one could mistake you for a lad."

She met his gaze over her shoulder. "It is not a disguise."

The full impact of her statement hardened his expression. "*Et tū, Brūte?* You are *deletoris.*"

"*Deletrix,* female, first of my kind."

His husky laugh was bitter. "I should marvel if there were a single person at that court aside from my doltish self not in pursuit of the Ancient."

"But you were in pursuit of the Ancient."

"Not really, not consciously. Certes, you were the craftiest player, attaching yourself to the one creature who could steal it for you, a vampire in ignorance and a meacock wretch withal! And then you purloin it off him! Your sedulity is worthy of applause, madame. You took no half measures but persevered with constancy in effort and application, went as far as whoring yourself lavishly to win the prize. . . . I would clap were my hands unbound."

His words, hurled with malicious intent, scourged her, racked her with contrition. His venom found all her sore spots. "You mock me, while I never mocked you."

All traces of irony—splenetic, setaceous, or otherwise—vanished from Michael's face. "I do not mock you, Renée. I was on fire with love for you. You broke my heart."

His valediction, delivered with cool finality, was the fatal twist of the dagger. She strode to the bolt-hole and lifted the bar from its brackets, wishing it were a sanctuary door knocker and that absolution awaited her on the other side. She should not care so much that Michael despised her so. She had accomplished an impossible assignment. She was returning to France victorious. She would have freedom, her mother's duchy, and Raphael. She had fought the battle of her life and won. Michael was a pawn in the game, a providential development, a lucky toss of the dice, a means to an end. What did it matter that she had run foul of him? She crumpled. *Sweet Jesu!*

"Get back here, you little witch! I cannot lay a hand on you!" Michael growled at her back. "But you shall do me the courtesy of explaining yourself, madame, as I mentally wring your deceitful neck!"

She swiped at her tears and whipped around. "I did not know you were clueless! How could I? A vampire that does not know he is a vampire! I only realized you were unaware when—"

His blue eyes glinted murderously. "Verily a lamentable and risible thing, a witless animal is, harnessed to the plow when the soil needs sowing and butchered when the snow comes."

She cried plaintively. "I do not think of you as an animal, Michael."

"Did you have a good laugh at my slavishness, shrew-witch? Did you rejoice in bringing me to my knees with your honeyed falseness?"

She shook her head adamantly. "I never laughed at you!"

Ruthlessly he forbore listening and plunged on. "How you must congratulate yourself for snaring the beast, neatly trussed in your seductive wiles. What price for carnal services rendered by a princess of the blood? Will they bestow you with a kingdom for your pains?"

"I am not a whore!" Renée sobbed, wounded and despaired, wanting to crawl into a ball and die. "I do care for you, Michael. By Christ's blessed body, not all was a lie."

"Then you have cut off your nose to spite your face, lady."

His statement, apt and simply delivered, tidied her mind, clearing the pin and web from her eyes. "Here is the thing," she breathed with restored confidence. "The man who made love to me last night, I adore him. The vampire who lusted for my blood and near bit my neck, I serve those who would have it vanquished. Were our roles reversed, what would you have done?"

"Spare me the witty equivocations and the artful excuses. Whom do you serve?"

She straightened her wobbly spine. "I serve my king and Cardinal Medici, the future pope."

"So you stole the Ancient for a rival cardinal. Fascinating. I imagine Holy Church considers the poxy thing, whatever it is, a card of ten. How did you become enmeshed in papal politics?"

"I do not give one jot about their politics! I did it to save my life and gain my freedom!"

"You are prevaricating again. You have your life as well as the universally coveted prize. You could purchase freedom anywhere. What hold do they have on you?"

"The queen my mother's inheritance, the duchy of Brittany. The king my father stole it from her. If I do not return to France with the Ancient, I will forfeit the title and the lands."

"Ah. Land is priceless. You got an excellent value in exchange for your . . ." He perused her. "What did you sell, Princess? I detect neither heart nor soul. Were you simply amusing yourself playing the game?" His mouth hardened. "Incidentally, you do not look amused anymore."

"You are one to talk! You serve a Vesper overlord! You were stealing the Ancient to bring it to a blood-sucking monster! A foul thing that wants to put mankind in pens and feed on us!"

He stared at her in thundering silence. His voice was a quiet rasp. "I stole the Ancient to stop a killer. Mind, I would have done it anyway, for I was unwittingly ordered to steal the silver box. As for duty, I believed I served the generous earl who had taken a bastard urchin from the stews, a boy like Christopher, whose father was a dead traitor and his mother a dead nun and a whore, and given him shelter, nutriment, affection, learning, pride in himself, a worthy future. I did not know my Lord Tyrone was a centuries-old vampire count until this very day."

"Then it is Tyrone. I suspected as much. A powerful lord in command of a lawless island, a man of mystery few have encountered . . . What is he like? Did you not notice any distinguishing vagaries in his behavior? Vampires, as a rule, do not move in sunlight. They do not eat or drink as normal human beings do. They feed on blood. They are ageless heretics, perennial . . ."

"You are wrong. They do go out in the daylight and devour victuals as any mortal being."

"You are special, Michael. I do not know by what means you were turned into a vampire. Think, have you ever seen your lord strut gaily in the sun or enter a church or devour meat?"

"Yes, in full armor or a cowl; no; and . . . I do not remember." He frowned. "He drinks wine."

"Wine and blood are both red. And his face? Has it aged since you came to live with him?"

"My lord is very old. Few more crinkles would make little difference." He blinked in sudden concentration. "You are correct. They do not age with years. I did not notice. As a boy growing up, I imagine I expected them to remain the same. . . ."

"Them?" She flinched. "Do you mean to tell me there is a whole country of them?"

"A couple of dozens I am personally acquainted with. I do not know about their families."

"Oh, Michael." She sank down on the edge of the bed beside him and clasped her fingers in her lap to keep from touching him. Holy Anne, she missed him already, which made no sense, as he was right here in front of her. And yet an abyss lay betwixt them now. "What did you plan on doing once you had the silver box? Shin it light-fast back to Ireland?"

"First, I would open it. Do you know what is secreted inside? Why it is called *the Ancient*?"

"I know nothing, and frankly, I do not care to be enlightened. I will be happy to hand it over to Cardinal Medici and be done with this infernal business."

"I imagine this 'infernal business' includes me. Well, I need answers. I hate what I am, what was done to me. My memory is a thresher. I need to know why and how I was transformed into a foul, blood-sucking monster."

She winced. "Your pardon. I did not mean—"

"You spoke the truth, and now hear mine. I swear to you, I do not want the poxy thing. You may have it, but please help me find answers before you hand it over to your cardinal."

"I, eh . . . cannot. I dare not rupture it before it is delivered."

"I will be careful. Unchain me. Let me look inside."

"No. I am sorry."

His eyes glinted compellingly. "Let me go, honeymouse. You do not hate me, do you?"

He was trying to spell-stop her with his dominant mind, seduce her into servile compliance, but his vampiric trick was not working on her. "Of course I do not hate you," she muttered. "But you know very well I cannot release you . . . yet."

He arched against the bed. "They will torture me, Renée! They will put me in a cage!"

"No. . . ." She shuddered. Her hand reached out to soothe and fell. "I will not allow it."

"Will you let the bloodhounds give me a right dusting and tip me off the Tarpeian, or down an oubliette, or better yet, install me in a catacomb in Rome, all mine to twiddle my thumbs there for five hundred years? No, wait. I have it! A heap of talshides in the marketplace! A heroine of the people you will be hailed, Saint Joan of Arc!"

She glowered at him. "She was burnt at the stake. Cease striving to bend my mind to your fiendish will! And stop suggesting all those horrible punishments! I would never do that to you! I am not taking you to be tortured by Holy Church. After I report to King Francis, I will set you free. I swear!"

His expression darkened, sobered. "I would not recommend it. Better kill me quick."

She froze. Tendrils of dread rimed her spine. "You would come after me?"

"Oh yes." He pinned her in his hard glittering gaze. "With a vengeance. You should have left me behind. Why didn't you?"

She made the mistake of allowing her gaze to roam his beautiful golden body. At his smirk, she looked up. "You would have come after me anyway," she replied in a small voice.

"True. But I would have been merciful. Now . . ." He surveyed his shackled, sprawled, near-naked frame. "Seeing as how I am pinioned to your bed like some paynim love slave, helpless to do aught but service when Your Grace fancies a ride on a golden stallion—"

"I fancy no such thing!" Cursing his uncanny ability to read her mind, she got up and paced the hold. Her cheeks were aflame. She had taken perverse pleasure in undressing him earlier with gentleness and care, had even stolen a few kisses and caresses. She could not help herself. Her weak flesh craved him. Her spirit pined for him. "Would you rather be chained on deck for the entire voyage, subjected to the elements? I thought you would be more comfortable here."

"Hold me fast, the harpy has a heart."

His sarcasm was her due penance. "Daring me to panic by threatening to exact revenge from me will not unlock your chains."

"Fickle and forever changing is a woman." He sighed. "Look at me, marmoset."

Reluctantly she did. His gaze glided appreciatively over her well-fitting masculine raiment. Stitched to fit her like a glove, the doublet and hose were made of soft black leather embroidered with gold thread, with snowy sleeves popping out from gilt-limned slashes, gold knops running down the front in rows *a là militaire*, and a gold crucifix sewn across her heart. Slim black boots hugged her calves and flared with a gilded fold above the knees. She had earned the right to proudly wear this uniform with pain and sweat.

"Come closer," Michael said.

"I am not sure I ought to. You look dangerous enough from where I stand."

"Indulge me. Look"—he rattled his chains again and gave a hiss of pain—"I am harmless."

"Ha!" She fleered and approached him against her better judgment. "What do you want?"

"Were we subjects of Master Thomas More's *Utopia*, you would remove your attire slowly and mount me," he drawled. "However, as I am your humble beast and you my warden, I beg two things. First, I would you give me a kiss; then I would you tell me the truth."

"What truth?" she inquired warily.

"I know you are not a whore. You enjoyed my company. You enjoyed my body. You could have killed me in the orchard or had your *deletoris* cut off my head. You chose not to. A woman either loves or hates, there is no third course, to quote Publilius Syrus. So I ask you, what hold do they have on you? What can I do to eliminate the threat? I am a vampire." He quirked a mirthless grin. "Put my talents to good use. Let me help you. I will free you from their yoke."

Renée fidgeted. Telling him the truth, how she had exploited his tender feelings in order to free Raphael, would be the end of everything, would obliterate what little affection he still bore her, and would irreversibly turn him into her mortal—worse, immortal—enemy. She should never have let him read the letter. "I told you. The queen my mother's duchy."

He transfixed her with his focused gaze, the sharp intelligence behind the charm surfacing in full force. The abrupt stillness of his countenance made her catch her breath. "You did it for him, your painter, Raphael. *Le Triomphe d'Amour.* The Triumph of Love. Is he in prison?"

Oh God. He saw right through her.

"Do not bother lying, Renée. I eavesdrop on your deepest thoughts."

"How do you do that?" Trepidation pitched her voice. "You were unable to do so before!"

"You did not love me before. You do now. And I cannot bend your mind to my will for the same reason. I still love you. Why are you going back to him, in the name of wonder?"

He still loved her. "They will execute him if I do not return with the box."

"The pox to him! Let him rot! What an artist he will die, just like Nero. Set me free, Renée! Grasp the nettle, light of my eyes! We could find happiness together—"

"I cannot let him rot in prison for me!" She paced about, hot and cold, shaking all over.

"So, this is the difficulty, this is the trouble," he bit out angrily. "It is easy to go down to the underworld; it is getting up to the upper world that is the problem. You think you still love him!"

It was true. She felt that she did. Ugh, she did not know any-more. . . .

"Oh, wretched minds of men; oh, their blind hearts . . . I could winkle him from prison—"

"I am not asking you to."

"—but I won't," he clipped vengefully, glancing at the dirk she held in her fist. "The appeal of killing this Michelangelo you lan-guish for would override all reason. If you choose the plaguey painter over me, best kill me now. You cannot set me free, Renée. *Ever.* And I cannot be caged like a beast. So I beg you. Use your lit-tle dagger on me." He growled. "Give me the misericord!"

She shrank back, staring at the V opening of his shirt: Burnished skin, hard muscle, rising and falling with his heartbeat. The prey was begging the huntress to take his life. "I cannot."

"Give me the merciful dagger, Renée. Administer the death stroke, as if I were a terminally wounded knight. Give quarter, honeymouse. Do not let them practice on me. Show me you are kind and merciful. Surely you can do this one thing for me."

His pleading tone, the hopelessness in his eyes, wrenched her heart. She knelt by the bed.

"Renée." He strained toward her. He emanated heat like a fur-nace. Desperate eyes implored her mercy. "Give me the kiss of peace and plunge the dirk into my heart."

"No, Michael. I could never kill you. . . ." She raised her hand to caress his cheek.

He recoiled from her touch with disgust, as if she had cast spu-tum on him. "Go ahead! Frolic in bed with your lover while you sentence me to hell! I shall still be spitted upon silver prongs when your great-grandsons and great-granddaughters inherit the earth."

Tears flooded her eyes, distorting her vision. "I will set you free in France."

"I will come for you." There was darkness in his voice, a sinister promise. "No bastion will keep you from me, Renée de Valois. I will drag you to the edge of the world and feast on your blood. You will never see the painter again. You will become the vampire's concubine, my love slave, my trove of earthly pleasures . . ."

"God's pity, you mean it!" She jumped rearward and collapsed on her backside.

"Aye, I mean it. Do away with me now. Quick! It would be an act of charity, I promise you. Put me out of this misery. Put the world out of my misery. *Please!*"

"No! I—cannot!" She tossed her dagger aside and pushed back across the floor on hands and heels. She shook violently, chilled and miserable. Her whole body hurt. What had she done?

"Never say I did not give you a fair chance." With a guttural roar, he jerked his arms, tearing the silver manacles from the chains. Renée jumped to her feet and stumbled back. Slack-jawed, she watched him peel the cuffs from bloody wrists and ankles, as if the silver were marchpane, and toss the bits on the floor. He stood. Their gazes clashed. He looked primed to pounce.

"Afraid now?" Michael's wickedly satisfied smile made her think of a dragon gloating over a hoard. His blue eyes sparkled with draconian mischief, the desire to incinerate her alternating with the temptation to make a meal of her. Her chances did not look good. She ran for the bolt-hole. He was behind her in a flash. She jabbed an elbow into the dimple beneath his breastbone.

Michael grunted, doubling over. "You she-devil!"

Before he caught her, she squatted, rolled aside, and kicked his feet from under him. He fell down with a booming thud, grunting in stupefaction. She was on her feet and towering over his sprawled form as he raised himself on his elbows and stared at her, as if she had grown horns.

"Hoa, my spirited little Amazon!" He smiled broadly. "Pax!"

Her heeled boot was already in the air, primed to smash into his face. The kick should afford her the instant she needed to stab him with a sharp piece of silver and place him *hors de combat*. Her dirk was across the room, but she had something else just as lethal to a vampire. The silver rose, his archery prize, was on a table a pace to her left. Then his sword to cut off his head—

Renée froze. All her training and she could not do it. She could not boot-mark his handsome face. She could not tread upon the appealing mouth grinning at her with challenging adoration. She staggered, devastated. "H-how did you . . . ?" Her gaze bounced between him and the meshed chain links scattered all over the floor. The bloody scratches on his wrists and ankles had healed already. "You had the power to free yourself all along, and yet you asked me to kill you. . . ."

"Let us just say I have a friend in this hold, and it is not you." He lunged up. She shrieked. Suddenly he was behind her, his hand on her mouth. His steely arm seized her. "If you scream, I will tear apart your men, limb from limb. What I cannot do to you I will do to them. Do you want to watch me strop my fangs on your *deletoris*? I shall relish using them for a whetstone."

She shook her head forcefully.

"Good. We understand each other." He carried her across the hold and flung her facedown upon the bed. He bestrode her backside and pinned her wrists above her head with one hand. He used the other to rip the back of her doublet and peel it from her body. She screeched in protest. "Scream, my pretty odalisque, if you so wish. Remember my promise." Her cambric shirt shared the fate of the doublet. He stripped her torso bare, pulled her tight maunches from her arms, and used the shredded cambric strips to tie her wrists together above her head.

Renée grumbled and wriggled in vain under his crushing bulk. "Get off me, you fat troll!"

"Fat troll?" He ran his fingertip along her bare arm, from her wrist to her exposed armpit.

"*Arrêtez!* Stop, stop!" she squeaked, cringing at the needling tickles. "Unscrupulous fiend! Do not tickle me! I hate it!"

Michael chuckled and did it again. "You should not reveal royal secrets to the enemy, love."

Renée fumed, grunted, and twitched. "I spared your face—and you punish me for it?"

"How ferocious you are, my wild mare," he whispered. "Do not try to unhorse me. Tougher combatants than you have tried . . . and failed." He pushed his hand beneath her, smoothed his open palm over her heaving torso, and cupped her breast. His gentle fondling knocked the air out of her lungs. She squirmed as sparkly frissons of arousal skittered through her incapacitated body. He rolled a finger over her stiff nipple, thrumming her lute strings, increasing and expanding the sensations. A pulse of desire took effect between her thighs. Michael groaned. "You want me."

"You said you would not lay a hand on me, heathen!" she gasped as her breast rubbed itself sensuously into the warm loving hand.

"Learn your lesson, love. Foul, blood-sucking monsters lie." He latched his sultry mouth to her naked shoulder, kissing and licking, as his cunning hand moved on to the neglected breast and plied the nipple to raging sensitivity. She could not keep her bottom from swiveling beneath him. The tighter she squeezed her thighs together to keep from shifting, the more stimulated she became. She buried low moans in the bed linen, her shame terrible and complete. "You like that."

"I did not give you leave to ravish me," she objected woefully, cursing her wanton response. His masterful ministrations lit balefires in her body until it forgot how to fight.

Michael lifted his weight to turn her around, still pinning her bound wrists above her head. "Did you really think manipulating and misusing a vampire was good for your health? Did you expect to abduct me to France and reach your destination unravished? I think not." He laughed.

"Lecherous demon!" She scowled petulantly. "I cannot fathom this. I took every precaution to bind you properly."

Amazement expanded his irises. "Your Grace shall have to pardon my impertinence. I swear I did not set out deliberately to frustrate her royal plans, except I do not enjoy smarting under acidic metal." His gaze settled on her little breasts, thrust high with her arms stretched above her head. "I particularly do not enjoy panting for a confectionary shrew who would rather tease than bestride my bedridden, aching loins." He dipped his head and sucked a jutting nipple into his mouth. Lightning shot to her curling toes and fingertips. With a deplorably purring complaint, she arched beneath him, inadvertently offering more to his worshipful mouth.

It was divine torture, the tremolo he played with the tip of his tongue on her sensitive nipple. She writhed like a feeble worm, hating and loving what he did to her in the same breath, gasping, wanting more. The instant he let go of her wrists to mold her breasts with his hands and lavish them with generous suckling, she delved her fingers in his hair and yanked with all her might.

"Ouch!" His eyes came up glowering. "Sheathe your quills, angry porpentine! You will have me baldpated within a week!"

"A week? Ha! Your hair will be off by daylight!" Her haughtily delivered barb ended with a harrumph when he flipped her over again. His hands gripped the waistline of her hose and ripped it apart with the linen strossers underneath. Renée grunted and struggled furiously as he shredded her raiment and pulled off her boots as well, leaving her nude and utterly defenseless. "You have ruined my costume, villain! It was new!"

Warm, large hands caressed the cool cheeks of her derrière with blatant approval. A brazen finger slid along the cleft. She clamped her thighs together against the imminent assault upon her secret folds and moaned at the sensations it aroused. The tight squeezing excited her, brought her closer to cresting despite the forcible manhandling. Reveling in her power, she cursed him under her breath. He chuckled deep in his throat. "This is all for effect, love. You would not want your men to know you have surrendered your body willingly to the despicable leech, would you?"

"Willingly?" She craned her head aside to glare at him. "I am not willing, hell spawn! Cease and desist at once, I say!"

A shade of resentment and vengeance passed across the usually doting brow. "Not willing?" He stretched her arms high, hovered over her, and slid his hand beneath her all the way toward her *mons generis*. She stiffened at the light touch of fingers upon the damp curls. He caressed the tender cleft with his fingertips but did not go any farther. Her heartbeat escalated to a roaring in her ears. The faint petting was steadily and methodically reducing her to a molten, quaking pulp of lust. The longer he delayed deepening his butterfly touch, the hotter her flesh burned for it. She swallowed squeals of frustration. Too strong to dislodge and too enraged to oblige her stifled pleas, the colossus breathing in the crook of her neck was not the indulgent lover of last night, anticipating her every desire and deftly answering her every need. This was comeuppance for her treachery, quid pro quo for the undeserved maltreatment of him, for the pain administered to his trusting heart and to his body, and for the insults she kept lobbing in his face.

Renée shut her eyes and wheeled her thoughts away from the gentle battering her ramparts were undergoing. A conciliatory attitude was called for until the how to clap him in chains again was revealed to her. It was the last lucid thought in her head. Pleasure whammed her as the slow fingers slid deeper, parting the florets, and rubbed her slippery, throbbing flesh to blissful relief. She cried with helpless excitement as his thumb circled the seat of her delight with tantalizing patience intended to prologue her climactic, gratifying convulsions, rendering her soft and pliant for his designs. Oh, this was heresy. Her faithless body, enchanted with a lustful vampire, melted in anticipation of ravishment; her overemotional mind filled with wonder and yearning.

Michael groaned at the dewy invitation. He spread the warm moisture around her corolla, making her crave his ultimate possession. He plunged two long fingers inside her and hooked them to stroke an astoundingly, marvelously tender spot. Sweetness welled up in her with shuddering force. Bubbles eddied and rippled and burst in a radiant unending flow of contentment. Her inner muscles fluttered and pulsed around his fingers, the rapturous sensation saturating her whole being. His thumb swirled around her little hill of Venus, pressing, insisting, and swiftly milking another whirlpool of jolting pleasure that shot to the tips of her hair and fingernails. She fizzed and juddered, sobbing as the glow descended upon her.

"Not willing?" He lifted his glistening hand to her view, resting his chin on her arm. "What would you call this?" Heat brightened his eyes. He pressed his fingers to his nose, inhaling deeply. His bold, unapologetic carnality shocked her, thrilled her. "Your natural perfume intoxicates me, did you know that? The scent of your desire betrays you every time I come near you, Renée."

"Then we are both betrayed," she whispered dolorously. "You are a vampire."

Hurt and frustration etched his eyes. He moved back and knocked her legs apart, shoving his knees between them. His forcefulness left her vulnerable and exposed. She pulled her tied wrists to her mouth and tugged on the knot with her teeth. He was always tying her. "Hoo!" She gasped when he hoicked up her bottom, positioning her on her hands and knees. He yanked her rearward and climbed off the bed to stand behind her. Holding her thighs, he sultrily kissed her derrière.

"Michael! You shameless, licentious lunatic, release me!"

"I am not nearly done with you yet, my lush love delicacy." He playfully bit her bottom and laughed at her fulminating yelps. He splayed his hand on her back and gently pushed to arch her spine so that her bottom thrust upward. He clasped her thighs, knelt down, and put his mouth to the flower of her sex. Squeaks of mortified excitement trilled her throat as he sucked the river of fire between her legs. He opened her with his fingers to grant him better access and rumbled like a bear lapping at a bowl of honey. His tongue rasped, licked, and titillated her Venus sweetness, plying her profoundest pleasure points with unerring, unhurried proficiency. She sagged, burying her hot face in her tied wrists, yielding to the sinful sensations like an epicurean sultan indulging his appetites at an extravagant feast of rare delicacies served on jeweled gold plate. Liquid heat flowed and shone through her as he suckled and pleasured her with tender skill.

He went at her untiringly, determined to extract her ultimate capitulation; soft lips kissing, tongue flicking, swirling, and playing with all her needful spots. He pushed her higher, brought her so close, and then eased her down again. The heat pooling in her belly condensed into a tight, pulsing ball of fire; then it swelled and blazed into a gigantic cannonball. She begged for mercy.

Michael shoved a clever finger inside her, lit the fuse, and the gun went off, explosively. Hot, concentrated pleasure spurted through her, drenching her mind and body, wrenching jarring tremors of swift, intense, delicious contentment from the epicenter of her being, a fluid torrent of luxurious delight. She vibrated in pure, mindless abandon, peaking and falling like tidal waves.

"Whoa . . ." Michael murmured in awe. "Volcano of honey."

Renée collapsed on the bed, boneless and satiated, vivid colors swimming before her eyes.

Michael looped his arm around her waist and hefted the soft, quivering lump of wetness that she was higher up the bed. He divested himself of his shirt and slops and climbed in beside her. He flipped her onto her back, undid her bindings, scattered kisses on her sweaty cheeks, eyelids, and lips, and sank in between her thighs, opening them wide apart. He lay atop her, damp and hot. "My fey love goddess," he whispered. "No man will love you as I do. It is impossible, a fact of nature. Remember this when you see your painter again."

In her senseless lassitude, she felt the thick, blunt head of his turgid penis prodding her sex. She mumbled a feeble plea for peace, but he ignored it. His hand reached down between them to lightly tease the little hill of Venus into granting him admittance. It was wholly unnecessary. Her body, lubricious and supple from his erotic, all-dissolving lovemaking, played lascivious traitor; she could do naught but succumb to the imposed intoxication of the senses. She wrapped her arms and legs around him and kissed his mouth. It was a long, aching, deep, and tender kiss.

A kiss of peace.

She felt him blaze with longing as he glided heavily, slickly into her molten sheath, all the way to the root. He was a firebrand, hard and immense, within her. Squeezing her muscles against the invasion amplified her enjoyment, and his. He pulled out and thrust in, impaling her slowly, deeply, stirring and stroking her into a mewling, trembling, muddled tangle of sensations all over again. He took her with maddening ease, staring into her eyes. She undulated harder, spurring him with her body, with aching insistence, demanding more, panting and clawing for release.

He captured her mouth, his hot tongue plundering and dueling with hers. His motion became fast and furious, a charge. Lance couched, muscles taut, he slammed into her, joining her in the wild storm. Her insides coiled into a tight, throbbing fist. The vortex pulling, pulling . . .

Michael growled in savage torment. The sound, feral and ominous, made her open her eyes. His eyes were silvery, his fangs long and sharp. A scream of terror clogged her throat but would not come out. The bottle in his sporran was empty; she had checked. The sun would rise any moment now. It was his time. They stared at each other, unmoving.

Michael was still lodged deep inside her, his skin awash with sweat, burning with fever. Agony furrowed his face. He radiated pain. He cupped her chin and brushed her tangled mass of hair off the side of her neck. Panic possessed her. "No, Michael . . . Do not . . ."

"I am sorry . . . Do not hate me. . . ." He shifted her chin aside. His breath fanned the vulnerable hollow of her neck; his tongue licked her frantic pulse.

Shaking with unspent passion, with apprehension, she recognized his words as her own.

His reprisal.

Renée strained, cried, and wiggled, but he would not stop. And she knew: in treating him as a vampire she had unleashed the vampire. Steeling herself for the excruciating pain, she shut her eyes on a silent prayer. She felt cool pressure slowly invade her neck. There was no pain. Blood jetted from her vein straight into his receptive, sucking maw, and a surge of delicious heat jolted her, flooded the pit of her stomach, rekindling her desire to blazing intensity, divine delirium. . . .

A pleasing madness or rapture? she wondered hazily. *Passion. This is passion.*

Michael moved inside her, plunging and sliding, feeding her passion as he fed on her blood, groaning his contentment. She lost all touch with the present. Intense pleasure rushed and pounded through her, plangent surf of rippling, explosive rapture, gathering force, soaring . . . and finally crashing. She crested brighter, higher, farther, a star in the heavens, iridescent, lightless, languorously floating adrift on a shimmering sea of unimaginable bliss, stardust, and dreams.

❧ 26 ❧

We are ashes and shadows.

—Horace: *Odes*

The bloodlust emerged with a roar, worse than before. In the space of several heartbeats—an eternity—Michael had become a raging, ravening vampire, vacant of thought, driven by instinct, with a single bridling impulse to gentle his assault on Renée's neck.

But then the pleasure . . . heady sweetness, luscious heat, divinity flooded and engulfed him in a tremendous, continuous flow of delight, its force, duration, and intensity the stuff of dreams.

Renée's blood filled his mouth with delicious richness. He was inside her mind, her body, an omniscient god merging with his goddess. They were one, her pleasure equaling and nourishing his own. Her long-drawn-out climax milked his all-consuming, wrenching release, blowing him apart, depleting his powers. He felt spent and replete at the same time. *Blissful.*

Michael flopped aside and pulled her petite, strong body into his embrace.

"Michael," she murmured, bewildered, wiggling closer. "You did not hurt me."

It did not diminish his guilt. He stared at the beams, ashamed. He never thought he would do that to her. His threats had not been spoken with intent. The full realization of what he was finally sank in. He was a vampire, doomed to walk the earth in the dark, an outsider, feared and despised, alone, for centuries upon centuries. The sun was rising. Renée was fast asleep.

Michael marveled that Renée should sleep peacefully in his arms, her back nestled against his chest, after he had abused her petal-soft body, gorging himself on her like a grisly swine.

A foul, blood-sucking, ravishing monster.

Two hours later, his body still pulsated like a plucked bowstring vibrating into place.

Careful not to wake her, he swept her fragrant ebony locks aside and examined the bite mark he had inflicted on her delicate neck. Not as awful as he had imagined. Bless the gods. A pair of tiny bodkin holes, not gruesome, not the craters Ferdinand had left on his victims. Extraordinary, he thought, that even in his blood-thirsting rampage, the instinct to protect her—even from his vengeful, humiliated, despicable, unnatural self—had overridden aught else.

Still, it did not diminish his terrible guilt.

"You bit me," she murmured drowsily, wakening.

"I am sorry." His voice was gruff with remorse. He felt abashed.

"Do not be a hypocrite. Your voice is hoarse from shouting your pleasure."

Michael flushed hotly. Merely thinking about it was having an embarrassing effect on the part of his anatomy lodged against the enticing cleft of her perfect, lush bottom. He pulled away. She stopped him, lifting his hand to her lips. "Do not leave me. I—I enjoyed it."

He kissed her milky cheek. "I know, but I should not have bled you. Never again."

"Do not speak promises you cannot keep. How will you survive the rest of the crossing?"

"You are my warden. I thought you might have a few sheep stowed aboard."

"Your pardon." She craned her head, chuckling. "I neglected to consider your preferred diet when supplying the ship with the necessary provisions. A thoughtless omission on my part."

"Leastways you are joking about it instead of reaching for silver blades."

"You are not angry with me anymore. I feel . . . you have forgiven me. This makes me smile."

"I forgave you when you would not stab me to death despite my goading threats. Besides"—he grinned—"lovers' quarrels are a renewal of love."

Her gemlike eyes widened in accusation. "You were testing me? Michael! You are a fiend! Certes, you knew you had the power to break free any moment."

He pondered it. "I would not have been able to free myself in time had you been unhesitant."

She scrutinized him closely. Her eyes darkened at the truth she found. "You wanted to die."

He averted his gaze, lovingly combing his fingers through her soft, scented tresses.

"Michael, you must come to terms with what you are. Your condition is unalterable."

"I know." He sailed his hand along her nude, silken body, marveling at the perfect dips and rises. He could linger over her forever and not have enough. "You need to take me back, Renée."

Gloominess etched her enchanting violet eyes. "You do not want to come with me?"

"As a husband?" he challenged her doubtingly. "A lover? A fool? Your painter's apprentice, perhaps? Tell me, what role do you see me play in your life?"

"A friend?" the sharp-witted malapert bandied instantly, her courtier's visor in place.

His heart, emaciated after last night's revelations, shriveled some more. Softly he recited:

> *"No beauty could be better wrought.*
> *When to bed she's blithely brought,*
> *Happy for him who knows her thought,*
> *That creature fair!*
> *But well I know she loves me not,*
> *To my despair."*

His hand, cushioning her cheek, moistened. "You cry, marmoset? I am the one within rights to shed tears over our star-crossed fate. You have forfeited your entitlement."

"You are an immortal vampire," she said poignantly. "I am a woman with a little lifetime. What future do we have together? And supposing we stay like this, how long before you notice I am withering before your very eyes? Years from now, you will still be young and beautiful as you are today, and I will be an old crone with white hair. Would you have an Adele for a wife?"

He could never transform her to be like him, suffer his fate, even if she asked him to, which she clearly did not. "Young, old, rich, poor, healthy, ill, I do not care. You are my heart, Renée."

"When I die, you will go on living. Your happiness cannot depend entirely upon me."

"That is my predicament. Not yours." He would not live a day after her.

"Vampires cannot sire children. I want babies. Will you hire out peasants to breed me?"

"No," he stated vehemently, the idea of her with another man so hateful to him that he spoke without thinking. Her logic wrecked him, though. She was right. "We have no future."

"We have the present." She flipped around, pushed him to his back, and slithered atop him. His hands cruised along the graceful curve of her back and cupped her bottom. She flung her hair back and leaned in to kiss him. Her soft, moist kiss stilled his heart. He rolled on top of her and kissed her, exploring her honeyed mouth, soothing his despair in her clinging embrace. He had two options: abduct her or leave her at her port of destination. He would not subject himself to the torture of watching her reunite with her painter. He might as well use her vicious silver dirk on himself straightaway. As for abducting her, a dream he would save for the cold, dark, endless nights ahead, for he could never deprive her of the joy of motherhood.

"How long does it take to reach France?" he asked.

"Sometimes days, sometimes weeks, depends on the weather."

"Then we have no time to spare." He pushed down along her lithe, delectable body and gave her stuff to dream about and wallow in for the entire duration of the little lifetime she planned on spending with her plaguey artist.

Renée sent a scouting hand over the wrinkled sheet and found no warm muscle to caress. She sat up with a start. Her gaze located Michael at the porthole, brooding at the waves splashing by. He stood at an ominously rigid stance, legs braced apart, muscles taut, arms folded across his chest, his naked, suntanned, gorgeous body silhouetted against the vivid purplish hues of sunset.

Badly in need of nourishment, she polished off the last sweet cake left on the platter on the bedside console and drained a flagon of Bordeaux, commenting on Cardinal Medici's caravel, a floating luxury, furnished in antique Italianate style with silk hangings and lacquered fixtures.

"Michael?" she said when a while had passed and her chatter left him unresponsive.

"I have changed my mind." His voice was frigid. Not a hair on his head stirred. "We are not sailing to France. We are returning to England."

"You jest! I escaped that island by the skin of my teeth. I am still not out of the dark wood yet. Nor will I be until I deliver the Ancient."

"I opened the silver box."

"What?" She leaped from the bed, got tangled in the sheet, and would have splashed across the floorboards if Michael had not whooshed to her rescue, frightening the dust on the furniture. Grateful though she was, she would never get used to his moving like a gust of air.

As soon as he steadied her, he returned to his former vantage point. She went to search her cloak-bag. The box was gone. "God spare you, Michael, what did you do with it?"

"I hid it where you will never find it."

Cold panic gripped her. "Please tell me you did not toss it over-board!"

"I did not toss it overboard. Are you not interested to know what I found inside the box?"

She glared at his broad, uncompromising back. "Well?" She

dreaded to hear his response. If he told her the box contained air, she would toss herself overboard.

"Tell me how they recruited you first."

His attitude harried her. "Why are you so cold and hostile to me?"

He was silent for a long count. "You speak in your sleep."

"You are not making sense," she muttered. "Tell me what you found in the box."

"You moaned," he uttered sternly. "You said . . ."

She lost her patience. "What the devil did I say to make you so disagreeable?"

"Raphael."

Merde. Renée drew up behind his formidable frame. She caressed the arrogant backbone. His skin was warm velvet beneath her gliding hands. "It was my conscience speaking," she said softly. "He is rotting in a rat-infested dungeon while I am losing myself in you." She pressed her mouth to his shoulder, indulging her sensual infatuation with his body, and slid her hands around his waist to splay them over the fretwork of hard sinew shaping his torso. She rose on tiptoe and kissed the dip of heady scents and smoothness beneath the gilt spun ribands. "I am enraptured by you," she breathed. "Can you not tell?"

He peeled her hands from his body. "You would say anything, do anything, to convince me to give you back the Ancient."

Smiling at his grumpiness, she rubbed her cheek against his shoulder blade like a pleasure-seeking cat. She had never had a man throw a jealous fit of temper over her. But his resentment could cost her a great deal, everything! So she did the most uncharacteristic thing. She told him her life history, leading up to their encounter in the undercroft at King Henry's court.

Michael listened attentively, riveted, asking questions, commenting. Every little detail drew a response from him—a frown, a sound, a smile, nods, remarks. He truly, wholeheartedly cared.

She could see in his eyes that he was committing everything to memory, the epitaph of her he would carry in his heart and mind for centuries henceforward.

The idea of him left alone in the world saddened her beyond belief.

"You need protection," he said when she finished her narration. "And an ace in your sleeve. They may renege on their promises, and you will be left with nothing. The *deletoris* serve the cardinal. The duchies are within your king's realm. Your sister is powerless. Soubise is a swine and a danger that needs to be disposed of. And your painter is a spineless nobody."

She smiled knowingly. "Are you implying I need you?"

He shrugged. "You do not want me, but you still need protection, an advantage, something wherewith to force their hand."

"The Ancient."

"Cardinal Medici told you it is a powerful weapon against vampires. Maybe there is more, a card to renegotiate with. Why hand it over to him without looking inside, blithely, trustingly? Do not think I am selfishly trying to manipulate you. I am speaking my mind. Yes, I should like to unlock the Ancient's secrets. Yes, I think you have much to gain as well. Therefore, I propose a bargain. Let us return to England, investigate this thing, find illumination. Possession is yours. No tricks. We will collaborate as partners, hopefully find answers, and afterward, you leave with the Ancient to France. I stay behind and confront mine own demons. We part in friendship."

His integrity and sharp intelligence were rare and precious qualities, but his complete lack of guile in all his dealings with her won her over, shook her world. He kept proving, over and over again, that her well-being was his primary concern. "I trust you." The admission burst out of her. "And I do not trust anyone!" she admitted. "I feel I can be truthful with you, as I have not been with another living soul, aside from Adele and the queen my mother who knew me as a girl."

His eyes were sorrowful, guilt-ridden. "You trust me, after what I did to you?"

"Even in your bloodlust you were my ever-gentle vampire." Feelings gushed from a deep, forgotten place inside her, whirling and bursting, pouring out, flooding, uncontainable, watery. "Aristophanes tells us that humans were created with four arms, four legs, and a single head made of two faces, and that Zeus, fearful of their power, split them all in half, condemning them to spending their lives . . . "

"Searching for the other half to complete them," Michael finished solemnly.

Jesu. All she saw were his eyes, honest and adoring. The feelings kept gushing like a spring. Thoughts, dreams, fears, hurts . . . She dissolved. Soul-wrenched sobs racked her body. Her face pressed into Michael's chest; his arms came around her, cloaking her with strength and warmth.

The crying went on forever. She could not stanch the downpour of emotional upheaval. He lifted her in his arms, her limbs twining around him like a vine, and sat down on the bed, holding and soothing her patiently as she exhausted herself. It was a cleansing. Refuse and rubbish fell away, leaving her small, bright, and weepy. She rubbed her face against his neck. She wanted to live in this warm nook, hide here forever, never emerge. She felt cherished and precious and safe.

By the time she raised her head, Michael was slippery wet with her tears. She tightened the clasp of her arms and legs around him. "I love you with all of my heart and soul," she confessed to him and to herself. She had fallen in love with him. When had that happened? Gradually, from the start. *My soul mate, my love mate, my truth. Do not leave me. Never leave me.*

"Never," he promised, burrowing his face against her hair.

When Renée finally found the will and fortitude to lift her face from his shoulder and tackle the world, she was moistly smeared with all the humors of her eyes and nose. Michael grabbed the edge of the sheet and wiped her clean, as one would a child. He smiled. "Pretty baby."

She cupped his face, sought his sea-hued eyes for foul falseness, found none, and kissed him deeply, mellifluously. "I am preposterously stupid," she whispered in between indulgent kisses.

"There is nothing preposterous about you. You were brought up in a world of suffocating intrigue and deceit. You were clever and knew how to negotiate the web woven by your father. The price, however, was steep. Your pelt thickened protectively, and you disappeared within."

"Why, Michael." She smiled bemusedly. "How insightful of you!"

"You told me everything. Your words. Your feelings."

"My Ancient," she reminded him pertly. "Where did you conceal it, vampire?"

"Look beneath your pillow, witch."

She did not leave her perch in his lap. She enjoyed holding him, kissing his face. "Tell me."

He fell back on the bed and reached beneath her pillow. Still holding her, he sat up. She took the cloth-wrapped box from his hand and dispensed with the covering. Masterfully wrought, the silver box depicted the story of St. Michael slaying the Serpent. "One would think it belongs to you, or that you were meant to have it," she said. "St. Michael, the Serpent slayer."

"You are forgetting, sweetheart, that I am the Serpent in the fable. Captain Luzio of Cardinal Campeggio's body of *deletoris* told me about the she-devils and their Vesper babies."

"Cardinal Medici enlightened me about that, as well. Oh, but there is no lid. How did you open it? Ah, I see. The box is covered with argent dots. The combination, how did you divine it? Did the box hum the cipher key to you?"

"Something like that." He grinned. "I guessed. Look, the angel has four dots. I decided that he was the positive character in the fable and therefore has the key."

"He has two on his face, one over his heart, and one in his hand."

"Right. So I thought: mouth for breath, for soul, then heart for blood, for spirit, then brow for thought, for truth, and then hand for strength, for duty."

She tried it—and an invisible lid popped open. "Michael! You are stupendously clever!"

He shrugged. "Mayhap you were right and the box hummed to me. I cannot fathom how—"

"You may have been inspired, but your gumption did the rest." A trifle frightened, she lifted the lid with reverence. She set the box aside and took out the shiny bale of metal that lay inside. "This is the Ancient, a metal scroll? How peculiar. I thought it might be the relics of a saint. When we were in Wolsey's chapel, for a moment I thought the statue would come to life and that Our Lord and Our Lady would lift and embrace me."

"Actually, it is quite brilliant, this thing, and I suspect very old. This is copper, soft metal, easily rolled, long-lasting, and I can touch it. It needs warming before unfurling lest it breaks. Fire will melt it, though. Here, I will warm it with my hands for you."

"You did not open it? You waited for me?" She stared at him in astonishment. Beautiful, kind, compassionate, bright, truthful, courageous, a sweet lover . . . "You are an angel."

"Vampire, honeymouse. Half demon, half human. Be not confused."

The roll, sufficiently heated, unfurled of its own volition. "Strange markings," Renée observed. "What do you suppose they are? A cryptic language?"

Michael examined the scroll. "I have seen such markings before. . . ."

"Where? You must remember! I know your memory is frayed—"

Michael rubbed the gold ring on his forefinger. "I do remember. In my lord's library."

"Oh." Her enthusiasm diminished. "It is a vampiric language."

"No, it is not. And I know just the person who might be able to interpret it for us."

❧ 27 ❧

May you arise from my bones,
O my unknown avenger!

—Virgil: *Aeneid*

King Henry scrubbed his chin with the heavily jeweled left hand—a very bad sign. Suddenly the hand slammed on the table, jacking the councilors out of their chairs and the bearers of the terrible tidings to the corner of the chamber. "This is disastrous! An army of demons?"

"A small one, Your Majesty," stammered Sir Walter Devereaux. The king gave him a blank look, as if surprised that the wall had spoken, and Sir Francis Bryan gave him a silencing nudge.

King Henry's damning glare swerved toward Wolsey with a pointed jeweled finger. "This is your doing! You and your gouty friend from Rome—you brought them here!"

Cardinal Wolsey, of a mind that hosting the entire panicky court in his newfangled palace of Hampton Court was sufficient penance, dutifully bowed his impenitent head. The Ancient was gone, stolen along with his future as pope. His king's fury barely tickled his own supreme rage.

The Duke of Buckingham cleared his throat. "We should rally troops with all speed and meet this army—"

"Where?" the king demanded brusquely. "For aught we know they may land on this roof!"

The Duke of Norfolk, pleased to see his rival squirming at the king's rebuke, said, "Cardinal Campeggio's abrupt leave-taking has left us somewhat in the lurch. However, it has come to my attention that while in my Lord Chancellor's residence at York Place, Campeggio's special army of vampire destroyers had bestowed some goodly training in supernatural warfare on His Grace's yeomen of the guard. Perhaps His Grace would kindly consent to lend us his expert troops. . . ."

That drew blood. Wolsey cursed the ancient duke. It was his line! Scheduled to be delivered at the opportune moment; after all the noddies made their unhelpful utterances and no solution was in the offing, he was to sweep in and save the day. The odious Norfolk, preempting him, put him in the worst light possible. He smiled at the king. "I would not have it any other way, Your Majesty! My Lord Norfolk was stating the obvious." *God rot his soul!*

"Why are they coming?" King Henry demanded in rhetorical fashion, as if addressing the Almighty. "What do they want with us?"

"Your Majesty, if I may." Sir Walter Devereaux took a step toward the table. "I have reason to believe that they are coming for Sir Michael Devereaux, although I cannot fathom why."

Wolsey could. They wanted the Ancient! Clearly his ill-chosen protégé had turned rogue vampire *and* was still in London, possibly with his princess. Ergo, the demons were not planning a bloodsucking fest along the Thames. They were hunting down one of their own.

If Wolsey ran the rogue to the ground before the vampires did, he would set up a trap for the entire vampire horde, obliterate the lot of them at a blow, and reclaim the Ancient—and with it the promised chair of St. Peter. Certes, finding a vampire who did not want to be found was no easy feat; his own kind, equipped with better snouts, saw fit to descend in numbers. Then again, Wolsey knew something that the vampires did not: Michael Devereaux was in love. It was a good thing that Wolsey possessed just the snout to sniff out French princesses.

They were back in London.

Renée was beside herself with misgivings. Her soles burned upon the ground, as though she were treading brimstone. Only Michael's hand, reassuringly squeezing hers, lent her courage. Guised in black cloaks complete with cowls, drawn low over their eyes, they were accompanied by her dutiful *deletoris*. The Ancient was concealed inside the breast of Michael's doublet.

"This is the house," he said, surveying the dark, run-down abode meanly situated between a tavern and London Bridge on the bankside of the Southwark stews.

Bawdy laughter, lewd women, boisterous drunks, and glittering lights ruled every lane. Only the sad little house, ensconced in a nook, seemed to frown at and recoil from the vulgar revelry.

Michael sought her hooded gaze. "Sweetheart, shall we knock?"

She gave a brisk nod and walked with him to the door. The old man who invited them inside the dusty, cluttered house and offered them wine was pleasantly surprised to see Michael.

"My dear boy, come in, come in. And who might this be? Your lady, Sir Michael?"

With a radiant smile, Michael locked his arms around her. "My lady love, Abraham. Behold the light of my life, the best of mine, the chatelaine of my heart and soul."

"I am an old man but can still appreciate your devoted attachment to this lovely creature. Welcome to my humble residence, my lady. Please, be seated."

Abraham Wiseman, Michael had told her, was a lone fugitive *marrano* from Spain. He had sheltered Michael after his poor mother had died. Michael had confided in her all about his early years in the stews, recent discoveries of his. They had no secrets between them, not anymore.

The days and nights spent in the luxury hold on the ship had been the best of her life. Glittering magical moments. They shared confidences, made love, laughed at silly things, ate, slept, and at dawn he would inexorably wake her to feed the untamed shade lurking inside him. Ever gentle, he apologized for his thirst with sweet, easy lovemaking and held her tenderly in his arms for hours afterward. It was easy to forget that a whole world of dangers lay beyond their little haven. Yet she was unable to ignore the gloominess Michael hid behind a careful visor of optimism. He was aching inside. This afternoon, when he made love to her be-

fore they left the ship, he was fire, reducing her to a state of forget-
fulness of all save him, taking her with a passion so raw and desperate that she felt as if he were conveying a message he dared not
put into words.

It felt as though he were saying good-bye.

On their way over, they had made a stop at Westminster Abbey
to see Christopher and the two servants. Michael assured them
that all was well and that he would be returning to collect them
soon. His promise had not assuaged Renée's steadily escalating sense
of foreboding.

"How may I serve you?" Abraham inquired when they were sitting at his table, sipping sweet wine of excellent quality. Abraham,
Renée suspected, was richer than his living suggested.

"Abraham, I need must ask you to perform an act of kindness to
me," Michael said. "But I should warn you first. My very presence
in your house endangers your well-being. I have become a hunted
man, a pariah among my fellow Englishmen, a creature to be slain.
I shan't imperil you further by narrating the events that have led to
this dismal situation. Suffice it to say that your refusal will be understood and forgiven. I will not take offense. I—"

"Enough waffling, dear boy, I am for you, one pariah to another,
one hunted soul reaching out to his fellow man in need. Pray tell
me how I may ease your burden."

Michael produced the red metal scroll, warmed it between his
hands, and let it unfurl on the baize cloth covering the untidy
worktable. "Can you translate this document for me?"

Abraham brought the candlestick closer, leaned in, squinted at
the odd lettering. He recoiled, expression thunderous. Black eyes,
sharp as burning ambers, stared at Michael. "Do you know what
this is?"

Renée slid her icy hand into Michael's under the table. Warm
fingers wrapped around hers.

Michael sustained Abraham's gaze. "Hebrew."

Abraham's voice was a faint murmur. Tears trembled in his eyes.
"The last time I saw these letters was eight days after the birth of
my son. We sealed his covenant with God in a ceremony in an under-

ground cellar by a single candlelight. We whispered. I read the blessing . . ."

Renée's throat constricted. The yawning pain the old man emanated filtered through her skin like the heat and smoke and stench of the church fires, burning God's creatures in the name of God. Religion, Lucretius lamented, had been able to lead men to commit so many evils.

"If this is too difficult for you," Michael began gently.

Abraham drew a shuddering breath. "Let me see." He absorbed himself in the document. His eyes lifted. "Good God, Michael! This is no tally stick. Have you a notion what you have here?"

Michael grinned sheepishly. "If we did, we would not be here."

"This . . ." Abraham's hands floated over the scroll reverently, not touching. He read: "'We, the White Sicarii of the Hebrews of Jerusalem and of Qumran, Soldiers of God, vanquishers of Evil, do commit the truth of our war against Darkness and the children of Darkness, spawned into this world by means of foulness and trickery, to the safekeeping of our offspring and their issue in the time of the greatest of all upheavals.'" He swallowed. "Titled *The Last Testament*."

Renée shivered, gooseflesh all over, and burrowed closer up to Michael. Immediately he put his arm around her, nestling her against his heat. "How old is it, do you suppose?"

Abraham puffed out air. "Older than Our Lord Christ, methinks. Shall I continue?"

"Please."

"'In pure soul, true heart, sound mind, and strong hand, faithful servants of *Aur Ain Soph*, Limitless Light, Light Without End . . .' They mean the God of the Hebrews, Michael. 'We who are sworn to sweep the world created unto us of Devourers, Evil Demons of Matter and the shells of the Dead, breed of the One Adorned With Fire, who seek to waste the substance and thought of Creation, and their creatures, Those Who Go Forth into the Place Empty of God, commend the Sword of Justice of the Angel Who Is Like God . . .' The angel's name translates to Michael in English. 'Branded with the blood of *Shedim* . . .' They mean shade, devils.

'To help protect the faithful against the powers of these spirits henceforward . . .' The document is long."

"Can you summarize it for us?" Michael asked.

"Yes, of course. Be advised, though. These are the secrets within the secrets of the Hebrew faith. They define the inner meaning and the significance of all things. To know this may put you in graver danger than you already are, for it may incur the wrath of God and of the Evil One."

Michael sought Renée's gaze. "You decide, honeymouse. Your possession."

You are the inner meaning and the significance of all things for me, her mind whispered to him with all the love in her heart. "You need to know, Michael. Let us go on."

"Well, then." Abraham paused to read some more. "They tell us that God created the world through Ten Utterances, ten divine perfections, called *Sephirot*, that illuminate the divine plan as it unfolds in the process of creation. At the same time, the world received ten shells, primeval husks of impurity and evil forces, called *Qeliphot*. The process takes place with perfect parallels, listed here. Then they tell us that as God tempted Adam with Eve, so did Satan tempt Adam with Lilith, a demon queen. Their ungodly union bred a creature called Night Spirit."

Renée looked at Michael. *Vesper.*

"This creature is half man and half demon, a living dead, with a soul, a body, but bereft of spirit to bind the soul to the body. Hence it must steal the spirit of man, which flows in his veins, the blood of man. The White Sicarii narrate their longtime war against this creature and its creatures. There were more, as the demon queen sent her, well, ladies-in-waiting to tempt other men and fill the world with their evil eggs. In retribution for the havoc they had wreaked, God cleansed the world of all the she-demons but one, the queen who hid. It is said of her, 'Her house sinks down to death, her gates are gates of death, she wanders at night, vexing the sons of men.'"

"We know the story of the angel Michael and the she-dragon. Pray go on."

"The she-demons were destroyed. Their blood-sucking children remained. The White Sicarii hunted them down for ages and destroyed all but ten, who fled into the unknown in the shape of night mist. Now comes the part of the sword. The archangel Michael appeared before the leader of the White Sicarii. He bestowed him with the bloody Sword of Justice that had slain Lilith and commanded him to conceal it well so that future generations would have the ultimate weapon to fight the ten night spirits who had vanished should they resurface in the world. The White Sicarii melted the Sword, bespotted with the queen-demon's blood, and created this document from it."

"A sword of copper, not silver," Michael said, bemused. "Mysterious."

"How does one recreate the sword?" Renée asked pragmatically.

"Ah, here is the thing, one does not. The power of the Sword can be extracted. Once. It will manifest in the extractor. He will become the Sword of Justice. And the scroll will lose the power. But there is a proviso. The Sword was tinctured with the queen-demon's blood. Hence, the extractor must have the blood of the night spirits flowing in his veins. It is a Divine Test. The extractor must be chosen with special care. He must revere the ten divine perfections, none of the ten impurities. If the extractor is impure, or is Night Spirit, mankind will perish. The archangel Michael is depicted as the Great Prince Who Stands Up for the Children of God. The bearer of his sword is expected to follow this legacy, protect the men and women created in God's image."

"An oxymoron," Michael stated. "A night spirit that is not Night Spirit, loyal to mankind, not to its kind."

"No, it is not." Renée commanded his gaze. "The Night Spirits are the Vespers. You are not a Vesper."

Reading her intention, Michael grew pale.

"Michael, do not balk. If your lord comes looking for this, you have to be prepared. He is so powerful. You told me that I needed an advantage, a card of ace. Now I tell you the same. You need the Sword."

"If I do this, if it is at all possible, then you will return to France with a worthless scroll. Do you honestly think I would countenance your putting yourself in mortal danger?"

"I am not returning to France."

Michael took her face in his hands. "Yes, you are. What life will you have with me? Always on the run. I cannot return to Ireland, I have lost my place at court. Cardinal Campeggio will call for a crusade against me. I will have to go into hiding. How will I protect you? What life will you have with me, my sweet princess?"

"So it is true. You planned to leave me. I felt it." Her eyes pooled with tears.

"I love you. I want you to have a worthy, secure life, with a home and babes. Abraham"—he turned to their avid spectator—"what sort of life may a refugee expect?"

"Fear of darkness, destitution, loneliness, shame."

Her spirit rebelled. "No, listen well. Extract the power of the Sword, Michael, vanquish your foes, win glory, and you shall have love. For love and glory, the ultimate triumph."

He was thinking. "Abraham, please list the ten divine perfections."

Abraham's eyes twinkled. "I should like to state that I concur with your lady. Well. The first perfection is *Crown*, the power of the Creator; two is the Power of Wisdom; three, the Power of Love—understanding, repentance, reason; four, the Power of Vision—mercy, grace; five, the Power of Intention—judgment, strength, determination; six, Creative Power—symmetry, balance and compassion; seven, the Power of the Eternal Now—contemplation, persistence, initiative; eight, the Power of the Intellect and Observation—surrender, sincerity, and steadfastness; nine, the Power of Manifesting—foundation, wholly remembering, coherent knowledge; and ten, the Power of Healing and of Accomplishment—kingdom, physical presence, vision, and illusion."

"And the ten impurities?" Michael demanded.

"One, Satan—Adversary King; two, Confusion of the Power of God—wickedness; three is Concealment of God—darkness; four, One of the Flock—wastefulness; five, the Destroying God—fire, the burning of bodies; six, Lord of the Dead—those bellow grief and tears; seven, Ravens of the Burning of God—makers of sharp weapons; eight, the Desolation of God—filth and displeasure; nine, Night Specter—vileness; and ten, Whisperers—sorcery."

"Michael." Renée gripped his doublet. "You can do it. You have none of those impurities."

"How does one go about extracting the power?" Michael asked Abraham. "Does it say?"

Abraham concentrated. "No, I cannot find instructions. You must divine it yourself."

They fell silent. Then Michael asked Abraham to read some more and repeat the ten good and bad qualities. "Why is ten the repetitive number?" Renée asked. "Surely it is significant."

Abraham raised his hands. "Ten fingers. It is the number of creation."

"Ten fingers!" Renée exclaimed. "Place your hands on the scroll and see if aught happens."

Michael did as she suggested. His hands flew up as he gave a hissing breath. "It burned me. I told you the thing hates me."

Abraham eyed the scroll. "Try to place each finger on the ten names of the good qualities. Here, I will show you: Crown, Wisdom, Love, Mercy . . ."

This time, only Michael's right hand came up. "It scorched my finger."

"Just one finger?" Abraham asked. "Which one? Ah, the Crown."

"What does it mean?" Renée asked.

Abraham considered Michael. "Are you a faithful Christian?"

"He is pagan," Renée muttered, vexed and despaired. "He does not believe in God."

Michael looked abashed, forlorn. "I was too young when my mother died. My protector was . . . pagan."

Abraham patted his hand. "Come with me."

Abraham led Michael to the window. "Look outside. What do you see?"

Michael stared at the alleys, at the river, at the rooftops, at the sky. "I see night."

"Look wider, higher, see the whole world. What do you see?"

Michael looked but he saw nothing. He was dying inside. After tonight, he would never see her again. It was a vow he had made to himself. To let her go, to give her a fair chance at life. He stared at the sky. Dark blue, clouds. He wanted to growl at . . . "I see night that wraps everything."

"A divine blanket. Good. Now look inside yourself. Deeply as you can. What do you see?"

Nothing. All Tyrone had taught him left him at that moment. All he saw was . . . "Love."

"What color is it?"

"Abraham, your questions . . ." Michael exhaled with exasperation. The love was enormous, colossal. So much love, in a small place, deep inside himself. "Flame. White. Gold. Sunshine."

"Limitless Light?" Abraham asked shrewdly. "Light Without End—would this describe the love you feel inside yourself for your lady?"

"Yes," Michael whispered wretchedly. He felt drained.

"This is God, your God. The dark night that encompasses you, the white light of love you feel and carry inside. The wholeness within and the wholeness beyond. *Ehyeh Asher Ehyeh.* I AM THAT I AM. That is God. Forget the legends, the symbols. You do not ask your mind whether it believes—you feel God here!" Abraham punched himself between heart and stomach.

Michael felt the fist, as if it knocked the air of his own lungs. He breathed deeply. Strength permeated and imbued him with courage. "Again. I will try again."

He returned to his place at the table beside Renée and gathered her into his arms. "Hold me."

She did, filling him, completing him. He tilted her head back, stared into her glittering violet eyes. *So beautiful. His.* Surely God— her Creator—loved him. Holding her head in his hand, he kissed her mouth tenderly. Feelings overflowed. *Surrender. Grace. Generosity.*

When he lifted his head, he felt ready. He drew the scroll closer. Splayed his fingers over the words: *Crown, Wisdom, Love, Mercy, Courage, Balance, Contemplation, Sincerity, Foundation, Kingdom . . .* Bright white light poured through him, flooded him, blinded him.

Visions—fantastic, chaotic, tremendous, colorful, floating—pummeled his brain. Beating. Pain. Roger Vise and the boys kicking his face. Lord Tyrone stepping out of the mist, with silvery eyes and snarling fangs, ripping throats, drinking blood, staring down, seeing him. *"Fair little boy, have you a place? No place? Come with me, then."* Rain. Thunder. Ireland. *"Pledge, cleave to me. Do for me as I did for you."* Knife. Blood. Gold cup. Laughter. *"Drink poison from a cup of gold. Laugh if you are wise. Sin strongly. Death is nothing to us."* Pain. *"Let justice be done, even though the heavens fall."* Rain. Irons. Naked on the floor. Cold. Dawn. Burning skin. Fire. Sun.

Michael opened his eyes. "I remember! Everything!" He felt alive, bright and bursting. Free.

Renée and Abraham beheld him in stupefaction, with apprehension.

"What?" Michael asked. He was on his feet. But did not recall rising. "Am I different?"

Renée stood up beside him. She touched his chest, his face. "You are . . . aglow."

He looked at his hands and saw nothing out of the ordinary. "I feel . . . healthy."

"You were shouting. You disappeared in a pillar of blinding white light. The whole house was swallowed by the luminosity. The thick white light burst out from you. We saw nothing but I trow the entire city perceived the powerful radiance. The window is open."

Premonition pounded through him. His lord was coming. The vampires. "We need to go. Abraham." He took the old man's hand in his. "My thanks. You are a true friend."

Renée wrapped the scroll and offered it to him. Michael took it from her hand, opened her cloak, and pushed it in her purse. "Take it to France. My lord is coming. You leave without me. Now." He grabbed her hand and ushered her outside, blocking out her protests.

The *deletoris* were waiting. Renée assured her sergeant that all was well.

"There is no time," Michael insisted. "They are coming." He urged them toward the barge and told them to clamber inside. He drew Renée into his arms. "My sweetheart . . ."

She searched his eyes. "You leave me, Michael? You promised you never would."

"You are leaving me, marmoset. You are returning to your life. I will always be for you. The scroll has no power. Use that if they renege. Take my ring." He shoved his signet ring onto her forefinger. "Remember we were at court one moment and in Wolsey's library the next? I had left the ring there beforehand. So long as you have my ring, I could always reach you in a heartbeat. If you have need of me, just speak it. I will know. Be happy, marmoset. Do not look back." He hugged her tightly and kissed her. "My love is yours for eternity."

"Lovers are mad," she muttered. She wrapped her hands around his neck and meshed their mouths together sweetly, despondently, instilling her heart and soul into the touch of her lips.

He broke them apart and handed her into the barge. Her face was awash with tears.

"Leave now, Renée. Men, take her away."

The river mist sucked the barge into its folds.

Shattered into innumerable, invisible aching pieces, Michael soundlessly recited:

> *I think my heart will break in two*
> *With sighs and care.*
> *With God's own greeting may she go,*
> *So white, so fair!*

"*Michael . . .*" Renée whispered to him. *Be well, be well, my love.*
. . .

Michael stood on the bankside, watching the fog, the river, the night . . .

He felt the instant the vampires arrived.

For the blood that we spilled
For the hero we killed
Toil and woe, toil and woe,
Till the doom is fulfilled!

—P. W. Joyce: *Old Celtic Romances,*
Tales from Irish Mythology:
The Quest for the Eric-Fine

"How far, Michael, will you abuse my patience?" They dropped from the sky in the form of black birds of prey, turning to wolves. His face to the river, his back exposed and surrounded, Michael recalled the old Roman saying: in front a precipice, behind wolves. He whipped around, light-footed, barely touching the ground.

Lord Tyrone, his withered face ashen, gave a bellow that discharged leaves from trees. His clawed hands smashed into Michael's chest. "Thief! Deceiver! Recreant traitor! You fooled me!"

Michael was a rock. "You sent Ferdinand to destroy me. You hurt my feelings."

"You betrayed me, thrall! I made you with my blood, and you stole the Sword! Curse you!" He roared at the dark blue welkin, disturbing the river, battering the rickety brackets hard by.

The wolves transformed into familiar faces: knights, centuries old, silvery eyed, fanged, snarling. An unbeatable army. *I serve those who would have it vanquished.*

A thin whistle cut the wind. *Thud.* A dart hit the back of Michael's thigh. Fire shot through his body. He fell on the ground as a barrage of silver-tipped arrows slammed into the vampires in front of him. They were under attack. From the river. His injured thigh burning like the dickens, he shifted on the ground. True enough, as the mist parted, he saw the longboats slithering closer like giant eels upon the water, lined with archers, knights, men-at-arms. The king's army.

The vampires flitted for shelter. Michael felt a strong hand heft him from the ground. "Come on, get up!" Tyrone growled. He yanked the dart from Michael's thigh and dragged him into an alley. The silver cross-bolts kept pelting them like a hailstorm. Some of the vampires leaped onto the boats, ripping throats, tearing limbs, wielding their fangs and claws better than daggers.

Michael kneaded his wounded thigh. After Renée had stabbed him with silver, he had fallen unconscious for hours. This time his body fought the poison; the burning was ebbing. He stared at his lord, his mentor, the only father he had ever known. "You saved me. Again."

"I sent Sir Ferdinand to watch your back, but his hatred and hunger got the better of him. He decided to take the Sword for himself. Whom Jupiter wishes to destroy, he first makes mad."

"Who will guard the guardians themselves, eh?" Michael said flatly.

"My human body has rotten, my shade powers are fading. I trusted you. You were my hope. The Sword's force would have granted me more centuries. What creature is not thirsty for life?"

"You transformed me in the eyrie the night we supposedly fell ill with the Sweat. Did you bite me, take my blood? It is the one thing I do not recall."

Tyrone smiled. "No, Michael. I gave you *my* blood in a cup of gold. The sun did the rest. I did not want to transform you. You were meant to be human. You lack the ruthlessness necessary to bleed men of life in order to feed your needs and desires. But you were disheartened as Ferdinand basted you right and left. You felt incompetent, unworthy, as most men do when confronted with the superiority of my species. The lessons were learned but not implemented."

"Why did you conceal the truth from me? You sent me out an ignoramus."

"There was no time to apprentice you. The cardinals were about to fight for the Sword. I was wrong to alter my decision at the last moment. I baffled you, fool that I am. But you fathomed the secrets on your own. The powers, the weaknesses, the prize . . ."

"You have walked the earth for centuries, hundreds of years. Whence did you come?"

Tyrone laughed. "Hundreds of years? Thousands, Michael. When the world was pagan and men were illiterate. You took the power, you know the fable."

"You are a Vesper, one of the ten the White Sicarii could not destroy."

"Oh, there were many more of us. Vespers, unlike vampire men, procreate. I came from the land between the rivers Euphrates and the Tigris. I knew not my father, my mother was a spirit. I was like you. We had a purpose on this earth. We were the keepers of wisdom. We immortalized scholars, craftsmen, beauty. Then the Hebrews came with their one jealous God, intolerant of creatures they perceived as foul and ungodly. They understood not our duty. They butchered us, the Romans butchered them, and I fled with my brethren to Regio X on the northeastern border of Italy. We prospered, continued our mission, all was well. Until the pestilent faith spread in a new form: Christianity. They were fanatical slaughterers. Crusaders. The Church had the Sword. War raged between the priests and the empire. The emperor came to me with a bargain. I slay his foes, he delivers the Sword. I trusted him. We fought and nearly won. The new emperor recanted. Instead of fulfilling the promise, he and the pope initiated the Decimation. They were good. They knew our secret weaknesses. Vampire men who had suckled the cross from their mothers' teats were vulnerable. None remained. My brother Vespers were captured by trickery and burned."

"None remained but you, my nameless lord, English but not English."

"My name you cannot pronounce. I live in Spain a year and I am Spanish. My powers you cannot fathom. But you may hear my name. It is . . ." He said his name.

Verily, Michael could not pronounce it. The king's army, having repelled the vampires from the riverbank, was disembarking to sweep the stews clean of the beasts. They were walking into a trap. The vampires were regrouping, shape-shifting, converging, as Tyrone had taught Michael.

"Shall we finish the battle?"

Michael hesitated. "They are the king's men."

"They perceive you as a vampire. You are not one of them anymore. Fight with us."

And then what? Michael wondered. Where would he go? What would he be?

"Return to Ireland with me," Tyrone replied. "We will rebel, throw the English banners to the sea. Finish this war with me, Michael. Take blood. You owe me that."

"The vampires have no quarrel with the king's men. We should leave. Rally them."

"No!" The fangs and the silvery eyes emerged. "Vampires take blood. Fight!"

Michael found himself in the midst of the melee, sword in hand, feinting right and left. The English surpassed the vampires in numbers tenfold but had slim chances of survival. Shadows flashed amongst them, snatching flesh from bone, fanging necks, shredding bodies, devouring, gorging themselves on their victims' blood. Ravening, mindless fiends, they burst into brothels, spreading death, feeding demonically, feverishly, ravaging, plundering, murdering for pleasure.

It was a massacre.

The senseless butchery sickened Michael, but the scent of fresh blood filling his nostrils was a heady inducement for the vampire within. Bloodlust pounded through his veins, embruting his features. *Take blood*, husked a voice in his head. *Feast on the humans. Feed. They are nothing.*

The Great Prince Who Stands Up for the Children of God.

The bearer of the Sword protects the men and women created in God's image.

A body of armored knights pounced on him from every direction. Silver blades slashed his arms and back. His flesh burned. Loath to be overpowered and captured, Michael fought back.

He came up against a burly soldier, silver-suited cap-à-pie. He saw the colors. *Stanley.*

"Hoa!" exclaimed his horrified courtly companion, raising his visor, recognition etching his eyes. Michael felt ashamed. Stanley regarded him curiously. "Friend or foe?"

Michael, aware that his moonstone eyes and sharp fangs were all too visible, was stunned by Stanley's chivalrous address—and in the midst of the carnage. The decision was made. "Friend!"

"Welcome back, runt." Stanley hooked his plated forearm with Michael's sleeved one in a knightly handshake. "Help me find Suffolk. Two fiends pounced on him, and he disappeared."

Michael found His mighty Grace battling two vampires with his back to the Cardinal's Hat Inn. As Stanley rammed into the one on the right, Michael attacked the one on the left. It was Sir Henry, Tyrone's dues collector, silvery eyes glinting. The white power of the Sword quickened inside Michael and shot through his eyes, incinerating the vampire on the spot. *Hoa!* Michael staggered back. The other vampire whipped around. Michael saw the argent eyes— and the white rays shot out again. The vampire collapsed in a heap of ash.

Suffolk, bewildered yet healthy, beheld Michael in astonishment. "God's teeth!"

Michael grinned crookedly. "How now, I am friend—Your Grace?"

"My Grace is friendly, very friendly!" Suffolk laughed, and hooked their forearms as Stanley had done. "Stanley, saw you what I did? God's might, what cheerful fiendishness is this?"

"Aye, my knees have turned to water!" Stanley laughed.

Michael found himself flanked and recruited. "Let us find more vampires to flay," Suffolk proposed merrily. "This lost battle has just become a lot more interesting."

It was. Once Michael had made the choice to protect, he manifested the power of the Sword. The white rays fired with precision at the figures he wanted destroyed. Blades and darts squashed against his body and bounced off. The vampires soon indentified him as their primary adversary. They came at him as wolves, as raptors, as hairy beasts. He eliminated them systematically, and when they fled, he snatched raptors from the sky and ran the absconding wolves to earth.

Sunrise was approaching by the time the stews were neatly scoured and cleaned of vampires.

And then there were only two.

Fat mist swirled to engulf Michael. *Thief, deceiver*, husked his former lord and mentor. *Are you stronger than I?* The mist eddied, caressed, and dispersed. *I shall expect you in Ireland. . . . Do not tarry . . . or you will be too late. . . . Do not arrive late. . . .*

"For what?" Michael demanded of the fleeing mist.

There was no answer. Sunrays shone in Michael's eyes.

❧ 29 ❧

Yet, if you knew me well, you would not
  shun
My love, but to my wished embraces run:
Would languish in your turn, and court
  my stay;
And much repent of your unwise delay.

—Ovid: *Metamorphosis XIII*

Renée sank before King Francis with a flounce of dusty skirts. "Your Majesty." She offered him the silver box on the open palm of her hand. "Your prize."

Cardinal Medici, sitting by the king, snatched the box and vanished into a private closet. He returned a moment later, beaming. "Impressive, Princess! Words fail me. I thank you."

"Your Grace is welcome." She smiled. "My king, have I your leave to repair to Brittany?"

"*Hein* . . ." King Francis looked mystified, pleased, and ill at ease all at once. He extended his hand to gallantly lift her to her feet and then snapped his fingers for a chair for her. "There is the matter of your betrothal to the noble heir of His Grace the Duke of Este to be discussed. . . ."

Renée sat down gracefully on the edge of the tall-backed chair and accepted a goblet of rosé. They had made excellent speed. She was exhausted. She did not feel triumphant. Her world had upturned itself while she was in the hold with Michael. Now she felt bereft, like Eve, booted out of the Garden of Eden after tempting Adam with the apple. She had truth. She did not have Michael. "I hope Your Majesty will forgive my answer. I cannot be married to the duke's worthy son."

"The contract and the indentures have been signed. Have you not received our letter?"

Renée rubbed the large gold ring perched on her gloved forefinger. "Letter, Your Grace?"

"The duchy of Este is an excellent settlement, rich as Brittany, a most advantageous match. You should be pleased. The marriage will be celebrated on *Assomption*, the fifteenth day of August, by proxy, and shortly thereafter you will repair to the demesne of your lord husband."

It saddened her that Michael was right; she would have liked her king to keep his word. "Am I to be stripped of my title as Duchess of Brittany, sire? Is our agreement null and void?"

Cardinal Medici eyed King Francis with a cocked eyebrow, curious to see how Long-Nose would excuse his violation of the contract he had gleefully signed in this very chamber.

"You may be interested to know," Long-Nose waffled, pleasantness larding his voice, "that we have released your artist friend from prison. Oh, and early this morning the Duke de Soubise suffered a tragic accident at the hunt. A wild boar charged at him from nowhere and fanged him right brutally. The varlets were useless with fear. Soubise died screaming in agony."

Renée gasped. Fanged! Was Michael here? She came to her feet. "My king, have I the queen my mother's bequest, as was promised to me on parchment sealed with the arms of France?"

King Francis did not respond. His silence fell between them like a great void.

Renée stiffened her spine. The time had come for her to give this epigone of King Louis XII and his holy banker a taste of the dish they had shoved down her throat and see how they liked it. "Your Majesty, I cannot marry d'Este because I already have a husband. I was handfasted with Sir Michael Devereaux in England." She showed him the ring. "The ceremony is sanctioned by Holy Church and is binding, as my good cardinal may attest." To nip plots of annulment in the bud, she put a hand on her belly and blithely lied, "The first fruit of our union is well on its way."

King Francis exploded from his throne, spattering furiously. He

shouted and reproached and called her many unpleasant things—
and she relished every moment of it.

The scroll has no power. Use that if they renege.

"My lord cardinal." She smiled with vengeful satisfaction, remembering his demand that she should strip before them. "Your
scroll is empty of power. The Sword of the archangel Michael was
absorbed into my husband. Now he embodies it, and he is a vampire. Astonishing, is it not?"

The cardinal grasped at his chest with both hands, shouting the
Paternoster.

"Pray do not be afeared, Your Grace," she went on composedly.
"He is a virtuous vampire."

Cardinal Medici's thunderous glower swerved toward Long-
Nose. "Our contract is null and void! You have contracted a she-
demon!"

"Oh, but, Your Grace, I have done my duty," Renée assured
him. "I have stolen the Ancient from Cardinal Wolsey's house,
under Cardinal Campeggio's watchful nose. They are ruined in
Rome. Your future seat is secure, the competition eliminated. The
French treasury has earned your generous contribution." She
aimed a menacing glare at King Francis. "All dues will be paid in
full, Your Graces, or I shall invoke hell!" She let her armed threat
fester in their minds. "Your spies in England will corroborate my
tidings. Frantic accounts of the affair are not far behind me, I trow.
I shall leave court for Brittany at once. I give Your Graces good
day." She curtsied prettily and strode out of the royal privy chamber, grinning victoriously, after all.

"Adele, pack all! We are leaving Amboise, never to return!"
Renée skidded to a startled halt inside her luxurious apartment,
nearly toppling over the trunks brought from the ship.

"You have a visitor." Adele gestured at the timid, dark-haired,
untidy young man standing quietly by the window.

"Raphael."

He gave a shy bow, paint-smeared fingers kneading a worn velvet cap. "My lady, I came as soon as news of your arrival reached
the salon of Madame Marguerite. God's greeting to you."

Renée swallowed. He looked pale and thin and . . . the way he always did. She felt awkward. Had she ever been in love with him? Had she been blind? So uninspiring, so dull. Not Michael. She rallied and offered her hand gracefully. It mattered not that he had signed the false statement and that he might or might not have been conspiring with the witch Marguerite. She did not want him anymore. She just wanted to be rid of him. Swiftly, cleanly, politely. Painlessly, if possible.

Her silence augmented his discomfiture. He waited for her cue.

Suddenly it did matter to Renée that Raphael had sworn he had had no carnal knowledge of her. Surely he had known his statement would be used to procure her a husband. He had given up while she had been risking everything—her life—for a chance at a future for them, the coward.

Your king may have every prince in the world, from Catai to Hispaniola, queued up for your hand, but it will not make a plaguey difference. Do you know why? I have fallen in love with you.

Michael, a bastard from the stews, the son of an attainted traitor, dared to hopelessly love the lawful daughter of King Louis XII and would have fought to the death to be with her had he not cared so deeply for her comfort and happiness. Fearless and true.

In comparison, Raphael's love was frumenty.

"I am for the Loire." She floated around the room, tidying naught in particular. "I—I am married. I am to meet up with my lord husband. Have you been painting?"

"Madame de Chevreuse has commissioned two murals for her lord husband's new palace."

"This is wondrous! Your star will shine. Raphael." She stopped before him. "I am sorry."

He smiled sadly. He stepped closer to kiss her hand. "My Muse. God keep you."

"Your Majesty." Michael knelt before King Henry VIII. The king, Michael noticed wryly, was embedded in a ring of silver-armed bodyguards. Everyone dreaded the supervampire.

Suffolk, Cardinal Wolsey, Stanley, and several other familiars flanked the throne. His mates were smiling, the cardinal was contemplating how best to employ Michael's powers in pursuit of his own agenda, the king was intimidated, fascinated, and slightly jealous of Michael's powers. Their minds whispered to him faintly, chaotically, a farrago of fears, cunning, doubts, hope, lies, wishes, approval, praises, a medley of muddled sentiments. With time he might come to master his new abilities. He had all the time in the world. Centuries, mayhap millennia. God help him.

"Sir Michael Devereaux!" the king exclaimed. "We have received a papal bull on your behalf that lauds your triumph over the demons in the Battle of the Stews. Holy Church has seen fit to bestow you with these titles." He read: "'*Redemptor Mundi*, Redeemer of the World, Defender of Christendom; *Gonfaloniere*, Captain General and Admiral of the Holy Roman Church in the Holy Fight against the Forces of Evil; and *Gladius Invictus*, Invincible Sword in the service of the Good People of the Faith.' What say you?"

Michael smiled. The words *in the service of* were not lost on him. A cunning strategy, he granted. They lavished him with honors, recruited his allegiance, and established their authority over him, the vast scarlet pall of Holy Church, all in one bull. "I am honored." He inclined his head. "However, if Your Grace will permit, I am English and proud of my heritage. Naturally I shall do my sacred duty by the world, but I serve and cleave to one king—the King of England and France, Protector of the Faith, Defender of the Realm, Henry Tudor." He sank to one knee, head bent in deference to the king's grace, and awaited King Henry's pleasure—and verdict. He took care to observe the tiniest detail of proper protocol, make no sudden movements, for he was still being measured in the king's balance.

This was his second interview with King Henry since the Battle of the Stews. The first had taken place in the guard room immediately after the battle. Stanley and Suffolk had insisted. He had been tired, gory, and miserable. He had hardly paid attention to what was being said to him. He had gotten back his lodging in the palace, complete with his equipage and casket of bottles, and instantly went to collect Christopher and his servants from Westminster Abbey. Afterward, he had returned to the stews to look for the other four little boys. He had not found them.

The next day, he had left for France—and come back.

Renée was well. He had made sure. And she was better off without him.

King Henry handed the bull to his secretary, who handed it to Michael. "We have decided to ennoble you. You shall be the Duke of Tyrone and serve England as Lord Lieutenant of Ireland."

Michael pushed to his feet with a sinking sense of glum disappointment. Polite banishment. While it suited him perfectly—court life held no interest for him whatsoever, there was naught for him here; the intrigues, power plays, and deceit would go on ad nausea—he had enjoyed his stay here, being a part of something bigger than himself, history. He had made friends that were good and true, like Stanley, grinning at him, all puffed up like a pigeon with brotherly pride, and Suffolk, winking at him. He had enjoyed hunting, feasting, jousting, plotting, and fighting with all of them, even with Cardinal Wolsey. It was hurtful to be discarded. Nevertheless, Rome had spoken, King Henry had spoken. All that remained was for Michael to take his dignified leave. He sketched a bow. "I am Your Majesty's most grateful servant."

As he walked out of the privy chamber, King Henry called after him, "My Lord Tyrone!"

Michael turned around. The king regarded him ambiguously. "I trust we shall see you on St. George's Day . . . next year?" A rakish smile curled the royal lips. "Break spears together?"

Michael grinned. Not banished, after all. "With pleasure, Your Majesty!" He brandished his arm and strode out in a much better humor, sword rattling against his hip. He had done it—what he had come here to achieve. He had asserted his mettle, plucked a laurel leaf of glory, and found a place in the ranks of his brethren. He had found pride in himself.

Ireland was home, Michael decided as he flew past rolling pastures teeming with deer, blue lakes shimmering under the sun, stone villages rich with produce, wild hills carpeted with vivid flowers, and emerald woods as far as the eye could see. Birds shrieked a fond salute overhead. Christopher was delighted with everything, just as Michael had been twenty years ago, brought to a genuine home—of a vampire. Except that Christopher knew his secret, as did the rest of Christianity whose dominions he had sworn to protect in a ceremony orchestrated by the Right Reverend Cardinal of York. His allegiance had been signed and sealed. Like his fate.

Castle Tyrone, watchfully presiding over its rebellious environs, soared gray and formidable at the top of a lush rise. Michael knew his lord was there, awaiting him, even before he heard the faint husk in his head, *You come at last . . . Thief, deceiver . . . My foundling son . . .*

Michael left Christopher with Cáit, who burst into tears of joy upon seeing him, and headed for the lord's chamber. Out of the common gaze he flew up the stairwell and emerged a heartbeat later in the darkened stone realm of the Vesper whose name he could not pronounce.

The former Earl of Tyrone was abed. His skin was sallow and rutted. He had aged decades, it seemed, since last they met. "Aye, I am dying. Giving you my blood weakened me."

Michael rolled up his sleeve, knelt beside the bed, and offered his forearm. An act of charity to repay many kindnesses. His lord waved his hand feebly. "No. My time has come. I am tired." He considered Michael with purposeful severity. "You will continue my office, serve this world, as I have? You are the last keeper of wisdom, Michael. You have a sacred duty."

"Sacred, my lord? To feed on mankind and inflict my foulness on them?"

His lord roared. "You have understood . . . learned . . . *nothing*! That God, that jealous, wrathful God in whose name my species was decimated—do you not deem Him all-powerful?"

"I do."

"And the Divine Thought of Creation—flawless or flawed?"

"Flawless."

The last Night Spirit pushed up his decomposing flesh and bone on his elbow, his powers of Shade fading rapidly, and directed his last spark of life at Michael. "Then how can I be a flaw? Was I not created with this world? Am I not its servant, as all creatures are? The Great Flood, did it not breed creation? Preserve wisdom and beauty, Michael. That is my testament unto you."

Michael was cast in silence. *Keeper of wisdom.* The invaluable libraries, the universal works of artists, of scholars, of healers, of men in service of humanity, so easily destroyed in wars. The duty to preserve the limitless lore of humankind for future generations was sacred indeed.

"Do something for me," his lord murmured. "Take me to the eyrie. I would see the sun."

"It would burn you." As it burned him, in the ephemeral moments when his human body had fought the Vesper blood he had consumed. He remembered that rainy night. His lord had led him to a table laden with an empty gold chalice. *"Come. Let us observe the proper rite of initiation."* His lord had slashed open a wrist vein and filled the chalice with his thick, dark Vesper blood. Michael, moonstruck, had consumed it obediently. He had stripped naked at his lord's command, let his lord clap him in irons on the gilt gridiron set in the black marble floor beneath the center skylight in the eyrie's dome, and lay beneath the icy-cold waterfall like Isaac on Mt. Moriah, awaiting the sun to rise and burn him into immortality.

"You remember," his lord said.

"Why did you that? Why did you let the sun burn me, when you could have drained me of blood before I drank of yours?"

His lord smiled weakly. "Sunflower, I could not deprive you of all you loved."

All he loved . . . was in France. "It might not have worked." Michael's tone was accusatory. A war of pain had raged in his body between the sun, the water, and the Night Spirit's blood.

"The sun, she is my greatest enemy. She spared you. Her painting you in her colors was her message to me. My time has come. Now I would see her, the fire goddess. Laugh at her as I die, as I reunite with my son. He has been waiting a long time in the underworld of the Shade. Take me to the eyrie, Michael."

Michael shoved his hands beneath the large but frail body and lifted him in his arms. "You never spoke of your son, only mentioned him," he said as he carried his lord to the tower.

"I loved a daughter of Eve once, an Egyptian courtesan. She was beautiful. I was enthralled. She gave me a son, my only son.

Vespers mate for life, Michael. We love once. She loved many. She betrayed me. Her new lover, a king, told her to stab my heart with a silver dagger. She tried and died for it. There!" his lord said as they entered the eyrie. "Put me where I put you, under the skylight in the dome."

"Enthrall but do not love. How did your son die?" He placed him on the floor.

A cloud blocked the sun. "The Guelph ambushed us. Silver darts flying. The sun was rising. We had not taken blood in days. I dissolved into mist. Emiliano tarried. They destroyed him." His lord cursed the cloud, and the frightened thing fled. "Ah! There she is! The fire goddess . . ."

Michael started. "Emiliano? No! He is not dead! He is in Rome, a prisoner!" He reached for his lord, to pull him away from the sun, to save him. "Your son lives!" he kept shouting. "Live!"

It was too late.

A hiss of anguish filtered through the thin lips as they turned to ash. "Save him . . . for me. . . ."

Michael dropped to his knees at the heap of ash and stared at it for a long time afterward.

Michael had not come to Renée in Amboise. Nor had he been waiting for her in Brittany. News of his supernatural feats of valor in the Battle of the Stews was the litany of the world. As a result, Holy Church disbanded its purposeless army of *deletoris*. Michael was hailed the new Defender of Christendom and was minted the first Duke of Tyrone, Lord Lieutenant of Ireland.

Michael had glory.

Days turned to weeks as Renée repined for him, in vain. She called for him all the time, but he would not come to her. Glory, it seemed, was sufficient reward for her vampire.

She resolved to travel through her estates, act the chatelaine, accompanied by Francesco, her new marshal. She initiated repairs in her demesnes, hired proficient stewards, and visited with her Breton relations and tenants. Ultimately she retired to the coastline, the longest in France.

As spring warmed into summer, she took long walks along the cliffs, admiring the delicate blending of pink and orange hues in the rocks, the blue and green in the clear water of the sea.

The sea soothed her. She was so lonely. At times she wished she had never known the strong emotions involved in loving a man with the heart, body, and soul of a woman. The tenderness Raphael had briefly inspired in her was the light puffs of foam upon the enormous sea of her love for Michael Devereaux. He believed he was doing her a good turn. He was wrong, so wrong . . .

"Be patient," Adele would say. "Love will come."

"When?" *When will he come?*

"When you least expect it."

The man she least expected waited for her in the garden one afternoon upon her return from a walk along the cliff. It was not Rougé, whose letters from England she kept returning unopened.

"Your Grace." She sank in a curtsey. Her guest reclined on a cushioned settle, gobbling fruit and pastries and sipping lambig, his plush scarlet robes billowing gently at the hem.

Cardinal Medici smiled. "Barefoot, madame?"

"I came from the beach," she explained negligently, and sat on a stool across from him.

"You are not curious to learn the reason for my impromptu visit?"

"I am certain Your Grace will enlighten me in good time."

"Your lord husband, the duke, I hear he is in Ireland."

"So he is."

His intrusive gaze probed her lap. "No babe under the kirtle. Most unfortunate that vampire men cannot sire children. Do you expect him sometime soon . . . ?"

Her temper flared. "Do not think he will countenance any threats made—"

"No threats. I come in peace. I have something for you." He chuckled as she narrowed her eyes on him. "We fear the Greeks even when they bring gifts." He indicated the large traveling box on the end of the table. "The thing itself speaks."

Renée removed the leather wrap of the parcel resting inside the box. It was an old tome.

"This book is the property of Holy Church. I had it delivered from Rome, especially for you, on loan, of course. I marked the correct page. Read the postscript at the bottom."

Renée unclasped and opened the embossed leather cover on the ribbon-marked page. The tiny hand scrawl was difficult to decipher. *The blood of a young man executed for his faith has the power to heal* . . . Her eyes jerked up to find the cardinal's amused gaze on her.

"Five centuries ago, a dedicated monk by the name of Agapitus was infected by a vampire and became one himself. Agapitus, a faithful servant of Our Lord Christ, hated his ailment as it removed him from the Cross. He absorbed himself in searching for a cure. It took him decades of experiments until finally he stumbled upon it. The blood of a saint executed for his faith will turn a man-vampire back into man. Agapitus drank the blood and returned to his human form."

"The blood of a saint," Renée hissed angrily. "Do you sell such indulgences in Rome?"

"No." The cardinal lost his smile. He leaned closer, whispering, "But I know where you may find a cupful of a saint's blood. The cathedral in Naples safeguards a glass vessel that contains the blood of St. Januarius, a young man executed for his faith. Should your lord husband drink this blood, he will be a healthy man again. You would like that, would you not, madame?"

"If he drinks this blood, he will lose the powers of the Sword." She scrutinized him sharply. So he had fathomed her. He sensed her unrequited craving for the "husband" who could not be all hers. "How kind and magnanimous Your Grace is. You would grant my heart's desire, gratis."

He opened his hands in a humbly concurring gesture. How benevolent, indeed.

"Except that Your Grace is aught but selfless," she plowed on ruthlessly. "Michael Devereaux has stolen the Power, and if you cannot have it . . . then—by God!—no one else should." His sly maneuver had caught her off guard like a hot poker in the belly. "This is why you took the trouble."

"You have touched the thing with a needle." He shrugged. "I do not deny it."

"But the vampires . . ."

"All vanquished. None remained, expect . . . Michael."

More powerful than all his predecessors put together, Renée read the unspoken words. "Two and a half centuries ago Holy Church claimed the Vespers were all destroyed. They returned."

"The vampires and their Vesper overlords are all gone, including the one who styled himself Earl of Tyrone. My sources are reliable. The Vesper perished in his castle. Michael was there."

Of course the fox would have spies in Michael's household. But—*merciful Jesu!*—a cure! Renée was beside herself, tempted. If Michael were human again, they would be able to enjoy a normal life as husband and wife, have babies, love each other freely, and grow old together. . . .

The cardinal rose from the settle. "I leave the book, and the decision, in your capable hands. The Sword has served its purpose. The world, I promise you, will not fall into upheaval should you choose to have your husband in your loving bosom again. I give you good day."

❧ 30 ❧

I recognize the return of the old fires.

—Virgil: *Aeneid*

County Tyrone, Ireland, Lammastide, 1518

Horsemen were approaching from behind.
"We are being followed," Michael said. They were traveling to the festival of *Lughnasadh* at the nearby village. Christopher was bouncing up and down in front of him, prattling about toads, worms, and Nurse Cáit. Clearly the mild-mannered serving wench loved the boy if she tolerated his god-awful pranks. In contrast, Michael had been getting the baleful eye. Since his return, he had neglected to invite her to his bed. Not once. Not even when he was lying awake, burning. It was not her fault. He was simply not interested in women who were not Renée de Valois.

"Vampire instinct, my lord?" Pippin asked hopefully.

"Yes—and no, Pippin, I will not turn you into a vampire. Take Christopher." He handed the boy into his manservant's arms. "Wait here. I will be back shortly." He turned Archangel around and kneed the stallion into a gallop. He moved a lot faster on foot, in the air, but he endeavored to lead as normal a life as possible. His blood-lust was enough to struggle with as it was.

Lush green swards, dotted with patches of multicolored flowers, rushed on either side of him as he flew back toward the castle. The thundering in his chest grew mightier as the riders came into view. He had fought his heart's desire for so long and so hard—and now she was here. The die was cast. He would not let her go. Not again. Not ever. She had made her decision.

A lone horseman broke from the company and rode out to meet him halfway. *Renée.*

The love of his life glowed in a riding habit of snow-white velvet with a plumed hat perched stylishly atop her head, unbound ebony locks whipping at her back. "Sir!" she called out to him, rosy-cheeked, violet eyes sparkling. "Would you please point the way to the festival?"

They circled each other on horseback. He was grinning doltishly. "My lady comes to wager on the horse races?"

Her roseate lips pouted like a waterspout. "Horse races? I have not thought of that. I come in search of a husband—for a twelve-month and a day."

He could not wait. He swung a leg over Archangel's head, slid from the saddle, and grabbed her palfrey's reins. He looked up at her, yearning. "Only for a twelvemonth and a day?"

She extended her hands in a silent request. Michael clasped her waist and lifted her from the saddle. Her hands moved from his shoulders to his nape as she slowly glided the length of his body. Her fragrant breath caressed his lips. "Know you of fair Irishmen in want of a bride?"

"No, my lady." He embraced her, feeling her fingers sink into his hair. "They are all taken."

Renée's adorable face filled his vision. "And you, sir? Are you taken?"

"Most definitely." He touched his lips to hers, savoring the first contact. *How sweet you are*, his mind whispered to her as he tasted her mouth. *My sweet-and-twenty.*

"Michael." She melted into him, his beautiful princess. "I have you fast now. To be in love and wise is scarce granted even to a god."

He laughed and kissed her heartily. "And goddesses—are they wise in love?"

She smiled pertly. "Females are always wise. It is a fact of nature. Is Christopher with you? I would greet him. Adele misses him, too."

"I see you have brought your entire court with you, madame." He did not even have to look. He smelled them, heard their chatter in his ears. "Have you carted Raphael, as well, muzzled? He may paint a mural for our bedchamber: *The Triumph of Vampires over Plaguey Artists.*"

She tightened her lips against a smile. "Soubise was devoured by a wild boar. Very cruel."

"So you guessed. The filthy swine deserved it. I felt no remorse. As for your painter—"

She caressed his cheek. "Paled in comparison. I knew that before I returned to France. I love you, *Michel.* You should have come for me. I waited. Did you not hear me calling?"

"I heard. I wanted to . . . God knows how much I love you, but the things you said on the ship were sensible. You deserve a husband who will give you babes and not take your blood."

"Would you be that husband if you could?"

He opened himself entirely to her gaze. "What do you think, marmoset?"

She gave him a curl of lip. "I have a cure. The Cure! Hear me out."

Renée laced her fingers over Michael's chest and rested her chin on her hands. "Summers in Ireland, winters in Brittany, autumns in Chartres, and springtime with the court in England. How does my timetabling appeal to Your Grace of Tyrone and of Brittany and Chartres?"

Michael's gaze was far away, contemplating the moon shining outside the open window, his hand caressing her bare hip. "My Grace of Brittany and Chartres as well?" he asked distractedly.

"*Jure uxoris*, in right of wife."

"I want to have a little lifetime with you. I do not want to be a vampire."

"But you have doubts."

"The Vespers are not all gone. He lied to you. They have one locked underground in Rome. Count Emiliano, my erstwhile lord's son. He has been incarcerated there three centuries now."

Renée's head came up. "Count Emiliano?"

Michael looked at her. "You have heard of him."

"Yes. So?"

"So . . . three hundred years in a small room under the world, no clothes, no company, no air. They feed him rats' blood tinctured with silver to keep him tame. He lies on his back on the floor and speaks to the ceiling. They say he is raving mad. I think he is fighting to keep his sanity." He shut his eyes. "Sometimes, I hear him growling from the depths of hell, calling for a savior."

She shuddered. "You may be imagining it."

"I know I am. It does not make a plaguey difference. My old lord's dying wish was for me to set his son free. If we set out to Naples—and I imagine we shall have to steal the saint's blood as your cardinal will not give it to us—do I liberate Emiliano before, after . . . never? The powers of the Sword will be lost forever. The power of procreation will return. I want to do this for you."

"Michael, if you liberate this powerful Vesper . . . Three hundred years of captivity breed a lot of revenge. You will have to kill him in the end."

"Death would be merciful compared with living an eternal nightmare."

"My darling lord." She kissed him. "Your kind heart humbles me."

"Renée." Michael swept her hair back. "You came back to me. *To you my life belongs.*"

"Think upon it, then. I will accept whatever you decide." She dangled the scarlet ribbon he had tied around her wrist at the pagan ceremony, felt the weight of the gold ring he had bestowed on her finger in a quiet church service. "We are trothplighted for good or bad."

He rolled onto her. "You think upon it, my wise goddess, while I worship at your shrine. . . ."

RESOURCES

Bindoff, S. T. *Pelican History of England: Tudor England*. Penguin, 1993.

Clough, C. H. *Francis I and the Courtiers of Castiglione's Courtier.* European Studies Review. Vol. viii, 1978.

Elton, G. R. *England under the Tudors*. Methuen, 1955.

Erickson, Carolly. *Great Harry*. St. Martin's Griffin, 1980.

Goold, G. P. *Propertius*. Loeb Classical Library, Harvard University Press, 1990.

Henderson, Paula. *The Tudor House and Garden*. Yale University Press, 2005.

Jourda, Pierre. *Une princesse de Renaissance, Marguerite d'Angoulême, Reine de Navarre, 1492–1549*. Genève, Slatkine Reprints, 1973.

Kelly, Henry Ansgar. *Bishops, Prioresses, and Bawds in the Stews of Southwark*. Medieval Academy of America, 2000.

Knecht, R. J. *Renaissance Warrior and Patron: The Reign of Francis I*. Cambridge: Cambridge University Press, 1994.

Kramer, Samuel Noah. *Gilgamesh and the Huluppu-Tree: A Reconstructed Sumerian Text*. Assyriological Studies of the Oriental Institute of the University of Chicago, 1938.

Mazo Karras, Ruth. *Working Together in the Middle Ages: The Regulation of Brothels in Later Medieval England*. The University of Chicago Press, 1989.

Mikhaila, Ninya; Malcolm-Davis, Jane. *The Tudor Tailor. Techniques and Patterns for Making Historically Accurate Period Clothing*. Batsford, 2006.

Morwood, James. *A Dictionary of Latin Words and Phrases*. Oxford University Press, 1998.

Mozley, J. H. (Revised by G. P. Goold). *Ovid: The Art of Love and Other Poems*. Loeb Classical Library, Harvard University Press, 1979.

Patai, Raphael. *Adam ve-Adama*. Jerusalem: The Hebrew Press Association, 1941–1942.

Regardie, Israel. *A Garden of Pomegranates*. Llewellyn Publications, 1999.

Regardie, Israel. *Tree of Life*. Red Wheel-Weiser Publication, 2000.

Schmidt, Alexander. *Shakespeare Lexicon and Quotation Dictionary*. Dover Publications, Inc., 1971.

Schwartz, Howard. *Lilith's Cave: Jewish Tales of the Supernatural*. San Francisco: Harper & Row, 1988.

Starkey, David. *The Reign of Henry VIII, Personalities and Politics*. G. Philip, 1985.

Stone, Brian. *Medieval English Verse*. Penguin Classics, 1964.

Summers, Montague. *Vampire: His Kith and Kin*. Kessinger Publishing, 2003.

The works of Bill Heidrick and his Qabalistic analysis. http://www.billheidrick.com.

Thurley, Simon. *The Royal Palaces of Tudor England*. Yale University Press, 1993.

Weir, Alison. *Henry VIII the King and His Court*. Random House, 2001.

Wolkstein, Diane, and Samuel Noah Kramer. *Inanna: Queen of Heaven and Earth*. Harper & Row, New York, 1983.